GULLIVER'S TRAVELS AND
OTHER WRITINGS

JONATHAN SWIFT

GULLIVER'S TRAVELS AND OTHER WRITINGS

EDITED BY

LOUIS A. LANDA

OXFORD UNIVERSITY PRESS
LONDON OXFORD
1976

Oxford University Press

LONDON OXFORD GLASGOW NEW YORK
TORONTO MELBOURNE WELLINGTON CAPE TOWN
IBADAN NAIROBI DAR ES SALAAM LUSAKA ADDIS ABABA
KUALA LUMPUR SINGAPORE JAKARTA HONG KONG TOKYO
DELHI BOMBAY CALCUTTA MADRAS KARACHI

ISBN 0 19 281206 8

First published in the United States of America by Houghton Mifflin Company, Boston, Mass., U.S.A. First issued as an Oxford University Press paperback by Oxford University Press, London, 1976.

CONTENTS

INTRODUCTION

Louis A. Landa

"I have observed," wrote Mr. Spectator in 1711, "that a reader seldom peruses a book with pleasure 'till he knows whether the writer of it be a black or fair man, of a mild or choleric disposition, married or a bachelor, with other particulars of the like nature, that conduce very much to the right understanding of an author." This insistence on the value of biography for the appreciation of literature applies with peculiar force to Jonathan Swift because he was one of the most *personal* of authors. What manner of man was he? Legends have swirled about him and facts have been so stubbornly resisted that the true lineaments of his complex and compelling personality have all too often been left obscure. Let us begin his story, not as custom decrees, with his birth, but, perversely, with his epitaph. He penned his own epitaph (a pleasant practice now sadly fallen into desuetude), intent on embodying in a few pungent phrases the essential aspect of his character, that special vision he had of himself and wished posterity to respect. Although Dr. Johnson once remarked that "in lapidary inscriptions a man is not upon oath," one feels the incontestable rightness of the commemorative words which Swift wrote into his will, with the request that they be inscribed in black marble, "in large letters, deeply cut, and strongly gilded."

"You remember how it goes," William Butler Yeats wrote. "It is almost finer in English than in Latin: 'He has gone where fierce indignation can lacerate his heart no more' [*Ubi Saeva Indignatio/Ulterius/Cor Lacerare Nequit*]." But it is not these words alone, striking as they are, which made Yeats say that "Swift sleeps under the greatest epitaph in history." There is also a spirited Latin injunction to the wayfarer to imitate, if he can, what Swift did in behalf of liberty: *Abi Viator/Et Imitare Si Poteris/Strenuum Pro Virili/Libertatis Vindicatorem. Libertatis*, we may be certain, in no narrow sense, as Professor Maurice Johnson has remarked in an excellent comment on Swift's epitaph. Swift had in mind a larger liberation, not merely political (though that would be included), but a freeing of the human mind from error and the human spirit from baseness. Now, we need not make him more noble than he was. His ideals doubtless were at times, as his enemies loudly insisted, the prey of crass circumstances; and when his deeper convictions were affronted, he could be relentless and hard. He was perhaps more apt to exercise than suffer the proud man's contumely. Nevertheless, his vision of himself, as suggested by the epitaph, is no misrepresentation. Many of his works and much of his career testify to an abiding concern for the plight of man. Fierce indignation did lacerate his heart as he observed the shackled human spirit. The *saeva indignatio* hints at the wrathful moralist, one utterly incapable of looking at the world with detachment. Any conception of Swift as a man of letters withdrawn from the world and registering his wrath, contempt, and despair merely in words is completely false. Like so many other literary geniuses of the eighteenth century, he was a man of action, anything but aloof from the stresses and strains of local and national life. His public career lasted for almost three decades, from 1710, when he was a prolific political journalist in England for a period of almost four years, to about 1739, when ill health and age had drained his energies. For over two decades following 1714, he was one of Ireland's great men, a zealous churchman in control of a great cathedral and a vigorous participant in the affairs of the nation. Swift was, in fact, a practical reformer, as ready with deeds as with his pen.

He would not have felt a dichotomy between the man of action and the satirist. Nor would he grant the validity of a later-day assessment of satire as something merely negative. To the great satirists of the period satire was an affirmative thing, with constructive intentions. It seemed to offer the best corrective to the vices and follies of man and society as no other literary mode could; and if Swift's ironic wit derives mainly from the bent of his mind and temperament, he was fortunately born in an age that cherished and nourished this quality. "The satirist," Henry Fielding once wrote, "is to be regarded as our physician, not our enemy." Although there was some vocal dissent from this view even in Swift's day, we owe to a later period the extreme conviction that the satirist is somehow an offensive person, at his worst a misanthrope, at his best a cynic, and in either case a man with little or no compassion and hope. The fierce, dark, and violent rhetoric of Swift's major satires, the mingling of acerbity, wit, gloom, and anguish, has often been disconcerting to critics and has unbalanced their judgments of him as a man. Thus Thackeray and other Victorians could view him as living constantly in a raging compound of madness, malignity, and misanthropy, a portrait curiously oblivious to that extensive portion of Swift's works in which comedy and intellectual play prevail, untouched by a darker note. Swift as a smiling satirist should be given his due, the author of the *Bickerstaff Papers* and of many witty poems, for example, one who would tickle mankind into good manners or laugh men out of their favorite follies. It is not easy to release Swift from the legend of the gloomy dean which has been so firmly established. His life, it has been said, "was a long disease, with its disappointments, its self-torture, its morbid recriminations." This is as false as it is theatrical. Philosophically, certainly, he was inclined to an astringent and realistic view of life (habitually expressed in comic terms), but that his personal existence was one of prolonged agony is nonsense.

It is true that Swift's letters in the 1730's show an increase in gloomy pronouncements, a result in good part of his bad health. He knew what it was to suffer from poor eyesight, giddiness, and nausea, the last two of these stemming from a malady which had afflicted him from his early years, Ménière's Syndrome. His correspondents hear much of his ill health in this decade. One of the most frequently quoted letters dates from July, 1740:

> I have been very miserable all night, and today extremely deaf and full of pain. I am so stupid and confounded, that I cannot express the mortification I am under both in body and mind. All I can say is, that I am not in torture, but I daily and hourly expect it. Pray let me know how your health is and your family. I hardly understand one word I write. I am sure my days will be very few; few and miserable they must be. I am, for those few days,
>
> > Yours entirely,
> > J. Swift.
> If I do not blunder, it is Saturday, July 26, 1740. If I live till Monday, I shall hope to see you, perhaps for the last time.

This is indeed the outcry of a wretched man, one of a number of such letters written to friends in Swift's later years. If gathered together by an assiduous critic predisposed to theatricalism, he could use them well in support of a theory of "agony and rage and self-torture." But the letter just quoted belongs to Swift's seventy-third year, and it, along with others in the 1730's, should be kept in their proper perspective. By 1735 Swift was approaching seventy, in an age when medical science could not bring either cure or relief to ills which now yield easily to treatment. Men had to live with their maladies, and endure them as well as they could. It is possible that Swift, who was no stoic, was more vocal than others on the subject of pain and misery or that he merely used, characteristically, unrestrained language. But granted that he did undergo in his later years a considerable agony of body and spirit, the point is that this has been excessively dramatized, made to represent the whole man, read back into his earlier years, and used crudely in interpreting his works.

"Good night, I hope I shall never see you again" — this is reported as Swift's manner in later years of bidding farewell to friends, to illustrate a presumed characteristic bitterness and an anguished wish for release by death. If he actually used this remark, if he used it seriously, clearly some weight would attach to it; but I should want to know to whom he used it and in what tone and spirit. It sounds very much like his usual banter, the transparent friendly insult and genial vituperation, which so often distinguishes his letters and his manner to friends who understood his ironic turn and his liking for the inverted compliment. His biographers have displayed a naïve susceptibility to such casual remarks and incidents, his supposed habit, to instance one more, of reading the Book of Job regularly on his birthday — a habit that he himself mentioned only once, on his seventy-first birthday. It has been said of Dr. Johnson that everyone thinks of him as an old man, a fate that not infrequently happens to writers who live beyond the allotted biblical span; and Swift too has suffered from being mirrored in the minds of later generations by selected details from his declining years. But there is another Swift, the man described (even in the 1730's) as a person of "infinite spirits" and "very good humour." There is the Swift who wrote delightful light verse, the punster, the genial, witty companion of Queen Anne's Lord Treasurer and her Secretary of State from 1710 to 1714, the Swift who was an eagerly sought guest at great houses, the Swift who had a genius for friendship with both sexes (to balance his competence in making, usually, the right enemies), and the Swift whose letters, squibs, poems, and daily activities give evidence of vitality, playfulness of mind, and many wholesome satisfactions. These aspects of the man should be taken into account, to bring the picture into proper proportions.

Biography and criticism have reciprocal influences; and the conception of Swift as a man has been greatly influenced by the criticism of *Gulliver's Travels*. The masterpiece became the man. One might enter a caveat against selecting a single work of an author who wrote many, over a period of forty years, and finding in that particular work a final explanation of his personality. But the range and the volume of Swift's work have to many critics seemed of little weight; and not even the whole of *Gulliver's Travels* has been thought necessary for a full understanding. The Fourth Book, with its contrasting pictures of Yahoo and Houyhnhnm, has been thought ample. Here the critics of the past (and a dwindling few of these times) found all they needed to construct the horrendous image of the man, though they have been adept at selecting precisely the right biographical fact or myth to enforce their conception, including his few scatalogical poems, whose purport they have abysmally failed to understand. We are more recently emerging into a period of sounder criticism and fuller comprehension of the man and his genius, but for almost two hundred

years most readers were prevented from viewing either Swift or
Gulliver's Travels in a perspective that did justice to either. The book
became an ethical or psychological case history, or both, of its author,
in which the presumed intolerable misanthropy of Part IV, its debase-
ment of humankind, showed — as Swift's first biographer maintained
— that Swift himself was the degenerate Yahoo he had so infamously
depicted as representative of man. Other commentators of the later
eighteenth century took a similar high moral line. A man who could
thus libel human nature must be reflecting, it seemed, his own moral
deformity and defiled imagination. Inevitably, and unconsciously, the
degraded nature of the author had a subtle influence on literary
judgment. The ethical culpability of the writer lent strength to the
view that the Fourth Voyage is an artistic failure, as though a Buddhist
should deny the literary worth of Dante's *Divine Comedy* or Milton's
Paradise Lost because they are doctrinally unsound. Yet it ought to
be said to the honor of the eighteenth-century commentators that they
paid the author of *Gulliver's Travels* the compliment of believing him
a sane man. It remained for the nineteenth-century critics to take
a new tack and elaborate a less defensible charge. Though they readily accepted the view that Part IV could be explained in terms of a
depraved author, they added that it might well be explained in terms
of a mad one. Early in the century Sir Walter Scott, repelled by
"this horrible outline of mankind degraded to a bestial state," thought
it must be the result of "the first impressions of . . . incipient mental
disease." The theory of malignancy was supplemented by the theory
of lunacy. It was then only a step to Thackeray's advice to his
audience, when he was lecturing on the eighteenth-century humorists,
that Part IV should not be read. Pass over it, he counselled his
hearers, and hoot its author for this portion of the book — "filthy in
word, filthy in thought, furious, raging, obscene." Similarly Edmund
Gosse, a product of the second half of the nineteenth century, whose
prolific criticism spanned the Victorian period and the first three
decades of the twentieth century, found evidence of a diseased brain
in the Fourth Voyage, which banished it from decent households.
It is not surprising that in our century the psychoanalysts have seized
on so attractive a subject as Swift; and now we find *Gulliver* explained
in terms of neuroses and complexes. Witness these words from *The
Psychoanalytic Review* (1942): *Gulliver's Travels* "may be viewed
as a neurotic phantasy with coprophilia as its main content." It
furnishes

> abundant evidence of the neurotic make up of the author and
> discloses in him a number of perverse trends indicative of fixation
> at the anal sadistic stage of libidinal development. Most con-
> spicuous among those perverse trends is that of coprophilia,

although the work furnishes evidence of numerous other related neurotic characteristics accompanying the general picture of psychosexual infantilism and emotional immaturity.

By a diligent search the psychoanalyst was able to discover "evidence" that the author was afflicted with a formidable variety of neurotic tendencies, including misogyny, mysophilia, mysophobia, voyeurism, exhibitionism, and compensatory potency reactions. This indeed is helpful! And it carries conviction in direct proportion to its helpfulness. If the psychoanalytic approach seems to have in it an element of absurdity, we should recognize that it is only a logical extension of the disordered-intellect theory of the nineteenth century, the chief difference being that the terminology has changed and that the psychoanalyst frankly sees *Gulliver's Travels* as a case history, whereas many earlier critics were presumably making a literary appraisal.

Perhaps these crude and amateur attempts deserve little attention, yet they are a phenomenon that the serious reader of Swift can hardly ignore in the light of their recurrence and their effectiveness in perpetuating myths. And they sometimes come with persuasiveness and literary flavor, as in Aldous Huxley's essay on Swift in *Do What You Will* (1929), where Huxley arrives at an amazingly over-simplified explanation of Swift's genius: "Swift's greatness," he writes, "lies in the intensity, the almost insane violence, of that 'hatred of bowels' which is the essence of his misanthropy and which underlies the whole of his work." The critics who have relied on a theory of insanity or disordered intellect to explain Swift have vitiated their case by resorting to *ex post facto* reasoning. The failure of Swift's faculties towards the end of his life, some fifteen or sixteen years *after* the publication of *Gulliver's Travels*, has been seized upon to explain something the critics neither liked nor understood. It seemed to them valid to push his "insanity" back in time, to look retrospectively at the intolerable Fourth Voyage of *Gulliver*, and to infer that he must have been at least incipiently mad when he wrote it. Yet the same commentators who observe manifestations of a disordered intellect in Part IV have not thought to question the intellect behind the Third Voyage, which we now know was composed in point of time after the Fourth. These same commentators have nothing but praise for the vigor, the keenness, the sanity, and the humanity of the mind that produced the *Drapier's Letters*, the first of which Swift was writing only a month after completing a draft of Part IV of *Gulliver*.

This is not to deny that a central fact in Swift's life and his works is his pessimism. If we reject the extreme view that his life was compounded of bitter malignity, raging madness, and black misanthropy, or even the more moderate tradition that misery and gloom were pervasive in his daily existence, we still must grant that his pessimism was real and ample. The burning phrases of the epitaph, the fierce indignation and the lacerated heart, are not to be discounted, as I have already suggested. The problem is to explain his pessimism in less melodramatic terms and to substitute for mere speculation a due regard for the known facts of his life and for any other influences, intellectual and social ones, for example, which may be relevant. In the external aspects of his career, even when soberly examined, one can observe a pattern of frustration that took its toll of his spirits, or somehow left him scarred. His early years in Ireland, of which all too little is known, probably left no ineffaceable scars. Born in Ireland in 1667, a posthumous child in an Anglo-Irish family of little means, he nevertheless was fortunate enough to receive a good education through the aid of a relative. He first attended Kilkenny School, and then, aged 14, entered Trinity College, Dublin, where (as he later misleadingly said) "he was stopped of his degree for dullness and insufficiency." Actually, though his record was indifferent, he was graduated a Bachelor of Arts in 1686 and remained at Trinity College until early in 1689, when the disruptions of the Revolution of 1688 succeeded the disruptions of post-Cromwellian Ireland. Reflecting on this period much later, in his *Autobiographical Fragment* (c. 1727), he recalled the ill treatment of his relatives, the neglect of his studies, and his sunken spirits; yet his university days certainly did not sour his nature, and in the decade that followed 1689 the years were brighter. He passed a considerable portion of his time in England, in the household of Sir William Temple as the secretary of that distinguished Whig statesman and diplomat. Here, at Moor Park in Surrey, Swift moved in an atmosphere of culture and enlightenment; he read widely and fruitfully, and came to know several prominent men who later entered significantly into his life. Not least of all, it was here that he first met Esther Johnson, the Stella of his poems and his *Journal*. At Moor Park also his literary inclinations were nourished and stimulated, to result in *A Tale of a Tub* and *The Battle of the Books*.

In an interval in his residence with Temple, Swift took an important step. In 1694 he went into holy orders. There had been a rift with his patron, in what was at best a makeshift relationship, and his decision to enter orders resulted less from deep conviction that the Church was his mission in life than from the necessity of settling himself, an attitude that the eighteenth century did not find strange. He had been promised a good appointment. Instead he found himself, in what must have seemed banishment, relegated to the bleak northeastern coast of Ireland as a country vicar of three small run-down parishes, the chief of which was Kilroot. Here, in a diocese recently shaken by scandal, in which the bishop had been deprived and a number of clergymen excommunicated or suspended for such varied offenses as fornication, adultery, drunkenness, neglect of cures, and simony, Swift began his long clerical career of half a century, fully exposed to the spiritual and physical dry rot of the Anglican Establishment in Ireland. His parish churches were in decay; the temporalities of the Church had been alienated to laymen, and he had only a handful of parishioners to serve. In striking contrast to his own moribund benefices was the flourishing Presbyterian Kirk. The circumstances were highly appropriate for developing his detestation of nonconformity and his fear of its power; and we must recollect that his brilliant *Tale of a Tub*, with its satiric attack on religious dissent, dates from this period of Swift's career, when the experience of Ulster Presbyterianism was fresh enough to give a dark and bitter tinge to that work.

It was an inauspicious and barren beginning for the youthful clergyman, bound to leave lasting impressions. He was soon to suffer another disappointment. Leaving his desolate parishes behind, he returned to the household of Temple in 1696 with expectations of a good appointment in England, though not necessarily in the Church. But Temple's death in 1699 ended his hopes and once again he returned to Ireland, this time as domestic chaplain to the Earl of Berkeley, one of the Irish Lord Justices. Even now Swift thought that he had excellent prospects, preferment to a lucrative deanery, only to find that he was put off with three insignificant country parishes, united under the name of Laracor, and soon afterwards, perhaps as a conciliatory gesture, the prebend of Dunlavin in St. Patrick's Cathedral. Later in his career, as he looked retrospectively at these early frustrations, Swift remarked on them with some bitterness; but in 1700, at the age of 33, he had enough youthful buoyancy and ambition to look forward without undue brooding over past disappointments. In the next few years he solidified his position as a canon of St. Patrick's Cathedral and came to be looked upon as a rising clergyman in the Church of Ireland. At the same time he was maintaining his English connections. He published in 1701, in London, where he was then visiting, the first of his political pamphlets, *A Discourse of the Contests and Dissensions between the Nobles and the Commons in Athens and Rome*. Although this tract has some interest for Swift's political theory, it is more significant for personal reasons. By means of it he achieved influence and reputation with powerful leaders of the Whigs. Several of the Whig statesmen, among them Lord Somers, to whom the *Tale of a Tub* was later dedicated, had been impeached by the House of Commons. Taking advantage of the situation, Swift came to their defense, thus strengthening his friendly relations with the Whigs which had begun during his residence with Sir William Temple.

And with the Whigs in power in 1707, he became a logical emissary to represent the bishops of the Irish Church in a matter of moment — a plea to Queen Anne for remission of certain clerical taxes paid to the English Crown, the First Fruits and Twentieth Parts, imposts that fell heavily on the already impoverished Irish clergymen. The importance of this mission in Swift's life cannot be over-estimated. In a significant sense this was the beginning of his public career. He appeared in England to make his plea to the Whig leaders, and received encouragement from such powerful statesmen as Halifax, Somers, Pembroke, and Sunderland. But the most powerful of all, the Earl of Godolphin, the Lord Treasurer, he did not win over — for political reasons. Godolphin, and in fact the Whig government, wished the clergy of the Irish Establishment to support legislation in Ireland removing the Test Act, an act designed to preserve the exclusive political position of the Anglican Church in that country by excluding all except Anglican communicants from holding public offices. If the clergymen of Ireland lent their endeavors to this political manoeuvre, which was intended to ease the lot of the dissenters, Queen Anne's first minister indicated to Swift that he would influence the Queen to remit the First Fruits and Twentieth Parts. Swift's deepest convictions never received a more severe test. Throughout his life he believed that the Anglican Church as established by law should be *the* Church of England and Ireland, firmly protected against political encroachments from the dissenters, though he granted the nonconformists the right of conscience and the practice of their beliefs. He never forgot what had happened to the Anglican Establishment under the rule of Cromwell and the Puritans; and the removal of the Test Act he conceived to be a significant step towards returning dissenters to power. Much of the intensity of feeling against nonconformity in *A Tale of a Tub* and the *Argument Against Abolishing Christianity* derives from his fear that this might occur again. In this respect he was possibly more a man of the seventeenth than of the eighteenth century. In any case, at this critical moment in his career, his loyalty to the Church he served remained firm, at the expense of his personal fortune. He expected preferment from the Whigs, and had a right to expect it. But he never wavered in his rejection of the terms proposed by the Lord Treasurer. And in what unquestionably were acts of self-abnegation, he wrote several pamphlets opposing the policy of the Whig ministry and defining the true principles of a Church-of-England man as he conceived them. But the incident left him bitter and disappointed. At the same time it helps to explain why his enemies, who occasionally gibed without justice at his religious faith, never mocked at his devotion to the Church — a man, one of them declared, "whose affection to the Church was never doubted, tho' his Christianity was ever question'd." In this period, from 1707 to 1710, Swift grew familiar with the scheming methods of courts and statesmen and with the pointless delays and manoeuvres that could envelop an honorable project. Unquestionably some of the cynicism about the political tribe so pervasive in his writing stems from these years. But there were other experiences in these busy months, more satisfying ones, as the widening of his friendships, which included Addison and Steele, the publication of the *Bickerstaff Papers*, and the contributions to *The Tatler*.

The late fall of 1710 proved a decisive point in Swift's career. It brought his shift in political allegiance from Whig to Tory, something his enemies never permitted him to forget though it was logical in all of its aspects. He watched with more pleasure than concern the fall of the Whig statesmen who had rebuffed him and the accession to power of moderate Tories under the leadership of Robert Harley, later the Earl of Oxford, destined to figure so prominently in Swift's life. Early in October he was received by Harley, to whom he now made his plea in behalf of the Irish clergy. Harley listened sympathetically, promised his support, and, with a keen eye for the practical uses of literary genius, turned Swift to political journalism in defense of the new Tory ministry. What is more, in a mere two weeks the Queen, at Harley's suggestion, acted favorably on Swift's mission, in contrast to three years of futile effort under the Whigs. It was all very gratifying; and he immediately wrote to Stella with obvious pleasure that Queen Anne would soon inform the bishops in Ireland and would take notice that "it was done upon a memorial from me." "I believe," he added, "never any thing was compassed so soon, and purely done by my personal credit with Mr. Harley." At this very moment, by one of those minor ironies that are sometimes big with consequences, the Irish bishops who had commissioned him decided that he was not, after all, the appropriate person for the task. Before word of his success reached Dublin, he was informed of their lack of faith in his endeavors and their desire to work through other channels. Swift's reaction may easily be imagined! Then, to compound the injury, when notification came from the throne, the bishops gave formal thanks to the Queen, to Harley, and to the recently appointed Lord Lieutenant of Ireland (who had played no part) without any reference to Swift himself. It was a slight, deliberate, ungenerous, and ungrateful, one that left him bitterly resentful and helps to explain perhaps the contempt for bishops which later animated him. The whole situation was hardly calculated to sweeten his nature. He had nursed the project carefully over a period of years and seen it clearly as something bound up with his personal ambitions and fortunes. For almost three years the Whigs in England had kept him in suspense with constant promises of advancement in the Church. It never came; and to this grievous frustration of personal hopes was added the intolerable and ungracious behavior of the bishops in Ireland.

There were, however, balms for his wounded feelings. His new political alignment, with the Tories, was congenial in its personal relationships and promising for his future. Moreover, it was based upon those very convictions and principles relating to church and state which had made his alliance with the Whigs an uneasy one. In November, 1710, he was made editor of *The Examiner*, a journal founded to defend the policies of Harley, Bolingbroke, and the Tory ministry. The position of power and trust he now occupied gave him a sense of exhilaration and released his energies. The years 1710 to 1713 represented for him a full tide of excitement and achievement. Political verses and pamphlets flowed from his pen. He struck out with consummate skill at Godolphin, at the Duke of Marlborough, the famous general and statesman, at the Duchess of Somerset (the Queen's confidante), at disgruntled Whigs and deists, at recalcitrant Tories and stubborn Scots. He found new friends — and inevitably in his position became himself a frequent political target. The friendship with those staunch Whigs, Addison and Steele, cooled, to be replaced by intimacy with authors inclined to the Tories, the poets Pope, Gay, and Prior, the dramatist Congreve, and the brilliant scientist and literary man who was physician to Queen Anne, John Arbuthnot. Swift moved about among the statesmen, court officials, titled aristocrats, and other dignitaries with aplomb and satisfaction, with a special sense that he was seeing history made, and with a special gusto for the incidents of each day. It is all zestily detailed in the *Journal to Stella*, that intimate revelation of his thoughts and actions mailed back to Ireland for the eyes of Esther Johnson. One gets from his letters and other writings in these years a vivid impression of unfolding dramatic events, events which swirled around him and are now part of the history of Queen Anne's final years — the undermining of the influence of the Duke and Duchess of Marlborough, the attempted assassination of Robert Harley, Jacobite intrigue, the secret negotiations to end the War of the Spanish Succession, and many lesser occurrences, all of which have as he presents them a dimension and color that coldly objective history does not attain because Swift assesses these matters as a participant — and indeed as a partisan whose judgment of personalities and motives must be scanned.

By the early part of 1713 clouds were gathering. It became clear that the divisions among the Tories and the bitter rift between Harley and Bolingbroke would have disastrous effects. Swift watched with despair as the ministry went to its destruction. Its fall and the death of Queen Anne in 1714 closed what he considered the most brilliant chapter in his life. For him personally the future was to be "exile" in Ireland, with only two visits to England in the long years ahead. Fortunately, before the Tories fell from power he was given the long-deferred advancement in the Church, though it was after all an appointment that to him and to his friends seemed less than his deserts. He had devoutly hoped to remain in England, not necessarily as a bishop or a dean, as he had some reason to expect in the light of contemporary custom. A canonry at Windsor or Westminster would have satisfied him. But the Queen and the Archbishop of York were set against it; and there were others, the Duchess of Somerset, for example, whose enmity may have influenced the Queen, not to mention the culpability of his friend Harley, whose aggrandizement of his own family led him to bestow bishoprics that might with more justice have gone to Swift. It was particularly disconcerting that he stood by month after month in expectation of preferment, as he had with the Whigs, listening to promises and rumors, while deaneries and bishoprics fell vacant and were filled by the appointment of others. His anger and resentment mounted, and finally in April 1713, he informed Harley that he would no longer endure the embarrassment of remaining in England unless he received an honorable preferment. This brought action, not however without some wrangling, and he was made Dean of St. Patrick's on April 23, 1713.

"My enemies [are] busy," Swift wrote to Stella at this time. They continued to be busy. The news of his appointment to a deanery made them clamorous. Legend has it that the following lines were affixed to the door of the cathedral on the day of his installation:

> Look down, St. Patrick, look, we pray,
>   On thine own Church and steeple;
> Convert thy Dean, on this great day;
>   Or else God help the people.

The violence of the Whig attack on Swift, as a turncoat, an obscene and irreverent clergyman, a party scribbler and hireling, suggests how effective he had been as a political journalist. Even in parliament he was denounced — as "a divine hardly suspected of being a Christian, but in a fair way of being a bishop." Now as a dignitary of the Church he was to continue in the realm of controversy. As he took up his decanal duties in 1714, he was confronted with formidable opposition from politically inclined members of the cathedral and from the influential Archbishop of Dublin, William King, a staunch Whig with whom Swift fought fiercely at times but with whom he also joined on occasions in defense of the Church and of Ireland. No small part of his energies in the two decades following 1714 went into struggles for the welfare of the Anglican Establishment in Ireland. He was one

of the few who had the courage to fight the powerful bishops when
they endeavored to take advantage of the lower clergy. He was a
leader of the clergy in their perpetual economic warfare with laymen
who resisted payment of tithes or unscrupulously benefited from
church lands; and he kept close watch over the Irish parliament, to
prevent legislation unfavorable to the vulnerable clergy. This phase
of his career is well exhibited in his church tracts, so little read in
modern times because they are concerned with outmoded matters,
though they were of vast importance to his age. His greatness as a
churchman, universally acknowledged, does not derive from defense
of theological doctrine. This was not his métier. He was, all the
evidence shows, a man of deep and untroubled faith, who thought
it folly to enter into controversies about the infallible doctrines of
Christianity. His efforts were directed instead to the support of the
privileged position of the Anglican religion and of its temporal prosperity, so necessary in his eyes if a reasonable and moderate Christianity was to survive. The threats as he conceived them were social,
economic, religious, and political, and both from within and without
the Church. He combatted them where he could, often with notable
success. But in this sphere, as elsewhere, he had many moments of
despair and pessimism. As he approached his seventieth year he wrote
gloomily, "I have long given up all hopes of Church or Christianity."

The debility of the Church was matched by the debility of the
Irish economy; and Swift's struggle for the Anglican Establishment
was paralleled by his endeavors in behalf of the impoverished, oppressed nation. For the first few years after his return to Ireland
in 1714, sunken in spirits and weighed down with other matters, he
did not play a vital part in public affairs. The events in England subsequent to the fall of the Harley cabinet were hardly to be borne. Harley was imprisoned; Bolingbroke, accused of Jacobite intrigue, fled
to France; other friends were dispersed or out of power, and Swift
himself was under suspicion. His mail was intercepted, and he was
in danger of being brought to England to testify, perhaps to stand trial.
These events, which Swift later wove into the political allegory in
Gulliver's Travels, resulted from the determination of the Whigs,
restored to power by the accession of George I, to punish those who
had thrown away the fruits of Marlborough's victories on the Continent by making peace with France. Swift, as journalist for the
Harley ministry, had defended the peace, attacked Marlborough, and
made himself obnoxious to the Whigs. Fortunately the turbulent
feelings calmed down. The disquieting personal threat he faced with
courage and dignity, but the situation in England from 1714 to 1717,
added to the atmosphere of political hostility in Ireland, tended to
immobilize him. By 1718 his spirits had revived and he was beginning

to concern himself with (in his own phrase) "the wretched condition of Ireland." For two decades thereafter he produced what we now call the Irish tracts, addressed frequently to England as well as to Ireland. The materials of these are economic, political, broadly social, but many of them are not mere documents of the times. They are transformed by greatness of style, irony, wit, and anguish of spirit. One of them, *A Modest Proposal*, is with justice acclaimed the greatest short satire in the language. Perhaps in this brief work best of all we can see how appropriate was his use of the phrase, the lacerated heart. Here, underneath the irony, one finds anger, indignation, and humanity — qualities that generated and gave force to his pessimism. In the years following 1719, when he was writing *Gulliver's Travels*, he was also producing some of these lesser works quite consonant in spirit with his great masterpiece, similarly bitter and despairing. England's opprobrious treatment of Ireland he brought under scathing attack, for example, in the first of the Irish tracts, *A Proposal for the Universal Use of Irish Manufacture* (1720), a plea to the people of Ireland to attempt a measure of economic self sufficiency. The same motive in part animated *The Drapier's Letters* (1724), where he combatted the notion that Ireland was merely a colony of England, existing for the profit of the mother country. He appraised with a clear vision the cold mercantilism of the times by which Ireland's powerful neighbor restricted the trade and agriculture of the hapless Irish. At the same time he lashed the people of Ireland — the absentees for draining the wealth of the country, the tradesmen for dishonesty, the nobility for indifference, the strolling beggars for sloth, the men and women of fashion for shortsighted indulgences. Not surprisingly, the language of these tracts is sometimes that of despair, hopelessness, and disillusionment, yet it is notable that he persisted to the end of his active life in his efforts to achieve reforms and relieve the people of Ireland. Here was no withdrawal to nurse cynical indifference or misanthropy. The emotional coloring and strong rhetoric of the Irish tracts are appropriate to the purpose in hand, quite proper from a reformer bent on seeing maladjustments corrected and human weakness moderated. Swift's clerical profession, his position as dean and dignitary, not only gave him the opportunity, it imposed upon him the obligation to take cognizance of public and private distress. This duty he never scanted, either as a private citizen willingly using his own money or as a public figure with the prestige of his office. It was thus that he became an embodiment of the voice and conscience of Ireland, and was popularly hailed as the Hibernian Patriot. Yeats would have it that Swift's heart "dragged him down into mankind," by which he means (I suppose) that Swift had a compulsion to express his humanity by sharing man's agonies. This suggests what one cannot miss in reading the Irish tracts, their remarkable kinship to *Gulliver's Travels*. Although these lesser works are lamentations over one hapless country, directed at specific evils in the social and economic order, we are always left with a strong sense that basically the troubles derive from the irrational nature of man — his ill use, in the language of *Gulliver's Travels*, of that "small pittance" of reason which has fallen to him "to aggravate [his] *natural* corruptions, and to acquire new ones which Nature had not given [him]."

The many external facts of Swift's career which help to explain his pessimism are not to be divorced from the intellectual currents of his time, certain philosophical and theological influences, which may have shaped his conception of man and the world. It would seem reasonable, for example, to expect that his thinking as a Christian divine might have a strong influence. Were there elements in the traditional Christian view of the nature of man, or its modifications, from which his pessimism was partially derived, or which reinforced it? We get a clue that this approach may be fruitful from the words of Swift's relative and biographer, Deane Swift, who wrote that the Christian conception of the evil nature of man appears to be "the groundwork of the whole satire contained in the voyage to the Houyhnhnms." This is indeed a far cry from the view that the Fourth Voyage grew out of Swift's malignity, personal bitterness, or madness. "Dr. Swift," Deane Swift added, "was not the first preacher whose writings import this kind of philosophy." Deane Swift could easily have pointed to scores of clergymen in the seventeenth and eighteenth centuries who, like their predecessors, expatiated on the corruption of human nature. If they recognized the existence of a divine spark, they seldom forgot that other aspect of man — and in a rhetoric every bit as harsh as Swift's. That mild Anglican, Jeremy Taylor, could remark, "What is man but a vessel of dung, a stink of corruption, and by birth, a slave to the devil" — a remark that his listeners would accept acquiescently as not in the least misanthropic and nothing more than a conventional homiletic reflection on the depravity of man. Even in the "benevolent" Christianity of the early eighteenth century this language did not disappear; and Jeremy Taylor's gnomic description of man in its theological context is a parallel for Gulliver's equally gnomic description — "a lump of deformity and diseases both in body and mind" — in its ethical context. This is that violent rhetoric of denunciation which in its line of descent can be traced back to the medieval preachers as they described proud, lecherous, gluttonous man, a traditional anathematism; and as such it remained a vital element in Christian homiletic literature.

Swift probably would have thought an optimistic divine a contradiction in terms; and his own pessimism is at least consonant with the pessimism at the heart of Christianity. One of his sermons begins:

> The holy Scripture is full of expressions to set forth the miserable condition of man during the whole progress of his life; his weakness, pride, and vanity; his unmeasurable desires, and perpetual disappointments; the prevalence of his passions, and the corruptions of his reason; his deluding hopes . . .; his natural and artificial wants; his cares and anxieties; the diseases of his body, and the diseases of his mind; the shortness of his life; his dread of a future state, with his carelessness to prepare for it: and the wise men of all ages have made the same reflections.

If Swift had written his own comment on *Gulliver's Travels*, he might well have used the words of this sermon. That great work is obviously concerned to set forth the miserable condition of man, his weakness, pride, and vanity, his unmeasurable desires, the prevalency of his passions, the corruption of his reason, and so on through the catalogue. Some of Swift's surviving sermons, as well as those of his fellow divines, could easily be used to annotate *Gulliver's Travels*. It seems clear that there is an affinity between this work and many of the quite conventional sermons on depraved human nature and the evils of this life. The satirist and the divine tend to merge, or at the very least to come together in striking compatibility as they envisage man. If Swift sounds like those whose emphasis on man's depravity derives from Augustinian and Calvinistic roots, this is a result of the intensity of his attack and his extreme rhetoric and not, it must be firmly stated, the result of his agreement with the doctrines which buttressed the Augustinian view or the Calvinistic restatement of it. He felt too keenly man's moral responsibility, and would have been embarrassed, had he been alive at mid-century, to hear John Wesley approve his conception of man's corruption. Soon after the publication of *Gulliver's Travels*, a Dublin essayist, commenting on the theme of human corruption, complained that it had been preached upon to the point of exhaustion, yet continues to be "a darling theme [among] great numbers of grave and orthodox divines." They hold the doctrine of man's depravity, he added, to be of the utmost importance in religion, and belief in it "absolutely necessary to denominate a man a good Christian."

Swift's sermons indicate that he was one of these "grave and orthodox divines" who reaffirmed the taint in man's nature as a cardinal principle of Christian theology. He reaffirmed it all the more strongly because, it may be, he scented heresy in the air; or, if heresy is too extreme a term, he felt uneasily a threat to Christianity in a host of writers who were showing only "the fair side of human nature in Adam's posterity" and asserting man's natural goodness. A moderated Pelagianism was current, a heresy which St. Augustine had combatted in the 5th century A.D., draining the doctrine of original sin of its full efficacy and, as a consequence, weakening the doctrines of redemption and grace. Article IX of the Anglican Church, on original sin, formally signified the "infection of nature" in man and referred to the vain talk of Pelagians. But there were "mighty softeners" (Deane Swift's phrase) of this doctrine in Swift's day, John Locke, for example, who denied, without raising much serious protest, that the fall of Adam implied the corruption of human nature in Adam's posterity (*The Reasonableness of Christianity*, 1695). Theologians joined with others in panegyrics on human nature, in showing it "in its proper dignity" and affirming man's natural goodness, an aspect of that current of thought which we now label "sentimentalism." In two of his sermons, *On the Testimony of the Conscience* and *Upon the Excellence of Christianity*, Swift considers those who express this theory of human nature. He finds their views both false and dangerous, false in that they minimize the powerful defect in man's will, dangerous in that they reflect an "undue conceit of human sufficiency." To the extent that they endow man, they take away from God. They tend towards a secular ethics, a freeing of man from the restraints of a religious conscience which alone can ensure right behavior since, as he maintains, "there is no other tie [other than religion] thro' which the pride, or lust, or avarice, or ambition of mankind will not certainly break at one time or other." Thus Swift topples over "these mighty softeners" of man's corrupt nature — the sentimental proponents of "benevolent" man, the neo-stoics who hypothesized a proud, magnanimous man sufficient unto himself, the theorists who had created "the man of honor" and the "mere moral man" with a capacity for virtue for virtue's own sake, and the deists with their rational man. By contrast Swift depicts man as he is, a creature of passions, pride, and self-love, a frail and sinful being in need of redemption and anything but self-sufficient or inclined by his nature to virtue.

Even though the view of man as formulated in *Gulliver's Travels* may have received both coloring and substance from the currents of traditional Christian thought, we are obviously not to conceive of the work as a religious tract or as concerned with doctrine. *Gulliver's Travels* is secular, an exploration of man's social and moral nature in non-theological terms, done in the allegorical mode and embedded in fantasy. Nevertheless we may reasonably suppose that Swift's thinking as a divine had a yeasty influence, however difficult it is to define that influence precisely or indicate its full extent. It seems to go beyond the obvious use of the traditional symbols of sin — that is, those figures and images of the flesh which he utilizes in describing the Yahoos. The noisome putridity of these creatures, their envelopment in stench and dungy vileness, is, of course, emblematic of their moral natures. Swift has employed an old device abundant in Christian literature (though not only there) — the metaphorical association of physical corruption with moral corruption. And it is this same device which has disturbed many critics in their reading of his anti-sentimental, anti-Petrarchan poems, those few scatalogical verses out of several hundred he composed, such as *A Beautiful Young Nymph Going to Bed, The Lady's Dressing Room,* and *Strephon and Chloe.* Here indeed he has employed an extreme naturalistic language, occasional flashes of which we find also in *Gulliver's Travels.* Our more fastidious age has found these unwholesome, an "obsessive . . . preoccupation" one critic has said, "with the visceral and excrementitious"; and another, after peeping into the depths of Swift's subconscious, has endowed him with "an excremental vision" — an explanation that needs an explanation. The language itself might well have seemed to an eighteenth-century reader not excessively shocking. Taboo words go in and out of fashion. Words concerned with bodily functions, dirt, disease, squalor in general, jarred the sensibilities less in Swift's day, as did the facts they described. But apart from the mere uninhibited language he uses, the privilege of any satirist, Swift reflects traditional views in these scatalogical poems. Their staple is woman as the embodiment of vice, her hypocrisy, her deceptiveness, her filthiness beneath a fair exterior. The tradition is both classical and Christian. The Latin satirist Juvenal (of the Sixth satire) and a medieval church father descanting on womankind as the devil incarnate tend to sound alike on this subject; and Swift sounds like both of them. There are as well other, more purely literary traditions to which Swift strongly reacted, "the high raptures and romantic flights" of pastoral writers and Petrarchan sonneteers, for example. The difficulty of disentangling the traditions is clear enough, but both overtly and implicitly Swift reflects a basic religious idea, the dichotomy of body and soul, and the implications which flow from this idea. The romantic glorification of what, after all, is only flesh and blood, the exaltation of values concerned with the body, exterior beauty — his corrosive attack on this way of thinking has a strong ethical intention such as we find enduringly in homiletic literature. How base it is, said a contemporary preacher, "to serve an Idol of flesh and blood; a paunch of guts, that's full of filth and excrements within, and the skin itself, the cleanest part, is ashamed to be uncovered." Are this clergyman and Swift coprophilous, as the psychoanalyst would have it? Or are they concerned with a vital and perennial notion about the dual nature of man?

The difficulty in separating the strands of influence is further complicated by the prevalence in contemporary thought of a libertine strain in which the denigration of human nature was no less severe than that of the divines in their Augustinian and Calvinistic moods. This vilification of man in "modish French authors" and in "loose and profligate writers" in England was uncomfortably close in language, however different in purpose, to the language of "grave and orthodox divines." When Addison, in *The Tatler*, No. 108, praised the ancient moralists for exhibiting the "natural grandeur" of man, he contrasts them with those recent writers who basely depreciate human nature, such as La Rochefoucauld, the celebrated author of the *Maximes*, who does not distinguish, so Addison complained, between "the species of men and brutes." Swift, on the other hand, pays a tribute to La Rochefoucauld at the opening of the *Verses on the Death of Dr. Swift* (1731):

> As Rochefoucault his maxims drew
> From nature, I believe 'em true:
> They argue no corrupted mind
> In him; the fault is in mankind.

Even more significant, as *Gulliver's Travels* was nearing completion in 1725, Pope's announced intention of writing maxims in opposition to La Rochefoucauld found no favor in Swift's eyes. Rochefoucauld, he wrote to Pope, "is my favorite, because I found my whole character in him." Here then is another current of thought, stressing man's egoistic and subrational nature, reflected most baldly in such widely read writers as La Rochefoucauld, Bayle, Rochester, Hobbes, and Mandeville, which merits consideration as a formative influence on Swift. This *libertin* appraisal of human nature existed in a worldly and secular context quite opposed in spirit and intention to the orthodox Christian conception, which was concerned with man's ultimate salvation. Both served Swift's satiric purposes. That he was disturbed by the contradiction in spirit between the two views or felt the need to reconcile them is not evident. This need not surprise us, as it would not surprise him, who wrote: "How inconsistent is man with himself!"

Finally, it may help us to assess Swift more competently if we rob him of a little of his uniqueness (though not of his literary greatness) in viewing the age. Envision him as one of a collective body of eighteenth-century Jeremiahs whose lamentations were filling the air. The Tory wits, as Professor Louis Bredvold has so persuasively shown in his excellent essay, "The Gloom of the Tory Satirists," reflected, even generated, their fair share of the gloom-thickened atmosphere of the period of Queen Anne and the first Georges. But in this limited respect there was nothing singular, except their talents, about Swift and his friends — Pope, Gay, Prior, Arbuthnot, and

Parnell. "We are doomed to be undone," wrote Bishop George Berkeley in 1721, in his tract significantly titled, *An Essay towards Preventing the Ruin of Great Britain*, one of numerous dark pictures of the character and destiny of the British. Many looked about and saw widely prevailing infection, a culture losing its vigor and its better values, under the impact of bribery, luxury, political faction, deteriorated education, an immoral stage, ostentatious fashions, a dissolute and slothful poor, an irresponsible aristocracy, loss of public spirit, imitation of French and Italian fopperies, the vulgarization of the arts, and a dozen other such evils. But only a person of the rarest gifts, such as Swift, could transmute these into an imperishable imaginative comment on the nature of man and society.

A CHRONOLOGICAL TABLE

Swift born in Dublin of English parents	Nov. 30, 1667
Attended Kilkenny Grammar School	c. 1673–1682
Esther Johnson [Stella] born	Mar. 13, 1681
Swift entered Trinity College, Dublin	April 24, 1682
B. A. degree, *speciali gratia.* Continued at Trinity College, Dublin	Feb. 15, 1686
Left Ireland for England as a result of troubles incident to the fall of James II. Lived with his mother	1688 or early in 1689
Entered household of Sir William Temple. Probably first acquaintance with Stella.	1689
Returned to Ireland	May, 1690
Returned to England (August) and to Temple in Moor Park. Early poems, 1690–93	Dec. (?), 1691
M. A. degree, Hart Hall, University of Oxford	July 5, 1692
Ordained in Ireland: (1) Deacon and	Oct. 28, 1694
(2) Priest	Jan. 13, 1695
Appointed to the prebend of Kilroot, near Belfast, (Jan. 28) and began to reside in Kilroot	March, 1695
Returned to Moor Park. (Temple's death, 1699)	1696
Domestic chaplain to Lord Berkeley (Lord Justice of Ireland) in Dublin	Summer, 1699
Presented to livings of Laracor and two other country parishes	Feb. 1700
Installed prebendary of St. Patrick's Cathedral, Dublin	Oct. 22, 1700
To England with Lord Berkeley. Soon published first political tract, in defence of impeached Whig statesmen, *Contests and Dissensions . . . in Athens and Rome*	April, 1701
Doctor of Divinity degree, Trinity College, Dublin	Feb. 1702
A Tale of a Tub and *The Battle of the Books* published	1704
Emissary of Church of Ireland to seek remission of First Fruits from Queen Anne. Resident in London. Wrote tracts on church and state, including *Argument Against Abolishing Christianity* (pub. 1711). Published *Bickerstaff Papers.* Failed to win support of Whig cabinet for his mission or to win preferment in the Church. Returned to Ireland, June, 1709	Nov., 1707– May, 1709
To England again seeking remission of First Fruits.	Sept. 1710
Journal to Stella. Letters to Esther Johnson in Ireland begin, to continue until June, 1713	Sept. 1710

Swift met Robert Harley, head of Queen Anne's new   Oct. 4, 1710
ministry (Tory). Harley supports his project. Swift
joined Tories, became editor of *The Examiner* (Nov.
2, 1710), a Tory journal.

Active as political journalist. Wrote poems and tracts   1710–14
in support of the Tory ministry. Attacked Marlborough and other Whigs. Friendship with Addison
and Steele cools. Friendship with Gay, Pope, Congreve, Arbuthnot, and Esther Vanhomrigh (Vanessa)
developed.

Installed as Dean of St. Patrick's Cathedral, Dublin.   June 13, 1713
Returned to London, Sept. 9, 1713

Returned to Ireland to take up duties as Dean after   Sept. 1714
the fall of the Harley cabinet (July) and death of
Anne (Aug. 1, 1714).

Ill-founded rumors report his marriage to Stella   1716

Published *A Proposal for the Universal Use of Irish*   1720
Manufacture, first of the significant Irish tracts

The Drapier's Letters. Swift became the Hibernian   1724
Patriot. Reward offered by English authorities for
the discovery of the Drapier

Visited England. Stayed with Pope at Twickenham   March–Aug.,
(summer)   1726

Discussed Irish problems with Sir Robert Walpole, Lord   April 27, 1726
Treasurer, to no avail

Cadenus and Vanessa published. This poem tells of the   May, 1726
relationship between Swift and Esther Vanhomrigh,
who had died June 2, 1723.

Gulliver's Travels published in London soon after Swift   Oct. 28, 1726
returned to Ireland

Last visit to England (April–Sept.)   1727

Death of Stella   Jan. 28, 1728

Conducts *The Intelligencer*, with Sheridan   1728

A Modest Proposal published   1729

Verses on the Death of Dr. Swift composed (pub. 1739)   1731

Wrote *The Legion Club*, a violent attack on the Irish   1736
House of Commons

Found to be "of unsound mind and memory"   Aug. 17, 1742

Death. Buried in St. Patrick's Cathedral, Oct. 22. Left   Oct. 19, 1745
the greater part of his estate for the founding of a
hospital for the insane

TRAVELS

INTO SEVERAL

Remote NATIONS

OF THE

WORLD.

In FOUR PARTS.

By *LEMUEL GULLIVER*,
First a Surgeon, and then a Captain of several SHIPS.

VOL. I.

LONDON:

Printed for Benj. Motte, *at the*
Middle Temple-Gate *in* Fleet-street.
MDCCXXVI.

Title-page of the First Edition, 1726

A LETTER FROM CAPT. GULLIVER
TO HIS COUSIN SYMPSON.

I hope you will be ready to own publicly, whenever you shall be called to it, that by your great and frequent urgency you prevailed on me to publish a very loose and uncorrect account of my travels; with direction to hire some young gentlemen of either university to put them in order, and correct the style, as my cousin Dampier did by my advice, in his book called *A Voyage round the World*. But I do not remember I gave you power to consent, that any thing should be omitted, and much less that any thing should be inserted: therefore, as to the latter, I do here renounce every thing of that kind; particularly a paragraph about her Majesty the late Queen Anne, of most pious and glorious memory; although I did reverence and esteem her more than any of human species. But you, or your interpolator, ought to have considered, that as it was not my inclination, so was it not decent to praise any animal of our composition before my master Houyhnhnm: and besides, the fact was altogether false; for to my knowledge, being in England during some part of her Majesty's reign, she did govern by a chief minister; nay, even by two successively; the first whereof was the Lord of Godolphin, and the second the Lord of Oxford; so that you have made me *say the thing that was not*. Likewise, in the account of the Academy of Projectors, and several passages of my discourse to my master Houyhnhnm, you have either omitted some material circumstances, or minced or changed them in such a manner, that I do hardly know mine own work. When I formerly hinted to you something of this in a letter, you were pleased to answer, that you were afraid of giving offence; that people in power were very watchful over the press, and apt not only to interpret, but to punish every thing which looked like an *innuendo* (as I think you called it). But pray, how could that which I spoke so many years ago, and at above five thousand leagues distance, in another reign, be applied to any of the yahoos who now are said to govern the herd; especially at a time when I little thought on or feared the unhappiness of living under them? Have not I the most reason to complain, when I see these very yahoos carried by Houyhnhnms in a vehicle, as if these were brutes, and those the rational creatures? And, indeed, to avoid so monstrous and detestable a sight was one principal motive of my retirement hither.

Thus much I thought proper to tell you in relation to your self, and to the trust I reposed in you.

I do in the next place complain of my own great want of judgment, in being prevailed upon by the intreaties and false reasonings of you and some others, very much against mine own opinion, to suffer my travels to be published. Pray bring to your mind how often I desired you to consider, when you insisted on the motive of public good, that the yahoos were a species of animals utterly incapable of amendment by precepts or examples, and so it hath proved; for instead of seeing a full stop put to all abuses and corruptions, at least in this little island, as I had reason to expect: behold, after above six months' warning, I cannot learn that my book hath produced one single effect according to mine intentions: I desired you would let me know by a letter, when party and faction were extinguished; judges learned and upright; pleaders honest and modest, with some tincture of common sense; and Smithfield blazing with pyramids of law-books; the young nobility's education entirely changed; the physicians banished; the female yahoos abounding in virtue, honour, truth and good sense; courts and levees of great ministers thoroughly weeded and swept; wit, merit and learning rewarded; all disgracers of the press in prose and verse condemned to eat nothing but their own cotton, and quench their thirst with their own ink. These, and a thousand other reformations, I firmly counted upon by your encouragement; as indeed they were plainly deducible from the precepts delivered in my book. And, it must be owned, that seven months were a sufficient time to correct every vice and folly to which yahoos are subject, if their natures had been capable of the least disposition to virtue or wisdom; yet so far have you been from answering mine expectation in any of your letters, that on the contrary you are loading our carrier every week with libels, and keys, and reflections, and memoirs, and second parts; wherein I see myself accused of reflecting upon great states-folk; of degrading human nature (for so they have still the confidence to style it), and of abusing the female sex. I find likewise, that the writers of those bundles are not agreed among themselves; for some of them will not allow me to be author of mine own travels; and others make me author of books to which I am wholly a stranger.

I find likewise that your printer hath been so careless as to confound the times, and mistake the dates of my several voyages and returns, neither assigning the true year, or the true month, or day of the month; and I hear the original manuscript is all destroyed since the publication of my book. Neither have I any copy left;

however, I have sent you some corrections, which you may insert if ever there should be a second edition: and yet I cannot stand to them, but shall leave that matter to my judicious and candid readers, to adjust it as they please.

I hear some of our sea-yahoos find fault with my sea-language, as not proper in many parts, nor now in use. I cannot help it. In my first voyages, while I was young, I was instructed by the oldest mariners, and learned to speak as they did. But I have since found that the sea-yahoos are apt, like the land ones, to become new-fangled in their words; which the latter change every year, insomuch as I remember upon each return to mine own country, their old dialect was so altered that I could hardly understand the new. And I observe, when any yahoo comes from London out of curiosity to visit me at mine own house, we neither of us are able to deliver our conceptions in a manner intelligible to the other.

If the censure of yahoos could any way affect me, I should have great reason to complain that some of them are so bold as to think my book of travels a mere fiction out of mine own brain; and have gone so far as to drop hints that the Houyhnhnms and yahoos have no more existence than the inhabitants of Utopia.

Indeed I must confess, that as to the people of Lilliput, Brobdingrag (for so the word should have been spelt, and not erroneously 'Brobdingnag') and Laputa, I have never yet heard of any yahoo so presumptuous as to dispute their being, or the facts I have related concerning them; because the truth immediately strikes every reader with conviction. And is there less probability in my account of the Houyhnhnms or yahoos, when it is manifest as to the latter, there are so many thousands even in this city, who only differ from their brother brutes in Houyhnhnmland, because they use a sort of a jabber, and do not go naked? I wrote for their amendment, and not their approbation. The united praise of the whole race would be of less consequence to me than the neighing of those two degenerate Houyhnhnms I keep in my stable; because from these, degenerate as they are, I still improve in some virtues, without any mixture of vice.

Do these miserable animals presume to think that I am so far degenerated as to defend my veracity? Yahoo as I am, it is well known through all Houyhnhnmland, that by the instructions and example of my illustrious master, I was able in the compass of two years (although I confess with the utmost difficulty) to remove that infernal habit of lying, shuffling, deceiving, and equivocating, so deeply rooted in the very souls of all my species, especially the Europeans.

I have other complaints to make upon this vexatious occasion; but I forbear troubling myself or you any further. I must freely confess, that since my last return some corruptions of my yahoo nature have revived in me by conversing with a few of your species, and particularly those of mine own family, by an unavoidable necessity; else I should never have attempted so absurd a project as that of reforming the yahoo race in this kingdom; but I have now done with all such visionary schemes for ever.

April 2, 1727.

THE PUBLISHER TO THE READER

The author of these *Travels*, Mr. Lemuel Gulliver, is my ancient and intimate friend; there is likewise some relation between us by the mother's side. About three years ago Mr. Gulliver, growing weary of the concourse of curious people coming to him at his house in Redriff, made a small purchase of land, with a convenient house, near Newark in Nottinghamshire, his native country; where he now lives retired, yet in good esteem among his neighbours.

Although Mr. Gulliver was born in Nottinghamshire, where his father dwelt, yet I have heard him say, his family came from Oxfordshire; to confirm which, I have observed in the churchyard at Banbury, in that county, several tombs and monuments of the Gullivers.

Before he quitted Redriff, he left the custody of the following papers in my hands, with the liberty to dispose of them as I should think fit. I have carefully perused them three times: the style is very plain and simple; and the only fault I find is, that the author, after the manner of travellers, is a little too circumstantial. There is an air of truth apparent through the whole; and indeed, the author was so distinguished for his veracity, that it became a sort of proverb among his neighbours at Redriff, when any one affirmed a thing, to say, it was as true as if Mr. Gulliver had spoke it.

By the advice of several worthy persons, to whom, with the author's permission, I communicated these papers, I now venture to send them into the world, hoping they may be at least, for some time, a better entertainment to our young noblemen than the common scribbles of politics and party.

This volume would have been at least twice as large, if I had not made bold to strike out innumerable passages relating to the winds and tides, as well as to the variations and bearings in the several voyages; together with the minute descriptions of the management of the ship in storms, in the style of sailors: likewise the account of the longitudes and latitudes; wherein I have reason to apprehend that Mr. Gulliver may be a little dissatisfied: but I was resolved to fit the work as much as possible to the general capacity of readers. However, if my own ignorance in sea-affairs shall have led me to commit some mistakes, I alone am answerable for them: and if any traveller hath a curiosity to see the whole work at large, as it came from the hand of the author, I will be ready to gratify him.

As for any further particulars relating to the author, the reader will receive satisfaction from the first pages of the book.

RICHARD SYMPSON.

THE
CONTENTS.

PART I.

[A VOYAGE TO LILLIPUT]

9

PART II.

[A VOYAGE TO BROBDINGNAG]

PART III.

[A VOYAGE TO LAPUTA, BALNIBARBI, GLUBBDUBDRIB, LUGGNAGG, AND JAPAN]

PART IV.

[A VOYAGE TO THE COUNTRY OF THE HOUYHNHNMS]

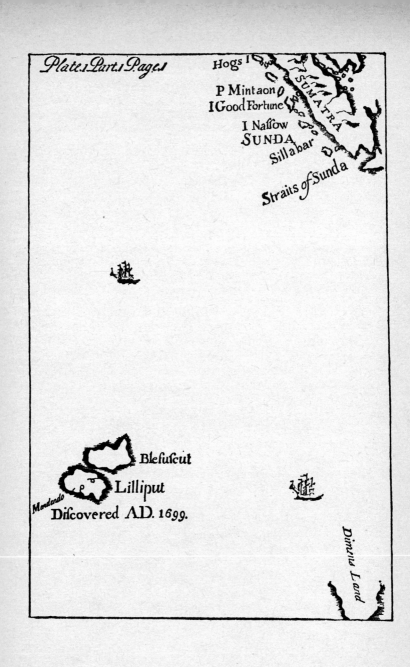

Plate.1 Part.1 Page.1

Hogs I

SUMATRA

P Mintaon
I Good Fortune

I Naſſow
SUNDA
Sillabar

Straits of Sunda

Blefuſcut

Mordendo Lilliput

Discovered A.D. 1699.

Dimrus Land

TRAVELS.

PART I

A VOYAGE TO LILLIPUT.

CHAPTER I.

*The author gives some account of himself and family; his first induce-
ments to travel. He is shipwrecked, and swims for his life, gets
safe on shore in the country of Lilliput, is made a prisoner, and
carried up the country.*

MY father had a small estate in Nottinghamshire; I was the
third of five sons. He sent me to Emanuel College in
Cambridge, at fourteen years old, where I resided three
years, and applied my self close to my studies: but the charge of
maintaining me (although I had a very scanty allowance) being
too great for a narrow fortune, I was bound apprentice to Mr.
James Bates, an eminent surgeon in London, with whom I continued four years; and my father now and then sending me small
sums of money, I laid them out in learning navigation, and other
parts of the mathematics, useful to those who intend to travel, as
I always believed it would be some time or other my fortune to
do. When I left Mr. Bates, I went down to my father; where, by
the assistance of him and my uncle John, and some other relations I got forty pounds, and a promise of thirty pounds a year
to maintain me at Leyden: there I studied physic two years and
seven months, knowing it would be useful in long voyages.

Soon after my return from Leyden, I was recommended, by
my good master Mr. Bates, to be surgeon to the *Swallow*, Captain Abraham Pannell commander; with whom I continued three
years and a half, making a voyage or two into the Levant, and
some other parts. When I came back, I resolved to settle in London, to which Mr. Bates, my master, encouraged me, and by him
I was recommended to several patients. I took part of a small
house in the Old Jury; and being advised to alter my condition,
I married Mrs. Mary Burton, second daughter to Mr. Edmond
Burton hosier in Newgate Street, with whom I received four
hundred pounds for a portion.

But, my good master Bates dying in two years after, and I having few friends, my business began to fail; for my conscience
would not suffer me to imitate the bad practice of too many
among my brethren. Having therefore consulted with my wife,
and some of my acquaintance, I determined to go again to sea.
I was surgeon successively in two ships, and made several voyages, for six years, to the East and West Indies, by which I got
some addition to my fortune. My hours of leisure I spent in
reading the best authors ancient and modern, being always provided with a good number of books; and when I was ashore, in
observing the manners and dispositions of the people, as well as
learning their language, wherein I had a great facility by the
strength of my memory.

The last of these voyages not proving very fortunate, I grew
weary of the sea, and intended to stay at home with my wife and
family. I removed from the Old Jury to Fetter Lane, and from
thence to Wapping, hoping to get business among the sailors; but
it would not turn to account. After three years' expectation that
things would mend, I accepted an advantageous offer from Captain William Prichard, master of the *Antelope*, who was making
a voyage to the South Sea. We set sail from Bristol May 4th,
1699, and our voyage at first was very prosperous.

It would not be proper, for some reasons, to trouble the reader
with the particulars of our adventures in those seas: let it suffice
to inform him, that in our passage from thence to the East Indies
we were driven by a violent storm to the northwest of Van Diemen's Land. By an observation, we found ourselves in the latitude
of 30 degrees 2 minutes south. Twelve of our crew were dead by
immoderate labour, and ill food, the rest were in a very weak
condition. On the fifth of November, which was the beginning
of summer in those parts, the weather being very hazy, the seamen spied a rock, within half a cable's length of the ship; but the
wind was so strong, that we were driven directly upon it, and
immediately split. Six of the crew, of whom I was one, having
let down the boat into the sea, made a shift to get clear of the
ship, and the rock. We rowed by my computation about three
leagues, till we were able to work no longer, being already spent
with labour while we were in the ship. We therefore trusted ourselves to the mercy of the waves, and in about half an hour the
boat was overset by a sudden flurry from the north. What became of my companions in the boat, as well as of those who escaped on the rock, or were left in the vessel, I cannot tell; but
conclude they were all lost. For my own part, I swam as fortune
directed me, and was pushed forward by wind and tide. I often

let my legs drop, and could feel no bottom: but when I was almost gone and able to struggle no longer, I found myself within my depth; and by this time the storm was much abated. The declivity was so small, that I walked near a mile before I got to the shore, which I conjectured was about eight o'clock in the evening. I then advanced forward near half a mile, but could not discover any sign of houses or inhabitants; at least I was in so weak a condition, that I did not observe them. I was extremely tired, and with that, and the heat of the weather, and about half a pint of brandy that I drank as I left the ship, I found myself much inclined to sleep. I lay down on the grass, which was very short and soft, where I slept sounder than ever I remember to have done in my life, and, as I reckoned, above nine hours; for when I awaked, it was just daylight. I attempted to rise, but was not able to stir: for as I happened to lie on my back, I found my arms and legs were strongly fastened on each side to the ground; and my hair, which was long and thick, tied down in the same manner. I likewise felt several slender ligatures across my body, from my armpits to my thighs. I could only look upwards, the sun began to grow hot, and the light offended my eyes. I heard a confused noise about me, but, in the posture I lay, could see nothing except the sky. In a little time I felt something alive moving on my left leg, which advancing gently forward over my breast, came almost up to my chin; when, bending my eyes downwards as much as I could, I perceived it to be a human creature not six inches high, with a bow and arrow in his hands, and a quiver at his back. In the mean time, I felt at least forty more of the same kind (as I conjectured) following the first. I was in the utmost astonishment, and roared so loud, that they all ran back in a fright; and some of them, as I was afterwards told, were hurt with the falls they got by leaping from my sides upon the ground. However, they soon returned, and one of them, who ventured so far as to get a full sight of my face, lifting up his hands and eyes by way of admiration, cried out in a shrill, but distinct voice, *Hekinah degul:* the others repeated the same words several times, but I then knew not what they meant. I lay all this while, as the reader may believe, in great uneasiness: at length, struggling to get loose, I had the fortune to break the strings and wrench out the pegs that fastened my left arm to the ground; for, by lifting it up to my face, I discovered the methods they had taken to bind me; and, at the same time, with a violent pull, which gave me excessive pain, I a little loosened the strings that tied down my hair on the left side, so that I was just able to turn my head about two inches.

But the creatures ran off a second time, before I could seize them; whereupon there was a great shout in a very shrill accent, and after it ceased, I heard one of them cry aloud, *Tolgo phonac*; when in an instant I felt above an hundred arrows discharged on my left hand, which pricked me like so many needles; and besides they shot another flight into the air, as we do bombs in Europe, whereof many, I suppose, fell on my body (though I felt them not) and some on my face, which I immediately covered with my left hand. When this shower of arrows was over, I fell a groaning with grief and pain, and then striving again to get loose, they discharged another volley larger than the first, and some of them attempted with spears to stick me in the sides; but, by good luck, I had on me a buff jerkin, which they could not pierce. I thought it the most prudent method to lie still, and my design was to continue so till night, when, my left hand being already loose, I could easily free myself: and as for the inhabitants, I had reason to believe I might be a match for the greatest armies they could bring against me, if they were all of the same size with him that I saw. But fortune disposed otherwise of me. When the people observed I was quiet, they discharged no more arrows: but by the noise increasing, I knew their numbers were greater; and about four yards from me, over-against my right ear, I heard a knocking for above an hour, like people at work; when, turning my head that way, as well as the pegs and strings would permit me, I saw a stage erected about a foot and a half from the ground, capable of holding four of the inhabitants, with two or three ladders to mount it: from whence one of them, who seemed to be a person of quality, made me a long speech, whereof I understood not one syllable. But I should have mentioned, that before the principal person began his oration, he cried out three times, *Langro dehul san*: (these words and the former were afterwards repeated and explained to me). Whereupon immediately about fifty of the inhabitants came, and cut the strings that fastened the left side of my head, which gave me the liberty of turning it to the right, and of observing the person and gesture of him who was to speak. He appeared to be of a middle age, and taller than any of the other three who attended him, whereof one was a page who held up his train, and seemed to be somewhat longer than my middle finger; the other two stood one on each side to support him. He acted every part of an orator, and I could observe many periods of threatenings, and others of promises, pity and kindness. I answered in a few words, but in the most submissive manner, lifting up my left hand and both eyes to the sun, as calling him for a witness; and being almost

famished with hunger, having not eaten a morsel for some hours
before I left the ship, I found the demands of nature so strong
upon me, that I could not forbear showing my impatience (perhaps against the strict rules of decency) by putting my finger
frequently on my mouth, to signify that I wanted food. The
Hurgo (for so they call a great lord, as I afterwards learnt)
understood me very well. He descended from the stage, and
commanded that several ladders should be applied to my sides,
on which above an hundred of the inhabitants mounted, and
walked towards my mouth, laden with baskets full of meat,
which had been provided and sent thither by the King's orders
upon the first intelligence he received of me. I observed there
was the flesh of several animals, but could not distinguish them
by the taste. There were shoulders, legs and loins shaped like
those of mutton, and very well dressed, but smaller than the
wings of a lark. I eat them by two or three at a mouthful, and
took three loaves at a time, about the bigness of musket bullets.
They supplied me as fast as they could, showing a thousand
marks of wonder and astonishment at my bulk and appetite. I
then made another sign that I wanted drink. They found by my
eating that a small quantity would not suffice me, and being a
most ingenious people, they slung up with great dexterity one of
their largest hogsheads, then rolled it towards my hand, and beat
out the top; I drank it off at a draught, which I might well do, for
it hardly held half a pint, and tasted like a small wine of Burgundy, but much more delicious. They brought me a second
hogshead, which I drank in the same manner, and made signs for
more, but they had none to give me. When I had performed
these wonders, they shouted for joy, and danced upon my breast,
repeating several times as they did at first, *Hekinah degul.* They
made me a sign that I should throw down the two hogsheads,
but first warned the people below to stand out of the way, crying
aloud, *Borach mivola*, and when they saw the vessels in the air,
there was an universal shout of *Hekinah degul.* I confess I was
often tempted, while they were passing backwards and forwards
on my body, to seize forty or fifty of the first that came in my
reach, and dash them against the ground. But the remembrance
of what I had felt, which probably might not be the worst they
could do, and the promise of honour I made them, for so I interpreted my submissive behaviour, soon drove out those imaginations. Besides, I now considered my self as bound by the laws
of hospitality to a people who had treated me with so much expense and magnificence. However, in my thoughts I could not
sufficiently wonder at the intrepidity of these diminutive mortals,

who durst venture to mount and walk on my body, while one of my hands was at liberty, without trembling at the very sight of so prodigious a creature as I must appear to them. After some time, when they observed that I made no more demands for meat, there appeared before me a person of high rank from his Imperial Majesty. His Excellency, having mounted on the small of my right leg, advanced forwards up to my face, with about a dozen of his retinue. And producing his credentials under the Signet Royal, which he applied close to my eyes, spoke about ten minutes, without any signs of anger, but with a kind of determinate resolution; often pointing forwards, which, as I afterwards found, was towards the capital city, about half a mile distant, whither it was agreed by his Majesty in council that I must be conveyed. I answered in few words, but to no purpose, and made a sign with my hand that was loose, putting it to the other (but over his Excellency's head, for fear of hurting him or his train) and then to my own head and body, to signify that I desired my liberty. It appeared that he understood me well enough, for he shook his head by way of disapprobation, and held his hand in a posture to show that I must be carried as a prisoner. However, he made other signs to let me understand that I should have meat and drink enough, and very good treatment. Whereupon I once more thought of attempting to break my bonds, but again, when I felt the smart of their arrows upon my face and hands, which were all in blisters, and many of the darts still sticking in them, and observing likewise that the number of my enemies encreased, I gave tokens to let them know that they might do with me what they pleased. Upon this the *Hurgo* and his train withdrew with much civility and cheerful countenances. Soon after I heard a general shout, with frequent repetitions of the words, *Peplom selan*, and I felt great numbers of the people on my left side relaxing the cords to such a degree, that I was able to turn upon my right, and to ease myself with making water; which I very plentifully did, to the great astonishment of the people, who conjecturing by my motions what I was going to do, immediately opened to the right and left on that side to avoid the torrent which fell with such noise and violence from me. But before this, they had daubed my face and both my hands with a sort of ointment very pleasant to the smell, which in a few minutes removed all the smart of their arrows. These circumstances, added to the refreshment I had received by their victuals and drink, which were very nourishing, disposed me to sleep. I slept about eight hours, as I was afterwards assured; and it was no wonder, for the physicians, by the Emperor's order, had mingled a sleeping potion in the hogsheads of wine.

It seems that upon the first moment I was discovered sleeping on the ground after my landing, the Emperor had early notice of it by an express, and determined in council that I should be tied in the manner I have related (which was done in the night while I slept), that plenty of meat and drink should be sent me, and a machine prepared to carry me to the capital city.

This resolution perhaps may appear very bold and dangerous, and I am confident would not be imitated by any prince in Europe on the like occasion; however, in my opinion, it was extremely prudent as well as generous. For supposing these people had endeavoured to kill me with their spears and arrows while I was asleep, I should certainly have awaked with the first sense of smart, which might so far have roused my rage and strength, as to enable me to break the strings wherewith I was tied; after which, as they were not able to make resistance, so they could expect no mercy.

These people are most excellent mathematicians, and arrived to a great perfection in mechanics by the countenance and encouragement of the Emperor, who is a renowned patron of learning. This prince hath several machines fixed on wheels for the carriage of trees and other great weights. He often builds his largest men of war, whereof some are nine foot long, in the woods where the timber grows, and has them carried on these engines three or four hundred yards to the sea. Five hundred carpenters and engineers were immediately set at work to prepare the greatest engine they had. It was a frame of wood raised three inches from the ground, about seven foot long and four wide, moving upon twenty-two wheels. The shout I heard was upon the arrival of this engine, which it seems set out in four hours after my landing. It was brought parallel to me as I lay. But the principal difficulty was to raise and place me in this vehicle. Eighty poles, each of one foot high, were erected for this purpose, and very strong cords of the bigness of packthread were fastened by hooks to many bandages, which the workmen had girt round my neck, my hands, my body, and my legs. Nine hundred of the strongest men were employed to draw up these cords by many pulleys fastened on the poles, and thus, in less than three hours, I was raised and slung into the engine, and there tied fast. All this I was told, for while the whole operation was performing, I lay in a profound sleep, by the force of that soporiferous medicine infused into my liquor. Fifteen hundred of the Emperor's largest horses, each about four inches and a half high,

were employed to draw me towards the metropolis, which, as I
said, was half a mile distant.

About four hours after we began our journey, I awaked by a
very ridiculous accident; for, the carriage being stopped a while
to adjust something that was out of order, two or three of the
young natives had the curiosity to see how I looked when I was
asleep; they climbed up into the engine, and advancing very
softly to my face, one of them, an officer in the guards, put the
sharp end of his half-pike a good way up into my left nostril,
which tickled my nose like a straw, and made me sneeze violently: whereupon they stole off unperceived, and it was three
weeks before I knew the cause of my awaking so suddenly. We
made a long march the remaining part of the day, and rested at
night with five hundred guards on each side of me, half with
torches, and half with bows and arrows, ready to shoot me if I
should offer to stir. The next morning at sunrise we continued
our march, and arrived within two hundred yards of the city
gates about noon. The Emperor and all his court came out to
meet us, but his great officers would by no means suffer his
Majesty to endanger his person by mounting on my body.

At the place where the carriage stopped, there stood an ancient
temple, esteemed to be the largest in the whole kingdom, which
having been polluted some years before by an unnatural murder,
was, according to the zeal of those people, looked on as profane,
and therefore had been applied to common use, and all the ornaments and furniture carried away. In this edifice it was determined I should lodge. The great gate fronting to the north was
about four foot high, and almost two foot wide, through which
I could easily creep. On each side of the gate was a small window not above six inches from the ground: into that on the left
side, the King's smiths conveyed fourscore and eleven chains,
like those that hang to a lady's watch in Europe, and almost as
large, which were locked to my left leg with six and thirty pad-
locks. Over against this temple, on the other side of the great
highway, at twenty foot distance, there was a turret at least five
foot high. Here the Emperor ascended with many principal
lords of his court, to have an opportunity of viewing me, as I
was told, for I could not see them. It was reckoned that above
an hundred thousand inhabitants came out of the town upon the
same errand; and in spite of my guards, I believe there could not
be fewer than ten thousand, at several times, who mounted upon
my body by the help of ladders. But a proclamation was soon
issued to forbid it upon pain of death. When the workmen found
it was impossible for me to break loose, they cut all the strings

that bound me; whereupon I rose up with as melancholy a disposition as ever I had in my life. But the noise and astonishment of the people at seeing me rise and walk are not to be expressed. The chains that held my left leg were about two yards long, and gave me not only the liberty of walking backwards and forwards in a semicircle; but, being fixed within four inches of the gate, allowed me to creep in, and lie at my full length in the temple.

CHAPTER II.

The Emperor of Lilliput, attended by several of the nobility, comes to see the author in his confinement. The Emperor's person and habit described. Learned men appointed to teach the author their language. He gains favour by his mild disposition. His pockets are searched, and his sword and pistols taken from him.

When I found myself on my feet, I looked about me, and must confess I never beheld a more entertaining prospect. The country round appeared like a continued garden, and the inclosed fields, which were generally forty foot square, resembled so many beds of flowers. These fields were intermingled with woods of half a stang, and the tallest trees, as I could judge, appeared to be seven foot high. I viewed the town on my left hand, which looked like the painted scene of a city in a theatre.

I had been for some hours extremely pressed by the necessities of nature; which was no wonder, it being almost two days since I had last disburthened myself. I was under great difficulties between urgency and shame. The best expedient I could think on, was to creep into my house, which I accordingly did; and shutting the gate after me, I went as far as the length of my chain would suffer, and discharged my body of that uneasy load. But this was the only time I was ever guilty of so uncleanly an action; for which I cannot but hope the candid reader will give some allowance, after he hath maturely and impartially considered my case, and the distress I was in. From this time my constant practice was, as soon as I rose, to perform that business in open air, at the full extent of my chain, and due care was taken every morning before company came, that the offensive matter should be carried off in wheelbarrows by two servants appointed for that purpose. I would not have dwelt so long upon a circumstance, that perhaps at first sight may appear not very momentous, if I had not thought it necessary to justify my character in point of cleanliness to the world; which I am told some of my maligners have been pleased, upon this and other occasions, to call in question.

When this adventure was at an end, I came back out of my house, having occasion for fresh air. The Emperor was already descended from the tower, and advancing on horseback towards me, which had like to have cost him dear; for the beast, although very well trained, yet wholly unused to such a sight, which appeared as if a mountain moved before him, reared up on his hinder feet: but that prince, who is an excellent horseman, kept his seat, until his attendants ran in, and held the bridle, while his Majesty had time to dismount. When he alighted, he surveyed me round with great admiration, but kept beyond the length of my chains. He ordered his cooks and butlers, who were already prepared, to give me victuals and drink, which they pushed forward in a sort of vehicles upon wheels until I could reach them. I took these vehicles, and soon emptied them all; twenty of them were filled with meat, and ten with liquor; each of the former afforded me two or three good mouthfuls, and I emptied the liquor of ten vessels, which was contained in earthen vials, into one vehicle, drinking it off at a draught, and so I did with the rest. The Empress, and young princes of the blood, of both sexes, attended by many ladies, sat at some distance in their chairs; but upon the accident that happened to the Emperor's horse, they alighted, and came near his person, which I am now going to describe. He is taller, by almost the breadth of my nail, than any of his court, which alone is enough to strike an awe into the beholders. His features are strong and masculine, with an Austrian lip and arched nose, his complexion olive, his countenance erect, his body and limbs well proportioned, all his motions graceful, and his deportment majestic. He was then past his prime, being twenty-eight years and three quarters old, of which he had reigned about seven, in great felicity, and generally victorious. For the better convenience of beholding him, I lay on my side, so that my face was parallel to his, and he stood but three yards off: however, I have had him since many times in my hand, and therefore cannot be deceived in the description. His dress was very plain and simple, and the fashion of it between the Asiatic and the European; but he had on his head a light helmet of gold, adorned with jewels, and a plume on the crest. He held his sword drawn in his hand, to defend himself, if I should happen to break loose; it was almost three inches long, the hilt and scabbard were gold enriched with diamonds. His voice was shrill, but very clear and articulate, and I could distinctly hear it when I stood up. The ladies and courtiers were all most magnificently clad, so that the spot they stood upon seemed to resemble a petticoat spread on the ground, embroidered with figures of gold and silver. His Imperial Majesty spoke often to me, and I returned answers, but neither of us could understand a syllable. There were several of his priests and lawyers present (as I conjectured by their habits) who were commanded to address themselves to me, and I spoke to them in as many languages as I had the least smattering of, which were High and Low Dutch, Latin, French, Spanish, Italian, and Lingua Franca; but all to no purpose. After about two hours the court retired, and I was left with a strong guard, to prevent the impertinence, and probably the malice of the rabble, who were very impatient to crowd about me as near as they durst, and some of them had the impudence to shoot their arrows at me as I sat on the ground by the door of my house, whereof one very narrowly missed my left eye. But the colonel ordered six of the ringleaders to be seized, and thought no punishment so proper as to deliver them bound into my hands, which some of his soldiers accordingly did, pushing them forwards with the butt-ends of their pikes into my reach; I took them all in my right hand, put five of them into my coat-pocket, and as to the sixth, I made a countenance as if I would eat him alive. The poor man squalled terribly, and the colonel and his officers were in much pain, especially when they saw me take out my penknife: but I soon put them out of fear; for, looking mildly, and immediately cutting the strings he was bound with, I set him gently on the ground, and away he ran; I treated the rest in the same manner, taking them one by one out of my pocket, and I observed both the soldiers and people were highly obliged at this mark of my clemency, which was represented very much to my advantage at court.

Towards night I got with some difficulty into my house, where I lay on the ground, and continued to do so about a fortnight; during which time the Emperor gave orders to have a bed prepared for me. Six hundred beds of the common measure were brought in carriages, and worked up in my house; an hundred and fifty of their beds sewn together made up the breadth and length, and these were four double, which however kept me but very indifferently from the hardness of the floor, that was of smooth stone. By the same computation they provided me with sheets, blankets, and coverlets, tolerable enough for one who had been so long enured to hardships as I.

As the news of my arrival spread through the kingdom, it brought prodigious numbers of rich, idle, and curious people to

see me; so that the villages were almost emptied, and great neglect of tillage and household affairs must have ensued, if his Imperial Majesty had not provided by several proclamations and
orders of state against this inconveniency. He directed that those
who had already beheld me should return home, and not presume to come within fifty yards of my house without licence
from court: whereby the secretaries of state got considerable
fees.

In the mean time, the Emperor held frequent councils to debate what course should be taken with me; and I was afterwards
assured by a particular friend, a person of great quality, who was
as much in the secret as any, that the court was under many difficulties concerning me. They apprehended my breaking loose,
that my diet would be very expensive, and might cause a famine. Sometimes they determined to starve me, or at least to shoot
me in the face and hands with poisoned arrows, which would
soon dispatch me: but again they considered, that the stench of
so large a carcase might produce a plague in the metropolis, and
probably spread through the whole kingdom. In the midst of
these consultations, several officers of the army went to the door
of the great council-chamber; and two of them being admitted,
gave an account of my behaviour to the six criminals above-mentioned, which made so favourable an impression in the breast of
his Majesty and the whole board in my behalf, that an imperial
commission was issued out, obliging all the villages nine hundred
yards round the city to deliver in every morning six beeves,
forty sheep, and other victuals for my sustenance; together with
a proportionable quantity of bread, and wine, and other liquors:
for the due payment of which his Majesty gave assignments upon
his treasury. For this prince lives chiefly upon his own demesnes,
seldom except upon great occasions raising any subsidies upon
his subjects, who are bound to attend him in his wars at their
own expense. An establishment was also made of six hundred
persons to be my domestics, who had board-wages allowed for
their maintenance, and tents built for them very conveniently
on each side of my door. It was likewise ordered, that three hundred tailors should make me a suit of clothes after the fashion of
the country: that six of his Majesty's greatest scholars should be
employed to instruct me in their language: and, lastly, that the
Emperor's horses, and those of the nobility and troops of guards,
should be exercised in my sight, to accustom themselves to me.
All these orders were duly put in execution, and in about three
weeks I made a great progress in learning their language; during
which time the Emperor frequently honoured me with his visits,

and was pleased to assist my masters in teaching me. We began already to converse together in some sort; and the first words I learnt were to express my desire that he would please to give me my liberty, which I every day repeated on my knees. His answer, as I could apprehend was, that this must be a work of time, not to be thought on without the advice of his council, and that first I must *lumos kelmin pesso desmar lon emposo;* that is, swear a peace with him and his kingdom. However, that I should be used with all kindness, and he advised me to acquire, by my patience, and discreet behaviour, the good opinion of himself and his subjects. He desired I would not take it ill, if he gave orders to certain proper officers to search me; for probably I might carry about me several weapons, which must needs be dangerous things, if they answered the bulk of so prodigious a person. I said, his Majesty should be satisfied, for I was ready to strip myself, and turn up my pockets before him. This I delivered part in words, and part in signs. He replied, that by the laws of the kingdom I must be searched by two of his officers; that he knew this could not be done without my consent and assistance; that he had so good an opinion of my generosity and justice, as to trust their persons in my hands: that whatever they took from me should be returned when I left the country, or paid for at the rate which I would set upon them. I took up the two officers in my hands, put them first into my coat-pockets, and then into every other pocket about me, except my two fobs, and another secret pocket which I had no mind should be searched, wherein I had some little necessaries of no consequence to any but myself. In one of my fobs there was a silver watch, and in the other a small quantity of gold in a purse. These gentlemen, having pen, ink and paper about them, made an exact inventory of every thing they saw; and when they had done, desired I would set them down, that they might deliver it to the Emperor. This inventory I afterwards translated into English, and is word for word as follows.

Imprimis, In the right coat-pocket of the Great Man-Mountain (for so I interpret the words *Quinbus Flestrin*) after the strictest search, we found only one great piece of coarse cloth, large enough to be a foot-cloth for your Majesty's chief room of state. In the left pocket, we saw a huge silver chest, with a cover of the same metal, which we the searchers were not able to lift. We desired it should be opened, and one of us, stepping into it, found himself up to the mid leg in a sort of dust, some part whereof, flying up to our faces, set us both a sneezing for several times together. In his right waistcoat-pocket, we found a prodigious

bundle of white thin substances, folded one over another, about
the bigness of three men, tied with a strong cable, and marked
with black figures; which we humbly conceive to be writings,
every letter almost half as large as the palm of our hands. In the
left, there was a sort of engine, from the back of which were extended twenty long poles, resembling the palisados before your
Majesty's court; wherewith we conjecture the Man-Mountain
combs his head, for we did not always trouble him with questions, because we found it a great difficulty to make him understand us. In the large pocket on the right side of his middle
cover (so I translate the word *ranfu-lo*, by which they meant my
breeches) we saw a hollow pillar of iron, about the length of a
man, fastened to a strong piece of timber, larger than the pillar;
and upon one side of the pillar were huge pieces of iron sticking
out, cut into strange figures, which we know not what to make
of. In the left pocket, another engine of the same kind. In the
smaller pocket on the right side, were several round flat pieces of
white and red metal, of different bulk; some of the white, which
seemed to be silver, were so large and heavy, that my comrade
and I could hardly lift them. In the left pocket were two black
pillars irregularly shaped: we could not, without difficulty, reach
the top of them as we stood at the bottom of his pocket. One of
them was covered, and seemed all of a piece: but at the upper end
of the other, there appeared a white round substance, about twice
the bigness of our heads. Within each of these was inclosed a
prodigious plate of steel; which, by our orders, we obliged him
to show us, because we apprehended they might be dangerous
engines. He took them out of their cases, and told us, that in his
own country his practice was to shave his beard with one of
these, and to cut his meat with the other. There were two
pockets which we could not enter: these he called his fobs; they
were two large slits cut into the top of his middle cover, but
squeezed close by the pressure of his belly. Out of the right fob
hung a great silver chain, with a wonderful kind of engine at the
bottom. We directed him to draw out whatever was at the end
of that chain; which appeared to be a globe, half silver, and half
of some transparent metal: for on the transparent side we saw
certain strange figures circularly drawn, and thought we could
touch them, until we found our fingers stopped with that lucid
substance. He put this engine to our ears, which made an inces-
sant noise like that of a watermill. And we conjecture it is either
some unknown animal, or the god that he worships: but we are
more inclined to the latter opinion, because he assured us (if we
understood him right, for he expressed himself very imper-

fectly), that he seldom did any thing without consulting it. He called it his oracle, and said it pointed out the time for every action of his life. From the left fob he took out a net almost large enough for a fisherman, but contrived to open and shut like a purse, and served him for the same use: we found therein several massy pieces of yellow metal, which, if they be of real gold, must be of immense value.

Having thus, in obedience to your Majesty's commands, diligently searched all his pockets, we observed a girdle about his waist made of the hide of some prodigious animal; from which, on the left side, hung a sword of the length of five men, and on the right, a bag or pouch divided into two cells, each cell capable of holding three of your Majesty's subjects. In one of these cells were several globes or balls of a most ponderous metal, about the bigness of our heads, and required a strong hand to lift them: the other cell contained a heap of certain black grains, but of no great bulk or weight, for we could hold above fifty of them in the palms of our hands.

This is an exact inventory of what we found about the body of the Man-Mountain, who used us with great civility, and due respect to your Majesty's commission. Signed and sealed on the fourth day of the eighty-ninth moon of your Majesty's auspicious reign.

CLEFREN FRELOCK, MARSI FRELOCK.

When this inventory was read over to the Emperor, he directed me to deliver up the several particulars. He first called for my scimitar, which I took out, scabbard and all. In the mean time he ordered three thousand of his choicest troops (who then attended him) to surround me at a distance, with their bows and arrows just ready to discharge: but I did not observe it, for my eyes were wholly fixed upon his Majesty. He then desired me to draw my scimitar, which, although it had got some rust by the sea-water, was in most parts exceeding bright. I did so, and immediately all the troops gave a shout between terror and surprise; for the sun shone clear, and the reflection dazzled their eyes as I waved the scimitar to and fro in my hand. His Majesty, who is a most magnanimous prince, was less daunted than I could expect; he ordered me to return it into the scabbard, and cast it on the ground as gently as I could, about six foot from the end of my chain. The next thing he demanded was one of the hollow iron pillars, by which he meant my pocket-pistols. I drew it out, and at his desire, as well as I could, expressed to him the use of it; and charging it only with powder, which by the closeness of my pouch happened to escape wetting in the sea (an inconvenience that all prudent mariners take special care to provide against), I first cautioned the Emperor not to be afraid, and then I let it off in the air. The astonishment here was much greater than at the sight of my scimitar. Hundreds fell down as if they had been struck dead; and even the Emperor, although he stood his ground, could not recover himself in some time. I delivered up both my pistols in the same manner as I had done my scimitar, and then my pouch of powder and bullets; begging him that the former might be kept from the fire, for it would kindle with the smallest spark, and blow up his imperial palace into the air. I likewise delivered up my watch, which the Emperor was very curious to see, and commanded two of his tallest yeomen of the guards to bear it on a pole upon their shoulders, as draymen in England do a barrel of ale. He was amazed at the continual noise it made, and the motion of the minute-hand, which he could easily discern; for their sight is much more acute than ours: he asked the opinions of his learned men about him, which were various and remote, as the reader may well imagine without my repeating; although indeed I could not very perfectly understand them. I then gave up my silver and copper money, my purse with nine large pieces of gold, and some smaller ones; my knife and razor, my comb and silver snuff-box, my handkerchief and journal book. My scimitar, pistols, and pouch, were conveyed in carriages to his Majesty's stores; but the rest of my goods were returned me.

I had, as I before observed, one private pocket which escaped their search, wherein there was a pair of spectacles (which I sometimes use for the weakness of my eyes), a pocket perspective, and several other little conveniences; which, being of no consequence to the Emperor, I did not think my self bound in honour to discover, and I apprehended they might be lost or spoiled if I ventured them out of my possession.

CHAPTER III.

The author diverts the Emperor and his nobility of both sexes in a very uncommon manner. The diversions of the court of Lilliput described. The author hath his liberty granted him upon certain conditions.

My gentleness and good behaviour had gained so far on the Emperor and his court, and indeed upon the army and people in general, that I began to conceive hopes of getting my liberty in a short time. I took all possible methods to cultivate this favourable disposition. The natives came by degrees to be less apprehensive of any danger from me. I would sometimes lie down, and let five or six of them dance on my hand. And at last the boys and girls would venture to come and play at hide and seek in my hair. I had now made a good progress in understanding and speaking their language. The Emperor had a mind one day to entertain me with several of the country shows, wherein they exceed all nations I have known, both for dexterity and magnificence. I was diverted with none so much as that of the rope-dancers, performed upon a slender white thread, extended about two foot, and twelve inches from the ground. Upon which I shall desire liberty, with the reader's patience, to enlarge a little.

This diversion is only practised by those persons who are candidates for great employments, and high favour, at court. They are trained in this art from their youth, and are not always of noble birth, or liberal education. When a great office is vacant either by death or disgrace (which often happens) five or six of those candidates petition the Emperor to entertain his Majesty and the court with a dance on the rope, and whoever jumps the highest without falling, succeeds in the office. Very often the chief ministers themselves are commanded to show their skill, and to convince the Emperor that they have not lost their faculty. Flimnap, the Treasurer, is allowed to cut a caper on the strait rope, at least an inch higher than any other lord in the whole empire. I have seen him do the summerset several times together upon a trencher fixed on the rope, which is no thicker than a common packthread in England. My friend Reldresal, Principal Secretary for Private Affairs, is, in my opinion, if I am not partial, the second after the Treasurer; the rest of the great officers are much upon a par.

These diversions are often attended with fatal accidents, whereof great numbers are on record. I my self have seen two or three candidates break a limb. But the danger is much greater when the ministers themselves are commanded to show their dexterity; for by contending to excel themselves and their fellows, they strain so far, that there is hardly one of them who hath not received a fall, and some of them two or three. I was assured that a year or two before my arrival, Flimnap would have infallibly broke his neck, if one of the King's cushions, that accidentally lay on the ground, had not weakened the force of his fall.

There is likewise another diversion, which is only shown before the Emperor and Empress, and first minister, upon particular occasions. The Emperor lays on a table three fine silken threads of six inches long. One is blue, the other red, and the third green. These threads are proposed as prizes for those persons whom the Emperor hath a mind to distinguish by a peculiar mark of his favour. The ceremony is performed in his Majesty's great chamber of state, where the candidates are to undergo a trial of dexterity very different from the former, and such as I have not observed the least resemblance of in any other country of the old or the new world. The Emperor holds a stick in his hands, both ends parallel to the horizon, while the candidates, advancing one by one, sometimes leap over the stick, sometimes creep under it backwards and forwards several times, according as the stick is advanced or depressed. Sometimes the Emperor holds one end of the stick, and his first minister the other; sometimes the minister has it entirely to himself. Whoever performs his part with most agility, and holds out the longest in leaping and creeping, is rewarded with the blue-coloured silk; the red is given to the next, and the green to the third, which they all wear girt twice round about the middle; and you see few great persons about this court who are not adorned with one of these girdles.

The horses of the army, and those of the royal stables, having been daily led before me, were no longer shy, but would come up to my very feet without starting. The riders would leap them over my hand as I held it on the ground, and one of the Emperor's huntsmen, upon a large courser, took my foot, shoe and all; which was indeed a prodigious leap. I had the good fortune to divert the Emperor one day after a very extraordinary manner. I desired he would order several sticks of two foot high, and the thickness of an ordinary cane, to be brought me; whereupon his Majesty commanded the master of his woods to give directions accordingly, and the next morning six woodmen arrived with as many carriages, drawn by eight horses to each. I took nine of these sticks, and fixing them firmly in the ground in a quadrangular figure, two foot and a half square, I took four other sticks, and tied them parallel at each corner, about two foot from the ground; then I fastened my handkerchief to the nine sticks that stood erect, and extended it on all sides till it was as tight as the top of a drum; and the four parallel sticks, rising about five inches higher than the handkerchief, served as ledges on each side. When I had finished my work, I desired the Emperor to let a troop of his best horse, twenty-four in number, come and exercise upon this plain. His Majesty approved of the proposal, and I took them up one by one in my hands, ready mounted and armed, with the proper officers to exercise them. As soon as they got into order, they divided into two parties, performed mock skirmishes, discharged blunt arrows, drew their swords, fled and pursued, attacked and retired, and in short discovered the best military discipline I ever beheld. The parallel sticks secured them and their horses from falling over the stage; and the Emperor was so much delighted, that he ordered this entertainment to be repeated several days, and once was pleased to be lifted up, and give the word of command; and, with great difficulty, persuaded even the Empress her self to let me hold her in her close chair within two yards of the stage, from whence she was able to take a full view of the whole performance. It was my good fortune that no ill accident happened in these entertainments, only once a fiery horse that belonged to one of the captains pawing with his hoof struck a hole in my handkerchief, and his foot slipping, he overthrew his rider and himself; but I immediately relieved them both, for covering the hole with one hand, I set down the troop with the other, in the same manner as I took them up. The horse that fell was strained in the left shoulder, but the rider got no hurt, and I repaired my handkerchief as well as I could; however, I would not trust to the strength of it any more in such dangerous enterprises.

About two or three days before I was set at liberty, as I was entertaining the court with these kinds of feats, there arrived an express to inform his Majesty that some of his subjects, riding near the place where I was first taken up, had seen a great black substance lying on the ground, very oddly shaped, extending its edges round as wide as his Majesty's bedchamber, and rising up in the middle as high as a man; that it was no living creature, as they at first apprehended, for it lay on the grass without motion, and some of them had walked round it several times; that by mounting upon each others' shoulders, they had got to the top, which was flat and even, and stamping upon it they found it was hollow within; that they humbly conceived it might be something belonging to the Man-Mountain, and if his Majesty pleased, they would undertake to bring it with only five horses. I presently knew what they meant, and was glad at heart to receive this intelligence. It seems upon my first reaching the shore after our shipwreck, I was in such confusion, that before I came to the place where I went to sleep, my hat, which I had fastened with a string to my head while I was rowing, and had stuck on all the time I was swimming, fell off after I came to land; the string, as I conjecture, breaking by some accident which I never observed, but thought my hat had been lost at sea. I entreated his Imperial Majesty to give orders it might be brought to me as soon as possible, describing to him the use and the nature of it: and the next day the waggoners arrived with it, but not in a very good condition; they had bored two holes in the brim, within an inch and half of the edge, and fastened two hooks in the holes; these hooks were tied by a long cord to the harness, and thus my hat was dragged along for above half an English mile: but the ground in that country being extremely smooth and level, it received less damage than I expected.

Two days after this adventure, the Emperor having ordered that part of his army which quarters in and about his metropolis to be in a readiness, took a fancy of diverting himself in a very singular manner. He desired I would stand like a colossus, with my legs as far asunder as I conveniently could. He then commanded his general (who was an old experienced leader, and a great patron of mine) to draw up the troops in close order, and march them under me, the foot by twenty-four in a breast, and the horse by sixteen, with drums beating, colours flying, and pikes advanced. This body consisted of three thousand foot, and a thousand horse. His Majesty gave orders, upon pain of death, that every soldier in his march should observe the strictest decency with regard to my person; which, however, could not prevent some of the younger officers from turning up their eyes as they passed under me. And, to confess the truth, my breeches were at that time in so ill a condition, that they afforded some opportunities for laughter and admiration.

I had sent so many memorials and petitions for my liberty, that his Majesty at length mentioned the matter, first in the cabinet, and then in a full council; where it was opposed by none, except Skyresh Bolgolam, who was pleased, without any provocation, to be my mortal enemy. But it was carried against him by the whole board, and confirmed by the Emperor. That minister was *Galbet*, or Admiral of the Realm, very much in his master's confidence, and a person well versed in affairs, but of a morose and sour complexion. However, he was at length persuaded to comply; but prevailed that the articles and conditions upon which I should be set free, and to which I must swear, should be drawn up by himself. These articles were brought to me by Skyresh Bolgolam in person, attended by two under-secretaries, and several persons of distinction. After they were read, I was demanded to swear to the performance of them; first in the manner of my own country, and afterwards in the method prescribed by their laws; which was to hold my right foot in my left hand, to place the middle finger of my right hand on the crown of my head, and my thumb on the tip of my right ear. But because the reader may perhaps be curious to have some idea of the style and manner of expression peculiar to that people, as well as to know the articles upon which I recovered my liberty, I have made a translation of the whole instrument word for word, as near as I was able, which I here offer to the public.

GOLBASTO MOMAREN EVLAME GURDILO SHEFIN MULLY ULLY GUE, most mighty Emperor of Lilliput, delight and terror of the universe, whose dominions extend five thousand blustrugs (about twelve miles in circumference) to the extremities of the globe; monarch of all monarchs, taller than the sons of men; whose feet press down to the center, and whose head strikes against the sun: at whose nod the princes of the earth shake their knees; pleasant as the spring, comfortable as the summer, fruitful as autumn, dreadful as winter. His most sublime Majesty proposeth to the Man-Mountain, lately arrived at our celestial dominions, the following articles, which by a solemn oath he shall be obliged to perform.

First, The Man-Mountain shall not depart from our dominions, without our licence under our great seal.

Secondly, He shall not presume to come into our metropolis, without our express order; at which time the inhabitants shall have two hours warning to keep within their doors.

Thirdly, The said Man-Mountain shall confine his walks to our principal high roads, and not offer to walk or lie down in a meadow or field of corn.

Fourthly, As he walks the said roads, he shall take the utmost care not to trample upon the bodies of any of our loving subjects, their horses, or carriages, nor take any of our said subjects into his hands, without their own consent.

Fifthly, If an express require extraordinary dispatch, the Man-Mountain shall be obliged to carry in his pocket the messenger and horse a six days' journey once in every moon, and return the said messenger back (if so required) safe to our Imperial Presence.

Sixthly, He shall be our ally against our enemies in the island of Blefuscu, and do his utmost to destroy their fleet, which is now preparing to invade us.

Seventhly, That the said Man-Mountain shall, at his times of leisure, be aiding and assisting to our workmen, in helping to raise certain great stones, towards covering the wall of the principal park, and other our royal buildings.

Eighthly, That the said Man-Mountain shall, in two moons' time, deliver in an exact survey of the circumference of our dominions by a computation of his own paces round the coast.

Lastly, That upon his solemn oath to observe all the above articles, the said Man-Mountain shall have a daily allowance of meat and drink sufficient for the support of 1728 of our subjects, with free access to our Royal Person, and other marks of our favour. Given at our palace at Belfaborac the twelfth day of the ninety-first moon of our reign.

I swore and subscribed to these articles with great cheerfulness and content, although some of them were not so honourable as I could have wished; which proceeded wholly from the malice of Skyresh Bolgolam the High Admiral: whereupon my chains were immediately unlocked, and I was at full liberty; the Emperor himself in person did me the honour to be by at the whole ceremony. I made my acknowledgements by prostrating myself at his Majesty's feet: but he commanded me to rise; and after many gracious expressions, which, to avoid the censure of vanity, I shall not repeat, he added, that he hoped I should prove a useful servant, and well deserve all the favours he had already conferred upon me, or might do for the future.

The reader may please to observe, that in the last article for the recovery of my liberty, the Emperor stipulates to allow me a quantity of meat and drink sufficient for the support of 1728 Lilliputians. Some time after, asking a friend at court how they came to fix on that determinate number, he told me, that his Majesty's mathematicians, having taken the height of my body by the help of a quadrant, and finding it to exceed theirs in the proportion of twelve to one, they concluded from the similarity of their bodies, that mine must contain at least 1728 of theirs, and consequently would require as much food as was necessary to support that number of Lilliputians. By which the reader may conceive an idea of the ingenuity of that people, as well as the prudent and exact œconomy of so great a prince.

Chapter IV.

Mildendo, the metropolis of Lilliput, described, together with the Emperor's palace. A conversation between the author and a principal secretary, concerning the affairs of that empire; the author's offers to serve the Emperor in his wars.

The first request I made after I had obtained my liberty, was, that I might have licence to see Mildendo, the metropolis; which the Emperor easily granted me, but with a special charge to do no hurt, either to the inhabitants, or their houses. The people had notice by proclamation of my design to visit the town. The wall which encompassed it is two foot and an half high, and at least eleven inches broad, so that a coach and horses may be driven very safely round it; and it is flanked with strong towers at ten foot distance. I stepped over the great western gate, and passed very gently, and sideling through the two principal streets, only in my short waistcoat, for fear of damaging the roofs and eaves of the houses with the skirts of my coat. I walked with the utmost circumspection, to avoid treading on any stragglers, who might remain in the streets, although the orders were very strict, that all people should keep in their houses, at their own peril. The garret windows and tops of houses were so crowded with spectators, that I thought in all my travels I had not seen a more populous place. The city is an exact square, each side of the wall being five hundred foot long. The two great streets, which run cross and divide it into four quarters, are five foot wide. The lanes and alleys, which I could not enter, but only viewed them as I passed, are from twelve to eighteen inches. The town is capable of holding five hundred thousand souls. The houses are from three to five stories. The shops and markets well provided.

The Emperor's palace is in the center of the city, where the two great streets meet. It is inclosed by a wall of two foot high, and twenty foot distant from the buildings. I had his Majesty's permission to step over this wall; and the space being so wide between that and the palace, I could easily view it on every side. The outward court is a square of forty foot, and includes two other courts: in the inmost are the royal apartments, which I was very desirous to see, but found it extremely difficult; for the great gates, from one square into another, were but eighteen inches high, and seven inches wide. Now the buildings of the outer court were at least five foot high, and it was impossible for me to stride over them, without infinite damage to the pile, although the walls were strongly built of hewn stone, and four inches thick. At the same time the Emperor had a great desire that I should see the magnificence of his palace; but this I was not able to do till three days after, which I spent in cutting down with my knife some of the largest trees in the royal park, about an hundred yards distant from the city. Of these trees I made two stools, each about three foot high, and strong enough to bear my weight. The people having received notice a second time, I went again through the city to the palace, with my two stools in my hands. When I came to the side of the outer court, I stood upon one stool, and took the other in my hand: this I lifted over the roof,

and gently set it down on the space between the first and second
court, which was eight foot wide. I then stepped over the buildings very conveniently from one stool to the other, and drew up
the first after me with a hooked stick. By this contrivance I got
into the inmost court; and lying down upon my side, I applied
my face to the windows of the middle stories, which were left
open on purpose, and discovered the most splendid apartments
that can be imagined. There I saw the Empress, and the young
princes in their several lodgings, with their chief attendants about
them. Her Imperial Majesty was pleased to smile very graciously
upon me, and gave me out of the window her hand to kiss.

But I shall not anticipate the reader with farther descriptions of
this kind, because I reserve them for a greater work, which is
now almost ready for the press, containing a general description
of this empire, from its first erection, through a long series of
princes, with a particular account of their wars and politics, laws,
learning, and religion; their plants and animals, their peculiar
manners and customs, with other matters very curious and useful;
my chief design at present being only to relate such events and
transactions as happened to the public, or to myself, during a residence of about nine months in that empire.

One morning, about a fortnight after I had obtained my liberty,
Reldresal, Principal Secretary (as they style him) of Private
Affairs, came to my house, attended only by one servant. He ordered his coach to wait at a distance, and desired I would give
him an hour's audience; which I readily consented to, on account
of his quality, and personal merits, as well as of the many good
offices he had done me during my solicitations at court. I offered
to lie down, that he might the more conveniently reach my ear;
but he chose rather to let me hold him in my hand during our
conversation. He began with compliments on my liberty, said he
might pretend to some merit in it; but, however, added, that if it
had not been for the present situation of things at court, perhaps
I might not have obtained it so soon. For, said he, as flourishing
a condition as we appear to be in to foreigners, we labour under
two mighty evils; a violent faction at home, and the danger of an
invasion by a most potent enemy from abroad. As to the first,
you are to understand, that for above seventy moons past, there
have been two struggling parties in the empire, under the names
of *Tramecksan* and *Slamecksan*, from the high and low heels on
their shoes, by which they distinguish themselves. It is alleged
indeed, that the high heels are most agreeable to our ancient constitution: but however this be, his Majesty hath determined to
make use of only low heels in the administration of the govern-

ment and all offices in the gift of the crown, as you cannot but observe; and particularly, that his Majesty's imperial heels are lower at least by a *drurr* than any of his court; (*drurr* is a measure about the fourteenth part of an inch). The animosities between these two parties run so high, that they will neither eat nor drink, nor talk with each other. We compute the *Tramecksan*, or High-Heels, to exceed us in number; but the power is wholly on our side. We apprehend his Imperial Highness, the heir to the crown, to have some tendency towards the High-Heels; at least we can plainly discover one of his heels higher than the other, which gives him a hobble in his gait. Now, in the midst of these intestine disquiets, we are threatened with an invasion from the island of Blefuscu, which is the other great empire of the universe, almost as large and powerful as this of his Majesty. For as to what we have heard you affirm, that there are other kingdoms and states in the world, inhabited by human creatures as large as yourself, our philosophers are in much doubt, and would rather conjecture that you dropped from the moon, or one of the stars; because it is certain, that an hundred mortals of your bulk would, in a short time, destroy all the fruits and cattle of his Majesty's dominions. Besides, our histories of six thousand moons make no mention of any other regions, than the two great empires of Lilliput and Blefuscu. Which two mighty powers have, as I was going to tell you, been engaged in a most obstinate war for six and thirty moons past. It began upon the following occasion. It is allowed on all hands, that the primitive way of breaking eggs before we eat them, was upon the larger end: but his present Majesty's grandfather, while he was a boy, going to eat an egg, and breaking it according to the ancient practice, happened to cut one of his fingers. Whereupon the Emperor his father published an edict, commanding all his subjects, upon great penalties, to break the smaller end of their eggs. The people so highly resented this law, that our histories tell us there have been six rebellions raised on that account; wherein one emperor lost his life, and another his crown. These civil commotions were constantly fomented by the monarchs of Blefuscu; and when they were quelled, the exiles always fled for refuge to that empire. It is computed, that eleven thousand persons have, at several times, suffered death, rather than submit to break their eggs at the smaller end. Many hundred large volumes have been published upon this controversy: but the books of the Big-Endians have been long forbidden, and the whole party rendered incapable by law of holding employments. During the course of these troubles, the emperors of Blefuscu did frequently expostulate by their ambassadors, accus-

ing us of making a schism in religion, by offending against a fundamental doctrine of our great prophet Lustrog, in the fifty-
fourth chapter of the *Brundecral* (which is their Alcoran). This,
however, is thought to be a mere strain upon the text: for the
words are these; That all true believers shall break their eggs at
the convenient end: and which is the convenient end, seems, in
my humble opinion, to be left to every man's conscience, or at
least in the power of the chief magistrate to determine. Now the
Big-Endian exiles have found so much credit in the Emperor of
Blefuscu's court, and so much private assistance and encouragement from their party here at home, that a bloody war hath been
carried on between the two empires for six and thirty moons with
various success; during which time we have lost forty capital
ships, and a much greater number of smaller vessels, together
with thirty thousand of our best seamen and soldiers; and the
damage received by the enemy is reckoned to be somewhat
greater than ours. However, they have now equipped a numerous fleet, and are just preparing to make a descent upon us; and
his Imperial Majesty, placing great confidence in your valour and
strength, hath commanded me to lay this account of his affairs
before you.

I desired the Secretary to present my humble duty to the Emperor, and to let him know, that I thought it would not become
me, who was a foreigner, to interfere with parties; but I was
ready, with the hazard of my life, to defend his person and state
against all invaders.

Chapter V.

*The author by an extraordinary stratagem prevents an invasion. A
high title of honour is conferred upon him. Ambassadors arrive
from the Emperor of Blefuscu, and sue for peace. The Empress's
apartment on fire by an accident; the author instrumental in saving the rest of the palace.*

The empire of Blefuscu is an island situated to the north-
northeast side of Lilliput, from whence it is parted only by a
channel of eight hundred yards wide. I had not yet seen it, and
upon this notice of an intended invasion, I avoided appearing on
that side of the coast, for fear of being discovered by some of the
enemy's ships, who had received no intelligence of me, all intercourse between the two empires having been strictly forbidden
during the war, upon pain of death, and an embargo laid by our

Emperor upon all vessels whatsoever. I communicated to his Majesty a project I had formed of seizing the enemy's whole fleet; which, as our scouts assured us, lay at anchor in the harbour ready to sail with the first fair wind. I consulted the most experienced seamen upon the depth of the channel, which they had often plumbed, who told me, that in the middle at high water it was seventy *glumgluffs* deep, which is about six foot of European measure; and the rest of it fifty *glumgluffs* at most. I walked to the northeast coast over against Blefuscu; where, lying down behind a hillock, I took out my small pocket perspective-glass, and viewed the enemy's fleet at anchor, consisting of about fifty men of war, and a great number of transports: I then came back to my house, and gave order (for which I had a warrant) for a great quantity of the strongest cable and bars of iron. The cable was about as thick as packthread, and the bars of the length and size of a knitting-needle. I trebled the cable to make it stronger, and for the same reason I twisted three of the iron bars together, bending the extremities into a hook. Having thus fixed fifty hooks to as many cables, I went back to the northeast coast, and putting off my coat, shoes, and stockings, walked into the sea in my leathern jerkin, about half an hour before high water. I waded with what haste I could, and swam in the middle about thirty yards until I felt ground; I arrived at the fleet in less than half an hour. The enemy was so frighted when they saw me, that they leaped out of their ships, and swam to shore, where there could not be fewer than thirty thousand souls. I then took my tackling, and fastening a hook to the hole at the prow of each, I tied all the cords together at the end. While I was thus employed, the enemy discharged several thousand arrows, many of which stuck in my hands and face; and besides the excessive smart, gave me much disturbance in my work. My greatest apprehension was for my eyes, which I should have infallibly lost, if I had not suddenly thought of an expedient. I kept among other little necessaries a pair of spectacles in a private pocket, which, as I observed before, had escaped the Emperor's searchers. These I took out and fastened as strongly as I could upon my nose, and thus armed went on boldly with my work in spite of the enemy's arrows, many of which struck against the glasses of my spectacles, but without any other effect, further than a little to discompose them. I had now fastened all the hooks, and taking the knot in my hand, began to pull; but not a ship would stir, for they were all too fast held by their anchors, so that the boldest part of my enterprise remained. I therefore let go the cord, and leaving the hooks fixed to the ships, I resolutely cut with my knife the cables that fastened the anchors, receiving above two hundred shots in my face and hands; then I took up the knotted end of the cables to which my hooks were tied, and with great ease drew fifty of the enemy's largest men-of-war after me.

The Blefuscudians, who had not the least imagination of what I intended, were at first confounded with astonishment. They had seen me cut the cables, and thought my design was only to let the ships run adrift, or fall foul on each other: but when they perceived the whole fleet, moving in order, and saw me pulling at the end, they set up such a scream of grief and despair, that it is almost impossible to describe or conceive. When I had got out of danger, I stopped a while to pick out the arrows that stuck in my hands and face, and rubbed on some of the same ointment that was given me at my first arrival, as I have formerly mentioned. I then took off my spectacles, and waiting about an hour until the tide was a little fallen, I waded through the middle with my cargo, and arrived safe at the royal port of Lilliput.

The Emperor and his whole court stood on the shore expecting the issue of this great adventure. They saw the ships move forward in a large half-moon, but could not discern me, who was up to my breast in water. When I advanced to the middle of the channel, they were yet more in pain, because I was under water to my neck. The Emperor concluded me to be drowned, and that the enemy's fleet was approaching in a hostile manner: but he was soon eased of his fears, for, the channel growing shallower every step I made, I came in a short time within hearing, and holding up the end of the cable by which the fleet was fastened, I cried in a loud voice, Long live the most puissant Emperor of Lilliput! This great prince received me at my landing with all possible encomiums, and created me a *Nardac* upon the spot, which is the highest title of honour among them.

His Majesty desired I would take some other opportunity of bringing all the rest of his enemy's ships into his ports. And so unmeasureable is the ambition of princes, that he seemed to think of nothing less than reducing the whole empire of Blesfuscu into a province, and governing it by a viceroy; of destroying the Big-Endian exiles, and compelling that people to break the smaller end of their eggs, by which he would remain sole monarch of the whole world. But I endeavoured to divert him from this design, by many arguments drawn from the topics of policy as well as justice: and I plainly protested, that I would never be an instrument of bringing a free and brave people into slavery. And when the matter was debated in council, the wisest part of the ministry were of my opinion.

This open bold declaration of mine was so opposite to the schemes and politics of his Imperial Majesty, that he could never forgive me; he mentioned it in a very artful manner at council, where I was told that some of the wisest appeared, at least, by their silence, to be of my opinion; but others, who were my secret enemies, could not forbear some expressions, which by a side-wind reflected on me. And from this time began an intrigue between his Majesty and a junta of ministers maliciously bent against me, which broke out in less than two months, and had like to have ended in my utter destruction. Of so little weight are the greatest services to princes, when put into the balance with a refusal to gratify their passions.

About three weeks after this exploit, there arrived a solemn embassy from Blefuscu, with humble offers of a peace; which was soon concluded upon conditions very advantageous to our Emperor, wherewith I shall not trouble the reader. There were six ambassadors, with a train of about five hundred persons, and their entry was very magnificent, suitable to the grandeur of their master, and the importance of their business. When their treaty was finished, wherein I did them several good offices by the credit I now had, or at least appeared to have at court, their Excellencies, who were privately told how much I had been their friend, made me a visit in form. They began with many compliments upon my valour and generosity, invited me to that kingdom in the Emperor their master's name, and desired me to show them some proofs of my prodigious strength, of which they had heard so many wonders; wherein I readily obliged them, but shall not interrupt the reader with the particulars.

When I had for some time entertained their Excellencies to their infinite satisfaction and surprise, I desired they would do me the honour to present my most humble respects to the Emperor their master, the renown of whose virtues had so justly filled the whole world with admiration, and whose royal person I resolved to attend before I returned to my own country: accordingly, the next time I had the honour to see our Emperor, I desired his general licence to wait on the Blefuscudian monarch, which he was pleased to grant me, as I could plainly perceive, in a very cold manner; but could not guess the reason, till I had a whisper from a certain person, that Flimnap and Bolgolam had represented my intercourse with those ambassadors as a mark of disaffection, from which I am sure my heart was wholly free. And this was the first time I began to conceive some imperfect idea of courts and ministers.

It is to be observed, that these ambassadors spoke to me by an interpreter, the languages of both empires differing as much from each other as any two in Europe, and each nation priding itself upon the antiquity, beauty, and energy of their own tongues, with an avowed contempt for that of their neighbour; yet our Emperor, standing upon the advantage he had got by the seizure of their fleet, obliged them to deliver their credentials, and make their speech, in the Lilliputian tongue. And it must be confessed, that from the great intercourse of trade and commerce between both realms, from the continual reception of exiles, which is mutual among them, and from the custom in each empire to send their young nobility and richer gentry to the other, in order to polish themselves, by seeing the world, and understanding men and manners, there are few persons of distinction, or merchants, or seamen, who dwell in the maritime parts, but what can hold conversation in both tongues; as I found some weeks after, when I went to pay my respects to the Emperor of Blefuscu, which in the midst of great misfortunes, through the malice of my enemies, proved a very happy adventure to me, as I shall relate in its proper place.

The reader may remember, that when I signed those articles upon which I recovered my liberty, there were some which I disliked upon account of their being too servile, neither could any thing but an extreme necessity have forced me to submit. But being now a *Nardac*, of the highest rank in that empire, such offices were looked upon as below my dignity, and the Emperor (to do him justice) never once mentioned them to me. However, it was not long before I had an opportunity of doing his Majesty, at least as I then thought, a most signal service. I was alarmed at midnight with the cries of many hundred people at my door; by which being suddenly awaked, I was in some kind of terror. I heard the word *burglum* repeated incessantly: several of the Emperor's court, making their way through the crowd, intreated me to come immediately to the palace, where her Imperial Majesty's apartment was on fire, by the carelessness of a maid of honour, who fell asleep while she was reading a romance. I got up in an instant; and orders being given to clear the way before me, and it being likewise a moonshine night, I made a shift to get to the palace without trampling on any of the people. I found they had already applied ladders to the walls of the apartment, and were well provided with buckets, but the water was at some distance. These buckets were about the size of a large thimble, and the poor people supplied me with them as fast as they could; but the flame was so violent that they did little good. I might easily have stifled it with my coat, which I unfortunately left behind me for haste, and came away only in my leathern jerkin. The case seemed wholly desperate and deplorable, and this magnificent palace would have infallibly been burnt down to the ground, if, by a presence of mind, unusual to me, I had not suddenly thought of an expedient. I had the evening before drank plentifully of a most delicious wine, called *glimigrim* (the Blefuscudians call it *flunec*, but ours is esteemed the better sort), which is very diuretic. By the luckiest chance in the world, I had not discharged myself of any part of it. The heat I had contracted by coming very near the flames, and by my labouring to quench them, made the wine begin to operate by urine; which I voided in such a quantity, and applied so well to the proper places, that in three minutes the fire was wholly extinguished, and the rest of that noble pile, which had cost so many ages in erecting, preserved from destruction.

It was now daylight, and I returned to my house, without waiting to congratulate with the Emperor; because, although I had done a very eminent piece of service, yet I could not tell how his Majesty might resent the manner by which I had performed it: for, by the fundamental laws of the realm, it is capital in any person, of what quality soever, to make water within the precints of the palace. But I was a little comforted by a message from his Majesty, that he would give orders to the Grand Justiciary for passing my pardon in form; which, however, I could not obtain. And I was privately assured, that the Empress, conceiving the greatest abhorrence of what I had done, removed to the most distant side of the court, firmly resolved that those buildings should never be repaired for her use; and, in the presence of her chief confidents, could not forbear vowing revenge.

Chapter VI.

Of the inhabitants of Lilliput; their learning, laws, and customs, the manner of educating their children. The author's way of living in that country. His vindication of a great lady.

Although I intend to leave the description of this empire to a particular treatise, yet in the mean time I am content to gratify the curious reader with some general ideas. As the common size of the natives is somewhat under six inches, so there is an exact proportion in all other animals, as well as plants and trees: for instance, the tallest horses and oxen are between four and five inches in height, the sheep an inch and a half, more or less; their

geese about the bigness of a sparrow, and so the several gradations downwards, till you come to the smallest, which, to my
sight, were almost invisible; but nature hath adapted the eyes of
the Lilliputians to all objects proper for their view: they see with
great exactness, but at no great distance. And to show the sharpness of their sight towards objects that are near, I have been
much pleased with observing a cook pulling a lark, which was
not so large as a common fly; and a young girl threading an
invisible needle with invisible silk. Their tallest trees are about
seven foot high; I mean some of those in the great royal park, the
tops whereof I could but just reach with my fist clenched. The
other vegetables are in the same proportion; but this I leave to the
reader's imagination.

I shall say but little at present of their learning, which for
many ages hath flourished in all its branches among them: but
their manner of writing is very peculiar, being neither from the
left to the right, like the Europeans; nor from the right to the
left, like the Arabians; nor from up to down, like the Chinese;
nor from down to up, like the Cascagians, but aslant from one
corner of the paper to the other, like ladies in England.

They bury their dead with their heads directly downwards,
because they hold an opinion that in eleven thousand moons they
are all to rise again, in which period the earth (which they conceive to be flat) will turn upside down, and by this means they
shall, at their resurrection, be found ready standing on their feet.
The learned among them confess the absurdity of this doctrine,
but the practice still continues, in compliance to the vulgar.

There are some laws and customs in this empire very peculiar,
and if they were not so directly contrary to those of my own
dear country, I should be tempted to say a little in their justification. It is only to be wished, that they were as well executed.
The first I shall mention relates to informers. All crimes against
the state are punished here with the utmost severity; but if the
person accused make his innocence plainly to appear upon his
trial, the accuser is immediately put to an ignominious death; and
out of his goods or lands, the innocent person is quadruply
recompensed for the loss of his time, for the danger he underwent, for the hardship of his imprisonment, and for all the
charges he hath been at in making his defence. Or, if that fund
be deficient, it is largely supplied by the crown. The Emperor
doth also confer on him some public mark of his favour, and
proclamation is made of his innocence through the whole city.

They look upon fraud as a greater crime than theft, and therefore seldom fail to punish it with death; for they allege, that

care and vigilance, with a very common understanding, may preserve a man's goods from thieves, but honesty hath no fence against superior cunning: and since it is necessary that there should be a perpetual intercourse of buying and selling, and dealing upon credit, where fraud is permitted and connived at, or hath no law to punish it, the honest dealer is always undone, and the knave gets the advantage. I remember when I was once interceding with the King for a criminal who had wronged his master of a great sum of money, which he had received by order, and ran away with; and happening to tell his Majesty, by way of extenuation, that it was only a breach of trust; the Emperor thought it monstrous in me to offer, as a defence, the greatest aggravation of the crime: and truly I had little to say in return, farther than the common answer, that different nations had different customs; for, I confess, I was heartily ashamed.

Although we usually call reward and punishment the two hinges upon which all government turns, yet I could never observe this maxim to be put in practice by any nation except that of Lilliput. Whoever can there bring sufficient proof that he hath strictly observed the laws of his country for seventy-three moons, hath a claim to certain privileges, according to his quality and condition of life, with a proportionable sum of money out of a fund appropriated for that use: he likewise acquires the title of *Snilpall*, or *Legal*, which is added to his name, but doth not descend to his posterity. And these people thought it a prodigious defect of policy among us, when I told them that our laws were enforced only by penalties without any mention of reward. It is upon this account that the image of Justice, in their courts of judicature, is formed with six eyes, two before, as many behind, and on each side one, to signify circumspection; with a bag of gold open in her right hand, and a sword sheathed in her left, to show she is more disposed to reward than to punish.

In choosing persons for all employments, they have more regard to good morals than to great abilities; for, since government is necessary to mankind, they believe that the common size of human understandings is fitted to some station or other, and that Providence never intended to make the management of public affairs a mystery, to be comprehended only by a few persons of sublime genius, of which there seldom are three born in an age: but they suppose truth, justice, temperance, and the like, to be in every man's power; the practice of which virtues, assisted by experience and a good intention, would qualify any man for the service of his country, except where a course of study is required. But they thought the want of moral virtues was so far from being supplied by superior endowments of the minds, that employments could never be put into such dangerous hands as those of persons so qualified; and at least, that the mistakes committed by ignorance in a virtuous disposition would never be of such fatal consequence to the public weal, as the practices of a man whose inclinations led him to be corrupt, and had great abilities to manage, to multiply, and defend his corruptions.

In like manner, the disbelief of a divine Providence renders a man uncapable of holding any public station; for since kings avow themselves to be the deputies of Providence, the Lilliputians think nothing can be more absurd than for a prince to employ such men as disown the authority under which he acts.

In relating these and the following laws, I would only be understood to mean the original institutions, and not the most scandalous corruptions into which these people are fallen by the degenerate nature of man. For as to that infamous practice of acquiring great employments by dancing on the ropes, or badges of favour and distinction by leaping over sticks, and creeping under them, the reader is to observe, that they were first introduced by the grandfather of the Emperor now reigning, and grew to the present height by the gradual increase of party and faction.

Ingratitude is among them a capital crime, as we read it to have been in some other countries; for they reason thus, that whoever makes ill returns to his benefactor, must needs be a common enemy to the rest of mankind, from whom he hath received no obligation, and therefore such a man is not fit to live.

Their notions relating to the duties of parents and children differ extremely from ours. For, since the conjunction of male and female is founded upon the great law of nature, in order to propagate and continue the species, the Lilliputians will needs have it, that men and women are joined together like other animals, by the motives of concupiscence; and that their tenderness towards their young proceeds from the like natural principle: for which reason they will never allow, that a child is under any obligation to his father for begetting him, or to his mother for bringing him into the world; which, considering the miseries of human life, was neither a benefit in itself, nor intended so by his parents, whose thoughts in their love-encounters were otherwise employed. Upon these, and the like reasonings, their opinion is, that parents are the last of all others to be trusted with the education of their own children: and therefore they have in every town public nurseries, where all parents, except cottagers and labourers, are obliged to send their infants of both sexes to be reared and educated when they come to the age of twenty moons, at which time they are supposed to have some rudiments of docility. These schools are of several kinds, suited to different qualities, and to both sexes. They have certain professors well skilled in preparing children for such a condition of life as befits the rank of their parents, and their own capacities as well as inclinations. I shall first say something of the male nurseries, and then of the female.

The nurseries for males of noble or eminent birth are provided with grave and learned professors, and their several deputies. The clothes and food of the children are plain and simple. They are bred up in the principles of honour, justice, courage, modesty, clemency, religion, and love of their country; they are always employed in some business, except in the times of eating and sleeping, which are very short, and two hours for diversions, consisting of bodily exercises. They are dressed by men until four years of age, and then are obliged to dress themselves, although their quality be ever so great; and the women attendants, who are aged proportionably to ours at fifty, perform only the most menial offices. They are never suffered to converse with servants, but go together in small or greater numbers to take their diversions, and always in the presence of a professor, or one of his deputies; whereby they avoid those early bad impressions of folly and vice to which our children are subject. Their parents are suffered to see them only twice a year; the visit is not to last above an hour. They are allowed to kiss the child at meeting and parting; but a professor, who always stands by on those occasions, will not suffer them to whisper, or use any fondling expressions, or bring any presents of toys, sweetmeats, and the like.

The pension from each family for the education and entertainment of a child, upon failure of due payment, is levied by the Emperor's officers.

The nurseries for children of ordinary gentlemen, merchants, traders, and handicrafts, are managed proportionably after the same manner; only those designed for trades are put out apprentices at seven years old, whereas those of persons of quality continue in their nurseries till fifteen, which answers to one and twenty with us: but the confinement is gradually lessened for the last three years.

In the female nurseries, the young girls of quality are educated much like the males, only they are dressed by orderly servants of their own sex, but always in the presence of a professor or deputy, until they come to dress themselves, which is at five years old. And if it be found that these nurses ever presume to entertain the girls with frightful or foolish stories, or the common follies practiced by chambermaids among us, they are publicly whipped thrice about the city, imprisoned for a year, and banished for life to the most desolate parts of the country. Thus the young ladies there are as much ashamed of being cowards and fools as the men, and despise all personal ornaments beyond decency and cleanliness: neither did I perceive any difference in their education, made by their difference of sex, only that the exercises of the females were not altogether so robust, and that some rules were given them relating to domestic life, and a smaller compass of learning was enjoined them: for their maxim is, that among people of quality, a wife should be always a reasonable and agreeable companion, because she cannot always be young. When the girls are twelve years old, which among them is the marriageable age, their parents or guardians take them home, with great expressions of gratitude to the professors, and seldom without tears of the young lady and her companions.

In the nurseries of females of the meaner sort, the children are instructed in all kinds of works proper for their sex, and their several degrees: those intended for apprentices are dismissed at seven years old, the rest are kept to eleven.

The meaner families who have children at these nurseries are obliged, besides their annual pension, which is as low as possible, to return to the steward of the nursery a small monthly share of their gettings, to be a portion for the child; and therefore all parents are limited in their expenses by the law. For the Lilliputians think nothing can be more unjust, than that people, in subservience to their own appetites, should bring children into the world, and leave the burthen of supporting them on the public. As to persons of quality, they give security to appropriate a certain sum for each child, suitable to their condition; and these funds are always managed with good husbandry, and the most exact justice.

The cottagers and labourers keep their children at home, their business being only to till and cultivate the earth, and therefore their education is of little consequence to the public; but the old and diseased among them are supported by hospitals: for begging is a trade unknown in this empire.

And here it may perhaps divert the curious reader, to give some account of my domestic, and my manner of living in this country, during a residence of nine months and thirteen days. Having a head mechanically turned, and being likewise forced by necessity, I had made for myself a table and chair convenient enough, out of the largest trees in the royal park. Two hundred sempstresses were employed to make me shirts, and linen for my bed and table, all of the strongest and coarsest kind they could get; which, however, they were forced to quilt together in several folds, for the thickest was some degrees finer than lawn. Their linen is usually three inches wide, and three foot make a piece. The sempstresses took my measure as I lay on the ground, one standing at my neck, and another at my midleg, with a strong cord extended, that each held by the end, while the third measured the length of the cord with a rule of an inch long. Then they measured my right thumb, and desired no more; for by a mathematical computation, that twice round the thumb is once round the wrist, and so on to the neck and the waist, and by the help of my old shirt, which I displayed on the ground before them for a pattern, they fitted me exactly. Three hundred tailors were employed in the same manner to make me clothes; but they had another contrivance for taking my measure. I kneeled down, and they raised a ladder from the ground to my neck; upon this ladder one of them mounted, and let fall a plumb-line from my collar to the floor, which just answered the length of my coat; but my waist and arms I measured myself. When my clothes were finished, which was done in my house (for the largest of theirs would not have been able to hold them) they looked like the patchwork made by the ladies in England, only that mine were all of a colour.

I had three hundred cooks to dress my victuals, in little convenient huts built about my house, where they and their families lived, and prepared me two dishes apiece. I took up twenty waiters in my hand, and placed them on the table; an hundred more attended below on the ground, some with dishes of meat, and some with barrels of wine, and other liquors, slung on their shoulders; all which the waiters above drew up as I wanted, in a very ingenious manner, by certain cords, as we draw the bucket up a well in Europe. A dish of their meat was a good mouthful, and a barrel of their liquor a reasonable draught. Their mutton yields to ours, but their beef is excellent. I have had a sirloin so large, that I have been forced to make three bits of it; but this is rare. My servants were astonished to see me eat it bones and all, as in our country we do the leg of a lark. Their geese and turkeys I usually eat at a mouthful, and I must confess they far exceed ours. Of their smaller fowl I could take up twenty or thirty at the end of my knife.

One day his Imperial Majesty, being informed of my way of living, desired that himself and his royal consort, with the young

princes of the blood of both sexes, might have the happiness (as
he was pleased to call it) of dining with me. They came accordingly, and I placed them upon chairs of state on my table, just
over-against me, with their guards about them. Flimnap the
Lord High Treasurer attended there likewise, with his white
staff; and I observed he often looked on me with a sour countenance, which I would not seem to regard, but eat more than
usual, in honour to my dear country, as well as to fill the court
with admiration. I have some private reasons to believe, that this
visit from his Majesty gave Flimnap an opportunity of doing me
ill offices to his master. That minister had always been my secret
enemy, although he outwardly caressed me more than was usual
to the moroseness of his nature. He represented to the Emperor
the low condition of his treasury; that he was forced to take up
money at great discount; that exchequer bills would not circulate
under nine per cent below par; that I had cost his Majesty above
a million and a half of *sprugs* (their greatest gold coin, about the
bigness of a spangle); and upon the whole, that it would be ad-
visable in the Emperor to take the first fair occasion of dismissing
me.

I am here obliged to vindicate the reputation of an excellent
lady, who was an innocent sufferer upon my account. The
Treasurer took a fancy to be jealous of his wife, from the malice
of some evil tongues, who informed him that her Grace had
taken a violent affection for my person, and the court-scandal ran
for some time, that she once came privately to my lodging. This
I solemnly declare to be a most infamous falsehood, without any
grounds, farther than that her Grace was pleased to treat me
with all innocent marks of freedom and friendship. I own she
came often to my house, but always publicly, nor ever without
three more in the coach, who were usually her sister and young
daughter, and some particular acquaintance; but this was common to many other ladies of the court. And I still appeal to my
servants round, whether they at any time saw a coach at my door
without knowing what persons were in it. On those occasions,
when a servant had given me notice, my custom was to go immediately to the door; and, after paying my respects, to take up
the coach and two horses very carefully in my hands (for if there
were six horses, the postillion always unharnessed four) and place
them on a table, where I had fixed a moveable rim quite round, of
five inches high, to prevent accidents. And I have often had four
coaches and horses at once on my table full of company, while
I sat in my chair leaning my face towards them; and when I was
engaged with one set, the coachmen would gently drive the

others round my table. I have passed many an afternoon very agreeably in these conversations. But I defy the Treasurer, or his two informers (I will name them, and let them make their best of it) Clustril and Drunlo, to prove that any person ever came to me *incognito*, except the Secretary Reldresal, who was sent by express command of his Imperial Majesty, as I have before related. I should not have dwelt so long upon this particular, if it had not been a point wherein the reputation of a great lady is so nearly concerned, to say nothing of my own; although I had the honour to be a *Nardac*, which the Treasurer himself is not; for all the world knows he is only a *Clumglum*, a title inferior by one degree, as that of a marquis is to a duke in England, yet I allow he preceded me in right of his post. These false informations, which I afterwards came to the knowledge of, by an accident not proper to mention, made the Treasurer show his lady for some time an ill countenance, and me a worse; for although he was at last undeceived and reconciled to her, yet I lost all credit with him, and found my interest decline very fast with the Emperor himself, who was indeed too much governed by that favourite.

Chapter VII.

The author, being informed of a design to accuse him of high treason, makes his escape to Blefuscu. His reception there.

Before I proceed to give an account of my leaving this kingdom, it may be proper to inform the reader of a private intrigue which had been for two months forming against me.

I had been hitherto all my life a stranger to courts, for which I was unqualified by the meanness of my condition. I had indeed heard and read enough of the dispositions of great princes and ministers; but never expected to have found such terrible effects of them in so remote a country, governed, as I thought, by very different maxims from those in Europe.

When I was just preparing to pay my attendance on the Emperor of Blefuscu, a considerable person at court (to whom I had been very serviceable at a time when he lay under the highest displeasure of his Imperial Majesty) came to my house very privately at night in a close chair, and without sending his name, desired admittance: the chairmen were dismissed; I put the chair, with his Lordship in it, into my coat-pocket; and giving orders to a trusty servant to say I was indisposed and gone to sleep, I fastened the door of my house, placed the chair on the table, according to my usual custom, and sat down by it. After the common salutations were over, observing his Lordship's countenance full of concern, and enquiring into the reason, he desired I would hear him with patience in a matter that highly concerned my honour and my life. His speech was to the following effect, for I took notes of it as soon as he left me.

You are to know, said he, that several committees of council have been lately called in the most private manner on your account: and it is but two days since his Majesty came to a full resolution.

You are very sensible that Skyresh Bolgolam (*Galbet*, or High Admiral) hath been your mortal enemy almost ever since your arrival. His original reasons I know not, but his hatred is much encreased since your great success against Blefuscu, by which his glory, as Admiral, is obscured. This lord, in conjunction with Flimnap the High Treasurer, whose enmity against you is notorious on account of his lady, Limtoc the General, Lalcon the Chamberlain, and Balmuff the Grand Justiciary, have prepared articles of impeachment against you, for treason, and other capital crimes.

This preface made me so impatient, being conscious of my own merits and innocence, that I was going to interrupt; when he entreated me to be silent, and thus proceeded.

Out of gratitude for the favours you have done me, I procured information of the whole proceedings, and a copy of the articles, wherein I venture my head for your service.

Articles of Impeachment against Quinbus Flestrin
(*the* Man-Moutain).

ARTICLE I.

Whereas, by a statute made in the reign of his Imperial Majesty Calin Deffar Plune, it is enacted, that whoever shall make water within the precincts of the royal palace shall be liable to the pains and penalties of high treason: notwithstanding, the said Quinbus Flestrin, in open breach of the said law, under colour of extinguishing the fire kindled in the apartment of his Majesty's most dear imperial consort, did maliciously, traitorously, and devilishly, by discharge of his urine, put out the said fire kindled in the said apartment, lying and being within the precincts of the said royal palace, against the statute in that case provided, etc., against the duty, etc.

ARTICLE II.

That the said Quinbus Flestrin, having brought the imperial fleet of Blefuscu into the royal port, and being afterwards commanded by his Imperial Majesty to seize all the other ships of the said empire of Blefuscu, and reduce that empire to a province, to be governed by a viceroy from hence, and to destroy and put to death not only all the Big-Endian exiles, but likewise all the people of that empire who would not immediately forsake the Big-Endian heresy: he, the said Flestrin, like a false traitor against his most Auspicious, Serene, Imperial Majesty, did petition to be excused from the said service, upon pretence of unwillingness to force the consciences, or destroy the liberties and lives of an innocent people.

ARTICLE III.

That, whereas certain ambassadors arrived from the court of Blefuscu to sue for peace in his Majesty's court: he the said Flestrin did, like a false traitor, aid, abet, comfort, and divert the said ambassadors, although he knew them to be servants to a prince who was lately an open enemy to his Imperial Majesty, and in open war against his said Majesty.

ARTICLE IV.

That the said Quinbus Flestrin, contrary to the duty of a faithful subject, is now preparing to make a voyage to the court and empire of Blefuscu, for which he hath received only verbal licence from his Imperial Majesty; and under colour of the said licence, doth falsely and traitorously intend to take the said voyage, and thereby to aid, comfort, and abet the Emperor of Blefuscu, so late an enemy, and in open war with his Imperial Majesty aforesaid.

There are some other articles, but these are the most important, of which I have read you an abstract.

In the several debates upon this impeachment, it must be confessed that his Majesty gave many marks of his great lenity, often urging the services you had done him, and endeavouring to extenuate your crimes. The Treasurer and Admiral insisted that you should be put to the most painful and ignominious death, by setting fire on your house at night, and the General was to attend with twenty thousand men armed with poisoned

arrows to shoot you on the face and hands. Some of your servants were to have private orders to strew a poisonous juice on
your shirts and sheets, which would soon make you tear your
own flesh, and die in the utmost torture. The General came into
the same opinion, so that for a long time there was a majority
against you. But his Majesty resolving, if possible, to spare your
life, at last brought off the Chamberlain.

Upon this incident, Reldresal, Principal Secretary for Private
Affairs, who always approved himself your true friend, was commanded by the Emperor to deliver his opinion, which he accordingly did; and therein justified the good thoughts you have of
him. He allowed your crimes to be great, but that still there was
room for mercy, the most commendable virtue in a prince, and
for which his Majesty was so justly celebrated. He said the
friendship between you and him was so well known to the world,
that perhaps the most honourable board might think him partial:
however, in obedience to the command he had received, he
would freely offer his sentiments. That if his Majesty, in consideration of your services, and pursuant to his own merciful
disposition, would please to spare your life, and only give order
to put out both your eyes, he humbly conceived, that by this
expedient justice might in some measure be satisfied, and all the
world would applaud the lenity of the Emperor, as well as the
fair and generous proceedings of those who have the honour to
be his counsellors. That the loss of your eyes would be no im-
pediment to your bodily strength, by which you might still be
useful to his Majesty. That blindness is an addition to courage,
by concealing dangers from us; that the fear you had for your
eyes was the greatest difficulty in bringing over the enemy's
fleet, and it would be sufficient for you to see by the eyes of the
ministers, since the greatest princes do no more.

This proposal was received with the utmost disapprobation by
the whole board. Bolgolam, the Admiral, could not preserve his
temper; but rising up in fury, said, he wondered how the Secretary durst presume to give his opinion for preserving the life
of a traitor: that the services you had performed were, by all
true reasons of state, the great aggravation of your crimes; that
you, who were able to extinguish the fire by discharge of urine
in her Majesty's apartment (which he mentioned with horror),
might, at another time, raise an inundation by the same means, to
drown the whole palace; and the same strength which enabled you
to bring over the enemy's fleet might serve, upon the first discontent, to carry it back: that he had good reasons to think you
were a Big-Endian in your heart; and as treason begins in the

heart before it appears in overt acts, so he accused you as a traitor on that account, and therefore insisted you should be put to death.

The Treasurer was of the same opinion; he showed to what straits his Majesty's revenue was reduced by the charge of maintaining you, which would soon grow insupportable: that the Secretary's expedient of putting out your eyes was so far from being a remedy against this evil, that it would probably increase it, as it is manifest from the common practice of blinding some kind of fowl, after which they fed the faster, and grew sooner fat: that his sacred Majesty, and the council, who are your judges, were in their own consciences fully convinced of your guilt, which was a sufficient argument to condemn you to death, without the formal proofs required by the strict letter of the law.

But his Imperial Majesty, fully determined against capital punishment, was graciously pleased to say, that since the council thought the loss of your eyes too easy a censure, some other may be inflicted hereafter. And your friend the Secretary humbly desiring to be heard again, in answer to what the Treasurer had objected concerning the great charge his Majesty was at in maintaining you, said, that his Excellency, who had the sole disposal of the Emperor's revenue, might easily provide against this evil, by gradually lessening your establishment; by which, for want of sufficient food, you would grow weak and faint, and lose your appetite, and consequently decay and consume in a few months; neither would the stench of your carcass be then so dangerous, when it should become more than half diminished; and immediately upon your death, five or six thousand of his Majesty's subjects might, in two or three days, cut your flesh from your bones, take it away by cart-loads, and bury it in distant parts to prevent infection, leaving the skeleton as a monument of admiration to posterity.

Thus by the great friendship of the Secretary, the whole affair was compromised. It was strictly enjoined, that the project of starving you by degrees should be kept a secret, but the sentence of putting out your eyes was entered on the books; none dissenting except Bolgolam the Admiral, who being a creature of the Empress, was perpetually instigated by her Majesty to insist upon your death, she having borne perpetual malice against you, on account of that infamous and illegal method you took to extinguish the fire in her apartment.

In three days your friend the Secretary will be directed to come to your house, and read before you the articles of impeachment; and then to signify the great lenity and favour of his Maj-

esty and council, whereby you are only condemned to the loss
of your eyes, which his Majesty doth not question you will
gratefully and humbly submit to; and twenty of his Majesty's
surgeons will attend, in order to see the operation well performed, by discharging very sharp-pointed arrows into the balls
of your eyes, as you lie on the ground.

I leave to your prudence what measures you will take; and to
avoid suspicion, I must immediately return in as private a manner
as I came.

His Lordship did so, and I remained alone, under many doubts
and perplexities of mind.

It was a custom introduced by this prince and his ministry
(very different, as I have been assured, from the practices of
former times) that after the court had decreed any cruel execution, either to gratify the monarch's resentment, or the malice of
a favourite, the Emperor always made a speech to his whole
council, expressing his great lenity and tenderness, as qualities
known and confessed by all the world. This speech was immediately published through the kingdom; nor did any thing
terrify the people so much as those encomiums on his Majesty's
mercy; because it was observed, that the more these praises were
enlarged and insisted on, the more inhuman was the punishment,
and the sufferer more innocent. Yet as to myself, I must confess,
having never been designed for a courtier either by my birth or
education, I was so ill a judge of things, that I could not discover
the lenity and favour of this sentence, but conceived it (perhaps
erroneously) rather to be rigorous than gentle. I sometimes
thought of standing my trial, for although I could not deny the
facts alleged in the several articles, yet I hoped they would admit
of some extenuations. But having in my life perused many state
trials, which I ever observed to terminate as the judges thought
fit to direct, I durst not rely on so dangerous a decision, in so
critical a juncture, and against such powerful enemies. Once I
was strongly bent upon resistance, for while I had liberty, the
whole strength of that empire could hardly subdue me, and I
might easily with stones pelt the metropolis to pieces; but I
soon rejected that project with horror, by remembering the oath
I had made to the Emperor, the favours I received from him, and
the high title of *Nardac* he conferred upon me. Neither had I so
soon learned the gratitude of courtiers, to persuade myself that
his Majesty's present severities acquitted me of all past obligations.

At last I fixed upon a resolution, for which it is probable I
may incur some censure, and not unjustly; for I confess I owe

the preserving my eyes, and consequently my liberty, to my own great rashness and want of experience: because if I had then known the nature of princes and ministers, which I have since observed in many other courts, and their methods of treating criminals less obnoxious than myself, I should with great alacrity and readiness have submitted to so easy a punishment. But hurried on by the precipitancy of youth, and having his Imperial Majesty's licence to pay my attendance upon the Emperor of Blefuscu, I took this opportunity, before the three days were elapsed, to send a letter to my friend the Secretary, signifying my resolution of setting out that morning for Blefuscu pursuant to the leave I had got; and without waiting for an answer, I went to that side of the island where our fleet lay. I seized a large man of war, tied a cable to the prow, and, lifting up the anchors, I stripped myself, put my clothes (together with my coverlet, which I carried under my arm) into the vessel, and drawing it after me between wading and swimming, arrived at the royal port of Blefuscu, where the people had long expected me; they lent me two guides to direct me to the capital city, which is of the same name. I held them in my hands until I came within two hundred yards of the gate, and desired them to signify my arrival to one of the secretaries, and let him know, I there waited his Majesty's commands. I had an answer in about an hour, that his Majesty, attended by the royal family, and great officers of the court, was coming out to receive me. I advanced a hundred yards. The Emperor, and his train, alighted from their horses, the Empress and ladies from their coaches, and I did not perceive they were in any fright or concern. I lay on the ground to kiss his Majesty's and the Empress's hand. I told his Majesty that I was come according to my promise, and with the licence of the Emperor my master, to have the honour of seeing so mighty a monarch, and to offer him any service in my power, consistent with my duty to my own prince; not mentioning a word of my disgrace, because I had hitherto no regular information of it, and might suppose myself wholly ignorant of any such design; neither could I reasonably conceive that the Emperor would discover the secret while I was out of his power: wherein, however, it soon appeared I was deceived.

I shall not trouble the reader with the particular account of my reception at this court, which was suitable to the generosity of so great a prince; nor of the difficulties I was in for want of a house and bed, being forced to lie on the ground, wrapped up in my coverlet.

Chapter VIII.

The author, by a lucky accident, finds means to leave Blefuscu; and, after some difficulties, returns safe to his native country.

Three days after my arrival, walking out of curiosity to the northeast coast of the island, I observed, about half a league off, in the sea, somewhat that looked like a boat overturned. I pulled off my shoes and stockings, and wading two or three hundred yards, I found the object to approach nearer by force of the tide, and then plainly saw it to be a real boat, which I supposed might, by some tempest, have been driven from a ship; whereupon I returned immediately towards the city, and desired his Imperial Majesty to lend me twenty of the tallest vessels he had left after the loss of his fleet, and three thousand seamen under the command of his Vice-Admiral. This fleet sailed round, while I went back the shortest way to the coast where I first discovered the boat; I found the tide had driven it still nearer. The seamen were all provided with cordage, which I had beforehand twisted to a sufficient strength. When the ships came up, I stripped myself, and waded till I came within an hundred yards of the boat, after which I was forced to swim till I got up to it. The seamen threw me the end of the cord, which I fastened to a hole in the fore-part of the boat, and the other end to a man of war: but I found all my labour to little purpose; for being out of my depth, I was not able to work. In this necessity, I was forced to swim behind, and push the boat forwards as often as I could, with one of my hands; and the tide favouring me, I advanced so far, that I could just hold up my chin and feel the ground. I rested two or three minutes, and then gave the boat another shove, and so on till the sea was no higher than my armpits; and now the most laborious part being over, I took out my other cables, which were stowed in one of the ships, and fastening them first to the boat, and then to nine of the vessels which attended me; the wind being favourable the seamen towed, and I shoved till we arrived within forty yards of the shore, and waiting till the tide was out, I got dry to the boat, and by the assistance of two thousand men, with ropes and engines, I made a shift to turn it on its bottom, and found it was but little damaged.

I shall not trouble the reader with the difficulties I was under by the help of certain paddles, which cost me ten days making, to get my boat to the royal port of Blefuscu, where a mighty concourse of people appeared upon my arrival, full of wonder at the sight of so prodigious a vessel. I told the Emperor that my good fortune had thrown this boat in my way, to carry me to some place from whence I might return into my native country, and begged his Majesty's orders for getting materials to fit it up, together with his licence to depart; which, after some kind expostulations, he was pleased to grant.

I did very much wonder, in all this time, not to have heard of any express relating to me from our Emperor to the court of Blefuscu. But I was afterwards given privately to understand, that his Imperial Majesty, never imagining I had the least notice of his designs, believed I was only gone to Blefuscu in performance of my promise, according to the licence he had given me, which was well known at our court, and would return in a few days when that ceremony was ended. But he was at last in pain at my long absence; and after consulting with the Treasurer, and the rest of that cabal, a person of quality was dispatched with the copy of the articles against me. This envoy had instructions to represent to the monarch of Blefuscu the great lenity of his master, who was content to punish me no further than with the loss of my eyes; that I had fled from justice, and if I did not return in two hours, I should be deprived of my title of *Nardac*, and declared a traitor. The envoy further added, that in order to maintain the peace and amity between both empires, his master expected, that his brother of Blefuscu would give orders to have me sent back to Lilliput, bound hand and foot, to be punished as a traitor.

The Emperor of Blefuscu, having taken three days to consult, returned an answer consisting of many civilities and excuses. He said, that as for sending me bound, his brother knew it was impossible; that although I had deprived him of his fleet, yet he owed great obligations to me for many good offices I had done him in making the peace. That however both their Majesties would soon be made easy; for I had found a prodigious vessel on the shore, able to carry me on the sea, which he had given order to fit up with my own assistance and direction, and he hoped in a few weeks both empires would be freed from so insupportable an incumbrance.

With this answer the envoy returned to Lilliput, and the monarch of Blefuscu related to me all that had passed, offering me at the same time (but under the strictest confidence) his gracious protection if I would continue in his service; wherein although I believed him sincere, yet I resolved never more to put any confidence in princes or ministers, where I could possibly avoid it; and therefore, with all due acknowledgements for his favourable intentions, I humbly begged to be excused. I told him, that since fortune, whether good or evil, had thrown a vessel in my way, I was resolved to venture myself in the ocean, rather than be an occasion of difference between two such mighty monarchs. Neither did I find the Emperor at all displeased; and I discovered by a certain accident, that he was very glad of my resolution, and so were most of his ministers.

These considerations moved me to hasten my departure somewhat sooner than I intended; to which the court, impatient to have me gone, very readily contributed. Five hundred workmen were employed to make two sails to my boat, according to my directions, by quilting thirteen fold of their strongest linen together. I was at the pains of making ropes and cables, by twisting ten, twenty or thirty of the thickest and strongest of theirs. A great stone that I happened to find, after a long search by the seashore, served me for an anchor. I had the tallow of three hundred cows for greasing my boat, and other uses. I was at incredible pains in cutting down some of the largest timber trees for oars and masts, wherein I was, however, much assisted by his Majesty's ship-carpenters, who helped me in smoothing them, after I had done the rough work.

In about a month, when all was prepared, I sent to receive his Majesty's commands, and to take my leave. The Emperor and royal family came out of the palace; I lay down on my face to kiss his hand, which he very graciously gave me: so did the Empress, and young princes of the blood. His Majesty presented me with fifty purses of two hundred *sprugs* apiece, together with his picture at full length, which I put immediately into one of my gloves, to keep it from being hurt. The ceremonies at my departure were too many to trouble the reader with at this time.

I stored the boat with the carcasses of an hundred oxen, and three hundred sheep, with bread and drink proportionable, and as much meat ready dressed as four hundred cooks could provide. I took with me six cows and two bulls alive, with as many ewes and rams, intending to carry them into my own country, and propagate the breed. And to feed them on board, I had a good bundle of hay, and a bag of corn. I would gladly have taken a dozen of the natives, but this was a thing the Emperor would by no means permit; and besides a diligent search into my pockets, his Majesty engaged my honour not to carry away any of his subjects, although with their own consent and desire.

Having thus prepared all things as well as I was able, I set sail on the twenty-fourth day of September, 1701, at six in the morning; and when I had gone about four leagues to the northward, the wind being at southeast, at six in the evening, I descried a small island about half a league to the northwest. I advanced forward, and cast anchor on the lee-side of the island, which seemed to be uninhabited. I then took some refreshment, and went to my rest. I slept well, and as I conjecture at least six hours, for I found the day broke in two hours after I awaked. It was a clear night. I eat my breakfast before the sun was up; and heaving anchor, the wind being favourable, I steered the same course that I had done the day before, wherein I was directed by my pocket-compass. My intention was to reach, if possible, one of those islands which I had reason to believe lay to the northeast of Van Diemen's Land. I discovered nothing all that day; but upon the next, about three in the afternoon, when I had by my computation made twenty-four leagues from Blefuscu, I descried a sail steering to the southeast; my course was due east. I hailed her, but could get no answer; yet I found I gained upon her, for the wind slackened. I made all the sail I could, and in half an hour she spied me, then hung out her ancient, and discharged a gun. It is not easy to express the joy I was in upon the unexpected hope of once more seeing my beloved country, and the dear pledges I had left in it. The ship slackened her sails, and I came up with her between five and six in the evening, September 26; but my heart leapt within me to see her English colours. I put my cows and sheep into my coat-pockets, and got on board with all my little cargo of provisions. The vessel was an English merchantman, returning from Japan by the North and South Seas; the captain, Mr. John Biddel of Deptford, a very civil man, and an excellent sailor. We were now in the latitude of 30 degrees south; there were about fifty men in the ship; and here I met an old comrade of mine, one Peter Williams, who gave me a good character to the captain. This gentleman treated me with kindness, and desired I would let him know what place I came from last, and whither I was bound; which I did in few words, but he thought I was raving, and that the dangers I underwent had disturbed my head; whereupon I took my black cattle and sheep out of my pocket, which, after great astonishment, clearly convinced him of my veracity. I then showed him the gold given me by the Emperor of Blefuscu, together with his Majesty's picture at full length, and some other rarities of that country. I gave him two purses of two hundred *sprugs* each, and promised, when we arrived in England, to make him a present of a cow and a sheep big with young.

I shall not trouble the reader with a particular account of this voyage, which was very prosperous for the most part. We arrived in the Downs on the 13th of April, 1702. I had only one misfortune, that the rats on board carried away one of my sheep; I found her bones in a hole, picked clean from the flesh. The rest of my cattle I got safe on shore, and set them a grazing in a bowling-green at Greenwich, where the fineness of the grass made them feed very heartily, though I had always feared the contrary; neither could I possibly have preserved them in so long a voyage, if the captain had not allowed me some of his best biscuit, which, rubbed to powder, and mingled with water, was their constant food. The short time I continued in England, I made a considerable profit by showing my cattle to many persons of quality, and others: and before I began my second voyage, I sold them for six hundred pounds. Since my last return, I find the breed is considerably increased, especially the sheep; which I hope will prove much to the advantage of the woollen manufacture, by the fineness of the fleeces.

I stayed but two months with my wife and family; for my insatiable desire of seeing foreign countries would suffer me to continue no longer. I left fifteen hundred pounds with my wife, and fixed her in a good house at Redriff. My remaining stock I carried with me, part in money, and part in goods, in hopes to improve my fortunes. My eldest uncle John had left me an estate in land, near Epping, of about thirty pounds a year; and I had a long lease of the Black Bull in Fetter Lane, which yielded me as much more: so that I was not in any danger of leaving my family upon the parish. My son Johnny, named so after his uncle, was at the grammar school, and a towardly child. My daughter Betty (who is now well married, and has children) was then at her needlework. I took leave of my wife, and boy and girl with tears on both sides, and went on board the *Adventure*, a merchant-ship of three hundred tons, bound for Surat, Captain John Nicholas of Liverpool, commander. But my account of this voyage must be referred to the second part of my *Travels*.

THE END OF THE FIRST PART.

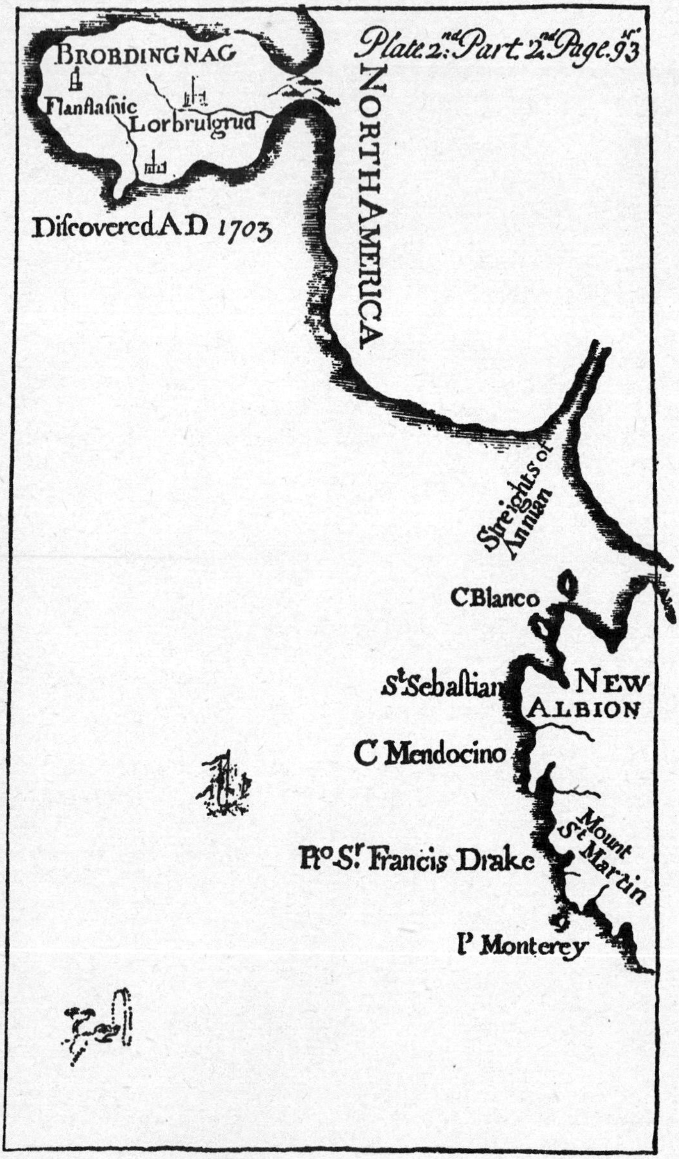

BRORDINGNAG

Flanflasnic

Lorbrulgrud

Discovered A.D. 1703

Plate 2.nd Part 2.nd Page 93.r

NORTH AMERICA

Streights of Annian

C Blanco

S.t Sebastian

NEW ALBION

C. Mendocino

P.to S.r Francis Drake

Mount S.t Martin

P. Monterey

TRAVELS.

PART II.

A VOYAGE TO BROBDINGNAG.

CHAPTER I.

A great storm described. The longboat sent to fetch water, the author
goes with it to discover the country. He is left on shore, is seized
by one of the natives, and carried to a farmer's house. His re-
ception there, with several accidents that happened there. A de-
scription of the inhabitants.

HAVING been condemned by nature and fortune to an
active and restless life, in two months after my return I
again left my native country, and took shipping in the
Downs on the 20th day of June, 1702, in the *Adventure*, Capt.
John Nicholas, a Cornish man, commander, bound for Surat. We
had a very prosperous gale till we arrived at the Cape of Good
Hope, where we landed for fresh water, but discovering a leak
we unshipped our goods, and wintered there; for the captain falling sick of an ague, we could not leave the Cape till the end of
March. We then set sail, and had a good voyage till we passed the
Straits of Madagascar; but having got northward of that island,
and to about five degrees south latitude, the winds, which in those
seas are observed to blow a constant equal gale between the north
and west from the beginning of December to the beginning of
May, on the 19th of April began to blow with much greater violence, and more westerly than usual, continuing so for twenty
days together, during which time we were driven a little to the
east of the Molucca Islands, and about three degrees northward of
the Line, as our captain found by an observation he took the 2nd
of May, at which time the wind ceased, and it was a perfect calm,
whereat I was not a little rejoiced. But he, being a man well
experienced in the navigation of those seas, bid us all prepare
against a storm, which accordingly happened the day following:
for a southern wind, called the southern monsoon, began to set in.

Finding it was like to overblow, we took in our spritsail, and
stood by to hand the foresail; but making foul weather, we

looked the guns were all fast, and handed the missen. The ship
lay very broad off, so we thought it better spooning before the
sea, than trying or hulling. We reefed the foresail and set him.
we hauled aft the fore-sheet; the helm was hard a weather. The
ship wore bravely. We belayed the fore-downhaul; but the sail
was split, and we hauled down the yard, and got the sail into the
ship, and unbound all the things clear of it. It was a very fierce
storm; the sea broke strange and dangerous. We hauled off upon
the lanyard of the whipstaff, and helped the man at helm. We
would not get down our topmast, but let all stand, because she
scudded before the sea very well, and we knew that the topmast
being aloft, the ship was the wholesomer, and made better way
through the sea, seeing we had searoom. When the storm was
over, we set foresail and mainsail, and brought the ship to. Then
we set the missen, main-topsail and the fore-topsail. Our course
was east-northeast, the wind was at southwest. We got the starboard tacks aboard, we cast off our weatherbraces and lifts; we
set in the lee braces, and hauled forward by the weather bowl-
ings, and hauled them tight, and belayed them, and hauled over
the missen tack to windward, and kept her full and by as near as
she would lie.

During this storm, which was followed by a strong wind
west-southwest, we were carried by my computation about five
hundred leagues to the east, so that the oldest sailor on board
could not tell in what part of the world we were. Our provisions held out well, our ship was staunch, and our crew all in
good health; but we lay in the utmost distress for water. We
thought it best to hold on the same course rather than turn more
northerly, which might have brought us to the northwest parts
of Great Tartary, and into the frozen sea.

On the 16th day of June, 1703, a boy on the topmast discovered land. On the 17th we came in full view of a great island
or continent (for we knew not whether) on the south side
whereof was a small neck of land jutting out into the sea, and a
creek too shallow to hold a ship of above one hundred tons. We
cast anchor within a league of this creek, and our captain sent a
dozen of his men well armed in the longboat, with vessels for
water if any could be found. I desired his leave to go with them,
that I might see the country, and make what discoveries I could.
When we came to land we saw no river or spring, nor any sign
of inhabitants. Our men therefore wandered on the shore to
find out some fresh water near the sea, and I walked alone about
a mile on the other side, where I observed the country all barren
and rocky. I now began to be weary, and seeing nothing to en-

tertain my curiosity, I returned gently down towards the creek; and the sea being full in my view, I saw our men already got into the boat, and rowing for life to the ship. I was going to hollow after them, although it had been to little purpose, when I observed a huge creature walking after them in the sea, as fast as he could: he waded not much deeper than his knees, and took prodigious strides: but our men had the start of him half a league, and the sea thereabouts being full of sharp pointed rocks, the monster was not able to overtake the boat. This I was afterwards told, for I durst not stay to see the issue of that adventure; but ran as fast as I could the way I first went; and then climbed up a steep hill which gave me some prospect of the country. I found it fully cultivated; but that which first surprised me was the length of the grass, which in those grounds that seemed to be kept for hay was above twenty foot high.

I fell into a high road, for so I took it to be, although it served to the inhabitants only as a footpath through a field of barley. Here I walked on for some time, but could see little on either side, it being now near harvest, and the corn rising at least forty foot. I was an hour walking to the end of this field, which was fenced in with a hedge of at least one hundred and twenty foot high, and the trees so lofty that I could make no computation of their altitude. There was a stile to pass from this field into the next. It had four steps, and a stone to cross over when you came to the uppermost. It was impossible for me to climb this stile, because every step was six foot high, and the upper stone above twenty. I was endeavouring to find some gap in the hedge, when I discovered one of the inhabitants in the next field advancing towards the stile, of the same size with him whom I saw in the sea pursuing our boat. He appeared as tall as an ordinary spire-steeple, and took about ten yards at every stride, as near as I could guess. I was struck with the utmost fear and astonishment, and ran to hide my self in the corn, from whence I saw him at the top of the stile, looking back into the next field on the right hand, and heard him call in a voice many degrees louder than a speaking-trumpet; but the noise was so high in the air, that at first I certainly thought it was thunder. Whereupon seven monsters like himself came towards him with reaping-hooks in their hands, each hook about the largeness of six scythes. These people were not so well clad as the first, whose servants or labourers they seemed to be. For, upon some words he spoke, they went to reap the corn in the field where I lay. I kept from them at as great a distance as I could, but was forced to move with extreme difficulty, for the stalks of the corn were sometimes not above a foot distant, so that I could hardly squeeze my body betwixt them. However, I made a shift to go forward till I came to a part of the field where the corn had been laid by the rain and wind. Here it was impossible for me to advance a step: for the stalks were so interwoven that I could not creep through, and the beards of the fallen ears so strong and pointed that they pierced through my clothes into my flesh. At the same time I heard the reapers not above an hundred yards behind me. Being quite dispirited with toil, and wholly overcome by grief and despair, I lay down between two ridges, and heartily wished I might there end my days. I bemoaned my desolate widow, and fatherless children. I lamented my own folly and wilfulness in attempting a second voyage against the advice of all my friends and relations. In this terrible agitation of mind I could not forbear thinking of Lilliput, whose inhabitants looked upon me as the greatest prodigy that ever appeared in the world: where I was able to draw an imperial fleet in my hand, and perform those other actions which will be recorded for ever in the chronicles of that empire, while posterity shall hardly believe them, although attested by millions. I reflected what a mortification it must prove to me to appear as inconsiderable in this nation as one single Lilliputian would be among us. But this I conceived was to be the least of my misfortunes: for, as human creatures are observed to be more savage and cruel in proportion to their bulk, what could I expect but to be a morsel in the mouth of the first among these enormous barbarians who should happen to seize me? Undoubtedly philosophers are in the right when they tell us, that nothing is great or little otherwise than by comparison. It might have pleased fortune to let the Lilliputians find some nation, where the people were as diminutive with respect to them, as they were to me. And who knows but that even this prodigious race of mortals might be equally overmatched in some distant part of the world, whereof we have yet no discovery?

Scared and confounded as I was, I could not forbear going on with these reflections, when one of the reapers, approaching within ten yards of the ridge where I lay, made me apprehend that with the next step I should be squashed to death under his foot, or cut in two with his reaping hook. And therefore, when he was again about to move, I screamed as loud as fear could make me. Whereupon the huge creature trod short, and looking round about under him for some time, at last espied me as I lay on the ground. He considered a while with the caution of one who endeavours to lay hold on a small dangerous animal in such a manner that it shall not be able either to scratch or to bite him, as I my self have sometimes done with a weasel in England. At length he ventured to take me up behind by the middle between his forefinger and thumb, and brought me within three yards of his eyes, that he might behold my shape more perfectly. I guessed his meaning, and my good fortune gave me so much presence of mind, that I resolved not to struggle in the least as he held me in the air above sixty foot from the ground, although he grievously pinched my sides, for fear I should slip through his fingers. All I ventured was to raise my eyes towards the sun, and place my hands together in a supplicating posture, and to speak some words in an humble melancholy tone, suitable to the condition I then was in. For I apprehended every moment that he would dash me against the ground, as we usually do any little hateful animal which we have a mind to destroy. But my good star would have it, that he appeared pleased with my voice and gestures, and began to look upon me as a curiosity, much wondering to hear me pronounce articulate words, although he could not understand them. In the mean time I was not able to forbear groaning and shedding tears, and turning my head towards my sides; letting him know, as well as I could, how cruelly I was hurt by the pressure of his thumb and finger. He seemed to apprehend my meaning; for, lifting up the lappet of his coat, he put me gently into it, and immediately ran along with me to his master, who was a substantial farmer, and the same person I had first seen in the field.

The farmer, having (as I supposed by their talk) received such an account of me as his servant could give him, took a piece of a small straw, about the size of a walking staff, and therewith lifted up the lappets of my coat; which it seems he thought to be some kind of covering that nature had given me. He blew my hairs aside to take a better view of my face. He called his hinds about him, and asked them (as I afterwards learned) whether they had ever seen in the fields any little creature that resembled me. He then placed me softly on the ground upon all four, but I got immediately up, and walked slowly backwards and forwards, to let those people see I had no intent to run away. They all sat down in a circle about me, the better to observe my motions. I pulled off my hat, and made a low bow towards the farmer. I fell on my knees, and lifted up my hands and eyes, and spoke several words as loud as I could: I took a purse of gold out of my pocket, and humbly presented it to him. He received it on the palm of his hand, then applied it close to his eye, to see what it was, and afterwards turned it several times with the point of a pin (which he took out of his sleeve), but could make nothing of it. Whereupon I made a sign that he should place his hand on the ground. I then took the purse, and opening it, poured all the gold into his palm. There were six Spanish pieces of four pistoles each, beside twenty or thirty smaller coins. I saw him wet the tip of his little finger upon his tongue, and take up one of my largest pieces, and then another, but he seemed to be wholly ignorant what they were. He made me a sign to put them again into my purse, and the purse again into my pocket, which after offering to him several times, I thought it best to do.

The farmer by this time was convinced I must be a rational creature. He spoke often to me, but the sound of his voice pierced my ears like that of a watermill, yet his words were articulate enough. I answered as loud as I could, in several languages, and he often laid his ear within two yards of me, but all in vain, for we were wholly unintelligible to each other. He then sent his servants to their work, and taking his handkerchief out of his pocket, he doubled and spread it on his left hand, which he placed flat on the ground, with the palm upwards, making me a sign to step into it, as I could easily do, for it was not above a foot in thickness. I thought it my part to obey, and for fear of falling, laid my self at full length upon the handkerchief, with the remainder of which he lapped me up to the head for further security, and in this manner carried me home to his house. There he called his wife, and showed me to her; but she screamed and ran back as women in England do at the sight of a toad or a spider. However, when she had a while seen my behaviour, and how well I observed the signs her husband made, she was soon reconciled, and by degrees grew extremely tender of me.

It was about twelve at noon, and a servant brought in dinner. It was only one substantial dish of meat (fit for the plain condition of an husbandman) in a dish of about four and twenty foot diameter. The company were the farmer and his wife, three children, and an old grandmother: when they were sat down, the farmer placed me at some distance from him on the table, which was thirty foot high from the floor. I was in a terrible fright, and kept as far as I could from the edge for fear of falling. The wife minced a bit of meat, then crumbled some bread on a trencher, and placed it before me. I made her a low bow, took out my knife and fork, and fell to eat, which gave them exceeding delight. The mistress sent her maid for a small dram cup, which held about two gallons, and filled it with drink; I took up the vessel with much difficulty in both hands, and in a most respectful manner drank to her ladyship's health, expressing the words as loud as I could in English, which made the company laugh so heartily, that I was almost deafened with the noise. This liquor tasted like a small cider, and was not unpleasant. Then the master made me a sign to come to his trencher side; but as I walked on the table, being in great surprise all the time, as the indulgent reader will easily conceive and excuse, I happened to stumble against a crust, and fell flat on my face, but received no hurt. I got up immediately, and observing the good people to be in much concern, I took my hat (which I held under my arm out of good manners) and waving it over my head, made three huzzas to show I had got no mischief by the fall. But advancing forwards toward my master (as I shall henceforth call him) his youngest son who sat next him, an arch boy of about ten years old, took me up by the legs, and held me so high in the air, that I trembled every limb; but his father snatched me from him, and at the same time gave him such a box on the left ear, as would have felled an European troop of horse to the earth, ordering him to be taken from the table. But being afraid the boy might owe me a spite, and well remembering how mischievous all children among us naturally are to sparrows, rabbits, young kittens, and puppy dogs, I fell on my knees, and pointing to the boy, made my master understand, as well as I could, that I desired his son might be pardoned. The father complied, and the lad took his seat again; whereupon I went to him and kissed his hand, which my master took, and made him stroke me gently with it.

In the midst of dinner, my mistress's favourite cat leapt into her lap. I heard a noise behind me like that of a dozen stocking-weavers at work; and turning my head I found it proceeded from the purring of this animal, who seemed to be three times larger than an ox, as I computed by the view of her head, and one of her paws, while her mistress was feeding and stroking her. The fierceness of this creature's countenance altogether discomposed me; although I stood at the further end of the table, above fifty foot off, and although my mistress held her fast for fear she might give a spring, and seize me in her talons. But it happened there was no danger; for the cat took not the least notice of me when my master placed me within three yards of her. And as I have been always told, and found true by experience in my travels, that flying, or discovering fear before a fierce animal, is a certain way to make it pursue or attack you, so I resolved in this dangerous juncture to show no manner of concern. I walked with intrepidity five or six times before the very head of the cat, and came within half a yard of her; whereupon she drew her self back, as if she were more afraid of me: I had less apprehension concerning the dogs, whereof three or four came into the room, as it is usual in farmers' houses; one of which was a mastiff equal in bulk to four elephants, and a greyhound somewhat taller than the mastiff, but not so large.

When dinner was almost done, the nurse came in with a child of a year old in her arms, who immediately spied me, and began a squall that you might have heard from London Bridge to Chelsea, after the usual oratory of infants, to get me for a plaything. The mother out of pure indulgence took me up, and put me towards the child, who presently seized me by the middle, and got my head in his mouth, where I roared so loud that the urchin was frighted, and let me drop, and I should infallibly have broke my neck if the mother had not held her apron under me. The nurse to quiet her babe made use of a rattle, which was a kind of hollow vessel filled with great stones, and fastened by a cable to the child's waist: but all in vain, so that she was forced to apply the last remedy by giving it suck. I must confess no object ever disgusted me so much as the sight of her monstrous breast, which I cannot tell what to compare with, so as to give the curious reader an idea of its bulk, shape and colour. It stood prominent six foot, and could not be less than sixteen in circumference. The nipple was about half the bigness of my head, and the hue both of that and the dug so varified with spots, pimples and freckles, that nothing could appear more nauseous: for I had a near sight of her, she sitting down the more conveniently to give suck, and I standing on the table. This made me reflect upon the fair skins of our English ladies, who appear so beautiful to us, only because they are of our own size, and their defects not to be seen but through a magnifying glass, where we find by experiment that the smoothest and whitest skins look rough and coarse, and ill coloured.

I remember when I was at Lilliput, the complexions of those diminutive people appeared to me the fairest in the world; and talking upon this subject with a person of learning there, who was an intimate friend of mine, he said that my face appeared much fairer and smoother when he looked on me from the ground, than it did upon a nearer view when I took him up in my hand, and brought him close, which he confessed was at first a very shocking sight. He said he could discover great holes in my skin, that the stumps of my beard were ten times stronger than the bristles of a boar, and my complexion made up of several colours altogether disagreeable: although I must beg leave to say for my self, that I am as fair as most of my sex and country, and very little sunburnt by all my travels. On the other side, discoursing of the ladies in that emperor's court, he used to tell me, one had freckles, another too wide a mouth, a third too large a nose, nothing of which I was able to distinguish. I confess this reflection was obvious enough; which however I could not forbear, lest the reader might think those vast creatures were actually deformed: for I must do them justice to say they are a comely race of people; and particularly the features of my master's countenance, although he were but a farmer, when I beheld him from the height of sixty foot, appeared very well proportioned.

When dinner was done, my master went out to his labourers, and, as I could discover by his voice and gesture, gave his wife a strict charge to take care of me. I was very much tired and disposed to sleep, which my mistress perceiving, she put me on her own bed, and covered me with a clean white handkerchief, but larger and coarser than the mainsail of a man of war.

I slept about two hours, and dreamed I was at home with my wife and children, which aggravated my sorrows when I awaked and found my self alone in a vast room, between two and three hundred foot wide, and above two hundred high, lying in a bed twenty yards wide. My mistress was gone about her household affairs, and had locked me in. The bed was eight yards from the floor. Some natural necessities required me to get down; I durst not presume to call, and if I had, it would have been in vain with such a voice as mine at so great a distance from the room where I lay to the kitchen where the family kept. While I was under these circumstances two rats crept up the curtains, and ran smelling backwards and forwards on the bed. One of them came up almost to my face, whereupon I rose in a fright, and drew out my hanger to defend my self. These horrible animals had the boldness to attack me on both sides, and one of them held his fore-feet at my collar; but I had the good fortune to rip up his belly before he could do me any mischief. He fell down at my feet, and the other, seeing the fate of his comrade, made his escape, but not without one good wound on the back, which I gave him as he fled, and made the blood run trickling from him. After this exploit, I walked gently to and fro on the bed, to recover my breath and loss of spirits. These creatures were of the size of a large mastiff, but infinitely more nimble and fierce, so that if I had taken off my belt before I went to sleep, I must have infallibly been torn to pieces and devoured. I measured the tail of the dead rat, and found it to be two yards long wanting an inch; but it went against my stomach to drag the carcass off the bed, where it lay still bleeding; I observed it had yet some life, but with a strong slash cross the neck I thoroughly dispatched it.

Soon after my mistress came into the room, who seeing me all bloody, ran and took me up in her hand. I pointed to the dead rat, smiling and making other signs to show I was not hurt, whereat she was extremely rejoiced, calling the maid to take up the dead rat with a pair of tongs, and throw it out of the window. Then she set me on a table, where I showed her my hanger all bloody, and wiping it on the lappet of my coat, returned it to the scabbard. I was pressed to do more than one thing which another could not do for me, and therefore endeavoured to make my mistress understand that I desired to be set down on the floor; which after she had done, my bashfulness would not suffer me to express my self farther than by pointing to the door, and bowing several times. The good woman with much difficulty at last perceived what I would be at, and taking me up again in her hand, walked into the garden, where she set me down. I went on one side about two hundred yards, and beckoning to her not to look or to follow me, I hid myself between two leaves of sorrel, and there discharged the necessities of nature.

I hope the gentle reader will excuse me for dwelling on these and the like particulars, which, however insignificant they may appear to grovelling vulgar minds, yet will certainly help a philosopher to enlarge his thoughts and imagination, and apply them to the benefit of public as well as private life, which was my sole design in presenting this and other accounts of my travels to the world; wherein I have been chiefly studious of truth, without affecting any ornaments of learning or of style. But the whole scene of this voyage made so strong an impression on my mind, and is so deeply fixed in my memory, that in committing it to paper I did not omit one material circumstance: however, upon a strict review, I blotted out several passages of less moment which were in my first copy, for fear of being censured as tedious and trifling, whereof travellers are often, perhaps not without justice, accused.

Chapter II.

A description of the farmer's daughter. The author carried to a market-town, and then to the metropolis. The particulars of his journey.

My mistress had a daughter of nine years old, a child of forward parts for her age, very dextrous at her needle, and skilful in dressing her baby. Her mother and she contrived to fit up the baby's cradle for me against night: the cradle was put into a small drawer of a cabinet, and the drawer placed upon a hanging shelf for fear of the rats. This was my bed all the time I stayed with those people, although made more convenient by degrees, as I began to learn their language, and make my wants known. This young girl was so handy, that after I had once or twice pulled off my clothes before her, she was able to dress and undress me, although I never gave her that trouble when she would let me do either my self. She made me seven shirts, and some other linen, of as fine cloth as could be got, which indeed was coarser than sackcloth; and these she constantly washed for me with her own hands. She was likewise my school-mistress to teach me the language: when I pointed to any thing, she told me the name of it in her own tongue, so that in a few days I was able to call for whatever I had a mind to. She was very good natured, and not above forty foot high, being little for her age. She gave me the name of *Grildrig*, which the family took up, and afterwards the whole kingdom. The word imports what the Latins call *nanunculus*, the Italians *homunceletino*, and the English *manni-kin*. To her I chiefly owe my preservation in that country: we never parted while I was there; I called her my *glumdalclitch*, or 'little nurse': and I should be guilty of great ingratitude if I omitted this honourable mention of her care and affection towards me, which I heartily wish it lay in my power to requite as she deserves, instead of being the innocent but unhappy instrument of her disgrace, as I have too much reason to fear.

It now began to be known and talked of in the neighbourhood, that my master had found a strange animal in the field, about the bigness of a *splacknuck*, but exactly shaped in every part like a human creature; which it likewise imitated in all its actions; seemed to speak in a little language of its own, had already learned several words of theirs, went erect upon two legs, was tame and gentle, would come when it was called, do whatever it was bid, had the finest limbs in the world, and a complexion fairer than a nobleman's daughter of three years old. Another farmer who lived hard by, and was a particular friend of my master, came on a visit on purpose to enquire into the truth of this story. I was immediately produced, and placed upon a table, where I walked as I was commanded, drew my hanger, put it up again, made my reverence to my master's guest, asked him in his own language how he did, and told him he was welcome, just as my little nurse had instructed me. This man, who was old and dim-sighted, put on his spectacles to behold me better, at which

I could not forbear laughing very heartily, for his eyes appeared like the full moon shining into a chamber at two windows. Our people, who discovered the cause of my mirth, bore me company in laughing, at which the old fellow was fool enough to be angry and out of countenance. He had the character of a great miser, and to my misfortune he well deserved it, by the cursed advice he gave my master to show me as a sight upon a market-day in the next town, which was half an hour's riding, about two and twenty miles from our house. I guessed there was some mischief contriving, when I observed my master and his friend whispering long together, sometimes pointing at me; and my fears made me fancy that I overheard and understood some of their words. But the next morning Glumdalclitch my little nurse told me the whole matter, which she had cunningly picked out from her mother. The poor girl laid me on her bosom, and fell a weeping with shame and grief. She apprehended some mischief would happen to me from rude vulgar folks, who might squeeze me to death, or break one of my limbs by taking me in their hands. She had also observed how modest I was in my nature, how nicely I regarded my honour, and what an indignity I should conceive it to be exposed for money as a public spectacle to the meanest of the people. She said, her papa and mamma had promised that Grildrig should be hers, but now she found they meant to serve her as they did last year, when they pretended to give her a lamb, and yet, as soon as it was fat, sold it to a butcher. For my own part, I may truly affirm that I was less concerned than my nurse. I had a strong hope, which never left me, that I should one day recover my liberty; and as to the ignominy of being carried about for a monster, I considered my self to be a perfect stranger in the country, and that such a misfortune could never be charged upon me as a reproach if ever I should return to England; since the King of Great Britain himself, in my condition, must have undergone the same distress.

My master, pursuant to the advice of my friend, carried me in a box the next market-day to the neighbouring town, and took along with him his little daughter my nurse upon a pillion behind him. The box was close on every side, with a little door for me to go in and out, and a few gimlet-holes to let in air. The girl had been so careful to put the quilt of her baby's bed into it, for me to lie down on. However, I was terribly shaken and discomposed in this journey, although it were but of half an hour. For the horse went about forty foot at every step, and trotted so high, that the agitation was equal to the rising and falling of a ship in a great storm, but much more frequent: our journey was somewhat further than from London to St. Albans. My master alighted at an inn which he used to frequent; and after consulting a while with the inn-keeper, and making some necessary preparations, he hired the *Grultrud*, or crier, to give notice through the town of a strange creature to be seen at the Sign of the Green Eagle, not so big as a *splacknuck* (an animal in that country very finely shaped, about six foot long) and in every part of the body resembling an human creature, could speak several words, and perform an hundred diverting tricks.

I was placed upon a table in the largest room of the inn, which might be near three hundred foot square. My little nurse stood on a low stool close to the table, to take care of me, and direct what I should do. My master, to avoid a crowd, would suffer only thirty people at a time to see me. I walked about on the table as the girl commanded; she asked me questions as far as she knew my understanding of the language reached, and I answered them as loud as I could. I turned about several times to the company, paid my humble respects, said they were welcome, and used some other speeches I had been taught. I took up a thimble filled with liquor, which Glumdalclitch had given me for a cup, and drank their health. I drew out my hanger, and flourished with it after the manner of fencers in England. My nurse gave me part of a straw, which I exercised as a pike, having learned the art in my youth. I was that day shown to twelve sets of company, and as often forced to go over again with the same fopperies, till I was half dead with weariness and vexation. For those who had seen me made such wonderful reports, that the people were ready to break down the doors to come in. My master for his own interest would not suffer any one to touch me except my nurse; and, to prevent danger, benches were set round the table at such a distance as put me out of every body's reach. However, an unlucky school-boy aimed a hazel nut directly at my head, which very narrowly missed me; otherwise, it came with so much violence that it would have infallibly knocked out my brains, for it was almost as large as a small pumpion: but I had the satisfaction to see the young rogue well beaten, and turned out of the room.

My master gave public notice, that he would show me again the next market-day, and in the mean time he prepared a more convenient vehicle for me, which he had reason enough to do; for I was so tired with my first journey, and with entertaining company for eight hours together, that I could hardly stand upon my legs, or speak a word. It was at least three days before I recovered my strength; and that I might have no rest at home, all the neighbouring gentlemen from an hundred miles round, hearing of my fame, came to see me at my master's own house. There could not be fewer than thirty persons with their wives and children (for the country is very populous); and my master demanded the rate of a full room whenever he showed me at home, although it were only to a single family. So that for some time I had but little ease every day of the week (except Wednesday, which is their Sabbath) although I were not carried to the town.

My master, finding how profitable I was like to be, resolved to carry me to the most considerable cities of the kingdom. Having therefore provided himself with all things necessary for a long journey, and settled his affairs at home, he took leave of his wife, and upon the 17th of August, 1703, about two months after my arrival, we set out for the metropolis, situated near the middle of that empire, and about three thousand miles distance from our house: my master made his daughter Glumdalclitch ride behind him. She carried me on her lap in a box tied about her waist. The girl had lined it on all sides with the softest cloth she could get, well quilted underneath, furnished it with her baby's bed, provided me with linen and other necessaries, and made every thing as convenient as she could. We had no other company but a boy of the house, who rode after us with the luggage.

My master's design was to show me in all the towns by the way, and to step out of the road for fifty or an hundred miles, to any village or person of quality's house where he might expect custom. We made easy journeys of not above seven or eightscore miles a day: for Glumdalclitch, on purpose to spare me, complained she was tired with the trotting of the horse. She often took me out of my box at my own desire, to give me air, and show me the country, but always held me fast by leading-strings. We passed over five or six rivers many degrees broader and deeper than the Nile or the Ganges; and there was hardly a rivulet so small as the Thames at London Bridge. We were ten weeks in our journeys, and I was shown in eighteen large towns, besides many villages and private families.

On the 26th day of October, we arrived at the metropolis, called in their language *Lorbrulgrud*, or *Pride of the Universe*. My master took a lodging in the principal street of the city, not far from the royal palace, and put out bills in the usual form, containing an exact description of my person and parts. He hired a large room between three and four hundred foot wide. He provided a table sixty foot in diameter, upon which I was to act my part, and palisadoed it round three feet from the edge, and as many high, to prevent my falling over. I was shown ten times a day to the wonder and satisfaction of all people. I could now speak the language tolerably well, and perfectly understood every word that was spoken to me. Besides, I had learnt their alphabet, and could make a shift to explain a sentence here and there; for Glumdalclitch had been my instructor while we were at home, and at leisure hours during our journey. She carried a little book in her pocket, not much larger than a Sanson's *Atlas*; it was a common treatise for the use of young girls, giving a short account of their religion; out of this she taught me my letters, and interpreted the words.

CHAPTER III.

The author sent for to court. The Queen buys him of his master the farmer, and presents him to the King. He disputes with his Majesty's great scholars. An apartment at court provided for the author. He is in high favour with the Queen. He stands up for the honour of his own country. His quarrels with the Queen's dwarf.

The frequent labours I underwent every day made in a few weeks a very considerable change in my health: the more my master got by me, the more unsatiable he grew. I had quite lost my stomach, and was almost reduced to a skeleton. The farmer observed it, and concluding I soon must die, resolved to make as good a hand of me as he could. While he was thus reasoning and resolving with himself, a *slardral*, or gentleman usher, came from court, commanding my master to bring me immediately thither for the diversion of the Queen and her ladies. Some of the latter had already been to see me, and reported strange things of my beauty, behaviour, and good sense. Her Majesty and those who attended her were beyond measure delighted with my demeanor. I fell on my knees, and begged the honour of kissing her imperial foot; but this gracious princess held out her little finger towards me (after I was set on a table) which I embraced in both my arms, and put the tip of it, with the utmost respect, to my lip. She made me some general questions about my country and my travels, which I answered as distinctly and in as few words as I could. She asked whether I would be content to live at court. I bowed down to the board of the table, and humbly answered that I was my master's slave, but if I were at my own disposal, I should be proud to devote my life to her Majesty's service. She then asked my master whether he were willing to sell me at a good price. He, who apprehended I could not live a month, was ready enough to part with me, and demanded a thousand pieces of gold, which were ordered him on the spot, each piece being about the bigness of eight hundred moidores; but, allowing for the proportion of all things between that country and Europe, and the high price of gold among them, was hardly so great a sum as a thousand guineas would be in England. I then said to the Queen, since I was now her Majesty's most humble creature and vassal, I must beg the favour, that Glumdalclitch, who had always tended me with so much care and kindness, and understood to do it so well, might be admitted into her service, and continue to be my nurse and instructor. Her Majesty agreed to my petition, and easily got the farmer's consent, who was glad enough to have his daughter preferred at court: and the poor girl herself was not able to hide her joy: my late master withdrew, bidding me farewell, and saying he had left me in a good service; to which I replied not a word, only making him a slight bow.

The Queen observed my coldness, and when the farmer was gone out of the apartment, asked me the reason. I made bold to tell her Majesty that I owed no other obligation to my late master, than his not dashing out the brains of a poor harmless creature found by chance in his field; which obligation was amply recompensed by the gain he had made in showing me through half the kingdom, and the price he had now sold me for. That the life I had since led was laborious enough to kill an animal of ten times my strength. That my health was much impaired by the continual drudgery of entertaining the rabble every hour of the day, and that if my master had not thought my life in danger, her Majesty perhaps would not have got so cheap a bargain. But as I was out of all fear of being ill treated under the protection of so great and good an empress, the Ornament of Nature, the Darling of the World, the Delight of her Subjects, the Phoenix of the Creation; so, I hoped, my late master's apprehensions would appear to be groundless, for I already found my spirits to revive by the influence of her most august presence.

This was the sum of my speech, delivered with great improprieties and hesitation; the latter part was altogether framed in the style peculiar to that people, whereof I learned some phrases from Glumdalclitch, while she was carrying me to court.

The Queen, giving great allowance for my defectiveness in speaking, was however surprised at so much wit and good sense in so diminutive an animal. She took me in her own hand, and carried me to the King, who was then retired to his cabinet. His Majesty, a prince of much gravity, and austere countenance, not well observing my shape at first view, asked the Queen after a cold manner, how long it was since she grew fond of a *splack-nuck;* for such it seems he took me to be, as I lay upon my breast in her Majesty's right hand. But this princess, who hath an infinite deal of wit and humour, set me gently on my feet upon the scrutore, and commanded me to give his Majesty an account of my self, which I did in a very few words; and Glumdalclitch, who attended at the cabinet door, and could not endure I should be out of her sight, being admitted, confirmed all that had passed from my arrival at her father's house.

The King, although he be as learned a person as any in his dominions, had been educated in the study of philosophy, and particularly mathematics; yet when he observed my shape exactly, and saw me walk erect, before I began to speak, conceived I might be a piece of clock-work (which is in that country arrived to a very great perfection), contrived by some ingenious artist. But, when he heard my voice, and found what I delivered to be regular and rational, he could not conceal his astonishment. He was by no means satisfied with the relation I gave him of the manner I came into his kingdom, but thought it a story concerted between Glumdalclitch and her father, who had taught me a set of words to make me sell at a higher price. Upon this imagination he put several other questions to me, and still received rational answers, no otherwise defective than by a foreign accent, and an imperfect knowledge in the language, with some rustic phrases which I had learned at the farmer's house, and did not suit the polite style of a court.

His Majesty sent for three great scholars who were then in their weekly waiting (according to the custom in that country). These gentlemen, after they had a while examined my shape with much nicety, were of different opinions concerning me. They all agreed that I could not be produced according to the regular laws of nature, because I was not framed with a capacity of preserving my life, either by swiftness, or climbing of trees, or digging holes in the earth. They observed by my teeth, which they viewed with great exactness, that I was a carnivorous animal; yet most quadrupeds being an overmatch for me, and field mice, with some others, too nimble, they could not imagine how I should be able to support my self, unless I fed upon snails and other insects, which they offered by many learned arguments to evince that I could not possibly do. One of them seemed to think that I might be an embryo, or abortive birth. But this opinion was rejected by the other two, who observed my limbs to be perfect and finished, and that I had lived several years, as it was manifested from my beard, the stumps whereof they plainly discovered through a magnifying-glass. They would not allow me to be a dwarf, because my littleness was beyond all degrees of comparison; for the Queen's favourite dwarf, the smallest ever known in that kingdom, was near thirty foot high. After much debate, they concluded unanimously that I was only *relplum scalcath*, which is interpreted literally, *lusus naturæ;* a determination exactly agreeable to the modern philosophy of Europe, whose professors, disdaining the old evasion of occult causes, whereby the followers of Aristotle endeavour in vain to disguise their ignorance, have invented this wonderful solution of all difficulties to the unspeakable advancement of human knowledge.

After this decisive conclusion, I entreated to be heard a word or two. I applied myself to the King, and assured his Majesty that I came from a country which abounded with several millions of both sexes, and of my own stature; where the animals, trees, and houses were all in proportion, and where by consequence I might be as able to defend my self, and to find sustenance, as any of his Majesty's subjects could do here; which I took for a full answer to those gentlemen's arguments. To this they only replied with a smile of contempt, saying, that the farmer had instructed me very well in my lesson. The King, who had a much better understanding, dismissing his learned men, sent for the farmer, who by good fortune was not yet gone out of town; having therefore first examined him privately, and then confronted him with me and the young girl, his Majesty began to think that what we told him might possibly be true. He desired the Queen to order that a particular care should be taken of me, and was of opinion, that Glumdalclitch should still continue in her office of tending me, because he observed we had a great affection for each other. A convenient apartment was provided for her at court; she had a sort of governess appointed to take care of her education, a maid to dress her, and two other servants for menial offices; but the care of me was wholly appropriated to her self. The Queen commanded her own cabinet-maker to contrive a box that might serve me for a bed-chamber, after the model that Glumdalclitch and I should agree upon. This man was a most ingenious artist, and according to my directions, in three weeks finished for me a wooden chamber of sixteen foot square, and twelve high, with sash-windows, a door, and two closets, like a London bed-chamber. The board that made the ceiling was to be lifted up and down by two hinges, to put in a bed ready furnished by her Majesty's upholsterer, which Glumdalclitch took out every day to air, made it with her own hands, and letting it down at night, locked up the roof over me. A nice workman, who was famous for little curiosities, undertook to make me two chairs, with backs and frames, of a substance not unlike ivory, and two tables, with a cabinet to put my things in. The room was quilted on all sides, as well as the floor and the ceiling, to prevent any accident from the carelessness of those who carried me, and to break the force of a jolt when I went in a coach. I desired a lock for my door to prevent rats and mice from coming in: the smith after several attempts made the smallest that was ever seen among them, for I have known a larger at the gate of a gentleman's house in England. I made a shift to keep the key in a pocket of my own, fearing Glumdal-clitch might lose it. The Queen likewise ordered the thinnest silks that could be gotten, to make me clothes, not much thicker than an English blanket, very cumbersome till I was accustomed to them. They were after the fashion of the kingdom, partly resembling the Persian, and partly the Chinese, and are a very grave decent habit.

The Queen became so fond of my company, that she could not dine without me. I had a table placed upon the same at which her Majesty eat, just at her left elbow, and a chair to sit on. Glumdalclitch stood upon a stool on the floor, near my table, to assist and take care of me. I had an entire set of silver dishes and plates, and other necessaries, which, in proportion to those of the Queen, were not much bigger than what I have seen in a London toy-shop, for the furniture of a baby-house: these my little nurse kept in her pocket, in a silver box, and gave me at meals as I wanted them, always cleaning them her self. No person dined with the Queen but the two princesses royal, the elder sixteen years old, and the younger at that time thirteen and a month. Her Majesty used to put a bit of meat upon one of my dishes, out of which I carved for my self; and her diversion was to see me eat in miniature. For the Queen (who had indeed but a weak stomach) took up at one mouthful as much as a dozen English farmers could eat at a meal, which to me was for some time a very nauseous sight. She would craunch the wing of a lark, bones and all, between her teeth, although it were nine times as large as that of a full-grown turkey; and put a bit of bread in her mouth, as big as two twelve-penny loaves. She drank out of a golden cup, above a hogshead at a draught. Her knives were twice as long as a scythe set straight upon the handle. The spoons, forks, and other instruments were all in the same proportion. I remember when Glumdalclitch carried me out of curiosity to see some of the tables at court, where ten or a dozen of these enormous knives and forks were lifted up together, I thought I had never till then beheld so terrible a sight.

It is the custom that every Wednesday (which, as I have before observed, was their Sabbath) the King and Queen, with the royal issue of both sexes, dine together in the apartment of his Majesty, to whom I was now become a favourite; and at these times my little chair and table were placed at his left hand before one of the salt-cellars. This prince took a pleasure in conversing with me, enquiring into the manners, religion, laws, government, and learning of Europe, wherein I gave him the best account I was able. His apprehension was so clear, and his judgment so exact, that he made very wise reflections and observations upon all I said. But I confess, that after I had been a little too copious in talking of my own beloved country, of our trade, and wars by sea and land, of our schisms in religion, and parties in the state, the prejudices of his education prevailed so far, that he could not forbear taking me up in his right hand, and stroking me gently with the other, after an hearty fit of laughing, asked me whether I were a Whig or a Tory. Then turning to his first minister, who waited behind him with a white staff, near as tall as the main-mast of the *Royal Sovereign*, he observed how contemptible a thing was human grandeur, which could be mimicked by such diminutive insects as I: And yet, said he, I dare engage, those creatures have their titles and distinctions of honour, they contrive little nests and burrows, that they call houses and cities; they make a figure in dress and equipage; they love, they fight, they dispute, they cheat, they betray. And thus he continued on, while my colour came and went several times, with indignation to hear our noble country, the mistress of arts and arms, the scourge of France, the arbitress of Europe, the seat of virtue, piety, honour and truth, the pride and envy of the world, so contemptuously treated.

But, as I was not in a condition to resent injuries, so, upon mature thoughts, I began to doubt whether I were injured or no. For, after having been accustomed several months to the sight and converse of this people, and observed every object upon which I cast my eyes to be of proportionable magnitude, the horror I had first conceived from their bulk and aspect was so far worn off, that if I had then beheld a company of English lords and ladies in their finery and birthday clothes, acting their several parts in the most courtly manner of strutting, and bowing, and prating, to say the truth, I should have been strongly tempted to laugh as much at them as this king and his grandees did at me. Neither indeed could I forbear smiling at my self, when the

Queen used to place me upon her hand towards a looking-glass, by which both our persons appeared before me in full view together; and there could nothing be more ridiculous than the comparison: so that I really began to imagine my self dwindled many degrees below my usual size.

Nothing angered and mortified me so much as the Queen's dwarf, who being of the lowest stature that was ever in that country (for I verily think he was not full thirty foot high) became so insolent at seeing a creature so much beneath him, that he would always affect to swagger and look big as he passed by me in the Queen's antechamber, while I was standing on some table talking with the lords or ladies of the court, and he seldom failed of a smart word or two upon my littleness; against which I could only revenge my self by calling him brother, challenging him to wrestle, and such repartees as are usual in the mouths of court pages. One day at dinner this malicious little cub was so nettled with something I had said to him, that raising himself upon the frame of her Majesty's chair, he took me up by the middle, as I was sitting down, not thinking any harm, and let me drop into a large silver bowl of cream, and then ran away as fast as he could. I fell over head and ears, and if I had not been a good swimmer, it might have gone very hard with me; for Glumdalclitch in that instant happened to be at the other end of the room, and the Queen was in such a fright that she wanted presence of mind to assist me. But my little nurse ran to my relief, and took me out, after I had swallowed above a quart of cream. I was put to bed; however I received no other damage than the loss of a suit of clothes, which was utterly spoiled. The dwarf was soundly whipped, and as a further punishment, forced to drink up the bowl of cream into which he had thrown me; neither was he ever restored to favour: for, soon after, the Queen bestowed him to a lady of high quality, so that I saw him no more, to my very great satisfaction; for I could not tell to what extremities such a malicious urchin might have carried his resentment.

He had before served me a scurvy trick, which set the Queen a laughing, although at the same time she were heartily vexed, and would have immediately cashiered him, if I had not been so generous as to intercede. Her Majesty had taken a marrow-bone upon her plate, and after knocking out the marrow, placed the bone again in the dish erect as it stood before; the dwarf watching his opportunity, while Glumdalclitch was gone to the sideboard, mounted the stool she stood on to take care of me at meals, took me up in both hands, and squeezing my legs together, wedged them into the marrow-bone above my waist, where I stuck for some time, and made a very ridiculous figure. I believe it was near a minute before any one knew what was become of me, for I thought it below me to cry out. But, as princes seldom get their meat hot, my legs were not scalded, only my stockings and breeches in a sad condition. The dwarf at my entreaty had no other punishment than a sound whipping.

I was frequently rallied by the Queen upon account of my fearfulness, and she used to ask me whether the people of my country were as great cowards as my self. The occasion was this. The kingdom is much pestered with flies in summer, and these odious insects, each of them as big as a Dunstable lark, hardly gave me any rest while I sat at dinner, with their continual humming and buzzing about my ears. They would sometimes alight upon my victuals, and leave their loathsome excrement or spawn behind, which to me was very visible, although not to the natives of that country, whose large optics were not so acute as mine in viewing smaller objects. Sometimes they would fix upon my nose or forehead, where they stung me to the quick, smelling very offensively, and I could easily trace that viscous matter, which our naturalists tell us enables those creatures to walk with their feet upwards upon a ceiling. I had much ado to defend my self against these detestable animals, and could not forbear starting when they came on my face. It was the common practice of the dwarf to catch a number of these insects in his hand as schoolboys do among us, and let them out suddenly under my nose on purpose to frighten me, and divert the Queen. My remedy was to cut them in pieces with my knife as they flew in the air, wherein my dexterity was much admired.

I remember one morning when Glumdalclitch had set me in my box upon a window, as she usually did in fair days to give me air (for I durst not venture to let the box be hung on a nail out of the window, as we do with cages in England) after I had lifted up one of my sashes, and sat down at my table to eat a piece of sweet cake for my breakfast, above twenty wasps, allured by the smell, came flying into the room, humming louder than the drones of as many bagpipes. Some of them seized my cake, and carried it piecemeal away, others flew about my head and face, confounding me with the noise, and putting me in the utmost terror of their stings. However I had the courage to rise and draw my hanger, and attack them in the air. I dispatched four of them, but the rest got away, and I presently shut my window. These insects were as large as partridges: I took out their stings, found them an inch and a half long, and as sharp as needles. I carefully preserved them all, and having since shown them with some other curiosities in several parts of Europe, upon my return to England I gave three of them to Gresham College, and kept the fourth for my self.

CHAPTER IV.

The country described. A proposal for correcting modern maps. The King's palace, and some account of the metropolis. The author's way of travelling. The chief temple described.

I now intend to give the reader a short description of this country, as far as I travelled in it, which was not above two thousand miles round Lorbrulgrud the metropolis. For the Queen, whom I always attended, never went further when she accompanied the King in his progresses, and there stayed till his Majesty returned from viewing his frontiers. The whole extent of this prince's dominions reacheth about six thousand miles in length, and from three to five in breadth. From whence I cannot but conclude that our geographers of Europe are in a great error, by supposing nothing but sea between Japan and California; for it was ever my opinion, that there must be a balance of earth to counterpoise the great continent of Tartary; and therefore they ought to correct their maps and charts, by joining this vast tract of land to the northwest parts of America, wherein I shall be ready to lend them my assistance.

The kingdom is a peninsula, terminated to the northeast by a ridge of mountains thirty miles high, which are altogether impassable by reason of the volcanoes upon the tops. Neither do the most learned know what sort of mortals inhabit beyond these mountains, or whether they be inhabited at all. On the three other sides it is bounded by the ocean. There is not one seaport in the whole kingdom, and those parts of the coasts into which the rivers issue are so full of pointed rocks, and the sea generally so rough, that there is no venturing with the smallest of their boats, so that these people are wholly excluded from any commerce with the rest of the world. But the large rivers are full of vessels, and abound with excellent fish, for they seldom get any from the sea, because the sea-fish are of the same size with those in Europe, and consequently not worth catching; whereby it is manifest, that nature in the production of plants and animals of so extraordinary a bulk is wholly confined to this continent, of which I leave the reasons to be determined by philosophers.

However, now and then they take a whale that happens to be dashed against the rocks, which the common people feed on heartily. These whales I have known so large that a man could hardly carry one upon his shoulders; and sometimes for curiosity they are brought in hampers to Lorbrulgrud: I saw one of them in a dish at the King's table, which passed for a rarity, but I did not observe he was fond of it; for I think indeed the bigness disgusted him, although I have seen one somewhat larger in Greenland.

The country is well inhabited, for it contains fifty-one cities, near an hundred walled towns, and a great number of villages. To satisfy my curious reader, it may be sufficient to describe Lorbrulgrud. This city stands upon almost two equal parts on each side the river that passes through. It contains above eighty thousand houses, and about six hundred thousand inhabitants. It is in length three *glonglungs* (which make about fifty-four English miles) and two and a half in breadth, as I measured it my self in the royal map made by the King's order, which was laid on the ground on purpose for me, and extended an hundred feet; I paced the diameter and circumference several times barefoot, and computing by the scale, measured it pretty exactly.

The King's palace is no regular edifice, but an heap of buildings about seven miles round: the chief rooms are generally two hundred and forty foot high, and broad and long in proportion. A coach was allowed to Glumdalclitch and me, wherein her governess frequently took her out to see the town, or go among the shops; and I was always of the party, carried in my box; although the girl at my own desire would often take me out, and hold me in her hand, that I might more conveniently view the houses and the people as we passed along the streets. I reckoned our coach to be about a square of Westminster Hall, but not altogether so high; however, I cannot be very exact. One day the governess ordered our coachman to stop at several shops, where the beggars, watching their opportunity, crowded to the sides of the coach, and gave me the most horrible spectacles that ever an European eye beheld. There was a woman with a cancer in her breast, swelled to a monstrous size, full of holes, in two or three of which I could have easily crept, and covered my whole body. There was a fellow with a wen in his neck, larger than five woolpacks, and another with a couple of wooden legs, each about twenty foot high. But the most hateful sight of all was the lice crawling on their clothes. I could see distinctly the limbs of these vermin with my naked eye, much better than those of an European louse through a microscope, and their snouts with which they rooted like swine. They were the first I had ever beheld, and I should have been curious enough to dissect one of them, if I had proper instruments (which I unluckily left behind me in the ship) although indeed the sight was so nauseous, that it perfectly turned my stomach.

Beside the large box in which I was usually carried, the Queen ordered a smaller one to be made for me, of about twelve foot square, and ten high, for the convenience of travelling, because the other was somewhat too large for Glumdalclitch's lap, and cumbersome in the coach; it was made by the same artist, whom I directed in the whole contrivance. This travelling closet was an exact square with a window in the middle of three of the squares, and each window was latticed with iron wire on the outside, to prevent accidents in long journeys. On the fourth side, which had no window, two strong staples were fixed, through which the person that carried me, when I had a mind to be on horseback, put in a leathern belt, and buckled it about his waist. This was always the office of some grave trusty servant in whom I could confide, whether I attended the King and Queen in their progresses, or were disposed to see the gardens, or pay a visit to some great lady or minister of state in the court, when Glumdalclitch happened to be out of order: for I soon began to be known and esteemed among the greatest officers, I suppose more upon account of their Majesties' favour than any merit of my own. In journeys, when I was weary of the coach, a servant on horseback would buckle my box, and place it on a cushion before him; and there I had a full prospect of the country on three sides from my three windows. I had in this closet a field-bed and a hammock hung from the ceiling, two chairs and a table, neatly screwed to the floor, to prevent being tossed about by the agitation of the horse or the coach. And having been long used to sea-voyages, those motions, although sometimes very violent, did not much discompose me.

Whenever I had a mind to see the town, it was always in my travelling-closet, which Glumdalclitch held in her lap in a kind of open sedan, after the fashion of the country, borne by four men, and attended by two others in the Queen's livery. The people, who had often heard of me, were very curious to crowd about the sedan, and the girl was complaisant enough to make the bearers stop, and to take me in her hand that I might be more conveniently seen.

I was very desirous to see the chief temple, and particularly the tower belonging to it, which is reckoned the highest in the kingdom. Accordingly one day my nurse carried me thither, but

I may truly say I came back disappointed; for the height is not above three thousand foot, reckoning from the ground to the highest pinnacle top; which, allowing for the difference between the size of those people and us in Europe, is no great matter for admiration, nor at all equal in proportion (if I rightly remember) to Salisbury steeple. But, not to detract from a nation to which during my life I shall acknowledge my self extremely obliged, it must be allowed that whatever this famous tower wants in height is amply made up in beauty and strength. For the walls are near an hundred foot thick, built of hewn stone, whereof each is about forty foot square, and adorned on all sides with statues of gods and emperors cut in marble larger than the life, placed in their several niches. I measured a little finger which had fallen down from one of these statues, and lay unperceived among some rubbish, and found it exactly four foot and an inch in length. Glumdalclitch wrapped it up in a handkerchief, and carried it home in her pocket to keep among other trinkets, of which the girl was very fond, as children at her age usually are.

The King's kitchen is indeed a noble building, vaulted at top, and about six hundred foot high. The great oven is not so wide by ten paces as the cupola at St. Paul's: for I measured the latter on purpose after my return. But if I should describe the kitchen-grate, the prodigious pots and kettles, the joints of meat turning on the spits, with many other particulars, perhaps I should be hardly believed; at least a severe critic would be apt to think I enlarged a little, as travellers are often suspected to do. To avoid which censure, I fear I have run too much into the other extreme; and that if this treatise should happen to be translated into the language of Brobdingnag (which is the general name of that kingdom) and transmitted thither, the King and his people would have reason to complain that I had done them an injury by a false and diminutive representation.

His Majesty seldom keeps above six hundred horses in his stables: they are generally from fifty-four to sixty foot high. But, when he goes abroad on solemn days, he is attended for state by a militia guard of five hundred horse, which indeed I thought was the most splendid sight that could be ever beheld, till I saw part of his army in battalia, whereof I shall find another occasion to speak.

CHAPTER V.

Several adventures that happened to the author. The execution of a criminal. The author shows his skill in navigation.

I should have lived happy enough in that country, if my lit-tleness had not exposed me to several ridiculous and troublesome accidents, some of which I shall venture to relate. Glumdalclitch often carried me into the gardens of the court in my smaller box, and would sometimes take me out of it and hold me in her hand, or set me down to walk. I remember, before the dwarf left the Queen, he followed us one day into those gardens, and my nurse having set me down, he and I being close together, near some dwarf apple-trees, I must needs show my wit by a silly allusion between him and the trees, which happens to hold in their lan-guage as it doth in ours. Whereupon the malicious rogue, watch-ing his opportunity, when I was walking under one of them, shook it directly over my head, by which a dozen apples, each of them near as large as a Bristol barrel, came tumbling about my ears; one of them hit me on the back as I chanced to stoop, and knocked me down flat on my face, but I received no other hurt, and the dwarf was pardoned at my desire, because I had given the provocation.

Another day Glumdalclitch left me on a smooth grass-plot to divert my self while she walked at some distance with her governess. In the mean time there suddenly fell such a violent shower of hail, that I was immediately by the force of it struck to the ground: and when I was down, the hailstones gave me such cruel bangs all over the body, as if I had been pelted with tennis-balls; however I made a shift to creep on all four, and shelter my self by lying flat on my face on the lee-side of a border of lemon thyme, but so bruised from head to foot that I could not go abroad in ten days. Neither is this at all to be wondered at, because nature in that country observing the same proportion through all her operations, a hailstone is near eighteen hundred times as large as one in Europe, which I can assert upon experience, having been so curious to weigh and measure them.

But a more dangerous accident happened to me in the same garden, when my little nurse, believing she had put me in a secure place, which I often entreated her to do, that I might enjoy my own thoughts, and having left my box at home to avoid the trouble of carrying it, went to another part of the gardens with her governess and some ladies of her acquaintance. While she was absent and out of hearing, a small white spaniel

belonging to one of the chief gardeners, having got by accident
into the garden, happened to range near the place where I lay.
The dog, following the scent, came directly up, and taking me
in his mouth ran straight to his master, wagging his tail, and set
me gently on the ground. By good fortune he had been so well
taught, that I was carried between his teeth without the least
hurt, or even tearing my clothes. But the poor gardener, who
knew me well, and had a great kindness for me, was in a terrible
fright. He gently took me up in both his hands, and asked me
how I did; but I was so amazed and out of breath, that I could
not speak a word. In a few minutes I came to my self, and he
carried me safe to my little nurse, who by this time had returned
to the place where she left me, and was in cruel agonies when
I did not appear, nor answer when she called: she severely reprimanded the gardener on account of his dog. But the thing
was hushed up, and never known at court; for the girl was afraid
of the Queen's anger, and truly as to my self, I thought it would
not be for my reputation that such a story should go about.

This accident absolutely determined Glumdalclitch never to
trust me abroad for the future out of her sight. I had been long
afraid of this resolution, and therefore concealed from her some
little unlucky adventures that happened in those times when I was
left by my self. Once a kite hovering over the garden made a
stoop at me, and if I had not resolutely drawn my hanger, and
run under a thick espalier, he would have certainly carried me
away in his talons. Another time walking to the top of a fresh
mole-hill, I fell to my neck in the hole through which that animal
had cast up the earth, and coined some lie not worth remembering,
to excuse my self for spoiling my clothes. I likewise broke my
right shin against the shell of a snail, which I happened to stumble
over, as I was walking alone, and thinking on poor England.

I cannot tell whether I were more pleased or mortified to observe in those solitary walks, that the smaller birds did not appear
to be at all afraid of me, but would hop about within a yard
distance, looking for worms and other food with as much indifference and security as if no creature at all were near them. I
remember a thrush had the confidence to snatch out of my hand
with his bill a piece of cake that Glumdalclitch had just given me
for my breakfast. When I attempted to catch any of these birds,
they would boldly turn against me, endevouring to pick my
fingers, which I durst not venture within their reach; and then
they would hop back unconcerned to hunt for worms or snails,
as they did before. But one day I took a thick cudgel, and threw
it with all my strength so luckily at a linnet, that I knocked him

down, and seizing him by the neck with both my hands, ran with him in triumph to my nurse. However, the bird, who had only been stunned, recovering himself, gave me so many boxes with his wings on both sides of my head and body, although I held him at arm's length, and was out of the reach of his claws, that I was twenty times thinking to let him go. But I was soon relieved by one of our servants, who wrung off the bird's neck, and I had him next day for dinner by the Queen's command. This linnet, as near as I can remember, seemed to be somewhat larger than an English swan.

The maids of honour often invited Glumdalclitch to their apartments, and desired she would bring me along with her, on purpose to have the pleasure of seeing and touching me. They would often strip me naked from top to toe, and lay me at full length in their bosoms; wherewith I was much disgusted; because, to say the truth, a very offensive smell came from their skins; which I do not mention or intend to the disadvantage of those excellent ladies, for whom I have all manner of respect; but I conceive that my sense was more acute in proportion to my littleness, and that those illustrious persons were no more disagreeable to their lovers, or to each other, than people of the same quality are with us in England. And, after all, I found their natural smell was much more supportable than when they used perfumes, under which I immediately swooned away. I cannot forget that an intimate friend of mine in Lilliput took the freedom, in a warm day, when I had used a good deal of exercise, to complain of a strong smell about me, although I am as little faulty that way as most of my sex: but I suppose his faculty of smelling was as nice with regard to me, as mine was to that of this people. Upon this point, I cannot forbear doing justice to the Queen my mistress, and Glumdalclitch my nurse, whose persons were as sweet as those of any lady in England.

That which gave me most uneasiness among these maids of honour, when my nurse carried me to visit them, was to see them use me without any manner of ceremony, like a creature who had no sort of consequence. For they would strip themselves to the skin, and put on their smocks in my presence, while I was placed on their toilet directly before their naked bodies, which, I am sure, to me was very far from being a tempting sight, or from giving me any other emotions than those of horror and disgust. Their skins appeared so coarse and uneven, so variously coloured, when I saw them near, with a mole here and there as broad as a trencher, and hairs hanging from it thicker than pack-threads; to say nothing further concerning the rest of their persons. Neither did they at all scruple while I was by to discharge what they had drunk, to the quantity of at least two hogsheads, in a vessel that held above three tuns. The handsomest among these maids of honour, a pleasant frolicsome girl of sixteen, would sometimes set me astride upon one of her nipples, with many other tricks, wherein the reader will excuse me for not being over particular. But I was so much displeased, that I entreated Glumdalclitch to contrive some excuse for not seeing that young lady any more.

One day a young gentleman, who was nephew to my nurse's governess, came and pressed them both to see an execution. It was of a man who had murdered one of that gentleman's intimate acquaintance. Glumdalclitch was prevailed on to be of the company, very much against her inclination, for she was naturally tender-hearted: and as for my self, although I abhorred such kind of spectacles, yet my curiosity tempted me to see something that I thought must be extraordinary. The malefactor was fixed in a chair upon a scaffold erected for the purpose, and his head cut off at one blow with a sword of about forty foot long. The veins and arteries spouted up such a prodigious quantity of blood, and so high in the air, that the great *jet d'eau* at Versailles was not equal for the time it lasted; and the head, when it fell on the scaffold floor, gave such a bounce as made me start, although I was at least an English mile distant.

The Queen, who often used to hear me talk of my sea-voyages, and took all occasions to divert me when I was melancholy, asked me whether I understood how to handle a sail or an oar, and whether a little exercise of rowing might not be convenient for my health. I answered that I understood both very well. For although my proper employment had been to be surgeon or doctor to the ship, yet often, upon a pinch, I was forced to work like a common mariner. But I could not see how this could be done in their country, where the smallest wherry was equal to a first rate man of war among us, and such a boat as I could manage would never live in any of their rivers: her Majesty said, if I would contrive a boat, her own joiner should make it, and she would provide a place for me to sail in. The fellow was an ingenious workman, and by my instructions in ten days finished a pleasure-boat with all its tackling, able conveniently to hold eight Europeans. When it was finished, the Queen was so delighted, that she ran with it in her lap to the King, who ordered it to be put in a cistern full of water, with me in it, by way of trial, where I could not manage my two sculls or little oars for want of room. But the Queen had before contrived another project. She ordered the joiner to make a wooden trough of three hundred foot long, fifty broad, and eight deep; which being well pitched to prevent leaking, was placed on the floor along the wall, in an outer room of the palace. It had a cock near the bottom to let out the water when it began to grow stale, and two servants could easily fill it in half an hour. Here I often used to row for my diversion, as well as that of the Queen and her ladies, who thought themselves agreeably entertained with my skill and agility. Sometimes I would put up my sail, and then my business was only to steer, while the ladies gave me a gale with their fans; and when they were weary, some of the pages would blow my sail forward with their breath, while I showed my art by steering starboard or larboard as I pleased. When I had done, Glumdalclitch always carried back my boat into her closet, and hung it on a nail to dry.

In this exercise I once met an accident which had like to have cost me my life. For, one of the pages having put my boat into the trough, the governess who attended Glumdalclitch very officiously lifted me up to place me in the boat, but I happened to slip through her fingers, and should have infallibly fallen down forty foot upon the floor if, by the luckiest chance in the world, I had not been stopped by a corking-pin that stuck in the good gentlewoman's stomacher; the head of the pin passed between my shirt and the waistband of my breeches, and thus I was held by the middle in the air till Glumdalclitch ran to my relief.

Another time, one of the servants, whose office it was to fill my trough every third day with fresh water, was so careless to let a huge frog (not perceiving it) slip out of his pail. The frog lay concealed till I was put into my boat, but then seeing a resting place, climbed up, and made it lean so much on one side, that I was forced to balance it with all my weight on the other, to prevent overturning. When the frog was got in, it hopped at once half the length of the boat, and then over my head, backwards and forwards, daubing my face and clothes with its odious slime. The largeness of its features made it appear the most deformed animal that can be conceived. However, I desired Glumdalclitch to let me deal with it alone. I banged it a good while with one of my sculls, and at last forced it to leap out of the boat.

But the greatest danger I ever underwent in that kingdom was from a monkey, who belonged to one of the clerks of the kitchen. Glumdalclitch had locked me up in her closet, while she went somewhere upon business or a visit. The weather being very warm, the closet window was left open, as well as the windows and the door of my bigger box, in which I usually lived, because of its largeness and conveniency. As I sat quietly meditating at my table, I heard something bounce in at the closet window, and skip about from one side to the other; whereat, although I were much alarmed, yet I ventured to look out, but not stirring from my seat; and then I saw this frolicsome animal, frisking and leaping up and down till at last he came to my box, which he seemed to view with great pleasure and curiosity, peeping in at the door and every window. I retreated to the farther corner of my room, or box, but the monkey, looking in at every side, put me into such a fright, that I wanted presence of mind to conceal my self under the bed, as I might easily have done. After some time spent in peeping, grinning, and chattering, he at last espied me, and reaching one of his paws in at the door, as a cat does when she plays with a mouse, although I often shifted place to avoid him, he at length seized the lappet of my coat (which being made of that country silk, was very thick and strong) and dragged me out. He took me up in his right forefoot, and held me as a nurse does a child she is going to suckle, just as I have seen the same sort of creature do with a kitten in Europe: and when I offered to struggle, he squeezed me so hard, that I thought it more prudent to submit. I have good reason to believe that he took me for a young one of his own species, by his often stroking my face very gently with his other paw. In these diversions he was interrupted by a noise at the closet door, as if some body were opening it; whereupon he suddenly leaped up to the window at which he had come in, and thence upon the leads and gutters, walking upon three legs, and holding me in the fourth, till he clambered up to a roof that was next to ours. I heard Glumdalclitch give a shriek at the moment he was carrying me out. The poor girl was almost distracted: that quarter of the palace was all in an uproar; the servants ran for ladders; the monkey was seen by hundreds in the court sitting upon the ridge of a building, holding me like a baby in one of his fore-paws, and feeding me with the other, by cramming into my mouth some victuals he had squeezed out of the bag on one side of his chaps, and patting me when I would not eat; whereat many of the rabble below could not forbear laughing; neither do I think they justly ought to be blamed, for without question the sight was ridiculous enough to every body but my self. Some of the people threw up stones, hoping to drive the monkey down; but this was strictly forbidden, or else very probably my brains had been dashed out.

The ladders were now applied, and mounted by several men,

which the monkey observing, and finding himself almost encompassed, not being able to make speed enough with his three legs, let me drop on a ridge tile, and made his escape. Here I sat for some time five hundred yards from the ground, expecting every moment to be blown down by the wind, or to fall by my own giddiness, and come tumbling over and over from the ridge to the eaves. But an honest lad, one of my nurse's footmen, climbed up, and putting me into his breeches pocket, brought me down safe.

I was almost choked with the filthy stuff the monkey had crammed down my throat; but my dear little nurse picked it out of my mouth with a small needle, and then I fell a vomiting, which gave me great relief. Yet I was so weak and bruised in the sides with the squeezes given me by this odious animal, that I was forced to keep my bed a fortnight. The King, Queen and all the court sent every day to enquire after my health, and her Majesty made me several visits during my sickness. The monkey was killed, and an order made that no such animal should be kept about the palace.

When I attended the King after my recovery, to return him thanks for his favours, he was pleased to rally me a good deal upon this adventure. He asked me what my thoughts and speculations were while I lay in the monkey's paw, how I liked the victuals he gave me, his manner of feeding, and whether the fresh air on the roof had sharpened my stomach. He desired to know what I would have done upon such an occasion in my own country. I told his Majesty, that in Europe we had no monkeys, except such as were brought for curiosities from other places, and so small, that I could deal with a dozen of them together, if they presumed to attack me. And as for that monstrous animal with whom I was so lately engaged (it was indeed as large as an elephant), if my fears had suffered me to think so far as to make use of my hanger (looking fiercely and clapping my hand upon the hilt as I spoke) when he poked his paw into my chamber, perhaps I should have given him such a wound as would have made him glad to withdraw it with more haste than he put it in. This I delivered in a firm tone, like a person who was jealous lest his courage should be called in question. However, my speech produced nothing else besides a loud laughter, which all the respect due to his Majesty from those about him could not make them contain. This made me reflect how vain an attempt it is for a man to endeavour doing himself honour among those who are out of all degree of equality or comparison with him. And yet I have seen the moral of my own behaviour very frequent in England since my return, where a little contemptible varlet, without the least title to birth, person, wit, or common sense, shall presume to look with importance, and put himself upon a foot with the greatest persons of the kingdom.

I was every day furnishing the court with some ridiculous story; and Glumdalclitch, although she loved me to excess, yet was arch enough to inform the Queen whenever I committed any folly that she thought would be diverting to her Majesty. The girl, who had been out of order, was carried by her governess to take the air about an hour's distance, or thirty miles from town. They alighted out of the coach near a small footpath in a field, and Glumdalclitch setting down my travelling box, I went out of it to walk. There was a cow-dung in the path, and I must needs try my activity by attempting to leap over it. I took a run, but unfortunately jumped short, and found my self just in the middle up to my knees. I waded through with some difficulty, and one of the footmen wiped me as clean as he could with his handkerchief; for I was filthily bemired, and my nurse confined me to my box till we returned home; where the Queen was soon informed of what had passed, and the footmen spread it about the court, so that all the mirth, for some days, was at my expense.

Chapter VI.

Several contrivances of the author to please the King and Queen. He shows his skill in music. The King enquires into the state of Europe, which the author relates to him. The King's observations thereon.

I used to attend the King's levee once or twice a week, and had often seen him under the barber's hand, which indeed was at first very terrible to behold. For the razor was almost twice as long as an ordinary scythe. His Majesty according to the custom of the country was only shaved twice a week. I once prevailed on the barber to give me some of the suds or lather, out of which I picked forty or fifty of the strongest stumps of hair. I then took a piece of fine wood, and cut it like the back of a comb, making several holes in it at equal distance with as small a needle as I could get from Glumdalclitch. I fixed in the stumps so artificially, scraping and sloping them with my knife towards the points, that I made a very tolerable comb; which was a seasonable supply, my own being so much broken in the teeth, that it was almost useless: neither did I know any artist in that country so nice and exact, as would undertake to make me another.

And this puts me in mind of an amusement wherein I spent many of my leisure hours. I desired the Queen's woman to save for me the combings of her Majesty's hair, whereof in time I got a good quantity, and consulting with my friend the cabinet-maker, who had received general orders to do little jobs for me, I directed him to make two chair-frames, no larger than those I had in my box, and then to bore little holes with a fine awl round those parts where I designed the backs and seats; through these holes I wove the strongest hairs I could pick out, just after the manner of cane-chairs in England. When they were finished, I made a present of them to her Majesty, who kept them in her cabinet, and used to show them for curiosities, as indeed they were the wonder of every one who beheld them. The Queen would have had me sit upon one of these chairs, but I absolutely refused to obey her, protesting I would rather die a thousand deaths than place a dishonourable part of my body on those precious hairs that once adorned her Majesty's head. Of these hairs (as I had always a mechanical genius) I likewise made a neat little purse about five foot long, with her Majesty's name deciphered in gold letters, which I gave to Glumdalclitch, by the Queen's consent. To say the truth, it was more for show than use, being not of strength to bear the weight of the larger coins, and therefore she kept nothing in it, but some little toys that girls are fond of.

The King, who delighted in music, had frequent concerts at court, to which I was sometimes carried, and set in my box on a table to hear them: but the noise was so great, that I could hardly distinguish the tunes. I am confident that all the drums and trumpets of a royal army, beating and sounding together just at your ears, could not equal it. My practice was to have my box removed from the places where the performers sat, as far as I could, then to shut the doors and windows of it, and draw the window curtains; after which I found their music not disagreeable.

I had learned in my youth to play a little upon the spinet. Glumdalclitch kept one in her chamber, and a master attended twice a week to teach her: I call it a spinet, because it somewhat resembled that instrument, and was played upon in the same manner. A fancy came into my head that I would entertain the King and Queen with an English tune upon this instrument. But this appeared extremely difficult: for the spinet was near sixty foot long, each key being almost a foot wide, so that, with my arms extended, I could not reach to above five keys, and to press them down required a good smart stroke with my fist, which would be too great a labour, and to no purpose. The method I contrived was this. I prepared two round sticks about the bigness of common cudgels; they were thicker at one end than the other, and I covered the thicker ends with a piece of a mouse's skin, that by rapping on them I might neither damage the tops of the keys, nor interrupt the sound. Before the spinet a bench was placed about four foot below the keys, and I was put upon the bench. I ran sideling upon it that way and this, as fast as I could, banging the proper keys with my two sticks, and made a shift to play a jig to the great satisfaction of both their Majesties: but it was the most violent exercise I ever underwent, and yet I could not strike above sixteen keys, nor, consequently, play the bass and treble together, as other artists do; which was a great disadvantage to my performance.

The King, who, as I before observed, was a prince of excellent understanding, would frequently order that I should be brought in my box, and set upon the table in his closet. He would then command me to bring one of my chairs out of the box, and sit down within three yards distance upon the top of the cabinet, which brought me almost to a level with his face. In this manner I had several conversations with him. I one day took the freedom to tell his Majesty, that the contempt he discovered towards Europe, and the rest of the world, did not seem answerable to those excellent qualities of mind he was master of. That reason did not extend it self with the bulk of the body: on the contrary, we observed in our country that the tallest persons were usually least provided with it. That among other animals, bees and ants had the reputation of more industry, art and sagacity than many of the larger kinds. And that, as inconsiderable as he took me to be, I hoped I might live to do his Majesty some signal service. The King heard me with attention, and began to conceive a much better opinion of me than he had ever before. He desired I would give him as exact an account of the government of England as I possibly could; because, as fond as princes commonly are of their own customs (for so he conjectured of other monarchs by my former discourses), he should be glad to hear of any thing that might deserve imitation.

Imagine with thy self, courteous reader, how often I then wished for the tongue of Demosthenes or Cicero, that might have enabled me to celebrate the praise of my own dear native country in a style equal to its merits and felicity.

I began my discourse by informing his Majesty that our dominions consisted of two islands, which composed three mighty kingdoms under one sovereign, besides our plantations in America. I dwelt long upon the fertility of our soil, and the temperature of our climate. I then spoke at large upon the constitution of an English parliament, partly made up of an illustrious body called the House of Peers, persons of the noblest blood, and of the most ancient and ample patrimonies. I described that extraordinary care always taken of their education in arts and arms, to qualify them for being counsellors born to the king and kingdom, to have a share in the legislature, to be members of the highest court of judicature from whence there could be no appeal; and to be champions always ready for the defence of their prince and country by their valour, conduct and fidelity. That these were the ornament and bulwark of the kingdom, worthy followers of their most renowned ancestors, whose honour had been the reward of their virtue, from which their posterity were never once known to degenerate. To these were joined several holy persons, as part of that assembly, under the title of bishops, whose peculiar business it is to take care of religion, and of those who instruct the people therein. These were searched and sought out through the whole nation, by the prince and wisest counsellors, among such of the priesthood as were most deservedly distinguished by the sanctity of their lives, and the depth of their erudition; who were indeed the spiritual fathers of the clergy and the people.

That the other part of the parliament consisted of an assembly called the House of Commons, who were all principal gentlemen, freely picked and culled out by the people themselves, for their great abilities, and love of their country, to represent the wisdom of the whole nation. And these two bodies make up the most august assembly in Europe, to whom, in conjunction with the prince, the whole legislature is committed.

I then descended to the courts of justice, over which the judges, those venerable sages and interpreters of the law, presided, for determining the disputed rights and properties of men, as well as for the punishment of vice, and protection of innocence. I mentioned the prudent management of our treasury, the valour and achievements of our forces by sea and land. I computed the number of our people, by reckoning how many millions there might be of each religious sect, or political party among us. I did not omit even our sports and pastimes, or any other particular which I thought might redound to the honour of my country. And I finished all with a brief historical account of affairs and events in England for about an hundred years past.

This conversation was not ended under five audiences, each of several hours, and the King heard the whole with great attention, frequently taking notes of what I spoke, as well as memorandums of what questions he intended to ask me.

When I had put an end to these long discourses, his Majesty in a sixth audience, consulting his notes, proposed many doubts, queries, and objections, upon every article. He asked, what methods were used to cultivate the minds and bodies of our young nobility, and in what kind of business they commonly spent the first and teachable part of their lives. What course was taken to supply that assembly when any noble family became extinct. What qualifications were necessary in those who are to be created new lords: whether the humour of the prince, a sum of money to a court-lady, or a prime minister, or a design of strengthening a party opposite to the public interest, ever happened to be motives in those advancements. What share of knowledge these lords had in the laws of their country, and how they came by it, so as to enable them to decide the properties of their fellow-subjects in the last resort. Whether they were always so free from avarice, partialities, or want, that a bribe, or some other sinister view, could have no place among them. Whether those holy lords I spoke of were constantly promoted to that rank upon account of their knowledge in religious matters, and the sanctity of their lives; had never been compliers with the times while they were common priests, or slavish prostitute chaplains to some nobleman, whose opinions they continued servilely to follow after they were admitted into that assembly.

He then desired to know what arts were practised in electing those whom I called commoners. Whether a stranger with a strong purse might not influence the vulgar voters to choose him before their own landlords, or the most considerable gentleman in the neighbourhood. How it came to pass, that people were so violently bent upon getting into this assembly, which I allowed to be a great trouble and expense, often to the ruin of their families, without any salary or pension: because this appeared such an exalted strain of virtue and public spirit, that his Majesty seemed to doubt it might possibly not be always sincere: and he desired to know whether such zealous gentlemen could have any views of refunding themselves for the charges and trouble they were at, by sacrificing the public good to the designs of a weak and vicious prince in conjunction with a corrupted ministry. He multiplied his questions, and sifted me thoroughly upon every part of this head, proposing numberless enquiries and objections, which I think it not prudent or convenient to repeat.

Upon what I said in relation to our courts of justice, his Majesty desired to be satisfied in several points: and this I was the better able to do, having been formerly almost ruined by a long suit in chancery, which was decreed for me with costs. He asked, what time was usually spent in determining between right and wrong, and what degree of expense. Whether advocates and orators had liberty to plead in causes manifestly known to be unjust, vexatious, or oppressive. Whether party in religion or politics were observed to be of any weight in the scale of justice. Whether those pleading orators were persons educated in the general knowledge of equity, or only in provincial, national, and other local customs. Whether they or their judges had any part in penning those laws which they assumed the liberty of interpreting and glossing upon at their pleasure. Whether they had ever at different times pleaded for and against the same cause, and cited precedents to prove contrary opinions. Whether they were a rich or a poor corporation. Whether they received any pecuniary reward for pleading or delivering their opinions. And particularly whether they were ever admitted as members in the lower senate.

He fell next upon the management of our treasury; and said, he thought my memory had failed me, because I computed our taxes at about five or six millions a year, and when I came to mention the issues, he found they sometimes amounted to more than double; for the notes he had taken were very particular in this point, because he hoped, as he told me, that the knowledge of our conduct might be useful to him, and he could not be deceived in his calculations. But, if what I told him were true, he was still at a loss how a kingdom could run out of its estate like a private person. He asked me, who were our creditors; and where we found money to pay them. He wondered to hear me talk of such chargeable and extensive wars; that certainly we must be a quarrelsome people, or live among very bad neighbours, and that our generals must needs be richer than our kings. He asked what business we had out of our own islands, unless upon the score of trade or treaty, or to defend the coasts with our fleet. Above all, he was amazed to hear me talk of a mercenary standing army in the midst of peace, and among a free people. He said if we were governed by our own consent in the persons of our representatives, he could not imagine of whom we were afraid, or against whom we were to fight, and would hear my opinion, whether a private man's house might not better be defended by himself, his children, and family, than by a half a dozen rascals picked up at a venture in the streets, for small wages, who might get an hundred times more by cutting their throats.

He laughed at my odd kind of arithmetic (as he was pleased to call it) in reckoning the numbers of our people by a computation drawn from the several sects among us in religion and politics. He said, he knew no reason, why those who entertain opinions prejudicial to the public should be obliged to change, or should not be obliged to conceal them. And as it was tyranny in any government to require the first, so it was weakness not to enforce the second: for a man may be allowed to keep poisons in his closets, but not to vend them about as cordials.

He observed, that among the diversions of our nobility and gentry I had mentioned gaming. He desired to know at what age this entertainment was usually taken up, and when it was laid down. How much of their time it employed; whether it ever went so high as to affect their fortunes. Whether mean vicious people by their dexterity in that art might not arrive at great riches, and sometimes keep our very nobles in dependence, as well as habituate them to vile companions, wholly take them from the improvement of their minds, and force them, by the losses they received, to learn and practice that infamous dexterity upon others.

He was perfectly astonished with the historical account I gave him of our affairs during the last century, protesting it was only an heap of conspiracies, rebellions, murders, massacres, revolutions, banishments, the very worst effects that avarice, faction, hypocrisy, perfidiousness, cruelty, rage, madness, hatred, envy, lust, malice, and ambition could produce.

His Majesty in another audience was at the pains to recapitulate the sum of all I had spoken, compared the questions he made with the answers I had given; then taking me into his hands, and stroking me gently, delivered himself in these words, which I shall never forget, nor the manner he spoke them in: My little friend Grildrig, you have made a most admirable panegyric upon your country. You have clearly proved that ignorance, idleness and vice are the proper ingredients for qualifying a legislator. That laws are best explained, interpreted, and applied by those whose interest and abilities lie in perverting, confounding, and eluding them. I observe among you some lines of an institution, which in its original might have been tolerable, but these half erased, and the rest wholly blurred and blotted by corruptions. It doth not appear from all you have said, how any one perfection is required towards the procurement of any one station among you, much less that men are ennobled on account of their virtue, that priests are advanced for their piety or learning, soldiers for their conduct or valour, judges for their integrity, senators for the love of their country, or counsellors for their wisdom. As for yourself, continued the King, who have spent the greatest part of your life in travelling, I am well disposed to hope you may hitherto have escaped many vices of your country. But, by what I have gathered from your own relation, and the answers I have with much pains wringed and extorted from you, I cannot but conclude the bulk of your natives to be the most pernicious race of little odious vermin that nature ever suffered to crawl upon the surface of the earth.

CHAPTER VII.

The author's love of his country. He makes a proposal of much advantage to the King, which is rejected. The King's great ignorance in politics. The learning of that country very imperfect and confined. Their laws, and military affairs, and parties in the state.

Nothing but an extreme love of truth could have hindered me from concealing this part of my story. It was in vain to discover my resentments, which were always turned into ridicule; and I was forced to rest with patience while my noble and most beloved country was so injuriously treated. I am heartily sorry as any of my readers can possibly be, that such an occasion was given: but this prince happened to be so curious and inquisitive upon every particular, that it could not consist either with gratitude or good manners to refuse giving him what satisfaction I was able. Yet thus much I may be allowed to say in my own vindication, that I artfully eluded many of his questions, and gave to every point a more favourable turn by many degrees than the strictness of truth would allow. For I have always borne that laudable partiality to my own country, which Dionysius Halicarnassensis with so much justice recommends to an historian. I would hide the frailties and deformities of my political mother, and place her virtues and beauties in the most advantageous light. This was my sincere endeavour in those many discourses I had with that mighty monarch, although it unfortunately failed of success.

But great allowances should be given to a king who lives wholly secluded from the rest of the world, and must therefore be altogether unacquainted with the manners and customs that most prevail in other nations: the want of which knowledge will ever produce many prejudices, and a certain narrowness of thinking, from which we and the politer countries of Europe are wholly exempted. And it would be hard indeed, if so remote a prince's notions of virtue and vice were to be offered as a standard for all mankind.

To confirm what I have now said, and further to show the miserable effects of a confined education, I shall here insert a passage which will hardly obtain belief. In hopes to ingratiate my self farther into his Majesty's favour, I told him of an invention discovered between three and four hundred years ago, to make a certain powder, into an heap of which the smallest spark of fire falling, would kindle the whole in a moment, although it were as big as a mountain, and make it all fly up in the air together, with a noise and agitation greater than thunder. That a proper quantity of this powder rammed into an hollow tube of brass or iron, according to its bigness, would drive a ball of iron or lead with such violence and speed as nothing was able to sustain its force. That the largest balls, thus discharged, would not only destroy whole ranks of an army at once, but batter the strongest walls to the ground, sink down ships, with a thousand men in each, to the bottom of the sea; and when linked together by a chain, would cut through masts and rigging, divide hundreds of bodies in the middle, and lay all waste before them. That we often put this powder into large hollow balls of iron, and discharged them by an engine into some city we were besieging, which would rip up the pavement, tear the houses to pieces, burst and throw splinters on every side, dashing out the brains of all who came near. That I knew the ingredients very well, which were cheap, and common; I understood the manner of compounding them, and could direct his workmen how to make those tubes of a size proportionable to all other things in his Majesty's kingdom, and the largest need not be above two hundred foot long; twenty or thirty of which tubes, charged with the proper quantity of powder and balls, would batter down the walls of the strongest town in his dominions in a few hours, or destroy the whole metropolis, if ever it should pretend to dispute his absolute commands. This I humbly offered to his Majesty as a small tribute of acknowledgment in return of so many marks that I had received of his royal favour and protection.

The King was struck with horror at the description I had given of those terrible engines, and the proposal I had made. He was amazed how so impotent and groveling an insect as I (these were his expressions) could entertain such inhuman ideas, and in so familiar a manner as to appear wholly unmoved at all the scenes of blood and desolation, which I had painted as the common effects of those destructive machines, whereof he said, some evil genius, enemy to mankind, must have been the first contriver. As for himself, he protested, that although few things delighted him so much as new discoveries in art or in nature, yet he would rather lose half his kingdom than be privy to such a secret, which he commanded me, as I valued my life, never to mention any more.

A strange effect of narrow principles and short views! that a prince possessed of every quality which procures veneration, love, and esteem; of strong parts, great wisdom and profound learning, endued with admirable talents for government, and almost adored by his subjects, should from a nice unnecessary scruple, whereof in Europe we can have no conception, let slip an opportunity put into his hands, that would have made him absolute master of the lives, the liberties, and the fortunes of his people. Neither do I say this with the least intention to detract from the many virtues of that excellent king, whose character I am sensible will on this account be very much lessened in the opinion of an English reader: but I take this defect among them to have risen from their ignorance, by not having hitherto reduced politics into a science, as the more acute wits of Europe have done. For I remember very well, in a discourse one day with the King, when I happened to say there were several thousand books among us written upon the art of government, it gave him (directly contrary to my intention) a very mean opinion of our understandings. He professed both to abominate and despise all mystery, refinement, and intrigue, either in a prince or a minister. He could not tell what I meant by secrets of state, where an enemy or some rival nation were not in the case. He confined the knowledge of governing within very narrow bounds; to common sense and reason, to justice and lenity, to the speedy determination of civil and criminal causes; with some other obvious topics which are not worth considering. And he gave it for his opinion, that whoever could make two ears of corn, or two blades of grass to grow upon a spot of ground where only one grew before, would deserve better of mankind, and do more essential service to his country, than the whole race of politicians put together.

The learning of this people is very defective, consisting only in morality, history, poetry, and mathematics, wherein they must be allowed to excel. But the last of these is wholly applied to what may be useful in life, to the improvement of agriculture and all mechanical arts; so that among us it would be little esteemed. And as to ideas, entities, abstractions and transcendentals, I could never drive the least conception into their heads.

No law of that country must exceed in words the number of letters in their alphabet, which consists only of two and twenty. But indeed, few of them extend even to that length. They are expressed in the most plain and simple terms, wherein those people are not mercurial enough to discover above one interpretation. And to write a comment upon any law is a capital crime. As to the decision of civil causes, or proceedings against criminals, their precedents are so few, that they have little reason to boast of any extraordinary skill in either.

They have had the art of printing, as well as the Chinese, time out of mind. But their libraries are not very large; for that of the King's, which is reckoned the largest, doth not amount to above a thousand volumes, placed in a gallery of twelve hundred foot long, from whence I had liberty to borrow what books I pleased. The Queen's joiner had contrived in one of Glumdalclitch's rooms a kind of wooden machine five and twenty foot high, formed like a standing ladder; the steps were each fifty foot long. It was indeed a moveable pair of stairs, the lowest end placed at ten foot distance from the wall of the chamber. The book I had a mind to read was put up leaning against the wall. I first mounted to the upper step of the ladder, and turning my face towards the book, began at the top of the page, and so walking to the right and left about eight or ten paces, according to the length of the lines, till I had gotten a little below the level of my eyes, and then descending gradually till I came to the bottom: after which I mounted again, and began the other page in the same manner, and so turned over the leaf, which I could easily do with both my hands, for it was as thick and stiff as a pasteboard, and in the largest folios not above eighteen or twenty foot long.

Their style is clear, masculine, and smooth, but not florid, for they avoid nothing more than multiplying unnecessary words, or using various expressions. I have perused many of their books, especially those in history and morality. Among the latter I was much diverted with a little old treatise, which always lay in Glumdalclitch's bedchamber, and belonged to her governess, a grave elderly gentlewoman, who dealt in writings of morality and devotion. The book treats of the weakness of human kind, and is in little esteem except among women and the vulgar. However, I was curious to see what an author of that country could say upon such a subject. This writer went through all the usual topics of European moralists, showing how diminutive, contemptible, and helpless an animal was man in his own nature; how unable to defend himself from the inclemencies of the air, or the fury of wild beasts. How much he was excelled by one creature in strength, by another in speed, by a third in foresight, by a fourth in industry. He added, that nature was degenerated in these latter declining ages of the world, and could now produce only small abortive births in comparison of those in ancient times. He said it was very reasonable to think, not only that the species of men were originally much larger, but also that there must have been giants in former ages, which, as it is asserted by history and tradition, so it hath been confirmed by huge bones and skulls casually dug up in several parts of the kingdom, far exceeding the common dwindled race of man in our days. He argued, that the very laws of nature absolutely required we should have been made, in the beginning, of a size more large and robust, not so liable to destruction from every little accident of a tile falling from an house, or a stone cast from the hand of a boy, or of being drowned in a little brook. From this way of reasoning the author drew several moral applications useful in the conduct of life, but needless here to repeat. For my own part, I could not avoid reflecting how universally this talent was spread of drawing lectures in morality, or indeed rather matter of discontent and repining, from the quarrels we raise with nature. And, I believe, upon a strict enquiry those quarrels might be shown as ill-grounded among us as they are among that people.

As to their military affairs, they boast that the King's army consists of an hundred and seventy-six thousand foot, and thirty-two thousand horse, if that may be called an army which is made up of tradesmen in the several cities, and farmers in the country, whose commanders are only the nobility and gentry without pay or reward. They are indeed perfect enough in their exercises, and under very good discipline, wherein I saw no great merit; for how should it be otherwise, where every farmer is under the command of his own landlord, and every citizen under that of the principal men in his own city, chosen after the manner of Venice by ballot?

I have often seen the militia of Lorbrulgrud drawn out to exercise in a great field near the city, of twenty miles square. They were in all not above twenty-five thousand foot, and six thousand horse; but it was impossible for me to compute their number, considering the space of ground they took up. A cavalier mounted on a large steed might be about ninety foot high. I have seen this whole body of horse upon the word of command draw their swords at once, and brandish them in the air. Imagination can figure nothing so grand, so surprising and so astonishing. It looked as if ten thousand flashes of lightning were darting at the same time from every quarter of the sky.

I was curious to know how this prince, to whose dominions there is no access from any other country, came to think of armies, or to teach his people the practice of military discipline. But I was soon informed, both by conversation, and reading their histories. For in the course of many ages they have been troubled with the same disease to which the whole race of mankind is subject; the nobility often contending for power, the people for liberty, and the King for absolute dominion. All which, however happily tempered by the laws of that kingdom, have been sometimes violated by each of the three parties, and have more than once occasioned civil wars, the last whereof was happily put an end to by this prince's grandfather in a general composition; and the militia then settled with common consent hath been ever since kept in the strictest duty.

Chapter VIII.

The King and Queen make a progress to the frontiers. The author attends them. The manner in which he leaves the country very particularly related. He returns to England.

I had always a strong impulse that I should sometime recover my liberty, although it was impossible to conjecture by what means, or to form any project with the least hope of succeeding. The ship in which I sailed was the first ever known to be driven within sight of that coast, and the King had given strict orders, that if at any time another appeared, it should be taken ashore, and with all its crew and passengers brought in a tumbril to Lorbrulgrud. He was strongly bent to get me a woman of my own size, by whom I might propagate the breed: but I think I should rather have died than undergone the disgrace of leaving a posterity to be kept in cages like tame canary birds, and perhaps in time sold about the kingdom to persons of quality for curiosities. I was indeed treated with much kindness; I was the favourite of a great king and queen, and the delight of the whole court, but it was upon such a foot as ill became the dignity of human kind. I could never forget those domestic pledges I had left behind me. I wanted to be among people with whom I could converse upon even terms, and walk about the streets and fields without fear of being trod to death like a frog or young puppy. But my deliverance came sooner than I expected, and in a manner not very common: the whole story and circumstances of which I shall faithfully relate.

I had now been two years in this country; and about the beginning of the third, Glumdalclitch and I attended the King and Queen in a progress to the south coast of the kingdom. I was carried as usual in my travelling-box, which, as I have already described, was a very convenient closet of twelve foot wide. I had ordered a hammock to be fixed by silken ropes from the four corners at the top, to break the jolts, when a servant carried me before him on horseback, as I sometimes desired, and would often sleep in my hammock while we were upon the road. On the roof of my closet, just over the middle of the hammock, I ordered the joiner to cut out a hole of a foot square to give me air in hot weather as I slept, which hole I shut at pleasure with a board that drew backwards and forwards through a groove.

When we came to our journey's end, the King thought proper to pass a few days at a palace he hath near Flanflasnic, a city within eighteen English miles of the seaside. Glumdalclitch and I were much fatigued; I had gotten a small cold, but the poor girl was so ill as to be confined to her chamber. I longed to see the ocean, which must be the only scene of my escape, if ever it should happen. I pretended to be worse than I really was, and desired leave to take the fresh air of the sea, with a page whom I was very fond of, and who had sometimes been trusted with me. I shall never forget with what unwillingness Glumdalclitch consented, nor the strict charge she gave the page to be careful of me, bursting at the same time into a flood of tears, as if she had some foreboding of what was to happen. The boy took me out in my box about half an hour's walk from the palace towards the rocks on the seashore. I ordered him to set me down, and lifting up one of my sashes, cast many a wistful melancholy look towards the sea. I found my self not very well, and told the page that I had a mind to take a nap in my hammock, which I hoped would do me good. I got in, and the boy shut the window close down to keep out the cold. I soon fell asleep, and all I can conjecture is, that while I slept, the page, thinking no danger could happen, went among the rocks to look for birds' eggs, having before observed him from my window searching about, and picking up one or two in the clefts. Be that as it will, I found my self suddenly awaked with a violent pull upon the ring which was fastened at the top of my box for the conven-

iency of carriage. I felt the box raised very high in the air, and
then borne forward with prodigious speed. The first jolt had like
to have shaken me out of my hammock, but afterwards the
motion was easy enough. I called out several times as loud as I
could raise my voice, but all to no purpose. I looked towards my
windows, and could see nothing but the clouds and sky. I heard
a noise just over my head like the clapping of wings, and then
began to perceive the woful condition I was in; that some eagle
had got the ring of my box in his beak, with an intent to let it fall
on a rock like a tortoise in a shell, and then pick out my body
and devour it. For the sagacity and smell of this bird enable him
to discover his quarry at a great distance, although better concealed than I could be within a two-inch board.

In a little time I observed the noise and flutter of wings to
encrease very fast, and my box was tossed up and down like a
signpost in a windy day. I heard several bangs or buffets, as I
thought, given to the eagle (for such I am certain it must have
been that held the ring of my box in his beak) and then all on a
sudden felt my self falling perpendicularly down for above a
minute, but with such incredible swiftness that I almost lost my
breath. My fall was stopped by a terrible squash, that sounded
louder to my ears than the cataract of Niagara; after which I was
quite in the dark for another minute, and then my box began to
rise so high that I could see light from the tops of my windows.
I now perceived that I was fallen into the sea. My box, by the
weight of my body, the goods that were in, and the broad plates
of iron fixed for strength at the four corners of the top and bottom, floated about five foot deep in water. I did then, and do
now suppose that the eagle which flew away with my box was
pursued by two or three others, and forced to let me drop while
he was defending himself against the rest, who hoped to share
in the prey. The plates of iron fastened at the bottom of the box
(for those were the strongest) preserved the balance while it fell,
and hindered it from being broken on the surface of the water.
Every joint of it was well grooved, and the door did not move
on hinges, but up and down like a sash, which kept my closet so
tight that very little water came in. I got with much difficulty
out of my hammock, having first ventured to draw back the
slip-board on the roof already mentioned, contrived on purpose
to let in air, for want of which I found my self almost stifled.

How often did I then wish my self with my dear Glumdalclitch, from whom one single hour had so far divided me! And
I may say with truth, that in the midst of my own misfortune I
could not forbear lamenting my poor nurse, the grief she would

suffer for my loss, the displeasure of the Queen, and the ruin of her fortune. Perhaps many travellers have not been under greater difficulties and distress than I was at this juncture, expecting every moment to see my box dashed in pieces, or at least overset by the first violent blast, or a rising wave. A breach in one single pane of glass would have been immediate death: nor could any thing have preserved the windows but the strong lattice wires placed on the outside against accidents in travelling. I saw the water ooze in at several crannies, although the leaks were not considerable, and I endeavoured to stop them as well as I could. I was not able to lift up the roof of my closet, which otherwise I certainly should have done, and sat on the top of it, where I might at least preserve my self from being shut up, as I may call it, in the hold. Or, if I escaped these dangers for a day or two, what could I expect but a miserable death of cold and hunger! I was four hours under these circumstances, expecting and indeed wishing every moment to be my last.

I have already told the reader, that there were two strong staples fixed upon the side of my box which had no window, and into which the servant who used to carry me on horseback would put a leathern belt, and buckle it about his waist. Being in this disconsolate state, I heard or at least thought I heard some kind of grating noise on that side of my box where the staples were fixed, and soon after I began to fancy that the box was pulled or towed along in the sea; for I now and then felt a sort of tugging which made the waves rise near the tops of my windows, leaving me almost in the dark. This gave me some faint hopes of relief, although I was not able to imagine how it could be brought about. I ventured to unscrew one of my chairs, which were always fastened to the floor; and having made a hard shift to screw it down again directly under the slipping-board that I had lately opened, I mounted on the chair, and putting my mouth as near as I could to the hole, I called for help in a loud voice, and in all the languages I understood. I then fastened my handkerchief to a stick I usually carried, and thrusting it up the hole, waved it several times in the air, that if any boat or ship were near, the seamen might conjecture some unhappy mortal to be shut up in the box.

I found no effect from all I could do, but plainly perceived my closet to be moved along; and in the space of an hour, or better, that side of the box where the staples were, and had no window, struck against something that was hard. I apprehended it to be a rock, and found my self tossed more than ever. I plainly heard a noise upon the cover of my closet, like that of a cable, and the grating of it as it passed through the ring. I then found my self hoisted up by degrees at least three foot higher than I was before. Whereupon I again thrust up my stick and handkerchief, calling for help till I was almost hoarse. In return to which, I heard a great shout repeated three times, giving me such transports of joy as are not to be conceived but by those who feel them. I now heard a trampling over my head, and somebody calling through the hole with a loud voice in the English tongue, If there be any body below let them speak. I answered, I was an Englishman, drawn by ill fortune into the greatest calamity that ever any creature underwent, and begged, by all that was moving, to be delivered out of the dungeon I was in. The voice replied, I was safe, for my box was fastened to their ship; and the carpenter should immediately come, and saw an hole in the cover, large enough to pull me out. I answered, that was needless, and would take up too much time, for there was no more to be done, but let one of the crew put his finger into the ring, and take the box out of the sea into the ship, and so into the captain's cabin. Some of them upon hearing me talk so wildly thought I was mad; others laughed; for indeed it never came into my head that I was now got among people of my own stature and strength. The carpenter came, and in a few minutes sawed a passage about four foot square, then let down a small ladder, upon which I mounted, and from thence was taken into the ship in a very weak condition.

The sailors were all in amazement, and asked me a thousand questions, which I had no inclination to answer. I was equally confounded at the sight of so many pigmies, for such I took them to be, after having so long accustomed my eyes to the monstrous objects I had left. But the captain, Mr. Thomas Wilcocks, an honest worthy Shropshire man, observing I was ready to faint, took me into his cabin, gave me a cordial to comfort me, and made me turn in upon his own bed, advising me to take a little rest, of which I had great need. Before I went to sleep I gave him to understand that I had some valuable furniture in my box, too good to be lost; a fine hammock, an handsome field-bed, two chairs, a table and a cabinet: that my closet was hung on all sides, or rather quilted, with silk and cotton: that if he would let one of the crew bring my closet into his cabin, I would open it there before him, and show him my goods. The captain, hearing me utter these absurdities, concluded I was raving: however (I suppose to pacify me), he promised to give order as I desired, and going upon deck sent some of his men down into my closet, from whence (as I afterwards found) they drew up all my goods, and stripped off the quilting; but the chairs, cabinet and bedstead, being screwed to the floor, were much damaged by the ignorance of the seamen, who tore them up by force. Then they knocked off some of the boards for the use of the ship, and when they had got all they had a mind for, let the hulk drop into the sea, which, by reason of many breaches made in the bottom and sides, sunk to rights. And indeed I was glad not to have been a spectator of the havoc they made; because I am confident it would have sensibly touched me, by bringing former passages into my mind, which I had rather forget.

I slept some hours, but perpetually disturbed with dreams of the place I had left, and the dangers I had escaped. However, upon waking I found my self much recovered. It was now about eight o'clock at night, and the captain ordered supper immediately, thinking I had already fasted too long. He entertained me with great kindness, observing me not to look wildly, or talk inconsistently; and when we were left alone, desired I would give him a relation of my travels, and by what accident I came to be set adrift in that monstrous wooden chest. He said, that about twelve o'clock at noon, as he was looking through his glass, he spied it at a distance, and thought it was a sail, which he had a mind to make, being not much out of his course, in hopes of buying some biscuit, his own beginning to fall short. That upon coming nearer, and finding his error, he sent out his longboat to discover what I was; that his men came back in a fright, swearing they had seen a swimming house. That he laughed at their folly, and went himself in the boat, ordering his men to take a strong cable along with them. That the weather being calm, he rowed round me several times, observed my windows, and the wire lattices that defended them. That he discovered two staples upon one side, which was all of boards, without any passage for light. He then commanded his men to row up to that side, and fastening a cable to one of the staples, ordered his men to tow my chest (as he called it) towards the ship. When it was there, he gave directions to fasten another cable to the ring fixed in the cover, and to raise up my chest with pulleys, which all the sailors were not able to do above two or three foot. He said, they saw my stick and handkerchief thrust out of the hole, and concluded that some unhappy man must be shut up in the cavity. I asked whether he or the crew had seen any prodigious birds in the air about the time he first discovered me. To which he answered, that discoursing this matter with the sailors while I was asleep, one of them said he had observed three eagles flying towards the north, but remarked nothing of their being larger than the

usual size, which I suppose must be imputed to the great height
they were at: and he could not guess the reason of my question.
I then asked the captain how far he reckoned we might be from
land; he said, by the best computation he could make, we were
at least an hundred leagues. I assured him, that he must be mistaken by almost half, for I had not left the country from whence
I came above two hours before I dropped into the sea. Whereupon he began again to think that my brain was disturbed, of
which he gave me a hint, and advised me to go to bed in a cabin
he had provided. I assured him I was well refreshed with his
good entertainment and company, and as much in my senses as
ever I was in my life. He then grew serious, and desired to ask
me freely whether I were not troubled in mind by the consciousness of some enormous crime, for which I was punished at the
command of some prince, by exposing me in that chest, as great
criminals in other countries have been forced to sea in a leaky
vessel without provisions: for although he should be sorry to
have taken so ill a man into his ship, yet he would engage his
word to set me safe on shore in the first port where we arrived.
He added, that his suspicions were much increased by some very
absurd speeches I had delivered at first to the sailors, and afterwards to himself, in relation to my closet or chest, as well as by
my odd looks and behaviour while I was at supper.

I begged his patience to hear me tell my story, which I faithfully did from the last time I left England to the moment he first
discovered me. And, as truth always forceth its way into rational minds, so this honest worthy gentleman, who had some
tincture of learning, and very good sense, was immediately
convinced of my candor and veracity. But further to confirm
all I had said, I entreated him to give order that my cabinet should
be brought, of which I kept the key in my pocket (for he had
already informed me how the seamen disposed of my closet);
I opened it in his presence, and showed him the small collection
of rarities I made in the country from whence I had been so
strangely delivered. There was the comb I had contrived out of
the stumps of the King's beard, and another of the same materials, but fixed into a paring of her Majesty's thumb-nail, which
served for the back. There was a collection of needles and pins
from a foot to half a yard long. Four wasp-stings, like joiners'
tacks: some combings of the Queen's hair: a gold ring which one
day she made me a present of in a most obliging manner, taking
it from her little finger, and throwing it over my head like a
collar. I desired the captain would please to accept this ring in
return of his civilities, which he absolutely refused. I showed

him a corn that I had cut off with my own hand from a maid of honour's toe; it was about the bigness of a Kentish pippin, and grown so hard, that when I returned to England, I got it hollowed into a cup and set in silver. Lastly, I desired him to see the breeches I had then on, which were made of a mouse's skin.

I could force nothing on him but a footman's tooth, which I observed him to examine with great curiosity, and found he had a fancy for it. He received it with abundance of thanks, more than such a trifle could deserve. It was drawn by an unskilful surgeon in a mistake from one of Glumdalclitch's men, who was afflicted with the toothache, but it was as sound as any in his head. I got it cleaned, and put it into my cabinet. It was about a foot long, and four inches in diameter.

The captain was very well satisfied with this plain relation I had given him; and said, he hoped, when we returned to England I would oblige the world by putting it in paper, and making it public. My answer was, that I thought we were already over-stocked with books of travels: that nothing could now pass which was not extraordinary, wherein I doubted some authors less consulted truth than their own vanity or interest, or the diversion of ignorant readers. That my story could contain little besides common events, without those ornamental descriptions of strange plants, trees, birds, and other animals, or of the barbarous customs and idolatry of savage people, with which most writers abound. However, I thanked him for his good opinion, and promised to take the matter into my thoughts.

He said he wondered at one thing very much, which was to hear me speak so loud, asking me whether the King or Queen of that country were thick of hearing. I told him it was what I had been used to for above two years past, and that I admired as much at the voices of him and his men, who seemed to me only to whisper, and yet I could hear them well enough. But when I spoke in that country, it was like a man talking in the street to another looking out from the top of a steeple, unless when I was placed on a table, or held in any person's hand. I told him I had likewise observed another thing, that when I first got into the ship, and the sailors stood all about me, I thought they were the most little contemptible creatures I had ever beheld. For, indeed, while I was in that prince's country, I could never endure to look in a glass after my eyes had been accustomed to such prodigious objects, because the comparison gave me so despicable a conceit of my self. The captain said, that while we were at supper, he observed me to look at every thing with a sort of wonder, and that I often seemed hardly able to contain my laughter, which he knew not well how to take, but imputed it to some disorder in my brain. I answered, it was very true, and I wondered how I could forbear, when I saw his dishes of the size of a silver threepence, a leg of pork hardly a mouthful, a cup not so big as a nutshell: and so I went on, describing the rest of his household-stuff and provisions after the same manner. For although the Queen had ordered a little equipage of all things necessary for me while I was in her service, yet my ideas were wholly taken up with what I saw on every side of me, and I winked at my own littleness as people do at their own faults. The captain understood my raillery very well, and merrily replied with the old English proverb, that he doubted my eyes were bigger than my belly, for he did not observe my stomach so good, although I had fasted all day; and continuing in his mirth, protested he would have gladly given an hundred pounds to have seen my closet in the eagle's bill, and afterwards in its fall from so great an height into the sea; which would certainly have been a most astonishing object, worthy to have the description of it transmitted to future ages: and the comparison of Phaeton was so obvious, that he could not forbear applying it, although I did not much admire the conceit.

The captain, having been at Tonquin, was in his return to England driven northeastward to the latitude of 44 degrees, and of longitude 143. But meeting a trade wind two days after I came on board him, we sailed southward a long time, and coasting New Holland kept our course west-southwest, and then south-southwest till we doubled the Cape of Good Hope. Our voyage was very prosperous, but I shall not trouble the reader with a journal of it. Tht captain called in at one or two ports and sent in his longboat for provisions and fresh water, but I never went out of the ship till we came into the Downs, which was on the 3d day of June, 1706, about nine months after my escape. I offered to leave my goods in security for payment of my freight; but the captain protested he would not receive one farthing. We took kind leave of each other, and I made him promise he would come to see me at my house in Redriff. I hired a horse and guide for five shillings, which I borrowed of the captain.

As I was on the road, observing the littleness of the houses, the trees, the cattle and the people, I began to think my self in Lilliput. I was afraid of trampling on every traveller I met, and often called aloud to have them stand out of the way, so that I had like to have gotten one or two broken heads for my impertinence.

When I came to my own house, for which I was forced to

enquire, one of the servants opening the door, I bent down to go in (like a goose under a gate) for fear of striking my head. My wife ran out to embrace me, but I stooped lower than her knees, thinking she could otherwise never be able to reach my mouth. My daughter kneeled to ask me blessing, but I could not see her till she arose, having been so long used to stand with my head and eyes erect to above sixty foot; and then I went to take her up with one hand, by the waist. I looked down upon the servants and one or two friends who were in the house, as if they had been pigmies, and I a giant. I told my wife she had been too thrifty, for I found she had starved herself and her daughter to nothing. In short, I behaved my self so unaccountably, that they were all of the captain's opinion when he first saw me, and concluded I had lost my wits. This I mention as an instance of the great power of habit and prejudice.

In a little time I and my family and friends came to a right understanding: but my wife protested I should never go to sea any more; although my evil destiny so ordered that she had not power to hinder me, as the reader may know hereafter. In the mean time I here conclude the second part of my unfortunate voyages.

THE END of the SECOND PART.

Plate III. Part III.   *Page 190.*

Parts Unknown

LAND OF
St. James Bay
Robbin I
IESSO
Salmon B.
Canal

Sea of Core

Sando I.
Tsiroui

Meaco
Iedo

Japon

Afana Quinego

Tonsa I.
Bungo I.
Dunetris Strats
I Tanaxama

C. Patience
Straits of the Vries

Companys

Land
Stats I.

Tou Pt.
Reid Pt.
Bosho Pt.
Barnevelts

Ongolukig I.
South I.

Sialo
Glangurin
Maldoneda

I Deserta

Glubdubdnb

Urac
Tunal

LUGN-AGG
th Whaldragdul

Clanrynig

Laputa

BALNIBARBI
Lagado

Dicovered A.D. 1701

TRAVELS.

PART III.

A VOYAGE TO LAPUTA, BALNIBARBI, GLUBBDUBDRIB, LUGGNAGG, AND JAPAN.

CHAPTER I.

The author sets out on his third voyage. Is taken by pirates. The malice of a Dutchman. His arrival at an island. He is received into Laputa.

I had not been at home above ten days, when Captain William Robinson, a Cornish man, commander of the *Hope-well*, a stout ship of three hundred tons, came to my house. I had formerly been surgeon of another ship where he was master, and a fourth part owner, in a voyage to the Levant; he had always treated me more like a brother than an inferior officer, and hearing of my arrival made me a visit, as I apprehended, only out of friendship, for nothing passed more than what is usual after long absence. But repeating his visits often, expressing his joy to find me in good health, asking whether I were now settled for life, adding that he intended a voyage to the East Indies, in two months, at last plainly invited me, although with some apologies, to be surgeon of the ship; that I should have another surgeon under me besides our two mates; that my salary should be double to the usual pay; and that having experienced my knowledge in sea-affairs to be at least equal to his, he would enter into any engagement to follow my advice, as much as if I had share in the command.

He said so many other obliging things, and I knew him to be so honest a man, that I could not reject his proposal; the thirst I had of seeing the world, notwithstanding my past misfortunes, continuing as violent as ever. The only difficulty that remained was to persuade my wife, whose consent however I at last obtained, by the prospect of advantage she proposed to her children.

We set out the 5th day of August, 1706, and arrived at Fort St. George the 11th of April, 1707. We stayed there three weeks to refresh our crew, many of whom were sick. From thence we went to Tonquin, where the captain resolved to continue some time, because many of the goods he intended to buy were not ready, nor could he expect to be dispatched in several months. Therefore in hopes to defray some of the charges he must be at, he bought a sloop, loaded it with several sorts of goods, where-with the Tonquinese usually trade to the neighbouring islands, and putting fourteen men on board, whereof three were of the country, he appointed me master of the sloop, and gave me power to traffic while he transacted his affairs at Tonquin.

We had not sailed above three days, when, a great storm arising, we were driven five days to the north-northeast, and then to the east, after which we had fair weather, but still with a pretty strong gale from the west. Upon the tenth day we were chased by two pirates, who soon overtook us; for my sloop was so deep loaden, that she sailed very slow, neither were we in a condition to defend our selves.

We were boarded about the same time by both the pirates, who entered furiously at the head of their men, but finding us all prostrate upon our faces (for so I gave order), they pinioned us with strong ropes, and setting a guard upon us, went to search the sloop.

I observed among them a Dutchman, who seemed to be of some authority, although he was not commander of either ship. He knew us by our countenances to be Englishmen, and jab-bering to us in his own language, swore we should be tied back to back, and thrown into the sea. I spoke Dutch tolerably well; I told him who we were, and begged him in consideration of our being Christians and Protestants, of neighbouring countries, in strict alliance, that he would move the captains to take some pity on us. This inflamed his rage, he repeated his threatenings, and turning to his companions, spoke with great vehemence, in the Japanese language, as I suppose, often using the word *Christianos*.

The largest of the two pirate ships was commanded by a Japanese captain, who spoke a little Dutch, but very imperfectly. He came up to me, and after several questions, which I answered in great humility, he said we should not die. I made the captain a very low bow, and then turning to the Dutchman, said, I was sorry to find more mercy in a heathen, than in a brother Chris-tian. But I had soon reason to repent those foolish words; for that malicious reprobate, having often endeavoured in vain to persuade both the captains that I might be thrown into the sea (which they would not yield to after the promise made me, that

I should not die), however prevailed so far as to have a punishment inflicted on me, worse in all human appearance than death it self. My men were sent by an equal division into both the pirate ships, and my sloop new manned. As to my self, it was determined that I should be set adrift in a small canoe, with paddles and a sail, and four days' provisions, which last the Japanese captain was so kind to double out of his own stores, and would permit no man to search me. I got down into the canoe, while the Dutchman, standing upon the deck, loaded me with all the curses and injurious terms his language could afford.

About an hour before we saw the pirates, I had taken an observation, and found we were in the latitude of 46 N. and of longitude 183. When I was at some distance from the pirates, I discovered by my pocket-glass several islands to the southeast. I set up my sail, the wind being fair, with a design to reach the nearest of those islands, which I made a shift to do in about three hours. It was all rocky; however I got many birds' eggs, and striking fire I kindled some heath and dry seaweed, by which I roasted my eggs. I eat no other supper, being resolved to spare my provisions as much as I could. I passed the night under the shelter of a rock, strowing some heath under me, and slept pretty well.

The next day I sailed to another island, and thence to a third and fourth, sometimes using my sail, and sometimes my paddles. But not to trouble the reader with a particular account of my distresses, let it suffice that on the 5th day I arrived at the last island in my sight, which lay south-southeast to the former.

This island was at a greater distance than I expected, and I did not reach it in less than five hours. I encompassed it almost round before I could find a convenient place to land in, which was a small creek, about three times the wideness of my canoe. I found the island to be all rocky, only a little intermingled with tufts of grass, and sweet-smelling herbs. I took out my small provisions, and after having refreshed myself, I secured the remainder in a cave, whereof there were great numbers. I gathered plenty of eggs upon the rocks, and got a quantity of dry seaweed, and parched grass, which I designed to kindle the next day, and roast my eggs as well as I could. (For I had about me my flint, steel, match, and burning-glass.) I lay all night in the cave where I had lodged my provisions. My bed was the same dry grass and seaweed which I intended for fuel. I slept very little, for the disquiets of my mind prevailed over my weariness, and kept me awake. I considered how impossible it was to preserve my life in so desolate a place, and how miserable my end must be. Yet I found my self so listless and desponding, that I had not the heart to rise, and before I could get spirits enough to creep out of my cave, the day was far advanced. I walked a while among the rocks; the sky was perfectly clear, and the sun so hot, that I was forced to turn my face from it: when all on a sudden it became obscured, as I thought, in a manner very different from what happens by the interposition of a cloud. I turned back, and perceived a vast opaque body between me and the sun, moving forwards towards the island: it seemed to be about two miles high, and hid the sun six or seven minutes, but I did not observe the air to be much colder, or the sky more darkened, than if I had stood under the shade of a mountain. As it approached nearer over the place where I was, it appeared to be a firm substance, the bottom flat, smooth, and shining very bright from the reflection of the sea below. I stood upon a height about two hundred yards from the shore, and saw this vast body descending almost to a parallel with me, at less than an English mile distance. I took out my pocket-perspective, and could plainly discover numbers of people moving up and down the sides of it, which appeared to be sloping, but what those people were doing I was not able to distinguish.

The natural love of life gave me some inward motions of joy, and I was ready to entertain a hope, that this adventure might some way or other help to deliver me from the desolate place and condition I was in. But at the same time the reader can hardly conceive my astonishment, to behold an island in the air, inhabited by men, who were able (as it should seem) to raise, or sink, or put it into a progressive motion, as they pleased. But not being at that time in a disposition to philosophize upon this phenomenon, I rather chose to observe what course the island would take, because it seemed for a while to stand still. Yet soon after it advanced nearer, and I could see the sides of it, encompassed with several gradations of galleries, and stairs, at certain intervals, to descend from one to the other. In the lowest gallery, I beheld some people fishing with long angling rods, and others looking on. I waved my cap (for my hat was long since worn out)and my handkerchief towards the island; and upon its nearer approach, I called and shouted with the utmost strength of my voice; and then looking circumspectly, I beheld a crowd gathered to that side which was most in my view. I found by their pointing towards me and to each other, that they plainly discovered me, although they made no return to my shouting. But I could see four or five men running in great haste up the stairs to the top of the island, who then disappeared. I happened rightly to conjecture, that these were sent for orders to some person in authority upon this occasion.

The number of people increased, and in less than half an hour the island was moved and raised in such a manner, that the lowest gallery appeared in a parallel of less than an hundred yards' distance from the height where I stood. I then put my self into the most supplicating postures, and spoke in the humblest accent, but received no answer. Those who stood nearest over-against me seemed to be persons of distinction, as I supposed by their habit. They conferred earnestly with each other, looking often upon me. At length one of them called out in a clear, polite, smooth dialect, not unlike in sound to the Italian; and therefore I returned an answer in that language, hoping at least that the cadence might be more agreeable to his ears. Although neither of us understood the other, yet my meaning was easily known, for the people saw the distress I was in.

They made signs for me to come down from the rock, and go towards the shore, which I accordingly did; and the flying island being raised to a convenient height, the verge directly over me, a chain was let down from the lowest gallery, with a seat fastened to the bottom, to which I fixed my self, and was drawn up by pulleys.

CHAPTER II.

The humours and dispositions of the Laputans described. An account of their learning. Of the King and his court. The author's reception there. The inhabitants subject to fears and disquietudes. An account of the women.

At my alighting I was surrounded by a crowd of people, but those who stood nearest seemed to be of better quality. They beheld me with all the marks and circumstances of wonder, neither indeed was I much in their debt, having never till then seen a race of mortals so singular in their shapes, habits, and countenances. Their heads were all reclined either to the right, or the left; one of their eyes turned inward, and the other directly up to the zenith. Their outward garments were adorned with the figures of suns, moons, and stars, interwoven with those of fiddles, flutes, harps, trumpets, guitars, harpsichords, and many more instruments of music, unknown to us in Europe. I observed here and there many in the habits of servants, with a blown bladder fastened like a flail to the end of a short stick, which they carried in their hands. In each bladder was a small quantity of dried pease or little pebbles (as I was afterwards informed). With these bladders they now and then flapped the mouths and ears of those who stood near them, of which practice I could not then conceive the meaning; it seems, the minds of these people are so taken up with intense speculations, that they neither can speak, nor attend to the discourses of others, without being roused by some external taction upon the organs of speech and hearing; for which reason those persons who are able to afford it always keep a flapper (the original is *climenole*) in their family, as one of their domestics, nor ever walk abroad or make visits without him. And the business of this officer is, when two or more persons are in company, gently to strike with his bladder the mouth of him who is to speak, and the right ear of him or them to whom the speaker addresseth himself. This flapper is likewise employed diligently to attend his master in his walks, and upon occasion to give him a soft flap on his eyes, because he is always so wrapped up in cogitation, that he is in manifest danger of falling down every precipice, and bouncing his head against every post, and in the streets, of jostling others or being jostled himself into the kennel.

It was necessary to give the reader this information, without which he would be at the same loss with me, to understand the proceedings of these people, as they conducted me up the stairs, to the top of the island, and from thence to the royal palace. While we were ascending, they forgot several times what they were about, and left me to my self, till their memories were again roused by their flappers; for they appeared altogether unmoved by the sight of my foreign habit and countenance, and by the shouts of the vulgar, whose thoughts and minds were more disengaged.

At last we entered the palace, and proceeded into the chamber of presence, where I saw the King seated on his throne, attended on each side by persons of prime quality. Before the throne was a large table filled with globes and spheres, and mathematical instruments of all kinds. His Majesty took not the least notice of us, although our entrance was not without sufficient noise, by the concourse of all persons belonging to the court. But he was then deep in a problem, and we attended at least an hour before he could solve it. There stood by him, on each side, a young page, with flaps in their hands, and when they saw he was at leisure, one of them gently struck his mouth, and the other his right ear, at which he started like one awaked on the sudden, and looking towards me, and the company I was in, recollected the occasion of our coming, whereof he had been informed before. He spoke some words, whereupon immediately a young man with a flap came up to my side, and flapped me gently on the right ear; but I made signs as well as I could, that I had no occasion for such an instrument; which as I afterwards found gave his Majesty and the whole court a very mean opinion of my understanding. The King, as far as I could conjecture, asked me several questions, and I addressed my self to him in all the languages I had. When it was found that I could neither understand nor be understood, I was conducted by his order to an apartment in his palace (this prince being distinguished above all his predecessors for his hospitality to strangers), where two servants were appointed to attend me. My dinner was brought, and four persons of quality, whom I remembered to have seen very near the King's person, did me the honour to dine with me. We had two courses, of three dishes each. In the first course there was a shoulder of mutton, cut into an equilateral triangle, a piece of beef into a rhomboides, and a pudding into a cycloid. The second course was two ducks, trussed up into the form of fiddles; sausages and puddings resembling flutes and hautboys, and a breast of veal in the shape of a harp. The servants cut our bread into cones, cylinders, parallelograms, and several other mathematical figures.

While we were at dinner, I made bold to ask the names of several things in their language, and those noble persons, by the assistance of their flappers, delighted to give me answers, hoping to raise my admiration of their great abilities, if I could be brought to converse with them. I was soon able to call for bread and drink, or whatever else I wanted.

After dinner my company withdrew, and a person was sent to me by the King's order, attended by a flapper. He brought with him pen, ink, and paper, and three or four books, giving me to understand by signs, that he was sent to teach me the language. We sat together four hours, in which time I wrote down a great number of words in columns, with the translations over against them. I likewise made a shift to learn several short sentences. For my tutor would order one of my servants to fetch something, to turn about, to make a bow, to sit, or stand, or walk and the like. Then I took down the sentence in writing. He showed me also in one of his books the figures of the sun, moon, and stars, the zodiac, the tropics, and polar circles, together with the denominations of many figures of planes and solids. He gave me the names and descriptions of all the musical instruments, and the general terms of art in playing on each of them. After he had left me, I placed all my words with their interpretations in alphabetical order. And thus in a few days, by the help of a very faithful memory, I got some insight into their language.

The word which I interpret the *Flying* or *Floating Island* is in the original *Laputa*, whereof I could never learn the true etymology. *Lap* in the old obsolete language signifieth *high*, and *untuh* a *governor*, from which they say by corruption was derived *Laputa*, from *Lapuntuh*. But I do not approve of this derivation, which seems to be a little strained. I ventured to offer to the learned among them a conjecture of my own, that *Laputa* was *quasi Lap outed*; *Lap* signifying properly the dancing of the sunbeams in the sea, and *outed* a wing, which however I shall not obtrude, but submit to the judicious reader.

Those to whom the King had entrusted me, observing how ill I was clad, ordered a tailor to come next morning, and take my measure for a suit of clothes. This operator did his office after a different manner from those of his trade in Europe. He first took my altitude by a quadrant, and then, with rule and compasses, described the dimensions and outlines of my whole body, all which he entered upon paper, and in six days brought my clothes very ill made, and quite out of shape, by happening to mistake a figure in the calculation. But my comfort was, that I observed such accidents very frequent and little regarded.

During my confinement for want of clothes, and by an indisposition that held me some days longer, I much enlarged my dictionary; and when I went next to court, was able to understand many things the King spoke, and to return him some kind of answers. His Majesty had given orders that the island should move northeast and by east, to the vertical point over Lagado, the metropolis of the whole kingdom below upon the firm earth. It was about ninety leagues distant, and our voyage lasted four days and an half. I was not in the least sensible of the progressive motion made in the air by the island. On the second morning about eleven o'clock, the King himself in person, attended by his nobility, courtiers, and officers, having prepared all their musical instruments, played on them for three hours without intermission, so that I was quite stunned with the noise; neither could I possibly guess the meaning till my tutor informed me. He said that the people of their island had their ears adapted to hear the music of the spheres, which always played at certain periods, and the court was now prepared to bear their part in what ever instrument they most excelled.

In our journey towards Lagado, the capital city, his Majesty ordered that the island should stop over certain towns and villages, from whence he might receive the petitions of his subjects.

And to this purpose several packthreads were let down with small weights at the bottom. On these packthreads the people strung their petitions, which mounted up directly like the scraps of paper fastened by schoolboys at the end of the string that holds their kite. Sometimes we received wine and victuals from below, which were drawn up by pulleys.

The knowledge I had in mathematics gave me great assistance in acquiring their phraseology, which depended much upon that science and music; and in the latter I was not unskilled. Their ideas are perpetually conversant in lines and figures. If they would, for example, praise the beauty of a woman or any other animal, they describe it by rhombs, circles, parallelograms, ellipses, and other geometrical terms, or else by words of art drawn from music, needless here to repeat. I observed in the King's kitchen all sorts of mathematical and musical instruments, after the figures of which they cut up the joints that were served to his Majesty's table.

Their houses are very ill built, the walls bevil, without one right angle in any apartment, and this defect ariseth from the contempt they bear for practical geometry, which they despise as vulgar and mechanic, those instructions they give being too refined for the intellectuals of their workmen, which occasions perpetual mistakes. And although they are dextrous enough upon a piece of paper in the management of the rule, the pencil, and the divider, yet in the common actions and behaviour of life I have not seen a more clumsy, awkward, and unhandy people, nor so slow and perplexed in their conceptions upon all other subjects, except those of mathematics and music. They are very bad reasoners, and vehemently given to opposition, unless when they happen to be of the right opinion, which is seldom their case. Imagination, fancy, and invention, they are wholly strangers to, nor have any words in their language by which those ideas can be expressed; the whole compass of their thoughts and mind being shut up within the two forementioned sciences.

Most of them, and especially those who deal in the astronomical part, have great faith in judicial astrology, although they are ashamed to own it publicly. But what I chiefly admired, and thought altogether unaccountable, was the strong disposition I observed in them towards news and politics, perpetually enquiring into public affairs, giving their judgments in matters of state, and passionately disputing every inch of a party opinion. I have indeed observed the same disposition among most of the mathematicians I have known in Europe, although I could never discover the least analogy between the two sciences; unless those people suppose, that because the smallest circle hath as many degrees as the largest, therefore the regulation and management of the world require no more abilities than the handling and turning of a globe. But I rather take this quality to spring from a very common infirmity of human nature, inclining us to be more curious and conceited in matters where we have least concern, and for which we are least adapted either by study or nature.

These people are under continual disquietudes, never enjoying a minute's peace of mind; and their disturbances proceed from causes which very little affect the rest of mortals. Their apprehensions arise from several changes they dread in the celestial bodies. For instance; that the earth, by the continual approaches of the sun towards it, must in course of time be absorbed or swallowed up. That the face of the sun will by degrees be encrusted with its own effluvia, and give no more light to the world. That the earth very narrowly escaped a brush from the tail of the last comet, which would have infallibly reduced it to ashes; and that the next, which they have calculated for one and thirty years hence, will probably destroy us. For, if in its perihelion it should approach within a certain degree of the sun (as by their calculations they have reason to dread), it will conceive a degree of heat ten thousand times more intense than that of red-hot glowing iron; and in its absence from the sun, carry a blazing tail ten hundred thousand and fourteen miles long; through which if the earth should pass at the distance of one hundred thousand miles from the nucleus or main body of the comet, it must in its passage be set on fire, and reduced to ashes. That the sun daily spending its rays without any nutriment to supply them, will at last be wholly consumed and annihilated; which must be attended with the destruction of this earth, and of all the planets that receive their light from it.

They are so perpetually alarmed with the apprehensions of these and the like impending dangers, that they can neither sleep quietly in their beds, nor have any relish for the common pleasures or amusements of life. When they meet an acquaintance in the morning, the first question is about the sun's health, how he looked at his setting and rising, and what hopes they have to avoid the stroke of the approaching comet. This conversation they are apt to run into with the same temper that boys discover in delighting to hear terrible stories of sprites and hobgoblins, which they greedily listen to, and dare not go to bed for fear.

The women of the island have abundance of vivacity; they contemn their husbands, and are exceedingly fond of strangers, whereof there is always a considerable number from the continent below, attending at court, either upon affairs of the several towns and corporations, or their own particular occasions, but are much despised, because they want the same endowments. Among these the ladies choose their gallants: but the vexation is, that they act with too much ease and security, for the husband is always so rapt in speculation, that the mistress and lover may proceed to the greatest familiarities before his face, if he be but provided with paper and implements, and without his flapper at his side.

The wives and daughters lament their confinement to the island, although I think it the most delicious spot of ground in the world; and although they live here in the greatest plenty and magnificence, and are allowed to do whatever they please, they long to see the world, and take the diversions of the metropolis, which they are not allowed to do without a particular licence from the King; and this is not easy to be obtained because the people of quality have found by frequent experience how hard it is to persuade their women to return from below. I was told that a great court lady, who had several children, is married to the prime minister, the richest subject in the kingdom, a very graceful person, extremely fond of her, and lives in the finest palace of the island, went down to Lagado, on the pretence of health, there hid her self for several months, till the King sent a warrant to search for her, and she was found in an obscure eating house all in rags, having pawned her clothes to maintain an old deformed footman, who beat her every day, and in whose company she was taken much against her will. And although her husband received her with all possible kindness, and without the least reproach, she soon after contrived to steal down again with all her jewels, to the same gallant, and hath not been heard of since.

This may perhaps pass with the reader rather for an European or English story, than for one of a country so remote. But he may please to consider, that the caprices of womankind are not limited by any climate or nation, and that they are much more uniform than can be easily imagined.

In about a month's time I had made a tolerable proficiency in their language, and was able to answer most of the King's questions, when I had the honour to attend him. His Majesty discovered not the least curiosity to enquire into the laws, government, history, religion, or manners of the countries where I had been, but confined his questions to the state of mathematics, and received the account I gave him with great contempt and indifference, though often roused by his flapper on each side.

CHAPTER III

A phenomenon solved by modern philosophy and astronomy. The
Laputians' great improvements in the latter. The King's method
of suppressing insurrections.

I desired leave of this prince to see the curiosities of the island,
which he was graciously pleased to grant, and ordered my tutor
to attend me. I chiefly wanted to know to what cause in art or in
nature it owed its several motions, whereof I will now give a
philosophical account to the reader.

The Flying or Floating Island is exactly circular, its diameter
7,837 yards, or about four miles and an half, and consequently
contains ten thousand acres. It is three hundred yards thick.
The bottom or under surface, which appears to those who view it
from below, is one even regular plate of adamant, shooting up to
the height of about two hundred yards. Above it lie the several
minerals in their usual order, and over all is a coat of rich mould
ten or twelve foot deep. The declivity of the upper surface,
from the circumference to the center, is the natural cause why
all the dews and rains which fall upon the island are conveyed in
small rivulets towards the middle, where they are emptied into
four large basons, each of about half a mile in circuit, and two
hundred yards distant from the center. From these basons the
water is continually exhaled by the sun in the day time, which
effectually prevents their overflowing. Besides, as it is in the
power of the monarch to raise the island above the region of
clouds and vapours, he can prevent the falling of dews and rains
when ever he pleases. For the highest clouds cannot rise above
two miles, as naturalists agree, at least they were never known to
do so in that country.

At the center of the island there is a chasm about fifty yards in
diameter, from whence the astronomers descend into a large
dome, which is therefore called *Flandona Gagnole*, or the *Astron-*
omer's Cave, situated at the depth of an hundred yards beneath
the upper surface of the adamant. In this cave are twenty lamps
continually burning, which from the reflection of the adamant
cast a strong light into every part. The place is stored with great
variety of sextants, quadrants, telescopes, astrolabes, and other
astronomical instruments. But the greatest curiosity, upon which
the fate of the island depends, is a loadstone of a prodigious size,
in shape resembling a weaver's shuttle. It is in length six yards,
and in the thickest part at least three yards over. This magnet
is sustained by a very strong axle of adamant passing through its
middle, upon which it plays, and is poised so exactly that the

weakest hand can turn it. It is hooped round with an hollow cylinder of adamant, four foot deep, as many thick, and twelve yards in diameter, placed horizontally, and supported by eight adamantine feet, each six yards high. In the middle of the concave side there is a groove twelve inches deep, in which the extremities of the axle are lodged, and turned round as there is occasion.

The stone cannot be moved from its place by any force, because the hoop and its feet are one continued piece with that body of adamant which constitutes the bottom of the island.

By means of this loadstone, the island is made to rise and fall, and move from one place to another. For, with respect to that part of the earth over which the monarch presides, the stone is endued at one of its sides with an attractive power, and at the other with a repulsive. Upon placing the magnet erect with its attracting end towards the earth, the island descends; but when the repelling extremity points downwards, the island mounts directly upwards. When the position of the stone is oblique, the motion of the island is so too. For in this magnet the forces always act in lines parallel to its direction.

By this oblique motion the island is conveyed to different parts of the monarch's dominions. To explain the manner of its progress, let *A B* represent a line drawn cross the dominions of Balnibarbi, let the line *c d* represent the loadstone, of which let *d* be the repelling end, and *c* the attracting end, the island being over *C;* let the stone be placed in the position *c d* with its repelling end downwards; then the island will be driven upwards obliquely towards *D*. When it is arrived at *D*, let the stone be turned upon its axle till its attracting end points towards *E*, and then the island will be carried obliquely towards *E;* where if the stone be again turned upon its axle till it stands in the position *E F*, with its repelling point downwards, the island will rise obliquely towards *F*, where by directing the attracting end towards *G*, the island may be carried to *G*, and from *G* to *H*, by turning the stone, so as to make its repelling extremity point directly downwards. And thus by changing the situation of the stone as often as there is occasion, the island is made to rise and fall by turns in an oblique direction, and by those alternate risings and fallings (the obliquity being not considerable) is conveyed from one part of the dominions to the other.

But it must be observed, that this island cannot move beyond the extent of the dominions below, nor can it rise above the height of four miles. For which the astronomers (who have

Plate 4. Part 3.   Page 218.

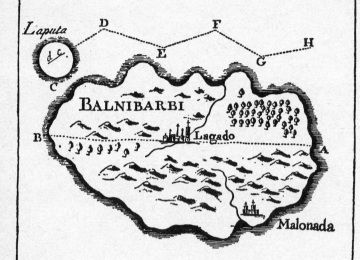

written large systems concerning the stone) assign the following reason: that the magnetic virtue does not extend beyond the distance of four miles, and that the mineral which acts upon the stone in the bowels of the earth, and in the sea about six leagues distant from the shore, is not diffused through the whole globe, but terminated with the limits of the King's dominions; and it was easy, from the great advantage of such a superior situation, for a prince to bring under his obedience whatever country lay within the attraction of that magnet.

When the stone is put parallel to the plane of the horizon, the island standeth still; for in that case, the extremities of it, being at equal distance from the earth, act with equal force, the one in drawing downwards, the other in pushing upwards, and consequently no motion can ensue.

This loadstone is under the care of certain astronomers, who from time to time give it such positions as the monarch directs. They spend the greatest part of their lives in observing the celestial bodies, which they do by the assistance of glasses far excelling ours in goodness. For although their largest telescopes do not exceed three feet, they magnify much more than those of a hundred with us, and at the same time show the stars with greater clearness. For this advantage hath enabled them to extend their discoveries much farther than our astronomers in Europe. They have made a catalogue of ten thousand fixed stars, whereas the largest of ours do not contain above one third part of that number. They have likewise discovered two lesser stars, or 'satellites', which revolve about Mars, whereof the innermost is distant from the center of the primary planet exactly three of his diameters, and the outermost five; the former revolves in the space of ten hours, and the latter in twenty-one and an half; so that the squares of their periodical times are very near in the same proportion with the cubes of their distance from the center of Mars, which evidently shows them to be governed by the same law of gravitation, that influences the other heavenly bodies.

They have observed ninety-three different comets, and settled their periods with great exactness. If this be true (and they affirm it with great confidence) it is much to be wished that their observations were made public, whereby the theory of comets, which at present is very lame and defective, might be brought to the same perfection with other parts of astronomy.

The King would be the most absolute prince in the universe, if he could but prevail on a ministry to join with him; but these having their estates below on the continent, and considering that the office of a favourite hath a very uncertain tenure, would never consent to the enslaving their country.

If any town should engage in rebellion or mutiny, fall into violent factions, or refuse to pay the usual tribute, the King hath two methods of reducing them to obedience. The first and the mildest course is by keeping the island hovering over such a town, and the lands about it, whereby he can deprive them of the benefit of the sun and the rain, and consequently afflict the inhabitants with dearth and diseases. And if the crime deserve it they are at the same time pelted from above with great stones, against which they have no defence but by creeping into cellars or caves, while the roofs of their houses are beaten to pieces. But if they still continue obstinate, or offer to raise insurrections, he proceeds to the last remedy, by letting the island drop directly upon their heads, which makes a universal destruction both of houses and men. However, this is an extremity to which the prince is seldom driven, neither indeed is he willing to put it in execution, nor dare his ministers advise him to an action which, as it would render them odious to the people, so it would be a great damage to their own estates, that lie all below, for the island is the King's demesne.

But there is still indeed a more weighty reason, why the kings of this country have been always averse from executing so terrible an action, unless upon the utmost necessity. For if the town intended to be destroyed should have in it any tall rocks, as it generally falls out in the larger cities, a situation probably chosen at first with a view to prevent such a catastrophe; or if it abound in high spires or pillars of stone, a sudden fall might endanger the bottom or under surface of the island, which although it consist, as I have said, of one entire adamant two hundred yards thick, might happen to crack by too great a shock, or burst by approaching too near the fires from the houses below, as the backs both of iron and stone will often do in our chimneys. Of all this the people are well apprised, and understand how far to carry their obstinacy, where their liberty or property is concerned. And the King, when he is highest provoked, and most determined to press a city to rubbish, orders the island to descend with great gentleness, out of a pretence of tenderness to his people, but indeed for fear of breaking the adamantine bottom; in which case it is the opinion of all their philosophers, that the loadstone could no longer hold it up, and the whole mass would fall to the ground.

About three years before my arrival among them, while the King was in his progress over his dominions, there happened an extraordinary accident which had like to have put a period to the fate of that monarchy, at least as it is now instituted. Lindalino, the second city in the kingdom, was the first his Majesty visited in his progress. Three days after his departure, the inhabitants, who had often complained of great oppressions, shut the town gates, seized on the governor, and with incredible speed and labour erected four large towers, one at every corner of the city (which is an exact square), equal in height to a strong pointed rock that stands directly in the center of the city. Upon the top of each tower, as well as upon the rock, they fixed a great load-stone, and in case their design should fail, they had provided a vast quantity of the most combustible fuel, hoping to burst therewith the adamantine bottom of the island, if the loadstone project should miscarry.

It was eight months before the King had perfect notice that the Lindalinians were in rebellion. He then commanded that the island should be wafted over the city. The people were unanimous, and had laid in store of provisions, and a great river runs through the middle of the town. The King hovered over them several days to deprive them of the sun and the rain. He ordered many packthreads to be let down, yet not a person offered to send up a petition, but instead thereof, very bold demands, the redress of all their grievances, great immunities, the choice of their own governor, and other the like exorbitances. Upon which his Majesty commanded all the inhabitants of the island to cast great stones from the lower gallery into the town; but the citizens had provided against this mischief by conveying their persons and effects into the four towers, and other strong buildings, and vaults underground.

The King being now determined to reduce this proud people, ordered that the island should descend gently within forty yards of the top of the towers and rock. This was accordingly done; but the officers employed in that work found the descent much speedier than usual, and by turning the loadstone could not without great difficulty keep it in a firm position, but found the island inclining to fall. They sent the King immediate intelligence of this astonishing event and begged his Majesty's permission to raise the island higher; the King consented, a general council was called, and the officers of the loadstone ordered to attend. One of the oldest and expertest among them obtained leave to try an experiment. He took a strong line of an hundred yards, and the island being raised over the town above the attracting power they had felt, he fastened a piece of adamant to the end of his line which had in it a mixture of iron mineral, of the same nature with that whereof the bottom or lower surface of the island is composed, and from the lower gallery let it down slowly towards the top of the towers. The adamant was not descended four yards, before the officer felt it drawn so strongly downwards, that he could hardly pull it back. He then threw down several small pieces of adamant, and observed that they were all violently attracted by the top of the tower. The same experiment was made on the other three towers, and on the rock with the same effect.

This incident broke entirely the King's measures and (to dwell no longer on other circumstances) he was forced to give the town their own conditions.

I was assured by a great minister, that if the island had descended so near the town as not to be able to raise it self, the citizens were determined to fix it for ever, to kill the King and all his servants, and entirely change the government.

By a fundamental law of this realm, neither the King nor either of his two elder sons are permitted to leave the island, nor the Queen, till she is past child-bearing.

CHAPTER IV.

The author leaves Laputa, is conveyed to Balnibarbi, arrives at the metropolis. A description of the metropolis and the country adjoining. The author hospitably received by a great lord. His conversation with that lord.

Although I cannot say that I was ill treated in this island, yet I must confess I thought my self too much neglected, not without some degree of contempt. For neither prince nor people appeared to be curious in any part of knowledge, except mathematics and music, wherein I was far their inferior, and upon that account very little regarded.

On the other side, after having seen all the curiosities of the island, I was very desirous to leave it, being heartily weary of those people. They were indeed excellent in two sciences for which I have great esteem, and wherein I am not unversed, but at the same time so abstracted and involved in speculation that I never met with such disagreeable companions. I conversed only with women, tradesmen, flappers, and court-pages, during two months of my abode there, by which at last I rendered my self extremely contemptible, yet these were the only people from whom I could ever receive a reasonable answer.

I had obtained by hard study a good degree of knowledge in their language; I was weary of being confined to an island where I received so little countenance, and resolved to leave it with the first opportunity.

There was a great lord at court, nearly related to the King, and for that reason alone used with respect. He was universally reckoned the most ignorant and stupid person among them. He had performed many eminent services for the crown, had great natural and acquired parts, adorned with integrity and honour, but so ill an ear for music, that his detractors reported he had been often known to beat time in the wrong place; neither could his tutors without extreme difficulty teach him to demonstrate the most easy proposition in the mathematics. He was pleased to show me many marks of favour, often did me the honour of a visit, desired to be informed in the affairs of Europe, the laws and customs, the manners and learning of the several countries where I had travelled. He listened to me with great attention, and made very wise observations on all I spoke. He had two flappers attending him for state, but never made use of them except at court, and in visits of ceremony, and would always command them to withdraw when we were alone together.

I intreated this illustrious person to intercede in my behalf with his Majesty for leave to depart, which he accordingly did, as he was pleased to tell me, with regret: for indeed he had made me several offers very advantageous, which however I refused with expressions of the highest acknowledgement.

On the 16th day of February, I took leave of his Majesty and the court. The King made me a present to the value of about two hundred pounds English, and my protector his kinsman as much more, together with a letter of recommendation to a friend of his in Lagado, the metropolis; the island being then hovering over a mountain about two miles from it, I was let down from the lowest gallery, in the same manner as I had been taken up.

The continent, as far as it is subject to the monarch of the Flying Island, passes under the general name of Balnibarbi, and the metropolis, as I said before, is called Lagado. I felt some little satisfaction in finding my self on firm ground. I walked to the city without any concern, being clad like one of the natives, and sufficiently instructed to converse with them. I soon found out the person's house to whom I was recommended, presented my letter from his friend the grandee in the island, and was received with much kindness. This great lord, whose name was Munodi, ordered me an apartment in his own house, where I

continued during my stay, and was entertained in a most hospitable manner.

The next morning after my arrival he took me in his chariot
to see the town, which is about half the bigness of London, but
the houses very strangely built, and most of them out of repair.
The people in the streets walked fast, looked wild, their eyes
fixed, and were generally in rags. We passed through one of the
town gates, and went about three miles into the country, where
I saw many labourers working with several sorts of tools in the
ground, but was not able to conjecture what they were about,
neither did I observe any expectation either of corn or grass,
although the soil appeared to be excellent. I could not forbear
admiring at these odd appearances both in town and country,
and I made bold to desire my conductor, that he would be
pleased to explain to me what could be meant by so many busy
heads, hands, and faces, both in the streets and the fields, because
I did not discover any good effects they produced; but on the
contrary, I never knew a soil so unhappily cultivated, houses so
ill contrived and so ruinous, or a people whose countenances and
habit expressed so much misery and want.

This Lord Munodi was a person of the first rank, and had been
some years Governor of Lagado, but by a cabal of ministers was
discharged for insufficiency. However, the King treated him
with tenderness, as a well-meaning man, but of a low contemptible understanding.

When I gave that free censure of the country and its inhabitants, he made no further answer than by telling me that I had
not been long enough among them to form a judgment, and
that the different nations of the world had different customs,
with other common topics to the same purpose. But when we
returned to his palace, he asked me how I liked the building,
what absurdities I observed, and what quarrel I had with the
dress and looks of his domestics. This he might safely do, because every thing about him was magnificent, regular, and polite.
I answered that his Excellency's prudence, quality, and fortune
had exempted him from those defects which folly and beggary
had produced in others. He said if I would go with him to his
country house, about twenty miles distant, where his estate lay,
there would be more leisure for this kind of conversation. I
told his Excellency that I was entirely at his disposal, and accordingly we set out next morning.

During our journey, he made me observe the several methods
used by farmers in managing their lands, which to me were
wholly unaccountable, for, except in some very few places, I

could not discover one ear of corn or blade of grass. But in three hours travelling the scene was wholly altered; we came into a most beautiful country; farmers' houses at small distances, neatly built, the fields enclosed, containing vineyards, corn-grounds and meadows. Neither do I remember to have seen a more delightful prospect. His Excellency observed my countenance to clear up; he told me with a sigh, that there his estate began, and would continue the same till we should come to his house. That his countrymen ridiculed and despised him for managing his affairs no better, and for setting so ill an example to the kingdom, which however was followed by very few, such as were old and wilful, and weak like himself.

We came at length to the house, which was indeed a noble structure, built according to the best rules of ancient architecture. The fountains, gardens, walks, avenues, and groves were all disposed with exact judgment and taste. I gave due praises to every thing I saw, whereof his Excellency took not the least notice till after supper, when, there being no third companion, he told me with a very melancholy air, that he doubted he must throw down his houses in town and country, to rebuild them after the present mode, destroy all his plantations, and cast others into such a form as modern usage required, and give the same directions to all his tenants, unless he would submit to incur the censure of pride, singularity, affectation, ignorance, caprice, and perhaps encrease his Majesty's displeasure.

That the admiration I appeared to be under would cease or diminish when he had informed me of some particulars, which probably I never heard of at court, the people there being too much taken up in their own speculations to have regard to what passed here below.

The sum of his discourse was to this effect. That about forty years ago, certain persons went up to Laputa either upon business or diversion, and after five months continuance came back with a very little smattering in mathematics, but full of volatile spirits acquired in that airy region. That these persons upon their return began to dislike the management of every thing below, and fell into schemes of putting all arts, sciences, languages, and mechanics upon a new foot. To this end they procured a royal patent for erecting an academy of PROJECTORS in Lagado; and the humour prevailed so strongly among the people, that there is not a town of any consequence in the kingdom without such an academy. In these colleges the professors contrive new rules and methods of agriculture and building, and new instruments and tools for all trades and manufactures, whereby, as they undertake, one man shall do the work of ten; a palace may be built in a week, of materials so durable as to last for ever without repairing. All the fruits of the earth shall come to maturity at whatever season we think fit to choose, and increase an hundred fold more than they do at present, with innumerable other happy proposals. The only inconvenience is, that none of these projects are yet brought to perfection, and in the mean time the whole country lies miserably waste, the houses in ruins, and the people without food or clothes. By all which, instead of being discouraged, they are fifty times more violently bent upon prosecuting their schemes, driven equally on by hope and despair; that as for himself, being not of an enterprising spirit, he was content to go on in the old forms, to live in the houses his ancestors had built, and act as they did in every part of life without innovation. That some few other persons of quality and gentry had done the same, but were looked on with an eye of contempt and ill will, as enemies to art, ignorant, and ill commonwealth's-men, preferring their own ease and sloth before the general improvement of their country.

His Lordship added, that he would not by any further particulars prevent the pleasure I should certainly take in viewing the Grand Academy, whither he was resolved I should go. He only desired me to observe a ruined building upon the side of a mountain about three miles distant, of which he gave me this account. That he had a very convenient mill within half a mile of his house, turned by a current from a large river, and sufficient for his own family as well as a great number of his tenants. That about seven years ago a club of those projectors came to him with proposals to destroy this mill, and build another on the side of that mountain, on the long ridge whereof a long canal must be cut for a repository of water, to be conveyed up by pipes and engines to supply the mill: because the wind and air upon a height agitated the water, and thereby made it fitter for motion: and because the water descending down a declivity would turn the mill with half the current of a river whose course is more upon a level. He said, that being then not very well with the court, and pressed by many of his friends, he complied with the proposal; and after employing an hundred men for two years, the work miscarried, the projectors went off, laying the blame entirely upon him, railing at him ever since, and putting others upon the same experiment, with equal assurance of success, as well as equal disappointment.

In a few days we came back to town, and his Excellency, considering the bad character he had in the Academy, would not go with me himself, but recommended me to a friend of his to bear me company thither. My Lord was pleased to represent me as a great admirer of projects, and a person of much curiosity and easy belief, which indeed was not without truth, for I had my self been a sort of projector in my younger days.

Chapter V.

The author permitted to see the Grand Academy of Lagado. The Academy largely described. The arts wherein the professors employ themselves.

This academy is not an entire single building, but a continuation of several houses on both sides of a street, which growing waste was purchased and applied to that use.

I was received very kindly by the Warden, and went for many days to the Academy. Every room hath in it one or more projectors, and I believe I could not be in fewer than five hundred rooms.

The first man I saw was of a meagre aspect, with sooty hands and face, his hair and beard long, ragged and singed in several places. His clothes, shirt, and skin were all of the same colour. He had been eight years upon a project for extracting sunbeams out of cucumbers, which were to be put into vials hermetically sealed, and let out to warm the air in raw inclement summers. He told me, he did not doubt in eight years more that he should be able to supply the Governor's gardens with sunshine at a reasonable rate; but he complained that his stock was low, and entreated me to give him something as an encouragement to ingenuity, especially since this had been a very dear season for cucumbers. I made him a small present, for my Lord had furnished me with money on purpose, because he knew their practice of begging from all who go to see them.

I went into another chamber, but was ready to hasten back, being almost overcome with a horrible stink. My conductor pressed me forward, conjuring me in a whisper to give no offence, which would be highly resented, and therefore I durst not so much as stop my nose. The projector of this cell was the most ancient student of the Academy. His face and beard were of a pale yellow; his hands and clothes daubed over with filth. When I was presented to him, he gave me a very close embrace (a compliment I could well have excused). His employment from his first coming into the Academy was an operation to reduce human excrement to its original food, by separating the several parts, removing the tincture which it receives from the gall, making the odour exhale, and scumming off the saliva. He had a weekly allowance from the society of a vessel filled with human ordure, about the bigness of a Bristol barrel.

I saw another at work to calcine ice into gunpowder, who likewise showed me a treatise he had written concerning the malleability of fire, which he intended to publish.

There was a most ingenious architect who had contrived a new method for building houses, by beginning at the roof and working downwards to the foundation, which he justified to me by the like practice of those two prudent insects, the bee and the spider.

There was a man born blind, who had several apprentices in his own condition: their employment was to mix colours for painters, which their master taught them to distinguish by feeling and smelling. It was indeed my misfortune to find them at that time not very perfect in their lessons, and the professor himself happened to be generally mistaken; this artist is much encouraged and esteemed by the whole fraternity.

In another apartment I was highly pleased with a projector, who had found a device of plowing the ground with hogs, to save the charges of plows, cattle, and labour. The method is this: in an acre of ground you bury, at six inches distance, and eight deep, a quantity of acorns, dates, chestnuts, and other mast or vegetables whereof these animals are fondest: then you drive six hundred or more of them into the field, where in a few days they will root up the whole ground in search of their food, and make it fit for sowing, at the same time manuring it with their dung; it is true upon experiment they found the charge and trouble very great, and they had little or no crop. However, it is not doubted that this invention may be capable of great improvement.

I went into another room, where the walls and ceiling were all hung round with cobwebs, except a narrow passage for the artist to go in and out. At my entrance he called aloud to me not to disturb his webs. He lamented the fatal mistake the world had been so long in of using silkworms, while we had such plenty of domestic insects, who infinitely excelled the former, because they understood how to weave as well as spin. And he proposed farther, that by employing spiders the charge of dyeing silks would be wholly saved, whereof I was fully convinced when he showed me a vast number of flies most beautifully coloured, wherewith he fed his spiders, assuring us that the webs would take a tincture from them; and as he had them of all hues, he hoped to fit every body's fancy, as soon as he could find proper food for the flies, of certain gums, oils, and other glutinous matter, to give a strength and consistence to the threads.

There was an astronomer who had undertaken to place a sundial upon the great weathercock on the town-house, by adjusting the annual and diurnal motions of the earth and sun, so as to answer and coincide with all accidental turnings by the wind.

I was complaining of a small fit of the colic, upon which my conductor led me into a room, where a great physician resided, who was famous for curing that disease by contrary operations from the same instrument. He had a large pair of bellows with a long slender muzzle of ivory. This he conveyed eight inches up the anus, and drawing in the wind, he affirmed he could make the guts as lank as a dried bladder. But when the disease was more stubborn and violent, he let in the muzzle while the bellows were full of wind, which he discharged into the body of the patient, then withdrew the instrument to replenish it, clapping his thumb strongly against the orifice of the fundament; and this being repeated three or four times, the adventitious wind would rush out, bringing the noxious along with it (like water put into a pump) and the patient recovers. I saw him try both experiments upon a dog, but could not discern any effect from the former. After the latter, the animal was ready to burst, and made so violent a discharge, as was very offensive to me and my companions. The dog died on the spot, and we left the doctor endeavouring to recover him by the same operation.

I visited many other apartments, but shall not trouble my reader with all the curiosities I observed, being studious of brevity.

I had hitherto seen only one side of the Academy, the other being appropriated to the advancers of speculative learning, of whom I shall say something when I have mentioned one illustrious person more, who is called among them 'the universal artist'. He told us he had been thirty years employing his thoughts for the improvement of human life. He had two large rooms full of wonderful curiosities, and fifty men at work. Some were condensing air into a dry tangible substance, by extracting the nitre, and letting the aqueous or fluid particles percolate; others softening marble for pillows and pincushions; others petrifying the hoofs of a living horse to preserve them from foundering. The artist himself was at that time busy upon two great designs; the first, to sow land with chaff, wherein he affirmed the true seminal virtue to be contained, as he demonstrated by several experiments which I was not skilful enough to comprehend. The other was, by a certain composition of gums, minerals, and vegetables outwardly applied to prevent the growth of wool upon two young lambs; and he hoped in a reasonable time to propagate the breed of naked sheep all over the kingdom.

We crossed a walk to the other part of the Academy, where, as I have already said, the projectors in speculative learning resided.

The first professor I saw was in a very large room, with forty pupils about him. After salutation, observing me to look earnestly upon a frame, which took up the greatest part of both the length and breadth of the room, he said perhaps I might wonder to see him employed in a project for improving speculative knowledge by practical and mechanical operations. But the world would soon be sensible of its usefulness, and he flattered himself that a more noble, exalted thought never sprang in any other man's head. Every one knows how laborious the usual method is of attaining to arts and sciences; whereas by his contrivance the most ignorant person at a reasonable charge, and with a little bodily labour, may write books in philosophy, poetry, politics, law, mathematics and theology, without the least assistance from genius or study. He then led me to the frame, about the sides whereof all his pupils stood in ranks. It was twenty foot square, placed in the middle of the room. The superficies was composed of several bits of wood, about the bigness of a die, but some larger than others. They were all linked together by slender wires. These bits of wood were covered on every square with papers pasted on them, and on these papers were written all the words of their language in their several moods, tenses, and declensions, but without any order. The professor then desired me to observe, for he was going to set his engine at work. The pupils at his command took each of them hold of an iron handle, whereof there were forty fixed round the edges of the frame, and giving them a sudden turn, the whole disposition of the words was entirely changed. He then commanded six and thirty of the lads to read the several lines softly as they appeared upon the frame; and where they found three or four words together that might make part of a sentence, they dictated to the four remaining boys who were scribes. This work was repeated three or four times, and at every turn the engine was so contrived, that the words shifted into new places, as the square bits of wood moved upside down.

Plate 5 Part 3.

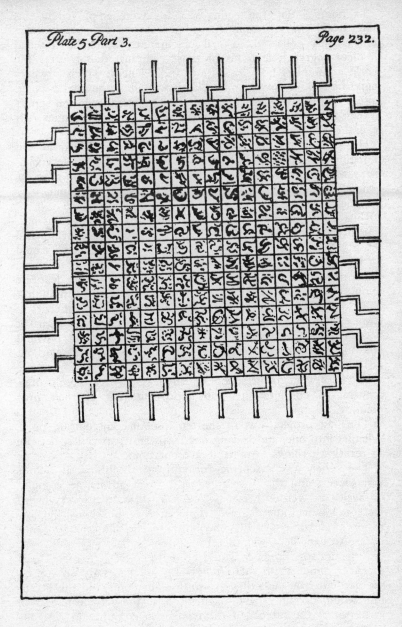

Six hours a day the young students were employed in this labour, and the professor showed me several volumes in large folio already collected, of broken sentences, which he intended to piece together, and out of those rich materials to give the world a complete body of all arts and sciences; which however might be still improved, and much expedited, if the public would raise a fund for making and employing five hundred such frames in Lagado, and oblige the managers to contribute in common their several collections.

He assured me, that this invention had employed all his thoughts from his youth, that he had emptied the whole vocabulary into his frame, and made the strictest computation of the general proportion there is in books between the numbers of particles, nouns, and verbs, and other parts of speech.

I made my humblest acknowledgements to this illustrious person for his great communicativeness, and promised if ever I had the good fortune to return to my native country, that I would do him justice, as the sole inventor of this wonderful machine; the form and contrivance of which I desired leave to delineate upon paper as in the figure here annexed. I told him, although it were the custom of our learned in Europe to steal inventions from each other, who had thereby at least this advantage, that it became a controversy which was the right owner, yet I would take such caution, that he should have the honour entire without a rival.

We next went to the school of languages, where three professors sat in consultation upon improving that of their own country.

The first project was to shorten discourse by cutting polysyllables into one, and leaving out verbs and participles, because in reality all things imaginable are but nouns.

The other was a scheme for entirely abolishing all words whatsoever; and this was urged as a great advantage in point of health as well as brevity. For it is plain, that every word we speak is in some degree a diminution of our lungs by corrosion, and consequently contributes to the shortening of our lives. An expedient was therefore offered, that since words are only names for *things*, it would be more convenient for all men to carry about them such *things* as were necessary to express the particular business they are to discourse on. And this invention would certainly have taken place, to the great ease as well as health of the subject, if the women in conjunction with the vulgar and illiterate had not threatened to raise a rebellion, unless they might be allowed the liberty to speak with their tongues, after the manner of their forefathers; such constant irreconcilable enemies to science are the common people. However, many of the most learned and wise adhere to the new scheme of expressing themselves by *things*, which hath only this inconvenience attending it, that if a man's business be very great, and of various kinds, he must be obliged in proportion to carry a greater bundle of *things* upon his back, unless he can afford one or two strong servants to attend him. I have often beheld two of those sages almost sinking under the weight of their packs, like pedlars among us; who when they met in the streets would lay down their loads, open their sacks and hold conversation for an hour together; then put up their implements, help each other to resume their burthens, and take their leave.

But for short conversations a man may carry implements in his pockets and under his arms, enough to supply him, and in his house he cannot be at a loss; therefore the room where company meet who practise this art is full of all *things* ready at hand, requisite to furnish matter for this kind of artificial converse.

Another great advantage proposed by this invention was that it would serve as an universal language to be understood in all civilised nations, whose goods and utensils are generally of the same kind, or nearly resembling, so that their uses might easily be comprehended. And thus ambassadors would be qualified to treat with foreign princes or ministers of state to whose tongues they were utter strangers.

I was at the mathematical school, where the master taught his pupils after a method scarce imaginable to us in Europe. The proposition and demonstration were fairly written on a thin wafer, with ink composed of a cephalic tincture. This the student was to swallow upon a fasting stomach, and for three days following eat nothing but bread and water. As the wafer digested, the tincture mounted to his brain, bearing the proposition along with it. But the success hath not hitherto been answerable, partly by some error in the *quantum* or composition, and partly by the perverseness of lads, to whom this bolus is so nauseous that they generally steal aside, and discharge it upwards before it can operate; neither have they been yet persuaded to use so long an abstinence as the prescription requires.

CHAPTER VI.

A further account of the Academy. The author proposes some improvements which are honourably received.

In the school of political projectors I was but ill entertained, the professors appearing in my judgment wholly out of their senses, which is a scene that never fails to make me melancholy. These unhappy people were proposing schemes for persuading monarchs to choose favourites upon the score of their wisdom, capacity and virtue; of teaching ministers to consult the public good; of rewarding merit, great abilities and eminent services; of instructing princes to know their true interest by placing it on the same foundation with that of their people: of choosing for employments persons qualified to exercise them; with many other wild impossible chimæras, that never entered before into the heart of man to conceive, and confirmed in me the old observation, that there is nothing so extravagant and irrational which some philosophers have not maintained for truth.

But, however, I shall so far do justice to this part of the Academy, as to acknowledge that all of them were not so visionary. There was a most ingenious doctor who seemed to be perfectly versed in the whole nature and system of government. This illustrious person had very usefully employed his studies in finding out effectual remedies for all diseases and corruptions to which the several kinds of public administration are subject by the vices or infirmities of those who govern, as well as by the licentiousness of those who are to obey. For instance: whereas all writers and reasoners have agreed, that there is a strict universal resemblance between the natural and the political body; can there be any thing more evident, than that the health of both must be preserved, and the diseases cured, by the same prescriptions? It is allowed that senates and great councils are often troubled with redundant, ebullient, and other peccant humours, with many diseases of the head, and more of the heart; with strong convulsions, with grievous contractions of the nerves and sinews in both hands, but especially the right; with spleen, flatus, vertigos and deliriums; with scrofulous tumours full of fœtid purulent matter; with sour frothy ructations, with canine appetites and crudeness of digestion, besides many others needless to mention. This doctor therefore proposed, that upon the meeting of a senate, certain physicians should attend at the three first days of their sitting, and, at the close of each day's debate, feel the pulses of every senator; after which, having maturely considered, and consulted upon the nature of the several maladies, and the methods of cure, they should on the fourth day return to the senate house, attended by their apothecaries stored with proper medicines, and before the members sat, administer to each of them lenitives, aperitives, abstersives, corrosives, restringents, palliatives, laxatives, cephalalgics, icterics, apophlegmatics, acoustics, as their several cases required; and according as these medicines should operate, repeat, alter, or omit them at the next meeting.

This project could not be of any great expense to the public, and might, in my poor opinion, be of much use for the dispatch of business in those countries where senates have any share in the legislative power, beget unanimity, shorten debates, open a few mouths which are now closed, and close many more which are now open; curb the petulancy of the young, and correct the positiveness of the old; rouse the stupid, and damp the pert.

Again, because it is a general complaint that the favourites of princes are troubled with short and weak memories, the same doctor proposed, that whoever attended a first minister, after having told his business with the utmost brevity, and in the plainest words, should at his departure give the said minister a tweak by the nose, or a kick in the belly, or tread on his corns, or lug him thrice by both ears, or run a pin into his breech, or pinch his arm black and blue, to prevent forgetfulness: and at every levee day repeat the same operation, till the business were done or absolutely refused.

He likewise directed, that every senator in the great council of a nation, after he had delivered his opinion, and argued in the defence of it, should be obliged to give his vote directly contrary; because if that were done, the result would infallibly terminate in the good of the public.

When parties in a state are violent, he offered a wonderful contrivance to reconcile them. The method is this. You take an hundred leaders of each party, you dispose them into couples of such whose heads are nearest of a size; then let two nice operators saw off the occiput of each couple at the same time, in such a manner that the brain may be equally divided. Let the occiputs thus cut off be interchanged, applying each to the head of his opposite party-man. It seems indeed to be a work that requireth some exactness, but the professor assured us, that if it were dextrously performed the cure would be infallible. For he argued thus; that the two half brains being left to debate the matter between themselves within the space of one skull, would soon come to a good understanding, and produce that moderation, as well as regularity of thinking, so much to be wished for in the heads of those who imagine they came into the world only to watch and govern its motion. and as to the difference of brains in quantity or quality, among those who are directors in faction, the doctor assured us from his own knowledge, that it was a perfect trifle.

I heard a very warm debate between two professors, about the most commodious and effectual ways and means of raising money without grieving the subject. The first affirmed the justest method would be to lay a certain tax upon vices and folly, and the sum fixed upon every man to be rated after the fairest manner by a jury of his neighbours. The second was of an opinion directly contrary, to tax those qualities of body and mind for which men chiefly value themselves, the rate to be more or less according to the degrees of excelling, the decision whereof should be left entirely to their own breast. The highest tax was upon men who are the greatest favourites of the other sex, and the assessments according to the number and natures of the favours they have received; for which they are allowed to be their own vouchers. Wit, valour, and politeness were likewise proposed to be largely taxed, and collected in the same manner, by every person's giving his own word for the quantum of what he possessed. But as to honour, justice, wisdom and learning, they should not be taxed at all, because they are qualifications of so singular a kind, that no man will either allow them in his neighbour, or value them in himself.

The women were proposed to be taxed according to their beauty and skill in dressing, wherein they had the same privilege with the men, to be determined by their own judgment. But constancy, chastity, good sense, and good nature were not rated, because they would not bear the charge of collecting.

To keep senators in the interest of the crown, it was proposed that the members should raffle for employments, every man first taking an oath, and giving security that he would vote for the court, whether he won or no, after which the losers had in their turn the liberty of raffling upon the next vacancy. Thus hope and expectation would be kept alive, none would complain of broken promises, but impute their disappointments wholly to Fortune, whose shoulders are broader and stronger than those of a ministry.

Another professor showed me a large paper of instructions for discovering plots and conspiracies against the government. He advised great statesmen to examine into the diet of all suspected persons; their times of eating; upon which side they lay in bed; with which hand they wiped their posteriors; to take a strict view of their excrements, and from the colour, the odour, the taste, the consistence, the crudeness or maturity of digestion, form a judgment of their thoughts and designs. Because men are never so serious, thoughtful, and intent, as when they are at stool, which he found by frequent experiment: for in such conjunctures, when he used merely as a trial to consider which was the best way of murdering the King, his ordure would have a tincture of green, but quite different when he thought only of raising an insurrection or burning the metropolis.

The whole discourse was written with great acuteness, containing many observations both curious and useful for politicians, but as I conceived not altogether complete. This I ventured to tell the author, and offered if he pleased to supply him with some additions. He received my proposition with more compliance than is usual among writers, especially those of the projecting species, professing he would be glad to receive farther information.

I told him, that in the kingdom of Tribnia, by the natives called Langden, where I had long sojourned, the bulk of the people consisted wholly of discoverers, witnesses, informers, accusers, prosecutors, evidences, swearers, together with their several subservient and subaltern instruments, all under the colours, the conduct, and pay of ministers and their deputies. The plots in that kingdom are usually the workmanship of those persons who desire to raise their own characters of profound politicians, to restore new vigour to a crazy administration, to stifle or divert general discontents, to fill their coffers with forfeitures, and raise or sink the opinion of public credit, as either shall best answer their private advantage. It is first agreed and settled among them what suspected persons shall be accused of a plot: then effectual care is taken to secure all their letters and other papers, and put the owners in chains. These papers are delivered to a set of artists, very dextrous in finding out the mysterious meanings of words, syllables, and letters. For instance, they can decipher a close-stool to signify a privy-council, a flock of geese a senate, a lame dog an invader, a codshead a ———, the plague a standing army, a buzzard a prime minister, the gout a high priest, a gibbet a secretary of state, a chamber-pot a committee of grandees, a sieve a court lady, a broom a revolution, a mousetrap an employment, a bottomless pit the treasury, a sink a court, a cap and bells a favourite, a broken reed a court of justice, an empty tun a general, a running sore the administration.

When this method fails, they have two others more ef-

fectual, which the learned among them call acrostics and anagrams. First they can decipher all initial letters into political
meanings. Thus N shall signify a plot, B a regiment of horse, L
a fleet at sea. Or secondly by transposing the letters of the
alphabet in any suspected paper, they can lay open the deepest
designs of a discontented party. So, for example, if I should say
in a letter to a friend, Our brother Tom has just got the piles, a
man of skill in this art would discover how the same letters
which compose that sentence may be analysed into the following
words: Resist — a plot is brought home — the tour. And this is
the anagrammatic method.

The professor made me great acknowledgments for communicating these observations, and promised to make honourable
mention of me in his treatise.

I saw nothing in this country that could invite me to a longer
continuance, and began to think of returning home to England.

CHAPTER VII.

*The author leaves Lagado, arrives at Maldonada. No ship ready. He
takes a short voyage to Glubbdubdrib. His reception by the
Governor.*

The continent of which this kingdom is a part extends itself,
as I have reason to believe, eastward to that unknown tract of
America, westward of California and north to the Pacific Ocean,
which is not above an hundred and fifty miles from Lagado,
where there is a good port and much commerce with the great
island of Luggnagg, situated to the northwest about 29 degrees
north latitude, and 140 longitude. This island of Luggnagg
stands southeastwards of Japan, about an hundred leagues distant. There is a strict alliance between the Japanese Emperor
and the King of Luggnagg, which affords frequent opportunities
of sailing from one island to the other. I determined therefore to
direct my course this way in order to my return to Europe. I
hired two mules with a guide to show me the way, and carry
my small baggage. I took leave of my noble protector, who had
shown me so much favour, and made me a generous present at
my departure.

My journey was without any accident or adventure worth relating. When I arrived at the port of Maldonada (for so it is called)
there was no ship in the harbour bound for Luggnagg, nor like to
be in some time. The town is about as large as Portsmouth. I

soon fell into some acquaintance, and was very hospitably received. A gentleman of distinction said to me, that since the
ships bound for Luggnagg could not be ready in less than a
month, it might be no disagreeable amusement for me to take a
trip to the little island of Glubbdubdrib, about five leagues off to
the southwest. He offered himself and a friend to accompany
me, and that I should be provided with a small convenient barque
for the voyage.

Glubbdubdrib, as nearly as I can interpret the word, signifies
The Island of *Sorcerers* or *Magicians*. It is about one third as
large as the Isle of Wight, and extremely fruitful: it is governed
by the head of a certain tribe, who are all magicians. This tribe
marries only among each other, and the eldest in succession is
prince or governor. He hath a noble palace and a park of about
three thousand acres, surrounded by a wall of hewn stone twenty
foot high. In this park are several smaller inclosures for cattle,
corn, and gardening.

The Governor and his family are served and attended by
domestics of a kind somewhat unusual. By his skill in necromancy, he hath power of calling whom he pleaseth from the
dead, and commanding their service for twenty-four hours, but
no longer; nor can he call the same persons up again in less than
three months, except upon very extraordinary occasions.

When we arrived at the island, which was about eleven in the
morning, one of the gentlemen who accompanied me went to the
Governor, and desired admittance for a stranger, who came on
purpose to have the honour of attending on his Highness. This
was immediately granted, and we all three entered the gate of the
palace between two rows of guards, armed and dressed after a
very antic manner, and something in their countenances that
made my flesh creep with a horror I cannot express. We passed
through several apartments between servants of the same sort,
ranked on each side as before, till we came to the chamber of
presence, where, after three profound obeisances, and a few general questions, we were permitted to sit on three stools near the
lowest step of his Highness's throne. He understood the language of Balnibarbi, although it were different from that of his
island. He desired me to give him some account of my travels;
and to let me see that I should be treated without ceremony, he
dismissed all his attendants with a turn of his finger, at which to
my great astonishment they vanished in an instant, like visions in
a dream, when we awake on a sudden. I could not recover my
self in some time, till the Governor assured me that I should
receive no hurt; and observing my two companions to be under

no concern, who had been often entertained in the same manner,
I began to take courage, and relate to his Highness a short history
of my several adventures, yet not without some hesitation, and
frequently looking behind me to the place where I had seen
those domestic spectres. I had the honour to dine with the
Governor, where a new set of ghosts served up the meat, and
waited at table. I now observed my self to be less terrified than
I had been in the morning. I stayed till sunset, but humbly desired his Highness to excuse me for not accepting his invitation of
lodging in the palace. My two friends and I lay at a private house
in the town adjoining, which is the captial of this little island; and
the next morning we returned to pay our duty to the Governor,
as he was pleased to command us.

After this manner we continued in the island for ten days,
most part of every day with the Governor, and at night in our
lodging. I soon grew so familiarized to the sight of spirits, that
after the third or fourth time they gave me no emotion at all; or
if I had any apprehensions left, my curiosity prevailed over them.
For his Highness the Governor ordered me to call up whatever
persons I would choose to name, and in whatever numbers
among all the dead from the beginning of the world to the present time, and command them to answer any questions I should
think fit to ask; with this condition, that my questions must be
confined within the compass of the times they lived in. And one
thing I might depend upon, that they would certainly tell me
truth, for lying was a talent of no use in the lower world.

I made my humble acknowledgements to his Highness for so
great a favour. We were in a chamber, from whence there was a
fair prospect into the park. And because my first inclination was
to be entertained with scenes of pomp and magnificence, I desired to see Alexander the Great, at the head of his army just
after the battle of Arbela, which upon a motion of the Governor's finger immediately appeared in a large field under the
window, where we stood. Alexander was called up into the
room: it was with great difficulty that I understood his Greek,
and had but little of my own. He assured me upon his honour
that he was not poisoned, but died of a fever by excessive
drinking.

Next I saw Hannibal passing the Alps, who told me he had not
a drop of vinegar in his camp.

I saw Cæsar and Pompey at the head of their troops, just ready
to engage. I saw the former in his last great triumph. I desired
that the Senate of Rome might appear before me in one large
chamber, and a modern representative in counterview in another.

The first seemed to be an assembly of heroes and demigods; the other a knot of pedlars, pickpockets, highwaymen and bullies.

The Governor at my request gave the sign for Cæsar and Brutus to advance towards us. I was struck with a profound veneration at the sight of Brutus, and could easily discover the most consummate virtue, the greatest intrepidity and firmness of mind, the truest love of his country and general benevolence for mankind in every lineament of his countenance. I observed with much pleasure that these two persons were in good intelligence with each other, and Cæsar freely confessed to me, that the greatest actions of his own life were not equal by many degrees to the glory of taking it away. I had the honour to have much conversation with Brutus; and was told, that his ancestor Junius, Socrates, Epaminondas, Cato the younger, Sir Thomas More and himself were perpetually together: a *sextumvirate* to which all the ages of the world cannot add a seventh.

It would be tedious to trouble the reader with relating what vast numbers of illustrious persons were called up, to gratify that insatiable desire I had to see the world in every period of antiquity placed before me. I chiefly fed my eyes with beholding the destroyers of tyrants and usurpers, and the restorers of liberty to oppressed and injured nations. But it is impossible to express the satisfaction I received in my own mind, after such a manner as to make it a suitable entertainment to the reader.

CHAPTER VIII.

A further account of Glubbdubdrib. Ancient and modern history corrected.

Having a desire to see those ancients who were most renowned for wit and learning, I set apart one day on purpose. I proposed that Homer and Aristotle might appear at the head of all their commentators; but these were so numerous that some hundreds were forced to attend in the court and outward rooms of the palace. I knew and could distinguish those two heroes at first sight, not only from the crowd, but from each other. Homer was the taller and comelier person of the two, walked very erect for one of his age, and his eyes were the most quick and piercing I ever beheld. Aristotle stooped much, and made use of a staff. His visage was meager, his hair lank and thin, and his voice hollow. I soon discovered that both of them were perfect strangers to the rest of the company, and had never seen or heard of them before. And I had a whisper from a ghost, who shall be nameless, that these commentators always kept in the most distant quarters from their principals in the lower world, through a consciousness of shame and guilt, because they had so horribly misrepresented the meaning of those authors to posterity. I introduced Didymus and Eustathius to Homer, and prevailed on him to treat them better than perhaps they deserved, for he soon found they wanted a genius to enter into the spirit of a poet. But Aristotle was out of all patience with the account I gave him of Scotus and Ramus, as I presented them to him, and he asked them whether the rest of the tribe were as great dunces as themselves.

I then desired the Governor to call up Descartes and Gassendi, with whom I prevailed to explain their systems to Aristotle. This great philosopher freely acknowledged his own mistakes in natural philosophy, because he proceeded in many things upon conjecture, as all men must do; and he found that Gassendi, who had made the doctrine of Epicurus as palatable as he could, and the *vortices* of Descartes, were equally exploded. He predicted the same fate to *attraction*, whereof the present learned are such zealous asserters. He said, that new systems of nature were but new fashions, which would vary in every age; and even those who pretend to demonstrate them from mathematical principles would flourish but a short period of time, and be out of vogue when that was determined.

I spent five days in conversing with many others of the ancient learned. I saw most of the first Roman emperors. I prevailed on the Governor to call up Eliogabalus's cooks to dress us a dinner, but they could not show us much of their skill, for want of materials. A helot of Agesilaus made us a dish of Spartan broth, but I was not able to get down a second spoonful.

The two gentlemen who conducted me to the island were pressed by their private affairs to return in three days, which I employed in seeing some of the modern dead who had made the greatest figure for two or three hundred years past in our own and other countries of Europe; and having been always a great admirer of old illustrious families, I desired the Governor would call up a dozen or two of kings with their ancestors in order for eight or nine generations. But my disappointment was grievous and unexpected. For instead of a long train with royal diadems, I saw in one family, two fiddlers, three spruce courtiers, and an Italian prelate. In another, a barber, an abbot, and two cardinals. I have too great a veneration for crowned heads to dwell any longer on so nice a subject. But as to counts, marquesses, dukes, earls, and the like, I was not so scrupulous. And I confess it was not without some pleasure that I found my self able to trace the particular features, by which certain families are distinguished, up to their originals. I could plainly discover from whence one family derives a long chin, why a second hath abounded with knaves for two generations, and fools for two more; why a third happened to be crack-brained, and a fourth to be sharpers. Whence it came what Polydore Virgil says of a certain great house, *Nec vir fortis, nec fœmina casta.* How cruelty, false-hood, and cowardice grew to be characteristics by which certain families are distinguished as much as by their coat of arms. Who first brought the pox into a noble house, which hath lineally descended in scrofulous tumours to their posterity. Neither could I wonder at all this, when I saw such an interruption of lineages by pages, lackeys, valets, coachmen, gamesters, fiddlers, players, captains, and pickpockets.

I was chiefly disgusted with modern history. For having strictly examined all the persons of greatest name in the courts of princes for an hundred years past, I found how the world had been misled by prostitute writers, to ascribe the greatest exploits in war to cowards, the wisest counsel to fools, sincerity to flatterers, Roman virtue to betrayers of their country, piety to atheists, chastity to sodomites, truth to informers. How many innocent and excellent persons had been condemned to death or banishment, by the practising of great ministers upon the corruption of judges, and the malice of factions. How many villains had been exalted to the highest places of trust, power, dignity, and profit: how great a share in the motions and events of courts, councils, and senates might be challenged by bawds, whores, pimps, parasites, and buffoons: how low an opinion I had of human wisdom and integrity, when I was truly informed of the springs and motives of great enterprises and revolutions in the world, and of the contemptible accidents to which they owed their success.

Here I discovered the roguery and ignorance of those who pretend to write *anecdotes*, or secret history, who send so many kings to their graves with a cup of poison; will repeat the discourse between a prince and chief minister, where no witness was by; unlock the thoughts and cabinets of ambassadors and secretaries of state, and have the perpetual misfortune to be mistaken. Here I discovered the true causes of many great events that have surprised the world, how a whore can govern the back-stairs, the back-stairs a council, and the council a senate. A general confessed in my presence, that he got a victory purely by the force of cowardice and ill conduct: and an admiral that for want of proper intelligence, he beat the enemy to whom he intended to betray the fleet. Three kings protested to me, that in their whole reigns they did never once prefer any person of merit, unless by mistake or treachery of some minister in whom they confided: neither would they do it if they were to live again; and they showed with great strength of reason, that the royal throne could not be supported without corruption, because that positive, confident, restive temper, which virtue infused into man, was a perpetual clog to public business.

I had the curiosity to enquire in a particular manner, by what method great numbers had procured to themselves high titles of honour, and prodigious estates; and I confined my enquiry to a very modern period: however, without grating upon present times, because I would be sure to give no offence even to foreigners (for I hope the reader need not be told that I do not in the least intend my own country in what I say upon this occasion) a great number of persons concerned were called up, and upon a very slight examination, discovered such a scene of infamy, that I cannot reflect upon it without some seriousness. Perjury, oppression, subornation, fraud, pandarism, and the like infirmities, were amongst the most excusable arts they had to mention, and for these I gave, as it was reasonable, due allowance. But when some confessed they owed their greatness and wealth to sodomy or incest, others to the prostituting of their own wives and daughters; others to the betraying their country or their prince; some to poisoning, more to the perverting of justice in order to destroy the innocent: I hope I may be pardoned if these discoveries inclined me a little to abate of that profound veneration which I am naturally apt to pay to persons of high rank, who ought to be treated with the utmost respect due to their sublime dignity, by us their inferiors.

I had often read of some great services done to princes and states, and desired to see the persons by whom those services were performed. Upon enquiry I was told that their names were to be found on no record, except a few of them whom history hath represented as the vilest rogues and traitors. As to the rest, I had never once heard of them. They all appeared with dejected looks, and in the meanest habit, most of them telling me they died in poverty and disgrace, and the rest on a scaffold or a gibbet.

Among others there was one person whose case appeared a little singular. He had a youth about eighteen years old standing by his side. He told me he had for many years been commander of a ship, and in the sea fight at Actium had the good fortune to break through the enemy's great line of battle, sink three of their capital ships, and take a fourth, which was the sole cause of Antony's flight, and of the victory that ensued; that the youth standing by him, his only son, was killed in the action. He added, that upon the confidence of some merit, the war being at an end, he went to Rome, and solicited at the court of Augustus to be preferred to a greater ship, whose commander had been killed; but without any regard to his pretensions, it was given to a boy who had never seen the sea, the son of a Libertina, who waited on one of the Emperor's mistresses. Returning back to his own vessel, he was charged with neglect of duty, and the ship given to a favourite page of Publicola the Vice-Admiral; whereupon he retired to a poor farm, at a great distance from Rome, and there ended his life. I was so curious to know the truth of this story, that I desired Agrippa might be called, who was admiral in that fight. He appeared and confirmed the whole account, but with much more advantage to the captain, whose modesty had extenuated or concealed a great part of his merit.

I was surprised to find corruption grown so high and so quick in that empire, by the force of luxury so lately introduced, which made me less wonder at many parallel cases in other countries, where vices of all kinds have reigned so much longer, and where the whole praise as well as pillage hath been engrossed by the chief commander, who perhaps had the least title to either.

As every person called up made exactly the same appearance he had done in the world, it gave me melancholy reflections to observe how much the race of human kind was degenerate among us, within these hundred years past. How the pox under all its consequences and denominations had altered every lineament of an English countenance, shortened the size of bodies, unbraced the nerves, relaxed the sinews and muscles, introduced a sallow complexion, and rendered the flesh loose and rancid.

I descended so low as to desire that some English yeomen of the old stamp might be summoned to appear, once so famous for the simplicity of their manners, diet and dress, for justice in their dealings, for their true spirit of liberty, for their valour and love of their country. Neither could I be wholly unmoved after comparing the living with the dead, when I considered how all these pure native virtues were prostituted for a piece of money by their grandchildren, who in selling their votes, and managing at elections, have acquired every vice and corruption that can possibly be learned in a court.

CHAPTER IX.

The author's return to Maldonada. Sails to the kingdom of Luggnagg.
The author confined. He is sent for to court. The manner of
his admittance. The King's great lenity to his subjects.

The day of our departure being come, I took leave of his
Highness the Governor of Glubbdubdrib, and returned with
my two companions to Maldonada, where after a fortnight's
waiting, a ship was ready to sail for Luggnagg. The two
gentlemen and some others were so generous and kind as to
furnish me with provisions, and see me on board. I was a month
in this voyage. We had one violent storm, and were under a
necessity of steering westward to get into the trade wind, which
holds for above sixty leagues. On the 21st of April, 1709, we
sailed in the river of Clumegnig, which is a seaport town, at
the southeast point of Luggnagg. We cast anchor within a league
of the town, and made a signal for a pilot. Two of them came
on board in less than half an hour, by whom we were guided
between certain shoals and rocks, which are very dangerous in
the passage, to a large basin, where a fleet may ride in safety
within a cable's length of the town wall.

Some of our sailors, whether out of treachery or inadvertence,
had informed the pilots that I was a stranger and a great
traveller, whereof these gave notice to a custom-house officer,
by whom I was examined very strictly upon my landing. This
officer spoke to me in the language of Balnibarbi, which by the
force of much commerce is generally understood in that town,
especially by seamen, and those employed in the customs. I
gave him a short account of some particulars, and made my
story as plausible and consistent as I could; but I thought it
necessary to disguise my country, and call my self a Hollander,
because my intentions were for Japan, and I knew the Dutch
were the only Europeans permitted to enter into that kingdom.
I therefore told the officer, that having been shipwrecked on
the coast of Balnibarbi, and cast on a rock, I was received up
into Laputa, or the Flying Island (of which he had often heard)
and was now endeavouring to get to Japan, from whence I
might find a convenience of returning to my own country. The
officer said I must be confined till he could receive orders from
court, for which he would write immediately, and hoped to
receive an answer in a fortnight. I was carried to a convenient
lodging, with a sentry placed at the door; however I had the
liberty of a large garden, and was treated with humanity enough,
being maintained all the time at the King's charge. I was visited

by several persons, chiefly out of curiosity, because it was reported I came from countries very remote of which they had never heard.

I hired a young man who came in the same ship to be an interpreter; he was a native of Luggnagg, but had lived some years at Maldonada, and was a perfect master of both languages. By his assistance I was able to hold a conversation with those that came to visit me; but this consisted only of their questions, and my answers.

The dispatch came from court about the time we expected. It contained a warrant for conducting me and my retinue to Traldragdubh or Trildrogdrib, for it is pronounced both ways as near as I can remember, by a party of ten horse. All my retinue was that poor lad for an interpreter, whom I persuaded into my service. At my humble request, we had each of us a mule to ride on. A messenger was dispatched half a day's journey before us, to give the King notice of my approach, and to desire that his Majesty would please to appoint a day and hour, when it would be his gracious pleasure that I might have the honour to 'lick the dust before his footstool.' This is the court style, and I found it to be more than matter of form. For upon my admittance two days after my arrival, I was commanded to crawl up on my belly, and lick the floor as I advanced; but on account of my being a stranger, care was taken to have it so clean that the dust was not offensive. However, this was a peculiar grace, not allowed to any but persons of the highest rank, when they desire an admittance. Nay, sometimes the floor is strewed with dust on purpose, when the person to be admitted happens to have powerful enemies at court. And I have seen a great lord with his mouth so crammed, that when he had crept to the proper distance from the throne, he was not able to speak a word. Neither is there any remedy, because it is capital for those who receive an audience to spit or wipe their mouths in his Majesty's presence. There is indeed another custom, which I cannot altogether approve of. When the King hath a mind to put any of his nobles to death in a gentle indulgent manner, he commands to have the floor strowed with a certain brown powder, of a deadly composition, which being licked up infallibly kills him in twenty-four hours. But in justice to this prince's great clemency, and the care he hath of his subjects' lives (wherein it were much to be wished that the monarchs of Europe would imitate him) it must be mentioned for his honour, that strict orders are given to have the infected parts of the floor well washed after every such execution, which if his domestics neglect, they are in danger of incurring his royal displeasure. I my self heard him give directions, that one of his pages should be whipped, whose turn it was to give notice about washing the floor after an execution, but maliciously had omitted it, by which neglect a young lord of great hopes coming to an audience, was unfortunately poisoned, although the King at that time had no design against his life. But this good prince was so gracious as to forgive the page his whipping, upon promise that he would do so no more, without special orders.

To return from this digression; when I had crept within four yards of the throne, I raised my self gently upon my knees, and then striking my forehead seven times against the ground, I pronounced the following words, as they had been taught me the night before, *Ickpling gloffthrobb squutserumm blhiop mlashnalt, zwin tnodbalkguffh slhiophad gurdlubh asht.* This is the compliment established by the laws of the land for all persons admitted to the King's presence. It may be rendered into English thus: May your Cœlestial Majesty outlive the sun, eleven moons and an half. To this the King returned some answer, which although I could not understand, yet I replied as I had been directed: *Fluft drin yalerick dwuldum prastrad mirplush,* which properly signifies, My tongue is in the mouth of my friend, and by this expression was meant that I desired leave to bring my interpreter; whereupon the young man already mentioned was accordingly introduced, by whose intervention I answered as many questions as his Majesty could put in above an hour. I spoke in the Balnibarbian tongue, and my interpreter delivered my meaning in that of Luggnagg.

The King was much delighted with my company, and ordered his *Bliffmarklub* or high chamberlain to appoint a lodging in the court for me and my interpreter, with a daily allowance for my table, and a large purse of gold for my common expenses.

I stayed three months in this country out of perfect obedience to his Majesty, who was pleased highly to favour me, and made me very honourable offers. But I thought it more consistent with prudence and justice to pass the remainder of my days with my wife and family.

CHAPTER X.

The Luggnaggians commended. A particular description of the struld-
bruggs, with many conversations between the author and some
eminent persons upon that subject.

The Luggnaggians are a polite and generous people, and
although they are not without some share of that pride which is
peculiar to all eastern countries, yet they show themselves
courteous to strangers, especially such who are countenanced by
the court. I had many acquaintance among persons of the best
fashion, and being always attended by my interpreter, the conversation we had was not disagreeable.

One day in much good company I was asked by a person of
quality, whether I had seen any of their *struldbruggs* or
immortals. I said I had not, and desired he would explain to me
what he meant by such an appellation applied to a mortal
creature. He told me, that sometimes, although very rarely, a
child happened to be born in a family with a red circular spot
in the forehead, directly over the left eyebrow, which was an infallible mark that it should never die. The spot, as he described
it, was about the compass of a silver three pence, but in the course
of time grew larger, and changed its colour; for at twelve years
old it became green, so continued till five and twenty, then
turned to a deep blue; at five and forty it grew coal black, and as
large as an English shilling, but never admitted any farther alteration. He said these births were so rare, that he did not believe
there could be above eleven hundred *struldbruggs* of both sexes
in the whole kingdom, of which he computed about fifty in the
metropolis, and among the rest a young girl born about three
years ago. That these productions were not peculiar to any
family, but a mere effect of chance, and the children of the
struldbruggs themselves were equally mortal with the rest of the
people.

I freely own my self to have been struck with inexpressible
delight upon hearing this account: and the person who gave it me
happening to understand the Balnibarbian language, which I
spoke very well, I could not forbear breaking out into expressions perhaps a little too extravagant. I cried out as in a rapture:
Happy nation where every child hath at least a chance for being
immortal! Happy people who enjoy so many living examples of
ancient virtue, and have masters ready to instruct them in the
wisdom of all former ages! But happiest beyond all comparison
are those excellent *struldbruggs*, who being born exempt from
that universal calamity of human nature, have their minds free

and disengaged, without the weight and depression of spirits caused by the continual apprehension of death. I discovered my admiration that I had not observed any of these illustrious persons at court, the black spot on the forehead being so remarkable a distinction, that I could not have easily overlooked it and it was impossible that his Majesty, a most judicious prince, should not provide himself with a good number of such wise and able counsellors. Yet perhaps the virtue of those reverend sages was too strict for the corrupt and libertine manners of a court. And we often find by experience that young men are too opinionative and volatile to be guided by the sober dictates of their seniors. However, since the King was pleased to allow me access to his royal person, I was resolved upon the very first occasion to deliver my opinion to him on this matter freely, and at large by the help of my interpreter; and whether he would please to take my advice or no, yet in one thing I was determined, that his Majesty having frequently offered me an establishment in this country, I would with great thankfulness accept the favour, and pass my life here in the conversation of those superior beings the *struldbruggs*, if they would please to admit me.

The gentleman to whom I addressed my discourse, because (as I have already observed) he spoke the language of Balnibarbi, said to me with a sort of a smile, which usually ariseth from pity to the ignorant, that he was glad of any occasion to keep me among them, and desired my permission to explain to the company what I had spoke. He did so, and they talked together for some time in their own language, whereof I understood not a syllable, neither could I observe by their countenances what impression my discourse had made on them. After a short silence the same person told me, that his friends and mine (so he thought fit to express himself) were very much pleased with the judicious remarks I had made on the great happiness and advantages of immortal life, and they were desirous to know in a particular manner, what scheme of living I should have formed to my self, if it had fallen to my lot to have been born a *struldbrugg*.

I answered, it was easy to be eloquent on so copious and delightful a subject, especially to me who have been often apt to amuse my self with visions of what I should do if I were a king, a general, or a great lord; and upon this very case I had frequently run over the whole system how I should employ my self and pass the time if I were sure to live for ever.

That if it had been my good fortune to come into the world a *struldbrugg*, as soon as I could discover my own happiness by understanding the difference between life and death, I would

first resolve by all arts and methods whatsoever to procure my
self riches. In the pursuit of which by thrift and management,
I might reasonably expect in about two hundred years to be the
wealthiest man in the kingdom. In the second place, I would
from my earliest youth apply myself to the study of arts and
sciences, by which I should arrive in time to excel all others in
learning. Lastly, I would carefully record every action and
event of consequence that happened in the public, impartially
draw the characters of the several successions of princes, and
great ministers of state, with my own observations on every point.
I would exactly set down the several changes in customs,
languages, fashions of dress, diet and diversions. By all which
acquirements, I should be a living treasury of knowledge and
wisdom, and certainly become the oracle of the nation.

I would never marry after threescore, but live in an
hospitable manner, yet still on the saving side. I would entertain
myself in forming and directing the minds of hopeful young
men, by convincing them from my own remembrance, experience and observation, fortified by numerous examples, of the usefulness of virtue in public and private life. But my choice and
constant companions should be a set of my own immortal
brotherhood, among whom I would elect a dozen from the most
ancient down to my own contemporaries. Where any of these
wanted fortunes, I would provide them with convenient lodges
round my own estate, and have some of them always at my
table, only mingling a few of the most valuable among you
mortals, whom length of time would harden me to lose with
little or no reluctance, and treat your posterity after the same
manner; just as a man diverts himself with the annual succession
of pinks and tulips in his garden, without regretting the loss of
those which withered the preceding year.

These *struldbruggs* and I would mutually communicate our
observations and memorials through the course of time, remark
the several gradations by which corruption steals into the world,
and oppose it in every step, by giving perpetual warning and
instruction to mankind; which, added to the strong influence of
our own example, would probably prevent that continual degeneracy of human nature so justly complained of in all ages.

Add to all this, the pleasure of seeing the various revolutions
of states and empires, the changes in the lower and upper world,
ancient cities in ruins, and obscure villages become the seats of
kings. Famous rivers lessening into shallow brooks, the ocean
leaving one coast dry, and overwhelming another; the discovery
of many countries yet unknown. Barbarity overrunning the

politest nations, and the most barbarous becoming civilized. I
should then see the discovery of the longitude, the perpetual
motion, the universal medicine, and many other great inventions
brought to the utmost perfection.

What wonderful discoveries should we make in astronomy,
by outliving and confirming our own predictions, by observing
the progress and returns of comets, with the changes of motion
in the sun, moon and stars.

I enlarged upon many other topics which the natural desire of
endless life and sublunary happiness could easily furnish me with.
When I had ended, and the sum of my discourse had been interpreted as before to the rest of the company, there was a good
deal of talk among them in the language of the country, not without some laughter at my expense. At last the same gentleman
who had been my interpreter said, he was desired by the rest
to set me right in a few mistakes, which I had fallen into through
the common imbecility of human nature, and upon that allowance
was less answerable for them. That this breed of *struldbruggs* was
peculiar to their country, for there were no such people either
in Balnibarbi or Japan, where he had the honour to be ambassador
from his Majesty, and found the natives in both those kingdoms
very hard to believe that the fact was possible, and it appeared
from my astonishment when he first mentioned the matter to me,
that I received it as a thing wholly new, and scarcely to be credited. That in the two kingdoms above mentioned, where during
his residence he had conversed very much, he observed long life to
be the universal desire and wish of mankind. That whoever had
one foot in the grave was sure to hold back the other as strongly
as he could. That the oldest had still hopes of living one day
longer, and looked on death as the greatest evil, from which
nature always prompted him to retreat; only in this island of
Luggnagg the appetite for living was not so eager, from the continual example of the *struldbruggs* before their eyes.

That the system of living contrived by me was unreasonable
and unjust, because it supposed a perpetuity of youth, health, and
vigour, which no man could be so foolish to hope, however
extravagant he might be in his wishes. That the question therefore was not whether a man would choose to be always in the
prime of youth, attended with prosperity and health, but how
he would pass a perpetual life under all the usual disadvantages
which old age brings along with it. For although few men will
avow their desires of being immortal upon such hard conditions,
yet in the two kingdoms before-mentioned of Balnibarbi and
Japan, he observed that every man desired to put off death for

some time longer, let it approach ever so late, and he rarely heard of any man who died willingly, except he were incited by the extremity of grief or torture. And he appealed to me whether in those countries I had travelled, as well as my own, I had not observed the same general disposition.

After this preface he gave me a particular account of the *struldbruggs* among them. He said they commonly acted like mortals, till about thirty years old, after which by degrees they grew melancholy and dejected, increasing in both till they came to fourscore. This he learned from their own confession; for otherwise there not being above two or three of that species born in an age, they were too few to form a general observation by. When they came to fourscore years, which is reckoned the extremity of living in this country, they had not only all the follies and infirmities of other old men, but many more which arose from the dreadful prospect of never dying. They were not only opinionative, peevish, covetous, morose, vain, talkative, but uncapable of friendship, and dead to all natural affection, which never descended below their grandchildren. Envy and impotent desires are their prevailing passions. But those objects against which their envy seems principally directed, are the vices of the younger sort, and the deaths of the old. By reflecting on the former, they find themselves cut off from all possibility of pleasure; and whenever they see a funeral, they lament and repine that others are gone to an harbour of rest, to which they themselves never can hope to arrive. They have no remembrance of any thing but what they learned and observed in their youth and middle age, and even that is very imperfect. And for the truth or particulars of any fact, it is safer to depend on common traditions than upon their best recollections. The least miserable among them appear to be those who turn to dotage and entirely lose their memories; these meet with more pity and assistance, because they want many bad qualities which abound in others.

If a *struldbrugg* happen to marry one of his own kind, the marriage is dissolved of course by the courtesy of the kingdom, as soon as the younger of the two comes to be fourscore. For the law thinks it a reasonable indulgence, that those who are condemned without any fault of their own to a perpetual continuance in the world, should not have their misery doubled by the load of a wife.

As soon as they have completed the term of eighty years, they are looked on as dead in law; their heirs immediately succeed to their estates, only a small pittance is reserved for their support, and the poor ones are maintained at the public charge. After that period they are held incapable of any employment of trust or profit; they cannot purchase lands or take leases, neither are they allowed to be witnesses in any cause, either civil or criminal, not even for the decision of meers and bounds.

At ninety they lose their teeth and hair, they have at that age no distinction of taste, but eat and drink whatever they can get, without relish or appetite. The diseases they were subject to still continue without encreasing or diminishing. In talking they forget the common appellation of things, and the names of persons, even of those who are their nearest friends and relations. For the same reason they never can amuse themselves with reading, because their memory will not serve to carry them from the beginning of a sentence to the end; and by this defect they are deprived of the only entertainment whereof they might otherwise be capable.

The language of this country being always upon the flux, the *struldbruggs* of one age do not understand those of another, neither are they able after two hundred years to hold any conversation (farther than by a few general words) with their neighbours the mortals, and thus they lie under the disadvantage of living like foreigners in their own country.

This was the account given me of the *struldbruggs*, as near as I can remember. I afterwards saw five or six of different ages, the youngest not above two hundred years old, who were brought to me at several times by some of my friends; but although they were told that I was a great traveller, and had seen all the world, they had not the least curiosity to ask me a question; only desired I would give them *slumskudask*, or a token of remembrance, which is a modest way of begging, to avoid the law that strictly forbids it, because they are provided for by the public, although indeed with a very scanty allowance.

They are despised and hated by all sorts of people; when one of them is born, it is reckoned ominous, and their birth is recorded very particularly; so that you may know their age by consulting the registry, which however hath not been kept above a thousand years past, or at least hath been destroyed by time or public disturbances. But the usual way of computing how old they are, is by asking them what kings or great persons they can remember, and then consulting history, for infallibly the last prince in their mind did not begin his reign after they were fourscore years old.

They were the most mortifying sight I ever beheld, and the women more horrible than the men. Besides the usual deformities in extreme old age, they acquired an additional ghastliness in proportion to their number of years, which is not to be described, and among half a dozen I soon distinguished which was the eldest, although there was not above a century or two between them.

The reader will easily believe, that from what I had heard and seen, my keen appetite for perpetuity of life was much abated. I grew heartily ashamed of the pleasing visions I had formed, and thought no tyrant could invent a death into which I would not run with pleasure from such a life. The King heard of all that had passed between me and my friends upon this occasion, and rallied me very pleasantly, wishing I would send a couple of *struldbruggs* to my own country, to arm our people against the fear of death; but this it seems is forbidden by the fundamental laws of the kingdom, or else I should have been well content with the trouble and expense of transporting them.

I could not but agree that the laws of this kingdom, relating to the *struldbruggs*, were founded upon the strongest reasons, and such as any other country would be under the necessity of enacting in the like circumstances. Otherwise, as avarice is the necessary consequent of old age, those immortals would in time become proprietors of the whole nation, and engross the civil power, which, for want of abilities to manage, must end in the ruin of the public.

CHAPTER XI.

The author leaves Luggnagg and sails to Japan. From thence he returns in a Dutch ship to Amsterdam, and from Amsterdam to England.

I thought this account of the *struldbruggs* might be some entertainment to the reader, because it seems to be a little out of the common way, at least, I do not remember to have met the like in any book of travels that hath come to my hands: and if I am deceived, my excuse must be, that it is necessary for travellers who describe the same country very often to agree in dwelling on the same particulars, without deserving the censure of having borrowed or transcribed from those who wrote before them.

There is indeed a perpetual commerce between this kingdom and the great empire of Japan, and it is very probable that the Japanese authors may have given some account of the *struldbruggs;* but my stay in Japan was so short, and I was so entirely a stranger to the language, that I was not qualified to make any enquiries. But I hope the Dutch upon this notice will be curious and able enough to supply my defects.

His Majesty having often pressed me to accept some employment in his court, and finding me absolutely determined to return to my native country, was pleased to give me his licence to depart, and honoured me with a letter of recommendation under his own hand to the Emperor of Japan. He likewise presented me with four hundred forty-four large pieces of gold (this nation delighting in even numbers) and a red diamond which I sold in England for eleven hundred pounds.

On the 6th day of May, 1709, I took a solemn leave of his Majesty, and all my friends. This prince was so gracious as to order a guard to conduct me to Glanguenstald, which is a royal port to the southwest part of the island. In six days I found a vessel ready to carry me to Japan, and spent fifteen days in the voyage. We landed at a small port-town called Xamoschi, situated on the southeast part of Japan; the town lies on the western part where there is a narrow strait, leading northward into a long arm of the sea, upon the northwest part of which Yedo, the metropolis stands. At landing I showed the custom-house officers my letter from the King of Luggnagg to his Imperial Majesty. They knew the seal perfectly well; it was as broad as the palm of my hand. The impression was, *a king lifting up a lame beggar from the earth*. The magistrates of the town, hearing of my letter, received me as a public minister; they provided me with carriages and servants, and bore my charges to Yedo, where I was admitted to an audience, and delivered my letter, which was opened with great ceremony, and explained to the Emperor by an interpreter, who gave me notice of his Majesty's order, that I should signify my request, and whatever it were, it should be granted for the sake of his royal brother of Luggnagg. This interpreter was a person employed to transact affairs with the Hollanders; he soon conjectured by my countenance that I was an European, and therefore repeated his Majesty's commands in Low Dutch, which he spoke perfectly well. I answered (as I had before determined) that I was a Dutch merchant, shipwrecked in a very remote country, from whence I travelled by sea and land to Luggnagg, and then took shipping for Japan, where I knew my countrymen often traded, and with some of these I hoped to get an opportunity of returning into Europe: I therefore most humbly entreated his royal favour to give order, that I should be conducted in safety to Nangasac: to this I added another petition, that for the sake of my patron the King of

Luggnagg, his Majesty would condescend to excuse my performing the ceremony imposed on my countrymen of *trampling upon the crucifix*, because I had been thrown into his kingdom by my misfortunes, without any intention of trading. When this latter petition was interpreted to the Emperor, he seemed a little surprised, and said he believed I was the first of my countrymen who ever made any scruple in this point, and that he began to doubt whether I was a real Hollander or no; but rather suspected I must be a Christian. However, for the reasons I had offered, but chiefly to gratify the King of Luggnagg, by an uncommon mark of his favour, he would comply with the singularity of my humour; but the affair must be managed with dexterity, and his officers should be commanded to let me pass as it were by forgetfulness. For he assured me, that if the secret should be discovered by my countrymen, the Dutch, they would cut my throat in the voyage. I returned my thanks by the interpreter for so unusual a favour, and some troops being at that time on their march to Nangasac, the commanding officer had orders to convey me safe thither, with particular instructions about the business of the crucifix.

On the 9th day of June, 1709, I arrived at Nangasac, after a very long and troublesome journey. I soon fell into company of some Dutch sailors belonging to the *Amboyna* of Amsterdam, a stout ship of 450 tons. I had lived long in Holland, pursuing my studies at Leyden, and I spoke Dutch well. The seamen soon knew from whence I came last; they were curious to enquire into my voyages and course of life. I made up a story as short and probable as I could, but concealed the greatest part. I knew many persons in Holland, I was able to invent names for my parents, whom I pretended to be obscure people in the province of Gelderland. I would have given the captain (one Theodorus Vangrult) what he pleased to ask for my voyage to Holland; but understanding I was a surgeon, he was contented to take half the usual rate, on condition that I would serve him in the way of my calling. Before we took shipping, I was often asked by some of the crew, whether I had performed the ceremony above-mentioned. I evaded the question by general answers, that I had satisfied the Emperor and court in all particulars. However, a malicious rogue of a skipper went to an officer, and pointing to me, told him, I had not yet *trampled on the crucifix* but the other, who had received instructions to let me pass, gave the rascal twenty strokes on the shoulders with a bamboo, after which I was no more troubled with such questions.

Nothing happened worth mentioning in this voyage. We sailed

with a fair wind to the Cape of Good Hope, where we stayed only to take in fresh water. On the 6th of April we arrived safely at Amsterdam, having lost only three men by sickness in the voyage, and a fourth who fell from the foremast into the sea, not far from the coast of Guinea. From Amsterdam I soon after set sail for England in a small vessel belonging to that city.

On the 10th of April, 1710, we put in at the Downs. I landed the next morning, and saw once more my native country after an absence of five years and six months complete. I went straight to Redriff, where I arrived the same day at two in the afternoon, and found my wife and family in good health.

THE END OF THE THIRD PART.

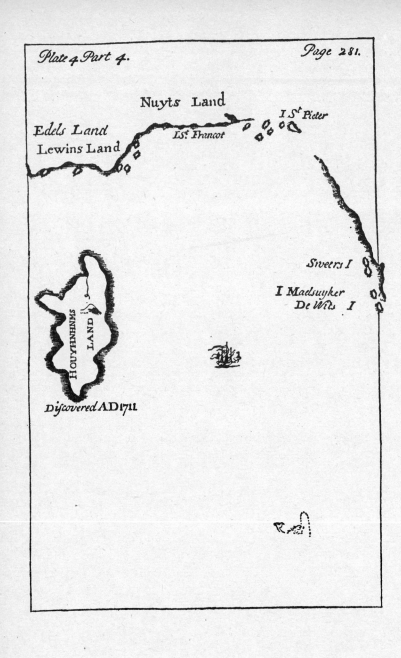

Plate 4 Part 4.

Page 281.

Nuyts Land

Edels Land
Lewins Land

I St Pieter

I St Francot

Siveers I

I Madsuyker
De Wits I

HOUYHNHNMS LAND

Discovered AD 1711.

TRAVELS.

PART IV.

A VOYAGE TO THE COUNTRY OF THE HOUYHNHNMS.

CHAPTER I.

The author sets out as captain of a ship. His men conspire against him, confine him a long time to his cabin, set him on shore in an unknown land. He travels up in the country. The yahoos, a strange sort of animal, described. The author meets two Houyhnhnms.

I continued at home with my wife and children about five months in a very happy condition, if I could have learned the lesson of knowing when I was well. I left my poor wife big with child, and accepted an advantageous offer made me to be captain of the *Adventure*, a stout merchantman of 350 tons: for I understood navigation well, and being grown weary of a surgeon's employment at sea, which however I could exercise upon occasion, I took a skilful young man of that calling, one Robert Purefoy, into my ship. We set sail from Portsmouth upon the 7th day of September, 1710; on the 14th, we met with Captain Pocock of Bristol, at Tenariff, who was going to the bay of Campechy, to cut logwood. On the 16th, he was parted from us by a storm; I heard since my return that his ship foundered, and none escaped, but one cabin-boy. He was an honest man, and a good sailor, but a little too positive in his own opinions, which was the cause of his destruction, as it hath been of several others. For if he had followed my advice, he might at this time have been safe at home with his family as well as myself.

I had several men died in my ship of calentures, so that I was forced to get recruits out of Barbadoes, and the Leeward Islands, where I touched by the direction of the merchants who employed me, which I had soon too much cause to repent; for I found afterwards that most of them had been buccaneers. I had fifty hands on board, and my orders were, that I should trade

with the Indians in the South Sea, and make what discoveries I
could. These rogues whom I had picked up debauched my other
men, and they all formed a conspiracy to seize the ship and secure
me; which they did one morning, rushing into my cabin, and
binding me hand and foot, threatening to throw me overboard,
if I offered to stir. I told them, I was their prisoner, and would
submit. This they made me swear to do, and then unbound me,
only fastening one of my legs with a chain near my bed, and
placed a sentry at my door with his piece charged, who was
commanded to shoot me dead if I attempted my liberty. They
sent me down victuals and drink, and took the government of the
ship to themselves. Their design was to turn pirates, and plunder
the Spaniards, which they could not do till they got more men.
But first they resolved to sell the goods in the ship, and then go
to Madagascar for recruits, several among them having died since
my confinement. They sailed many weeks, and traded with the
Indians, but I knew not what course they took, being kept close
prisoner in my cabin, and expecting nothing less than to be
murdered, as they often threatened me.

Upon the 9th day of May, 1711, one James Welch came
down to my cabin; and said he had orders from the captain to set
me ashore. I expostulated with him, but in vain; neither would
he so much as tell me who their new captain was. They forced
me into the long-boat, letting me put on my best suit of clothes,
which were as good as new, and a small bundle of linen, but no
arms except my hanger; and they were so civil as not to search
my pockets, into which I conveyed what money I had, with some
other little necessaries. They rowed about a league, and then set
me down on a strand. I desired them to tell me what country it
was. They all swore, they knew no more than myself, but said,
that the captain (as they called him) was resolved, after they had
sold the lading, to get rid of me in the first place where they discovered land. They pushed off immediately, advising me to
make haste, for fear of being overtaken by the tide, and bade me
farewell.

In this desolate condition I advanced forward, and soon got
upon firm ground, where I sat down on a bank to rest myself, and
consider what I had best to do. When I was a little refreshed I
went up into the country, resolving to deliver myself to the first
savages I should meet, and purchase my life from them by some
bracelets, glass rings, and other toys, which sailors usually provide themselves with in those voyages, and whereof I had some
about me: the land was divided by long rows of trees, not
regularly planted, but naturally growing; there was great plenty

of grass, and several fields of oats. I walked very circumspectly
for fear of being surprised, or suddenly shot with an arrow from
behind or on either side. I fell into a beaten road, where I saw
many tracks of human feet, and some of cows, but most of
horses. At last I beheld several animals in a field, and one or two
of the same kind sitting in trees. Their shape was very singular,
and deformed, which a little discomposed me, so that I lay down
behind a thicket to observe them better. Some of them coming
forward near the place where I lay, gave me an opportunity of
distinctly marking their form. Their heads and breasts were
covered with a thick hair, some frizzled and others lank; they
had beards like goats, and a long ridge of hair down their backs,
and the foreparts of their legs and feet, but the rest of their
bodies were bare, so that I might see their skins, which were of a
brown buff colour. They had no tails, nor any hair at all on their
buttocks, except about the anus; which, I presume, nature had
placed there to defend them as they sat on the ground; for this
posture they used, as well as lying down, and often stood on their
hind feet. They climbed high trees, as nimbly as a squirrel, for
they had strong extended claws before and behind, terminating
in sharp points, and hooked. They would often spring, and
bound, and leap with prodigious agility. The females were not
so large as the males; they had long lank hair on their heads, and
only a sort of down on the rest of their bodies, except about the
anus, and pudenda. Their dugs hung between their fore-feet,
and often reached almost to the ground as they walked. The hair
of both sexes was of several colours, brown, red, black, and yellow. Upon the whole, I never beheld in all my travels so
disagreeable an animal, or one against which I naturally conceived so strong antipathy. So that thinking I had seen enough,
full of contempt and aversion, I got up and pursued the beaten
road, hoping it might direct me to the cabin of some Indian. I
had not gone far when I met one of these creatures full in my
way, and coming up directly to me. The ugly monster, when
he saw me, distorted several ways every feature of his visage, and
stared as at an object he had never seen before; then approaching
nearer, lifted up his forepaw, whether out of curiosity or mischief, I could not tell. But I drew my hanger, and gave him a
good blow with the flat side of it, for I durst not strike him with
the edge, fearing the inhabitants might be provoked against me,
if they should come to know that I had killed or maimed any of
their cattle. When the beast felt the smart, he drew back, and
roared so loud, that a herd of at least forty came flocking about
me from the next field, howling and making odious faces; but I

ran to the body of a tree, and leaning my back against it, kept them off, by waving my hanger. Several of this cursed brood getting hold of the branches behind leaped up into the tree, from whence they began to discharge their excrements on my head: however, I escaped pretty well, by sticking close to the stem of a tree, but was almost stifled with the filth, which fell about me on every side.

In the midst of this distress, I observed them all to run away on a sudden as fast as they could, at which I ventured to leave the tree, and pursue the road, wondering what it was that could put them into this fright. But looking on my left hand, I saw a horse walking softly in the field, which my persecutors having sooner discovered, was the cause of their flight. The horse started a little when he came near me, but soon recovering himself, looked full in my face with manifest tokens of wonder: he viewed my hands and feet, walking round me several times. I would have pursued my journey, but he placed himself directly in the way, yet looking with a very mild aspect, never offering the least violence. We stood gazing at each other for some time; at last I took the boldness to reach my hand towards his neck, with a design to stroke it, using the common style and whistle of jockeys when they are going to handle a strange horse. But this animal, seeming to receive my civilities with disdain, shook his head, and bent his brows, softly raising up his left forefoot to remove my hand. Then he neighed three or four times, but in so different a cadence, that I almost began to think he was speaking to himself in some language of his own.

While he and I were thus employed, another horse came up; who applying himself to the first in a very formal manner, they gently struck each other's right hoof before, neighing several times by turns, and varying the sound, which seemed to be almost articulate. They went some paces off, as if it were to confer together, walking side by side, backward and forward, like persons deliberating upon some affair of weight, but often turning their eyes towards me, as it were to watch that I might not escape. I was amazed to see such actions and behaviour in brute beasts, and concluded with myself, that if the inhabitants of this country were endued with a proportionable degree of reason, they must needs be the wisest people upon earth. This thought gave me so much comfort, that I resolved to go forward until I could discover some house or village, or meet with any of the natives, leaving the two horses to discourse together as they pleased. But the first, who was a dapple grey, observing me to steal off, neighed after me in so expressive a tone, that I fancied myself to understand what he meant; whereupon I turned back, and came near him, to expect his farther commands. But concealing my fear as much as I could, for I began to be in some pain, how this adventure might terminate; and the reader will easily believe I did not much like my present situation.

The two horses came up close to me, looking with great earnestness upon my face and hands. The grey steed rubbed my hat all round with his right fore-hoof, and discomposed it so much, that I was forced to adjust it better, by taking it off, and settling it again; whereat both he and his companion (who was a brown bay) appeared to be much surprised; the latter felt the lappet of my coat, and finding it to hang loose about me, they both looked with new signs of wonder. He stroked my right hand, seeming to admire the softness, and colour; but he squeezed it so hard between his hoof and his pastern, that I was forced to roar; after which they both touched me with all possible tenderness. They were under great perplexity about my shoes and stockings, which they felt very often, neighing to each other, and using various gestures, not unlike those of a philosopher, when he would attempt to solve some new and difficult phænomenon.

Upon the whole, the behaviour of these animals was so orderly and rational, so acute and judicious, that I at last concluded, they must needs be magicians, who had thus metamorphosed themselves upon some design, and seeing a stranger in the way, were resolved to divert themselves with him; or perhaps were really amazed at the sight of a man so very different in habit, feature, and complexion from those who might probably live in so remote a climate. Upon the strength of this reasoning, I ventured to address them in the following manner: Gentlemen, if you be conjurers, as I have good cause to believe, you can understand any language; therefore I make bold to let your Worships know, that I am a poor distressed English man, driven by his misfortunes upon your coast, and I entreat one of you, to let me ride upon his back, as if he were a real horse, to some house or village, where I can be relieved. In return of which favour, I will make you a present of this knife and bracelet (taking them out of my pocket). The two creatures stood silent while I spoke, seeming to listen with great attention; and when I had ended, they neighed frequently towards each other, as if they were engaged in serious conversation. I plainly observed, that their language expressed the passions very well, and the words might with little pains be resolved into an alphabet more easily than the Chinese.

I could frequently distinguish the word *yahoo*, which was repeated by each of them several times; and although it was impossible for me to conjecture what it meant, yet while the two horses were busy in conversation, I endeavoured to practice this word upon my tongue; and as soon as they were silent, I boldly pronounced *yahoo* in a loud voice, imitating, at the same time, as near as I could, the neighing of a horse; at which they were both visibly surprised, and the grey repeated the same word twice, as if he meant to teach me the right accent, wherein I spoke after him as well as I could, and found myself perceivably to improve every time, although very far from any degree of perfection. Then the bay tried me with a second word, much harder to be pronounced; but reducing it to the English orthography, may be spelt thus, *Houyhnhnm*. I did not succeed in this so well as the former, but after two or three farther trials, I had better fortune; and they both appeared amazed at my capacity.

After some farther discourse, which I then conjectured might relate to me, the two friends took their leaves, with the same compliment of striking each other's hoof; and the grey made me signs that I should walk before him, wherein I thought it prudent to comply, till I could find a better director. When I offered to slacken my pace, he would cry *hhuun, hhuun;* I guessed his meaning, and gave him to understand, as well as I could, that I was weary, and not able to walk faster; upon which he would stand a while to let me rest.

Chapter II.

The author conducted by a Houyhnhnm to his house. The house described. The author's reception. The food of the Houyhnhnms. The author in distress for want of meat, is at last relieved. His manner of feeding in that country.

Having travelled about three miles, we came to a long kind of building, made of timber stuck in the ground, and wattled across; the roof was low, and covered with straw. I now began to be a little comforted, and took out some toys, which travellers usually carry for presents to the savage Indians of America and other parts, in hopes the people of the house would be thereby encouraged to receive me kindly. The horse made me a sign to go in first; it was a large room with a smooth clay floor, and a rack and manger extending the whole length on one side. There were three nags, and two mares, not eating, but some of them sitting down upon their hams, which I very much wondered at; but wondered more to see the rest employed in domestic business. They seemed but ordinary cattle; however, this confirmed my first opinion, that a people who could so far civilize brute animals must needs excel in wisdom all the nations of the world. The grey came in just after, and thereby prevented any ill treatment which the others might have given me. He neighed to them several times in a style of authority, and received answers.

Beyond this room there were three others, reaching the length of the house, to which you passed through three doors, opposite to each other, in the manner of a vista; we went through the second room towards the third; here the grey walked in first, beckoning me to attend: I waited in the second room, and got ready my presents for the master and mistress of the house: they were two knives, three bracelets of false pearl, a small looking-glass and a bead necklace. The horse neighed three or four times, and I waited to hear some answers in a human voice, but I heard no other returns than in the same dialect, only one or two a little shriller than his. I began to think that this house must belong to some person of great note among them, because there appeared so much ceremony before I could gain admittance. But that a man of quality should be served all by horses was beyond my comprehension. I feared my brain was disturbed by my sufferings and misfortunes: I roused myself, and looked about me in the room where I was left alone; this was furnished as the first, only after a more elegant manner. I rubbed my eyes often, but the same objects still occurred. I pinched my arms and sides, to awake myself, hoping I might be in a dream. I then absolutely concluded, that all these appearances could be nothing else but necromancy and magic. But I had no time to pursue these reflections; for the grey horse came to the door, and made me a sign to follow him into the third room, where I saw a very comely mare, together with a colt and foal, sitting on their haunches, upon mats of straw, not unartfully made, and perfectly neat and clean.

The mare, soon after my entrance, rose from her mat, and coming up close, after having nicely observed my hands and face, gave me a most contemptuous look; then turning to the horse, I heard the word *yahoo* often repeated betwixt them; the meaning of which word I could not then comprehend, although it were the first I had learned to pronounce; but I was soon better informed, to my everlasting mortification: for the horse beckoning to me with his head, and repeating the word *hhuun, hhuun,* as he did upon the road, which I understood was to attend him,

led me out into a kind of court, where was another building at
some distance from the house. Here we entered, and I saw three
of those detestable creatures, which I first met after my landing,
feeding upon roots, and the flesh of some animals, which I afterwards found to be that of asses and dogs, and now and then a
cow dead by accident or disease. They were all tied by the neck
with strong withes, fastened to a beam; they held their food
between the claws of their forefeet, and tore it with their teeth.

The master horse ordered a sorrel nag, one of his servants, to
untie the largest of these animals, and take him into the yard.
The beast and I were brought close together, and our countenances diligently compared, both by master and servant, who
thereupon repeated several times the word *yahoo*. My horror
and astonishment are not to be described, when I observed, in
this abominable animal, a perfect human figure; the face of it
indeed was flat and broad, the nose depressed, the lips large, and
the mouth wide. But these differences are common to all savage
nations, where the lineaments of the countenance are distorted
by the natives suffering their infants to lie grovelling on the
earth, or by carrying them on their backs, nuzzling with their
face against the mother's shoulders. The forefeet of the yahoo
differed from my hands in nothing else but the length of the
nails, the coarseness and brownness of the palms, and the hairiness on the backs. There was the same resemblance between
our feet, with the same differences, which I knew very well,
although the horses did not, because of my shoes and stockings;
the same in every part of our bodies, except as to hairiness and
colour, which I have already described.

The great difficulty that seemed to stick with the two horses,
was to see the rest of my body so very different from that of a
yahoo, for which I was obliged to my clothes, whereof they
had no conception: the sorrel nag offered me a root, which he
held (after their manner, as we shall describe in its proper place)
between his hoof and pastern; I took it in my hand, and having
smelt it, returned it to him as civilly as I could. He brought
out of the yahoo's kennel a piece of ass's flesh, but it smelt so
offensively that I turned from it with loathing: he then threw it
to the yahoo, by whom it was greedily devoured. He afterwards
showed me a wisp of hay, and a fetlock full of oats; but I shook
my head, to signify, that neither of these were food for me.
And indeed, I now apprehended, that I must absolutely starve,
if I did not get to some of my own species: for as to those filthy
yahoos, although there were few greater lovers of mankind, at
that time, than myself, yet I confess I never saw any sensitive

being so detestable on all accounts; and the more I came near them, the more hateful they grew, while I stayed in that country. This the master horse observed by my behaviour, and therefore sent the yahoo back to his kennel. He then put his fore-hoof to his mouth, at which I was much surprised, although he did it with ease, and with a motion that appeared perfectly natural, and made other signs to know what I would eat; but I could not return him such an answer as he was able to apprehend; and if he had understood me, I did not see how it was possible to contrive any way for finding myself nourishment. While we were thus engaged, I observed a cow passing by, whereupon I pointed to her, and expressed a desire to let me go and milk her. This had its effect; for he led me back into the house, and ordered a mare-servant to open a room, where a good store of milk lay in earthen and wooden vessels, after a very orderly and cleanly manner. She gave me a large bowl full, of which I drank very heartily, and found myself well refreshed.

About noon I saw coming towards the house a kind of vehicle drawn like a sledge by four yahoos. There was in it an old steed, who seemed to be of quality; he alighted with his hind feet forward, having by accident got a hurt in his left forefoot. He came to dine with our horse, who received him with great civility. They dined in the best room, and had oats boiled in milk for the second course, which the old horse eat warm, but the rest cold. Their mangers were placed circular in the middle of the room, and divided into several partitions, round which they sat on their haunches upon bosses of straw. In the middle was a large rack with angles answering to every partition of the manger. So that each horse and mare eat their own hay, and their own mash of oats and milk, with much decency and regularity. The behaviour of the young colt and foal appeared very modest, and that of the master and mistress extremely cheerful and complaisant to their guest. The grey ordered me to stand by him, and much discourse passed between him and his friend concerning me, as I found by the stranger's often looking on me, and the frequent repetition of the word *yahoo*.

I happened to wear my gloves, which the master grey observing, seemed perplexed, discovering signs of wonder what I had done to my forefeet; he put his hoof three or four times to them, as if he would signify, that I should reduce them to their former shape, which I presently did, pulling off both my gloves, and putting them into my pocket. This occasioned farther talk, and I saw the company was pleased with my behaviour, whereof I soon found the good effects. I was ordered to speak the few words I understood, and while they were at dinner, the master taught me the names for oats, milk, fire, water, and some others: which I could readily pronounce after him, having from my youth a great facility in learning languages.

When dinner was done, the master horse took me aside, and by signs and words made me understand the concern he was in, that I had nothing to eat. Oats in their tongue are called *hlunnh*. This word I pronounced two or three times; for although I had refused them at first, yet upon second thoughts, I considered that I could contrive to make of them a kind of bread, which might be sufficient with milk to keep me alive, till I could make my escape to some other country, and to creatures of my own species. The horse immediately ordered a white mare-servant of his family to bring me a good quantity of oats in a sort of wooden tray. These I heated before the fire as well as I could, and rubbed them till the husks came off, which I made a shift to winnow from the grain; I ground and beat them between two stones, then took water, and made them into a paste or cake, which I toasted at the fire, and eat warm with milk. It was at first a very insipid diet, although common enough in many parts of Europe, but grew tolerable by time; and having been often reduced to hard fare in my life, this was not the first experiment I had made how easily nature is satisfied. And I cannot but observe, that I never had one hour's sickness, while I stayed in this island. It is true, I sometimes made a shift to catch a rabbit, or bird, by springes made of yahoos' hairs, and I often gathered wholesome herbs, which I boiled, or eat as salads with my bread, and now and then, for a rarity, I made a little butter, and drank the whey. I was at first at a great loss for salt; but custom soon reconciled the want of it; and I am confident that the frequent use of salt among us is an effect of luxury, and was first introduced only as a provocative to drink; except where it is necessary for preserving of flesh in long voyages, or in places remote from great markets. For we observe no animal to be fond of it but man: and as to myself, when I left this country, it was a great while before I could endure the taste of it in anything that I eat.

This is enough to say upon the subject of my diet, wherewith other travellers fill their books, as if the readers were personally concerned whether we fared well or ill. However, it was necessary to mention this matter, lest the world should think it impossible that I could find sustenance for three years in such a country, and among such inhabitants.

When it grew towards evening, the master horse ordered a place for me to lodge in; it was but six yards from the house, and separated from the stable of the yahoos. Here I got some straw, and covering myself with my own clothes, slept very sound. But I was in a short time better accommodated, as the reader shall know hereafter, when I come to treat more particularly about my way of living.

CHAPTER III.

The author studious to learn the language, the Houyhnhnm his master assists in teaching him. The language described. Several Houyhnhnms of quality come out of curiosity to see the author. He gives his master a short account of his voyage.

My principal endeavour was to learn the language, which my master (for so I shall henceforth call him) and his children, and every servant of his house were desirous to teach me. For they looked upon it as a prodigy that a brute animal should discover such marks of a rational creature. I pointed to every thing, and enquired the name of it, which I wrote down in my journal-book when I was alone, and corrected my bad accent, by desiring those of the family to pronounce it often. In this employment, a sorrel nag, one of the under servants, was very ready to assist me.

In speaking, they pronounce through the nose and throat, and their language approaches nearest to the High Dutch or German, of any I know in Europe; but is much more graceful and significant. The Emperor Charles V made almost the same observation, when he said, that if he were to speak to his horse, it should be in High Dutch.

The curiosity and impatience of my master were so great, that he spent many hours of his leisure to instruct me. He was convinced (as he afterwards told me) that I must be a yahoo, but my teachableness, civility and cleanliness astonished him; which were qualities altogether so opposite to those animals. He was most perplexed about my clothes, reasoning sometimes with himself, whether they were a part of my body; for I never pulled them off till the family were asleep, and got them on before they waked in the morning. My master was eager to learn from whence I came, how I acquired those appearances of reason which I discovered in all my actions, and to know my story from my own mouth, which he hoped he should soon do by the great proficiency I made in learning and pronouncing their words and sentences. To help my memory, I formed all I learned into the English alphabet, and writ the words down with the translations. This last, after some time, I ventured to do in my master's presence. It cost me much trouble to explain to him what I was doing; for the inhabitants have not the least idea of books or literature.

In about ten weeks time I was able to understand most of his questions, and in three months could give him some tolerable answers. He was extremely curious to know from what part of the country I came, and how I was taught to imitate a rational creature, because the yahoos (whom he saw I exactly resembled in my head, hands and face, that were only visible), with some appearance of cunning, and the strongest disposition to mischief, were observed to be the most unteachable of all brutes. I answered, that I came over the sea, from a far place, with many others of my own kind, in a great hollow vessel made of the bodies of trees. That my companions forced me to land on this coast, and then left me to shift for myself. It was with some difficulty, and by the help of many signs, that I brought him to understand me. He replied, that I must needs be mistaken, or that I 'said the thing which was not.' (For they have no words in their language to express lying or falsehood.) He knew it was impossible that there could be a country beyond the sea, or that a parcel of brutes could move a wooden vessel whither they pleased upon water. He was sure no Houyhnhnm alive could make such a vessel, or would trust yahoos to manage it.

The word *Houyhnhnm*, in their tongue, signifies a *horse*, and in its etymology, *the perfection of nature*. I told my master, that I was at a loss for expression, but would improve as fast as I could; and hoped in a short time I should be able to tell him wonders: he was pleased to direct his own mare, his colt and foal, and the servants of the family to take all opportunities of instructing me, and every day for two or three hours he was at the same pains himself: several horses and mares of quality in the neighbourhood came often to our house upon the report spread of a wonderful yahoo, that could speak like a Houyhnhnm, and seemed in his words and actions to discover some glimmerings of reason. These delighted to converse with me; they put many questions, and received such answers as I was able to return. By all which advantages, I made so great a progress, that in five months from my arrival I understood whatever was spoke, and could express myself tolerably well.

The Houyhnhnms who came to visit my master, out of a design of seeing and talking with me, could hardly believe me to be a right yahoo, because my body had a different covering from others of my kind. They were astonished to observe me without the usual hair or skin except on my head, face, and hands; but

I discovered that secret to my master, upon an accident, which happened about a fortnight before.

I have already told the reader, that every night, when the family were gone to bed, it was my custom to strip and cover myself with my clothes: it happened one morning early, that my master sent for me, by the sorrel nag, who was his valet; when he came, I was fast asleep, my clothes fallen off on one side, and my shirt above my waist. I awaked at the noise he made, and observed him to deliver his message in some disorder; after which he went to my master, and in a great fright gave him a very confused acount of what he had seen: this I presently discovered; for going, as soon as I was dressed, to pay my attendance upon his Honour, he asked me the meaning of what his servant had reported, that I was not the same thing when I slept as I appeared to be at other times; that his valet assured him, some part of me was white, some yellow, at least not so white, and some brown.

I had hitherto concealed the secret of my dress, in order to distinguish myself as much as possible from that cursed race of yahoos; but now I found it in vain to do so any longer. Besides, I considered that my clothes and shoes would soon wear out, which already were in a declining condition, and must be supplied by some contrivance from the hides of yahoos or other brutes; whereby the whole secret would be known: I therefore told my master, that in the country from whence I came those of my kind always covered their bodies with the hairs of certain animals prepared by art, as well for decency, as to avoid inclemencies of air both hot and cold; of which, as to my own person, I would give him immediate conviction, if he pleased to command me; only desiring his excuse, if I did not expose those parts that nature taught us to conceal. He said my discourse was all very strange, but especially the last part; for he could not understand why nature should teach us to conceal what nature had given. That neither himself nor family were ashamed of any parts of their bodies; but however I might do as I pleased. Whereupon, I first unbuttoned my coat, and pulled it off. I did the same with my waistcoat; I drew off my shoes, stockings, and breeches. I let my shirt down to my waist, and drew up the bottom, fastening it like a girdle about my middle to hide my nakedness.

My master observed the whole performance with great signs of curiosity and admiration. He took up all my clothes in his pastern, one piece after another, and examined them diligently; he then stroked my body very gently and looked round me several times, after which he said, it was plain I must be a perfect

yahoo; but that I differed very much from the rest of my species,
in the whiteness and smoothness of my skin, my want of hair in
several parts of my body, the shape and shortness of my claws
behind and before, and my affectation of walking continually on
my two hinder feet. He desired to see no more, and gave me
leave to put on my clothes again, for I was shuddering with cold.

I expressed my uneasiness at his giving me so often the appellation of *yahoo*, an odious animal, for which I had so utter an
hatred and contempt; I begged he would forbear applying that
word to me, and take the same order in his family, and among his
friends whom he suffered to see me. I requested likewise, that
the secret of my having a false covering to my body might be
known to none but himself, at least as long as my present clothing should last; for as to what the sorrel nag his valet had
observed, his Honour might command him to conceal it.

All this my master very graciously consented to, and thus the
secret was kept till my clothes began to wear out, which I was
forced to supply by several contrivances, that shall hereafter be
mentioned. In the mean time, he desired I would go on with my
utmost diligence to learn their language, because he was more
astonished at my capacity for speech and reason than at the
figure of my body, whether it were covered or no; adding, that
he waited with some impatience to hear the wonders which I
promised to tell him.

From thenceforward he doubled the pains he had been at to
instruct me; he brought me into all company, and made them
treat me with civility, because, as he told them privately, this
would put me into good humour, and make me more diverting.

Every day when I waited on him, beside the trouble he was at
in teaching, he would ask me several questions concerning
myself, which I answered as well as I could; and by those means
he had already received some general ideas, although very imperfect. It would be tedious to relate the several steps by which
I advanced to a more regular conversation: but the first account I
gave of myself in any order and length, was to this purpose:

That I came from a very far country, as I already had
attempted to tell him, with about fifty more of my own species;
that we travelled upon the seas, in a great hollow vessel made
of wood, and larger than his Honour's house. I described the
ship to him in the best terms I could, and explained by the help of
my handkerchief displayed, how it was driven forward by the
wind. That upon a quarrel among us, I was set on shore on this
coast, where I walked forward without knowing whither, till he
delivered me from the persecution of those execrable yahoos. He

asked me, who made the ship, and how it was possible that the
Houyhnhnms of my country would leave it to the management
of brutes? My answer was, that I durst proceed no farther in my
relation, unless he would give me his word and honour that he
would not be offended, and then I would tell him the wonders I
had so often promised. He agreed; and I went on by assuring
him, that the ship was made by creatures like myself, who in all
the countries I had travelled, as well as in my own, were the only
governing, rational animals; and that upon my arrival hither, I
was as much astonished to see the Houyhnhnms act like rational
beings, as he or his friends could be in finding some marks of
reason in a creature he was pleased to call a yahoo, to which I
owned my resemblance in every part, but could not account for
their degenerate and brutal nature. I said farther, that if good
fortune ever restored me to my native country, to relate my
travels hither, as I resolved to do, every body would believe that
I 'said the thing which was not'; that I invented the story out of
my own head; and with all possible respect to himself, his family
and friends, and under his promise of not being offended, our
countrymen would hardly think it probable, that a Houyhnhnm
should be the presiding creature of a nation, and a yahoo the
brute.

CHAPTER IV.

*The Houyhnhnms' notion of truth and falsehood. The author's dis-
course disapproved by his master. The author gives a more particular account of himself, and the accidents of his voyage.*

My master heard me with great appearances of uneasiness in
his countenance, because *doubting* or *not believing*, are so little
known in this country, that the inhabitants cannot tell how to
behave themselves under such circumstances. And I remember
in frequent discourses with my master concerning the nature of
manhood, in other parts of the world, having occasion to talk of
lying and *false representation*, it was with much difficulty that he
comprehended what I meant, although he had otherwise a most
acute judgment. For he argued thus; that the use of speech was
to make us understand one another, and to receive information of
facts; now if any one *said the thing which was not*, these ends
were defeated; because I cannot properly be said to understand
him, and I am so far from receiving information, that he leaves
me worse than in ignorance, for I am led to believe a thing black

when it is white, and short when it is long. And these were all the notions he had concerning that faculty of lying, so perfectly well understood, and so universally practised among human creatures.

To return from this digression; when I asserted that the yahoos were the only governing animals in my country, which my master said was altogether past his conception, he desired to know, whether we had Houyhnhnms among us, and what was their employment: I told him, we had great numbers, that in summer they grazed in the fields, and in winter were kept in houses, with hay and oats, where yahoo servants were employed to rub their skins smooth, comb their manes, pick their feet, serve them with food, and make their beds. I understand you well, said my master, it is now very plain, from all you have spoken, that whatever share of reason the yahoos pretend to, the Houyhnhnms are your masters; I heartily wish our yahoos would be so tractable. I begged his Honour would please to excuse me from proceeding any farther, because I was very certain that the account he expected from me would be highly displeasing. But he insisted in commanding me to let him know the best and the worst: I told him, he should be obeyed. I owned, that the Houyhnhnms among us, whom we called horses, were the most generous and comely animal we had, that they excelled in strength and swiftness; and when they belonged to persons of quality, employed in travelling, racing, and drawing chariots, they were treated with much kindness and care, till they fell into diseases, or became foundered in the feet; but then they were sold, and used to all kind of drudgery till they died; after which their skins were stripped and sold for what they were worth, and their bodies left to be devoured by dogs and birds of prey. But the common race of horses had not so good fortune, being kept by farmers and carriers and other mean people, who put them to greater labour, and feed them worse. I described, as well as I could, our way of riding, the shape and use of a bridle, a saddle, a spur, and a whip, of harness and wheels. I added, that we fastened plates of a certain hard substance called 'iron' at the bottom of their feet, to preserve their hoofs from being broken by the stony ways on which we often travelled.

My master, after some expressions of great indignation, wondered how we dared to venture upon a Houyhnhnm's back, for he was sure that the weakest servant in his house would be able to shake off the strongest yahoo, or by lying down, and rolling upon his back, squeeze the brute to death. I answered, that our horses were trained up from three or four years old to the several uses we intended them for; that if any of them proved intolerably vicious, they were employed for carriages; that they were severely beaten while they were young, for any mischievous tricks; that the males, designed for the common use of riding or draught, were generally castrated about two years after their birth, to take down their spirits, and make them more tame and gentle; that they were indeed sensible of rewards and punishments; but his Honour would please to consider, that they had not the least tincture of reason any more than the yahoos in this country.

It put me to the pains of many circumlocutions to give my master a right idea of what I spoke; for their language doth not abound in variety of words, because their wants and passions are fewer than among us. But it is impossible to express his noble resentment at our savage treatment of the Houyhnhnm race, particularly after I had explained the manner and use of castrating horses among us, to hinder them from propagating their kind, and to render them more servile. He said, if it were possible there could be any country where yahoos alone were endued with reason, they certainly must be the governing animal, because reason will in time always prevail against brutal strength. But, considering the frame of our bodies, and especially of mine, he thought no creature of equal bulk was so ill contrived for employing that reason in the common offices of life; whereupon he desired to know whether those among whom I lived resembled me or the yahoos of his country. I assured him, that I was as well shaped as most of my age: but the younger and the females were much more soft and tender, and the skins of the latter generally as white as milk. He said, I differed indeed from other yahoos, being much more cleanly, and not altogether so deformed, but in point of real advantage he thought I differed for the worse. That my nails were of no use either to my fore or hinder feet; as to my forefeet, he could not properly call them by that name, for he never observed me to walk upon them; that they were too soft to bear the ground; that I generally went with them uncovered, neither was the covering I sometimes wore on them of the same shape or so strong as that on my feet behind. That I could not walk with any security, for if either of my hinder feet slipped, I must inevitably fall. He then began to find fault with other parts of my body, the flatness of my face, the prominence of my nose, my eyes placed directly in front, so that I could not look on either side without turning my head: that I was not able to feed myself without lifting one of my forefeet to my mouth: and therefore nature had placed those joints to answer that necessity. He knew not what could be the use of those several clefts and divisions in my feet behind; that these were too soft to bear the hardness and sharpness of stones without a covering made from the skin of some other brute; that my whole body wanted a fence against heat and cold, which I was forced to put on and off every day with tediousness and trouble. And lastly, that he observed every animal in this country naturally to abhor the yahoos, whom the weaker avoided, and the stronger drove from them. So that supposing us to have the gift of reason, he could not see how it were possible to cure that natural antipathy which every creature discovered against us; nor consequently, how we could tame and render them serviceable. However, he would (as he said) debate the matter no farther, because he was more desirous to know my own story, the country where I was born, and the several actions and events of my life before I came hither.

I assured him how extremely desirous I was that he should be satisfied in every point; but I doubted much, whether it would be possible for me to explain myself on several subjects whereof his Honour could have no conception, because I saw nothing in his country to which I could resemble them. That however, I would do my best, and strive to express myself by similitudes, humbly desiring his assistance when I wanted proper words; which he was pleased to promise me.

I said, my birth was of honest parents, in an island called England, which was remote from this country as many days' journey as the strongest of his Honour's servants could travel in the annual course of the sun. That I was bred a surgeon, whose trade is to cure wounds and hurts in the body, got by accident or violence; that my country was governed by a female man, whom we called *queen*. That I left it to get riches, whereby I might maintain myself and family when I should return. That in my last voyage I was commander of the ship, and had about fifty yahoos under me, many of which died at sea, and I was forced to supply them by others picked out from several nations. That our ship was twice in danger of being sunk; the first time by a great storm, and the second, by striking against a rock. Here my master interposed, by asking me, how I could persuade strangers out of different countries to venture with me, after the losses I had sustained, and the hazards I had run. I said, they were fellows of desperate fortunes, forced to fly from the places of their birth, on account of their poverty or their crimes. Some were undone by lawsuits; others spent all they had in drinking, whoring, and gaming; others fled for treason; many for murder, theft, poisoning, robbery, perjury, forgery, coining false money, for committing rapes or sodomy, for flying from their colours, or deserting to the enemy, and most of them had broken prison; none of these durst return to their native countries for fear of being hanged, or of starving in a jail; and therefore were under a necessity of seeking a livelihood in other places.

During this discourse, my master was pleased often to interrupt me; I had made use of many circumlocutions in describing to him the nature of the several crimes, for which most of our crew had been forced to fly their country. This labour took up several days' conversation before he was able to comprehend me. He was wholly at a loss to know what could be the use or necessity of practising those vices. To clear up which I endeavoured to give him some ideas of the desire of power and riches, of the terrible effects of lust, intemperance, malice and envy. All this I was forced to define and describe by putting of cases, and making suppositions. After which, like one whose imagination was struck with something never seen or heard of before, he would lift up his eyes with amazement and indignation. Power, government, war, law, punishment, and a thousand other things had no terms wherein that language could express them, which made the difficulty almost insuperable to give my master any conception of what I meant. But being of an excellent understanding, much improved by contemplation and converse, he at last arrived at a competent knowledge of what human nature in our parts of the world is capable to perform, and desired I would give him some particular account of that land which we call Europe, especially of my own country.

CHAPTER V.

The author, at his master's commands, informs him of the state of England. The causes of war among the princes of Europe. The author begins to explain the English constitution.

The reader may please to observe, that the following extract of many conversations I had with my master contains a summary of the most material points which were discoursed at several times for above two years; his Honour often desiring fuller satisfaction as I farther improved in the Houyhnhnm tongue. I laid before him, as well as I could, the whole state of Europe; I discoursed of trade and manufactures, of arts and sciences; and the answers I gave to all the questions he made, as they arose upon

several subjects, were a fund of conversation not to be exhausted. But I shall here only set down the substance of what passed
between us concerning my own country, reducing it into order
as well as I can, without any regard to time or other circumstances, while I strictly adhere to truth. My only concern is, that
I shall hardly be able to do justice to my master's arguments and
expressions, which must needs suffer by my want of capacity, as
well as by a translation into our barbarous English.

In obedience therefore to his Honour's commands, I related to
him the Revolution under the Prince of Orange; the long war
with France entered into by the said prince, and renewed by his
successor the present queen, wherein the greatest powers of
Christendom were engaged, and which still continued: I computed, at his request, that about a million of yahoos might have
been killed in the whole progress of it, and perhaps a hundred or
more cities taken, and five times as many ships burnt or sunk.

He asked me what were the usual causes or motives that made
one country go to war with another. I answered they were innumerable, but I should only mention a few of the chief. Sometimes the ambition of princes, who never think they have
land or people enough to govern: sometimes the corruption of
ministers, who engage their master in a war in order to stifle or
divert the clamour of the subjects against their evil administration. Difference in opinions hath cost many millions of lives: for
instance, whether flesh be bread, or bread be flesh; whether the
juice of a certain berry be blood or wine; whether whistling be
a vice or a virtue; whether it be better to kiss a post, or throw
it into the fire; what is the best colour for a coat, whether black,
white, red, or grey; and whether it should be long or short,
narrow or wide, dirty or clean, with many more. Neither are
any wars so furious and bloody, or of so long continuance, as
those occasioned by difference in opinion, especially if it be in
things indifferent.

Sometimes the quarrel between two princes is to decide which
of them shall dispossess a third of his dominions, where neither
of them pretend to any right. Sometimes one prince quarrelleth
with another, for fear the other should quarrel with him. Sometimes a war is entered upon, because the enemy is too strong,
and sometimes because he is too weak. Sometimes our neighbours want the things which we have, or have the things which
we want; and we both fight, till they take ours or give us theirs.
It is a very justifiable cause of war to invade a country after the
people have been wasted by famine, destroyed by pestilence, or
embroiled by factions amongst themselves. It is justifiable to

enter into a war against our nearest ally, when one of his towns lies convenient for us, or a territory of land, that would render our dominions round and compact. If a prince send forces into a nation where the people are poor and ignorant, he may lawfully put half of them to death, and make slaves of the rest, in order to civilize and reduce them from their barbarous way of living. It is a very kingly, honourable, and frequent practice, when one prince desires the assistance of another to secure him against an invasion, that the assistant, when he hath driven out the invader, should seize on the dominions himself, and kill, imprison or banish the prince he came to relieve. Alliance by blood or marriage is a sufficient cause of war between princes, and the nearer the kindred is, the greater is their disposition to quarrel: poor nations are hungry, and rich nations are proud, and pride and hunger will ever be at variance. For these reasons, the trade of a soldier is held the most honourable of all others: because a soldier is a yahoo hired to kill in cold blood as many of his own species, who have never offended him, as possibly he can.

There is likewise a kind of beggarly princes in Europe, not able to make war by themselves, who hire out their troops to richer nations, for so much a day to each man; of which they keep three fourths to themselves, and it is the best part of their maintenance; such are those in Germany and many northern parts of Europe.

What you have told me (said my master) upon the subject of war, does indeed discover most admirably the effects of that reason you pretend to: however, it is happy that the shame is greater than the danger; and that nature hath left you utterly uncapable of doing much mischief. For your mouths lying flat with your faces, you can hardly bite each other to any purpose, unless by consent. Then as to the claws upon your feet before and behind, they are so short and tender, that one of our yahoos would drive a dozen of yours before him. And therefore in recounting the numbers of those who have been killed in battle, I cannot but think that you have *said the thing which is not*.

I could not forbear shaking my head and smiling a little at his ignorance. And being no stranger to the art of war, I gave him a description of cannons, culverins, muskets, carabines, pistols, bullets, powder, swords, bayonets, battles, sieges, retreats, attacks, undermines, countermines, bombardments, sea-fights; ships sunk with a thousand men, twenty thousand killed on each side; dying groans, limbs flying in the air, smoke, noise, confusion, trampling to death under horses' feet; flight, pursuit, victory; fields strewed with carcases left for food to dogs, and wolves, and birds of prey; plundering, stripping, ravishing, burning and destroying. And to set forth the valour of my own dear countrymen, I assured him, that I had seen them blow up a hundred enemies at once in a siege, and as many in a ship, and beheld the dead bodies drop down in pieces from the clouds, to the great diversion of all the spectators.

I was going on to more particulars, when my master commanded me silence. He said, whoever understood the nature of yahoos might easily believe it possible for so vile an animal to be capable of every action I had named, if their strength and cunning equalled their malice. But as my discourse had increased his abhorrence of the whole species, so he found it gave him a disturbance in his mind, to which he was wholly a stranger before. He thought his ears being used to such abominable words, might by degrees admit them with less detestation. That although he hated the yahoos of this country, yet he no more blamed them for their odious qualities, than he did a *gnnayh* (a bird of prey) for its cruelty, or a sharp stone for cutting his hoof. But when a creature pretending to reason could be capable of such enormities, he dreaded lest the corruption of that faculty might be worse than brutality itself. He seemed therefore confident, that instead of reason, we were only possessed of some quality fitted to increase our natural vices; as the reflection from a troubled stream returns the image of an ill-shapen body, not only larger, but more distorted.

He added, that he had heard too much upon the subject of war, both in this and some former discourses. There was another point which a little perplexed him at present. I had said, that some of our crew left their country on account of being ruined by *law;* that I had already explained the meaning of the word; but he was at a loss how it should come to pass, that the *law* which was intended for every man's preservation, should be any man's ruin. Therefore he desired to be farther satisfied what I meant by *law,* and the dispensers thereof according to the present practice in my own country; because he thought nature and reason were sufficient guides for a reasonable animal, as we pretended to be, in showing us what we ought to do, and what to avoid.

I assured his Honour, that law was a science wherein I had not much conversed, further than by employing advocates in vain, upon some injustices that had been done me. However, I would give him all the satisfaction I was able.

I said there was a society of men among us, bred up from their youth in the art of proving by words multiplied for the purpose, that white is black, and black is white, according as they are paid. To this society all the rest of the people are slaves.

For example, if my neighbour hath a mind to my cow, he hires a lawyer to prove that he ought to have my cow from me. I must then hire another to defend my right, it being against all rules of law that any man should be allowed to speak for himself. Now in this case, I who am the true owner lie under two great disadvantages. First, my lawyer, being practiced almost from his cradle in defending falsehood, is quite out of his element when he would be an advocate for justice, which as an office unnatural, he always attempts with great awkwardness, if not with ill will. The second disadvantage is, that my lawyer must proceed with great caution, or else he will be reprimanded by the judges, and abhorred by his brethren, as one who would lessen the practice of the law. And therefore I have but two methods to preserve my cow. The first is to gain over my adversary's lawyer with a double fee, who will then betray his client by insinuating that he hath justice on his side. The second way is for my lawyer to make my cause appear as unjust as he can, by allowing the cow to belong to my adversary; and this if it be skilfully done will certainly bespeak the favour of the bench.

Now, your Honour is to know that these judges are persons appointed to decide all controversies of property, as well as for the trial of criminals, and picked out from the most dextrous lawyers who are grown old or lazy, and having been biassed all their lives against truth and equity, lie under such a fatal necessity of favouring fraud, perjury, and oppression, that I have known several of them refuse a large bribe from the side where justice lay, rather than injure the faculty by doing any thing unbecoming their nature or their office.

It is a maxim among these lawyers, that whatever hath been done before may legally be done again: and therefore they take special care to record all the decisions formerly made against common justice and the general reason of mankind. These, under the name of *precedents*, they produce as authorities, to justify the most iniquitous opinions; and the judges never fail of decreeing accordingly.

In pleading, they studiously avoid entering into the merits of the cause, but are loud, violent, and tedious in dwelling upon all circumstances which are not to the purpose. For instance, in the case already mentioned; they never desire to know what claim or title my adversary hath to my cow, but whether the said cow were red or black, her horns long or short; whether the field I

graze her in be round or square, whether she was milked at home
or abroad, what diseases she is subject to, and the like; after
which they consult precedents, adjourn the cause from time to
time, and in ten, twenty, or thirty years come to an issue.

It is likewise to be observed that this society hath a peculiar
cant and jargon of their own, that no other mortal can understand, and wherein all their laws are written, which they take
special care to multiply; whereby they have wholly confounded
the very essence of truth and falsehood, of right and wrong; so
that it will take thirty years to decide whether the field left me by
my ancestors for six generations belongs to me or to a stranger
three hundred miles off.

In the trial of persons accused for crimes against the state the
method is much more short and commendable: the judge first
sends to sound the disposition of those in power, after which he
can easily hang or save the criminal, strictly preserving all due
forms of law.

Here my master, interposing, said it was a pity, that creatures
endowed with such prodigious abilities of mind as these lawyers,
by the description I gave of them, must certainly be, were not
rather encouraged to be instructors of others in wisdom and
knowledge. In answer to which I assured his Honour, that in all
points out of their own trade they were usually the most ignorant and stupid generation among us, the most despicable in
common conversation, avowed enemies to all knowledge and
learning, and equally disposed to pervert the general reason of
mankind in every other subject of discourse, as in that of their
own profession.

Chapter VI.

A continuation of the state of England under Queen Anne. The char-
acter of a first minister in the courts of Europe.

My master was yet wholly at a loss to understand what motives could incite this race of lawyers to perplex, disquiet, and
weary themselves by engaging in a confederacy of injustice,
merely for the sake of injuring their fellow-animals; neither
could he comprehend what I meant in saying they did it for hire.
Whereupon I was at much pains to describe to him the use of
money, the materials it was made of, and the value of the metals;
that when a yahoo had got a great store of this precious substance, he was able to purchase whatever he had a mind to, the

finest clothing, the noblest houses, great tracts of land, the most costly meats and drinks, and have his choice of the most beautiful females. Therefore since money alone was able to perform all these feats, our yahoos thought they could never have enough of it to spend or to save, as they found themselves inclined from their natural bent either to profusion or avarice. That the rich man enjoyed the fruit of the poor man's labour, and the latter were a thousand to one in proportion to the former. That the bulk of our people were forced to live miserably, by labouring every day for small wages to make a few live plentifully. I enlarged myself much on these and many other particulars to the same purpose: but his Honour was still to seek, for he went upon a supposition that all animals had a title to their share in the productions of the earth, and especially those who presided over the rest. Therefore he desired I would let him know what these costly meats were, and how any of us happened to want them. Whereupon I enumerated as many sorts as came into my head, with the various methods of dressing them, which could not be done without sending vessels by sea to every part of the world, as well for liquors to drink, as for sauces, and innumerable other conveniencies. I assured him, that this whole globe of earth must be at least three times gone round, before one of our better female yahoos could get her breakfast, or a cup to put it in. He said, that must needs be a miserable country which cannot furnish food for its own inhabitants. But what he chiefly wondered at was how such vast tracts of ground as I described should be wholly without fresh water, and the people put to the necessity of sending over the sea for drink. I replied, that England (the dear place of my nativity) was computed to produce three times the quantity of food more than its inhabitants are able to consume, as well as liquors extracted from grain, or pressed out of the fruit of certain trees, which made excellent drink, and the same proportion in every other convenience of life. But in order to feed the luxury and intemperance of the males, and the vanity of the females, we sent away the greatest part of our necessary things to other countries, from whence in return we brought the materials of diseases, folly, and vice, to spend among ourselves. Hence it follows of necessity that vast numbers of our people are compelled to seek their livelihood by begging, robbing, stealing, cheating, pimping, forswearing, flattering, suborning, forging, gaming, lying, fawning, hectoring, voting, scribbling, star-gazing, poisoning, whoring, canting, libelling, free-thinking, and the like occupations: every one of which terms, I was at much pains to make him understand.

That wine was not imported among us from foreign countries to supply the want of water or other drinks, but because it was a sort of liquid which made us merry, by putting us out of our senses; diverted all melancholy thoughts, begat wild extravagant imaginations in the brain, raised our hopes, and banished our fears, suspended every office of reason for a time, and deprived us of the use of our limbs, until we fell into a profound sleep; although it must be confessed, that we always awaked sick and dispirited, and that the use of this liquor filled us with diseases, which made our lives uncomfortable and short.

But beside all this, the bulk of our people supported themselves by furnishing the necessities or conveniencies of life to the rich, and to each other. For instance, when I am at home and dressed as I ought to be, I carry on my body the workmanship of an hundred tradesmen; the building and furniture of my house employ as many more, and five times the number to adorn my wife.

I was going on to tell him of another sort of people, who get their livelihood by attending the sick, having upon some occasions informed his Honour that many of my crew had died of diseases. But here it was with the utmost difficulty that I brought him to apprehend what I meant. He could easily conceive that a Houyhnhnm grew weak and heavy a few days before his death, or by some accident might hurt a limb. But that Nature, who works all things to perfection, should suffer any pains to breed in our bodies, he thought impossible, and desired to know the reason of so unaccountable an evil. I told him, we fed on a thousand things which operated contrary to each other; that we eat when we were not hungry, and drank without the provocation of thirst; that we sat whole nights drinking strong liquors without eating a bit, which disposed us to sloth, enflamed our bodies, and precipitated or prevented digestion. That prostitute female yahoos acquired a certain malady, which bred rotteness in the bones of those who fell into their embraces; that this and many other diseases were propagated from father to son, so that great numbers come into the world with complicated maladies upon them; that it would be endless to give him a catalogue of all diseases incident to human bodies; for they could not be fewer than five or six hundred, spread over every limb and joint; in short, every part, external and intestine, having diseases appropriated to each. To remedy which, there was a sort of people bred up among us, in the profession or pretence of curing the sick. And because I had some skill in the faculty, I would, in gratitude to his Honour, let him know the whole mystery and method by which they proceed.

Their fundamental is, that all diseases arise from repletion, from whence they conclude that a great evacuation of the body is necessary, either through the natural passage, or upwards at the mouth. Their next business is, from herbs, minerals, gums, oils, shells, salts, juices, seaweed, excrements, barks of trees, serpents, toads, frogs, spiders, dead men's flesh and bones, birds, beasts and fishes, to form a composition for smell and taste the most abominable, nauseous and detestable that they can possibly contrive, which the stomach immediately rejects with loathing; and this they call a vomit; or else from the same storehouse, with some other poisonous additions, they command us to take in at the orifice above or below (just as the physician then happens to be disposed) a medicine equally annoying and disgustful to the bowels, which, relaxing the belly, drives down all before it, and this they call a purge or a clyster. For nature (as the physicians allege) having intended the superior anterior orifice only for the intromission of solids and liquids, and the inferior posterior for ejection, these artists ingeniously considering that in all diseases Nature is forced out of her seat, therefore to replace her in it, the body must be treated in a manner directly contrary, by interchanging the use of each orifice, forcing solids and liquids in at the anus, and making evacuations at the mouth.

But besides real diseases we are subject to many that are only imaginary, for which the physicians have invented imaginary cures; these have their several names, and so have the drugs that are proper for them, and with these our female yahoos are always infested.

One great excellency in this tribe is their skill at prognostics, wherein they seldom fail; their predictions in real diseases, when they rise to any degree of malignity, generally portending death, which is always in their power, when recovery is not: and therefore, upon any unexpected signs of amendment, after they have pronounced their sentence, rather than be accused as false prophets, they know how to approve their sagacity to the world by a seasonable dose.

They are likewise of special use to husbands and wives who are grown weary of their mates, to eldest sons, to great ministers of state, and often to princes.

I had formerly upon occasion discoursed with my master upon the nature of our government in general, and particularly of our own excellent constitution, deservedly the wonder and envy of the whole world. But having here accidentally mentioned a 'minister of state', he commanded me some time after to inform him, what species of yahoo I particularly meant by that appellation.

I told him that a first or chief minister of state, who was the person I intended to describe, was a creature wholly exempt from joy and grief, love and hatred, pity and anger; at least makes use of no other passions but a violent desire of wealth, power, and titles; that he applies his words to all uses, except to the indication of his mind; that he never tells a truth, but with an intent that you should take it for a lie; nor a lie, but with a design that you should take it for a truth; that those he speaks worst of behind their backs are in the surest way to preferment; and whenever he begins to praise you to others or to yourself, you are from that day forlorn. The worst mark you can receive is a promise, especially when it is confirmed with an oath; after which every wise man retires, and gives over all hopes.

There are three methods by which a man may rise to be chief minister: the first is, by knowing how with prudence to dispose of a wife, a daughter, or a sister: the second, by betraying or undermining his predecessor: and the third is, by a furious zeal in public assemblies against the corruptions of the court. But a wise prince would rather choose to employ those who practise the last of these methods; because such zealots prove always the most obsequious and subservient to the will and passions of their master. That these 'ministers' having all employments at their disposal, preserve themselves in power by bribing the majority of a senate or great council; and at last, by an expedient called an 'act of indemnity' (whereof I described the nature to him) they secure themselves from after reckonings, and retire from the public, laden with the spoils of the nation.

The palace of a chief minister is a seminary to breed up others in his own trade; the pages, lackeys, and porter, by imitating their master, become ministers of state in their several districts, and learn to excel in the three principal ingredients, of insolence, lying, and bribery. Accordingly, they have a subaltern court paid to them by persons of the best rank, and sometimes by the force of dexterity and impudence arrive through several gradations to be successors to their lord.

He is usually governed by a decayed wench or favourite foot-man, who are the tunnels through which all graces are conveyed, and may properly be called, in the last resort, the governors of the kingdom.

One day my master, having heard me mention the nobility of my country, was pleased to make me a compliment which I could not pretend to deserve: that he was sure I must have been born of some noble family, because I far exceeded in shape, colour, and cleanliness, all the yahoos of his nation, although I seemed to fail in strength and agility, which must be imputed to my different way of living from those other brutes, and besides, I was not only endowed with the faculty of speech, but likewise with some rudiments of reason, to a degree that with all his acquaintance I passed for a prodigy.

He made me observe, that among the Houyhnhnms, the white, the sorrel, and the iron-grey were not so exactly shaped as the bay, the dapple-grey, and the black; nor born with equal talents of the mind, or a capacity to improve them; and therefore continued always in the condition of servants, without ever aspiring to match out of their own race, which in that country would be reckoned monstrous and unnatural.

I made his Honour my most humble acknowledgments for the good opinion he was pleased to conceive of me; but assured him at the same time that my birth was of the lower sort, having been born of plain honest parents, who were just able to give me a tolerable education: that nobility among us was altogether a different thing from the idea he had of it; that our young noblemen are bred from their childhood in idleness and luxury; that as soon as years will permit, they consume their vigor and contract odious diseases among lewd females; and when their fortunes are almost ruined, they marry some woman of mean birth, disagreeable person, and unsound constitution, merely for the sake of money, whom they hate and despise. That the productions of such marriages are generally scrofulous, ricketty, or deformed children, by which means the family seldom continues above three generations, unless the wife takes care to provide a healthy father among her neighbours or domestics, in order to improve and continue the breed. That a weak diseased body, a meager countenance, and sallow complexion are the true marks of noble blood; and a healthy robust appearance is so disgraceful in a man of quality, that the world concludes his real father to have been a groom, or a coachman. The imperfections of his mind run parallel with those of his body, being a composition of spleen, dulness, ignorance, caprice, sensuality, and pride.

Without the consent of this illustrious body no law can be enacted, repealed, or altered, and these nobles have likewise the decision of all our possessions without appeal.

Chapter VII.

The author's great love of his native country. His master's observations upon the constitution and administration of England, as described by the author, with parallel cases and comparisons. His master's observations upon human nature.

The reader may be disposed to wonder how I could prevail on myself to give so free a representation of my own species, among a race of mortals who were already too apt to conceive the vilest opinion of human kind from that entire congruity betwixt me and their yahoos. But I must freely confess, that the many virtues of those excellent quadrupeds, placed in opposite view to human corruptions, had so far opened my eyes and enlarged my understanding, that I began to view the actions and passions of man in a very different light, and to think the honour of my own kind not worth managing; which, besides, it was impossible for me to do before a person of so acute a judgment as my master, who daily convinced me of a thousand faults in myself, whereof I had not the least perception before, and which with us would never be numbered even among human infirmities: I had likewise learned from his example an utter detestation of all falsehood or disguise; and truth appeared so amiable to me, that I determined upon sacrificing every thing to it.

Let me deal so candidly with the reader as to confess, that there was yet a much stronger motive for the freedom I took in my representation of things. I had not been a year in this country before I contracted such a love and veneration for the inhabitants, that I entered on a firm resolution never to return to human kind, but to pass the rest of my life among these admirable Houyhnhnms in the contemplation and practice of every virtue; where I could have no example or incitement to vice. But it was decreed by Fortune, my perpetual enemy, that so great a felicity should not fall to my share. However, it is now some comfort to reflect, that in what I said of my countrymen I extenuated their faults as much as I durst before so strict an examiner, and upon every article gave as favourable a turn as the matter would bear. For, indeed, who is there alive that will not be swayed by his bias and partiality to the place of his birth?

I have related the substance of several conversations I had with my master, during the greatest part of the time I had the honour to be in his service, but have indeed for brevity sake omitted much more than is here set down.

When I had answered all his questions, and his curiosity seemed to be fully satisfied, he sent for me one morning early.

and commanding me to sit down at some distance (an honour which he had never before conferred upon me), he said he had been very seriously considering my whole story, as far as it related both to myself and my country: that he looked upon us as a sort of animals to whose share, by what accident he could not conjecture, some small pittance of reason had fallen, whereof we made no other use than by its assistance to aggravate our natural corruptions, and to acquire new ones which Nature had not given us. That we disarmed ourselves of the few abilities she had bestowed, had been very successful in multiplying our original wants, and seemed to spend our whole lives in vain endeavours to supply them by our own inventions. That as to myself, it was manifest I had neither the strength or agility of a common yahoo, that I walked infirmly on my hinder feet, had found out a contrivance to make my claws of no use or defence, and to remove the hair from my chin, which was intended as a shelter from the sun and the weather. Lastly, that I could neither run with speed, nor climb trees like my brethren (as he called them) the yahoos in this country.

That our institutions of government and law were plainly owing to our gross defects in reason, and by consequence, in virtue; because reason alone is sufficient to govern a rational creature; which was therefore a character we had no pretence to challenge, even from the account I had given of my own people, although he manifestly perceived, that in order to favour them I had concealed many particulars, and often *said the thing which was not*.

He was the more confirmed in this opinion, because he observed, that as I agreed in every feature of my body with other yahoos, except where it was to my real disadvantage in point of strength, speed, and activity, the shortness of my claws, and some other particulars where nature had no part; so from the representation I had given him of our lives, our manners, and our actions, he found as near a resemblance in the disposition of our minds. He said the yahoos were known to hate one another more than they did any different species of animals; and the reason usually assigned was the odiousness of their own shapes, which all could see in the rest, but not in themselves. He had therefore begun to think it not unwise in us to cover our bodies, and, by that invention, conceal many of our deformities from each other, which would else be hardly supportable. But he now found he had been mistaken, and that the dissensions of those brutes in his country were owing to the same cause with ours, as I had described them. For if (said he) you throw among five yahoos as

much food as would be sufficient for fifty, they will, instead of
eating peaceably, fall together by the ears, each single one
impatient to have all to itself, and therefore a servant was usually
employed to stand by while they were feeding abroad, and those
kept at home were tied at a distance from each other; that if a
cow died of age or accident, before a Houyhnhnm could secure
it for his own yahoos, those in the neighbourhood would come in
herds to seize it, and then would ensue such a battle as I had
described, with terrible wounds made by their claws on both
sides, although they seldom were able to kill one another, for
want of such convenient instruments of death as we had invented. At other times the like battles have been fought between the
yahoos of several neighbourhoods without any visible cause; those
of one district watching all opportunities to surprise the next
before they are prepared. But if they find their project hath
miscarried, they return home, and, for want of enemies, engage in
what I call a civil war among themselves.

That in some fields of his country there are certain shining
stones of several colours, whereof the yahoos are violently fond,
and when part of these stones are fixed in the earth, as it sometimes happeneth, they will dig with their claws for whole days to
get them out, carry them away, and hide them by heaps in their
kennels; but still looking round with great caution, for fear their
comrades should find out their treasure. My master said, he
could never discover the reason of this unnatural appetite, or how
these stones could be of any use to a yahoo; but now he believed
it might proceed from the same principle of avarice which I had
ascribed to mankind; that he had once, by way of experiment,
privately removed a heap of these stones from the place where
one of his yahoos had buried it: whereupon the sordid animal,
missing his treasure, by his loud lamenting brought the whole
herd to the place, there miserably howled, then fell to biting and
tearing the rest, began to pine away, would neither eat, nor sleep,
nor work, till he ordered a servant privately to convey the stones
into the same hole and hide them as before; which when his
yahoo had found, he presently recovered his spirits and good
humour, but took care to remove them to a better hiding-place,
and hath ever since been a very serviceable brute.

My master farther assured me, which I also observed myself,
that in the fields where these shining stones abound, the fiercest
and most frequent battles are fought, occasioned by perpetual
inroads of the neighbouring yahoos.

He said, it was common, when two yahoos discovered such a
stone in a field, and were contending which of them should be

the proprietor, a third would take the advantage, and carry it away from them both; which my master would needs contend to have some resemblance with our suits at law; wherein I thought it for our credit not to undeceive him; since the decision he mentioned was much more equitable than many decrees among us: because the plaintiff and defendant there lost nothing beside the stone they contended for, whereas our courts of equity would never have dismissed the cause while either of them had any thing left.

My master, continuing his discourse, said, there was nothing that rendered the yahoos more odious than their undistinguishing appetite to devour every thing that came in their way, whether herbs, roots, berries, corrupted flesh of animals, or all mingled together: and it was peculiar in their temper, that they were fonder of what they could get by rapine or stealth at a greater distance, than much better food provided for them at home. If their prey held out, they would eat till they were ready to burst, after which Nature had pointed out to them a certain root that gave them a general evacuation.

There was also another kind of root very juicy, but somewhat rare and difficult to be found, which the yahoos sought for with much eagerness, and would suck it with great delight; and it produced in them the same effects that wine hath upon us. It would make them sometimes hug, and sometimes tear one another; they would howl and grin, and chatter, and reel, and tumble, and then fall asleep in the mud.

I did indeed observe, that the yahoos were the only animals in this country subject to any diseases; which, however, were much fewer than horses have among us, and contracted not by any ill treatment they meet with, but by the nastiness and greediness of that sordid brute. Neither has their language any more than a general appellation for those maladies, which is borrowed from the name of the beast, and called *hnea-yahoo*, or the *yahoo's-evil*, and the cure prescribed is a mixture of their own dung and urine forcibly put down the yahoo's throat. This I have since often known to have been taken with success, and do here freely recommend it to my countrymen, for the public good, as an admirable specific against all diseases produced by repletion.

As to learning, government, arts, manufactures, and the like, my master confessed he could find little or no resemblance between the yahoos of that country and those in ours. For he only meant to observe what parity there was in our natures. He had heard indeed some curious Houyhnhnms observe, that in most herds there was a sort of ruling yahoo (as among us there is generally some leading or principal stag in a park), who was always more deformed in body, and mischievous in disposition, than any of the rest. That this leader had usually a favourite as like himself as he could get, whose employment was to lick his master's feet and posteriors, and drive the female yahoos to his kennel; for which he was now and then rewarded with a piece of ass's flesh. This favourite is hated by the whole herd, and therefore, to protect himself, keeps always near the person of his leader. He usually continues in office till a worse can be found; but the very moment he is discarded, his successor, at the head of all the yahoos in that district, young and old, male and female, come in a body, and discharge their excrements upon him from head to foot. But how far this might be applicable to our courts and favourites, and ministers of state, my master said I could best determine.

I durst make no return to this malicious insinuation, which debased human understanding below the sagacity of a common hound, who has judgment enough to distinguish and follow the cry of the ablest dog in the pack, without being ever mistaken.

My master told me, there were some qualities remarkable in the yahoos, which he had not observed me to mention, or at least very slightly, in the accounts I had given him of human kind; he said, those animals, like other brutes, had their females in common; but in this they differed, that the she-yahoo would admit the male while she was pregnant, and that the hees would quarrel and fight with the females as fiercely as with each other. Both which practices were such degrees of infamous brutality, that no other sensitive creature ever arrived at.

Another thing he wondered at in the yahoos was their strange disposition to nastiness and dirt, whereas there appears to be a natural love of cleanliness in all other animals. As to the two former accusations, I was glad to let them pass without any reply, because I had not a word to offer upon them in defence of my species, which otherwise I certainly had done from my own inclinations. But I could have easily vindicated human kind from the imputation of singularity upon the last article, if there had been any swine in that country (as unluckily for me there were not), which, although it may be a sweeter quadruped than a yahoo, cannot, I humbly conceive, in justice pretend to more cleanliness; and so his Honour himself must have owned, if he had seen their filthy way of feeding, and their custom of wallowing and sleeping in the mud.

My master likewise mentioned another quality which his servants had discovered in several yahoos, and to him was wholly unaccountable. He said, a fancy would sometimes take a yahoo to retire into a corner, to lie down and howl, and groan, and spurn away all that came near him, although he were young and fat, and wanted neither food nor water; nor did the servants imagine what could possibly ail him. And the only remedy they found was to set him to hard work, after which he would infallibly come to himself. To this I was silent out of partiality to my own kind; yet here I could plainly discover the true seeds of spleen, which only seizeth on the lazy, the luxurious, and the rich; who, if they were forced to undergo the same regimen, I would undertake for the cure.

His Honour had farther observed, that a female yahoo would often stand behind a bank or a bush, to gaze on the young males passing by, and then appear, and hide, using many antic gestures and grimaces, at which time it was observed, that she had a most offensive smell; and when any of the males advanced, would slowly retire, looking often back, and with a counterfeit show of fear, run off into some convenient place where she knew the male would follow her.

At other times if a female stranger came among them, three or four of her own sex would get about her, and stare and chatter, and grin, and smell her all over, and then turn off with gestures that seemed to express contempt and disdain.

Perhaps my master might refine a little in these speculations, which he had drawn from what he observed himself, or had been told him by others: however, I could not reflect without some amazement, and much sorrow, that the rudiments of lewdness, coquetry, censure, and scandal, should have place by instinct in womankind.

I expected every moment that my master would accuse the yahoos of those unnatural appetites in both sexes, so common among us. But Nature, it seems, hath not been so expert a schoolmistress; and these politer pleasures are entirely the productions of art and reason, on our side of the globe.

CHAPTER VIII.

The author relates several particulars of the yahoos. The great virtues of the Houyhnhnms. The education and exercise of their youth. Their general assembly.

As I ought to have understood human nature much better than I supposed it possible for my master to do, so it was easy to apply the character he gave of the yahoos to myself and my

countrymen, and I believed I could yet make farther discoveries
from my own observation. I therefore often begged his Honour
to let me go among the herds of yahoos in the neighbourhood, to
which he always very graciously consented, being perfectly convinced that the hatred I bore those brutes would never suffer me
to be corrupted by them; and his Honour ordered one of his
servants, a strong sorrel nag, very honest and good-natured, to
be my guard, without whose protection I durst not undertake
such adventures. For I have already told the reader how much
I was pestered by those odious animals upon my first arrival.
And I afterwards failed very narrowly three or four times of falling into their clutches, when I happened to stray at any distance
without my hanger. And I have reason to believe they had some
imagination that I was of their own species, which I often assisted myself, by stripping up my sleeves, and showing my
naked arms and breast in their sight, when my protector was
with me. At which times they would approach as near as they
durst, and imitate my actions after the manner of monkeys, but
ever with great signs of hatred, as a tame jackdaw, with cap and
stockings, is always persecuted by the wild ones, when he happens to be got among them.

They are prodigiously nimble from their infancy; however, I
once caught a young male of three years old, and endeavoured by
all marks of tenderness to make it quiet; but the little imp fell a
squalling, and scratching, and biting with such violence, that
I was forced to let it go, and it was high time, for a whole troop
of old ones came about us at the noise, but finding the cub was
safe (for away it ran), and my sorrel nag being by, they durst not
venture near us. I observed the young animal's flesh to smell
very rank, and the stink was somewhat between a weasel and a
fox, but much more disagreeable. I forgot another circumstance
(and perhaps I might have the reader's pardon if it were wholly
omitted) that while I held the odious vermin in my hands, it
voided its filthy excrements of a yellow liquid substance all over
my clothes; but by good fortune there was a small brook hard
by, where I washed myself as clean as I could, although I durst
not come into my master's presence, until I were sufficiently
aired.

By what I could discover, the yahoos appear to be the most
unteachable of all animals, their capacities never reaching higher
than to draw or carry burthens. Yet I am of opinion this defect
ariseth chiefly from a perverse, restive disposition. For they are
cunning, malicious, treacherous and revengeful. They are
strong and hardy, but of a cowardly spirit, and by consequence

insolent, abject, and cruel. It is observed, that the redhaired of both sexes are more libidinous and mischievous than the rest, whom yet they much exceed in strength and activity.

The Houyhnhnms keep the yahoos for present use in huts not far from the house; but the rest are sent abroad to certain fields, where they dig up roots, eat several kinds of herbs, and search about for carrion, or sometimes catch weasels and *luhimuhs* (a sort of wild rat), which they greedily devour. Nature hath taught them to dig deep holes with their nails on the side of a rising ground, wherein they lie by themselves, only the kennels of the females are larger, sufficient to hold two or three cubs.

They swim from their infancy like frogs, and are able to continue long under water, where they often take fish, which the females carry home to their young. And upon this occasion, I hope the reader will pardon my relating an odd adventure.

Being one day abroad with my protector the sorrel nag, and the weather exceeding hot, I entreated him to let me bathe in a river that was near. He consented, and I immediately stripped myself stark naked, and went down softly into the stream. It happened that a young female yahoo, standing behind a bank, saw the whole proceeding, and inflamed by desire, as the nag and I conjectured, came running with all speed, and leaped into the water within five yards of the place where I bathed. I was never in my life so terribly frighted; the nag was grazing at some distance, not suspecting any harm. She embraced me after a most fulsome manner; I roared as loud as I could, and the nag came galloping towards me, whereupon she quitted her grasp, with the utmost reluctancy, and leaped upon the opposite bank, where she stood gazing and howling all the time I was putting on my clothes.

This was matter of diversion to my master and his family, as well as of mortification to myself. For now I could no longer deny that I was a real yahoo in every limb and feature, since the females had a natural propensity to me as one of their own species: neither was the hair of this brute of a red colour (which might have been some excuse for an appetite a little irregular) but black as a sloe, and her countenance did not make an appearance altogether so hideous as the rest of the kind; for, I think, she could not be above eleven years old.

Having already lived three years in this country, the reader I suppose will expect that I should, like other travellers, give him some account of the manners and customs of its inhabitants, which it was indeed my principal study to learn.

As these noble Houyhnhnms are endowed by nature with a

general disposition to all virtues, and have no conceptions or ideas of what is evil in a rational creature, so their grand maxim is, to cultivate reason, and to be wholly governed by it. Neither is reason among them a point problematical as with us, where men can argue with plausibility on both sides of a question; but strikes you with immediate conviction; as it must needs do where it is not mingled, obscured, or discoloured by passion and interest. I remember it was with extreme difficulty that I could bring my master to understand the meaning of the word *opinion*, or how a point could be disputable; because reason taught us to affirm or deny only where we are certain; and beyond our knowledge we cannot do either. So that controversies, wranglings, disputes, and positiveness in false or dubious propositions are evils unknown among the Houyhnhnms. In the like manner, when I used to explain to him our several systems of natural philosophy, he would laugh that a creature pretending to reason should value itself upon the knowledge of other people's conjectures, and in things where that knowledge, if it were certain, could be of no use. Wherein he agreed entirely with the sentiments of Socrates, as Plato delivers them; which I mention as the highest honour I can do that prince of philosophers. I have often since reflected what destruction such a doctrine would make in the libraries of Europe, and how many paths to fame would be then shut up in the learned world.

Friendship and benevolence are the two principal virtues among the Houyhnhnms, and these not confined to particular objects, but universal to the whole race. For a stranger from the remotest part is equally treated with the nearest neighbour, and wherever he goes, looks upon himself as at home. They preserve decency and civility in the highest degrees, but are altogether ignorant of ceremony. They have no fondness for their colts or foals, but the care they take in educating them proceeds entirely from the dictates of reason. And I observed my master to show the same affection to his neighbour's issue that he had for his own. They will have it that nature teaches them to love the whole species, and it is reason only that maketh a distinction of persons, where there is a superior degree of virtue.

When the matron Houyhnhnms have produced one of each sex, they no longer accompany with their consorts, except they lose one of their issue by some casualty, which very seldom happens: but in such a case they meet again, or when the like accident befalls a person whose wife is past bearing, some other couple bestows on him one of their own colts, and then go together a second time till the mother be pregnant. This caution is necessary to prevent the country from being overburthened with numbers. But the race of inferior Houyhnhnms bred up to be servants is not so strictly limited upon this article; these are allowed to produce three of each sex, to be domestics in the noble families.

In their marriages they are exactly careful to choose such colours as will not make any disagreeable mixture in the breed. Strength is chiefly valued in the male, and comeliness in the female, not upon the account of love, but to preserve the race from degenerating; for where a female happens to excel in strength, a consort is chosen with regard to comeliness. Courtship, love, presents, jointures, settlements, have no place in their thoughts, or terms whereby to express them in their language. The young couple meet and are joined, merely because it is the determination of their parents and friends: it is what they see done every day, and they look upon it as one of the necessary actions in a reasonable being. But the violation of marriage, or any other unchastity, was never heard of: and the married pair pass their lives with the same friendship and mutual benevolence that they bear to all others of the same species who come in their way; without jealousy, fondness, quarrelling, or discontent.

In educating the youth of both sexes, their method is admirable, and highly deserves our imitation. These are not suffered to taste a grain of oats, except upon certain days, till eighteen years old; nor milk, but very rarely; and in summer they graze two hours in the morning, and as many in the evening, which their parents likewise observe, but the servants are not allowed above half that time, and a great part of the grass is brought home, which they eat at the most convenient hours, when they can be best spared from work.

Temperance, industry, exercise and cleanliness, are the lessons equally enjoined to the young ones of both sexes: and my master thought it monstrous in us to give the females a different kind of education from the males, except in some articles of domestic management; whereby, as he truly observed, one half of our natives were good for nothing but bringing children into the world: and to trust the care of their children to such useless animals, he said, was yet a greater instance of brutality.

But the Houyhnhnms train up their youth to strength, speed, and hardiness, by exercising them in running races up and down steep hills, or over hard stony grounds, and when they are all in a sweat, they are ordered to leap over head and ears into a pond or a river. Four times a year the youth of certain districts meet to show their proficiency in running and leaping, and other feats of strength or agility, where the victor is rewarded with a song made in his or her praise. On this festival the servants drive a herd of yahoos into the field, laden with hay, and oats, and milk for a repast to the Houyhnhnms; after which these brutes are immediately driven back again, for fear of being noisome to the assembly.

Every fourth year, at the vernal equinox, there is a representative council of the whole nation, which meets in a plain about twenty miles from our house, and continues about five or six days. Here they inquire into the state and condition of the several districts; whether they abound or be deficient in hay or oats, or cows or yahoos. And wherever there is any want (which is but seldom) it is immediately supplied by unanimous consent and contribution. Here likewise the regulation of children is settled: as for instance, if a Houyhnhnm hath two males, he changeth one of them with another who hath two females: and when a child hath been lost by any casualty, where the mother is past breeding, it is determined what family in the district shall breed another to supply the loss.

CHAPTER IX.

A grand debate at the general assembly of the Houyhnhnms, and how it was determined. The learning of the Houyhnhnms. Their buildings. Their manner of burials. The defectiveness of their language.

One of these grand assemblies was held in my time, about three months before my departure, whither my master went as the representative of our district. In this council was resumed their old debate, and indeed, the only debate that ever happened in their country; whereof my master after his return gave me a very particular account.

The question to be debated was, whether the yahoos should be exterminated from the face of the earth. One of the members for the affirmative offered several arguments of great strength and weight, alleging, that as the yahoos were the most filthy, noisome, and deformed animal which nature ever produced, so they were the most restive and indocible, mischievous and malicious: they would privately suck the teats of the Houyhnhnms' cows, kill and devour their cats, trample down their oats and grass, if they were not continually watched, and commit a thousand other extravagancies. He took notice of a general tradition, that yahoos had not been always in their country: but that many ages ago two of these brutes appeared together upon a mountain, whether produced by the heat of the sun upon corrupted mud and slime, or from the ooze and froth of the sea, was never known. That these yahoos engendered, and their brood in a short time grew so numerous as to overrun and infest the whole nation. That the Houyhnhnms, to get rid of this evil, made a general hunting, and at last enclosed the whole herd; and destroying the older, every Houyhnhnm kept two young ones in a kennel, and brought them to such a degree of tameness, as an animal so savage by nature can be capable of acquiring; using them for draught and carriage. That there seemed to be much truth in this tradition, and that those creatures could not be *ylnhniamshy* (or *aborigines* of the land) because of the violent hatred the Houyhnhnms, as well as all other animals, bore them; which although their evil disposition sufficiently deserved, could never have arrived at so high a degree, if they had been aborigines, or else they would have long since been rooted out. That the inhabitants taking a fancy to use the service of the yahoos, had very imprudently neglected to cultivate the breed of asses, which were a comely animal, easily kept, more tame and orderly, without any offensive smell, strong enough for labour, although they yield to the other in agility of body; and if their braying be no agreeable sound, it is far preferable to the horrible howlings of the yahoos.

Several others declared their sentiments to the same purpose, when my master proposed an expedient to the assembly, whereof he had indeed borrowed the hint from me. He approved of the tradition, mentioned by the 'honourable member' who spoke before, and affirmed, that the two yahoos said to be first seen among them had been driven thither over the sea; that coming to land, and being forsaken by their companions, they retired to the mountains, and degenerating by degrees, became in process of time much more savage than those of their own species in the country from whence these two originals came. The reason of his assertion was, that he had now in his possession a certain wonderful yahoo (meaning myself) which most of them had heard of, and many of them had seen. He then related to them how he first found me; that my body was all covered with an artificial composure of the skins and hairs of other animals: that I spoke in a language of my own, and had thoroughly learned theirs: that I had related to him the accidents which brought me thither: that when he saw me without my covering, I was an exact yahoo in every part, only of a whiter colour, less hairy, and with shorter claws. He added, how I had endeavoured to persuade him, that in my own and other countries the yahoos acted as the governing, rational animal, and held the Houyhnhnms in servitude: that he observed in me all the qualities of a yahoo, only a little more civilized by some tincture of reason, which however was in a degree as far inferior to the Houyhnhnm race as the yahoos of their country were to me: that, among other things, I mentioned a custom we had of castrating Houyhnhnms when they were young, in order to render them tame; that the operation was easy and safe; that it was no shame to learn wisdom from brutes, as industry is taught by the ant, and building by the swallow. (For so I translate the word *lyhannh*, although it be a much larger fowl.) That this invention might be practised upon the younger yahoos here, which, besides rendering them tractable and fitter for use, would in an age put an end to the whole species without destroying life. That in the mean time the Houyhnhnms should be exhorted to cultivate the breed of asses, which, as they are in all respects more valuable brutes, so they have this advantage, to be fit for service at five years old, which the others are not till twelve.

This was all my master thought fit to tell me at that time of what passed in the grand council. But he was pleased to conceal one particular, which related personally to myself, whereof I soon felt the unhappy effect, as the reader will know in its proper place, and from whence I date all the succeeding misfortunes of my life.

The Houyhnhnms have no letters, and consequently their knowledge is all traditional. But there happening few events of any moment among a people so well united, naturally disposed to every virtue, wholly governed by reason, and cut off from all commerce with other nations, the historical part is easily preserved without burthening their memories. I have already observed, that they are subject to no diseases, and therefore can have no need of physicians. However, they have excellent medicines composed of herbs, to cure accidental bruises and cuts in the pastern or frog of the foot by sharp stones, as well as other maims and hurts in the several parts of the body.

They calculate the year by the revolution of the sun and the moon, but use no subdivisions into weeks. They are well enough acquainted with the motions of those two luminaries, and understand the nature of eclipses; and this is the utmost progress of their astronomy.

In poetry they must be allowed to excel all other mortals; wherein the justness of their similes, and the minuteness, as well as exactness of their descriptions, are indeed inimitable. Their verses abound very much in both of these, and usually contain either some exalted notions of friendship and benevolence, or the praises of those who were victors in races and other bodily exercises. Their buildings, although very rude and simple, are not inconvenient, but well contrived to defend them from all injuries of cold and heat. They have a kind of tree, which at forty years old loosens in the root, and falls with the first storm; it grows very straight, and being pointed like stakes with a sharp stone (for the Houyhnhnms know not the use of iron), they stick them erect in the ground about ten inches asunder, and then weave in oat-straw, or sometimes wattles betwixt them. The roof is made after the same manner, and so are the doors.

The Houyhnhnms use the hollow part between the pastern and the hoof of their forefeet as we do our hands, and this with greater dexterity than I could at first imagine. I have seen a white mare of our family thread a needle (which I lent her on purpose) with that joint. They milk their cows, reap their oats, and do all the work which requires hands, in the same manner. They have a kind of hard flints, which, by grinding against other stones, they form into instruments, that serve instead of wedges, axes, and hammers. With tools made of these flints they likewise cut their hay, and reap their oats, which there groweth naturally in several fields: the yahoos draw home the sheaves in carriages, and the servants tread them in certain covered huts, to get out the grain, which is kept in stores. They make a rude kind of earthen and wooden vessels, and bake the former in the sun.

If they can avoid casualties, they die only of old age, and are buried in the obscurest places that can be found, their friends and relations expressing neither joy nor grief at their departure; nor does the dying person discover the least regret that he is leaving the world, any more than if he were upon returning home from a visit to one of his neighbours; I remember my master having once made an appointment with a friend and his family to come to his house upon some affair of importance; on the day fixed, the mistress and her two children came very late; she made two excuses, first for her husband, who, as she said, happened that very morning to *lhnuwnh*. The word is strongly expressive in their language, but not easily rendered into English; it signifies, 'to retire to his first mother'. Her excuse for not coming sooner was, that her husband dying late in the morning, she was a good while consulting her servants about a convenient place where his body should be laid; and I observed she behaved herself at our house as cheerfully as the rest: she died about three months after.

They live generally to seventy or seventy-five years, very seldom to fourscore: some weeks before their death they feel a gradual decay, but without pain. During this time they are much visited by their friends, because they cannot go abroad with their usual ease and satisfaction. However, about ten days before their death, which they seldom fail in computing, they return the visits that have been made them by those who are nearest in the neighbourhood, being carried in a convenient sledge drawn by yahoos, which vehicle they use, not only upon this occasion, but when they grow old, upon long journeys, or when they are lamed by any accident. And therefore when the dying Houy-hnhnms return those visits, they take a solemn leave of their friends, as if they were going to some remote part of the country, where they designed to pass the rest of their lives.

I know not whether it may be worth observing, that the Houy-hnhnms have no word in their language to express any thing that is evil, except what they borrow from the deformities or ill qualities of the yahoos. Thus they denote the folly of a servant, an omission of a child, a stone that cuts their feet, a continuance of foul or unseasonable weather, and the like, by adding to each the epithet of *yahoo*. For instance, *hhnm yahoo, whnaholm yahoo, ynlhnmawihlma yahoo*, and an ill-contrived house *ynholmhnmrohlnw yahoo*.

I could with great pleasure enlarge farther upon the manners and virtues of this excellent people; but intending in a short time to publish a volume by itself expressly upon that subject, I refer the reader thither. And in the mean time, proceed to relate my own sad catastrophe.

Chapter X.

The author's œconomy and happy life among the Houyhnhnms. His great improvement in virtue, by conversing with them. Their conversations. The author has notice given him by his master that he must depart from the country. He falls into a swoon for grief, but submits. He contrives and finishes a canoe, by the help of a fellow-servant, and puts to sea at a venture.

I had settled my little œconomy to my own heart's content. My master had ordered a room to be made for me after their manner, about six yards from the house, the sides and floors of which I plastered with clay, and covered with rush mats of my own contriving; I had beaten hemp, which there grows wild, and made of it a sort of ticking: this I filled with the feathers of several birds I had taken with springes made of yahoos' hairs, and were excellent food. I had worked two chairs with my knife, the sorrel nag helping me in the grosser and more laborious part. When my clothes were worn to rags, I made myself others with the skins of rabbits, and of a certain beautiful animal about the same size, called *nnuhnoh*, the skin of which is covered with a fine down. Of these I likewise made very tolerable stockings. I soled my shoes with wood which I cut from a tree, and fitted to the upper leather, and when this was worn out, I supplied it with the skins of yahoos dried in the sun. I often got honey out of hollow trees, which I mingled with water, or eat it with my bread. No man could more verify the truth of these two maxims, *That nature is very easily satisfied*; and *That necessity is the mother of invention*. I enjoyed perfect health of body and tranquillity of mind; I did not feel the treachery or inconstancy of a friend, nor the injuries of a secret or open enemy. I had no occasion of bribing, flattering or pimping to procure the favour of any great man or of his minion. I wanted no fence against fraud or oppression; here was neither physician to destroy my body, nor lawyer to ruin my fortune; no informer to watch my words and actions, or forge accusations against me for hire: here were no gibers, censurers, backbiters, pickpockets, highwaymen, housebreakers, attorneys, bawds, buffoons, gamesters, politicians, wits, splenetics, tedious talkers, controvertists, ravishers, murderers, robbers, virtuosos: no leaders or followers of party and faction: no encouragers to vice, by seducement or examples: no dungeon, axes, gibbets, whipping-posts, or pillories: no cheating shopkeepers or mechanics: no pride, vanity, or affectation: no fops, bullies, drunkards, strolling whores, or poxes: no ranting, lewd, expensive wives: no stupid, proud pedants: no importunate, overbearing, quarrelsome, noisy, roaring, empty, conceited, swearing companions: no scoundrels, raised from the dust upon the merit of their vices, or nobility thrown into it on account of their virtues: no lords, fiddlers, judges or dancing-masters.

I had the favour of being admitted to several Houyhnhnms, who came to visit or dine with my master; where his Honour graciously suffered me to wait in the room, and listen to their discourse. Both he and his company would often descend to ask me questions, and receive my answers. I had also sometimes the honour of attending my master in his visits to others. I never presumed to speak, except in answer to a question, and then I did it with inward regret, because it was a loss of so much time for improving myself: but I was infinitely delighted with the station of an humble auditor in such conversations, where nothing passed but what was useful, expressed in the fewest and most significant words: where (as I have already said) the greatest decency was observed, without the least degree of ceremony; where no person spoke without being pleased himself, and pleasing his companions; where there was no interruptions, tediousness, heat, or difference of sentiments. They have a notion, that when people are met together, a short silence doth much improve conversation: this I found to be true; for during those little intermissions of talk, new ideas would arise in their minds, which very much enlivened the discourse. Their subjects are generally on friendship and benevolence, or order and œconomy, sometimes upon the visible operations of nature, or ancient traditions, upon the bounds and limits of virtue, upon the unerring rules of reason, or upon some determinations to be taken at the next great assembly, and often upon the various excellencies of poetry. I may add without vanity, that my presence often gave them sufficient matter for discourse, because it afforded my master an occasion of letting his friends into the history of me and my country, upon which they were all pleased to descant in a manner not very advantageous to human kind; and for that reason I shall not repeat what they said: only I may be allowed to observe, that his Honour, to my great admiration, appeared to understand the nature of yahoos much better than myself. He went through all our vices and follies, and discovered many which I had never mentioned to him, by only supposing what qualities a yahoo of their country, with a small proportion of reason, might be capable of exerting; and concluded, with too much probability, how vile as well as miserable such a creature must be.

I freely confess, that all the little knowledge I have of any value was acquired by the lectures I received from my master, and from hearing the discourses of him and his friends; to which I should be prouder to listen, than to dictate to the greatest and wisest assembly in Europe. I admired the strength, comeliness, and speed of the inhabitants; and such a constellation of virtues in such amiable persons produced in me the highest veneration. At first, indeed, I did not feel that natural awe which the yahoos and all other animals bear towards them; but it grew upon me by degrees, much sooner than I imagined, and was mingled with a respectful love and gratitude, that they would condescend to distinguish me from the rest of my species.

When I thought of my family, my friends, my countrymen, or human race in general, I considered them as they really were, yahoos in shape and disposition, only a little more civilized, and

qualified with the gift of speech, but making no other use of
reason than to improve and multiply those vices whereof their
brethren in this country had only the share that nature allotted
them. When I happened to behold the reflection of my own form
in a lake or fountain, I turned away my face in horror and detestation of myself, and could better endure the sight of a common
yahoo, than of my own person. By conversing with the Houyhnhnms, and looking upon them with delight, I fell to imitate
their gait and gesture, which is now grown into a habit, and my
friends often tell me in a blunt way that I 'trot like a horse';
which, however, I take for a great compliment: neither shall I
disown, that in speaking I am apt to fall into the voice and manner of the Houyhnhnms, and hear myself ridiculed on that account without the least mortification.

In the midst of all this happiness, when I looked upon myself
to be fully settled for life, my master sent for me one morning a
little earlier than his usual hour. I observed by his countenance
that he was in some perplexity, and at a loss how to begin what
he had to speak. After a short silence, he told me, he did not
know how I would take what he was going to say; that in the
last general assembly, when the affair of the yahoos was entered
upon, the representatives had taken offence at his keeping a yahoo
(meaning myself) in his family more like a Houyhnhnm than a
brute animal. That he was known frequently to converse with
me, as if he could receive some advantage or pleasure in my
company: that such a practice was not agreeable to reason or
nature, or a thing ever heard of before among them. The assembly did therefore exhort him, either to employ me like the
rest of my species, or command me to swim back to the place
from whence I came. That the first of these expedients was
utterly rejected by all the Houyhnhnms who had ever seen me at
his house or their own: for they alleged, that because I had some
rudiments of reason, added to the natural pravity of those animals, it was to be feared, I might be able to seduce them into
the woody and mountainous parts of the country, and bring them
in troops by night to destroy the Houyhnhnms' cattle, as being
naturally of the ravenous kind, and averse from labour.

My master added, that he was daily pressed by the Houyhnhnms of the neighbourhood to have the assembly's exhortation
executed, which he could not put off much longer. He doubted
it would be impossible for me to swim to another country, and
therefore wished I would contrive some sort of vehicle resembling those I had described to him, that might carry me on the
sea, in which work I should have the assistance of his own

servants, as well as those of his neighbours. He concluded, that for his own part he could have been content to keep me in his service as long as I lived, because he found I had cured myself of some bad habits and dispositions, by endeavouring, as far as my inferior nature was capable, to imitate the Houyhnhnms.

I should here observe to the reader, that a decree of the general assembly in this country is expressed by the word *hnhloayn*, which signifies an *exhortation*, as near as I can render it: for they have no conception how a rational creature can be compelled, but only advised or exhorted, because no person can disobey reason, without giving up his claim to be a rational creature.

I was struck with the utmost grief and despair at my master's discourse, and being unable to support the agonies I was under, I fell into a swoon at his feet; when I came to myself he told me that he concluded I had been dead. (For these people are subject to no such imbecilities of nature.) I answered, in a faint voice, that death would have been too great an happiness; that although I could not blame the assembly's exhortation, or the urgency of his friends, yet, in my weak and corrupt judgment, I thought it might consist with reason to have been less rigorous. That I could not swim a league, and probably the nearest land to theirs might be distant above an hundred; that many materials, necessary for making a small vessel to carry me off, were wholly wanting in this country, which, however, I would attempt in obedience and gratitude to his Honour, although I concluded the thing to be impossible, and therefore looked on my self as already devoted to destruction. That the certain prospect of an unnatural death was the least of my evils: for, supposing I should escape with life by some strange adventure, how could I think with temper of passing my days among yahoos, and relapsing into my old corruptions, for want of examples to lead and keep me within the paths of virtue? That I knew too well upon what solid reasons all the determinations of the wise Houyhnhnms were founded, not to be shaken by arguments of mine, a miserable yahoo; and therefore, after presenting him with my humble thanks for the offer of his servants' assistance in making a vessel, and desiring a reasonable time for so difficult a work, I told him I would endeavour to preserve a wretched being; and, if ever I returned to England, was not without hopes of being useful to my own species, by celebrating the praises of the renowned Houyhnhnms, and proposing their virtues to the imitation of mankind.

My master in a few words made me a very gracious reply, allowed me the space of two months to finish my boat; and ordered the sorrel nag, my fellow-servant (for so at this distance I may presume to call him) to follow my instructions, because I told my master, that his help would be sufficient, and I knew he had a tenderness for me.

In his company my first business was to go to that part of the coast where my rebellious crew had ordered me to be set on shore. I got upon a height, and looking on every side into the sea, fancied I saw a small island, towards the northeast: I took out my pocket-glass, and could then clearly distinguish it about five leagues off, as I computed; but it appeared to the sorrel nag to be only a blue cloud: for as he had no conception of any country beside his own, so he could not be as expert in distinguishing remote objects at sea as we who so much converse in that element.

After I had discovered this island, I considered no farther; but resolved it should, if possible, be the first place of my banishment, leaving the consequence to fortune.

I returned home, and consulting with the sorrel nag, we went into a copse at some distance, where I with my knife, and he with a sharp flint fastened very artificially after their manner, to a wooden handle, cut down several oak wattles about the thickness of a walking-staff, and some larger pieces. But I shall not trouble the reader with a particular description of my own mechanics; let it suffice to say that in six weeks' time, with the help of the sorrel nag, who performed the parts that required most labour, I finished a sort of Indian canoe, but much larger, covering it with the skins of yahoos well stitched together, with hempen threads of my own making. My sail was likewise composed of the skins of the same animal; but I made use of the youngest I could get, the older being too tough and thick, and I likewise provided myself with four paddles. I laid in a stock of boiled flesh, of rabbits and fowls, and took with me two vessels, one filled with milk, and the other with water.

I tried my canoe in a large pond near my master's house, and then corrected in it what was amiss; stopping all the chinks with yahoos' tallow, till I found it staunch, and able to bear me and my freight. And when it was as complete as I could possibly make it, I had it drawn on a carriage very gently by yahoos to the seaside, under the conduct of the sorrel nag and another servant.

When all was ready, and the day came for my departure, I took leave of my master and lady, and the whole family, my eyes flowing with tears, and my heart quite sunk with grief. But his Honour, out of curiosity, and perhaps (if I may speak it without vanity) partly out of kindness, was determined to see me in my canoe, and got several of his neighbouring friends to accompany him. I was forced to wait above an hour for the tide, and then observing the wind very fortunately bearing towards the island, to which I intended to steer my course, I took a second leave of my master: but as I was going to prostrate myself to kiss his hoof, he did me the honour to raise it gently to my mouth. I am not ignorant how much I have been censured for mentioning this last particular. Detractors are pleased to think it improbable, that so illustrious a person should descend to give so great a mark of distinction to a creature so inferior as I. Neither have I forgot how apt some travellers are to boast of extraordinary favours they have received. But if these censurers were better acquainted with the noble and courteous disposition of the Houyhnhnms, they would soon change their opinion.

I paid my respects to the rest of the Houyhnhnms in his Honour's company; then getting into my canoe, I pushed off from shore.

Chapter XI.

The author's dangerous voyage. He arrives at New Holland, hoping to settle there. Is wounded with an arrow by one of the natives. Is seized and carried by force into a Portuguese ship. The great civilities of the captain. The author arrives at England.

I began this desperate voyage on February 15, 1714–5, at 9 o'clock in the morning. The wind was very favourable; however, I made use at first only of my paddles, but considering I should soon be weary, and that the wind might probably chop about, I ventured to set up my little sail; and thus with the help of the tide I went at the rate of a league and a half an hour, as near as I could guess. My master and his friends continued on the shore till I was almost out of sight; and I often heard the sorrel nag (who always loved me) crying out, *Hnuy illa nyha maiah yahoo*, Take care of thyself, gentle yahoo.

My design was, if possible, to discover some small island uninhabited, yet sufficient by my labour to furnish me with the necessaries of life, which I would have thought a greater happiness than to be first minister in the politest court of Europe; so horrible was the idea I conceived of returning to live in the society and under the government of yahoos. For in such a solitude as I desired, I could at least enjoy my own thoughts, and reflect with delight on the virtues of those inimitable Houyhnhnms, without any opportunity of degenerating into the vices and corruptions of my own species.

The reader may remember what I related when my crew conspired aginst me, and confined me to my cabin. How I continued there several weeks, without knowing what course we took, and when I was put ashore in the long-boat, how the sailors told me with oaths, whether true or false, that they knew not in what part of the world we were. However, I did then believe us to be about ten degrees southward of the Cape of Good Hope, or about 45 degrees southern latitude, as I gathered from some general words I overheard among them, being I supposed to the southeast in their intended voyage to Madagascar. And although this were but little better than conjecture, yet I resolved to steer my course eastward, hoping to reach the southwest coast of New Holland, and perhaps some such island as I desired, lying westward of it. The wind was full west, and by six in the evening I computed I had gone eastward at least eighteen leagues, when I spied a very small island about half a league off, which I soon reached. It was nothing but a rock, with one creek, naturally arched by the force of tempests. Here I put in my canoe, and climbing a part of the rock, I could plainly discover land to the east, extending from south to north. I lay all night in my canoe, and repeating my voyage early in the morning, I arrived in seven hours to the southeast point of New Holland. This confirmed me in the opinion I have long entertained, that the maps and charts place this country at least three degrees more to the east than it really is; which thought I communicated many years ago to my worthy friend Mr. Herman Moll, and gave him my reasons for it, although he hath rather chosen to follow other authors.

I saw no inhabitants in the place where I landed, and being unarmed, I was afraid of venturing far into the country. I found some shellfish on the shore, and eat them raw, not daring to kindle a fire, for fear of being discovered by the natives. I continued three days feeding on oysters and limpets, to save my own provisions, and I fortunately found a brook of excellent water, which gave me great relief.

On the fourth day, venturing out early a little too far, I saw twenty or thirty natives upon a height, not above five hundred yards from me. They were stark naked, men, women, and children, round a fire, as I could discover by the smoke. One of them spied me, and gave notice to the rest; five of them advanced towards me, leaving the women and children at the fire. I made what haste I could to the shore, and getting into my canoe, shoved off: the savages observing me retreat, ran after me; and before I could get far enough into the sea, discharged an arrow, which wounded me deeply on the inside of my left knee

(I shall carry the mark to my grave). I apprehended the arrow might be poisoned, and paddling out of the reach of their darts (being a calm day), I made a shift to suck the wound, and dress it as well as I could.

I was at a loss what to do, for I durst not return to the same landing-place, but stood to the north, and was forced to paddle; for the wind, although very gentle, was against me, blowing northwest. As I was looking about for a secure landing-place, I saw a sail to the north-northeast, which appearing every minute more visible, I was in some doubt, whether I should wait for them or no; but at last my detestation of the yahoo race prevailed, and turning my canoe, I sailed and paddled together to the south, and got into the same creek from whence I set out in the morning, choosing rather to trust myself among these barbarians, than live with European yahoos. I drew up my canoe as close as I could to the shore, and hid myself behind a stone by the little brook, which, as I have already said, was excellent water.

The ship came within a half a league of this creek, and sent out her long-boat with vessels to take in fresh water (for the place it seems was very well known) but I did not observe it until the boat was almost on shore, and it was too late to seek another hiding-place. The seamen at their landing observed my canoe, and rummaging it all over, easily conjectured that the owner could not be far off. Four of them well armed searched every cranny and lurking-hole, till at last they found me flat on my face behind the stone. They gazed a while in admiration at my strange uncouth dress, my coat made of skins, my wooden-soled shoes, and my furred stockings; from whence, however, they concluded I was not a native of the place, who all go naked. One of the seamen in Portuguese bid me rise, and asked who I was. I understood that language very well, and getting upon my feet, said, I was a poor yahoo, banished from the Houyhnhnms, and desired they would please to let me depart. They admired to hear me answer them in their own tongue, and saw by my complexion I must be an European; but were at loss to know what I meant by yahoos and Houyhnhnms, and at the same time fell a laughing at my strange tone in speaking, which resembled the neighing of a horse. I trembled all the while betwixt fear and hatred: I again desired leave to depart, and was gently moving to my canoe; but they laid hold on me, desiring to know, what country I was of, whence I came, with many other questions. I told them I was born in England, from whence I came about five years ago, and then their country and ours were at peace. I therefore hoped they would not treat me as an enemy, since I meant them no harm, but was a poor yahoo, seeking some desolate place where to pass the remainder of his unfortunate life.

When they began to talk, I thought I never heard or saw any thing so unnatural; for it appeared to me as monstrous as if a dog or a cow should speak in England, or a yahoo in Houyhnhnm-land. The honest Portuguese were equally amazed at my strange dress, and the odd manner of delivering my words, which however they understood very well. They spoke to me with great humanity, and said they were sure their captain would carry me *gratis* to Lisbon, from whence I might return to my own country; that two of the seamen would go back to the ship, inform the captain of what they had seen, and receive his orders; in the mean time, unless I would give my solemn oath not to fly, they would secure me by force. I thought it best to comply with their proposal. They were very curious to know my story, but I gave them very little satisfaction; and they all conjectured that my misfortunes had impaired my reason. In two hours the boat, which went loaden with vessels of water, returned with the captain's commands to fetch me on board. I fell on my knees to preserve my liberty; but all was in vain, and the men having tied me with cords, heaved me into the boat, from whence I was taken into the ship, and from thence into the captain's cabin.

His name was Pedro de Mendez; he was a very courteous and generous person; he entreated me to give some account of my self, and desired to know what I would eat or drink; said, I should be used as well as himself, and spoke so many obliging things, that I wondered to find such civilities from a yahoo. However, I remained silent and sullen; I was ready to faint at the very smell of him and his men. At last I desired something to eat out of my own canoe; but he ordered me a chicken and some ex-cellent wine, and then directed that I should be put to bed in a very clean cabin. I would not undress myself, but lay on the bed-clothes, and in half an hour stole out, when I thought the crew was at dinner, and getting to the side of the ship was going to leap into the sea, and swim for my life, rather than continue among yahoos. But one of the seamen prevented me, and hav-ing informed the captain, I was chained to my cabin.

After dinner Don Pedro came to me, and desired to know my reason for so desperate an attempt: assured me he only meant to do me all the service he was able, and spoke so very movingly, that at last I descended to treat him like an animal which had some little portion of reason. I gave him a very short relation of my voyage, of the conspiracy against me by my own men, of the country where they set me on shore, and of my three years'

residence there. All which he looked upon as if it were a dream
or a vision; whereat I took great offence; for I had quite forgot
the faculty of lying, so peculiar to yahoos in all countries where
they preside, and, consequently, the disposition of suspecting
truth in others of their own species. I asked him, whether it
were the custom of his country to *say the thing that was not*. I
assured him I had almost forgot what he meant by falsehood, and
if I had lived a thousand years in Houyhnhnmland, I should
never have heard a lie from the meanest servant; that I was altogether indifferent whether he believed me or no; but however,
in return for his favours, I would give so much allowance to the
corruption of his nature as to answer any objection he would
please to make, and he might easily discover the truth.

The captain, a wise man, after many endeavours to catch me
tripping in some part of my story, at last began to have a better
opinion of my veracity. But he added, that since I professed so
inviolable an attachment to truth, I must give him my word of
honour to bear him company in this voyage without attempting
anything against my life, or else he would continue me a prisoner
till we arrived in Lisbon. I gave him the promise he required;
but at the same time protested that I would suffer the greatest
hardships rather than return to live among yahoos.

Our voyage passed without any considerable accident. In
gratitude to the captain I sometimes sat with him at his earnest
request, and strove to conceal my antipathy to human kind, although it often broke out, which he suffered to pass without observation. But the greatest part of the day, I confined myself to
my cabin, to avoid seeing any of the crew. The captain had often
entreated me to strip myself of my savage dress, and offered to
lend me the best suit of clothes he had. This I would not be
prevailed on to accept, abhorring to cover myself with anything
that had been on the back of a yahoo. I only desired he would
lend me two clean shirts, which having been washed since he
wore them, I believed would not so much defile me. These I
changed every second day, and washed them myself.

We arrived at Lisbon, Nov. 5, 1715. At our landing the captain forced me to cover myself with his cloak, to prevent the rabble from crowding about me. I was conveyed to his own house,
and, at my earnest request, he led me up to the highest room
backwards. I conjured him to conceal from all persons what I
had told him of the Houyhnhnms, because the least hint of such
a story would not only draw numbers of people to see me, but
probably put me in danger of being imprisoned, or burnt by the
Inquisition. The captain persuaded me to accept a suit of

clothes newly made, but I would not suffer the tailor to take my measure; however, Don Pedro being almost of my size, they fitted me well enough. He accoutred me with other necessaries all new, which I aired for twenty-four hours before I would use them.

The captain had no wife, nor above three servants, none of which were suffered to attend at meals, and his whole deportment was so obliging, added to very good *human* understanding, that I really began to tolerate his company. He gained so far upon me, that I ventured to look out of the back window. By degrees I was brought into another room, from whence I peeped into the street, but drew my head back in a fright. In a week's time he seduced me down to the door. I found my terror gradually lessened, but my hatred and contempt seemed to increase. I was at last bold enough to walk the street in his company, but kept my nose well stopped with rue, or sometimes with tobacco.

In ten days Don Pedro, to whom I had given some account of my domestic affairs, put it upon me as a point of honour and conscience, that I ought to return to my native country, and live at home with my wife and children. He told me, there was an English ship in the port just ready to sail, and he would furnish me with all things necessary. It would be tedious to repeat his arguments, and my contradictions. He said it was altogether impossible to find such a solitary island as I had desired to live in; but I might command in my own house, and pass my time in a manner as recluse as I pleased.

I complied at last, finding I could not do better. I left Lisbon the 24th day of November, in an English merchantman, but who was the master I never inquired. Don Pedro accompanied me to the ship, and lent me twenty pounds. He took kind leave of me, and embraced me at parting, which I bore as well as I could. During this last voyage I had no commerce with the master or any of his men, but pretending I was sick kept close in my cabin. On the fifth of December, 1715, we cast anchor in the Downs about nine in the morning, and at three in the afternoon I got safe to my house at Redriff.

My wife and family received me with great surprise and joy, because they concluded me certainly dead; but I must freely confess the sight of them filled me only with hatred, disgust and contempt, and the more by reflecting on the near alliance I had to them. For although, since my unfortunate exile from the Houyhnhnm country, I had compelled myself to tolerate the sight of yahoos, and to converse with Don Pedro de Mendez, yet my memory and imaginations were perpetually filled with the virtues and ideas of those exalted Houyhnhnms. And when I began to consider, that by copulating with one of the yahoo species I had become a parent of more, it struck me with the utmost shame, confusion, and horror.

As soon as I entered the house, my wife took me in her arms, and kissed me, at which, having not been used to the touch of that odious animal for so many years, I fell in a swoon for almost an hour. At the time I am writing it is five years since my last return to England: during the first year I could not endure my wife or children in my presence, the very smell of them was intolerable, much less could I suffer them to eat in the same room. To this hour they dare not presume to touch my bread, or drink out of the same cup, neither was I ever able to let one of them take me by the hand. The first money I laid out was to buy two young stone-horses, which I keep in a good stable, and next to them the groom is my greatest favourite; for I feel my spirits revived by the smell he contracts in the stable. My horses understand me tolerably well; I converse with them at least four hours every day. They are strangers to bridle or saddle; they live in great amity with me, and friendship to each other.

Chapter XII.

The author's veracity. His design in publishing this work. His censure of those travellers who swerve from the truth. The author clears himself from any sinister ends in writing. An objection answered. The method of planting colonies. His native country commended. The right of the crown to those countries described by the author is justified. The difficulty of conquering them. The author takes his last leave of the reader, proposeth his manner of living for the future, gives good advice, and concludes.

Thus, gentle reader, I have given thee a faithful history of my travels for sixteen years, and above seven months, wherein I have not been so studious of ornament as of truth. I could perhaps like others have astonished thee with strange improbable tales; but I rather chose to relate plain matter of fact in the simplest manner and style, because my principal design was to inform, and not to amuse thee.

It is easy for us who travel into remote countries, which are seldom visited by Englishmen or other Europeans, to form descriptions of wonderful animals both at sea and land. Whereas a traveller's chief aim should be to make men wiser and better,

and to improve their minds by the bad as well as good example
of what they deliver concerning foreign places.

I could heartily wish a law were enacted, that every traveller,
before he were permitted to publish his voyages, should be
obliged to make oath before the Lord High Chancellor that all he
intended to print was absolutely true to the best of his knowledge; for then the world would no longer be deceived as it
usually is, while some writers, to make their works pass the better
upon the public, impose the grossest falsities on the unwary
reader. I have perused several books of travels with great delight
in my younger days; but having since gone over most parts of the
globe, and been able to contradict many fabulous accounts from
my own observation, it hath given me a great disgust against this
part of reading, and some indignation to see the credulity of
mankind so impudently abused. Therefore since my acquaintance were pleased to think my poor endeavours might not be
unacceptable to my country, I imposed on myself as a maxim,
never to be swerved from, that I would *strictly adhere to truth*;
neither indeed can I be ever under the least temptation to vary
from it, while I retain in my mind the lectures and example of my
noble master, and the other illustrious Houyhnhnms, of whom I
had so long the honour to be an humble hearer.

—— *Nec si miserum Fortuna Sinonem*
Finxit, vanum etiam mendacemque improba finget.

I know very well how little reputation is to be got by writings
which require neither genius nor learning, nor indeed any other
talent, except a good memory or an exact journal. I know likewise, that writers of travels, like dictionary-makers, are sunk into
oblivion by the weight and bulk of those who come after, and
therefore lie uppermost. And it is highly probable, that such
travellers who shall hereafter visit the countries described in this
work of mine, may, by detecting my errors (if there be any),
and adding many new discoveries of their own, jostle me out of
vogue, and stand in my place, making the world forget that ever I
was an author. This indeed would be too great a mortification if
I wrote for fame: but, as my sole intention was the PUBLIC GOOD,
I cannot be altogether disappointed. For who can read of the
virtues I have mentioned in the glorious Houyhnhnms, without
being ashamed of his own vices, when he considers himself as the
reasoning, governing animal of his country? I shall say nothing
of those remote nations where yahoos preside, amongst which the
least corrupted are the Brobdingnagians, whose wise maxims in

morality and government it would be our happiness to observe. But I forbear descanting further, and rather leave the judicious reader to his own remarks and applications.

I am not a little pleased that this work of mine can possibly meet with no censurers: for what objections can be made against a writer who relates only plain facts that happened in such distant countries, where we have not the least interest with respect either to trade or negotiations? I have carefully avoided every fault with which common writers of travels are often too justly charged. Besides, I meddle not the least with any *party*, but write without passion, prejudice, or ill-will against any man or number of men whatsoever. I write for the noblest end, to inform and instruct mankind, over whom I may, without breach of modesty, pretend to some superiority from the advantages I received by conversing so long among the most accomplished Houyhnhnms. I write without any view towards profit or praise. I never suffer a word to pass that may look like reflection, or possibly give the least offence even to those who are most ready to take it. So that I hope I may with justice pronounce myself an author perfectly blameless, against whom the tribe of answerers, considerers, observers, reflecters, detecters, remarkers, will never be able to find matter for exercising their talents.

I confess, it was whispered to me that I was bound in duty, as a subject of England, to have given in a memorial to a secretary of state, at my first coming over; because, whatever lands are discovered by a subject belong to the crown. But I doubt whether our conquests in the countries I treat of would be as easy as those of Ferdinando Cortez over the naked Americans. The Lilliputians, I think, are hardly worth the charge of a fleet and army to reduce them, and I question whether it might be prudent or safe to attempt the Brobdingnagians. Or whether an English army would be much at their ease with the Flying Island over their heads. The Houyhnhnms, indeed, appear not to be so well prepared for war, a science to which they are perfect strangers, and especially against missive weapons. However, supposing myself to be a minister of state, I could never give my advice for invading them. Their prudence, unanimity, unacquaintedness with fear, and their love of their country would amply supply all defects in the military art. Imagine twenty thousand of them breaking into the midst of an European army, confounding the ranks, overturning the carriages, battering the warriors' faces into mummy, by terrible yerks from their hinder hoofs. For they would well deserve the character given to Augustus; *Recalcitrat undique tutus*. But instead of proposals

A VOYAGE TO THE HOUYHNHNMS 237

for conquering that magnanimous nation, I rather wish they were in a capacity or disposition to send a sufficient number of their inhabitants for civilizing Europe, by teaching us the first principles of honour, justice, truth, temperance, public spirit, fortitude, chastity, friendship, benevolence, and fidelity. The names of all which virtues are still retained among us in most languages, and are to be met with in modern as well as ancient authors; which I am able to assert from my own small reading.

But I had another reason which made me less forward to enlarge his Majesty's dominions by my discoveries. To say the truth, I had conceived a few scruples with relation to the distributive justice of princes upon those occasions. For instance, a crew of pirates are driven by a storm they know not whither, at length a boy discovers land from the topmast, they go on shore to rob and plunder, they see an harmless people, are entertained with kindness, they give the country a new name, they take formal possession of it for the king, they set up a rotten plank or a stone for a memorial, they murder two or three dozen of the natives, bring away a couple more by force for a sample, return home, and get their pardon. Here commences a new dominion acquired with a title by *divine right*. Ships are sent with the first opportunity, the natives driven out or destroyed, their princes tortured to discover their gold, a free license given to all acts of inhumanity and lust, the earth reeking with the blood of its inhabitants: and this execrable crew of butchers employed in so pious an expedition, is a modern colony sent to convert and civilize an idolatrous and barbarous people.

But this description, I confess, doth by no means affect the British nation, who may be an example to the whole world for their wisdom, care, and justice in planting colonies; their liberal endowments for the advancement of religion and learning; their choice of devout and able pastors to propagate Christianity; their caution in stocking their provinces with people of sober lives and conversations from this the mother kingdom; their strict regard to the distribution of justice, in supplying the civil administration through all their colonies with officers of the greatest abilities, utter strangers to corruption; and to crown all, by sending the most vigilant and virtuous governors, who have no other views than the happiness of the people over whom they preside, and the honour of the king their master.

But as those countries which I have described do not appear to have any desire of being conquered, and enslaved, murdered or driven out by colonies, nor abound either in gold, silver, sugar or tobacco; I did humbly conceive they were by no means proper objects of our zeal, our valour, or our interest. However, if those whom it may concern think fit to be of another opinion, I am ready to depose, when I shall be lawfully called, that no European did ever visit these countries before me. I mean, if the inhabitants ought to be believed; unless a dispute may arise about the two yahoos, said to have been seen many ages ago on a mountain in Houyhnhnmland, from whence the opinion is, that the race of those brutes hath descended; and these, for any thing I know, may have been English, which indeed I was apt to suspect from the lineaments of their posterity's countenances, although very much defaced. But, how far that will go to make out a title, I leave to the learned in colony-law.

But as to the formality of taking possession in my sovereign's name, it never came once into my thoughts; and if it had, yet as my affairs then stood, I should perhaps, in point of prudence and self-preservation, have put it off to a better opportunity.

Having thus answered the *only* objection than can ever be raised against me as a traveller, I here take a final leave of my courteous readers, and return to enjoy my own speculations in my little garden at Redriff, to apply those excellent lessons of virtue which I learned among the Houyhnhnms, to instruct the yahoos of my own family as far as I shall find them docible animals, to behold my figure often in a glass, and thus if possible habituate myself by time to tolerate the sight of a human creature; to lament the brutality of Houyhnhnms in my own country, but always treat their persons with respect, for the sake of my noble master, his family, his friends, and the whole Houy-hnhnm race, whom these of ours have the honour to resemble in all their lineaments, however their intellectuals came to degenerate.

I began last week to permit my wife to sit at dinner with me, at the farthest end of a long table, and to answer (but with the utmost brevity) the few questions I ask her. Yet the smell of a yahoo continuing very offensive, I always keep my nose well stopped with rue, lavender, or tobacco leaves. And although it be hard for a man late in life to remove old habits, I am not altogether out of hopes in some time to suffer a neighbour yahoo in my company without the apprehensions I am yet under of his teeth or his claws.

My reconcilement to the yahoo-kind in general might not be so difficult if they would be content with those vices and follies only which nature hath entitled them to. I am not in the least provoked at the sight of a lawyer, a pickpocket, a colonel, a fool, a lord, a gamester, a politician, a whoremonger, a physician, an evidence, a suborner, an attorney, a traitor, or the like; this is all according to the due course of things: but when I behold a lump of deformity and diseases both in body and mind, smitten with pride, it immediately breaks all the measures of my patience; neither shall I be ever able to comprehend how such an animal and such a vice could tally together. The wise and virtuous Houyhnhnms, who abound in all excellencies that can adorn a rational creature, have no name for this vice in their language, which hath no terms to express any thing that is evil, except those whereby they describe the detestable qualities of their yahoos, among which they were not able to distinguish this of pride, for want of thoroughly understanding human nature, as it showeth itself in other countries, where that animal presides. But I, who had more experience, could plainly observe some rudiments of it among the wild yahoos.

But the Houyhnhnms, who live under the government of reason, are no more proud of the good qualities they possess, than I should be for not wanting a leg or an arm, which no man in his wits would boast of, although he must be miserable without them. I dwell the longer upon this subject from the desire I have to make the society of an English yahoo by any means not insupportable, and therefore I here entreat those who have any tincture of this absurd vice, that they will not presume to appear in my sight.

FINIS

A TALE OF A TUB.

Written for the Univerſal Improvement of Mankind.

Diu multumque deſideratum.

To which is added,

An ACCOUNT of a BATTEL

BETWEEN THE

Antient and Modern BOOKS
in St. *James's* Library.

*Baſima eacabaſa eanaa irrauriſta, diarba da caeotaba
fobor camelanthi. Iren. Lib. 1. C. 18.*

*———— Juvatque novos decerpere flores,
Inſignemque meo capiti petere inde coronam,
Unde prius nulli velarunt tempora Muſæ.* Lucret.

The Fifth EDITION: With the Author's Apology and Explanatory Notes.
By *W. W--tt--n*, B. D. and others.

LONDON : Printed for *John Nutt*, near
Stationers-Hall. MDCCX.

Title-page of the Fifth Edition, 1710

Treatises wrote by the same Author, most of them mentioned in the following Discourses; which will be speedily published.

A Character of the present Set of Wits in this Island.

A panegyrical Essay upon the Number THREE.

A Dissertation upon the principal Productions of Grub Street.

Lectures upon a Dissection of Human Nature.

A Panegyric upon the World.

An analytical Discourse upon Zeal, histori-theo-physi-logically considered.

A general History of Ears.

A modest Defence of the Proceedings of the Rabble in all Ages.

A Description of the Kingdom of Absurdities.

A Voyage into England, by a Person of Quality in Terra Australis incognita, translated from the Original.

A critical Essay upon the Art of Canting, philosophically, physically, and musically considered.

AN APOLOGY

For the, &c.*

If good and ill nature equally operated upon Mankind I might have saved my self the trouble of this Apology; for it is manifest by the reception the following discourse hath met with, that those who approve it, are a great majority among the men of taste; yet there have been two or three treatises written expressly against it, besides many others that have flirted at it occasionally, without one syllable having been ever published in its defence or even quotation to its advantage, that I can remember, except by the polite author of a late discourse between a Deist and a Socinian.

Therefore, since the book seems calculated to live at least as long as our language and our taste admit no great alterations, I am content to convey some Apology along with it.

The greatest part of that book was finished above thirteen years since, 1696, which is eight years before it was published. The author was then young, his invention at the height, and his reading fresh in his head. By the assistance of some thinking, and much conversation, he had endeavoured to strip himself of as many real prejudices as he could; I say real ones, because, under the notion of prejudices, he knew to what dangerous heights some men have proceeded. Thus prepared, he thought the numerous and gross corruptions in Religion and Learning might furnish matter for a satire, that would be useful and diverting. He resolved to proceed in a manner that should be altogether new, the world having been already too long nauseated with endless repetitions upon every subject. The abuses in Religion, he proposed to set forth in the Allegory of the Coats and the three Brothers, which was to make up the body of the discourse. Those in learning he chose to introduce by way of digressions. He was then a young gentleman much in the world, and wrote to the taste of those who were like himself; therefore, in order to allure them, he gave a liberty to his pen, which might not suit with maturer years, or graver characters, and which he could have easily corrected with a very few blots, had he been master of his papers, for a year or two before their publication.

* For an explanation of this *Apology* and of the notes at the bottom of the following pages, see p. 519.

Not that he would have governed his judgment by the ill-placed cavils of the sour, the envious, the stupid, and the tasteless, which he mentions with disdain. He acknowledges there are several youthful sallies, which, from the grave and the wise, may deserve a rebuke. But he desires to be answerable no farther than he is guilty, and that his faults may not be multiplied by the ignorant, the unnatural, and uncharitable applications of those who have neither candour to suppose good meanings, nor palate to distinguish true ones. After which, he will forfeit his life, if any one opinion can be fairly deduced from that book, which is contrary to Religion or Morality.

Why should any clergyman of our church be angry to see the follies of fanaticism and superstition exposed, though in the most ridiculous manner; since that is perhaps the most probable way to cure them, or at least hinder them from farther spreading? Besides, though it was not intended for their perusal, it rallies nothing but what they preach against. It contains nothing to provoke them by the least scurrility upon their persons or their functions. It celebrates the Church of England as the most perfect of all others in discipline and doctrine, it advances no opinion they reject, nor condemns any they receive. If the clergy's resentments lay upon their hands, in my humble opinion they might have found more proper objects to employ them on: *nondum tibi defuit hostis*; I mean those heavy, illiterate scribblers, prostitute in their reputations, vicious in their lives, and ruined in their fortunes, who, to the shame of good sense as well as piety, are greedily read, merely upon the strength of bold, false, impious assertions, mixed with unmannerly reflections upon the priesthood, and openly intended against all Religion; in short, full of such principles as are kindly received, because they are levelled to remove those terrors that Religion tells men will be the consequence of immoral lives. Nothing like which is to be met with in this discourse, though some of them are pleased so freely to censure it. And I wish there were no other instance of what I have too frequently observed, that many of that reverend body are not always very nice in distinguishing between their enemies and their friends.

Had the author's intentions met with a more candid interpretation from some whom out of respect he forbears to name, he might have been encouraged to an examination of books written by some of those authors above described, whose errors, ignorance, dullness, and villainy, he thinks he could have detected and exposed in such a manner, that the persons who are most conceived to be infected by them, would soon lay them aside and be ashamed: But he has now given over those thoughts, since the weightiest men in the weightiest stations are pleased to think it a more dangerous point to laugh at those corruptions in Religion, which they themselves must disapprove, than to endeavour pulling up those very foundations, wherein all Christians have agreed.

He thinks it no fair proceeding, that any person should offer determinately to fix a name upon the author of this discourse, who hath all along concealed himself from most of his nearest friends: Yet several have gone a farther step, and pronounced another book [1] to have been the work of the same hand with this, which the author directly affirms to be a thorough mistake; he having yet never so much as read that discourse: a plain instance how little truth there often is in general surmises, or in conjectures drawn from a similitude of style, or way of thinking.

Had the author writ a book to expose the abuses in Law, or in Physic, he believes the learned professors in either faculty would have been so far from resenting it, as to have given him thanks for his pains, especially if he had made an honourable reservation for the true practice of either science. But Religion, they tell us, ought not to be ridiculed; and they tell us truth, yet surely the corruptions in it may; for we are taught by the tritest maxim in the world, that Religion being the best of things, its corruptions are likely to be the worst.

There is one thing which the judicious reader cannot but have observed, that some of those passages in this discourse, which appear most liable to objection, are what they call parodies, where the author personates the style and manner of other writers, whom he has a mind to expose. I shall produce one instance, it is in the two hundred and seventy-ninth page. Dryden, L'Estrange, and some others I shall not name, are here levelled at, who, having spent their lives in faction, and apostasies, and all manner of vice, pretended to be sufferers for Loyalty and Religion. So Dryden tells us in one of his prefaces of his merits and sufferings, thanks God that he *possesses his soul in patience;*[2] in other places he talks at the same rate; and L'Estrange often uses the like style; and I believe the reader may find more persons to give that passage an application: But this is enough to direct those who may have overlooked the author's intention.

There are three or four other passages which prejudiced or

---

[1] *Letter of Enthusiasm* [published in 1708 by Lord Shaftesbury].

[2] In the *Tale of a Tub*, Dryden is repeatedly mentioned with great disrespect, not only as a translator and original author, but a mean-spirited sycophant of the great. The passage here alluded to occurs in the *Essay on Satire*, which Dryden prefixed to his version of Juvenal. Scott.

ignorant readers have drawn by great force to hint at ill meanings, as if they glanced at some tenets in religion. In answer to all which, the author solemnly protests, he is entirely innocent; and never had it once in his thoughts, that anything he said, would in the least be capable of such interpretations, which he will engage to deduce full as fairly from the most innocent book in the world. And it will be obvious to every reader, that this was not any part of his scheme or design, the abuses he notes being such as all Church of England men agree in; nor was it proper for his subject to meddle with other points, than such as have been perpetually controverted since the Reformation.

To instance only in that passage about the three wooden machines mentioned in the Introduction: in the original manuscript there was a description of a fourth, which those who had the papers in their power, blotted out, as having something in it of satire, that I suppose they thought was too particular; and therefore they were forced to change it to the number Three, from whence some have endeavoured to squeeze out a dangerous meaning, that was never thought on. And, indeed, the conceit was half spoiled by changing the numbers; that of Four being much more cabalistic, and, therefore, better exposing the pretended virtue of Numbers, a superstition there intended to be ridiculed.

Another thing to be observed is, that there generally runs an irony through the thread of the whole book, which the men of taste will observe and distinguish, and which will render some objections that have been made, very weak and insignificant.

This Apology being chiefly intended for the satisfaction of future readers, it may be thought unnecessary to take any notice of such treatises as have been writ against this ensuing discourse, which are already sunk into waste paper and oblivion, after the usual fate of common answerers to books, which are allowed to have any merit: they are indeed like annuals, that grow about a young tree, and seem to vie with it for a summer but fall and die with the leaves in autumn, and are never heard of any more. When Dr. Eachard writ his book about the Contempt of the Clergy, numbers of those answerers immediately started up, whose memory, if he had not kept alive by his replies, it would now be utterly unknown that he were ever answered at all. There is indeed an exception, when any great genius thinks it worth his while to expose a foolish piece; so we still read Marvell's Answer to Parker with pleasure, though the book it answers be sunk long ago: so the Earl of Orrery's *Remarks* will be read with delight, when the *Dissertation* he exposes will neither be sought nor found: [3] but these are no enterprises for common hands, nor to be hoped for above once or twice in an age. Men would be more cautious of losing their time in such an undertaking, if they did but consider, that to answer a book effectually, requires more pains and skill, more wit, learning, and judgment, than were employed in the writing it. And the author assures those gentlemen, who have given themselves that trouble with him, that his discourse is the product of the study, the observation, and the invention of several years; that he often blotted out much more than he left, and if his papers had not been a long time out of his possession, they must have still undergone more severe corrections: and do they think such a building is to be battered with dirt-pellets, however envenomed the mouths may be that discharge them? He hath seen the productions but of two answerers, one of which first appeared as from an unknown hand, but since avowed by a person, who, upon some occasions, hath discovered no ill vein of humour. 'Tis a pity any occasion should put him under a necessity of being so hasty in his productions, which, otherwise, might often be entertaining. But there were other reasons obvious enough for his miscarriage in this; he writ against the conviction of his talent, and entered upon one of the wrongest attempts in nature, to turn into ridicule by a week's labour, a work which had cost so much time, and met with so much success in ridiculing others: the manner how he has handled his subject I have now forgot, having just looked it over when it first came out, as others did, merely for the sake of the title.

The other answer is from a person of a graver character, and is made up of half invective, and half annotation; [4] in the latter of which, he hath generally succeeded well enough. And the project at that time was not amiss, to draw in readers to his pamphlet, several having appeared desirous that there might be some explication of the more difficult passages. Neither can he be altogether blamed for offering at the invective part, because it is agreed on all hands that the author had given him sufficient provocation. The great objection is against his manner of treating it, very unsuitable to one of his function. It was determined by a fair majority, that this answerer had, in a way not to be pardoned, drawn his pen against a certain great man then alive, and universally reverenced for every good quality that

[3] Boyle's remarks upon *Bentley's Dissertation on the Epistles of Phalaris*. H.
[4] Wotton's *Defence of his Reflections upon Ancient and Modern Learning*. H.

could possibly enter into the composition of the most accomplished person; it was observed how he was pleased, and affected to have that noble writer called his adversary; and it was a point of satire well directed; for I have been told Sir W[illiam] T[emple] was sufficiently mortified at the term. All the men of wit and politeness were immediately up in arms through indignation, which prevailed over their contempt, by the consequences they apprehended from such an example; and it grew to be Porsenna's case; *idem trecenti juravimus*. In short, things were ripe for a general insurrection, till my Lord Orrery had a little laid the spirit, and settled the ferment. But his lordship being principally engaged with another antagonist,[5] it was thought necessary, in order to quiet the minds of men, that this opposer should receive a reprimand, which partly occasioned that discourse of *The Battle of the Books*; and the author was farther at the pains to insert one or two remarks on him, in the body of the book.

This answerer has been pleased to find fault with about a dozen passages, which the author will not be at the trouble of defending, farther than by assuring the reader, that, for the greater part, the reflecter is entirely mistaken, and forces interpretations which never once entered into the writer's head, nor will he is sure into that of any reader of taste and candour; he allows two or three at most, there produced, to have been delivered unwarily: for which he desires to plead the excuse offered already, of his youth, and frankness of speech, and his papers being out of his power at the time they were published.

But this answerer insists, and says, what he chiefly dislikes, is the design: what that was, I have already told, and I believe there is not a person in England who can understand that book, that ever imagined it to have been anything else, but to expose the abuses and corruptions in Learning and Religion.

But it would be good to know what design this reflecter was serving, when he concludes his pamphlet with a *Caution to Readers* to beware of thinking the author's wit was entirely his own: surely this must have had some allay of personal animosity, at least mixed with the design of serving the public by so useful a discovery; and it indeed touches the author in a very tender point, who insists upon it, that through the whole book he has not borrowed one single hint from any writer in the world; and he thought, of all criticisms, that would never have been one. He conceived it was never disputed to be an original, whatever faults it might have. However this answerer produces three

[5] Bentley, concerning Phalaris and Æsop. H.

instances to prove this author's wit is not his own in many places. The first is, that the names of Peter, Martin, and Jack, are borrowed from a letter of the late Duke of Buckingham. Whatever wit is contained in those three names, the author is content to give it up, and desires his readers will subtract as much as they placed upon that account; at the same time protesting solemnly, that he never once heard of that letter, except in this passage of the answerer: so that the names were not borrowed, as he affirms, though they should happen to be the same; which, however, is odd enough, and what he hardly believes, that of Jack being not quite so obvious as the other two. The second instance to show the author's wit is not his own, is Peter's banter (as he calls it in his Alsatia phrase) upon Transubstantiation, which is taken from the same duke's conference with an Irish priest, where a cork is turned into a horse. This the author confesses to have seen about ten years after his book was writ, and a year or two after it was published. Nay, the answerer overthrows this himself; for he allows the *Tale* was writ in 1697; and I think that pamphlet was not printed in many years after. It was necessary that corruption should have some allegory as well as the rest; and the author invented the properest he could, without inquiring what other people had writ; and the commonest reader will find, there is not the least resemblance between the two stories. The third instance is in these words; 'I have been assured, that the battle in St. James's Library is, *mutatis mutandis*, taken out of a French book, entitled, *Combat des Livres*, if I misremember not.' In which passage there are two clauses observable; 'I have been assured'; and, 'if I misremember not.' I desire first to know whether, if that conjecture proves an utter falsehood, those two clauses will be a sufficient excuse for this worthy critic. The matter is a trifle; but, would he venture to pronounce at this rate upon one of greater moment? I know nothing more contemptible in a writer than the character of a plagiary, which he here fixes at a venture; and this not for a passage, but a whole discourse, taken out from another book, only *mutatis mutandis*. The author is as much in the dark about this as the answerer; and will imitate him by an affirmation at random; that if there be a word of truth in this reflection, he is a paltry, imitating pedant; and the answerer is a person of wit, manners, and truth. He takes his boldness, from never having seen any such treatise in his life, nor heard of it before; and he is sure it is impossible for two writers, of different times and countries, to agree in their thoughts after such a manner, that two continued discourses shall be the same, only *mutatis mutandis*. Neither will he insist upon the mistake of the title, but let the answerer and his friend produce any book they please, he defies them to show one single particular, where the judicious reader will affirm he has been obliged for the smallest hint; giving only allowance for the accidental encountering of a single thought, which he knows may sometimes happen; though he has never yet found it in that discourse, nor has heard it objected by anybody else.

So that if ever any design was unfortunately executed, it must be that of this answerer; who, when he would have it observed that the author's wit is not his own, is able to produce but three instances, two of them mere trifles, and all three manifestly false. If this be the way these gentlemen deal with the world in those criticisms, where we have not leisure to defeat them, their readers had need be cautious how they rely upon their credit; and whether this proceeding can be reconciled to humanity or truth, let those who think it worth their while determine.

It is agreed, this answerer would have succeeded much better, if he had stuck wholly to his business as a commentator upon the *Tale of a Tub*, wherein it cannot be denied that he hath been of some service to the public, and has given very fair conjectures towards clearing up some difficult passages; but it is the frequent error of those men (otherwise very commendable for their labours), to make excursions beyond their talent and their office, by pretending to point out the beauties and the faults; which is no part of their trade, which they always fail in, which the world never expected from them, nor gave them any thanks for endeavouring at. The part of Minellius, or Farnaby,[6] would have fallen in with his genius, and might have been serviceable to many readers, who cannot enter into the abstruser parts of that discourse; but *optat ephippia bos piger*. The dull, unwieldy, ill-shaped ox would needs put on the furniture of a horse, not considering he was born to labour, to plough the ground for the sake of superior beings, and that he has neither the shape, mettle, nor speed, of that nobler animal he would affect to personate.

It is another pattern of this answerer's fair dealing to give us hints that the author is dead, and yet to lay the suspicion upon somebody, I know not who, in the country; to which can be only returned, that he is absolutely mistaken in all his conjectures; and surely conjectures are, at best, too light a pretence to allow a man to assign a name in public. He condemns a book, and consequently the author, of whom he is utterly ignorant;

---

[6] Low commentators who wrote notes upon classic authors for the use of schoolboys. H.

yet at the same time fixes in print what he thinks a disadvantageous character upon those who never deserved it. A man who receives a buffet in the dark, may be allowed to be vexed; but it is an odd kind of revenge, to go to cuffs in broad day with the first he meets with, and lay the last night's injury at his door. And thus much for this *discreet, candid, pious,* and *ingenious* answerer.

How the author came to be without his papers, is a story not proper to be told, and of very little use, being a private fact of which the reader would believe as little or as much as he thought good. He had, however, a blotted copy by him, which he intended to have writ over, with many alterations, and this the publishers were well aware of, having put it into the bookseller's preface, that they *apprehended a surreptitious copy, which was to be altered,* &c. This, though not regarded by readers, was a real truth, only the surreptitious copy was rather that which was printed; and they made all haste they could, which indeed was needless; the author not being at all prepared; but he has been told the bookseller was in much pain, having given a good sum of money for the copy.

In the author's original copy there were not so many chasms as appear in the book; and why some of them were left, he knows not; had the publication been trusted to him, he should have made several corrections of passages, against which nothing hath been ever objected. He should likewise have altered a few of those that seem with any reason to be excepted against; but to deal freely, the greatest number he should have left untouched, as never suspecting it possible any wrong interpretations could be made of them.

The author observes, at the end of the book there is a discourse called *A Fragment*, which he more wondered to see in print than all the rest. Having been a most imperfect sketch, with the addition of a few loose hints, which he once lent a gentleman, who had designed a discourse of somewhat the same subject; he never thought of it afterwards; and it was a sufficient surprise to see it pieced up together, wholly out of the method and scheme he had intended; for it was the ground-work of a much larger discourse, and he was sorry to observe the materials so foolishly employed.

There is one further objection made by those who have answered this book, as well as by some others, that Peter is frequently made to repeat oaths and curses. Every reader observes it was necessary to know that Peter did swear and curse. The oaths are not printed out, but only supposed, and the idea of an oath is not immoral, like the idea of a profane or immodest speech. A man may laugh at the Popish folly of cursing people to hell, and imagine them swearing, without any crime; but lewd words, or dangerous opinions though printed by halves, fill the reader's mind with ill ideas; and of these the author cannot be accused. For the judicious reader will find that the severest strokes of satire in his book are levelled against the modern custom of employing wit upon those topics; of which there is a remarkable instance in the three hundred and nineteenth page, as well as in several others, though perhaps once or twice expressed in too free a manner, excusable only for the reasons already alleged. Some overtures have been made by a third hand to the bookseller, for the author's altering those passages which he thought might require it. But it seems the bookseller will not hear of any such thing, being apprehensive it might spoil the sale of the book.

The author cannot conclude this apology without making this one reflection; that, as wit is the noblest and most useful gift of human nature, so humor is the most agreeable; and where these two enter far into the composition of any work, they will render it always acceptable to the world. Now, the great part of those who have no share or taste of either, but by their pride, pedantry, and ill manners, lay themselves bare to the lashes of both, think the blow is weak, because they are insensible; and, where wit hath any mixture of raillery, 'tis but calling it banter, and the work is done. This polite word of theirs was first borrowed from the bullies in White-Friars, then fell among the footmen, and at last retired to the pedants; by whom it is applied as properly to the productions of wit, as if I should apply it to Sir Isaac Newton's mathematics. But, if this bantering, as they call it, be so despisable a thing, whence comes it to pass they have such a perpetual itch towards it themselves? To instance only in the answerer already mentioned; it is grievous to see him, in some of his writings, at every turn going out of his way to be waggish, to tell us of a *cow that pricked up her tail;* and in his answer to this discourse, he says, *it is all a farce and a ladle;* with other passages equally shining. One may say of these *impedimenta literarum,* that wit owes them a shame; and they cannot take wiser counsel than to keep out of harm's way, or at least not to come till they are sure they are called.

To conclude: with those allowances above required, this book should be read; after which, the author conceives, few things will remain which may not be excused in a young writer. He wrote only to the men of wit and taste, and he thinks he is not mistaken in his accounts, when he says they have been all of his side, enough to give him the vanity of telling his name, wherein the world with all its wise conjectures, is yet very much in the dark; which circumstance is no disagreeable amusement either to the public or himself.

The author is informed, that the bookseller has prevailed on several gentlemen to write some explanatory notes; for the goodness of which he is not to answer, having never seen any of them, nor intends it, till they appear in print; when it is not unlikely he may have the pleasure to find twenty meanings which never entered into his imagination.
June 3, 1709.

POSTSCRIPT

SINCE the writing of this which was about a year ago, a prostitute bookseller hath published a foolish paper, under the name of Notes on the *Tale of a Tub*, with some account of the author: and, with an insolence which, I suppose, is punishable by law, hath presumed to assign certain names. It will be enough for the author to assure the world, that the writer of that paper is utterly wrong in all his conjectures upon that affair. The author farther asserts that the whole work is entirely of one hand, which every reader of judgment will easily discover. The gentleman who gave the copy to the bookseller, being a friend of the author, and using no other liberties besides that of expunging certain passages where now the chasms appear under the name of *desiderata*. But if any person will prove his claim to three lines in the whole book, let him step forth, and tell his name and titles; upon which, the bookseller shall have orders to prefix them to the next edition, and the claimant shall from henceforward be acknowledged the undisputed author.

JOHN
LORD SOMERS.[1]

My Lord,

Tho' the author has written a large Dedication, yet that being addressed to a prince, whom I am never likely to have the honor of being known to; a person besides, as far as I can observe, not at all regarded, or thought on by any of our present writers; and being wholly free from that slavery which booksellers usually lie under, to the caprices of authors; I think it a wise piece of presumption to inscribe these papers to your lordship, and to implore your lordship's protection of them. God and your lordship know their faults and their merits; for, as to my own particular, I am altogether a stranger to the matter; and tho' everybody else should be equally ignorant, I do not fear the sale of the book, at all the worse, upon that score. Your lordship's name on the front in capital letters will at any time get off one edition: neither would I desire any other help to grow an alderman, than a patent for the sole privilege of dedicating to your lordship.

I should now, in right of a dedicator, give your lordship a list of your own virtues, and, at the same time, be very unwilling to offend your modesty; but chiefly I should celebrate your liberality towards men of great parts and small fortunes, and give you broad hints that I mean myself. And I was just going on, in the usual method, to peruse a hundred or two of dedications, and transcribe an abstract, to be applied to your lordship; but I was diverted by a certain accident. For, upon the covers of these papers, I casually observed written in large letters the two following words, DETUR DIGNISSIMO; which, for aught I knew, might contain some important meaning. But it unluckily fell out, that none of the authors I employ understood Latin (though I have them often in pay to translate out of that language); I was therefore compelled to have recourse to the curate of our parish, who Englished it thus, *Let it be given to the worthiest*: and his comment was, that the author meant his work should be dedicated to the sublimest genius of the age for wit, learning, judgment, eloquence, and wisdom. I called at a poet's chamber (who works for my shop) in an alley hard by, showed

---

[1] John Lord Somers, Chancellor of England in 1697, was one of the greatest men of his age and nation, and a great patron of learning. ... 1720 ED.

him the translation, and desired his opinion, who it was that the author could mean; he told me, after some consideration, that vanity was a thing he abhorred; but by the description, he thought himself to be the person aimed at; and, at the same time, he very kindly offered his own assistance *gratis* towards penning a dedication to himself. I desired him, however, to give a second guess. Why, then, said he, it must be I, or my Lord Somers. From thence I went to several other wits of my acquaintance, with no small hazard and weariness to my person, from a prodigious number of dark, winding stairs; but found them all in the same story, both of your lordship and themselves. Now, your lordship is to understand, that this proceeding was not of my own invention; for I have somewhere heard, it is a maxim, that those to whom everybody allows the second place, have an undoubted title to the first.

This infallibly convinced me, that your lordship was the person intended by the author. But, being very unacquainted in the style and form of dedications, I employed those wits aforesaid to furnish me with hints and materials, towards a panegyric upon your lordship's virtues.

In two days they brought me ten sheets of paper, filled up on every side. They swore to me, that they had ransacked whatever could be found in the characters of Socrates, Aristides, Epaminondas, Cato, Tully, Atticus, and other hard names, which I cannot now recollect. However, I have reason to believe, they imposed upon my ignorance, because, when I came to read over their collections, there was not a syllable there, but what I and everybody else knew as well as themselves: therefore I grievously suspect a cheat; and that these authors of mine stole and transcribed every word, from the universal report of mankind. So that I look upon myself as fifty shillings out of pocket, to no manner of purpose.

If, by altering the title, I could make the same materials serve for another Dedication (as my betters have done) it would help to make up my loss; but I have made several persons dip here and there in those papers, and before they read three lines, they have all assured me plainly, that they cannot possibly be applied to any persons besides your lordship.

I expected, indeed, to have heard of your lordship's bravery at the head of an army; of your undaunted courage in mounting a breach, or scaling a wall; or to have had your pedigree traced in a lineal descent from the house of Austria; or of your wonderful talent at dress and dancing; or your profound knowledge in algebra, metaphysics, and the oriental tongues. But to ply the world with an old beaten story of your wit, and eloquence, and learning, and wisdom, and justice, and politeness, and candor, and evenness of temper in all scenes of life; of that great discernment in discovering, and readiness in favouring deserving men; with forty other common topics; I confess, I have neither conscience nor countenance to do it. Because there is no virtue, either of a public or private life, which some circumstances of your own have not often produced upon the stage of the world; and those few, which for want of occasions to exert them, might otherwise have passed unseen or unobserved by your friends, your enemies have at length brought to light.

'Tis true, I should be very loth, the bright example of your lordship's virtues should be lost to after-ages, both for their sake and your own; but chiefly because they will be so very necessary to adorn the history of a late reign; and that is another reason why I would forbear to make a recital of them here; because I have been told by wise men, that as dedications have run for some years past, a good historian will not be apt to have recourse thither in search of characters.

There is one point, wherein I think we dedicators would do well to change our measures; I mean, instead of running on so far upon the praise of our patrons' liberality, to spend a word or two in admiring their patience. I can put no greater compliment on your lordship's, than by giving you so ample an occasion to exercise it at present. Tho' perhaps I shall not be apt to reckon much merit to your lordship upon that score, who having been formerly used to tedious harangues, and sometimes to as little purpose, will be the readier to pardon this, especially, when it is offered by one, who is with all respect and veneration,
          My Lord,
                Your lordship's most obedient,
                     and most faithful servant,
                                    THE BOOKSELLER.

THE
BOOKSELLER
TO THE
READER

It is now six years since these papers came first to my hand, which seems to have been about a twelvemonth after they were writ; for the author tells us in his preface to the first treatise, that he hath calculated it for the year 1697, and in several passages of that Discourse, as well as the second, it appears they were written about that time.

As to the author, I can give no manner of satisfaction; however, I am credibly informed that this publication is without his knowledge; for he concludes the copy is lost, having lent it to a person, since dead, and being never in possession of it after: so that, whether the work received his last hand, or whether he intended to fill up the defective places, is like to remain a secret.

If I should go about to tell the reader, by what accident I became master of these papers, it would, in this unbelieving age, pass for little more than the cant or jargon of the trade. I therefore gladly spare both him and myself so unnecessary a trouble. There yet remains a difficult question, why I published them no sooner. I forbore upon two accounts: first, because I thought I had better work upon my hands; and secondly, because I was not without some hope of hearing from the author, and receiving his directions. But I have been lately alarmed with intelligence of a surreptitious copy, which a certain great wit had new polished and refined, or, as our present writers express themselves, *fitted to the humor of the age;* as they have already done, with great felicity, to Don Quixote, Boccalini, La Bruyère and other authors. However, I thought it fairer dealing to offer the whole work in its naturals. If any gentleman will please to furnish me with a key, in order to explain the more difficult parts, I shall very gratefully acknowledge the favour, and print it by itself.

THE EPISTLE DEDICATORY

TO
HIS ROYAL HIGHNESS

PRINCE POSTERITY [1]

SIR,

I here present your highness with the fruits of a very few leisure hours, stolen from the short intervals of a world of business,
and of an employment quite alien from such amusements as this,
the poor production of that refuse of time which has lain heavy
upon my hands, during a long prorogation of parliament, a
great dearth of foreign news, and a tedious fit of rainy weather;
for which, and other reasons, it cannot choose extremely to
deserve such a patronage as that of your highness, whose numberless virtues in so few years, make the world look upon you as
the future example to all princes, for although your highness is
hardly got clear of infancy, yet has the universal learned world
already resolved upon appealing to your future dictates with the
lowest and most resigned submission; fate having decreed you
sole arbiter of the productions of human wit, in this polite and
most accomplished age. Methinks, the number of appellants
were enough to shock and startle any judge of a genius less
unlimited than yours: but in order to prevent such glorious
trials, the person [2] (it seems) to whose care the education of
your highness is committed, has resolved (as I am told) to keep
you in almost an universal ignorance of our studies, which it is
your inherent birth-right to inspect.

It is amazing to me, that this person should have assurance in
the face of the sun, to go about persuading your highness, that
our age is almost wholly illiterate, and has hardly produced one
writer upon any subject. I know very well, that when your highness shall come to riper years, and have gone through the learning of antiquity, you will be too curious to neglect inquiring into

---

[1] The Citation out of Irenæus in the title-page, which seems to be all
gibberish, is a form of initiation used anciently by the Marcosian Heretics.
W. WOTTON.

It is the usual style of decried writers to appeal to Posterity, who is here
represented as a prince in his nonage, and Time as his governor, and the
author begins in a way very frequent with him, by personating other writers,
who sometimes offer such reasons and excuses for publishing their works as
they ought chiefly to conceal and be ashamed of.

[2] *Time* allegorically described as the tutor of Posterity. SCOTT.

the authors of the very age before you: and to think that this insolent, in the account he is preparing for your view, designs to reduce them to a number so insignificant as I am ashamed to mention; it moves my zeal and my spleen for the honor and interest of our vast flourishing body, as well as of myself, for whom I know by long experience, he has professed, and still continues a peculiar malice.

'Tis not unlikely, that when your highness will one day peruse what I am now writing, you may be ready to expostulate with your governor upon the credit of what I here affirm, and command him to show you some of our productions. To which he will answer (for I am well informed of his designs) by asking your highness, where they are? and what is become of them? and pretend it a demonstration that there never were any, because they are not then to be found. Not to be found! Who has mislaid them? Are they sunk in the abyss of things; 'Tis certain, that in their own nature they were light enough to swim upon the surface for all eternity. Therefore the fault is in him, who tied weights so heavy to their heels, as to depress them to the center. Is their very essence destroyed? Who has annihilated them? Were they drowned by purges or martyred by pipes? Who administered them to the posteriors of ———? But that it may no longer be a doubt with your highness, who is to be the author of this universal ruin, I beseech you to observe that large and terrible scythe which your governor affects to bear continually about him. Be pleased to remark the length and strength, the sharpness and hardness of his nails and teeth: consider his baneful, abominable breath, enemy to life and matter, infectious and corrupting: and then reflect whether it be possible for any mortal ink and paper of this generation to make a suitable resistance. Oh, that your highness would one day resolve to disarm this usurping *maître du palais* [3] of his furious engines, and to bring your empire *hors de page*. [4]

It were endless to recount the several methods of tyranny and destruction, which your governor is pleased to practise upon this occasion. His inveterate malice is such to the writings of our age, that of several thousands produced yearly from this renowned city, before the next revolution of the sun, there is not one to be heard of: unhappy infants, many of them barbarously destroyed, before they have so much as learnt their mother-tongue to beg for pity. Some he stifles in their cradles, others he frights into convulsions, whereof they suddenly die; some

---

[3] Comptroller.
[4] Out of guardianship.

he flays alive, others he tears limb from limb. Great numbers
are offered to Moloch, and the rest, tainted by his breath, die of a
languishing consumption.

But the concern I have most at heart, is for our corporation of
poets, from whom I am preparing a petition to your highness, to
be subscribed with the names of one hundred thirty-six of the
first rate; but whose immortal productions are never likely to
reach your eyes, though each of them is now an humble and an
earnest appellant for the laurel, and has large comely volumes
ready to show for a support to his pretensions. The never-
dying works of these illustrious persons, your governor, sir, has
devoted to unavoidable death, and your highness is to be made
believe, that our age has never arrived at the honor to produce
one single poet.

We confess *Immortality* to be a great and powerful goddess;
but in vain we offer up to her our devotions and our sacrifices, if
your highness's governor, who has usurped the priesthood,
must by an unparalleled ambition and avarice, wholly intercept
and devour them.

To affirm that our age is altogether unlearned, and devoid of
writers in any kind, seems to be an assertion so bold and so false,
that I have been some time thinking, the contrary may almost be
proved by uncontrollable demonstration. 'Tis true indeed, that
although their numbers be vast, and their productions numerous
in proportion, yet are they hurried so hastily off the scene, that
they escape our memory, and delude our sight. When I first
thought of this address, I had prepared a copious list of titles to
present your highness as an undisputed argument for what I
affirm. The originals were posted fresh upon all gates and corners of streets; but returning in a very few hours to take a review,
they were all torn down, and fresh ones in their places. I inquired after them among readers and booksellers, but I inquired
in vain; *the memorial of them was lost among men; their place
was no more to be found;* and I was laughed to scorn for a clown
and a pedant, without all taste and refinement, little versed in the
course of present affairs, and that knew nothing of what had
passed in the best companies of court and town. So that I can
only avow in general to your highness, that we do abound in
learning and wit; but to fix upon particulars, is a task too slippery for my slender abilities. If I should venture in a windy day
to affirm to your highness, that there is a large cloud near the
horizon in the form of a bear, another in the zenith with the head
of an ass, a third to the westward with claws like a dragon, and
your highness should in a few minutes think fit to examine the

truth, 'tis certain they would all be changed in figure and position, new ones would arise, and all we could agree upon would
be, that clouds there were, but that I was grossly mistaken in the
zoography and topography of them.

But your governor perhaps may still insist, and put the question: What is then become of those immense bales of paper,
which must needs have been employed in such numbers of
books? Can these also be wholly annihilate, and so of a sudden,
as I pretend? What shall I say in return of so invidious an objection? It ill befits the distance between your highness and me, to
send you for ocular conviction to a jakes or an oven, to the windows of a bawdy-house, or to a sordid lantern. Books, like men
their authors, have no more than one way of coming into the
world, but there are ten thousand to go out of it, and return no
more.

I profess to your highness, in the integrity of my heart, that
what I am going to say is literally true this minute I am
writing: what revolutions may happen before it shall be ready
for your perusal, I can by no means warrant; however, I beg you
to accept it as a specimen of our learning, our politeness, and our
wit. I do therefore affirm upon the word of a sincere man, that
there is now actually in being a certain poet called John Dryden,
whose translation of Virgil was lately printed in a large folio,
well bound, and if diligent search were made, for aught I know, is
yet to be seen. There is another called Nahum Tate, who is
ready to make oath that he has caused many reams of verse to be
published whereof both himself and his bookseller (if lawfully required) can still produce authentic copies, and therefore wonders why the world is pleased to make such a
secret of it. There is a third, known by the name of Tom Durfey, a poet of a vast comprehension, an universal genius, and
most profound learning. There are also one Mr. Rymer, and one
Mr. Dennis, most profound critics. There is a person styled Dr.
Bentley, who has written near a thousand pages of immense
erudition, giving a full and true account of a certain squabble of
wonderful importance between himself and a bookseller: he is a
writer of infinite wit and humour; no man rallies with a better
grace, and in more sprightly turns. Farther, I avow to your highness, that with these eyes I have beheld the person of William
Wotton, B.D., who has written a good sizeable volume against a
friend of your governor (from whom, alas! he must therefore
look for little favour)[5] in a most gentlemanly style, adorned with

---

[5] Sir William Temple, with whom Wotton was then engaged in the
controversy concerning ancient and modern learning. SCOTT.

utmost politeness and civility; replete with discoveries equally valuable for their novelty and use; and embellished with traits of wit so poignant and so apposite, that he is a worthy yokemate to his forementioned friend.

Why should I go upon farther particulars, which might fill a volume with the just eulogies of my contemporary brethren? I shall bequeath this piece of justice to a larger work, wherein I intend to write a character of the present set of wits in our nation: their persons I shall describe particularly and at length, their genius and understandings in miniature.

In the mean time, I do here make bold to present your highness with a faithful abstract drawn from the universal body of all arts and sciences, intended wholly for your service and instruction. Nor do I doubt in the least, but your highness will peruse it as carefully, and make as considerable improvements, as other young princes have already done by the many volumes of late years written for a help to their studies.

That your highness may advance in wisdom and virtue, as well as years, and at last outshine all your royal ancestors, shall be the daily prayer of,

        Sir,

           Your Highness's
            Most devoted, &c.

Decemb.
1697.

PREFACE.

THE wits of the present age being so very numerous and penetrating, it seems the grandees of Church and State begin to fall under horrible apprehensions, lest these gentlemen, during the intervals of a long peace, should find leisure to pick holes in the weak sides of Religion and Government. To prevent which, there has been much thought employed of late upon certain projects for taking off the force and edge of those formidable inquirers, from canvassing and reasoning upon such delicate points. They have at length fixed upon one, which will require some time as well as cost to perfect. Meanwhile, the danger hourly increasing, by new levies of wits, all appointed (as there is reason to fear) with pen, ink, and paper, which may at an hour's warning be drawn out into pamphlets, and other offensive weapons, ready for immediate execution, it was judged of absolute necessity, that some present expedient be thought on, till the main design can be brought to maturity. To this end, at a Grand Committee some days ago, this important discovery was made by a certain curious and refined observer — that seamen have a custom when they meet a whale, to fling him out an empty tub by way of amusement, to divert him from laying violent hands upon the ship. This parable was immediately mythologized; the whale was interpreted to be Hobbes's *Leviathan*, which tosses and plays with all other schemes of Religion and Government, whereof a great many are hollow, and dry, and empty, and noisy, and wooden, and given to rotation. This is the *Leviathan* from whence the terrible wits of our age are said to borrow their weapons. The ship in danger is easily understood to be its old antitype, the Commonwealth. But how to analyze the tub, was a matter of difficulty; when after long enquiry and debate, the literal meaning was preserved; and it was decreed, that in order to prevent these Leviathans from tossing and sporting with the Commonwealth (which of itself is too apt to fluctuate) they should be diverted from that game by a *Tale of a Tub*. And my genius being conceived to lie not unhappily that way, I had the honor done me to be engaged in the performance.

This is the sole design in publishing the following treatise, which I hope will serve for an *interim* of some months to employ those unquiet spirits, till the perfecting of that great work, into the secret of which it is reasonable the courteous reader should have some little light.

It is intended that a large Academy be erected, capable of containing nine thousand seven hundred forty and three persons; which by modest computation is reckoned to be pretty near the current number of wits in this island. These are to be disposed into the several schools of this academy, and there pursue those studies to which their genius most inclines them. The undertaker himself will publish his proposals with all convenient speed, to which I shall refer the curious reader for a more particular account, mentioning at present only a few of the principal schools. There is first a large Pæderastic School, with French and Italian masters. There is also the Spelling School, a very spacious building: the School of Looking glasses: the School of Swearing: the School of Critics: the School of Salivation: the School of Hobby-horses: the School of Poetry: the School of Tops[1]: the School of Spleen: the School of Gaming: with many others too tedious to recount. No person to be admitted member into any of these schools without an attestation under two sufficient persons' hands, certifying him to be a wit.

But, to return, I am sufficiently instructed in the principal duty of a preface, if my genius were capable of arriving at it. Thrice have I forced my imagination to make the tour of my invention, and thrice it has returned empty; the latter having been wholly drained by the following treatise. Not so, my more successful brethren the moderns, who will by no means let slip a preface or dedication without some notable distinguishing stroke to surprise the reader at the entry, and kindle a wonderful expectation of what is to ensue. Such was that of a most ingenious poet, who soliciting his brain for something new, compared himself to the hangman, and his patron to the patient: this was *insigne, recens, indictum ore alio*.[2] When I went through that necessary and noble course of study,[3] I had the happiness to observe many such egregious touches, which I shall not injure the authors by transplanting, because I have remarked, that nothing is so very tender as a modern piece of wit, and which is apt to suffer so much in the carriage. Some things are extremely witty to-day, or fasting, or in this place, or at eight o'clock, or over a bottle, or spoke by Mr. What d'y'call'm, or in a summer's morning: any of which, by the smallest transposal or misapplication, is utterly annihilate. Thus, wit has its walks and purlieus, out of which it may not stray the breadth of an hair, upon peril of

[1] This I think the author should have omitted, it being of the very same nature with the School of Hobby-horses, if one may venture to censure one who is so severe a censurer of others, perhaps with too little distinction.

[2] Horace. Something extraordinary, new and never hit upon before.

[3] Reading Prefaces, &c.

being lost. The moderns have artfully fixed this mercury, and reduced it to the circumstances of time, place, and person. Such a jest there is, that will not pass out of Covent-Garden; and such a one, that is nowhere intelligible but at Hyde-Park Corner. Now, though it sometimes tenderly affects me to consider, that all the towardly passages I shall deliver in the following treatise, will grow quite out of date and relish with the first shifting of the present scene, yet I must need subscribe to the justice of this proceeding: because, I cannot imagine why we should be at expense to furnish wit for succeeding ages, when the former have made no sort of provision for ours, wherein I speak the sentiment of the very newest, and consequently the most ortho-dox refiners, as well as my own. However, being extremely solicitous, that every accomplished person who has got into the taste of wit calculated for this present month of August, 1697, should descend to the very bottom of all the sublime throughout this treatise, I hold fit to lay down this general maxim: whatever reader desires to have a thorough comprehension of an author's thoughts, cannot take a better method, than by putting himself into the circumstances and postures of life, that the writer was in upon every important passage as it flowed from his pen, for this will introduce a parity and strict correspondence of ideas between the reader and the author. Now, to assist the diligent reader in so delicate an affair, as far as brevity will permit, I have recollected, that the shrewdest pieces of this treatise were con-ceived in bed in a garret; at other times (for a reason best known to myself) I thought fit to sharpen my invention with hunger; and in general, the whole work was begun, continued, and ended, under a long course of physic, and a great want of money. Now, I do affirm, it will be absolutely impossible for the candid peruser to go along with me in a great many bright passages, unless upon the several difficulties emergent, he will please to capacitate and prepare himself by these directions. And this I lay down as my principal *postulatum*.

Because I have professed to be a most devoted servant of all modern forms, I apprehend some curious wit may object against me, for proceeding thus far in a preface, without declaiming, according to the custom, against the multitude of writers, whereof the whole multitude of writers most reasonably com-plains. I am just come from perusing some hundreds of prefaces, wherein the authors do at the very beginning address the gentle reader concerning this enormous grievance. Of these I have pre-served a few examples, and shall set them down as near as my memory has been able to retain them.

One begins thus:

> *For a man to set up for a writer, when the press swarms with*, &c.

Another:

> *The tax upon paper does not lessen the number of scribblers, who daily pester*, &c.

Another:

> *When every little would-be-wit takes pen in hand, 'tis in vain to enter the lists*, &c.

Another:

> *To observe what trash the press swarms with*, &c.

Another:

> Sir, *It is merely in obedience to your commands that I venture into the public; for who upon a less consideration would be of a party with such a rabble of scribblers*, &c.

Now, I have two words in my own defence against this objection. First, I am far from granting the number of writers a nuisance to our nation, having strenuously maintained the contrary in several parts of the following discourse. Secondly, I do not well understand the justice of this proceeding because I observe many of these polite prefaces to be not only from the same hand, but from those who are most voluminous in their several productions. Upon which I shall tell the reader a short tale.

A mountebank in Leicester-fields had drawn a huge assembly about him. Among the rest, a fat unwieldy fellow, half stifled in the press, would be every fit crying out, Lord! what a filthy crowd is here, pray, good people, give way a little. Bless me! what a devil has raked this rabble together, z—ds! what squeezing is this! honest friend, remove your elbow. At last a weaver that stood next him, could hold no longer. A plague confound you (said he,) for an overgrown sloven; and who (in the devil's name) I wonder, helps to make up the crowd half so much as yourself? Don't you consider (with a pox,) that you take up more room with that carcass than any five here? Is not the place as free for us as for you? Bring your own guts to a reasonable compass (and be d—n'd) and then I'll engage we shall have room enough for us all.

There are certain common privileges of a writer, the benefit whereof, I hope, there will be no reason to doubt; particularly, that where I am not understood, it shall be concluded, that something very useful and profound is couched underneath; and again, that whatever word or sentence is printed in a different character, shall be judged to contain something extraordinary either of wit or sublime.

As for the liberty I have thought fit to take of praising myself, upon some occasions or none, I am sure it will need no excuse, if a multitude of great examples be allowed sufficient authority. For it is here to be noted, that praise was originally a pension paid by the world; but the moderns finding the trouble and charge too great in collecting it, have lately bought out the fee-simple; since which time, the right of presentation is wholly in ourselves. For this reason it is, that when an author makes his own eulogy, he uses a certain form to declare and insist upon his title, which is commonly in these or the like words, 'I speak without vanity'; which I think plainly shows it to be a matter of right and justice. Now, I do here once for all declare, that in every encounter of this nature through the following treatise, the form aforesaid is implied; which I mention, to save the trouble of repeating it on so many occasions.

'Tis a great ease to my conscience that I have writ so elaborate and useful a discourse without one grain of satire intermixed; which is the sole point wherein I have taken leave to dissent from the famous originals of our age and country. I have observed some satirists to use the public much at the rate that pedants do a naughty boy, ready horsed for discipline: first expostulate the case, then plead the necessity of the rod from great provocations, and conclude every period with a lash. Now, if I know anything of mankind, these gentlemen might very well spare their reproof and correction: for there is not, through all nature, another so callous and insensible a member as the world's posteriors, whether you apply to it the toe or the birch. Besides, most of our late satirists seem to lie under a sort of mistake, that because nettles have the prerogative to sting, therefore all other weeds must do so too. I make not this comparison out of the least design to detract from these worthy writers, for it is well known among mythologists, that weeds have the preeminence over all other vegetables; and therefore the first monarch of this island, whose taste and judgment were so acute and refined, did very wisely root out the roses from the collar of the Order, and plant the thistles in their stead as the nobler flower of the two. For which reason it is conjectured by profounder antiquaries, that the satirical itch, so prevalent in this part of our island, was first brought among us from beyond the Tweed. Here may it long flourish and abound; may it survive and neglect the scorn of the world, with as much ease and contempt, as the world is insensible to the lashes of it. May their own dullness, or that of their party, be no discouragement for the authors to proceed; but let them remember, it is with wits as with razors, which are never so apt to cut those they are employed on, as when they have lost their edge. Besides, those whose teeth are too rotten to bite are best of all others qualified to revenge that defect with their breath.

I am not like other men, to envy or undervalue the talents I cannot reach; for which reason I must needs bear a true honour to this large eminent sect of our British writers. And I hope this little panegyric will not be offensive to their ears, since it has the advantage of being only designed for themselves. Indeed, nature herself has taken order, that fame and honour should be purchased at a better pennyworth by satire, than by any other productions of the brain; the world being soonest provoked to praise by lashes, as men are to love. There is a problem in an ancient author, why dedications, and other bundles of flattery run all upon stale, musty topics, without the smallest tincture of anything new; not only to the torment and nauseating of the Christian reader, but (if not suddenly prevented) to the universal spreading of that pestilent disease, the lethargy, in this island: whereas there is very little satire which has not something in it untouched before. The defects of the former are usually imputed to the want of invention among those who are dealers in that kind; but, I think, with a great deal of injustice; the solution being easy and natural. For the materials of panegyric being very few in number, have been long since exhausted. For, as health is but one thing, and has been always the same, whereas diseases are by thousands, besides new and daily additions; so, all the virtues that have been ever in mankind, are to be counted upon a few fingers, but his follies and vices are innumerable, and time adds hourly to the heap. Now the utmost a poor poet can do, is to get by heart a list of the cardinal virtues, and deal them with his utmost liberality to his hero or his patron: he may ring the changes as far as it will go, and vary his phrase till he has talked round: but the reader quickly finds it is all pork,[4] with a little variety of sauce. For there is no inventing terms of art beyond our ideas; and when ideas are exhausted, terms of art must be so too.

But tho' the matter for panegyric were as fruitful as the topics of satire, yet would it not be hard to find out a sufficient reason why the latter will be always better received than the first. For, this being bestowed only upon one or a few persons at a time, is sure to raise envy, and consequently ill words from the rest, who have no share in the blessing; but satire being levelled at all, is never resented for an offence by any, since

[4] Plutarch.

every individual person makes bold to understand it of others, and very wisely removes his particular part of the burden upon the shoulders of the world, which are broad enough, and able to bear it. To this purpose, I have sometimes reflected upon the difference between Athens and England, with respect to the point before us. In the Attic commonwealth,[5] it was the privilege and birthright of every citizen and poet to rail aloud and in public, or to expose upon the stage by name, any person they pleased, though of the greatest figure, whether a Creon, an Hyperbolus, an Alcibiades, or a Demosthenes: but on the other side, the least reflecting word let fall against the people in general, was immediately caught up, and revenged upon the authors, however considerable for their quality or their merits. Whereas in England it is just the reverse of all this. Here, you may securely display your utmost rhetoric against mankind, in the face of the world; tell them, 'That all are gone astray: that there is none that doth good, no not one; that we live in the very dregs of time; that knavery and atheism are epidemic as the pox; that honesty is fled with Astræa'; with any other commonplaces equally new and eloquent, which are furnished by the *splendida bilis*.[6] And when you have done, the whole audience, far from being offended, shall return you thanks as a deliverer of precious and useful truths. Nay farther; it is but to venture your lungs, and you may preach in Covent-Garden against foppery and fornication, and something else: against pride, and dissimulation, and bribery, at Whitehall: you may expose rapine and injustice in the Inns of Court Chapel: and in a city pulpit be as fierce as you please against avarice, hypocrisy, and extortion. 'Tis but a ball bandied to and fro, and every man carries a racket about him to strike it from himself among the rest of the company. But on the other side, whoever should mistake the nature of things so far, as to drop but a single hint in public, how such a one starved half the fleet, and half-poisoned the rest: how such a one, from a true principle of love and honour, pays no debts but for wenches and play: how such a one has got a clap and runs out of his estate: how Paris bribed by Juno and Venus,[7] loth to offend either party, slept out the whole cause on the bench: or how such an orator makes long speeches in the senate with much thought, little sense, and to no purpose; whoever, I say, should

---

[5] *Vide* Xenophon.
[6] Horace. Spleen.
[7] Juno and Venus are money and a mistress, very powerful bribes to a judge, if scandal says true. I remember such reflections were cast about that time, but I cannot fix the person intended here.

venture to be thus particular, must expect to be imprisoned for *scandalum magnatum;* to have challenges sent him; to be sued for defamation; and to be brought before the bar of the house.

But I forget that I am expatiating on a subject wherein I have no concern, having neither a talent nor an inclination for satire. On the other side, I am so entirely satisfied with the whole present procedure of human things, that I have been for some years preparing materials towards *A Panegyric upon the World;* to which I intended to add a second part, entitled, *A modest Defence of the Proceedings of the Rabble in all Ages.* Both these I had thoughts to publish by way of appendix to the following treatise; but finding my common-place book fill much slower than I had reason to expect, I have chosen to defer them to another occasion. Besides, I have been unhappily prevented in that design by a certain domestic misfortune, in the particulars whereof, though it would be very seasonable, and much in the modern way, to inform the gentle reader, and would also be of great assistance towards extending this preface into the size now in vogue, which by rule ought to be large in proportion as the subsequent volume is small; yet I shall now dismiss our impatient reader from any farther attendance at the porch, and having duly prepared his mind by a preliminary discourse, shall gladly introduce him to the sublime mysteries that ensue.

A TALE

OF A

TUB, &c.

SECTION I

THE INTRODUCTION

WHOEVER hath an ambition to be heard in a crowd, must press, and squeeze, and thrust, and climb with indefatigable pains, till he has exalted himself to a certain degree of altitude above them. Now, in all assemblies, though you wedge them ever so close, we may observe this peculiar property, that over their heads there is room enough, but how to reach it is the difficult point; it being as hard to get quit of number, as of hell.

> —— *Evadere ad auras,*
> *Hoc opus, hic labor est.*[1]

To this end, the philosopher's way in all ages has been by erecting certain edifices in the air: but, whatever practice and reputation these kind of structures have formerly possessed, or may still continue in, not excepting even that of Socrates, when he was suspended in a basket to help contemplation, I think, with due submission, they seem to labour under two inconveniences. First, that the foundations being laid too high, they have been often out of sight, and ever out of hearing. Secondly, that the materials, being very transitory, have suffered much from inclemencies of air, especially in these north-west regions.

Therefore, towards the just performance of this great work, there remain but three methods that I can think on; whereof the

[1] But to return, and view the cheerful skies,
In this the task and mighty labour lies.

wisdom of our ancestors being highly sensible, has, to encourage all aspiring adventurers, thought fit to erect three wooden machines for the use of those orators who desire to talk much without interruption. These are, the pulpit, the ladder, and the stage-itinerant. For, as to the bar, though it be compounded of the same matter, and designed for the same use, it cannot however be well allowed the honor of a fourth, by reason of its level or inferior situation exposing it to perpetual interruption from collaterals. Neither can the bench itself, though raised to a proper eminency, put in a better claim, whatever its advocates insist on. For if they please to look into the original design of its erection, and the circumstances or adjuncts subservient to that design, they will soon acknowledge the present practice exactly correspondent to the primitive institution, and both to answer the etymology of the name, which in the Phœnician tongue is a word of great signification, importing, if literally interpreted, the place of sleep; but in common acceptation, a seat well bolstered and cushioned, for the repose of old and gouty limbs: *senes ut in otia tuta recedant.* Fortune being indebted to them this part of retaliation, that, as formerly they have long talked whilst others slept, so now they may sleep as long whilst others talk.

But if no other argument could occur to exclude the Bench and the Bar from the list of oratorial machines, it were sufficient that the admission of them would overthrow a number which I was resolved to establish, whatever argument it might cost me; in imitation of that prudent method observed by many other philosophers and great clerks, whose chief art in division has been to grow fond of some proper mystical number, which their imaginations have rendered sacred, to a degree, that they force common reason to find room for it in every part of nature; reducing, including, and adjusting every genus and species within that compass, by coupling some against their wills, and banishing others at any rate. Now among all the rest, the profound number THREE is that which hath most employed my sublimest speculations, nor ever without wonderful delight. There is now in the press (and will be published next term) a panegyrical essay of mine upon this number, wherein I have by most convincing proofs not only reduced the senses and the elements under its banner, but brought over several deserters from its two great rivals, SEVEN and NINE.[2]

Now, the first of these oratorial machines in place as well as

[2] The numbers *seven* and *nine* were supposed to have a certain inherent and fatal power attached to them, especially in computing the years of human life. SCOTT.

dignity, is the pulpit. Of pulpits there are in this island several sorts; but I esteem only that made of timber from the *sylva Caledonia*, which agrees very well with our climate. If it be upon its decay, 'tis the better both for conveyance of sound, and for other reasons to be mentioned by and by. The degree of perfection in shape and size, I take to consist in being extremely narrow, with little ornament, and best of all without a cover (for by ancient rule, it ought to be the only uncovered vessel in every assembly where it is rightfully used) by which means, from its near resemblance to a pillory, it will ever have a mighty influence on human ears.

Of ladders I need say nothing: 'tis observed by foreigners themselves, to the honor of our country, that we excel all nations in our practice and understanding of this machine. The ascending orators do not only oblige their audience in the agreeable delivery, but the whole world in their early publication of these speeches; which I look upon as the choicest treasury of our British eloquence, and whereof I am informed that worthy citizen and bookseller, Mr. John Dunton, hath made a faithful and a painful collection, which he shortly designs to publish in twelve volumes in folio, illustrated with copperplates. A work highly useful and curious, and altogether worthy of such a hand.

The last engine of orators is the stage itinerant,[3] erected with much sagacity, *sub Jove pluvio, in triviis & quadriviis*.[4] It is the great seminary of the two former, and its orators are sometimes preferred to the one, and sometimes to the other, in proportion to their deservings, there being a strict and perpetual intercourse between all three.

From this accurate deduction it is manifest, that for obtaining attention in public, there is of necessity required a superior position of place. But although this point be generally granted, yet the cause is little agreed in; and it seems to me, that very few philosophers have fallen into a true, natural solution of this phenomenon. The deepest account, and the most fairly digested of any I have yet met with, is this, that air being a heavy body, and therefore (according to the system of Epicurus[5]) continually descending must needs be more so, when loaden and pressed down by words; which are also bodies of much weight and gravity, as it is manifest from those deep impressions they make and leave upon us; and therefore must be delivered from a due

---

[3] Is the mountebank's stage, whose orators the author determines either to the gallows or a conventicle.

[4] In the open air, and in streets where the greatest resort is.

[5] Lucretius, Lib. 2.

altitude, or else they will neither carry a good aim, nor fall down with a sufficient force.

Corpoream quoque enim vocem constare fatendum est,
Et sonitum, quoniam possunt impellere sensus.[6]

LUCR. Lib. 4.

And I am the readier to favour this conjecture, from a common observation, that in the several assemblies of these orators, nature itself hath instructed the hearers to stand with their mouths open, and erected parallel to the horizon, so as they may be intersected by a perpendicular line from the zenith to the center of the earth. In which position, if the audience be well compact, every one carries home a share, and little or nothing is lost.

I confess there is something yet more refined in the contrivance and structure of our modern theatres. For, first, the pit is sunk below the stage with due regard to the institution above deduced; that whatever weighty matter shall be delivered thence (whether it be lead or gold) may fall plumb into the jaws of certain critics (as I think they are called) which stand ready open to devour them. Then, the boxes are built round, and raised to a level with the scene, in deference to the ladies, because, that large portion of wit laid out in raising pruriences and protuberances, is observed to run much upon a line, and ever in a circle. The whining passions, and little starved conceits, are gently wafted up by their own extreme levity, to the middle region, and there fix and are frozen by the frigid understandings of the inhabitants. Bombastry and buffoonery, by nature lofty and light, soar highest of all, and would be lost in the roof, if the prudent architect had not with much foresight contrived for them a fourth place, called the twelve-penny gallery, and there planted a suitable colony, who greedily intercept them in their passage.

Now this physico-logical scheme of oratorial receptacles or machines, contains a great mystery, being a type, a sign, an emblem, a shadow, a symbol, bearing analogy to the spacious commonwealth of writers, and to those methods by which they must exalt themselves to a certain eminency above the inferior world. By the pulpit are adumbrated the writings of our modern saints in Great Britain, as they have spiritualized and refined them from the dross and grossness of sense and human reason. The matter, as we have said, is of rotten wood, and that upon two considerations; because it is the quality of rotten wood to give light in the dark: and secondly, because its cavities are full of

[6] 'Tis certain then, that voice that thus can wound
Is all material; body every sound.

worms; which is a type with a pair of handles,[7] having a respect to the two principal qualifications of the orator, and the two different fates attending upon his works.

The ladder is an adequate symbol of faction and of poetry, to both of which so noble a number of authors are indebted for their fame. Of faction, because[8]   *   *   * *Hiatus in MS.*
* * * * * * * * * *
* * * * * * * * * *
* * * * *   Of poetry, because its orators do *perorare* with a song; and because climbing up by slow degrees, fate is sure to turn them off before they can reach within many steps of the top: and because it is a preferment attained by transferring of property, and a confounding of *meum* and *tuum*.

Under the stage-itinerant are couched those productions designed for the pleasure and delight of mortal man; such as Sixpenny-worth of Wit, Westminster Drolleries, Delightful Tales, Compleat Jesters, and the like; by which the writers of and for *Grub Street*, have in these latter ages so nobly triumphed over Time; have clipped his wings, pared his nails, filed his teeth, turned back his hour-glass, blunted his scythe, and drawn the hob-nails out of his shoes. It is under this classis I have presumed to list my present treatise, being just come from having the honor conferred upon me to be adopted a member of that illustrious fraternity.

Now, I am not unaware, how the productions of the Grub Street brotherhood, have of late years fallen under many prejudices, nor how it has been the perpetual employment of two junior start-up societies to ridicule them and their authors, as unworthy their established post in the commonwealth of wit and learning. Their own consciences will easily inform them, whom I mean; nor has the world been so negligent a looker-on, as not to observe the continual efforts made by the societies of Gresham,[9] and of Will's,[1] to edify a name and reputation upon the ruin of

[7] The two principal qualifications of a fanatic preacher are, his inward light, and his head full of maggots, and the two different fates of his writings are, to be burnt or worm-eaten.

[8] Here is pretended a defect in the manuscript, and this is very frequent with our author, either when he thinks he cannot say anything worth reading, or when he has no mind to enter on the subject, or when it is a matter of little moment, or perhaps to amuse his reader (whereof he is frequently very fond) or lastly, with some satirical intention.

[9] Gresham College was the place where the Royal Society then met. . . . H.

[1] Will's coffee-house was formerly the place where the poets usually met, which tho' it be yet fresh in memory, yet in some years may be forgot, and want this explanation.

OURS. And this is yet a more feeling grief to us upon the
regards of tenderness as well as of justice, when we reflect on
their proceedings not only as unjust, but as ungrateful, undutiful,
and unnatural. For how can it be forgot by the world or themselves (to say nothing of our own records, which are full and
clear in the point) that they both are seminaries not only of our
planting, but our watering too? I am informed, our two rivals
have lately made an offer to enter into the lists with united forces,
and challenge us to a comparison of books, both as to weight and
number. In return to which (with licence from our president)
I humbly offer two answers: first, we say, the proposal is like that
which Archimedes made upon a smaller affair,[2] including an impossibility in the practice; for where can they find scales of
capacity enough for the first, or an arithmetician of capacity
enough for the second? Secondly, we are ready to accept the
challenge, but with this condition, that a third indifferent person
be assigned, to whose impartial judgment it shall be left to decide,
which society each book, treatise, or pamphlet, do most properly
belong to. This point, God knows, is very far from being fixed
at present; for we are ready to produce a catalogue of some
thousands, which in all common justice ought to be entitled to
our fraternity, but by the revolted and new-fangled writers,
most perfidiously ascribed to the others. Upon all which, we
think it very unbecoming our prudence, that the determination
should be remitted to the authors themselves; when our adversaries, by briguing and caballing, have caused so universal a
defection from us, that the greatest part of our society hath
already deserted to them, and our nearest friends begin to stand
aloof, as if they were half-ashamed to own us.

This is the utmost I am authorized to say upon so ungrateful
and melancholy a subject; because we are extreme unwilling to
inflame a controversy, whose continuance may be so fatal to the
interests of us all, desiring much rather that things be amicably
composed; and we shall so far advance on our side, as to be ready
to receive the two prodigals with open arms, whenever they shall
think fit to return from their husks and their harlots; which I
think from the present course of their studies[3] they most
properly may be said to be engaged in; and like an indulgent parent, continue to them our affection and our blessing.

But the greatest maim given to that general reception, which
the writings of our society have formerly received (next to the
transitory state of all sublunary things) hath been a superficial

---

[2] *Viz.* About moving the earth.
[3] Virtuoso experiments, and modern comedies.

vein among many readers of the present age, who will by no
means be persuaded to inspect beyond the surface and the rind
of things; whereas wisdom is a fox, who after long hunting will
at last cost you the pains to dig out. 'Tis a cheese, which by how
much the richer, has the thicker, the homelier, and the coarser
coat; and whereof to a judicious palate, the maggots are the best.
'Tis a sack-posset, wherein the deeper you go, you will find it
the sweeter. Wisdom is a hen, whose cackling we must value
and consider, because it is attended with an egg. But then lastly,
'tis a nut, which unless you choose with judgment, may cost you
a tooth, and pay you with nothing but a worm. In consequence
of these momentous truths, the Grubæan Sages have always
chosen to convey their precepts and their arts, shut up within
the vehicles of types and fables, which having been perhaps more
careful and curious in adorning, than was altogether necessary,
it has fared with these vehicles after the usual fate of coaches
over-finely painted and gilt, that the transitory gazers have so
dazzled their eyes, and filled their imaginations with the outward
lustre, as neither to regard or consider the person or the parts of
the owner within. A misfortune we undergo with somewhat less
reluctancy, because it has been common to us with Pythagoras,
Æsop, Socrates, and other of our predecessors.

However, that neither the world nor our selves, may any
longer suffer by such misunderstandings, I have been prevailed
on, after much importunity from my friends, to travel in a complete and laborious dissertation upon the prime productions of
our society, which, beside their beautiful externals, for the
gratification of superficial readers, have darkly and deeply couched
under them the most finished and refined systems of all sciences
and arts; as I do not doubt to lay open by untwisting or unwind-
ing, and either to draw up by exantlation, or display by incision.

This great work was entered upon some years ago, by one of
our most eminent members: he began with the *History of Reynard the Fox*,[4] but neither lived to publish his essay, nor to
proceed farther in so useful an attempt, which is very much to be
lamented, because the discovery he made, and communicated
with his friends, is now universally received; nor do I think any
of the learned will dispute that famous treatise to be a complete
body of civil knowledge, and the revelation, or rather the apoca-
lypse of all State Arcana. But the progress I have made is much

---

[4] The Author seems here to be mistaken, for I have seen a Latin edition
of *Reynard the Fox*, above an hundred years old, which I take to be the
original; for the rest it has been thought by many people to contain some
satirical design in it.

greater, having already finished my annotations upon several dozens; from some of which I shall impart a few hints to the candid reader, as far as will be necessary to the conclusion at which I aim.

The first piece I have handled is that of *Tom Thumb*, whose author was a Pythagorean philosopher. This dark treatise contains the whole scheme of the Metempsychosis, deducing the progress of the soul through all her stages.

The next is *Dr. Faustus*, penned by Artephius, an author *bonæ notæ*, and an *adeptus;* he published it in the nine hundred-eighty-fourth year of his age;[5] this writer proceeds wholly by reincrudation, or in the *via humida;* and the marriage between Faustus and Helen does most conspicuously dilucidate the fermenting of the male and female dragon.

Whittington and his Cat is the work of that mysterious rabbi, Jehuda Hannasi, containing a defence of the Gemara of the Jerusalem Mishna,[6] and its just preference to that of Babylon, contrary to the vulgar opinion.

The Hind and Panther. This is the masterpiece of a famous writer now living,[7] intended for a complete abstract of sixteen thousand schoolmen from Scotus to Bellarmine.

Tommy Potts.[8] Another piece supposed by the same hand, by way of supplement to the former.

The Wise Men of Gotham, cum appendice. This is a treatise of immense erudition, being the great original and fountain of those arguments, bandied about both in France and England, for a just defence of the moderns' learning and wit, against the presumption, the pride, and the ignorance of the ancients. This unknown author hath so exhausted the subject, that a penetrating reader will easily discover whatever hath been written since upon that dispute, to be little more than repetition. An abstract of this treatise hath been lately published by a worthy member of our society.[9]

These notices may serve to give the learned reader an idea as well as a taste of what the whole work is likely to produce; wherein I have now altogether circumscribed my thoughts and my studies; and if I can bring it to a perfection before I die, shall

---

[5] He lived a thousand.

[6] The Gemara is the decision, explanation, or interpretation of the Jewish rabbis; and the Mishna is properly the code or body of the Jewish civil or common law. H.

[7] Viz. In the year 1698.

[8] A popular ballad, then the favourite of the vulgar. . . . SCOTT.

[9] This I suppose to be understood of Mr. W-tt-n's *Discourse of Ancient and Modern Learning*.

reckon I have well employed the poor remains of an unfortunate life.[1] This indeed is more than I can justly expect from a quill worn to the pith in the service of the state, in *pros* and *cons* upon Popish plots, and meal-tubs,[2] and exclusion bills, and passive obedience, and addresses of lives and fortunes, and prerogative, and property, and liberty of conscience, and letters to a friend: from an understanding and a conscience thread-bare and ragged with perpetual turning; from a head broken in a hundred places by the malignants of the opposite factions; and from a body spent with poxes ill cured, by trusting to bawds and surgeons, who (as it afterwards appeared) were professed enemies to me and the government, and revenged their party's quarrel upon my nose and shins. Fourscore and eleven pamphlets have I written under three reigns, and for the service of six and thirty factions. But finding the state has no farther occasion for me and my ink, I retire willingly to draw it out into speculations more becoming a philosopher, having, to my unspeakable comfort, passed a long life with a conscience void of offence.

But to return. I am assured from the reader's candor, that the brief specimen I have given, will easily clear all the rest of our society's productions from an aspersion grown, as it is manifest, out of envy and ignorance: that they are of little farther use or value to mankind, beyond the common entertainments of their wit and their style; for these I am sure have never yet been disputed by our keenest adversaries: in both which, as well as the more profound and mystical part, I have throughout this treatise closely followed the most applauded originals. And to render all complete, I have with much thought and application of mind, so ordered, that the chief title prefixed to it (I mean, that under which I design it shall pass in the common conversations of court and town) is modelled exactly after the manner peculiar to our society.

I confess to have been somewhat liberal in the business of titles,[3] having observed the humor of multiplying them, to bear great vogue among certain writers, whom I exceedingly reverence. And indeed it seems not unreasonable that books, the children of the brain, should have the honor to be christened with variety of names, as well as other infants of quality. Our famous

---

[1] Here the author seems to personate L'Estrange, Dryden, and some others, who after having passed their lives in vices, faction and falsehood, have the impudence to talk of merit and innocence and sufferings.

[2] In King Charles the Second's time, there was an account of a Presbyterian plot, found in a tub, which then made much noise.

[3] The title-page in the original was so torn, that it was not possible to recover several titles which the author here speaks of.

Dryden has ventured to proceed a point farther, endeavouring to introduce also a multiplicity of god-fathers;[4] which is an improvement of much more advantage, upon a very obvious account. 'Tis a pity this admirable invention has not been better cultivated, so as to grow by this time into general imitation, when such an authority serves it for a precedent. Nor have my endeavours been wanting to second so useful an example. But it seems there is an unhappy expense usually annexed to the calling of a god-father, which was clearly out of my head, as it is very reasonable to believe. Where the pinch lay, I cannot certainly affirm; but having employed a world of thoughts and pains to split my treatise into forty sections, and having entreated forty lords of my acquaintance, that they would do me the honor to stand, they all made it a matter of conscience, and sent me their excuses.

SECTION II

ONCE upon a time, there was a man who had three sons by one wife,[5] and all at a birth, neither could the midwife tell certainly which was the eldest. Their father died while they were young, and upon his deathbed, calling the lads to him, spoke thus:

'Sons, because I have purchased no estate, nor was born to any, I have long considered of some good legacies to bequeath you; and at last, with much care as well as expense, have provided each of you (here they are) a new coat.[6] Now, you are to understand, that these coats have two virtues contained in them: one is, that with good wearing, they will last you fresh and sound as long as you live; the other is, that they will grow in the same proportion with your bodies, lengthening and widening of themselves, so as to be always fit. Here, let me see them on you before I die. So, very well; pray children, wear them clean, and brush them often. You will find in my will[7] (here it is) full instructions in every particular concerning the wearing and management of your coats; wherein you must be very exact, to avoid the penalties I

---

[4] See Virgil translated, &c.
He dedicated the different parts of Virgil to different patrons. H.

[5] By these three sons, Peter, Martin, and Jack, Popery, the Church of England, and our Protestant dissenters are designed. W. WOTTON.

[6] By his coats which he gave his sons, the garments of the Israelites. W. WOTTON.
An error (with submission) of the learned commentator; for by the coats are meant the doctrine and faith of Christianity, by the wisdom of the Divine Founder fitted to all times, places and circumstances. LAMBIN.

[7] The New Testament.

have appointed for every transgression or neglect, upon which your future fortunes will entirely depend. I have also commanded in my will, that you should live together in one house like brethren and friends, for then you will be sure to thrive, and not otherwise.'

Here the story says, this good father died, and the three sons went all together to seek their fortunes.

I shall not trouble you with recounting what adventures they met for the first seven years, any farther than by taking notice, that they carefully observed their father's will, and kept their coats in very good order; that they travelled through several countries, encountered a reasonable quantity of giants, and slew certain dragons.

Being now arrived at the proper age for producing themselves, they came up to town, and fell in love with the ladies, but especially three, who about that time were in chief reputation: the Duchess d'Argent, Madame de Grands Titres, and the Countess d'Orgueil.[8] On their first appearance, our three adventurers met with a very bad reception; and soon with great sagacity guessing out the reason, they quickly began to improve in the good qualities of the town: they writ, and rallied, and rhymed, and sung, and said, and said nothing: they drank, and fought, and whored, and slept, and swore, and took snuff: they went to new plays on the first night, haunted the chocolate-houses, beat the watch, lay on bulks, and got claps: they bilked hackney-coachmen, ran in debt with shopkeepers, and lay with their wives: they killed bailiffs, kicked fiddlers down stairs, eat at Locket's, loitered at Will's: they talked of the drawing-room, and never came there: dined with lords they never saw: whispered a duchess, and spoke never a word: exposed the scrawls of their laundress for billet-doux of quality: came ever just from court, and were never seen in it: attended the Levee *sub dio:* got a list of peers by heart in one company, and with great familiarity retailed them in another. Above all, they constantly attended those Committees of Senators who are silent in the House, and loud in the coffee-house, where they nightly adjourn to chew the cud of politics, and are encompassed with a ring of disciples, who lie in wait to catch up their droppings. The three brothers had acquired forty other qualifications of the like stamp, too tedious to recount, and by consequence were justly reckoned the most accomplished persons in

---

[8] Their mistresses are the Duchess d'Argent, Mademoiselle de Grands Titres, and the Countess d'Orgueil, *i.e.* covetousness, ambition, and pride, which were the three great vices that the ancient Fathers inveighed against as the first corruptions of Christianity. W. WOTTON.

the town. But all would not suffice, and the ladies aforesaid continued still inflexible. To clear up which difficulty I must, with the reader's good leave and patience, have recourse to some points of weight, which the authors of that age have not sufficiently illustrated.

For about this time it happened a sect arose,[9] whose tenets obtained and spread very far, especially in the *grand monde*, and among everybody of good fashion. They worshipped a sort of idol,[1] who, as their doctrine delivered, did daily create men by a kind of manufactory operation. This idol they placed in the highest parts of the house, on an altar erected about three foot: he was shown in the posture of a Persian emperor, sitting on a superficies, with his legs interwoven under him. This god had a goose for his ensign; whence it is, that some learned men pretend to deduce his original from Jupiter Capitolinus. At his left hand, beneath the altar, Hell seemed to open, and catch at the animals the idol was creating; to prevent which, certain of his priests hourly flung in pieces of the uninformed mass, or substance, and sometimes whole limbs already enlivened, which that horrid gulf insatiably swallowed, terrible to behold. The goose was also held a subaltern divinity or *deus minorum gentium*, before whose shrine was sacrificed that creature, whose hourly food is human gore, and who is in so great renown abroad, for being the delight and favourite of the Ægyptian Cercopithecus.[2] Millions of these animals were cruelly slaughtered every day, to appease the hunger of that consuming deity. The chief idol was also worshipped as the inventor of the yard and the needle; whether as the god of seamen, or on account of certain other mystical attributes, hath not been sufficiently cleared.

The worshippers of this deity had also a system of their belief, which seemed to turn upon the following fundamental. They held the universe to be a large suit of clothes, which invests everything: that the earth is invested by the air; the air is invested by the stars; and the stars are invested by the *primum mobile*. Look on this globe of earth, you will find it to be a very complete and fashionable dress. What is that which some call land, but a fine coat faced with green? or the sea, but a waistcoat of water-tabby? Proceed to the particular works of the creation, you will find how curious Journeyman Nature hath been, to trim up the

[9] This is an occasional satire upon dress and fashion, in order to introduce what follows.

[1] By this idol is meant a tailor.

[2] The Ægyptians worshipped a monkey, which animal is very fond of eating lice, styled here creatures that feed on human gore.

vegetable beaux; observe how sparkish a periwig adorns the head of a beech, and what a fine doublet of white satin is worn by the birch. To conclude from all, what is man himself but a micro-coat,[3] or rather a complete suit of clothes with all its trimmings? As to his body, there can be no dispute; but examine even the acquirements of his mind, you will find them all contribute in their order towards furnishing out an exact dress. To instance no more: is not religion a cloak; honesty a pair of shoes worn out in the dirt; self-love a surtout; vanity a shirt; and conscience a pair of breeches; which, though a cover for lewdness as well as nasti-ness, is easily slipt down for the service of both?

These *postulata* being admitted, it will follow in due course of reasoning, that those beings which the world calls improperly suits of clothes, are in reality the most refined species of animals, or to proceed higher, that they are rational creatures, or men. For is it not manifest that they live, and move, and talk, and per-form all other offices of human life? Are not beauty, and wit, and mien, and breeding, their inseparable properties? In short, we see nothing but them, hear nothing but them. Is it not they who walk the streets, fill up parliament-, coffee-, play-, bawdy-houses? 'Tis true indeed, that these animals, which are vulgarly called suits of clothes, or dresses, do according to certain com-positions receive different appellations. If one of them be trimmed up with a gold chain, and a red gown, and a white rod, and a great horse, it is called a Lord-Mayor; if certain ermines and furs be placed in a certain position, we style them a Judge, and so an apt conjunction of lawn and black satin we entitle a Bishop.

Others of these professors, though agreeing in the main system, were yet more refined upon certain branches of it; and held that man was an animal compounded of two dresses, the natural and the celestial suit, which were the body and the soul: that the soul was the outward, and the body the inward clothing; that the latter was *ex traduce;* but the former of daily creation and circum-fusion. This last they proved by scripture, because in them we live, and move, and have our being; as likewise by philosophy, because they are all in all, and all in every part. Besides, said they, separate these two, and you will find the body to be only a sense-less unsavoury carcass. By all which it is manifest, that the out-ward dress must needs be the soul.

To this system of religion were tagged several subaltern doc-trines, which were entertained with great vogue, as particularly,

[3] Alluding to the word microcosm, or a little world. as man hath been called by philosophers.

the faculties of the mind were deduced by the learned among them in this manner: embroidery was sheer wit; gold fringe was agreeable conversation; gold lace was repartee; a huge long periwig was humor; and a coat full of powder was very good raillery: all which required abundance of *finesse* and *delicatesse* to manage with advantage, as well as a strict observance after times and fashions.

I have with much pains and reading, collected out of ancient authors, this short summary of a body of philosophy and divinity, which seems to have been composed by a vein and race of thinking, very different from any other systems, either ancient or modern. And it was not merely to entertain or satisfy the reader's curiosity, but rather to give him light into several circumstances of the following story, that knowing the state of dispositions and opinions in an age so remote, he may better comprehend those great events which were the issue of them. I advise therefore the courteous reader to peruse with a world of application, again and again, whatever I have written upon this matter. And so leaving these broken ends, I carefully gather up the chief thread of my story and proceed.[4]

These opinions therefore were so universal, as well as the practices of them, among the refined part of court and town, that our three brother-adventurers, as their circumstances then stood, were strangely at a loss. For, on the one side, the three ladies they addressed themselves to (whom we have named already) were ever at the very top of the fashion, and abhorred all that were below it but the breadth of a hair. On the other side, their father's will was very precise, and it was the main precept in it, with the greatest penalties annexed, not to add to, or diminish from their coats one thread, without a positive command in the will. Now, the coats their father had left them were, 'tis true, of very good cloth, and besides, so neatly sewn, you would swear they were all of a piece; but at the same time very plain, and with

---

[4] The first part of the *Tale* is the history of Peter; thereby Popery is exposed; everybody knows the Papists have made great additions to Christianity; that indeed is the great exception which the Church of England makes against them; accordingly Peter begins his pranks with adding a shoulder-knot to his coat. W. WOTTON.

His description of the cloth of which the coat was made, has a farther meaning than the words may seem to import: 'The coats their father had left them were of very good cloth, and besides so neatly sewn, you would swear it had been all of a piece, but at the same time very plain with little or no ornament.' This is the distinguishing character of the Christian religion. *Christiana religio absoluta et simplex*, was Ammianus Marcellinus's description of it, who was himself a heathen. W. WOTTON.

little or no ornament; and it happened, that before they were a month in town, great shoulder-knots [5] came up; straight all the world was shoulder-knots; no approaching the ladies' *ruelles* without the *quota* of shoulder-knots. That fellow, cries one, has no soul; where is his shoulder-knot? Our three brethren soon discovered their want by sad experience, meeting in their walks with forty mortifications and indignities. If they went to the play-house, the door-keeper showed them into the twelve-penny gallery. If they called a boat, says a waterman, I am first sculler. If they stepped to the Rose to take a bottle, the drawer would cry, Friend, we sell no ale. If they went to visit a lady, a footman met them at the door with, Pray send up your message. In this unhappy case, they went immediately to consult their father's will, read it over and over, but not a word of the shoulder-knot. What should they do? What temper should they find? Obedience was absolutely necessary, and yet shoulder-knots appeared extremely requisite. After much thought, one of the brothers who happened to be more book-learned than the other two, said, he had found an expedient. ''Tis true,' said he, 'there is nothing here in this will, *totidem verbis*,[6] making mention of shoulder-knots, but I dare conjecture we may find them *inclusive*, or *totidem syllabis*.' This distinction was immediately approved by all; and so they fell again to examine the will. But their evil star had so directed the matter, that the first syllable was not to be found in the whole writing. Upon which disappointment, he who found the former evasion, took heart and said, 'Brothers, there is yet hopes; for though we cannot find them *totidem verbis*, nor *totidem syllabis*, I dare engage we shall make them out, *tertio modo*, or *totidem literis*.' This discovery was also highly commended, upon which they fell once more to the scrutiny, and soon picked out S,H,O,U,L,D,E,R; when the same planet, enemy to their repose, had wonderfully contrived, that a K was not to be found. Here was a weighty difficulty! But the distinguishing brother (for whom we shall hereafter find a name) now his hand was in, proved by a very good argument, that K was a modern illegitimate letter, unknown to the learned ages, nor anywhere to be found in ancient manuscripts.[6] ''Tis true,' said he, 'the word

[5] By this is understood the first introducing of pageantry, and unnecessary ornaments in the Church, such as were neither for convenience nor edification, as a shoulder-knot, in which there is neither symmetry nor use.

[6] When the Papists cannot find any thing which they want in Scripture, they go to oral tradition: thus Peter is introduced satisfied with the tedious way of looking for all the letters of any word, which he has occasion for in the Will, when neither the constituent syllables, nor much less the whole word, were there *in terminis*. W. WOTTON.

Calendæ hath in *Q.V.C.*[7] been sometimes writ with a K, but erroneously, for in the best copies it has been ever spelt with a C. And by consequence it was a gross mistake in our language to spell Knot with a K, but that from henceforward he would take care it should be writ with a C.' Upon this all farther difficulty vanished; shoulder-knots were made clearly out to be *jure paterno,* and our three gentlemen swaggered with as large and as flaunting ones as the best.

But, as human happiness is of a very short duration, so in those days were human fashions, upon which it entirely depends. Shoulder-knots had their time, and we must now imagine them in their decline; for a certain lord came just from Paris, with fifty yards of gold lace upon his coat, exactly trimmed after the court fashion of that month. In two days all mankind appeared closed up in bars of gold lace: [8] whoever durst peep abroad without his compliment of gold lace, was as scandalous as a —, and as ill received among the women. What should our three knights do in this momentous affair? They had sufficiently strained a point already in the affair of shoulder-knots. Upon recourse to the will, nothing appeared there but *altum silentium.* That of the shoulder-knots was a loose, flying, circumstantial point; but this of gold lace seemed too considerable an alteration without better warrant. It did *aliquo modo essentiæ adhærere,* and therefore required a positive precept. But about this time it fell out, that the learned brother aforesaid had read *Aristotelis Dialectica,* and especially that wonderful piece *de Interpretatione,* which has the faculty of teaching its readers to find out a meaning in everything but itself, like commentators on the Revelations, who proceed prophets without understanding a syllable of the text. 'Brothers,' said he, 'you are to be informed,[9] that of wills *duo sunt genera,* nuncupatory [1] and scriptory; that in the scriptory will here before us, there is no precept or mention about gold lace, *conceditur:* but, *si idem affirmetur de nuncupatorio, negatur.* For brothers, if you remember, we heard a fellow say when we were boys, that he heard my father's man say, that he heard my father say, that he would advise his sons to get gold lace on their coats,

---

[7] Quibusdam veteribus codicibus: some ancient manuscripts.

[8] I cannot tell whether the author means any new innovation by this word, or whether it be only to introduce the new methods of forcing and perverting Scripture.

[9] The next subject of our author's wit is the glosses and interpretations of Scripture, very many absurd ones of which are allowed in the most authentic books of the Church of Rome. W. WOTTON.

[1] By this is meant tradition, allowed to have equal authority with the scripture, or rather greater.

as soon as ever they could procure money to buy it.' 'By G—, that is very true,' cries the other; 'I remember it perfectly well,' said the third. And so without more ado they got the largest gold lace in the parish, and walked about as fine as lords.

A while after there came up all in fashion a pretty sort of flame-coloured satin [2] for linings, and the mercer brought a pattern of it immediately to our three gentlemen, 'An please your worships,' said he,[3] 'my Lord C — and Sir J. W. had linings out of this very piece last night; it takes wonderfully, and I shall not have a remnant left enough to make my wife a pin-cushion by to-morrow morning at ten o'clock.' Upon this, they fell again to rummage the will, because the present case also required a positive precept, the lining being held by orthodox writers to be of the essence of the coat. After long search, they could fix upon nothing to the matter in hand, except a short advice of their father's in the will, to take care of fire, and put out their candles before they went to sleep.[4] This though a good deal for the purpose, and helping very far towards self-conviction, yet not seeming wholly of force to establish a command; and being resolved to avoid farther scruple, as well as future occasion for scandal, says he that was the scholar, 'I remember to have read in wills of a codicil annexed, which is indeed a part of the will, and what it contains hath equal authority with the rest. Now, I have been considering of this same will here before us, and I cannot reckon it to be complete for want of such a codicil. I will therefore fasten one in its proper place very dexterously; I have had it by me some time; it was written by a dog-keeper of my grand-father's,[5] and talks a great deal (as good luck would have it) of

[2] This is purgatory, whereof he speaks more particularly hereafter, but here only to show how Scripture was perverted to prove it, which was done by giving equal authority with the Canon to Apocrypha, called here a codicil annexed.

It is likely the author, in every one of these changes in the brothers' dresses, refers to some particular error in the Church of Rome, though it is not easy I think to apply them all, but by this of flame-coloured satin, is manifestly intended purgatory; by gold lace may perhaps be understood the lofty ornaments and plate in the churches; the shoulder-knots and silver fringe are not so obvious, at least to me; but the Indian figures of men, women and children plainly relate to the pictures in the Romish churches, of God like an old man, of the Virgin Mary, and our Saviour as a child.

[3] This shows the time the author writ, it being about fourteen years since those two persons were reckoned the fine gentlemen of the town.

[4] That is, to take care of hell, and, in order to do that, to subdue and extinguish their lusts.

[5] I believe this refers to that part of the Apocrypha where mention is made of Tobit and his dog.

this very flame-coloured satin.' The project was immediately approved by the other two; an old parchment scroll was tagged on according to art, in the form of a codicil annexed, and the satin bought and worn.

Next winter, a player, hired for the purpose by the corporation of fringe-makers, acted his part in a new comedy, all covered with silver fringe,[6] and according to the laudable custom gave rise to that fashion. Upon which, the brothers consulting their father's will, to their great astonishment found these words; 'Item, I charge and command my said three sons to wear no sort of silver fringe upon or about their said coats,' etc., with a penalty in case of disobedience, too long here to insert. However, after some pause the brother so often mentioned for his erudition, who was well skilled in criticisms, had found in a certain author, which he said should be nameless, that the same word which in the will is called fringe, does also signify a broomstick, and doubtless ought to have the same interpretation in this paragraph. This, another of the brothers disliked, because of that epithet silver, which could not, he humbly conceived, in propriety of speech be reasonably applied to a broom-stick; but it was replied upon him, that this epithet was understood in a mythological and allegorical sense. However, he objected again, why their father should forbid them to wear a broom-stick on their coats, a caution that seemed unnatural and impertinent; upon which he was taken up short, as one that spoke irreverently of a mystery, which doubtless was very useful and significant, but ought not to be over-curiously pried into, or nicely reasoned upon. And in short, their father's authority being now considerably sunk, this expedient was allowed to serve as a lawful dispensation for wearing their full proportion of silver fringe.

A while after was revived an old fashion, long antiquated, of embroidery with Indian figures of men, women, and children.[7] Here they had no occasion to examine the will. They remembered but too well how their father had always abhorred this fashion; that he made several paragraphs on purpose, importing his utter detestation of it, and bestowing his everlasting curse to his sons whenever they should wear it. For all this, in a few days they appeared higher in the fashion than anybody else in the town. But they solved the matter by saying, that these figures

---

[6] This is certainly the farther introducing the pomps of habit and ornament.

[7] The images of saints, the blessed Virgin, and our Saviour an infant.

Ibid. Images in the Church of Rome give him but too fair a handle. The brothers remembered, &c. The allegory here is direct. W. WOTTON.

were not at all the same with those that were formerly worn, and were meant in the will. Besides, they did not wear them in that sense, as forbidden by their father, but as they were a commendable custom, and of great use to the public. That these rigorous clauses in the will did therefore require some allowance, and a favourable interpretation, and ought to be understood *cum grano salis*.

But fashions perpetually altering in that age, the scholastic brother grew weary of searching farther evasions, and solving everlasting contradictions. Resolved therefore at all hazards to comply with the modes of the world, they concerted matters together, and agreed unanimously to lock up their father's will in a strong box,[8] brought out of Greece or Italy (I have forgot which) and trouble themselves no farther to examine it, but only refer to its authority whenever they thought fit. In consequence whereof, a while after it grew a general mode to wear an infinite number of points, most of them tagged with silver: upon which the scholar pronounced *ex cathedra*,[9] that points were absolutely *jure paterno*, as they might very well remember. 'Tis true, indeed, the fashion prescribed somewhat more than were directly named in the will; however, that they, as heirs-general of their father, had power to make and add certain clauses for public emolument, though not deducible, *totidem verbis*, from the letter of the will, or else *multa absurda sequerentur*. This was understood for canonical, and therefore on the following Sunday they came to church all covered with points.

The learned brother so often mentioned was reckoned the best scholar in all that, or the next street to it; insomuch as, having run something behind-hand with the world, he obtained the favour from a certain lord,[1] to receive him into his house, and

---

[8] The Papists formerly forbade the people the use of scripture in a vulgar tongue; Peter therefore locks up his father's will in a strong box, brought out of Greece or Italy. Those countries are named because the New Testament is written in Greek; and the vulgar Latin, which is the authentic edition of the Bible in the Church of Rome, is in the language of old Italy. W. WOTTON.

[9] The popes in their decretals and bulls have given their sanction to very many gainful doctrines which are now received in the Church of Rome that are not mentioned in scripture, and are unknown to the primitive church; Peter accordingly pronounces *ex cathedra*, that points tagged with silver were absolutely *jure paterno*, and so they wore them in great numbers. W. WOTTON.

[1] This was Constantine the Great, from whom the popes pretend a donation of St. Peter's patrimony, which they have been never able to produce.

Ibid. The bishops of Rome enjoyed their privileges in Rome at first by

to teach his children. A while after the lord died, and he, by long practice of his father's will, found the way of contriving a deed of conveyance of that house to himself and his heirs; upon which he took possession, turned the young squires out, and received his brothers in their stead.

SECTION III

A DIGRESSION CONCERNING CRITICS

THO' I have been hitherto as cautious as I could, upon all occasions, most nicely to follow the rules and methods of writing laid down by the example of our illustrious moderns; yet has the unhappy shortness of my memory led me into an error, from which I must immediately extricate myself, before I can decently pursue my principal subject. I confess with shame, it was an unpardonable omission to proceed so far as I have already done, before I had performed the due discourses, expostulatory, supplicatory, or deprecatory, with my good lords the critics. Towards some atonement for this grievous neglect, I do here make humbly bold to present them with a short account of themselves and their art, by looking into the original and pedigree of the word, as it is generally understood among us, and very briefly considering the ancient and present state thereof.

By the word critic, at this day so frequent in all conversations, there have sometimes been distinguished three very different species of mortal men, according as I have read in ancient books and pamphlets. For first, by this term was understood such persons as invented or drew up rules for themselves and the world, by observing which, a careful reader might be able to pronounce upon the productions of the learned, form his taste to a true relish of the sublime and the admirable, and divide every beauty of matter or of style from the corruption that apes it. In their common perusal of books, singling out the errors and defects, the nauseous, the fulsome, the dull, and the impertinent, with the caution of a man that walks through Edinburgh streets in a morning, who is indeed as careful as he can to watch diligently, and spy out the filth in his way; not that he is curious to observe the colour and complexion of the ordure, or take its dimensions, much less to be paddling in, or tasting it; but only with a design

wit

---

the favour of emperors, whom at last they shut out of their own capital city, and then forged a donation from Constantine the Great, the better to justify what they did. In imitation of this, Peter having run something behind-hand in the world, obtained leave of a certain lord, &c. W. WOTTON.

to come out as cleanly as he may. These men seem, though very erroneously, to have understood the appellation of critic in a literal sense; that one principal part of his office was to praise and acquit; and that a critic, who sets up to read only for an occasion of censure and reproof, is a creature as barbarous as a judge, who should take up a resolution to hang all men that came before him upon a trial.

Again, by the word critic have been meant the restorers of ancient learning from the worms, and graves, and dust of manuscripts.

Now, the races of these two have been for some ages utterly extinct; and besides, to discourse any farther of them would not be at all to my purpose.

The third, and noblest sort, is that of the TRUE CRITIC, whose original is the most ancient of all. Every true critic is a hero born, descending in a direct line from a celestial stem by Momus and Hybris, who begat Zoilus, who begat Tigellius, who begat Etcætera the Elder; who begat Bentley, and Rymer, and Wotton, and Perrault, and Dennis, who begat Etcætera the Younger.

And these are the critics from whom the commonwealth of learning has in all ages received such immense benefits, that the gratitude of their admirers placed their origin in Heaven, among those of Hercules, Theseus, Perseus, and other great deservers of mankind. But heroic virtue itself hath not been exempt from the obloquy of evil tongues. For it hath been objected, that those ancient heroes, famous for their combating so many giants, and dragons, and robbers, were in their own persons a greater nuisance to mankind, than any of those monsters they subdued; and therefore to render their obligations more complete, when all other vermin were destroyed, should in conscience have concluded with the same justice upon themselves as Hercules most generously did, and hath upon that score procured to himself more temples and votaries than the best of his fellows. For these reasons, I suppose it is, why some have conceived it would be very expedient for the public good of learning that every true critic, as soon as he had finished his task assigned, should immediately deliver himself up to ratsbane, or hemp, or from some convenient altitude; and that no man's pretensions to so illustrious a character should by any means be received, before that operation were performed.

Now, from this heavenly descent of criticism, and the close analogy it bears to heroic virtue, 'tis easy to assign the proper employment of a true ancient genuine critic; which is, to travel through this vast world of writings; to pursue and hunt those monstrous faults bred within them; to drag out the lurking errors like Cacus from his den; to multiply them like Hydra's heads; and rake them together like Augeas's dung. Or else drive away a sort of dangerous fowl, who have a perverse inclination to plunder the best branches of the tree of knowledge, like those Stymphalian birds that eat up the fruit.

These reasonings will furnish us with an adequate definition of a true critic: that he is a discoverer and collector of writers' faults. Which may be farther put beyond dispute by the following demonstration: that whoever will examine the writings in all kinds, wherewith this ancient sect has honoured the world, shall immediately find, from the whole thread and tenor of them, that the ideas of the authors have been altogether conversant and taken up with the faults and blemishes, and oversights, and mistakes of other writers; and let the subject treated on be whatever it will, their imaginations are so entirely possessed and replete with the defects of other pens, that the very quintessence of what is bad does of necessity distil into their own, by which means the whole appears to be nothing else but an abstract of the criticisms themselves have made.

Having thus briefly considered the original and office of a critic, as the word is understood in its most noble and universal acceptation, I proceed to refute the objections of those who argue from the silence and pretermission of authors; by which they pretend to prove, that the very art of criticism, as now exercised, and by me explained, is wholly modern; and consequently, that the critics of Great Britain and France have no title to an original so ancient and illustrious as I have deduced. Now, if I can clearly make out on the contrary, that the most ancient writers have particularly described both the person and the office of a true critic, agreeable to the definition laid down by me, their grand objection, from the silence of authors, will fall to the ground.

I confess to have for a long time borne a part in this general error; from which I should never have acquitted myself, but through the assistance of our noble moderns; whose most edifying volumes I turn indefatigably over night and day, for the improvement of my mind, and the good of my country. These have with unwearied pains made many useful searches into the weak sides of the ancients, and given us a comprehensive list of them.[2] Besides, they have proved beyond contradiction, that the very finest things delivered of old, have been long since invented, and brought to light by much later pens; and that the noblest

[2] See Wotton, Of Ancient and Modern Learning.

discoveries those ancients ever made, of art or of nature, have all been produced by the transcending genius of the present age. Which clearly shows, how little merit those ancients can justly pretend to; and takes off that blind admiration paid them by men in a corner, who have the unhappiness of conversing too little with present things. Reflecting maturely upon all this, and taking in the whole compass of human nature, I easily concluded, that these ancients, highly sensible of their many imperfections, must needs have endeavoured from some passages in their works, to obviate, soften, or divert the censorious reader, by satire, or panegyric upon the true critics, in imitation of their masters, the moderns. Now, in the commonplaces of both these,[3] I was plentifully instructed, by a long course of useful study in prefaces and prologues; and therefore immediately resolved to try what I could discover of either, by a diligent perusal of the most ancient writers, and especially those who treated of the earliest times. Here I found to my great surprise, that although they all entered, upon occasion, into particular descriptions of the true critic, according as they were governed by their fears or their hopes; yet whatever they touched of that kind, was with abundance of caution, adventuring no farther than mythology and hieroglyphic. This, I suppose, gave ground to superficial readers, for urging the silence of authors, against the antiquity of the true critic, though the types are so apposite, and the applications so necessary and natural, that it is not easy to conceive how any reader of a modern eye and taste could overlook them. I shall venture from a great number to produce a few, which I am very confident will put this question beyond dispute.

It well deserves considering, that these ancient writers in treating enigmatically upon the subject, have generally fixed upon the very same hieroglyph, varying only the story according to their affections or their wit. For first, Pausanias is of opinion, that the perfection of writing correct was entirely owing to the institution of critics; and that he can possibly mean no other than the true critic, is, I think, manifest enough from the following description. He says, they were a race of men, who delighted to nibble at the superfluities, and excrescencies of books; which the learned at length observing, took warning of their own accord, to lop the luxuriant, the rotten, the dead, the sapless, and the overgrown branches from their works. But now, all this he cunningly shades under the following allegory; that the Nauplians in Argia [4] learned the art of pruning their vines, by observ-

---

[3] Satire and panegyric upon critics.
[4] Lib. —— .

ing, that when an ASS had browsed upon one of them, it thrived
the better, and bore fairer fruit. But Herodotus [5] holding the
very same hieroglyph, speaks much plainer, and almost *in terminis*. He hath been so bold as to tax the true critics of ignorance
and malice; telling us openly, for I think nothing can be plainer,
that in the western part of Libya, there were ASSES with
HORNS: upon which relation Ctesias [6] yet refines, mentioning
the very same animal about India, adding, that whereas all other
ASSES wanted a gall, these horned ones were so redundant in
that part, that their flesh was not to be eaten because of its extreme bitterness.

Now, the reason why those ancient writers treated this subject
only by types and figures, was, because they durst not make open
attacks against a party so potent and so terrible, as the critics of
those ages were, whose very voice was so dreadful, that a legion of
authors would tremble, and drop their pens at the sound; for so
Herodotus tells us expressly in another place,[7] how a vast army
of Scythians was put to flight in a panic terror, by the braying of
an ASS. From hence it is conjectured by certain profound
philologers, that the great awe and reverence paid to a true critic,
by the writers of Britain, have been derived to us from those our
Scythian ancestors. In short, this dread was so universal, that in
process of time, those authors who had a mind to publish their
sentiments more freely, in describing the true critics of their
several ages, were forced to leave off the use of the former
hieroglyph, as too nearly approaching the prototype, and invented other terms instead thereof that were more cautious and
mystical; so Diodorus,[8] speaking to the same purpose, ventures
no farther than to say, that in the mountains of Helicon, there
grows a certain weed, which bears a flower of so damned a scent,
as to poison those who offer to smell it. Lucretius gives exactly
the same relation:

Est etiam in magnis Heliconis montibus arbos,
Floris odore hominem retro consueta necare.[9]

Lib. 6.

But Ctesias, whom we lately quoted, hath been a great deal
bolder; he had been used with much severity by the true critics

[5] Lib. 4.
[6] Vide excerpta ex eo apud Photium.
[7] Lib. 4.
[8] Lib.
[9] Near Helicon, and round the learned hill,
Grow trees, whose blossoms with their odour kill.

of his own age, and therefore could not forbear to leave behind him at least one deep mark of his vengeance against the whole tribe. His meaning is so near the surface, that I wonder how it possibly came to be overlooked by those who deny the antiquity of the true critics. For pretending to make a description of many strange animals about India, he hath set down these remarkable words: 'Amongst the rest,' says he, 'there is a serpent that wants teeth, and consequently cannot bite; but if its vomit (to which it is much addicted) happens to fall upon anything, a certain rottenness or corruption ensues. These serpents are generally found among the mountains where jewels grow, and they frequently emit a poisonous juice whereof whoever drinks, that person's brains fly out of his nostrils.'

There was also among the ancients a sort of critic, not distinguished in species from the former, but in growth or degree, who seem to have been only the tyros or junior scholars; yet, because of their differing employments, they are frequently mentioned as a sect by themselves. The usual exercise of these younger students, was to attend constantly at theatres, and learn to spy out the worst parts of the play, whereof they were obliged carefully to take note, and render a rational account to their tutors. Fleshed at these smaller sports, like young wolves, they grew up in time to be nimble and strong enough for hunting down large game. For it hath been observed both among ancients and moderns, that a true critic hath one quality in common with a whore and an alderman, never to change his title or his nature; that a gray critic has been certainly a green one, the perfections and acquirements of his age being only the improved talents of his youth; like hemp, which some naturalists inform us is bad for suffocations, though taken but in the seed. I esteem the invention, or at least the refinement of prologues, to have been owing to these younger proficients, of whom Terence makes frequent and honourable mention, under the name of *malevoli*.

Now, 'tis certain, the institution of the true critics was of absolute necessity to the commonwealth of learning. For all human actions seem to be divided like Themistocles and his company; one man can fiddle, and another can make a small town a great city; and he that cannot do either one or the other, deserves to be kicked out of the creation. The avoiding of which penalty has doubtless given the first birth to the nation of critics, and withal, an occasion for their secret detractors to report, that a true critic is a sort of mechanic, set up with a stock and tools for his trade, at as little expense as a tailor; and that there is much analogy between the utensils and abilities of both: that the tailor's

hell is the type of a critic's common-place book, and his wit and
learning held forth by the goose; that it requires at least as many
of these to the making up of one scholar, as of the others to the
composition of a man; that the valour of both is equal, and their
weapons near of a size. Much may be said in answer to those
invidious reflections; and I can positively affirm the first to be a
falsehood: for, on the contrary, nothing is more certain, than
that it requires greater layings out, to be free of the critic's company, than of any other you can name. For, as to be a true beggar, it will cost the richest candidate every groat he is worth; so,
before one can commence a true critic, it will cost a man all the
good qualities of his mind; which, perhaps, for a less purchase,
would be thought but an indifferent bargain.

Having thus amply proved the antiquity of criticism, and described the primitive state of it, I shall now examine the present
condition of this empire, and show how well it agrees with its
ancient self. A certain author,[1] whose works have many ages
since been entirely lost, does in his fifth book and eighth chapter,
say of critics, that their writings are the mirrors of learning. This
I understand in a literal sense, and suppose our author must mean,
that whoever designs to be a perfect writer, must inspect into the
books of critics, and correct his invention there as in a mirror.
Now, whoever considers, that the mirrors of the ancients were
made of brass, and *sine mercurio*, may presently apply the two
principal qualifications of a true modern critic, and consequently
must needs conclude, that these have always been, and must be
for ever the same. For brass is an emblem of duration, and when
it is skilfully burnished, will cast reflections from its own superficies, without any assistance of mercury from behind. All the
other talents of a critic will not require a particular mention, being included, or easily deducible to these. However, I shall conclude with three maxims, which may serve both as characteristics
to distinguish a true modern critic from a pretender, and will be
also of admirable use to those worthy spirits, who engage in so
useful and honourable an art.

The first is, that criticism, contrary to all other faculties of the
intellect, is ever held the truest and best, when it is the very
first result of the critic's mind; as fowlers reckon the first aim for
the surest, and seldom fail of missing the ma·k, if they stay for
a second.

Secondly, the true critics are known by their talent of swarm-
ing about the noblest writers, to which they are carried merely

---

[1] A quotation after the manner of a great author. *Vide* Bentley's *Dissertation, &c.*

by instinct, as a rat to the best cheese, or a wasp to the fairest fruit. So when the king is a horse-back, he is sure to be the dirtiest person of the company, and they that make their court best, are such as bespatter him most.

Lastly, a true critic, in the perusal of a book, is like a dog at a feast, whose thoughts and stomach are wholly set upon what the guests fling away, and consequently is apt to snarl most when there are the fewest bones.

Thus much, I think, is sufficient to serve by way of address to my patrons, the true modern critics, and may very well atone for my past silence, as well as that which I am like to observe for the future. I hope I have deserved so well of their whole body, as to meet with generous and tender usage at their hands. Supported by which expectation, I go on boldly to pursue those adventures already so happily begun.

SECTION IV

A TALE OF A TUB

I HAVE now with much pains and study conducted the reader to a period, where he must expect to hear of great revolutions. For no sooner had our learned brother, so often mentioned, got a warm house of his own over his head, than he began to look big, and to take mightily upon him; insomuch, that unless the gentle reader out of his great candour will please a little to exalt his idea, I am afraid he will henceforth hardly know the hero of the play, when he happens to meet him, his part, his dress, and his mien being so much altered.

He told his brothers, he would have them to know that he was their elder, and consequently his father's sole heir; nay, a while after, he would not allow them to call him brother, but Mr. PETER; and then he must be styled *Father* PETER; and sometimes, *My Lord* PETER. To support this grandeur, which he soon began to consider could not be maintained without a better *fonde* than what he was born to, after much thought, he cast about at last to turn projector and virtuoso, wherein he so well succeeded, that many famous discoveries, projects, and machines, which bear great vogue and practice at present in the world, are owing entirely to Lord Peter's invention. I will deduce the best account I have been able to collect of the chief amongst them, without considering much the order they came out in; because, I think, authors are not well agreed as to that point.

I hope, when this treatise of mine shall be translated into foreign languages (as I may without vanity affirm, that the labour of collecting, the faithfulness in recounting, and the great useful-ness of the matter to the public, will amply deserve that justice) that the worthy members of the several academies abroad, especially those of France and Italy, will favourably accept these humble offers, for the advancement of universal knowledge. I do also advertise the most reverend fathers, the Eastern Mission-aries, that I have, purely for their sakes, made use of such words and phrases, as will best admit an easy turn into any of the orien-tal languages, especially the Chinese. And so I proceed with great content of mind, upon reflecting, how much emolument this whole globe of Earth is like to reap by my labours.

The first undertaking of Lord Peter, was to purchase a large continent,[2] lately said to have been discovered in *Terra Australis Incognita*. This tract of land he bought at a very great penny-worth from the discoverers themselves (though some pretend to doubt whether they had ever been there) and then retailed it into several cantons to certain dealers, who carried over colonies, but were all shipwrecked in the voyage. Upon which Lord Peter sold the said continent to other customers again, and again, and again, and again, with the same success.

The second project I shall mention, was his sovereign remedy for the worms,[3] especially those in the spleen.[4] The patient was to eat nothing after supper for three nights: as soon as he went to bed, he was carefully to lie on one side, and when he grew weary, to turn upon the other. He must also duly confine his two eyes to the same object; and by no means break wind at both ends together, without manifest occasion. These prescriptions dili-gently observed, the worms would void insensibly by perspira-tion, ascending through the brain.

A third invention was the erecting of a whispering-office,[5] for the public good and ease of all such as are hypochondriacal, or troubled with the colic; as likewise of all eaves-droppers,

---

[2] That is, Purgatory.

[3] Penance and absolution are played upon under the notion of a sovereign remedy for the worms, especially in the spleen, which by observ-ing Peter's prescription would void sensibly by perspiration, ascending through the brain, &c. W. WOTTON.

[4] Here the author ridicules the penances of the Church of Rome, which may be made as easy to the sinner as he pleases, provided he will pay for them accordingly.

[5] By his whispering-office, for the relief of eaves-droppers, physicians, bawds, and privy-counsellors, he ridicules auricular confession, and the priest who takes it, is described by the ass's head. W. WOTTON.

physicians, midwives, small politicians, friends fallen out, repeating poets, lovers happy or in despair, bawds, privy-counsellors,
pages, parasites and buffoons: in short, of all such as are in danger
of bursting with too much wind. An ass's head was placed so
conveniently, that the party affected might easily with his mouth
accost either of the animal's ears; which he was to apply close
for a certain space, and by a fugitive faculty, peculiar to the ears
of that animal, receive immediate benefit, either by eructation, or
expiration, or evomition.

Another very beneficial project of Lord Peter's was an office of
insurance[6] for tobacco-pipes, martyrs of the modern zeal,
volumes of poetry, shadows, ———— and rivers: that these, nor
any of these shall receive damage by fire. From whence our
friendly societies may plainly find themselves to be only tran-
scribers from this original; though the one and the other have
been of great benefit to the undertakers, as well as of equal to the
public.

Lord Peter was also held the original author of puppets and
raree-shows;[7] the great usefulness whereof being so generally
known, I shall not enlarge farther upon this particular.

But another discovery for which he was much renowned was
his famous universal pickle.[8] For having remarked how your
common pickle[9] in use among housewives, was of no farther
benefit than to preserve dead flesh, and certain kinds of vegetables, Peter, with great cost as well as art, had contrived a pickle
proper for houses, gardens, towns, men, women, children, and
cattle; wherein he could preserve them as sound as insects in
amber. Now, this pickle to the taste, the smell, and the sight,
appeared exactly the same with what is in common service for
beef, and butter, and herring (and has been often that way applied with great success) but for its many sovereign virtues was
a quite different thing. For Peter would put in a certain quantity
of his powder *pimperlim pimp*,[1] after which it never failed of

[6] This I take to be the office of indulgences, the gross abuses whereof
first gave occasion for the Reformation.
[7] I believe are the monkeries and ridiculous processions, &c. among the
papists.
[8] Holy water, he calls an universal pickle, to preserve houses, gardens,
towns, men, women, children, and cattle, wherein he could preserve them as
sound as insects in amber. W. WOTTON.
[9] This is easily understood to be holy water, composed of the same ingredients with many other pickles.
[1] And because holy water differs only in consecration from common
water, therefore he tells us that his pickle by the powder of *pimperlimpimp*
receives new virtues, though it differs not in sight nor smell from the
common pickles, which preserve beef, and butter, and herrings. W. WOTTON.

success. The operation was performed by spargefaction[2] in a proper time of the moon. The patient who was to be pickled, if it were a house, would infallibly be preserved from all spiders, rats, and weasels; if the party affected were a dog, he should be exempt from mange, and madness, and hunger. It also infallibly took away all scabs and lice, and scalled heads from children, never hindering the patient from any duty, either at bed or board.

But of all Peter's rarities, he most valued a certain set of bulls,[3] whose race was by great fortune preserved in a lineal descent from those that guarded the golden fleece. Though some who pretended to observe them curiously, doubted the breed had not been kept entirely chaste; because they had degenerated from their ancestors in some qualities, and had acquired others very extraordinary, but a foreign mixture. The bulls of Colchos are recorded to have brazen feet; but whether it happened by ill pasture and running, by an allay from intervention of other parents, from stolen intrigues; whether a weakness in their progenitors had impaired the seminal virtue, or by a decline necessary through a long course of time, the originals of nature being depraved in these latter sinful ages of the world; whatever was the cause, 'tis certain that Lord Peter's bulls were extremely vitiated by the rust of time in the metal of their feet, which was now sunk into common lead. However, the terrible roaring, peculiar to their lineage was preserved; as likewise that faculty of breathing out fire from their nostrils; which notwithstanding many of their detractors took to be a feat of art; and to be nothing so terrible as it appeared; proceeding only from their usual course of diet, which was of squibs and crackers.[4] However, they had two peculiar marks which extremely distinguished them from the bulls of Jason, and which I have not met together in the description of any other monster, beside that in Horace:

Varias inducere plumas;
and
Atrum desinit in piscem.

For these had fishes' tails, yet upon occasion could outfly any

---

[2] Sprinkling. H.

[3] The papal bulls are ridiculed by name, so that here we are at no loss for the author's meaning. W. WOTTON.

Ibid. Here the author has kept the name, and means the pope's bulls, or rather his fulminations and excommunications of heretical princes, all signed with lead and the seal of the fisherman.

[4] These are the fulminations of the pope threatening hell and damnation to those princes who offend him.

bird in the air. Peter put these bulls upon several employs. Sometimes he would set them a-roaring to fright naughty boys,[5] and make them quiet. Sometimes he would send them out upon errands of great importance; where it is wonderful to recount, and perhaps the cautious reader may think much to believe it, an *appetitus sensibilis*, deriving itself through the whole family from their noble ancestors, guardians of the golden fleece, they continued so extremely fond of gold, that if Peter sent them abroad, though it were only upon a compliment, they would roar, and spit, and belch, and piss, and fart, and snivel out fire, and keep a perpetual coil, till you flung them a bit of gold; but then, *pulveris exigui jactu*, they would grow calm and quiet as lambs. In short, whether by secret connivance, or encouragement from their master, or out of their own liquorish affection to gold, or both, it is certain they were no better than a sort of sturdy, swaggering beggars; and where they could not prevail to get an alms, would make women miscarry, and children fall into fits, who to this very day, usually call sprites and hobgoblins by the name of bull-beggars. They grew at last so very troublesome to the neighbourhood, that some gentlemen of the north-west got a parcel of right English bull-dogs, and baited them so terribly, that they felt it ever after.

I must needs mention one more of Lord Peter's projects, which was very extraordinary, and discovered him to be master of a high reach, and profound invention. Whenever it happened that any rogue of Newgate was condemned to be hanged, Peter would offer him a pardon for a certain sum of money which when the poor caitiff had made all shifts to scrape up and send, his lordship would return a piece of paper in this form.[6]

'TO all mayors, sheriffs, jailors, constables, bailiffs, hangmen, &c. Whereas we are informed that A. B. remains in the hands of you, or any of you, under the sentence of death. We will and command you upon sight hereof, to let the said prisoner depart to his own habitation, whether he stands condemned for murder, sodomy, rape, sacrilege, incest, treason, blasphemy, &c., for which this shall be your sufficient warrant: and if you fail hereof, G— d—mn you and yours to all eternity. And so we bid you heartily farewell.

> Your most humble
> man's man,
> Emperor PETER.'

[5] That is, kings who incur his displeasure.
[6] This is a copy of a general pardon, signed *Servus Servorum*.
Ibid. Absolution *in articulo mortis;* and the tax *cameræ apostolicæ*, are jested upon in Emperor Peter's letter. W. WOTTON.

The wretches trusting to this lost their lives and money too.

I desire of those, whom the learned among posterity will appoint for commentators upon this elaborate treatise, that they will proceed with great caution upon certain dark points, wherein all who are not *verè adepti*, may be in danger to form rash and hasty conclusions, especially in some mysterious paragraphs, where certain *arcana* are joined for brevity sake, which in the operation must be divided. And I am certain, that future sons of art will return large thanks to my memory, for so grateful, so useful an *innuendo*.

It will be no difficult part to persuade the reader that so many worthy discoveries met with great success in the world; though I may justly assure him that I have related much the smallest number; my design having been only to single out such as will be of most benefit for public imitation, or which best served to give some idea of the reach and wit of the inventor. And therefore it need not be wondered, if by this time, Lord Peter was become exceeding rich. But alas, he had kept his brain so long and so violently upon the rack, that at last it shook itself, and began to turn round for a little ease. In short, what with pride, projects, and knavery, poor Peter was grown distracted, and conceived the strangest imaginations in the world. In the height of his fits (as it is usual with those who run mad out of pride) he would call himself God Almighty,[7] and sometimes monarch of the universe. I have seen him (says my author) take three old high-crowned hats,[8] and clap them all on his head three story high, with a huge bunch of keys at his girdle,[9] and an angling rod in his hand. In which guise, whoever went to take him by the hand in the way of salutation, Peter with much grace, like a well-educated spaniel, would present them with his foot,[1] and if they refused his civility, then he would raise it as high as their chops, and give them a damned kick on the mouth, which hath ever since been called a salute. Whoever walked by without paying him their compliments, having a wonderful strong breath, he would blow their hats off into the dirt. Meantime, his affairs at home went upside down; and his two brothers had a wretched

[7] The Pope is not only allowed to be the vicar of Christ, but by several divines is called God upon earth, and other blasphemous titles.

[8] The triple crown.

[9] The keys of the church.

Ibid. The Pope's universal monarchy, and his triple crown and fisher's ring. W. WOTTON.

[1] Neither does his arrogant way of requiring men to kiss his slipper escape reflection. W. WOTTON.

time; where his first *boutade*[2] was, to kick both their wives one
morning out of doors, and his own too;[3] and in their stead, gave
orders to pick up the first three strollers could be met with in the
streets. A while after he nailed up the cellar-door, and would not
allow his brothers a drop of drink to their victuals.[4] Dining one
day at an alderman's in the city, Peter observed him expatiating
after the manner of his brethren, in the praises of his sirloin of
beef. Beef, said the sage magistrate, is the king of meat; beef
comprehends in it the quintessence of partridge, and quail, and
venison, and pheasants, and plum-pudding, and custard. When
Peter came home, he would needs take the fancy of cooking up
this doctrine into use, and apply the precept in default of a sirloin, to his brown loaf: 'Bread,' says he, 'dear brothers, is the
staff of life; in which bread is contained, inclusive, the quintessence of beef, mutton, veal, venison, partridge, plum-pudding,
and custard: and to render all complete, there is intermingled a
due quantity of water, whose crudities are also corrected by
yeast or barm, through which means it becomes a wholesome
fermented liquor diffused through the mass of the bread.' Upon
the strength of these conclusions, next day at dinner was the
brown loaf served up in all the formality of a city feast. 'Come
brothers,' said Peter, 'fall to, and spare not; here is excellent good
mutton;[5] or hold, now my hand is in, I'll help you.' At which
word, in much ceremony, with fork and knife, he carves out two
good slices of a loaf, and presents each on a plate to his brothers.
The elder of the two not suddenly entering into Lord Peter's
conceit, began with very civil language to examine the mystery.
'My lord,' said he, 'I doubt, with great submission, there may be
some mistake.' 'What,' says Peter, 'you are pleasant; come then,
let us hear this jest your head is so big with.' 'None in the world,
my lord; but unless I am very much deceived, your lordship was
pleased a while ago to let fall a word about mutton, and I would
be glad to see it with all my heart.' 'How,' said Peter, appearing
in great surprise, 'I do not comprehend this at all.' — Upon which,
the younger interposing to set the business right, 'My lord,'

[2] This word properly signifies a sudden jerk, or lash of a horse, when you
do not expect it.

[3] The celibacy of the Romish clergy is struck at in Peter's beating his
own and brothers' wives out of doors. W. WOTTON.

[4] The Pope's refusing the cup to the laity, persuading them that the blood
is contained in the bread, and that the bread is the real and entire body of
Christ.

[5] Transubstantiation. Peter turns his bread into mutton, and according to
the popish doctrine of concomitants, his wine too, which in his way he
calls palming his damned crusts upon the brothers for mutton. W. WOTTON.

said he, 'my brother, I suppose, is hungry, and longs for the mutton your lordship hath promised us to dinner.' 'Pray,' said Peter, 'take me along with you; either you are both mad, or disposed to be merrier than I approve of; if you there do not like your piece, I will carve you another, though I should take that to be the choice bit of the whole shoulder.' 'What then, my lord,' replied the first, 'it seems this is a shoulder of mutton all this while.' 'Pray, sir,' says Peter, 'eat your victuals and leave off your impertinence, if you please, for I am not disposed to relish it at present.' But the other could not forbear, being over-provoked at the affected seriousness of Peter's countenance. 'By G—, my lord,' said he, 'I can only say, that to my eyes, and fingers, and teeth, and nose, it seems to be nothing but a crust of bread.' Upon which the second put in his word: 'I never saw a piece of mutton in my life so nearly resembling a slice from a twelve-penny loaf.' 'Look ye, gentlemen,' cries Peter in a rage, 'to convince you what a couple of blind, positive, ignorant, wilful puppies you are, I will use but this plain argument; by G—, it is true, good, natural mutton as any in Leadenhall market; and G — confound you both eternally, if you offer to believe otherwise.' Such a thundering proof as this left no farther room for objection: the two unbelievers began to gather and pocket up their mistake as hastily as they could. 'Why, truly,' said the first, 'upon more mature consideration'—'Ay,' says the other, interrupting him, 'now I have thought better on the thing, your lordship seems to have a great deal of reason.' 'Very well,' said Peter, 'here boy, fill me a beer-glass of claret. Here's to you both with all my heart.' The two brethren much delighted to see him so readily appeased returned their most humble thanks, and said they would be glad to pledge his lordship. 'That you shall,' said Peter, 'I am not a person to refuse you anything that is reasonable; wine moderately taken is a cordial; here is a glass a-piece for you; 'tis true natural juice from the grape, none of your damned vintners brewings.' Having spoke thus, he presented to each of them another large dry crust, bidding them drink it off, and not be bashful, for it would do them no hurt. The two brothers, after having performed the usual office in such delicate conjunctures, of staring a sufficient period at Lord Peter and each other, and finding how matters were like to go, resolved not to enter on a new dispute, but let him carry the point as he pleased; for he was now got into one of his mad fits, and to argue or expostulate further, would only serve to render him a hundred times more untractable.

I have chosen to relate this worthy matter in all its circumstances, because it gave a principal occasion to that great and famous rupture,[6] which happened about the same time among these brethren, and was never afterwards made up. But of that I shall treat at large in another section.

However, it is certain, that Lord Peter, even in his lucid intervals, was very lewdly given in his common conversation, extreme wilful and positive, and would at any time rather argue to the death, than allow himself to be once in an error. Besides, he had an abominable faculty of telling huge palpable lies upon all occasions; and swearing, not only to the truth, but cursing the whole company to hell, if they pretended to make the least scruple of believing him. One time he swore he had a cow[7] at home, which gave as much milk at a meal, as would fill three thousand churches; and what was yet more extraordinary, would never turn sour. Another time he was telling of an old sign-post[8] that belonged to his father, with nails and timber enough on it to build sixteen large men-of-war. Talking one day of Chinese waggons, which were made so light as to sail over mountains: 'Z—nds,' said Peter, 'where's the wonder of that? By G—, I saw a large house of lime and stone[9] travel over sea and land (granting that it stopped sometimes to bait) above two thousand German leagues.' And that which was the good of it, he would swear desperately all the while, that he never told a lie in his life; and at every word: 'By G—, gentlemen, I tell you nothing but the truth; and the D—l broil them eternally that will not believe me.'

In short, Peter grew so scandalous that all the neighbourhood began in plain words to say, he was no better than a knave. And his two brothers, long weary of his ill usage, resolved at last to leave him; but first they humbly desired a copy of their father's will, which had now lain by neglected time out of mind. Instead of granting this request, he called them damned sons of whores, rogues, traitors, and the rest of the vile names he could muster up.

---

[6] By this rupture is meant the Reformation.

[7] The ridiculous multiplying of the Virgin Mary's milk among the papists, under the allegory of a cow, which gave as much milk at a meal as would fill three thousand churches. W. WOTTON.

[8] By this sign-post is meant the cross of our Blessed Saviour.

[9] The chapel of Loretto. He falls here only upon the ridiculous inventions of popery: the Church of Rome intended by these things to gull silly, superstitious people, and rook them of their money; that the world had been too long in slavery, our ancestors gloriously redeemed us from that yoke. The Church of Rome therefore ought to be exposed, and he deserves well of mankind that does expose it. W. WOTTON.

Ibid. The chapel of Loretto, which travelled from the Holy Land to Italy.

However, while he was abroad one day upon his projects, the two
youngsters watched their opportunity, made a shift to come at
the will,[1] and took a *copia vera*, by which they presently saw
how grossly they had been abused; their father having left them
equal heirs, and strictly commanded, that whatever they got
should lie in common among them all. Pursuant to which, their
next enterprise was to break open the cellar-door and get a little
good drink[2] to spirit and comfort their hearts. In copying the
will, they had met another precept against whoring, divorce, and
separate maintenance; upon which their next work[3] was to discard their concubines, and send for their wives. Whilst all this
was in agitation, there enters a solicitor from Newgate, desiring
Lord Peter would please to procure a pardon for a thief that was
to be hanged to-morrow. But the two brothers told him, he was
a coxcomb to seek pardons from a fellow who deserved to be
hanged much better than his client; and discovered all the method
of that imposture, in the same form I delivered it a while ago, advising the solicitor to put his friend upon obtaining a pardon from
the king.[4] In the midst of all this clutter and revolution, in
comes Peter with a file of dragoons[5] at his heels, and gathering
from all hands what was in the wind, he and his gang, after several millions of scurrilities and curses, not very important here to
repeat, by main force very fairly kicks them both out of doors[6]
and would never let them come under his roof from that day
to this.

SECTION V

A DIGRESSION IN THE MODERN KIND

WE whom the world is pleased to honor with the title of modern authors, should never have been able to compass our great
design of an everlasting remembrance, and never-dying fame, if
our endeavours had not been so highly serviceable to the general
good of mankind. This, O universe, is the adventurous attempt
of me thy secretary:

—— Quemvis perferre laborem
Suadet, & inducit noctes vigilare serenas.

1 Translated the scriptures into the vulgar tongues.
2 Administered the cup to the laity at the communion.
3 Allowed the marriages of priests.
4 Directed penitents not to trust to pardons and absolutions procured
for money, but sent them to implore the mercy of God, from whence alone
remission is to be obtained.
5 By Peter's dragoons is meant the civil power which those princes who
were bigoted to the Romish superstition, employed against the reformers.
6 The Pope shuts all who dissent from him out of the Church.

To this end, I have some time since, with a world of pains and art, dissected the carcass of human nature, and read many useful lectures upon the several parts, both containing and contained; till at last it smelt so strong, I could preserve it no longer. Upon which, I have been at a great expense to fit up all the bones with exact contexture, and in due symmetry; so that I am ready to show a very complete anatomy thereof to all curious gentlemen and others. But not to digress farther in the midst of a digression, as I have known some authors enclose digressions in one another, like a nest of boxes; I do affirm, that having carefully cut up human nature, I have found a very strange, new, and important discovery, that the public good of mankind is performed by two ways, instruction and diversion. And I have farther proved in my said several readings (which perhaps the world may one day see, if I can prevail on any friend to steal a copy, or on certain gentlemen of my admirers to be very importunate) that as mankind is now disposed, he receives much greater advantage by being diverted than instructed; his epidemical diseases being fastidiosity, amorphy, and oscitation; whereas in the present universal empire of wit and learning, there seems but little matter left for instruction. However, in compliance with a lesson of great age and authority, I have attempted carrying the point in all its heights; and accordingly throughout this divine treatise, have skilfully kneaded up both together with a layer of *utile*, and a layer of *dulce*.

When I consider how exceedingly our illustrious moderns have eclipsed the weak glimmering lights of the ancients, and turned them out of the road of all fashionable commerce, to a degree, that our choice town wits,[7] of most refined accomplishments, are in grave dispute, whether there have been ever any ancients or no: in which point we are like to receive wonderful satisfaction from the most useful labours and lucubrations of that worthy modern, Dr. Bentley: I say, when I consider all this, I cannot but bewail, that no famous modern hath ever yet attempted an universal system in a small portable volume of all things that are to be known, or believed, or imagined, or practised in life. I am, however, forced to acknowledge, that such an enterprise was thought on some time ago by a great philosopher of O. Brazile.[8]

---

[7] The learned person here meant by our author, hath been endeavouring to annihilate so many ancient writers, that until he is pleased to stop his hand it will be dangerous to affirm, whether there have been [ever] any ancients in the world.

[8] This is an imaginary island, of kin to that which is called the Painters' Wives Island, placed in some unknown part of the ocean, merely at the fancy of the map-maker.

The method he proposed was by a certain curious receipt, a nostrum, which after his untimely death, I found among his papers, and do here out of my great affection to the modern learned, present them with it, not doubting it may one day encourage some worthy undertaker.

You take fair correct copies, well bound in calf's skin, and lettered at the back, of all modern bodies of arts and sciences whatsoever, and in what language you please. These you distil in balneo Mariæ, *infusing* quintessence of poppy Q.S., *together with three pints of* Lethe, *to be had from the apothecaries. You cleanse away carefully the* sordes *and* caput mortuum, *letting all that is volatile evaporate. You preserve only the first running, which is again to be distilled seventeen times, till what remains will amount to about two drams. This you keep in a glass vial, hermetically sealed, for one-and-twenty days. Then you begin your catholic treatise, taking every morning fasting (first shaking the vial), three drops of this* elixir, *snuffing it strongly up your nose. It will dilate itself about the brain (where there is any) in fourteen minutes, and you immediately perceive in your head an infinite number of* abstracts, summaries, compendiums, extracts, collections, medulas, excerpta quædams, florilegias *and the like, all disposed into great order, and reducible upon paper.*

I must needs own, it was by the assistance of this *arcanum,* that I, though otherwise *impar,* have adventured upon so daring an attempt, never achieved or undertaken before, but by a certain author called Homer, in whom, though otherwise a person not without some abilities, and for an ancient, of a tolerable genius, I have discovered many gross errors, which are not to be forgiven his very ashes, if, by chance any of them are left. For whereas we are assured he designed his work for a complete body of all knowledge,[9] human, divine, political, and mechanic, it is manifest he hath wholly neglected some, and been very imperfect in the rest. For, first of all, as eminent a cabalist as his disciples would represent him, his account of the *opus magnum* is extremely poor and deficient; he seems to have read but very superficially either Sendivogius, Behmen, or *Anthroposophia Theomagica.*[1] He is also quite mistaken about the *sphœra pyroplastica*, a neglect not to be atoned for; and (if the reader will admit so severe

[9] Homerus omnes res humanas poematis complexus est. — *Xenoph in conviv.*

[1] A treatise written about fifty years ago, by a Welsh gentleman of Cambridge; his name, as I remember, was Vaughan, as appears by the answer to it writ by the learned Dr. Henry More; it is a piece of the most unintelligible fustian, that, perhaps, was ever published in any language.

a censure), *vix crederem autorem hunc, unquam audivisse ignis vocem.* His failings are not less prominent in several parts of the mechanics. For, having read his writings with the utmost application usual among modern wits, I could never yet discover the least direction about the structure of that useful instrument, a save-all. For want of which, if the moderns had not lent their assistance, we might yet have wandered in the dark. But I have still behind, a fault far more notorious to tax this author with; I mean, his gross ignorance in the common laws of this realm, and in the doctrine as well as discipline of the Church of England.[2] A defect indeed, for which both he and all the ancients stand most justly censured, by my worthy and ingenious friend, Mr. Wotton, Bachelor of Divinity, in his incomparable treatise of *Ancient and Modern Learning*, a book never to be sufficiently valued, whether we consider the happy turns and flowings of the author's wit, the great usefulness of his sublime discoveries upon the subject of flies and spittle, or the laborious eloquence of his style. And I cannot forbear doing that author the justice of my public acknowledgments, for the great helps and liftings I had out of his incomparable piece, while I was penning this treatise.

But, besides these omissions in Homer already mentioned, the curious reader will also observe several defects in that author's writings, for which he is not altogether so accountable. For whereas every branch of knowledge has received such wonderful acquirements since his age, especially within these last three years, or thereabouts, it is almost impossible he could be so very perfect in modern discoveries as his advocates pretend. We freely acknowledge him to be the inventor of the compass, of gunpowder, and the circulation of the blood: but I challenge any of his admirers to show me in all his writings a complete account of the spleen. Does he not also leave us wholly to seek in the art of political wagering? What can be more defective and unsatisfactory than his long dissertation upon tea? And as to his method of salivation without mercury, so much celebrated of late, it is to my own knowledge and experience a thing very little to be relied on.

It was to supply such momentous defects, that I have been prevailed on after long solicitation, to take pen in hand; and I dare venture to promise, the judicious reader shall find nothing neglected here, that can be of use upon any emergency of life. I am confident to have included and exhausted all that human imagi-

---

[2] Mr. Wotton (to whom our author never gives any quarter) in his comparison of ancient and modern learning, numbers divinity, law, &c., among those parts of knowledge wherein we excel the ancients.

nation can rise or fall to. Particularly, I recommend to the perusal of the learned certain discoveries that are wholly untouched by others; whereof I shall only mention among a great many more, my *New Help of Smatterers, or the Art of being Deep-learned and Shallow-read; A Curious Invention about Mouse-Traps; An Universal Rule of Reason, or Every Man his own Carver;* together with a most useful engine for catching of owls. All which the judicious reader will find largely treated on in the several parts of this discourse.

I hold myself obliged to give as much light as is possible, into the beauties and excellencies of what I am writing, because it is become the fashion and humor most applauded among the first authors of this polite and learned age, when they would correct the ill nature of critical, or inform the ignorance of courteous readers. Besides, there have been several famous pieces lately published both in verse and prose, wherein, if the writers had not been pleased, out of their great humanity and affection to the public, to give us a nice detail of the sublime and the admirable they contain, it is a thousand to one whether we should ever have discovered one grain of either. For my own particular, I cannot deny, that whatever I have said upon this occasion, had been more proper in a preface, and more agreeable to the mode which usually directs it there. But I here think fit to lay hold on that great and honourable privilege of being the last writer. I claim an absolute authority in right, as the freshest modern, which gives me a despotic power over all authors before me. In the strength of which title, I do utterly disapprove and declare against that pernicious custom, of making the preface a bill of fare to the book. For I have always looked upon it as a high point of indiscretion in monster-mongers and other retailers of strange sights, to hang out a fair large picture over the door, drawn after the life, with a most eloquent description underneath. This hath saved me many a threepence, for my curiosity was fully satisfied, and I never offered to go in, though often invited by the urging and attending orator, with his last moving and standing piece of rhetoric: 'Sir, upon my word, we are just going to begin.' Such is exactly the fate, at this time, of Prefaces, Epistles, Advertisements, Introductions, Prolegomenas, Apparatuses, To-the-Readers. This expedient was admirable at first; our great Dryden has long carried it as far as it would go, and with incredible success. He has often said to me in confidence, that the world would have never suspected him to be so great a poet, if he had not assured them so frequently in his prefaces, that it was impossible they could either doubt or forget it. Perhaps it may

be so; however, I much fear, his instructions have edified out of
their place, and taught men to grow wiser in certain points, where
he never intended they should; for it is lamentable to behold,
with what a lazy scorn many of the yawning readers in our age, do
now-a-days twirl over forty or fifty pages of preface and dedication (which is the usual modern stint) as if it were so much
Latin. Tho' it must be also allowed on the other hand that a
very considerable number is known to proceed critics and wits,
by reading nothing else. Into which two factions, I think, all
present readers may justly be divided. Now, for myself, I profess
to be one of the former sort; and therefore having the modern inclination to expatiate upon the beauty of my own productions,
and display the bright parts of my discourse, I thought best to do
it in the body of the work, where, as it now lies, it makes a very
considerable addition to the bulk of the volume, a circumstance
by no means to be neglected by a skilful writer.

Having thus paid my due deference and acknowledgment to
an established custom of our newest authors, by a long digression
unsought for, and an universal censure unprovoked, by forcing
into the light, with much pains and dexterity, my own excellencies and other men's defaults, with great justice to myself and
candor to them, I now happily resume my subject, to the infinite
satisfaction both of the reader and the author.

SECTION VI

A TALE OF A TUB

We left Lord Peter in open rupture with his two brethren; both
for ever discarded from his house, and resigned to the wide
world, with little or nothing to trust to. Which are circumstances
that render them proper subjects for the charity of a writer's pen
to work on, scenes of misery ever affording the fairest harvest
for great adventures. And in this the world may perceive the
difference between the integrity of a generous author and that of
a common friend. The latter is observed to adhere close in prosperity, but on the decline of fortune to drop suddenly off.
Whereas the generous author, just on the contrary, finds his hero
on the dunghill, from thence by gradual steps raises him to a
throne, and then immediately withdraws, expecting not so much
as thanks for his pains, in imitation of which example, I have
placed Lord Peter in a noble house, given him a title to wear, and
money to spend. There I shall leave him for some time, returning
where common charity directs me, to the assistance of his broth-

ers, at their lowest ebb. However, I shall by no means forget my
character of an historian to follow the truth step by step, whatever happens, or wherever it may lead me.

The two exiles, so nearly united in fortune and interest, took a
lodging together, where, at their first leisure, they began to reflect on the numberless misfortunes and vexations of their life
past, and could not tell on the sudden, to what failure in their conduct they ought to impute them, when, after some recollection,
they called to mind the copy of their father's will, which they
had so happily recovered. This was immediately produced, and
a firm resolution taken between them, to alter whatever was
already amiss and reduce all their future measures to the strictest obedience prescribed therein. The main body of the will (as
the reader cannot easily have forgot) consisted in certain admirable rules about 'the wearing of their coats, in the perusal
whereof, the two brothers at every period duly comparing the
doctrine with the practice, there was never seen a wider difference between two things, horrible downright transgressions of
every point. Upon which they both resolved, without further
delay, to fall immediately upon reducing the whole, exactly
after their father's model.

But here it is good to stop the hasty reader, ever impatient to
see the end of an adventure, before we writers can duly prepare
him for it. I am to record, that these two brothers began to be
distinguished at this time by certain names. One of them desired
to be called MARTIN,[3] and the other took the appellation of
JACK.[4] These two had lived in much friendship and agreement
under the tyranny of their brother Peter, as it is the talent of fel-
low-sufferers to do; men in misfortune being like men in the
dark, to whom all colours are the same. But when they came
forward into the world, and began to display themselves to each
other, and to the light, their complexions appeared extremely different, which the present posture of their affairs gave them sudden opportunity to discover.

But here the severe reader may justly tax me as a writer of
short memory, a deficiency to which a true modern cannot but
of necessity be a little subject: because, memory being an employment of the mind upon things past, is a faculty for which the
learned in our illustrious age have no manner of occasion, who
deal entirely with invention, and strike all things out of themselves, or at least by collision from each other; upon which account, we think it highly reasonable to produce our great forget-

3 Martin Luther.
4 John Calvin.

fulness, as an argument unanswerable for our great wit. I ought
in method to have informed the reader about fifty pages ago of a
fancy Lord Peter took, and infused into his brothers, to wear on
their coats whatever trimmings came up in fashion; never pulling off any, as they went out of the mode, but keeping on all
together, which amounted in time to a medley the most antic you
can possibly conceive, and this to a degree, that upon the time of
their falling out there was hardly a thread of the original coat to
be seen, but an infinite quantity of lace, and ribbons, and fringe,
and embroidery, and points (I mean only those tagged with silver,[5]
for the rest fell off). Now this material circumstance having been
forgot in due place, as good fortune hath ordered, comes in very
properly here, when the two brothers are just going to reform
their vestures into the primitive state, prescribed by their father's
will.

They both unanimously entered upon this great work, looking
sometimes on their coats, and sometimes on the will. Martin laid
the first hand; at one twitch brought off a large handful of points;
and with a second pull, stripped away ten dozen yards of fringe.[6]
But when he had gone thus far, he demurred a while: he knew
very well there yet remained a great deal more to be done; however, the first heat being over, his violence began to cool, and he
resolved to proceed more moderately in the rest of the work;
having already very narrowly escaped a swinging rent in pulling
off the points, which being tagged with silver (as we have
observed before) the judicious workman had with much sagacity
double sewn, to preserve them from falling.[7] Resolving therefore to rid his coat of a huge quantity of gold lace, he picked up
the stitches with much caution, and diligently gleaned out all the
loose threads as he went, which proved to be a work of time.
Then he fell about the embroidered Indian figures of men, wom-
en, and children, against which, as you have heard in its due
place, their father's testament was extremely exact and severe:
these, with much dexterity and application, were after a while
quite eradicated, or utterly defaced.[8] For the rest, where he
observed the embroidery to be worked so close, so as not to be

[5] Points tagged with silver are those doctrines that promote the greatness
and wealth of the church, which have been therefore woven deepest in the
body of Popery.

[6] Alluding to the commencement of the Reformation in England, by
seizing on the abbey lands. SCOTT.

[7] The dissolution of the monasteries occasioned several insurrections, and
much convulsion, during the reign of Edward VI. SCOTT.

[8] The abolition of the worship of saints was the second step in English
Reformation. SCOTT.

got away without damaging the cloth, or where it served to hide or strengthen any flaw in the body of the coat, contracted by the perpetual tampering of workmen upon it; he concluded the wisest course was to let it remain, resolving in no case whatsoever that the substance of the stuff should suffer injury, which he thought the best method for serving the true intent and meaning of his father's will. And this is the nearest account I have been able to collect of Martin's proceedings upon this great revolution.

But his brother Jack, whose adventures will be so extraordinary, as to furnish a great part in the remainder of this discourse, entered upon the matter with other thoughts, and a quite different spirit. For the memory of Lord Peter's injuries produced a degree of hatred and spite, which had a much greater share of inciting him than any regards after his father's commands, since these appeared at best only secondary and subservient to the other. However, for this medley of humor, he made a shift to find a very plausible name, honoring it with the title of zeal; which is perhaps the most significant word that hath been ever yet produced in any language; as, I think, I have fully proved in my excellent analytical discourse upon that subject; wherein I have deduced a histori-theo-physi-logical account of zeal, showing how it first proceeded from a notion into a word, and from thence in a hot summer ripened into a tangible substance. This work, containing three large volumes in folio, I design very shortly to publish by the modern way of subscription, not doubting but the nobility and gentry of the land will give me all possible encouragement, having already had such a taste of what I am able to perform.

I record, therefore, that brother Jack, brimful of this miraculous compound, reflecting with indignation upon Peter's tyranny, and farther provoked by the despondency of Martin, prefaced his resolutions to this purpose. 'What,' said he, 'a rogue that locked up his drink, turned away our wives, cheated us of our fortunes, palmed his damned crusts upon us for mutton, and at last kicked us out of doors; must we be in his fashions, with a pox? A rascal, besides, that all the street cries out against.' Having thus kindled and inflamed himself as high as possible, and by consequence, in a delicate temper for beginning a reformation, he set about the work immediately, and in three minutes made more dispatch than Martin had done in as many hours. For (courteous reader) you are given to understand, that zeal is never so highly obliged, as when you set it a-tearing; and Jack, who doated on that quality in himself, allowed it at this time its full swing. Thus it happened, that stripping down a parcel of gold lace a little too hastily, he rent the main body of his coat from top to bottom; and whereas his talent was not of the happiest in taking up a stitch, he knew no better way than to darn it again with packthread and a skewer. But the matter was yet infinitely worse (I record it with tears) when he proceeded to the embroidery: for, being clumsy by nature, and of temper impatient; withal, beholding millions of stitches that required the nicest hand, and sedatest constitutions, to extricate; in a great rage he tore off the whole piece, cloth and all, and flung it into the kennel,[9] and furiously thus continuing his career: 'Ah, good brother Martin,' said he, 'do as I do, for the love of God; strip, tear, pull, rend, flay off all, that we may appear as unlike the rogue Peter as it is possible. I would not for a hundred pounds carry the least mark about me, that might give occasion to the neighbours of suspecting I was related to such a rascal.' But Martin, who at this time happened to be extremely phlegmatic and sedate, begged his brother, of all love, not to damage his coat by any means; for he never would get such another: desired him to consider, that it was not their business to form their actions by any reflection upon Peter, but by observing the rules prescribed in their father's will. That he should remember, Peter was still their brother, whatever faults or injuries he had committed; and therefore they should by all means avoid such a thought as that of taking measures for good and evil, from no other rule than of opposition to him. That it was true, the testament of their good father was very exact in what related to the wearing of their coats; yet was it no less penal and strict in prescribing agreement, and friendship, and affection between them. And therefore, if straining a point were at all dispensible, it would certainly be so rather to the advance of unity than increase of contradiction.

Martin had still proceeded as gravely as he began, and doubtless would have delivered an admirable lecture of morality, which might have exceedingly contributed to my reader's repose, both of body and mind (the true ultimate end of ethics); but Jack was already gone a flight-shot beyond his patience. And as in scholastic disputes, nothing serves to rouse the spleen of him that opposes, so much as a kind of pedantic affected calmness in the respondent; disputants being for the most part like unequal scales, where the gravity of one side advances the lightness of the other, and causes it to fly up and kick the beam; so it happened here that the weight of Martin's argument exalted Jack's levity, and made him fly out and spurn against his brother's modera-

---

[9] The presbyterians, in discarding forms of prayers, and unnecessary church ceremonies, disused even those founded in scripture. SCOTT.

tion. In short, Martin's patience put Jack in a rage; but that which most afflicted him was, to observe his brother's coat so well reduced into the state of innocence; while his own was either wholly rent to his shirt, or those places which had escaped his cruel clutches, were still in Peter's livery. So that he looked like a drunken beau, half rifled by bullies; or like a fresh tenant of Newgate, when he has refused the payment of garnish; or like a discovered shoplifter left to the mercy of Exchange women; [1] or like a bawd in her old velvet petticoat, resigned into the secular hands of the mobile. Like any or like all of these, a medley of rags, and lace, and rents, and fringes, unfortunately Jack did now appear: he would have been extremely glad to see his coat in the condition of Martin's, but infinitely gladder to find that of Martin's in the same predicament with his. However, since neither of these was likely to come to pass, he thought fit to lend the whole business another turn, and to dress up necessity into a virtue. Therefore, after as many of the fox's[2] arguments as he could muster up, for bringing Martin to reason, as he called it; or, as he meant it, into his own ragged, bobtailed condition; and observing he said all to little purpose; what, alas, was left for the forlorn Jack to do, but after a million of scurrilities against his brother, to run mad with spleen, and spite, and contradiction. To be short, here began a mortal breach between these two. Jack went immediately to new lodgings, and in a few days it was for certain reported, that he had run out of his wits. In a short time after he appeared abroad, and confirmed the report by falling into the oddest whimseys that ever a sick brain conceived.

And now the little boys in the streets began to salute him with several names. Sometimes they would call him Jack the Bald; [3] sometimes, Jack with a lantern;[4] sometimes, Dutch Jack;[5] sometimes, French Hugh;[6] sometimes, Tom the beggar;[7] and sometimes, Knocking Jack of the north.[8] And it was under one, or some, or all of these appellations (which I leave the learned reader to determine) that he hath given rise to the most illustrious and

[1] The galleries over the piazzas in the Royal Exchange were formerly filled with shops, kept chiefly by women. . . . H.

[2] The fox in the fable, who having been caught in a trap and lost his tail, used many arguments to persuade the rest to cut off theirs; that the irregularity of his deformity might not expose him to derision. H.

[3] That is, Calvin, from *calvus*, bald.

[4] All those who pretend to inward light.

[5] Jack of Leyden, who gave rise to the Anabaptists.

[6] The Huguenots.

[7] The Gueuses, by which name some Protestants in Flanders were called.

[8] John Knox, the reformer of Scotland.

epidemic sect of Æolists; who with honourable commemoration, do still acknowledge the renowed JACK for their author and founder. Of whose original, as well as principles, I am now advancing to gratify the world with a very particular account.

—— Mellæo contingens cuncta lepore.

SECTION VII

A DIGRESSION IN PRAISE OF DIGRESSIONS

I HAVE sometimes heard of an *Iliad* in a nutshell; but it hath been my fortune to have much oftener seen a nutshell in an *Iliad*. There is no doubt that human life has received most wonderful advantages from both; but to which of the two the world is chiefly indebted, I shall leave among the curious, as a problem worthy of their utmost inquiry. For the invention of the latter, I think the commonwealth of learning is chiefly obliged to the great modern improvement of digressions: the late refinements in knowledge, running parallel to those of diet in our nation, which among men of a judicious taste are dressed up in various compounds, consisting in soups and olios, fricassees, and ragouts.

'Tis true, there is a sort of morose, detracting, ill-bred people, who pretend utterly to disrelish these polite innovations; and as to the similitude from diet, they allow the parallel, but are so bold to pronounce the example itself, a corruption and degeneracy of taste. They tell us that the fashion of jumbling fifty things together in a dish, was at first introduced in compliance to a depraved and debauched appetite, as well as to a crazy constitution: and to see a man hunting through an olio, after the head and brains of a goose, a widgeon, or a woodcock, is a sign he wants a stomach and digestion for more substantial victuals. Farther, they affirm, that digressions in a book are like foreign troops in a state, which argue the nation to want a heart and hands of its own, and often either subdue the natives, or drive them into the most unfruitful corners.

But, after all that can be objected by these supercilious censors, 'tis manifest, the society of writers would quickly be reduced to a very inconsiderable number, if men were put upon making books, with the fatal confinement of delivering nothing beyond what is to the purpose. 'Tis acknowledged, that were the case the same among us, as with the Greeks and Romans, when learning was in its cradle, to be reared and fed, and clothed by invention, it would be an easy task to fill up volumes upon particular occasions, without farther expatiating from the subject than my moderate excursions, helping to advance or clear the main design. But with knowledge it has fared as with a numerous army, encamped in a fruitful country, which for a few days maintains itself by the product of the soil it is on; till provisions being spent, they send to forage many a mile, among friends or enemies, it matters not. Meanwhile, the neighbouring fields, trampled and beaten down, become barren and dry, affording no sustenance but clouds of dust.

The whole course of things being thus entirely changed between us and the ancients, and the moderns wisely sensible of it, we of this age have discovered a shorter, and more prudent method, to become scholars and wits, without the fatigue of reading or of thinking. The most accomplished way of using books at present is two-fold: either first, to serve them as some men do lords, learn their titles exactly, and then brag of their acquaintance. Or secondly, which is indeed the choicer, the profounder, and politer method, to get a thorough insight into the index, by which the whole book is governed and turned, like fishes by the tail. For, to enter the palace of learning at the great gate, requires an expense of time and forms; therefore men of much haste and little ceremony are content to get in by the back door. For the arts are all in a flying march, and therefore more easily subdued by attacking them in the rear. Thus physicians discover the state of the whole body, by consulting only what comes from behind. Thus men catch knowledge by throwing their wit on the posteriors of a book, as boys do sparrows with flinging salt upon their tails. Thus human life is best understood by the wise man's rule of regarding the end. Thus are the sciences found like Hercules's oxen, by tracing them backwards. Thus are old sciences unravelled like old stockings, by beginning at the foot.

Besides all this, the army of the sciences hath been of late, with a world of martial discipline, drawn into its close order, so that a view or a muster may be taken of it with abundance of expedition. For this great blessing we are wholly indebted to systems and abstracts, in which the modern fathers of learning, like prudent usurers, spent their sweat for the ease of us their children. For labor is the seed of idleness, and it is the peculiar happiness of our noble age to gather the fruit.

Now the method of growing wise, learned, and sublime, having become so regular an affair, and so established in all its forms, the numbers of writers must needs have increased accordingly, and to a pitch that has made it of absolute necessity for them to interfere continually with each other. Besides, it is reckoned, that there is not at this present, a sufficient quantity of new matter left in nature, to furnish and adorn any one particular subject to the extent of a volume. This I am told by a very skilful computer, who hath given a full demonstration of it from rules of arithmetic.

This, perhaps, may be objected against by those who maintain the infinity of matter, and therefore will not allow that any species of it can be exhausted. For answer to which, let us examine the noblest branch of modern wit or invention, planted and cultivated by the present age, and which, of all others, hath borne the most and the fairest fruit. For though some remains of it were left us by the ancients, yet have not any of those, as I remember, been translated or compiled into systems for modern use. Therefore we may affirm, to our own honor, that it has in some sort, been both invented and brought to a perfection by the same hands. What I mean is, that highly celebrated talent among the modern wits, of deducing similitudes, allusions, and applications, very surprising, agreeable, and apposite, from the *pudenda* of either sex, together with their proper uses. And truly, having observed how little invention bears any vogue, besides what is derived into these channels, I have sometimes had a thought, that the happy genius of our age and country was prophetically held forth by that ancient typical description of the Indian pigmies;[9] whose stature did not exceed above two foot; *sed quorum pudenda crassa, & ad talos usque pertingentia.* Now, I have been very curious to inspect the late productions, wherein the beauties of this kind have most prominently appeared. And although this vein hath bled so freely, and all endeavours have been used in the power of human breath to dilate, extend, and keep it open; like the Scythians,[1] who had a custom, and an instrument, to blow up the privities of their mares, that they might yield the more milk; yet I am under an apprehension it is near growing dry, and past all recovery; and that either some new *fonde* of wit should, if possible, be provided, or else that we must e'en be content with repetition here, as well as upon all other occasions.

This will stand as an uncontestable argument, that our modern wits are not to reckon upon the infinity of matter for a constant supply. What remains therefore, but that our last recourse must be had to large indexes, and little compendiums; quotations must be plentifully gathered, and booked in alphabet; to this end, though authors need be little consulted, yet critics, and com-

[9] Ctesiæ fragm. apud Photium.
[1] Herodot. L. 4.

mentators, and lexicons carefully must. But above all, those judicious collectors of bright parts, and flowers, and observandas, are to be nicely dwelt on, by some called the sieves and boulters of learning, though it is left undetermined, whether they dealt in pearls or meal, and consequently, whether we are more to value that which passed through, or what stayed behind.

By these methods, in a few weeks, there starts up many a writer, capable of managing the profoundest and most universal subjects. For, what though his head be empty, provided his commonplace book be full; and if you will bate him but the circumstances of method, and style, and grammar, and invention; allow him but the common privileges of transcribing from others, and digressing from himself, as often as he shall see occasion; he will desire no more ingredients towards fitting up a treatise, that shall make a very comely figure on a bookseller's shelf; there to be preserved neat and clean for a long eternity, adorned with the heraldry of its title fairly inscribed on a label; never to be thumbed or greased by students, nor bound to everlasting chains of darkness in a library; but when the fulness of time is come, shall haply undergo the trial of purgatory, in order to ascend the sky.

Without these allowances, how is it possible we modern wits should ever have an opportunity to introduce our collections, listed under so many thousand heads of a different nature? for want of which, the learned world would be deprived of infinite delight, as well as instruction, and we ourselves buried beyond redress in an inglorious and undistinguished oblivion.

From such elements as these, I am alive to behold the day, wherein the corporation of authors can outvie all its brethren in the guild. A happiness derived to us with a great many others, from our Scythian ancestors, among whom the number of pens was so infinite, that the Grecian [2] eloquence had no other way of expressing it, than by saying, that in the regions far to the north, it was hardly possible for a man to travel, the very air was so replete with feathers.

The necessity of this digression will easily excuse the length; and I have chosen for it as proper a place as I could readily find. If the judicious reader can assign a fitter, I do here empower him to remove it into any other corner he pleases. And so I return with great alacrity to pursue a more important concern.

[2] Herodot. L. 4.

SECTION VIII

A TALE OF A TUB

THE learned Æolists[3] maintain the original cause of all things to be wind, from which principle this whole universe was at first produced, and into which it must at last be resolved; that the same breath which had kindled, and blew *up* the flame of nature, should one day blow it *out:*

> Quod procul à nobis flectat Fortuna gubernans.

This is what the *adepti* understand by their *anima mundi;* that is to say, the spirit, or breath, or wind of the world; for examine the whole system by the particulars of nature, and you will find it not to be disputed. For whether you please to call the *forma informans* of man, by the name of *spiritus, animus, afflatus,* or *anima;* what are all these but several appellations for wind, which is the ruling element in every compound, and into which they all resolve upon their corruption? Farther, what is life itself, but as it is commonly called, the breath of our nostrils? Whence it is very justly observed by naturalists, that wind still continues of great emolument in certain mysteries not to be named, giving occasion for those happy epithets of *turgidas* and *inflatus,* applied either to the *emittent* or *recipient* organs.

By what I have gathered out of ancient records, I find the compass of their doctrine took in two-and-thirty points, wherein it would be tedious to be very particular. However, a few of their most important precepts, deducible from it, are by no means to be omitted; among which the following maxim was of much weight: that since wind had the master share, as well as operation in every compound, by consequence, those beings must be of chief excellence, wherein that *primordium* appears most prominently to abound, and therefore man is in highest perfection of all created things, as having by the great bounty of philosophers, been endued with three distinct *animas* or winds, to which the sage Æolists, with much liberality, have added a fourth of equal necessity as well as ornament with the other three, by this *quartum principium,* taking in the four corners of the world; which gave occasion to that renowned cabalist, Bumbastus,[4] of placing the body of a man in due position to the four cardinal points.

In consequence of this, their next principle was, that man

---

[3] All pretenders to inspiration whatsoever.
[4] This is one of the names of Paracelsus; he was called Christophorus, Theophrastus, Paracelsus, Bumbastus.

brings with him into the world a peculiar portion or grain of
wind, which may be called a *quinta essentia*, extracted from the
other four. This quintessence is of a catholic use upon all
emergencies of life, is improvable into all arts and sciences, and
may be wonderfully refined, as well as enlarged by certain
methods in education. This, when blown up to its perfection,
ought not to be covetously hoarded up, stifled, or hid under a
bushel, but freely communicated to mankind. Upon these reasons, and others of equal weight, the wise Æolists affirm the
gift of BELCHING to be the noblest act of a rational creature.
To cultivate which art, and render it more serviceable to mankind, they made use of several methods. At certain seasons of
the year, you might behold the priests amongst them, in vast
numbers, with their mouths[5] gaping wide against a storm. At
other times were to be seen several hundreds linked together in
a circular chain, with every man a pair of bellows applied to his
neighbour's breech, by which they blew up each other to the
shape and size of a tun; and for that reason, with great propriety
of speech, did usually call their bodies, their vessels. When, by
these and the like performances, they were grown sufficiently
replete, they would immediately depart, and disembogue for the
public good a plentiful share of their acquirements, into their
disciples' chaps. For we must here observe, that all learning was
esteemed among them to be compounded from the same principle. Because, first, it is generally affirmed, or confessed that
learning puffeth men up; and, secondly, they proved it by the
following syllogism: Words are but wind; and learning is nothing
but words; *ergo*, learning is nothing but wind. For this reason,
the philosophers among them did, in their schools, deliver to their
pupils, all their doctrines and opinions, by eructation, wherein
they had acquired a wonderful eloquence, and of incredible variety. But the great characteristic, by which their chief sages
were best distinguished, was a certain position of countenance,
which gave undoubted intelligence to what degree or proportion
the spirit agitated the inward mass. For, after certain gripings,
the wind and vapours issuing forth, having first, by their turbu-
lence and convulsions within, caused an earthquake in man's little
world, distorted the mouth, bloated the cheeks, and gave the
eyes a terrible kind of *relievo*.[6] At which junctures all their
belches were received for sacred, the sourer the better, and swal-

[5] This is meant of those seditious preachers, who blow up the seeds of
rebellion, &c.

[6] This alludes to the grimaces and contortions usual among inspired
teachers, and their tone in speaking through the nose. 1720 ED.

lowed with infinite consolation by their meagre devotees. And
to render these yet more complete, because the breath of man's
life is in his nostrils, therefore the choicest, most edifying, and
most enlivening belches, were very wisely conveyed through that
vehicle, to give them a tincture as they passed.

Their gods were the four winds, whom they worshipped, as
the spirits that pervade and enliven the universe, and as those
from whom alone all inspiration can properly be said to proceed.
However, the chief of these, to whom they performed the adora-
tion of *latria*,[7] was the *Almighty North*,[8] an ancient deity,
whom the inhabitants of Megalopolis in Greece had likewise in
highest reverence. *Omnium deorum Boream maxime celebrant.*[9]
This god, though endued with ubiquity, was yet supposed by the
profounder Æolists, to possess one peculiar habitation, or (to
speak in form) a *cœlum empyræum*, wherein he was more in-
timately present. This was situated in a certain region, well
known to the ancient Greeks, by them called Σκοτία, or the Land
of Darkness. And although many controversies have arisen upon
that matter; yet so much is undisputed, that from a region of the
like denomination, the most refined Æolists have borrowed their
original, from whence, in every age, the zealous among their
priesthood have brought over their choicest inspiration, fetching
it with their own hands from the fountain head in certain bladders, and disploding it among the sectaries in all nations, who
did, and do, and ever will, daily gasp and pant after it.

Now, their mysteries and rites were performed in this manner.
'Tis well known among the learned, that the virtuosos of former
ages had a contrivance for carrying and preserving winds in
casks or barrels, which was of great assistance upon long sea
voyages, and the loss of so useful an art at present is very much
to be lamented, though, I know not how, with great negligence
omitted by Pancirollus.[1] It was an invention ascribed to Æolus
himself, from whom this sect is denominated; and who in honour
of their founder's memory have to this day preserved great numbers of those barrels, whereof they fix one in each of their
temples, first beating out the top; into this barrel, upon solemn
days, the priest enters, where, having before duly prepared himself by the methods already described, a secret funnel is also

[7] Latria is that worship which is paid only to the supreme Deity.　H.
[8] The more zealous sectaries were the presbyterians of the Scottish
discipline.　Scott.
[9] Pausan. L. 8.
[1] An author who writ *De Artibus perditis*, &c., Of Arts lost, and of Arts
invented.

conveyed from his posteriors to the bottom of the barrel, which admits new supplies of inspiration from a northern chink or cranny. Whereupon, you behold him swell immediately to the shape and size of his vessel. In this posture he disembogues whole tempests upon his auditory, as the spirit from beneath gives him utterance, which, issuing *ex adytis* and *penetralibus* is not performed without much pain and gripings. And the wind in breaking forth deals with his face[2] as it does with that of the sea, first blackening, then wrinkling, and at last bursting it into a foam. It is in this guise the sacred Æolist delivers his oracular belches to his panting disciples; of whom some are greedily gaping after the sanctified breath, others are all the while hymning out the praises of the winds; and, gently wafted to and fro by their own humming, do thus represent the soft breezes of their deities appeased.

It is from this custom of the priests, that some authors maintain these Æolists to have been very ancient in the world. Because, the delivery of their mysteries, which I have just now mentioned, appears exactly the same with that of other ancient oracles, whose inspirations were owing to certain subterraneous effluviums of wind, delivered with the same pain to the priest, and much about the same influence on the people.[3] It is true indeed, that these were frequently managed and directed by female officers, whose organs were understood to be better disposed for the admission of those oracular gusts, as entering and passing up through a receptacle of greater capacity, and causing also a pruriency by the way, such as with due management hath been refined from a carnal into a spiritual ecstasy. And to strengthen this profound conjecture, it is farther insisted, that this custom of female priests[4] is kept up still in certain refined colleges of our modern Æolists, who are agreed to receive their inspiration, derived through the receptacle aforesaid, like their ancestors, the Sybils.

And whereas the mind of Man, when he gives the spur and bridle to his thoughts, doth never stop, but naturally sallies out into both extremes of high and low, of good and evil; his first flight of fancy commonly transports him to ideas of what is most perfect, finished, and exalted; till having soared out of his own reach and sight, not well perceiving how near the frontiers of height and depth border upon each other; with the same course

[2] This is an exact description of the changes made in the face by enthusiastic preachers.

[3] The oracles delivered by the Pythoness and other priestesses of Apollo. SCOTT.

[4] Quakers who suffer their women to preach and pray.

and wing, he falls down plumb into the lowest bottom of things, like one who travels the east into the west, or like a straight line drawn by its own length into a circle. Whether a tincture of malice in our natures makes us fond of furnishing every bright idea with its reverse; or whether reason, reflecting upon the sum of things, can, like the sun, serve only to enlighten one half of the globe, leaving the other half, by necessity, under shade and darkness; or, whether fancy, flying up to the imagination of what is highest and best, becomes over-shot, and spent, and weary, and suddenly falls like a dead bird of paradise to the ground.[5] Or whether after all these metaphysical conjectures, I have not entirely missed the true reason; the proposition, however, which has stood me in so much circumstance, is altogether true; that, as the most uncivilized parts of mankind have some way or other climbed up into the conception of a God, or Supreme Power, so they have seldom forgot to provide their fears with certain ghastly notions, which, instead of better, have served them pretty tolerably for a devil. And this proceeding seems to be natural enough; for it is with men, whose imaginations are lifted up very high, after the same rate as with those whose bodies are so; that, as they are delighted with the advantage of a nearer contemplation upwards, so they are equally terrified with the dismal prospect of the precipice below. Thus, in the choice of a devil, it hath been the usual method of mankind, to single out some being, either in act or in vision, which was in most antipathy to the god they had framed. Thus also the sect of Æolists possessed themselves with a dread, and horror, and hatred of two malignant natures, betwixt whom and the deities they adored perpetual enmity was established. The first of these was the chameleon,[6] sworn foe to inspiration, who in scorn devoured large influences of their god, without refunding the smallest blast by eructation. The other was a huge terrible monster, called Moulinavent, who, with four strong arms, waged eternal battle with all their divinities, dexterously turning to avoid their blows, and repay them with interest.

Thus furnished, and set out with gods, as well as devils, was the renowned sect of Æolists, which makes at this day so illustrious a figure in the world, and whereof that polite nation of Laplanders are, beyond all doubt, a most authentic branch; of

[5] It was an ancient belief that birds of paradise had no feet, but always continued on the wing until their death. SCOTT.

[6] I do not well understand what the Author aims at here, any more than by the terrible Monster, mentioned in the following lines, called *Moulinavent,* which is the French word for a windmill.

whom I therefore cannot, without injustice, here omit to make honourable mention, since they appear to be so closely allied in point of interest, as well as inclinations, with their brother Æolists among us, as not only to buy their winds by wholesale from the same merchants, but also to retail them after the same rate and method, and to customers much alike.

Now, whether this system here delivered was wholly compiled by Jack, or, as some writers believe, rather copied from the original at Delphos, with certain additions and emendations, suited to times and circumstances, I shall not absolutely determine. This I may affirm, that Jack gave it at least a new turn, and formed it into the same dress and model as it lies deduced by me.

I have long sought after this opportunity of doing justice to a society of men for whom I have a peculiar honour, and whose opinions, as well as practices, have been extremely misrepresented and traduced by the malice or ignorance of their adversaries. For I think it one of the greatest and best of human actions, to remove prejudices, and place things in their truest and fairest light: which I therefore boldly undertake, without any regards of my own, beside the conscience, the honour, and the thanks.

SECTION IX

A DIGRESSION CONCERNING THE ORIGINAL, THE USE, AND IMPROVEMENT OF MADNESS IN A COMMONWEALTH.

NOR shall it any ways detract from the just reputation of this famous sect, that its rise and institution are owing to such an author as I have described Jack to be, a person whose intellectuals were overturned, and his brain shaken out of its natural position; which we commonly suppose to be a distemper, and call by the name of madness or phrenzy. For, if we take a survey of the greatest actions that have been performed in the world, under the influence of single men, which are the establishment of new empires by conquest, the advance and progress of new schemes in philosophy, and the contriving, as well as the propagating, of new religions, we shall find the authors of them all to have been persons whose natural reason had admitted great revolutions from their diet, their education, the prevalency of some certain temper, together with the particular influence of air and climate. Besides, there is something individual in human minds, that easily kindles at the accidental approach and collision of certain circumstances, which, though of paltry and mean appearance, do often flame out into the greatest emergencies of life. For great turns are not always given by strong hands, but by lucky adaption, and at proper seasons; and it is of no import where the fire was kindled, if the vapour has once got up into the brain. For the upper region of man is furnished like the middle region of the air; the materials are formed from causes of the widest difference, yet produce at last the same substance and effect. Mists arise from the earth, steams from dunghills, exhalations from the sea, and smoke from fire; yet all clouds are the same in composition as well as consequences, and the fumes issuing from a jakes will furnish as comely and useful a vapour as incense from an altar. Thus far, I suppose, will easily be granted me; and then it will follow, that as the face of nature never produces rain but when it is overcast and disturbed, so human understanding, seated in the brain, must be troubled and overspread by vapours, ascending from the lower faculties to water the invention and render it fruitful. Now, although these vapours (as it hath been already said) are of as various original as those of the skies, yet the crop they produce differs both in kind and degree, merely according to the soil. I will produce two instances to prove and explain what I am now advancing.

A certain great prince [7] raised a mighty army, filled his coffers with infinite treasures, provided an invincible fleet, and all this without giving the least part of his design to his greatest ministers or his nearest favourites. Immediately the whole world was alarmed; the neighbouring crowns in trembling expectation towards what point the storm would burst; the small politicians everywhere forming profound conjectures. Some believed he had laid a scheme for universal monarchy; others, after much insight, determined the matter to be a project for pulling down the pope, and setting up the reformed religion, which had once been his own. Some, again, of a deeper sagacity, sent him into Asia to subdue the Turk, and recover Palestine. In the midst of all these projects and preparations, a certain state-surgeon,[8] gathering the nature of the disease by these symptoms, attempted the cure, at one blow performed the operation, broke the bag, and out flew the vapour; nor did anything want to render it a complete remedy, only that the prince unfortunately happened to die in the performance. Now, is the reader exceeding curious to learn from whence this vapour took its rise, which had so long set the nations at a gaze? What secret wheel, what hidden spring

[7] This was Harry the Great of France.
[8] Ravillac, who stabbed Henry the Great in his coach.

could put into motion so wonderful an engine? It was afterwards discovered that the movement of this whole machine had
been directed by an absent female, whose eyes had raised a protuberancy, and before emission, she was removed into an enemy's country. What should an unhappy prince do in such tick-
lish circumstances as these? He tried in vain the poet's never-
failing receipt of *corpora quœque;* for

> Idque petit corpus mens unde est saucia amore;
> Unde feritur, eo tendit, gestitq; coire. — Lucr.

Having to no purpose used all peaceable endeavours, the collected part of the semen, raised and inflamed, became adust, converted to choler, turned head upon the spinal duct, and ascended
to the brain. The very same principle that influences a bully to
break the windows of a whore who has jilted him, naturally stirs
up a great prince to raise mighty armies, and dream of nothing
but sieges, battles, and victories.

> —— Teterrima belli
> Causa ——

The other instance [9] is what I have read somewhere in a very
ancient author, of a mighty king, who, for the space of above
thirty years, amused himself to take and lose towns, beat
armies, and be beaten, drive princes out of their dominions;
fright children from their bread and butter; burn, lay waste,
plunder, dragoon, massacre subject and stranger, friend and foe,
male and female. 'Tis recorded, that the philosophers of each
country were in grave dispute upon causes natural, moral, and
political, to find out where they should assign an original solution of this phenomenon. At last the vapour or spirit, which animated the hero's brain, being in perpetual circulation, seized
upon that region of the human body, so renowned for furnishing
the *zibeta occidentalis,*[1] and gathering there into a tumor, left
the rest of the world for that time in peace. Of such mighty consequence it is where those exhalations fix, and of so little from

---

[9] This is meant of the present French king.
Lewis XIV was cut of a *fistula in ano.* 1734 ED.
[1] Paracelsus, who was so famous for chemistry, tried an experiment upon
human excrement, to make a perfume of it, which when he had brought to
perfection, he called *zibeta occidentalis,* or western-civet, the back parts of
man (according to his division mentioned by the author, page 321) being
the west.

whence they proceed. The same spirits which, in their superior progress would conquer a kingdom, descending upon the anus, conclude in a fistula.

Let us next examine the great introducers of new schemes in philosophy, and search till we can find from what faculty of the soul the disposition arises in mortal man, of taking it into his head to advance new systems with such an eager zeal, in things agreed on all hands impossible to be known; from what seeds this disposition springs, and to what quality of human nature these grand innovators have been indebted for their number of disciples. Because, it is plain, that several of the chief among them, both ancient and modern, were usually mistaken by their adversaries, and indeed by all except their own followers, to have been persons crazed, or out of their wits, having generally proceeded in the common course of their words and actions by a method very different from the vulgar dictates of unrefined reason; agreeing for the most part in their several models, with their present undoubted successors in the academy of modern Bedlam (whose merits and principles I shall farther examine in due place). Of this kind were *Epicurus, Diogenes, Apollonius, Lucretius, Paracelsus, Descartes*, and others, who, if they were now in the world, tied fast, and separate from their followers, would, in this our undistinguishing age, incur manifest danger of phlebotomy, and whips, and chains, and dark chambers, and straw. For what man in the natural state or course of thinking, did ever conceive it in his power to reduce the notions of all mankind exactly to the same length, and breadth, and height of his own? Yet this is the first humble and civil design of all innovators in the empire of reason. Epicurus modestly hoped, that one time or other a certain fortuitous concourse of all men's opinions, after perpetual justlings, the sharp with the smooth, the light and the heavy, the round and the square, would by certain clinamina unite in the notions of atoms and void, as these did in the originals of all things. Cartesius reckoned to see before he died the sentiments of all philosophers, like so many lesser stars in his romantic system, wrapped and drawn within his own vortex. Now, I would gladly be informed, how it is possible to account for such imaginations as these in particular men without recourse to my phenomenon of vapours, ascending from the lower faculties to overshadow the brain, and thence distilling into conceptions for which the narrowness of our mother-tongue has not yet assigned any other name besides that of madness or phrenzy. Let us therefore now conjecture how it comes to pass, that none of these great prescribers do ever fail providing themselves and their notions with a number of implicit disciples. And, I think, the reason is easy to be assigned: for there is a peculiar string in the harmony of human understanding, which in several individuals is exactly of the same tuning. This, if you can dexterously screw up to its right key, and then strike gently upon it, whenever you have the good fortune to light among those of the same pitch, they will, by a secret necessary sympathy, strike exactly at the same time. And in this one circumstance lies all the skill or luck of the matter; for if you chance to jar the string among those who are either above or below your own height, instead of subscribing to your doctrine, they will tie you fast, call you mad, and feed you with bread and water. It is therefore a point of the nicest conduct to distinguish and adapt this noble talent, with respect to the differences of persons and of times. Cicero understood this very well, when writing to a friend in England, with a caution, among other matters, to beware of being cheated by our hackney-coachmen (who, it seems, in those days were as arrant rascals as they are now) has these remarkable words: *Est quod gaudeas te in ista loca venisse, ubi aliquid sapere viderere*.[2] For, to speak a bold truth, it is a fatal miscarriage so ill to order affairs, as to pass for a fool in one company, when in another you might be treated as a philosopher. Which I desire some certain gentlemen of my acquaintance to lay up in their hearts, as a very seasonable innuendo.

This, indeed, was the fatal mistake of that worthy gentleman, my most ingenious friend, Mr. Wotton: a person, in appearance ordained for great designs, as well as performances; whether you will consider his notions or his looks. Surely no man ever advanced into the public with fitter qualifications of body and mind, for the propagation of a new religion. Oh, had those happy talents misapplied to vain philosophy been turned into their proper channels of dreams and visions, where distortion of mind and countenance are of such sovereign use, the base detracting world would not then have dared to report that something is amiss, that his brain hath undergone an unlucky shake; which even his brother modernists themselves, like ungrates, do whisper so loud, that it reaches up to the very garret I am now writing in.

Lastly, whosoever pleases to look into the fountains of enthusiasm, from whence, in all ages, have eternally proceeded such fattening streams, will find the springhead to have been as troubled and muddy as the current. Of such great emolument is a tincture of this vapour, which the world calls madness, that

[2] Epist. ad Fam. Trebatio.

without its help, the world would not only be deprived of those two great blessings, conquests and systems, but even all mankind would unhappily be reduced to the same belief in things invisible. Now, the former *postulatum* being held, that it is of no import from what originals this vapour proceeds, but either in what angles it strikes and spreads over the understanding, or upon what species of brain it ascends; it will be a very delicate point to cut the feather, and divide the several reasons to a nice and curious reader, how this numerical difference in the brain can produce effects of so vast a difference from the same vapour, as to be the sole point of individuation between Alexander the Great, Jack of Leyden, and Monsieur Des Cartes. The present argument is the most abstracted that ever I engaged in; it strains my faculties to their highest stretch; and I desire the reader to attend with utmost perpensity for I now proceed to unravel this knotty point.

There is in mankind a certain ³ *   *   *   *   *   *

*   *   *   *   *   *   *   *   *   *   *

Hic multa   *   *   *   *   *   *   *   *
desiderantur   *   *   *   *   *   *   *   *

*   *   * And this I take to be a clear solution of the matter.

Having therefore so narrowly passed through this intricate difficulty, the reader will, I am sure, agree with me in the conclusion, that if the moderns mean by madness, only a disturbance or transposition of the brain, by force of certain vapours issuing up from the lower faculties, then has this madness been the parent of all those mighty revolutions that have happened in empire, in philosophy, and in religion. For the brain, in its natural position and state of serenity, disposeth its owner to pass his life in the common forms, without any thought of subduing multitudes to his own power, his reasons, or his visions; and the more he shapes his understanding by the pattern of human learning, the less he is inclined to form parties after his particular notions, because that instructs him in his private infirmities, as well as in the stubborn ignorance of the people. But when a man's fancy gets astride on his reason, when imagination is at cuffs with the senses, and common understanding, as well as common sense, is kicked out of doors, the first proselyte he makes is himself; and when that is once compassed, the difficulty is not so great in bringing over others; a strong delusion always operating from

³ Here is another defect in the manuscript, but I think the author did wisely, and that the matter which thus strained his faculties, was not worth a solution; and it were well if all metaphysical cobweb problems were no otherwise answered.

without as vigorously as from within. For, cant and vision are to the ear and the eye, the same that tickling is to the touch. Those entertainments and pleasures we most value in life, are such as dupe and play the wag with the senses. For, if we take an examination of what is generally understood by happiness, as it has respect either to the understanding or the senses, we shall find all its properties and adjuncts will herd under this short definition, that it is a perpetual possession of being well deceived. And first, with relation to the mind or understanding, 'tis manifest what mighty advantages fiction has over truth; and the reason is just at our elbow, because imagination can build nobler scenes, and produce more wonderful revolutions than fortune or nature will be at expense to furnish. Nor is mankind so much to blame in his choice thus determining him, if we consider that the debate merely lies between things past and things conceived; and so the question is only this — whether things that have place in the imagination, may not as properly be said to exist, as those that are seated in the memory, which may be justly held in the affirmative, and very much to the advantage of the former, since this is acknowledged to be the womb of things, and the other allowed to be no more than the grave. Again, if we take this definition of happiness, and examine it with reference to the senses, it will be acknowledged wonderfully adapt. How fading and insipid do all objects accost us, that are not conveyed in the vehicle of delusion? How shrunk is everything, as it appears in the glass of nature? So that if it were not for the assistance of artificial mediums, false lights, refracted angles, varnish, and tinsel, there would be a mighty level in the felicity and enjoyments of mortal men. If this were seriously considered by the world, as I have a certain reason to suspect it hardly will, men would no longer reckon among their high points of wisdom, the art of exposing weak sides, and publishing infirmities; an employment, in my opinion, neither better nor worse than that of unmasking, which I think has never been allowed fair usage, either in the world or the play-house.

In the proportion that credulity is a more peaceful possession of the mind than curiosity; so far preferable is that wisdom, which converses about the surface, to that pretended philosophy which enters into the depth of things, and then comes gravely back with informations and discoveries, that in the inside they are good for nothing. The two senses, to which all objects first address themselves, are the sight and the touch; these never examine farther than the colour, the shape, the size, and whatever other qualities dwell, or are drawn by art upon the outward of bodies; and then comes reason officiously with tools for cutting, and opening, and mangling, and piercing, offering to demonstrate, that they are not of the same consistence quite through. Now, I take all this to be the last degree of perverting nature; one of whose eternal laws it is, to put her best furniture forward. And therefore, in order to save the charges of all such expensive anatomy for the time to come, I do here think fit to inform the reader, that in such conclusions as these, reason is certainly in the right, and that in most corporeal beings, which have fallen under my cognizance, the outside hath been infinitely preferable to the in; whereof I have been farther convinced from some late experiments. Last week I saw a woman flayed, and you will hardly believe how much it altered her person for the worse. Yesterday I ordered the carcass of a beau to be stripped in my presence, when we were all amazed to find so many unsuspected faults under one suit of clothes. Then I laid open his brain, his heart, and his spleen; but I plainly perceived at every operation, that the farther we proceeded, we found the defects increase upon us in number and bulk; from all which, I justly formed this conclusion to myself; that whatever philosopher or projector can find out an art to sodder and patch up the flaws and imperfections of nature, will deserve much better of mankind, and teach us a more useful science, than that so much in present esteem, of widening and exposing them (like him who held anatomy to be the ultimate end of physic). And he, whose fortunes and dispositions have placed him in a convenient station to enjoy the fruits of this noble art; he that can with Epicurus content his ideas with the films and images that fly off upon his senses from the superficies of things; such a man truly wise, creams off nature, leaving the sour and the dregs for philosophy and reason to lap up. This is the sublime and refined point of felicity, called, the possession of being well deceived; the serene peaceful state of being a fool among knaves.

But to return to madness. It is certain, that according to the system I have above deduced, every species thereof proceeds from a redundancy of vapours; therefore, as some kinds of phrenzy give double strength to the sinews, so there are of other species, which add vigor, and life, and spirit to the brain. Now, it usually happens, that these active spirits, getting possession of the brain, resemble those that haunt other waste and empty dwellings, which for want of business, either vanish, and carry away a piece of the house, or else stay at home and fling it all out of the windows. By which are mystically displayed the two principal branches of madness, and which some philosophers not considering so well as I, have mistook to be different in their causes, over-hastily assigning the first to deficiency, and the other to redundance.

I think it therefore manifest, from what I have here advanced, that the main point of skill and address is to furnish employment for this redundancy of vapour, and prudently to adjust the season of it; by which means it may certainly become of cardinal and catholic emolument in a commonwealth. Thus one man, choosing a proper juncture, leaps into a gulf, from thence proceeds a hero, and is called the saver of his country; another achieves the same enterprise, but unluckily timing it, has left the brand of madness fixed as a reproach upon his memory; upon so nice a distinction are we taught to repeat the name of Curtius with reverence and love, that of Empedocles with hatred and contempt. Thus also it is usually conceived, that the elder Brutus only personated the fool and madman for the good of the public; but this was nothing else than a redundancy of the same vapour long misapplied, called by the Latins, *ingenium par negotiis;* [4] or (to translate it as nearly as I can) a sort of phrenzy, never in its right element, till you take it up in business of the state.

Upon all which, and many other reasons of equal weight, though not equally curious, I do here gladly embrace an opportunity I have long sought for, of recommending it as a very noble undertaking to Sir Edward Seymour, Sir Christopher Musgrave, Sir John Bowls, John How, Esq., and other patriots concerned, that they would move for leave to bring in a bill for appointing commissioners to inspect into Bedlam, and the parts adjacent; who shall be empowered to send for persons, papers, and records, to examine into the merits and qualifications of every student and professor, to observe with utmost exactness their several dispositions and behaviour, by which means, duly distinguishing and adapting their talents, they might produce admirable instruments for the several offices in a state, * * * * * [5], civil, and military, proceeding in such methods as I shall here humbly propose. And I hope the gentle reader will give some allowance to my great solicitudes in this important affair, upon account of that high esteem I have ever borne that honourable society, whereof I had some time the happiness to be an unworthy member.

Is any student tearing his straw in piece-meal, swearing and

[4] Tacit.
[5] Ecclesiastical. H.

blaspheming, biting his grate, foaming at the mouth, and empty-
ing his piss-pot in the spectators' faces? Let the right worship-
ful the commissioners of inspection give him a regiment of dragoons, and send him into Flanders among the rest. Is another
eternally talking, sputtering, gaping, bawling, in a sound without
period or article? What wonderful talents are here mislaid! Let
him be furnished immediately with a green bag and papers, and
threepence in his pocket,[6] and away with him to Westminster
Hall. You will find a third gravely taking the dimensions of his
kennel, a person of foresight and insight, though kept quite in
the dark; for why, like Moses, *ecce cornuta* [7] *erat ejus facies*. He
walks duly in one pace, entreats your penny with due gravity and
ceremony, talks much of hard times, and taxes, and the whore of
Babylon, bars up the wooden window of his cell constantly at
eight o'clock, dreams of fire, and shoplifters, and court-cus-
tomers, and privileged places. Now, what a figure would all
these acquirements amount to, if the owner were sent into the
city among his brethren! Behold a fourth, in much and deep
conversation with himself, biting his thumbs at proper junctures,
his countenance checkered with business and design, sometimes
walking very fast, with his eyes nailed to a paper that he holds in
his hands; a great saver of time, somewhat thick of hearing, very
short of sight, but more of memory; a man ever in haste, a great
hatcher and breeder of business, and excellent at the famous art
of whispering nothing; a huge idolator of monosyllables and pro-
crastination, so ready to give his word to everybody, that he
never keeps it; one that has forgot the common meaning of
words, but an admirable retainer of the sound; extremely subject
to the looseness, for his occasions are perpetually calling him
away. If you approach his grate in his familiar intervals, 'Sir,'
says he, 'give me a penny, and I'll sing you a song; but give me
the penny first.' (Hence comes the common saying, and com-
moner practice of parting with money for a song.) What a complete system of court skill is here described in every branch of it,
and all utterly lost with wrong application. Accost the hole of
another kennel, first stopping your nose, you will behold a surly,
gloomy, nasty, slovenly mortal, raking in his own dung, and dab-
bling in his urine. The best part of his diet is the reversion of his
own ordure, which expiring into steams, whirls perpetually

[6] A lawyers coach-hire [when four together, from any of the Inns of
Court to Westminster — H.].
[7] Cornutus is either horned or shining, and by this term, Moses is described
in the vulgar Latin of the Bible.

about, and at last re-infunds. His complexion is of a dirty yellow, with a thin scattered beard, exactly agreeable to that of his diet upon its first declination, like other insects, who having their birth and education in an excrement, from thence borrow their colour and their smell. The student of this apartment is very sparing of his words, but somewhat over-liberal of his breath; he holds his hand out ready to receive your penny, and immediately upon receipt withdraws to his former occupations. Now, is it not amazing to think, the society of Warwick-lane should have no more concern for the recovery of so useful a member, who, if one may judge from these appearances, would become the greatest ornament to that illustrious body? Another student struts up fiercely to your teeth, puffing with his lips, half squeezing out his eyes, and very graciously holds you out his hand to kiss. The keeper desires you not to be afraid of this professor, for he will do you no hurt; to him alone is allowed the liberty of the antechamber, and the orator of the place gives you to understand, that this solemn person is a tailor run mad with pride. This considerable student is adorned with many other qualities, upon which, at present, I shall not farther enlarge- - - - - -*Hark in your ear* [8] - - - - - - I am strangely mistaken, if all his address, his motions, and his airs, would not then be very natural, and in their proper element.

I shall not descend so minutely, as to insist upon the vast number of beaux, fiddlers, poets, and politicians, that the world might recover by such a reformation; but what is more material, besides the clear gain redounding to the commonwealth, by so large an acquisition of persons to employ, whose talents and acquirements, if I may be so bold as to affirm it, are now buried, or at least misapplied; it would be a mighty advantage accruing to the public from this inquiry, that all these would very much excel, and arrive at great perfection in their several kinds; which, I think, is manifest from what I have already shown, and shall enforce by this one plain instance, that even I myself, the author of these momentous truths, am a person, whose imaginations are hard-mouthed, and exceedingly disposed to run away with his reason, which I have observed from long experience to be a very light rider, and easily shook off; upon which account, my friends will never trust me alone, without a solemn promise to vent my speculations in this, or the like manner, for the universal benefit of human kind; which perhaps the gentle, courteous, and candid reader, brimful of that modern charity and tenderness usually annexed to his office, will be very hardly persuaded to believe.

[8] I cannot conjecture what the author means here, or how this chasm could be filled, tho' it is capable of more than one interpretation

SECTION X

THE AUTHOR'S COMPLIMENT TO THE READERS, &C.

A FURTHER DIGRESSION

IT is an unanswerable argument of a very refined age, the
wonderful civilities that have passed of late years between the
nation of authors and that of readers. There can hardly pop out
a play, a pamphlet, or a poem, without a preface full of
acknowledgments to the world for the general reception and ap-
plause they have given it,[9] which the Lord knows where, or when,
or how, or from whom it received. In due deference to so laudable a custom, I do here return my humble thanks to his Majesty,
and both Houses of Parliament; to the Lords of the King's Most
Honourable Privy Council; to the reverend the Judges; to the
clergy, and gentry, and yeomanry of this land; but in a more
especial manner to my worthy brethren and friends at Will's
Coffee-house, and Gresham College, and Warwick Lane, and
Moorfields, and Scotland Yard, and Westminster Hall, and Guild-
hall; in short, to all inhabitants and retainers whatsoever, either
in court, or church, or camp, or city, or country, for their generous and universal acceptance of this divine treatise. I accept their
approbation and good opinion with extreme gratitude, and to the
utmost of my poor capacity, shall take hold of all opportunities
to return the obligation.

I am also happy, that fate has flung me into so blessed an age
for the mutual felicity of booksellers and authors, whom I may
safely affirm to be at this day the two only satisfied parties in
England. Ask an author how his last piece hath succeeded: Why,
truly, he thanks his stars, the world has been very favourable,
and he has not the least reason to complain: and yet, by G—, he
writ it in a week at bits and starts, when he could steal an hour
from his urgent affairs; as it is a hundred to one you may see
farther in the preface, to which he refers you, and for the rest, to
the bookseller. There you go as a customer, and make the same
question: he blesses his God the thing takes wonderfully, he is
just printing a second edition, and has but three left in his shop.
You beat down the price: 'Sir, we shall not differ,' and in hopes
of your custom another time, lets you have it as reasonable as
you please, 'and pray send as many of your acquaintance as you
will, I shall upon your account furnish them all at the same rate.'

Now, it is not well enough considered, to what accidents and
occasions the world is indebted for the greatest part of those

---

[9] This is literally true, as we may observe in the prefaces to most plays,
poems, &c.

noble writings, which hourly start up to entertain it. If it were
not for a rainy day, a drunken vigil, a fit of the spleen, a course of
physic, a sleepy Sunday, an ill run at dice, a long tailor's bill, a
beggar's purse, a factious head, a hot sun, costive diet, want of
books, and a just contempt of learning. But for these events, I
say, and some others too long to recite (especially a prudent neglect of taking brimstone inwardly) I doubt, the number of
authors and of writings would dwindle away to a degree most
woeful to behold. To confirm this opinion, hear the words of the
famous Troglodyte philosopher: ''Tis certain' (said he) 'some
grains of folly are of course annexed, as part of the composition
of human nature, only the choice is left us, whether we please
to wear them inlaid or embossed; and we need not go very far
to seek how that is usually determined, when we remember it
is with human faculties as with liquors, the lightest will be ever
at the top.'

There is in this famous island of Britain a certain paltry scribbler, very voluminous, whose character the reader cannot
wholly be a stranger to. He deals in a pernicious kind of writings,
called *Second Parts*, and usually passes under the name of the
Author of the First. I easily foresee, that as soon as I lay down
my pen, this nimble operator will have stole it, and treat me as
inhumanly as he hath already done Dr. Blackmore, L'Estrange,
and many others who shall here be nameless. I therefore fly for
justice and relief into the hands of that great rectifier of saddles,[1]
and lover of mankind, Dr. Bentley, begging he will take this
enormous grievance into his most modern consideration; and if
it should so happen, that the furniture of an ass, in the shape of a
second part, must for my sins be clapped by a mistake upon my
back, that he will immediately please, in the presence of the
world, to lighten me of the burden, and take it home to his own
house, till the true beast thinks fit to call for it.

In the meantime I do here give this public notice, that my resolutions are to circumscribe within this discourse the whole stock
of matter I have been so many years providing. Since my vein is
once opened, I am content to exhaust it all at a running, for the
peculiar advantage of my dear country, and for the universal
benefit of mankind. Therefore hospitably considering the number of my guests, they shall have my whole entertainment at a
meal; and I scorn to set up the leavings in the cupboard. What
the guests cannot eat may be given to the poor, and the dogs[2]
under the table may gnaw the bones. This I understand for a

---

[1] Alluding to the trite phrase, *place the saddle on the right horse*. H.

[2] By dogs, the author means common injudicious critics, as he explains
it himself before in his Digression upon Critics (p. 297).

more generous proceeding, than to turn the company's stomach, by inviting them again to-morrow to a scurvy meal of scraps.

If the reader fairly considers the strength of what I have advanced in the foregoing section, I am convinced it will produce a wonderful revolution in his notions and opinions; and he will be abundantly better prepared to receive and to relish the concluding part of this miraculous treatise. Readers may be divided into three classes, the superficial, the ignorant, and the learned: and I have with much felicity fitted my pen to the genius and advantage of each. The superficial reader will be strangely provoked to laughter; which clears the breast and the lungs, is sovereign against the spleen, and the most innocent of all diuretics. The ignorant reader (between whom and the former the distinction is extremely nice) will find himself disposed to stare; which is an admirable remedy for ill eyes, serves to raise and enliven the spirits, and wonderfully helps perspiration. But the reader truly learned, chiefly for whose benefit I wake when others sleep, and sleep when others wake, will here find sufficient matter to employ his speculations for the rest of his life. It were much to be wished, and I do here humbly propose for an experiment, that every prince in Christendom will take seven of the deepest scholars in his dominions, and shut them up close for seven years in seven chambers, with a command to write seven ample commentaries on this comprehensive discourse. I shall venture to affirm, that whatever difference may be found in their several conjectures, they will be all, without the least 'distortion, manifestly deducible from the text. Meantime, it is my earnest request, that so useful an undertaking may be entered upon (if their Majesties please) with all convenient speed; because I have a strong inclination, before I leave the world, to taste a blessing which we mysterious writers can seldom reach till we have got into our graves, whether it is, that fame, being a fruit grafted on the body, can hardly grow, and much less ripen, till the stock is in the earth, or whether she be a bird of prey, and is lured, among the rest, to pursue after the scent of a carcass: or whether she conceives her trumpet sounds best and farthest when she stands on a tomb, by the advantage of a rising ground, and the echo of a hollow vault.

'Tis true, indeed, the republic of dark authors, after they once found out this excellent expedient of dying, have been peculiarly happy in the variety, as well as extent of their reputation. For, night being the universal mother of things, wise philosophers hold all writings to be fruitful in the proportion they are dark; and therefore, the true illuminated [3] (that is to say, the darkest of

---

[3] A name of the Rosicrucians.

all) have met with such numberless commentators, whose scholastic midwifery hath delivered them of meanings, that the authors themselves perhaps never conceived, and yet may very justly be allowed the lawful parents of them, the words of such writers being like seed,[4] which, however scattered at random, when they light upon a fruitful ground, will multiply far beyond either the hopes or imagination of the sower.

And therefore in order to promote so useful a work, I will here take leave to glance a few innuendoes, that may be of great assistance to those sublime spirits, who shall be appointed to labor in a universal comment upon this wonderful discourse. And first,[5] I have couched a very profound mystery in the number of O's multiplied by seven, and divided by nine. Also, if a devout brother of the Rosy Cross will pray fervently for sixty-three mornings, with a lively faith, and then transpose certain letters and syllables according to prescription in the second and fifth section, they will certainly reveal into a full receipt of the *opus magnum*. Lastly, whoever will be at the pains to calculate the whole number of each letter in this treatise, and sum up the difference exactly between the several numbers, assigning the true natural cause for every such difference, the discoveries in the product will plentifully reward his labour. But then he must beware of Bythus and Sigè,[6] and be sure not to forget the qualities of Acamoth: *A cujus lacrymis humecta prodit substantia, à risu lucida, à tristitiâ solida, & à timore mobilis*, wherein Eugenius Philalethes[7] hath committed an unpardonable mistake.

[4] Nothing is more frequent than for commentators to force interpretation, which the author never meant.

[5] This is what the Cabalists among the Jews have done with the Bible, and pretend to find wonderful mysteries by it.

[6] I was told by an eminent divine, whom I consulted on this point, that these two barbarous words, with that of Acamoth and its qualities, as here set down, are quoted from Irenæus. This he discovered by searching that ancient writer for another quotation of our author, which he has placed in the title-page, and refers to the book and chapter; the curious were very inquisitive, whether those barbarous words, *basima eacabasa, &c.* are really in Irenæus, and upon enquiry 'twas found they were a sort of cant or jargon of certain heretics, and therefore very properly prefixed to such a book as this of our author.

[7] *Vid. Anima magica abscondita.* To the above-mentioned treatise, called *Anthroposophia Theomagica*, there is another annexed, called *Anima magica abscondita*, written by the same author, Vaughan, under the name of Eugenius Philalethes, but in neither of those treatises is there any mention of Acamoth or its qualities, so that this is nothing but amusement, and a ridicule of dark, unintelligible writers; only the words, *A cujus lacrymis, & c.* are as we have said, transcribed from Irenæus, though I know not from what part. I believe one of the author's designs was to set curious men a-hunting through indexes, and enquiring for books out of the common road.

SECTION XI

A TALE OF A TUB

AFTER so wide a compass as I have wandered, I do now gladly
overtake, and close in with my subject, and shall henceforth hold
on with it an even pace to the end of my journey, except some
beautiful prospect appears within sight of my way, whereof
though at present I have neither warning nor expectation, yet
upon such an accident, come when it will, I shall beg my
reader's favour and company, allowing me to conduct him
through it along with myself. For in writing it is as in travelling:
if a man is in haste to be at home (which I acknowledge to be
none of my case, having never so little business as when I am
there) if his horse be tired with long riding and ill ways, or be
naturally a jade, I advise him clearly to make the straightest and
the commonest road, be it ever so dirty. But then surely we must
own such a man to be a scurvy companion at best; he spatters
himself and his fellow-travellers at every step: all their thoughts,
and wishes, and conversation, turn entirely upon the subject of
their journey's end; and at every splash, and plunge, and
stumble, they heartily wish one another at the devil.

On the other side, when a traveller and his horse are in heart
and plight, when his purse is full, and the day before him, he
takes the road only where it is clean or convenient; entertains his
company there as agreeably as he can; but upon the first occasion,
carries them along with him to every delightful scene in view,
whether of art, of nature, or of both; and if they chance to refuse
out of stupidity or weariness, let them jog on by themselves and
be d—n'd; he'll overtake them at the next town, at which arriving,
he rides furiously through; the men, women, and children run
out to gaze; a hundred [8] noisy curs run barking after him, of
which, if he honors the boldest with a lash of his whip, it is rather
out of sport than revenge; but should some sourer mongrel dare
too near an approach, he receives a salute on the chaps by an
accidental stroke from the courser's heels (nor is any ground lost
by the blow) which sends him yelping and limping home.

I now proceed to sum up the singular adventures of my
renowned Jack, the state of whose dispositions and fortunes the
careful reader does, no doubt, most exactly remember, as I last
parted with them in the conclusion of a former section. Therefore, his next care must be from two of the foregoing to extract
a scheme of notions, that may best fit his understanding for a
true relish of what is to ensue.

---

[8] By these are meant what the author calls the true critics, pp. 296–7.

Jack had not only calculated the first revolutions of his brain so prudently, as to give rise to that epidemic sect of Æolists, but succeeding also into a new and strange variety of conceptions, the fruitfulness of his imagination led him into certain notions, which, although in appearance very unaccountable, were not without their mysteries and their meanings, nor wanted followers to countenance and improve them. I shall therefore be extremely careful and exact in recounting such material passages of this nature as I have been able to collect, either from undoubted tradition, or indefatigable reading; and shall describe them as graphically as it is possible, and as far as notions of that height and latitude can be brought within the compass of a pen. Nor do I at all question, but they will furnish plenty of noble matter for such, whose converting imaginations dispose them to reduce all things into types; who can make shadows, no thanks to the sun, and then mould them into substances, no thanks to philosophy; whose peculiar talent lies in fixing tropes and allegories to the letter, and refining what is literal into figure and mystery.

Jack had provided a fair copy of his father's will, engrossed in form upon a large skin of parchment; and resolving to act the part of a most dutiful son, he became the fondest creature of it imaginable. For although, as I have often told the reader, it consisted wholly in certain plain, easy directions about the management and wearing of their coats, with legacies and penalties, in case of obedience or neglect, yet he began to entertain a fancy that the matter was deeper and darker, and therefore must needs have a great deal more of mystery at the bottom. 'Gentlemen,' said he, 'I will prove this very skin of parchment to be meat, drink, and cloth, to be the philosopher's stone, and the universal medicine.' ⁹ In consequence of which raptures, he resolved to make use of it in the most necessary, as well as the most paltry, occasions of life. He had a way of working it into any shape he pleased; so that it served him for a nightcap when he went to bed, and for an umbrella in rainy weather. He would lap a piece of it about a sore toe, or when he had fits, burn two inches under his nose; or if anything lay heavy on his stomach, scrape off, and swallow as much of the powder as would lie on a silver penny — they were all infallible remedies. With analogy to these refinements, his common talk and conversation ran wholly in the phrase of his will,¹ and he circumscribed the utmost of his elo-

⁹ The author here lashes those pretenders to purity, who place so much merit in using Scripture phrase[s] on all occasions.

¹ The Protestant dissenters use Scripture phrases in their serious discourses and composures more than the Church of England men; accordingly Jack is introduced making his common talk and conversation to run wholly in the phrase of his will. W. WOTTON.

quence within that compass, not daring to let slip a syllable without authority from thence. Once at a strange house, he was suddenly taken short upon an urgent juncture, whereon it may not be allowed too particularly to dilate; and being not able to call to mind, with that suddenness the occasion required, an authentic phrase for demanding the way to the backside; he chose rather as the more prudent course to incur the penalty in such cases usually annexed. Neither was it possible for the united rhetoric of mankind to prevail with him to make himself clean again; because having consulted the will upon this emergency, he met with a passage [2] near the bottom (whether foisted in by the transcriber, is not known) which seemed to forbid it.

He made it a part of his religion, never to say grace to his meat,[3] nor could all the world persuade him, as the common phrase is, to eat his victuals like a Christian.[4]

He bore a strange kind of appetite to snap-dragon,[5] and to the livid snuffs of a burning candle, which he would catch and swallow with an agility wonderful to conceive; and by this procedure, maintained a perpetual flame in his belly, which issuing in a glowing steam from both his eyes, as well as his nostrils and his mouth, made his head appear in a dark night, like the skull of an ass, wherein a roguish boy had conveyed a farthing candle, to the terror of his Majesty's liege subjects. Therefore, he made use of no other expedient to light himself home, but was wont to say, that a wise man was his own lanthorn.

He would shut his eyes as he walked along the streets, and if he happened to bounce his head against a post, or fall into the kennel (as he seldom missed either to do one or both) he would tell the gibing prentices, who looked on, that he submitted with entire resignation, as to a trip, or a blow of fate, with whom he

[2] I cannot guess the author's meaning here, which I would be very glad to know, because it seems to be of importance.
'Incurring the penalty in such cases usually annexed,' wants no explanation. He would not make himself clean, because having consulted the will (i.e. the New Testament) he met with a passage near the bottom, i. e. in the eleventh verse of the last chapter of the Revelations, 'He which is filthy, let him be filthy still,' which seemed to forbid it. 'Whether foisted in by the transcriber,' is added, because this paragraph is wanting in the Alexandrian MS., the oldest and most authentic copy of the New Testament. H.

[3] The slovenly way of receiving the sacrament among the fanatics.

[4] This is a common phrase to express eating cleanlily, and is meant for an invective against that undecent manner among some people in receiving the sacrament, so in the lines before 'tis said, Jack would never say grace to his meat, which is to be understood of the Dissenters refusing to kneel at the sacrament.

[5] I cannot well find the author's meaning here, unless it be the hot, untimely, blind zeal of enthusiasts.

found, by long experience, how vain it was either to wrestle or to cuff; and whoever durst undertake to do either, would be sure to come off with a swinging fall, or a bloody nose. 'It was ordained,' said he, 'some few days before the creation, that my nose and this very post should have a rencounter; [6] and, therefore, providence thought fit to send us both into the world in the same age, and to make us countrymen and fellow-citizens. Now, had my eyes been open, it is very likely the business might have been a great deal worse; for how many a confounded slip is daily got by man with all his foresight about him? Besides, the eyes of the understanding see best, when those of the senses are out of the way; and therefore, blind men are observed to tread their steps with much more caution, and conduct, and judgment, than those who rely with too much confidence upon the virtue of the visual nerve, which every little accident shakes out of order, and a drop, or a film, can wholly disconcert; like a lanthorn among a pack of roaring bullies when they scour the streets, exposing its owner and itself to outward kicks and buffets, which both might have escaped, if the vanity of appearing would have suffered them to walk in the dark. But farther, if we examine the conduct of these boasted lights, it will prove yet a great deal worse than their fortune. 'Tis true, I have broke my nose against this post, because providence either forgot, or did not think it convenient to twitch me by the elbow, and give me notice to avoid it. But let not this encourage either the present age or posterity to trust their noses into the keeping of their eyes, which may prove the fairest way of losing them for good and all. For, O ye eyes, ye blind guides, miserable guardians are ye of our frail noses; ye, I say, who fasten upon the first precipice in view, and then tow our wretched willing bodies after you, to the very brink of destruction; but, alas, that brink is rotten, our feet slip, and we tumble down prone into a gulf, without one hospitable shrub in the way to break the fall — a fall, to which not any nose of mortal make is equal, except that of the giant Laurcalco,[7] who was lord of the silver bridge. Most properly therefore, O eyes, and with great justice, may you be compared to those foolish lights, which conduct men through dirt and darkness, till they fall into a deep pit or a noisome bog.'

This I have produced as a scantling of Jack's great eloquence, and the force of his reasoning upon such abstruse matters.

He was, besides, a person of great design and improve-

---

[6] Predestination, the favorite doctrine of most dissenters, is here exposed. Dr. Wotton calls this a direct profanation of the majesty of God. 1720 ED.
[7] Vide *Don Quixote*.

ment in affairs of devotion, having introduced a new deity, who hath since met with a vast number of worshippers, by some called Babel, by others Chaos;[8] who had an ancient temple of Gothic structure upon Salisbury plain, famous for its shrine, and celebration by pilgrims.

When he had some roguish trick to play,[9] he would down with his knees, up with his eyes, and fall to prayers, though in the midst of the kennel. Then it was that those who understood his pranks, would be sure to get far enough out of his way; and whenever curiosity attracted strangers to laugh, or to listen, he would of a sudden with one hand out with his gear, and piss full in their eyes, and with the other, all to bespatter them with mud.

In winter he went always loose and unbuttoned,[1] and clad as thin as possible, to let *in* the ambient heat; and in summer lapped himself close and thick to keep it *out*.

In all revolutions of government,[2] he would make his court for the office of hangman general; and in the exercise of that dignity, wherein he was very dextrous, would make use of no other vizard[3] than a long prayer.

He had a tongue so musculous and subtile, that he could twist it up into his nose, and deliver a strange kind of speech from thence. He was also the first in these kingdoms, who began to improve the Spanish accomplishment of braying; and having large ears, perpetually exposed and arrect, he carried his art to such a perfection, that it was a point of great difficulty to distinguish either by the view or the sound between the original and the copy.

He was troubled with a disease, reverse to that called the stinging of the tarantula; and would run dog-mad at the noise of music,[4] especially a pair of bagpipes. But he would cure himself again, by taking two or three turns in Westminster Hall, or Billingsgate, or in a boarding-school, or the Royal-Exchange, or a state coffee-house.

He was a person that feared no colours,[5] but mortally hated

8 The dissenters . . . as utter enemies to what we call order and regularity in matters of worship. 1720 ED.

9 The villainies and cruelties committed by enthusiasts and fanatics among us were all performed under the disguise of religion and long prayers.

1 They affect differences in habit and behaviour.

2 They are severe persecutors, and all in a form of cant and devotion.

3 Cromwell and his confederates went, as they called it, to seek God, when they resolved to murder the king.

4 This is to expose our Dissenters' aversion to instrumental music in churches. W. WOTTON.

5 They quarrel at the most innocent decency and ornament, and defaced the statues and paintings on all the churches in England.

all, and upon that account bore a cruel aversion to painters; inso-much, that in his paroxysms, as he walked the streets, he would have his pockets loaden with stones to pelt at the signs.

Having from this manner of living, frequent occasion to wash himself, he would often leap over head and ears into the water,[6] though it were in the midst of the winter, but was always observed to come out again much dirtier, if possible, than he went in.

He was the first that ever found out the secret of contriving a soporiferous medicine to be conveyed in at the ears;[7] it was a compound of sulphur and balm of Gilead, with a little pilgrim's salve.

He wore a large plaister of artificial caustics on his stomach, with the fervor of which, he could set himself a-groaning, like the famous board upon application of a red-hot iron.

He would stand in the turning of a street, and, calling to those who passed by, would cry to one, 'Worthy sir, do me the honour of a good slap in the chaps';[8] to another, 'Honest friend, pray favour me with a handsome kick on the arse'; 'Madam, shall I entreat a small box on the ear from your ladyship's fair hands?' 'Noble captain, lend a reasonable thwack, for the love of God, with that cane of yours over these poor shoulders.' And when he had by such earnest solicitations made a shift to procure a basting sufficient to swell up his fancy and his sides, he would return home extremely comforted, and full of terrible accounts of what he had undergone for the public good. 'Observe this stroke' (said he, showing his bare shoulders) 'a plaguy janissary gave it me this very morning at seven o'clock, as, with much ado, I was driving off the great Turk. Neighbours mine, this broken head deserves a plaister; had poor Jack been tender of his noddle, you would have seen the Pope and the French king, long before this time of day, among your wives and your warehouses. Dear Christians, the great Mogul was come as far as White-chapel, and you may thank these poor sides that he hath not (God bless us) already swallowed up man, woman, and child.'

It was highly worth observing the singular effects of that aver-sion,[9] or antipathy, which Jack and his brother Peter seemed,

[6] Baptism of adults by plunging. H.

[7] Fanatic preaching, composed either of hell and damnation, or a fulsome description of the joys of heaven; both in such a dirty, nauseous style, as to be well resembled to pilgrim's salve.

[8] The fanatics have always had a way of affecting to run into persecution, and count vast merit upon every little hardship they suffer.

[9] The papists and fanatics, tho' they appear the most averse to each

even to an affectation, to bear toward each other. Peter had lately done some rogueries, that forced him to abscond; and he seldom ventured to stir out before night, for fear of bailiffs. Their lodgings were at the two most distant parts of the town from each other; and whenever their occasions or humours called them abroad, they would make choice of the oddest unlikely times and most uncouth rounds they could invent, that they might be sure to avoid one another: yet, after all this, it was their perpetual fortune to meet. The reason of which is easy enough to apprehend; for, the phrenzy and the spleen of both having the same foundation, we may look upon them as two pair of compasses, equally extended, and the fixed foot of each remaining in the same center; which, though moving contrary ways at first, will be sure to encounter somewhere or other in the circumference. Besides, it was among the great misfortunes of Jack, to bear a huge personal resemblance with his brother Peter. Their humours and dispositions were not only the same, but there was a close analogy in their shape and size, and their mien. Insomuch as nothing was more frequent than for a bailiff to seize Jack by the shoulders, and cry, 'Mr. Peter, you are the king's prisoner.' Or, at other times, for one of Peter's nearest friends to accost Jack with open arms, 'Dear Peter, I am glad to see thee, pray send me one of your best medicines for the worms.' This we may suppose was a mortifying return of those pains and proceedings Jack had laboured in so long; and finding how directly opposite all his endeavours had answered to the sole end and intention which he had proposed to himself, how could it avoid having terrible effects upon a head and heart so furnished as his? However, the poor remainders of his coat bore all the punishment; the orient sun never entered upon his diurnal progress, without missing a piece of it. He hired a tailor to stitch up the collar so close, that it was ready to choke him, and squeezed out his eyes at such a rate, as one could see nothing but the white. What little was left of the main substance of the coat, he rubbed every day for two hours against a rough-cast wall, in order to grind away the remnants of lace and embroidery, but at the same time went on with so much violence, that he proceeded a heathen philoso-

---

other, yet bear a near resemblance in many things, as has been observed by learned men.

Ibid. The agreement of our dissenters and the papists in that which Bishop Stillingfleet called the fanaticism of the Church of Rome, is ludicrously described for several pages together by Jack's likeness to Peter, and their being often mistaken for each other, and their frequent meeting when they least intended it. W. WOTTON.

pher. Yet after all he could do of this kind, the success continued still to disappoint his expectation. For, as it is the nature of rags to bear a kind of mock resemblance to finery, there being a sort of fluttering appearance in both, which is not to be distinguished at a distance, in the dark, or by short-sighted eyes; so, in those junctures, it fared with Jack and his tatters, that they offered to the first view a ridiculous flaunting, which assisting the resemblance in person and air, thwarted all his projects of separation, and left so near a similitude between them, as frequently deceived the very disciples and followers of both.

* * * * * * * * * * *

* * * * * * * * * * *

Desunt non- * * * * * * * * *
nulla. * * * * * * * * *

* * * * * * * * * * *

* * * * * * * * * * *

The old Sclavonian proverb said well, that it is with men as with asses; whoever would keep them fast, must find a very good hold at their ears. Yet I think we may affirm, and it hath been verified by repeated experience, that,

> Effugiet tamen hæc sceleratus vincula Proteus.

It is good, therefore, to read the maxims of our ancestors, with great allowances to times and persons; for if we look into primitive records, we shall find, that no revolutions have been so great, or so frequent, as those of human ears. In former days, there was a curious invention to catch and keep them; which, I think, we may justly reckon among the *artes perditæ;* and how can it be otherwise, when in these latter centuries the very species is not only diminished to a very lamentable degree, but the poor remainder is also degenerated so far as to mock our skilfullest tenure? For, if the only slitting of one ear in a stag hath been found sufficient to propagate the defect through a whole forest, why should we wonder at the greatest consequences, from so many loppings and mutilations, to which the ears of our fathers, and our own, have been of late so much exposed? 'Tis true, indeed, that while this island of ours was under the dominion of grace, many endeavours were made to improve the growth of ears once more among us. The proportion of largeness was not only looked upon as an ornament of the outward man, but as a type of grace in the inward. Besides, it is held by naturalists, that if there be a protuberancy of parts in the superiour region of the body, as in the ears and nose, there must be a parity also in the inferior; and therefore in that truly pious age, the males in every assembly, according as they were gifted, appeared very forward in exposing their ears to view, and the regions about them; because Hippocrates tells us,[1] that when the vein behind the ear happens to be cut, a man becomes a eunuch: and the females were nothing backwarder in beholding and edifying by them; whereof those who had already used the means, looked about them with great concern, in hopes of conceiving a suitable off-spring by such a prospect; others, who stood candidates for benevolence, found there a plentiful choice, and were sure to fix upon such as discovered the largest ears, that the breed might not dwindle between them. Lastly, the devouter sisters, who looked upon all extraordinary dilatations of that member as protrusions of zeal, or spiritual excrescencies, were sure to honor every head they sat upon, as if they had been marks of grace; but especially that of the preacher, whose ears were usually of the prime magnitude; which upon that account, he was very frequent and exact in exposing with all advantages to the people: in his rhetorical paroxysms turning sometimes to hold forth the one, and sometimes to hold forth the other; from which custom, the whole operation of preaching is to this very day, among their professors, styled by the phrase of *holding forth*.

Such was the progress of the saints for advancing the size of that member; and it is thought the success would have been every way answerable, if in process of time a cruel king[2] had not arose, who raised a bloody persecution against all ears above a certain standard; upon which some were glad to hide their flourishing sprouts in a black border, others crept wholly under a periwig; some were slit, others cropped, and a great number sliced off to the stumps. But of this more hereafter in my general *History of Ears*, which I design very speedily to bestow upon the public.

From this brief survey of the falling state of ears in the last age, and the small care had to advance their ancient growth in the present, it is manifest, how little reason we can have to rely upon a hold so short, so weak, and so slippery; and that whoever desires to catch mankind fast, must have recourse to some other methods. Now, he that will examine human nature with circumspection enough, may discover several handles whereof the six[3] senses afford one apiece, beside a great number that are

[1] *Lib. de aëre locis & aquis.*
[2] This was King Charles the Second, who at his restoration turned out all the dissenting teachers that would not conform.
[3] Including Scaliger's.

screwed to the passions, and some few riveted to the intellect. Among these last, curiosity is one, and of all others affords the firmest grasp: curiosity, that spur in the side, that bridle in the mouth, that ring in the nose, of a lazy and impatient and a grunting reader. By this handle it is, that an author should seize upon his readers; which as soon as he has once compassed, all resistance and struggling are in vain, and they become his prisoners as close as he pleases, till weariness or dullness force him to let go his grip.

And therefore, I, the author of this miraculous treatise, having hitherto, beyond expectation, maintained by the aforesaid handle a firm hold upon my gentle reader, it is with great reluctance, that I am at length compelled to remit my grasp, leaving them in the perusal of what remains to that natural oscitancy inherent in the tribe. I can only assure thee, courteous reader, for both our comforts, that my concern is altogether equal to thine, for my unhappiness in losing, or mislaying among my papers the remaining part of these memoirs; which consisted of accidents, turns, and adventures, both new, agreeable, and surprising; and therefore calculated, in all due points, to the delicate taste of this our noble age. But, alas, with my utmost endeavours, I have been able only to retain a few of the heads. Under which, there was a full account, how Peter got a protection out of the King's Bench; and of a reconcilement[4] between Jack and him, upon a design they had in a certain rainy night, to trepan brother Martin into a spunging-house, and there strip him to the skin. How Martin, with much ado, showed them both a fair pair of heels. How a new warrant came out against Peter; upon which, how Jack left him in the lurch, stole his protection, and made use of it himself. How Jack's tatters came into fashion in court and city; how he got upon a great horse,[5] and eat custard.[6] But the particulars of all these, with several others, which have now slid out of my memory, are lost beyond all hopes of recovery. For which misfortune, leaving my readers to condole with each other,

[4] In the reign of King James the Second, the Presbyterians by the king's invitation, joined with the Papists, against the Church of England, and addressed him for repeal of the penal laws and tests. The king by his dispensing power gave liberty of conscience, which both Papists and Presbyterians made use of, but upon the Revolution, the Papists being down of course, the Presbyterians freely continued their assemblies, by virtue of King James's indulgence, before they had a toleration by law; this I believe the author means by Jack's stealing Peter's protection, and making use of it himself.

[5] Sir Humphry Edwyn, a Presbyterian, was some years ago Lord Mayor of London, and had the insolence to go in his formalities to a conventicle, with the ensigns of his office.

[6] Custard is a famous dish at a Lord Mayor's feast.

as far as they shall find it to agree with their several constitutions; but conjuring them by all the friendship that hath passed between us, from the title-page to this, not to proceed so far as to injure their healths for an accident past remedy; I now go on to the ceremonial part of an accomplished writer, and therefore, by a courtly modern, least of all others to be omitted.

THE CONCLUSION

GOING too long is a cause of abortion as effectual, though not so frequent, as going too short; and holds true especially in the labors of the brain. Well fare the heart of that noble Jesuit,[7] who first adventured to confess in print, that books must be suited to their several seasons, like dress, and diet, and diversions; and better fare our noble nation, for refining upon this among other French modes. I am living fast to see the time, when a book that misses its tide, shall be neglected, as the moon by day, or like mackerel a week after the season. No man hath more nicely observed our climate, than the bookseller who bought the copy of this work; he knows to a tittle what subjects will best go off in a dry year, and which it is proper to expose foremost, when the weather-glass is fallen to much rain. When he had seen this treatise, and consulted his almanack upon it, he gave me to understand, that he had maturely considered the two principal things, which were the bulk and the subject; and found it would never take but after a long vacation, and then only in case it should happen to be a hard year for turnips. Upon which I desired to know, considering my urgent necessities, what he thought might be acceptable this month. He looked westward, and said, 'I doubt we shall have a fit of bad weather; however, if you could prepare some pretty little banter (but not in verse) or a small treatise upon the —— it would run like wildfire. But, if it hold up, I have already hired an author to write something against Dr. Bentley, which, I am sure, will turn to account.'

At length we agreed upon this expedient; that when a customer comes for one of these, and desires in confidence to know the author, he will tell him very privately, as a friend, naming whichever of the wits shall happen to be that week in the vogue; and if Durfey's last play should be in course, I had as lieve he may be the person as Congreve. This I mention, because I am wonderfully well acquainted with the present relish of courteous

---

[7] Père d'Orleans.

readers; and have often observed, with singular pleasure, that a fly, driven from a honey-pot, will immediately, with very good appetite alight and finish his meal on an excrement.

I have one word to say upon the subject of profound writers, who are grown very numerous of late; and I know very well, the judicious world is resolved to list me in that number. I conceive therefore, as to the business of being profound, that it is with writers as with wells—a person with good eyes may see to the bottom of the deepest, provided any water be there; and that often, when there is nothing in the world at the bottom, besides dryness and dirt, though it be but a yard and half under ground, it shall pass, however, for wondrous deep, upon no wiser a reason than because it is wondrous dark.

I am now trying an experiment very frequent among modern authors; which is to write upon *Nothing;* when the subject is utterly exhausted, to let the pen still move on; by some called the ghost of wit, delighting to walk after the death of its body. And to say the truth, there seems to be no part of knowledge in fewer hands, than that of discerning when to have done. By the time that an author has writ out a book, he and his readers are become old acquaintants, and grow very loth to part; so that I have sometimes known it to be in writing, as in visiting, where the ceremony of taking leave has employed more time than the whole conversation before. The conclusion of a treatise resembles the conclusion of human life, which hath sometimes been compared to the end of a feast; where few are satisfied to depart, *ut plenus vitæ conviva:* for men will sit down after the fullest meal, though it be only to doze, or to sleep out the rest of the day. But, in this latter, I differ extremely from other writers, and shall be too proud, if by all my labours, I can have any ways contributed to the repose of mankind in times [8] so turbulent and unquiet as these. Neither do I think such an employment so very alien from the office of a wit as some would suppose. For among a very polite nation in Greece,[9] there were the same temples built and consecrated to Sleep and the Muses, between which two deities they believed the strictest friendship was established.

I have one concluding favour to request of my reader; that he will not expect to be equally diverted and informed by every line or every page of this discourse; but give some allowance to the author's spleen, and short fits or intervals of dullness, as well as his own; and lay it seriously to his conscience, whether, if he were walking the streets, in dirty weather or a rainy day, he

[8] This was writ before the peace of Ryswick.
[9] Trezenii. Pausan. l[ib]. 2.

would allow it fair dealing in folks at their ease from a window
to critic his gait, and ridicule his dress at such a juncture.

In my disposure of employments of the brain, I have thought
fit to make invention the master, and to give method and reason
the office of its lackeys. The cause of this distribution was, from
observing it my peculiar case, to be often under a temptation of
being witty upon occasions, where I could be neither wise nor
sound, nor anything to the matter in hand. And I am too much
a servant of the modern way to neglect any such opportunities,
whatever pains or improprieties I may be at, to introduce them.
For I have observed, that from a laborious collection of seven
hundred thirty-eight flowers and shining hints of the best modern authors, digested with great reading into my book of commonplaces, I have not been able after five years to draw, hook, or
force, into common conversation, any more than a dozen. Of
which dozen, the one moiety failed of success, by being dropped
among unsuitable company; and the other cost me so many
strains, and traps, and ambages to introduce, that I at length resolved to give it over. Now, this disappointment (to discover a
secret) I must own, gave me the first hint of setting up for an
author; and I have since found, among some particular friends,
that it is become a very general complaint, and has produced the
same effects upon many others. For I have remarked many a
towardly word to be wholly neglected or despised in discourse,
which has passed very smoothly, with some consideration and
esteem, after its preferment and sanction in print. But now, since
by the liberty and encouragement of the press, I am grown absolute master of the occasions and opportunities to expose the talents I have acquired, I already discover, that the issues of my
observanda begin to grow too large for the receipts. Therefore,
I shall here pause a while, till I find, by feeling the world's pulse
and my own, that it will be of absolute necessity for us both, to
resume my pen.

A

Full and True Account

OF THE

BATTEL

Fought laſt *FRIDAY*,

Between the

Antient and the *Modern*

BOOKS

I N

St. *JAMES*'s

LIBRARY.

LONDON:
Printed in the Year, MDCCX.

TITLE-PAGE, 1710 EDITION

THE
BOOKSELLER
TO THE
READER

THE following Discourse, as it is unquestionably of the same author, so it seems to have been written about the same time with the former, I mean the year 1697, when the famous dispute was on foot about ancient and modern learning. The controversy took its rise from an essay of Sir William Temple's upon that subject, which was answered by W. Wotton, B.D., with an Appendix by Dr. Bentley, endeavouring to destroy the credit of Æsop and Phalaris for authors, whom Sir William Temple had, in the essay before-mentioned, highly commended. In that appendix, the doctor falls hard upon a new edition of Phalaris, put out by the Honourable Charles Boyle (now Earl of Orrery) to which Mr. Boyle replied at large, with great learning and wit; and the doctor voluminously rejoined. In this dispute, the town highly resented to see a person of Sir William Temple's character and methods roughly used by the two reverend gentlemen aforesaid, and without any manner of provocation. At length, there appearing no end of the quarrel, our author tells us, that the Books in St. James's Library, looking upon themselves as parties principally concerned, took up the controversy, and came to a decisive battle; but the manuscript, by the injury of fortune or weather, being in several places imperfect, we cannot learn to which side the victory fell.

I must warn the reader to beware of applying to persons what is here meant only of books in the most literal sense. So, when Virgil is mentioned, we are not to understand the person of a famous poet called by that name, but only certain sheets of paper, bound up in leather, containing in print the works of the said poet, and so of the rest.

THE
PREFACE
OF THE
AUTHOR

Satire is a sort of glass, *wherein beholders do generally discover everybody's face but their own; which is the chief reason for that kind of reception it meets in the world, and that so very few are offended with it. But if it should happen otherwise, the danger is not great; and I have learned from long experience never to apprehend mischief from those understandings I have been able to provoke; for anger and fury, though they add strength to the* sinews *of the* body, *yet are found to relax those of the* mind, *and to render all its efforts feeble and impotent.*

There is a brain *that will endure but one* scumming; *let the owner gather it with discretion, and manage his little stock with husbandry; but of all things, let him beware of bringing it under the* lash *of his* betters, *because that will make it all bubble up into impertinence, and he will find no new supply: wit, without knowledge, being a sort of* cream, *which gathers in a night to the top, and, by a skilful hand, may be soon* whipped *into* froth; *but once scummed away, what appears underneath will be fit for nothing but to be thrown to the hogs.*

A FULL AND TRUE

ACCOUNT

OF THE

BATTLE

FOUGHT LAST FRIDAY, &c.

WHOEVER examines with due circumspection into the *Annual Records of Time* [1] will find it remarked, that war is the child of pride, and pride the daughter of riches. The former of which assertions may be soon granted, but one cannot so easily subscribe to the latter; for pride is nearly related to beggary and want, either by father or mother, and sometimes by both; and to speak naturally, it very seldom happens among men to fall out when all have enough; invasions usually travelling from north to south, that is to say from poverty upon plenty. The most ancient and natural grounds of quarrels are lust and avarice; which, though we may allow to be brethren or collateral branches of pride, are certainly the issues of want. For, to speak in the phrase of writers upon the politics, we may observe in the Republic of Dogs (which in its original seems to be an institution of the many) that the whole state is ever in the profoundest peace after a full meal; and that civil broils arise among them when it happens for one great bone to be seized on by some leading dog, who either divides it among the few, and then it falls to an oligarchy, or keeps it to himself, and then it runs up to a tyranny. The same reasoning also holds place among them in those dissensions we behold upon a turgescency in any of their females. For the right of possession lying in common (it being impossible to establish a property in so delicate a case) jealousies

---

[1] Riches produceth pride; pride is war's ground, &c. *Vide Ephem. de Mary Clarke;* opt. edit. [now called *Wing's Sheet Almanack*, and printed by J. Roberts for the Company of Stationers. H.] For the authorship of the notes, see p. 519.

and suspicions do so abound, that the whole commonwealth of that street is reduced to a manifest state of war, of every citizen against every citizen, till some one of more courage, conduct, or fortune than the rest, seizes and enjoys the prize; upon which naturally arises plenty of heart-burning, and envy, and snarling against the happy dog. Again, if we look upon any of these republics engaged in a foreign war, either of invasion or defence, we shall find the same reasoning will serve as to the grounds and occasions of each, and that poverty or want in some degree or other (whether real or in opinion, which makes no alteration in the case) has a great share, as well as pride, on the part of the aggressor.

Now, whoever will please to take this scheme, and either reduce or adapt it to an intellectual state, or commonwealth of learning, will soon discover the first ground of disagreement between the two great parties at this time in arms, and may form just conclusions upon the merits of either cause. But the issue or events of this war are not so easy to conjecture at; for the present quarrel is so inflamed by the warm heads of either faction, and the pretensions somewhere or other so exorbitant, as not to admit the least overtures of accommodation. This quarrel first began (as I have heard it affirmed by an old dweller in the neighbourhood) about a small spot of ground, lying and being upon one of the two tops of the hill Parnassus; the highest and largest of which had, it seems, been time out of mind in quiet possession of certain tenants, called the Ancients, and the other was held by the Moderns. But these disliking their present station, sent certain ambassadors to the Ancients, complaining of a great nuisance; how the height of that part of Parnassus quite spoiled the prospect of theirs, especially towards the *East;* [2] and therefore, to avoid a war, offered them the choice of this alternative; either that the Ancients would please to remove themselves and their effects down to the lower summity, which the Moderns would graciously surrender to them, and advance in their place; or else that the said Ancients will give leave to the Moderns to come with shovels and mattocks, and level the said hill as low as they shall think it convenient. To which the Ancients made answer: how little they expected such a message as this from a colony whom they had admitted out of their own free grace, to so near a neighbourhood. That, as to their own seat, they were aborigines of it,

[2] Sir William Temple affects to trace the progress of arts and sciences from east to west. Thus the moderns had only such knowledge of the learning of Chaldæa and Egypt as was conveyed to them through the medium of Grecian and Roman writers. SCOTT.

and therefore to talk with them of a removal or surrender, was a
language they did not understand. That if the height of the hill on
their side shortened the prospect of the Moderns, it was a disadvantage they could not help, but desired them to consider, whether
that injury (if it be any) were not largely recompensed by the
shade and shelter it afforded them. That, as to levelling or
digging down, it was either folly or ignorance to propose it, if
they did, or did not know, how that side of the hill was an entire rock, which would break their tools and hearts, without any
damage to itself. That they would therefore advise the Moderns
rather to raise their own side of the hill, than dream of pulling
down that of the Ancients, to the former of which they would
not only give licence, but also largely contribute. All this was
rejected by the Moderns with much indignation, who still insisted upon one of the two expedients; and so this difference
broke out into a long and obstinate war, maintained on the one
part by resolution, and by the courage of certain leaders and
allies; but on the other, by the greatness of their number, upon
all defeats, affording continual recruits. In this quarrel whole
rivulets of ink have been exhausted, and the virulence of both
parties enormously augmented. Now, it must here be understood, that ink is the great missive weapon in all battles of the
learned, which conveyed through a sort of engine called a quill,
infinite numbers of these are darted at the enemy, by the valiant
on each side, with equal skill and violence, as if it were an engagement of porcupines. This malignant liquor was compounded by
the engineer who invented it of two ingredients, which are gall
and copperas, by its bitterness and venom to suit in some degree,
as well as to foment, the genius of the combatants. And as the
Grecians, after an engagement, when they could not agree about
the victory, were wont to set up trophies on both sides, the
beaten party being content to be at the same expense, to keep
itself in countenance (a laudable and ancient custom, happily
revived of late, in the art of war) so the learned, after a sharp and
bloody dispute, do on both sides hang out their trophies too,
whichever comes by the worse. These trophies have largely inscribed on them the merits of the cause, a full impartial account
of such a battle, and how the victory fell clearly to the party that
set them up. They are known to the world under several names;
as disputes, arguments, rejoinders, brief considerations, answers,
replies, remarks, reflections, objections, confutations. For a very
few days they are fixed up in all public places, either by themselves or their representatives,[3] for passengers to gaze at; from

[3] Their title-pages.

whence the chiefest and largest are removed to certain magazines they call libraries, there to remain in a quarter purposely assigned them, and from thenceforth begin to be called Books of Controversy.

In these books is wonderfully instilled and preserved the spirit of each warrior, while he is alive; and after his death his soul transmigrates there to inform them. This, at least, is the more common opinion; but I believe it is with libraries as with other cemeteries, where some philosphers affirm that a certain spirit, which they call *brutum hominis*, hovers over the monument till the body is corrupted and turns to dust or to worms, but then vanishes or dissolves. So, we may say, a restless spirit haunts over every book, till dust or worms have seized upon it, which to some may happen in a few days, but to others later; and therefore, books of controversy being, of all others, haunted by the most disorderly spirits, have always been confined in a separate lodge from the rest; and for fear of mutual violence against each other, it was thought prudent by our ancestors to bind them to the peace with strong iron chains. Of which invention the original occasion was this: when the works of Scotus first came out, they were carried to a certain great library and had lodgings appointed them; but this author was no sooner settled than he went to visit his master Aristotle, and there both concerted together to seize Plato by main force, and turn him out from his ancient station among the divines, where he had peaceably dwelt near eight hundred years. The attempt succeeded, and the two usurpers have reigned ever since in his stead; but to maintain quiet for the future, it was decreed, that all polemics of the larger size should be held fast with a chain.

By this expedient, the public peace of libraries might certainly have been preserved, if a new species of controversial books had not arose of late years, instinct with a most malignant spirit, from the war above-mentioned between the learned, about the higher summit of Parnassus.

When these books were first admitted into the public libraries, I remember to have said upon occasion, to several persons concerned, how I was sure they would create broils wherever they came, unless a world of care were taken; and therefore I advised that the champions of each side should be coupled together, or otherwise mixed, that like the blending of contrary poisons their malignity might be employed among themselves. And it seems I was neither an ill prophet nor an ill counsellor; for it was nothing else but the neglect of this caution which gave occasion to the terrible fight that happened on Friday last between the ancient and modern books in the King's Library. Now, because the talk of this battle is so fresh in everybody's mouth, and the expectation of the town so great to be informed in the particulars, I, being possessed of all qualifications requisite in an historian, and retained by neither party, have resolved to comply with the urgent importunity of my friends, by writing down a full impartial account thereof.

The guardian of the regal library,[4] a person of great valor, but chiefly renowned for his humanity,[5] had been a fierce champion for the Moderns; and, in an engagement upon Parnassus, had vowed, with his own hands, to knock down two of the Ancient chiefs,[6] who guarded a small pass on the superior rock, but, endeavouring to climb up was cruelly obstructed by his own unhappy weight, and tendency towards his center, a quality to which those of the Modern party are extreme subject; for, being light-headed, they have in speculation a wonderful agility, and conceive nothing too high for them to mount, but in reducing to practice discover a mighty pressure about their posteriors and their heels. Having thus failed in his design, the disappointed champion bore a cruel rancour to the Ancients, which he resolved to gratify by showing all marks of his favour to the books of their adversaries, and lodging them in the fairest apartments; when at the same time, whatever book had the boldness to own itself for an advocate of the Ancients, was buried alive in some obscure corner, and threatened, upon the least displeasure, to be turned out of doors. Besides, it so happened, that about this time there was a strange confusion of place among all the books in the library; for which several reasons were assigned. Some imputed it to a great heap of learned dust, which a perverse wind blew off from a shelf of Moderns into the keeper's eyes. Others affirmed he had a humour to pick the worms out of the schoolmen, and swallow them fresh and fasting; whereof some fell upon his spleen, and some climbed up into his head, to the great perturbation of both. And lastly, others maintained that by walking much in the dark about the library, he had quite lost the situation of it out of his head; and therefore in replacing his books he was apt to mistake, and clap Descartes next to Aristotle; poor

[4] Dr. Bentley was appointed Royal Librarian, December 23, 1693. . . . Scott.

[5] The Honourable Mr. Boyle, in the preface to his edition of Phalaris, says he was refused a manuscript by the library keeper, *pro solita humanitate suâ.*

[6] Dr. Bentley aided Wotton in his *Reflections upon Ancient and Modern Learning,* by proving that the works of Phalaris and Æsop, authors extolled by Sir William Temple, were in reality spurious. Scott.

Plato had got between Hobbes and the Seven Wise Masters, and Virgil was hemmed in with Dryden on one side and Withers on the other.

Meanwhile those books that were advocates for the Moderns chose out one from among them to make a progress through the whole library, examine the number and strength of their party, and concert their affairs. This messenger performed all things very industriously, and brought back with him a list of their forces, in all fifty thousand, consisting chiefly of light-horse, heavy-armed foot, and mercenaries; whereof the foot were in general but sorrily armed, and worse clad; their horses large, but extremely out of case and heart; however, some few by trading among the Ancients had furnished themselves tolerably enough.

While things were in this ferment, discord grew extremely high, hot words passed on both sides, and ill blood was plentifully bred. Here a solitary Ancient, squeezed up among a whole shelf of Moderns, offered fairly to dispute the case, and to prove by manifest reasons, that the priority was due to them, from long possession, and in regard of their prudence, antiquity, and, above all, their great merits towards the Moderns. But these denied the premises, and seemed very much to wonder how the Ancients could pretend to insist upon their antiquity, when it was so plain (if they went to that) that the Moderns were much the more ancient [7] of the two. As for any obligations they owed to the Ancients, they renounced them all. ' 'Tis true,' said they, 'we are informed, some few of our party have been so mean to borrow their subsistence from you; but the rest, infinitely the greater number (and especially we French and English) were so far from stooping to so base an example, that there never passed, till this very hour, six words between us. For our horses are of our own breeding, our arms of our own forging, and our clothes of our own cutting out and sewing.' Plato was by chance upon the next shelf, and observing those that spoke to be in the ragged plight mentioned a while ago, their jades lean and foundered, their weapons of rotten wood, their armour rusty, and nothing but rags underneath, he laughed aloud, and in his pleasant way swore, by G— he believed them.

Now, the Moderns had not proceeded in their late negotiation with secrecy enough to escape the notice of the enemy. For those advocates, who had begun the quarrel by setting first on foot the dispute of precedency, talked so loud of coming to a battle, that Temple happened to overhear them, and gave immediate intelligence to the Ancients, who thereupon drew up their scat-

[7] According to the modern paradox.

tered troops together, resolving to act upon the defensive; upon which several of the Moderns fled over to their party, and among the rest Temple himself. This Temple, having been educated and long conversed among the Ancients, was, of all the Moderns, their greatest favorite, and became their greatest champion.

Things were at this crisis, when a material accident fell out. For, upon the highest corner of a large window, there dwelt a certain spider, swollen up to the first magnitude by the destruction of infinite numbers of flies, whose spoils lay scattered before the gates of his palace, like human bones before the cave of some giant. The avenues to his castle were guarded with turnpikes and palisadoes, all after the modern way of fortification.[8] After you had passed several courts, you came to the center, wherein you might behold the constable himself in his own lodgings, which had windows fronting to each avenue, and ports to sally out upon all occasions of prey or defence. In this mansion he had for some time dwelt in peace and plenty, without danger to his person by swallows from above, or to his palace by brooms from below, when it was the pleasure of fortune to conduct thither a wandering bee, to whose curiosity a broken pane in the glass had discovered itself, and in he went; where expatiating a while, he at last happened to alight upon one of the outward walls of the spider's citadel; which, yielding to the unequal weight, sunk down to the very foundation. Thrice he endeavoured to force his passage, and thrice the center shook. The spider within, feeling the terrible convulsion, supposed at first that nature was approaching to her final dissolution; or else that Beelzebub,[9] with all his legions, was come to revenge the death of many thousands of his subjects, whom his enemy had slain and devoured. However, he at length valiantly resolved to issue forth, and meet his fate. Meanwhile the bee had acquitted himself of his toils, and posted securely at some distance, was employed in cleansing his wings, and disengaging them from the ragged remnants of the cobweb. By this time the spider was adventured out, when beholding the chasms, and ruins, and dilapidations of his fortress, he was very near at his wit's end; he stormed and swore like a madman, and swelled till he was ready to burst. At length, casting his eye upon the bee, and wisely gathering causes from events (for they knew each other by sight), 'A plague split you,' said he, 'for a giddy son of a whore.

[8] Fortification was one of the arts, upon the improvement of which the argument in favour of the moderns was founded by their advocates. Scott.
[9] The Hebrew god of flies. Pate MS.

Is it you, with a vengeance, that have made this litter here? Could you not look before you, and be d—nd? Do you think I have nothing else to do (in the devil's name) but to mend and repair after your arse?' 'Good words, friend,' said the bee (having now pruned himself, and being disposed to droll) 'I'll give you my hand and word to come near your kennel no more; I was never in such a confounded pickle since I was born.' 'Sirrah,' replied the spider, 'if it were not for breaking an old custom in our family, never to stir abroad against an enemy, I should come and teach you better manners.' 'I pray have patience,' said the bee, 'or you will spend your substance, and for aught I see, you may stand in need of it all, towards the repair of your house.' 'Rogue, rogue,' replied the spider, 'yet methinks you should have more respect to a person, whom all the world allows to be so much your betters.' 'By my troth,' said the bee, 'the comparison will amount to a very good jest, and you will do me a favour to let me know the reasons that all the world is pleased to use in so hopeful a dispute.' At this the spider, having swelled himself into the size and posture of a disputant, began his argument in the true spirit of controversy, with a resolution to be heartily scurrilous and angry, to urge on his own reasons, without the least regard to the answers or objections of his opposite, and fully predetermined in his mind against all conviction.

'Not to disparage myself,' said he, 'by the comparison with such a rascal, what art thou but a vagabond without house or home, without stock or inheritance, born to no possession of your own, but a pair of wings and a drone-pipe? Your livelihood is an universal plunder upon nature; a freebooter over fields and gardens; and for the sake of stealing will rob a nettle as easily as a violet. Whereas I am a domestic animal, furnished with a native stock within myself. This large castle (to show my improvements in the mathematics[1]) is all built with my own hands, and the materials extracted altogether out of my own person.'

'I am glad,' answered the bee, 'to hear you grant at least that I am come honestly by my wings and my voice; for then, it seems, I am obliged to Heaven alone for my flights and my music; and Providence would never have bestowed on me two such gifts, without designing them for the noblest ends. I visit indeed all the flowers and blossoms of the field and the garden; but whatever I collect from thence enriches myself, without the least injury to their beauty, their smell, or their taste. Now, for you and your skill in architecture and other mathematics, I have little

---

[1] The improvements in mathematical science were (very justly) urged by those who contended for the excellence of modern learning. SCOTT.

to say: in that building of yours there might, for aught I know, have been labor and method enough, but by woful experience for us both, 'tis too plain, the materials are naught, and I hope you will henceforth take warning, and consider duration and matter as well as method and art. You boast, indeed, of being obliged to no other creature, but of drawing and spinning out all from yourself; that is to say, if we may judge of the liquor in the vessel by what issues out, you possess a good plentiful store of dirt and poison in your breast; and, tho' I would by no means lessen or disparage your genuine stock of either, yet I doubt you are somewhat obliged for an increase of both, to a little foreign assistance. Your inherent portion of dirt does not fail of acquisitions, by sweepings exhaled from below; and one insect furnishes you with a share of poison to destroy another. So that in short, the question comes all to this — which is the nobler being of the two, that which by a lazy contemplation of four inches round, by an overweening pride, feeding and engendering on itself, turns all into excrement and venom, produces nothing at last, but flybane and a cobweb; or that which, by an universal range, with long search, much study, true judgment, and distinction of things, brings home honey and wax.'

This dispute was managed with such eagerness, clamor, and warmth, that the two parties of books in arms below stood silent a while, waiting in suspense what would be the issue, which was not long undetermined, for the bee grown impatient at so much loss of time, fled straight away to a bed of roses, without looking for a reply, and left the spider like an orator, collected in himself and just prepared to burst out.

It happened upon this emergency, that Æsop broke silence first. He had been of late most barbarously treated by a strange effect of the regent's humanity, who[2] had tore off his title-page, sorely defaced one half of his leaves, and chained him fast among a shelf of Moderns. Where soon discovering how high the quarrel was like to proceed, he tried all his arts, and turned himself to a thousand forms. At length in the borrowed shape of an ass, the regent mistook him for a Modern; by which means he had time and opportunity to escape to the Ancients, just when the spider and the bee were entering into their contest, to which he gave his attention with a world of pleasure; and when it was ended, swore in the loudest key, that in all his life he had never known two cases so parallel and adapt to each other, as that in the window, and this upon the shelves. 'The disputants,' said he,

[2] Bentley, who denied the antiquity of Æsop, and the authenticity of the fables ascribed to him. SCOTT.

'have admirably managed the dispute between them, have taken in the full strength of all that is to be said on both sides, and exhausted the substance of every argument *pro* and *con*. It is but to adjust the reasonings of both to the present quarrel, then to compare and apply the labors and fruits of each as the bee has learnedly deduced them; and we shall find the conclusions fall plain and close upon the Moderns and us. For pray gentlemen, was ever anything so modern as the spider in his air, his turns, and his paradoxes? He argues in the behalf of you his brethren and himself, with many boastings of his native stock and great genius, that he spins and spits wholly from himself, and scorns to own any obligation or assistance from without. Then he displays to you his great skill in architecture, and improvement in the mathematics. To all this the bee, as an advocate retained by us the Ancients, thinks fit to answer; that if one may judge of the great genius or inventions of the Moderns by what they have produced, you will hardly have countenance to bear you out in boasting of either. Erect your schemes with as much method and skill as you please; yet if the materials be nothing but dirt, spun out of your own entrails (the guts of modern brains) the edifice will conclude at last in a cobweb, the duration of which, like that of other spiders' webs, may be imputed to their being forgotten, or neglected, or hid in a corner. For anything else of genuine that the Moderns may pretend to, I cannot recollect, unless it be a large vein of wrangling and satire, much of a nature and substance with the spider's poison; which, however, they pretend to spit wholly out of themselves, is improved by the same arts, by feeding upon the insects and vermin of the age. As for us the Ancients, we are content with the bee to pretend to nothing of our own, beyond our wings and our voice, that is to say, our flights and our language. For the rest, whatever we have got, has been by infinite labor and search, and ranging through every corner of nature; the difference is, that instead of dirt and poison, we have rather chose to fill our hives with honey and wax, thus furnishing mankind with the two noblest of things, which are sweetness and light.'

'Tis wonderful to conceive the tumult arisen among the books, upon the close of this long descant of Æsop; both parties took the hint, and heightened their animosities so on a sudden, that they resolved it should come to a battle. Immediately the two main bodies withdrew under their several ensigns, to the farther parts of the library, and there entered into cabals and consults upon the present emergency. The Moderns were in very warm debates upon the choice of their leaders; and nothing less than the fear impending from their enemies could have kept them from mutinies upon this occasion. The difference was greatest among the horse, where every private trooper pretended to the chief command, from Tasso and Milton to Dryden and Withers. The light-horse[3] were commanded by Cowley and Despréaux.[4] There came the bowmen[5] under their valiant leaders, Descartes, Gassendi, and Hobbes, whose strength was such that they could shoot their arrows beyond the atmosphere, never to fall down again, but turn like that of Evander, into meteors, or like the cannon-ball, into stars. Paracelsus brought a squadron of stink-pot-flingers from the snowy mountains of Rhætia. There came a vast body of dragoons, of different nations, under the leading of Harvey, their great aga, part armed with scythes, the weapons of death; part with lances and long knives, all steeped in poison; part shot bullets of a most malignant nature, and used white powder which infallibly killed without report. There came several bodies of heavy-armed foot, all mercenaries, under the ensigns of Guicciardini, Davila, Polydore Virgil, Buchanan, Mariana, Camden, and others. The engineers were commanded by Regiomontanus and Wilkins. The rest were a confused multitude, led by Scotus, Aquinas, and Bellarmine; of mighty bulk and stature, but without either arms, courage, or discipline. In the last place, came infinite swarms of calones,[6] a disorderly rout led by L'Estrange, rogues and ragamuffins, that follow the camp for nothing but the plunder, all without coats to cover them.

The army of the Ancients was much fewer in number; Homer led the horse, and Pindar the light-horse; Euclid was chief engineer; Plato and Aristotle commanded the bowmen; Herodotus and Livy the foot; Hippocrates the dragoons. The allies, led by Vossius and Temple, brought up the rear.

All things violently tending to a decisive battle, Fame, who much frequented, and had a large apartment formerly assigned her in the regal library, fled up straight to Jupiter, to whom she

---

[3] The epic poets were presented as full-armed horsemen; the lyrical bards as light horse. Scott.

[4] More commonly known by the name of Boileau. H.

[5] The philosophers, whether physical or metaphysical, are thus classed. Scott.

[6] These are pamphlets, which are not bound or covered.

By calling this disorderly rout *calones* the author points both his satire and contempt against all sorts of mercenary scribblers, who write as they are commanded by the leaders and patrons of sedition, faction, corruption, and every evil work: they are styled *calones* because they are the meanest and most despicable of all writers, as the *calones,* whether belonging to the army or private families, were the meanest of all slaves or servants whatsoever. H.

delivered a faithful account of all that passed between the two parties below. (For, among the gods, she always tells truth.) Jove, in great concern, convokes a council in the Milky Way. The senate assembled, he declares the occasion of convening them; a bloody battle just impendent between two mighty armies of Ancient and Modern creatures, called books, wherein the celestial interest was but too deeply concerned. Momus, the patron of the Moderns, made an excellent speech in their favor, which was answered by Pallas, the protectress of the Ancients. The assembly was divided in their affections; when Jupiter commanded the book of fate to be laid before him. Immediately were brought by Mercury three large volumes in folio, containing memoirs of all things past, present, and to come. The clasps were of silver, double gilt; the covers of celestial turkey leather; and the paper such as here on earth might almost pass for vellum. Jupiter, having silently read the decree, would communicate the import to none, but presently shut up the book.

Without the doors of this assembly, there attended a vast number of light, nimble gods, menial servants to Jupiter: these are his ministering instruments in all affairs below. They travel in a caravan, more or less together, and are fastened to each other like a link of galley-slaves, by a light chain, which passes from them to Jupiter's great toe; and yet in receiving or delivering a message, they may never approach above the lowest step of his throne, where he and they whisper to each other through a long hollow trunk. These deities are called by mortal men accidents or events; but the gods call them second causes. Jupiter having delivered his message to a certain number of these divinities, they flew immediately down to the pinnacle of the regal library, and, consulting a few minutes, entered unseen and disposed the parties according to their orders.

Meanwhile Momus, fearing the worst, and calling to mind an ancient prophecy, which bore no very good face to his children the Moderns, bent his flight to the region of a malignant deity, called Criticism. She dwelt on the top of a snowy mountain in Nova Zembla; there Momus found her extended in her den, upon the spoils of numberless volumes half devoured. At her right hand sat Ignorance, her father and husband, blind with age; at her left, Pride, her mother, dressing her up in the scraps of paper herself had torn. There was Opinion, her sister, light of foot, hoodwinked, and headstrong, yet giddy and perpetually turning. About her played her children, Noise and Impudence, Dulness and Vanity, Positiveness, Pedantry, and Ill-Manners. The goddess herself had claws like a cat; her head, and ears, and voice resembled those of an ass; her teeth fallen out before, her eyes turned inward, as if she looked only upon herself; her diet was the overflowing of her own gall; her spleen was so large, as to stand prominent like a dug of the first rate; nor wanted excrescencies in form of teats, at which a crew of ugly monsters were greedily sucking; and, what is wonderful to conceive, the bulk of spleen increased faster than the sucking could diminish it, 'Goddess,' said Momus, 'can you sit idly here while our devout worshippers, the Moderns, are this minute entering into a cruel battle, and perhaps now lying under the swords of their enemies? Who then hereafter will ever sacrifice or build altars to our divinities? Haste therefore to the British Isle, and, if possible, prevent their destruction, while I make factions among the gods, and gain them over to our party.'

Momus, having thus delivered himself, stayed not for an answer, but left the goddess to her own resentment. Up she rose in a rage, and as it is the form upon such occasions, began a soliloquy: ' 'Tis I' (said she) 'who give wisdom to infants and idiots; by me, children grow wiser than their parents. By me, beaux become politicians, and school-boys judges of philosophy. By me, sophisters debate, and conclude upon the depths of knowledge; and coffeehouse wits, instinct by me, can correct an author's style and display his minutest errors, without understanding a syllable of his matter or his language. By me, striplings spend their judgment, as they do their estate, before it comes into their hands. 'Tis I who have deposed wit and knowledge from their empire over poetry, and advanced myself in their stead. And shall a few upstart Ancients dare oppose me?—But come, my aged parents and you, my children dear, and thou my beauteous sister; let us ascend my chariot, and haste to assist our devout Moderns, who are now sacrificing to us a hecatomb, as I perceive by that grateful smell, which from thence reaches my nostrils.'

The goddess and her train having mounted the chariot, which was drawn by tame geese, flew over infinite regions, shedding her influence in due places, till at length she arrived at her beloved island of Britain; but in hovering over its metropolis, what blessings did she not let fall upon her seminaries of Gresham and Covent Garden? And now she reached the fatal plain of St. James's Library, at what time the two armies were upon the point to engage; where entering with all her caravan unseen, and landing upon a case of shelves, now desert, but once inhabited by a colony of virtuosos, she stayed a while to observe the posture of both armies.

But here the tender cares of a mother began to fill her thoughts, and move in her breast. For, at the head of a troop of Modern

Bowmen, she cast her eyes upon her son W-tt-n; to whom the fates had assigned a very short thread. W-tt-n, a young hero, whom an unknown father of mortal race begot by stolen embraces with this goddess. He was the darling of his mother above all her children, and she resolved to go and comfort him. But first, according to the good old custom of deities, she cast about to change her shape, for fear the divinity of her countenance might dazzle his mortal sight, and overcharge the rest of his senses. She therefore gathered up her person into an octavo compass; her body grew white and arid, and split in pieces with dryness; the thick turned into pasteboard, and the thin into paper, upon which her parents and children artfully strewed a black juice, or decoction of gall and soot, in form of letters; her head, and voice, and spleen, kept their primitive form, and that which before was a cover of skin, did still continue so. In which guise she marched on towards the Moderns, undistinguishable in shape and dress from the divine B-ntl-y, W-tt-n's dearest friend. 'Brave W-tt-n,' said the goddess, 'why do our troops stand idle here, to spend their present vigour, and opportunity of this day? Away, let us haste to the generals, and advise to give the onset immediately.' Having spoke thus, she took the ugliest of her monsters, full glutted from her spleen, and flung it invisibly into his mouth, which, flying straight up into his head, squeezed out his eye-balls, gave him a distorted look, and half overturned his brain. Then she privately ordered two of her beloved children, Dulness and Ill-Manners, closely to attend his person in all encounters. Having thus accoutred him, she vanished in a mist, and the hero perceived it was the goddess his mother.

The destined hour of fate being now arrived, the fight began; whereof, before I dare adventure to make a particular description, I must, after the example of other authors, petition for a hundred tongues, and mouths, and hands, and pens, which would all be too little to perform so immense a work. Say, goddess, that presidest over History, who it was that first advanced in the field of battle. Paracelsus, at the head of his dragoons, observing Galen in the adverse wing, darted his javelin with a mighty force, which the brave Ancient received upon his shield, the point breaking in the second fold.   *   *   *   *   *   *

Hic pauca   *   *   *   *   *   *
desunt.   *
*   *   *   *   *   *   *   *

They bore the wounded aga[7] on their shields to his chariot

[7] Dr. Harvey. It was not thought proper to name his antagonist, but only to intimate that he was wounded. . . H.

Desunt *   *   *   *   *   *   *

nonnulla *   *   *   *   *   *   *

*   *   *   *   *   *   *

Then Aristotle, observing Bacon advance with a furious mien, drew his bow to the head, and let fly his arrow, which missed the valiant Modern, and went hizzing over his head. But Descartes it hit; the steel point quickly found a defect in his head-piece; it pierced the leather and the pasteboard, and went in at his right eye. The torture of the pain whirled the valiant bowman round, till death, like a star of superior influence, drew him into his own vortex.[8] *   *   *   *   *   *

*   *   *   *   *   *   *

Ingens hiatus *   *   *   *   *   *

hic in MS *   *   *   *   *   *

*   *   *   *   *   *   *

when Homer appeared at the head of the cavalry, mounted on a furious horse, with difficulty managed by the rider himself, but which no other mortal durst approach; he rode among the enemy's ranks, and bore down all before him. Say, goddess, whom he slew first, and whom he slew last. First, Gondibert[9] advanced against him, clad in heavy armour, and mounted on a staid sober gelding, not so famed for his speed as his docility in kneeling, whenever his rider would mount or alight. He had made a vow to Pallas that he would never leave the field till he had spoiled Homer [1] of his armor; madman, who had never once seen the wearer, nor understood his strength. Him Homer overthrew, horse and man to the ground, there to be trampled and choked in the dirt. Then, with a long spear, he slew Denham,[2] a stout Modern, who from his father's side derived his lineage from Apollo, but his mother was of mortal race. He fell, and bit the earth. The celestial part Apollo took, and made it a star, but the terrestrial lay wallowing upon the ground. Then Homer slew W-sl-y[3] with a kick of his horse's heel; he took Perrault by mighty force out of his saddle, then hurled him at Fontenelle, with the same blow dashing out both their brains.

On the left wing of the horse, Virgil appeared in shining armor, completely fitted to his body; he was mounted on a dapple-gray steed, the slowness of whose pace was an effect of the

---

8 Alluding to his absurd system. SCOTT.

9 A heroic poem by Sir William Davenant, in stanzas of four lines. H.

1 *Vid*. Homer.

2 Sir John Denham's poems are very unequal, extremely good, and very indifferent; so that his detractors said he was not the real author of *Cooper's Hill*.

3 Mr. Wesley, who wrote the *Life of Christ*, in verse, &c. A wretched scribbler. SCOTT.

highest mettle and vigour. He cast his eye on the adverse wing, with a desire to find an object worthy of his valour, when behold, upon a sorrel gelding of a monstrous size, appeared a foe, issuing from among the thickest of the enemy's squadrons; but his speed was less than his noise; for his horse, old and lean, spent the dregs of his strength in a high trot, which though it made slow advances, yet caused a loud clashing of his armor, terrible to hear. The two cavaliers had now approached within the throw of a lance, when the stranger desired a parley, and lifting up the vizor of his helmet, a face hardly appeared from within, which after a pause was known for that of the renowned Dryden. The brave Ancient suddenly started, as one possessed with surprise and disappointment together; for the helmet was nine times too large for the head, which appeared situate far in the hinder part, even like the lady in a lobster, or like a mouse under a canopy of state, or like a shrivelled beau from within the penthouse of a modern periwig; and the voice was suited to the visage, sounding weak and remote. Dryden in a long harangue soothed up the good Ancient, called him father, and by a large deduction of genealogies, made it plainly appear that they were nearly related. Then he humbly proposed an exchange of armor, as a lasting mark of hospitality between them. Virgil consented (for the goddess Diffidence came unseen, and cast a mist before his eyes) though his was of gold,[4] and cost a hundred beeves, the other's but of rusty iron. However, this glittering armor became the Modern yet worse than his own. Then they agreed to exchange horses; but when it came to the trial, Dryden was afraid, and utterly unable to mount.* * * * * *
* * * * * * * * *
* * * * * * * *Alter hiatus*
* * * * * * * *in MS.*
* * * Lucan appeared upon a fiery horse of admirable shape, but headstrong, bearing the rider where he list over the field; he made a mighty slaughter among the enemy's horse; which destruction to stop, Blackmore, a famous Modern (but one of the mercenaries) strenuously opposed himself, and darted a javelin with a strong hand, which falling short of its mark, struck deep in the earth. Then Lucan threw a lance; but Æsculapius came unseen, and turned off the point. 'Brave Modern,' said Lucan, 'I perceive some god protects you,[5] for never did my arm so deceive me before; but what mortal can contend with a god?

---

[4] *Vid.* Homer.
[5] His skill as a physician atoned for his dulness as a poet. H.

Therefore, let us fight no longer, but present gifts to each other.'
Lucan then bestowed the Modern a pair of spurs, and Blackmore
gave Lucan a bridle. * * * * * *
* * * * * * * * *

Pauca de- * * * * * * *
sunt. * * * * * * *

Creech; but the goddess Dulness took a cloud, formed into the
shape of Horace, armed and mounted, and placed it in a flying
posture before him. Glad was the cavalier to begin a combat
with a flying foe, and pursued the image, threatening loud, till
at last it led him to the peaceful bower of his father Ogleby, by
whom he was disarmed, and assigned to his repose.

Then Pindar slew —, and —, and Oldham, and —, and Afra the
Amazon,[6] light of foot; never advancing in a direct line, but
wheeling with incredible agility and force, he made a terrible
slaughter among the enemy's light horse. Him when Cowley
observed, his generous heart burnt within him, and he advanced
against the fierce Ancient, imitating his address, and pace, and
career, as well as the vigour of his horse and his own skill would
allow. When the two cavaliers had approached within the length
of three javelins, first Cowley threw a lance, which missed Pindar, and passing into the enemy's ranks, fell ineffectual to the
ground. Then Pindar darted a javelin so large and weighty that
scarce a dozen cavaliers, as cavaliers are in our degenerate days,
could raise it from the ground; yet he threw it with ease, and it
went by an unerring hand singing through the air; nor could the
Modern have avoided present death, if he had not luckily opposed the shield that had been given him by Venus.[7] And now
both heroes drew their swords, but the Modern was so aghast
and disordered, that he knew not where he was; his shield
dropped from his hands; thrice he fled, and thrice he could not
escape; at last he turned, and lifting up his hands in the posture
of a suppliant: 'Godlike Pindar,' said he, 'spare my life, and possess my horse with these arms, besides the ransom which my
friends will give when they hear I am alive, and your prisoner.'
'Dog,' said Pindar, 'let your ransom stay with your friends; but
your carcass shall be left for the fowls of the air and the beasts
of the field.' With that he raised his sword, and with a mighty
stroke cleft the wretched Modern in twain, the sword pursuing
the blow; and one half lay panting on the ground, to be trod

6 Mrs. Aphra Behn, author of many plays, novels, and poems. H.
7 His poem called *The Mistress*. H.

in pieces by the horses' feet, the other half was borne by the frighted steed through the field. This Venus [8] took, washed it seven times in ambrosia, then struck it thrice with a sprig of amaranth; upon which the leather grew round and soft, and the leaves turned into feathers, and being gilded before, continued gilded still; so it became a dove, and she harnessed it to her chariot.   *   *   *   *   *   *   *   *
*   *   *   *   *   *   *   *   *   *
*   *   *   *   *   *   *   *Hiatus valdè de-*
*   *   *   *   *   *   *flendus* in MS.

Day being far spent, and the numerous forces of the Moderns half inclining to a retreat, there issued forth from a squadron of their heavy-armed foot, a captain, whose name was B-ntl-y, in The Episode person the most deformed of all the Moderns, tall, of B-ntl-y but without shape or comeliness; large but without and W-tt-n. strength or proportion. His armor was patched up of a thousand incoherent pieces, and the sound of it, as he marched, was loud and dry, like that made by the fall of a sheet of lead, which an Etesian wind blows suddenly down from the roof of some steeple. His helmet was of old rusty iron, but the vizor was brass, which, tainted by his breath, corrupted into copperas, nor wanted gall from the same fountain; so that, when-ever provoked by anger or labour, an atramentous quality, of most malignant nature, was seen to distil from his lips. In his right hand [9] he grasped a flail, and (that he might never be un-provided of an offensive weapon) a vessel full of ordure in his left: thus completely armed, he advanced with a slow and heavy pace where the Modern chiefs were holding consult upon the sum of things; who, as he came onwards, laughed to behold his crooked leg and hump shoulder, which his boot and armor, vainly endeavouring to hide, were forced to comply with and expose. The generals made use of him for his talent of railing, which, kept within government, proved frequently of great serv-ice to their cause, but at other times did more mischief than good; for at the least touch of offence, and often without any at all, he would, like a wounded elephant, convert it against his leaders. Such, at this juncture, was the disposition of B-ntl-y; grieved to see the enemy prevail, and dissatisfied with every-body's conduct but his own. He humbly gave the Modern gen-erals to understand, that he conceived, with great submission,

[8] I do not approve the author's judgment in this, for I think Cowley's *Pindarics* are much preferable to his *Mistress*.
[9] The person here spoken of is famous for letting fly at everybody with-out distinction, and using mean and foul scurrilities.

they were all a pack of rogues, and fools, and sons of whores, and d-mnd cowards, and confounded loggerheads, and illiterate whelps, and nonsensical scoundrels; that if himself had been constituted general, those presumptuous dogs,[1] the Ancients, would long before this have been beaten out of the field. 'You,' said he, 'sit here idle; but when I, or any other valiant Modern, kill an enemy, you are sure to seize the spoil. But I will not march one foot against the foe till you all swear to me, that, whomever I take or kill, his arms I shall quietly possess.' B-ntl-y having spoken thus, Scaliger, bestowing him a sour look: 'Miscreant prater,' said he, 'eloquent only in thine own eyes, thou railest without wit, or truth, or discretion; the malignity of thy temper perverteth nature, thy learning makes thee more barbarous, thy study of humanity more inhuman; thy converse amongst poets, more grovelling, miry, and dull. All arts of civilizing others render thee rude and untractable; courts have taught thee ill manners, and polite conversation has finished thee a pedant. Besides, a greater coward burdeneth not the army. But never despond; I pass my word, whatever spoil thou takest shall certainly be thy own, though, I hope, that vile carcass will first become a prey to kites and worms.'

B-ntl-y durst not reply, but half choked with spleen and rage, withdrew, in full resolution of performing some great achievement. With him, for his aid and companion, he took his beloved W-tt-n; resolving by policy or surprise, to attempt some neglected quarter of the Ancients' army. They began their march over carcasses of their slaughtered friends; then to the right of their own forces; then wheeled northward, till they came to Aldrovandus's tomb, which they passed on the side of the declining sun. And now they arrived with fear towards the enemy's outguards; looking about, if haply they might spy the quarters of the wounded, or some straggling sleepers, unarmed and remote from the rest. As when two mongrel curs, whom native greediness and domestic want provoke and join in partnership, though fearful, nightly to invade the folds of some rich grazier, they, with tails depressed, and lolling tongues, creep soft and slow; meanwhile, the conscious moon, now in her zenith, on their guilty heads darts perpendicular rays; nor dare they bark, though much provoked at her refulgent visage, whether seen in puddle by reflection, or in sphere direct; but one surveys the region round, while t'other scouts the plain, if haply to discover at distance from the flock, some carcass half devoured, the refuse of gorged wolves, or ominous ravens. So marched this lovely, lov-

[1] *Vid.* Homer, de Thersite.

ing pair of friends, nor with less fear and circumspection; when, at distance, they might perceive two shining suits of armor hanging upon an oak, and the owners not far off in a profound sleep. The two friends drew lots, and the pursuing of this adventure fell to B-ntl-y; on he went, and in his van Confusion and Amaze, while Horror and Affright brought up the rear. As he came near, behold two heroes of the Ancients' army, Phalaris and Æsop, lay fast asleep: B-ntl-y would fain have dispatched them both, and stealing close, aimed his flail at Phalaris's breast. But then the goddess Affright interposing, caught the Modern in her icy arms, and dragged him from the danger she foresaw; for both the dormant heroes happened to turn at the same instant, though soundly sleeping, and busy in a dream. For Phalaris[2] was just that minute dreaming how a most vile poetaster had lampooned him, and how he had got him roaring in his bull. And Æsop dreamed, that as he and the Ancient chiefs were lying on the ground, a wild ass broke loose, ran about trampling and kicking, and dunging in their faces. B-ntl-y, leaving the two heroes asleep, seized on both their armors, and withdrew in quest of his darling W-tt-n.

He, in the mean time, had wandered long in search of some enterprize, till at length he arrived at a small rivulet, that issued from a fountain hard by, called in the language of mortal men, Helicon. Here he stopped, and, parched with thirst, resolved to allay it in this limpid stream. Thrice with profane hands he essayed to raise the water to his lips, and thrice it slipped all through his fingers. Then he stooped prone on his breast, but ere his mouth had kissed the liquid crystal, Apollo came, and in the channel held his shield betwixt the Modern and the fountain, so that he drew up nothing but mud. For, altho' no fountain on earth can compare with the clearness of Helicon, yet there lies at bottom a thick sediment of slime and mud; for so Apollo begged of Jupiter, as a punishment to those who durst attempt to taste it with unhallowed lips, and for a lesson to all not to draw too deep or far from the spring.

At the fountain-head W-tt-n discerned two heroes; the one he could not distinguish, but the other was soon known for Temple, general of the allies to the Ancients. His back was turned, and he was employed in drinking large draughts in his helmet from the fountain, where he had withdrawn himself to rest from the toils of the war. W-tt-n, observing him, with quaking knees, and trembling hands, spoke thus to himself: 'Oh that I could kill this

[2] This is according to Homer, who tells the dreams of those who were killed in their sleep.

destroyer of our army, what renown should I purchase among the chiefs! But to issue out against him,[3] man for man, shield against shield, and lance against lance, what Modern of us dare? For he fights like a god, and Pallas or Apollo are ever at his elbow. But, Oh mother! if what Fame reports be true, that I am the son of so great a goddess, grant me to hit Temple with this lance, that the stroke may send him to hell, and that I may return in safety and triumph, laden with his spoils.' The first part of his prayer, the gods granted at the intercession of his mother and of Momus; but the rest by a perverse wind sent from Fate was scattered in the air. Then W-tt-n grasped his lance, and brandishing it thrice over his head, darted it with all his might, the goddess, his mother, at the same time, adding strength to his arm. Away the lance went hissing, and reached even to the belt of the averted Ancient, upon which lightly grazing, it fell to the ground. Temple neither felt the weapon touch him, nor heard it fall; and W-tt-n might have escaped to his army, with the honor of having remitted his lance against so great a leader, unrevenged; but Apollo, enraged that a javelin, flung by the assistance of so foul a goddess, should pollute his fountain, put on the shape of ——, and softly came to young Boyle, who then accompanied Temple. He pointed first to the lance, then to the distant Modern that flung it, and commanded the young hero to take immediate revenge.[4] Boyle, clad in a suit of armor, which had been given him by all the gods,[5] immediately advanced against the trembling foe, who now fled before him. As a young lion in the Libyan plains or Araby desert, sent by his aged sire to hunt for prey, or health, or exercise, he scours along, wishing to meet some tiger from the mountains, or a furious boar; if chance, a wild ass, with brayings importune, affronts his ear, the generous beast, though loathing to distain his claws with blood so vile, yet much provoked at the offensive noise which Echo, foolish nymph, like her ill-judging sex, repeats much louder, and with more delight than Philomela's song, he vindicates the honor of the forest, and hunts the noisy, long-eared animal. So W-tt-n fled, so Boyle pursued. But W-tt-n, heavy-armed and slow of foot, began to slack his course, when his lover B-ntl-y appeared, returning laden with the spoils of the two sleeping Ancients. Boyle observed him well,

[3] *Vid*. Homer.

[4] Boyle alleges in his preface, as his principal reason for entering into the controversy about Phalaris, his respect for Sir William Temple, who had been coarsely treated by Bentley. SCOTT.

[5] Boyle was assisted in this dispute by Dean Aldrich, Dr. Atterbury, afterwards Bishop of Rochester, and other persons at Oxford, celebrated for their genius and their learning, then called the Christ Church wits. H.

and soon discovering the helmet and shield of Phalaris, his friend, both which he had lately with his own hands new polished and gilded, rage sparkled in his eyes, and, leaving his pursuit after W-tt-n, he furiously rushed on against this new approacher. Fain would he be revenged on both; but both now fled different ways; and as a woman[6] in a little house that gets a painful livelihood by spinning,[7] if chance her geese be scattered o'er the common, she courses round the plain from side to side, compelling here and there the stragglers to the flock; they cackle loud, and flutter o'er the champaign. So Boyle pursued, so fled this pair of friends: finding at length their flight was vain, they bravely joined, and drew themselves in phalanx. First B-ntl-y threw a spear with all his force, hoping to pierce the enemy's breast; but Pallas came unseen, and in the air took off the point, and clapped on one of lead, which after a dead bang against the enemy's shield, fell blunted to the ground. Then Boyle observing well his time, took a lance of wondrous length and sharpness; and as this pair of friends compacted stood close side to side, he wheeled him to the right, and with unusual force, darted the weapon. B-ntl-y saw his fate approach, and flanking down his arms close to his ribs, hoping to save his body, in went the point, passing through arm and side, nor stopped or spent its force, till it had also pierced the valiant W-tt-n who, going to sustain his dying friend, shared his fate. As when a skilful cook has trussed a brace of woodcocks, he, with iron skewer, pierces the tender sides of both, their legs and wings close pinioned to their ribs; so was this pair of friends transfixed, till down they fell, joined in their lives, joined in their deaths, so closely joined that Charon will mistake them both for one, and waft them over Styx for half his fare. Farewell, beloved loving pair; few equals have you left behind: and happy and immortal shall you be, if all my wit and eloquence can make you.

   And, now   *   *   *   *   *   *   *
*   *   *   *   *   *   *   *   *
*   *   *   *   *   *   *   *   *
*   *   *Desunt cætera.*

FINIS.

[6] *Vid.* Homer.

[7] This is also after the manner of Homer; the woman's getting a painful livelihood by spinning, has nothing to do with the similitude, nor would be excusable without such an authority.

The Bickerstaff Papers

PREDICTIONS for the Year 1708

Wherein the Month, and Day of the Month, are set down,
the Persons named, and the great Actions and Events of
next Year particularly related as they will come to pass.
Written to prevent the People of England from being farther
imposed on by vulgar Almanack-Makers.

By Isaac Bickerstaff, Esq.

HAVING long considered the gross abuse of astrology in this
kingdom, upon debating the matter with my self, I could
not possibly lay the fault upon the art, but upon those
gross impostors, who set up to be the artists. I know several
learned men have contended, that the whole is a cheat; that it is
absurd and ridiculous to imagine the stars can have any influence
at all upon human actions, thoughts, or inclinations; and whoever
has not bent his studies that way may be excused for thinking so,
when he sees in how wretched a manner this noble art is treated,
by a few mean, illiterate traders between us and the stars; who
import a yearly stock of nonsense, lies, folly, and impertinence,
which they offer to the world as genuine from the planets,
although they descend from no greater a height than their own
brains.

I intend, in a short time, to publish a large and rational defence
of this art, and therefore shall say no more in its justification at
present, than that it hath been in all ages defended by many
learned men, and among the rest by Socrates himself, whom I
look upon as undoubtedly the wisest of uninspired mortals: to
which if we add, that those who have condemned this art,
although otherwise learned, having been such as either did not
apply their studies this way, or at least did not succeed in their
applications; their testimony will not be of much weight to its

disadvantage, since they are liable to the common objection of condemning what they did not understand.

Nor am I at all offended, or think it an injury to the art, when I see the common dealers in it, the *Students in astrology*, the *Philomaths*, and the rest of that tribe, treated by wise men with the utmost scorn and contempt; but I rather wonder, when I observe gentlemen in the country, rich enough to serve the nation in Parliament, poring in Partridge's Almanack, to find out the events of the year, at home and abroad; not daring to propose a hunting match, until Gadbury or he hath fixed the weather.

I will allow either of the two I have mentioned, or any other of the fraternity, to be not only astrologers, but conjurers too, if I do not produce an hundred instances in all their Almanacks, to convince any reasonable man, that they do not so much as understand grammar and syntax; that they are not able to spell any word out of the usual road, nor, even in their prefaces, to write common sense, or intelligible English. Then, for their observations and predictions, they are such as will equally suit any age or country in the world. "This month a certain great person will be threatened with death or sickness." This the newspaper will tell them, for there we find at the end of the year, that no month passes without the death of some person of note; and it would be hard, if it should be otherwise, when there are at least two thousand persons of note in this kingdom, many of them old, and the Almanack-maker has the liberty of choosing the sickliest season of the year, where he may fix his prediction. Again, "This month an eminent clergyman will be preferred;" of which there may be some hundreds, half of them with one foot in the grave. Then, "Such a planet in such a house shows great machinations, plots, and conspiracies, that may in time be brought to light:" after which, if we hear of any discovery the astrologer gets the honour; if not, his prediction still stands good. And at last, "God preserve King William from all his open and secret enemies, Amen." When, if the king should happen to have died, the astrologer plainly foretold it; otherwise it passes but for the pious ejaculation of a loyal subject: although it unluckily happened in some of their Almanacks, that poor King William was prayed for many months after he was dead, because it fell out, that he died about the beginning of the year.

To mention no more of their impertinent predictions, what have we to do with their advertisements about "pills and drink for the venereal disease," or their mutual quarrels in verse and prose of Whig and Tory, wherewith the stars have little to do?

Having long observed and lamented these, and a hundred other abuses of this art too tedious to repeat, I resolved to proceed in a new way, which I doubt not will be to the general satisfaction of the kingdom. I can this year produce but a specimen of what I design for the future; having employed most part of my time, in adjusting and correcting the calculations I made for some years past, because I would offer nothing to the world, of which I am not as fully satisfied, as that I am now alive. For these two last years I have not failed in above one or two particulars, and those of no very great moment. I exactly foretold the miscarriage at Toulon, with all its particulars; and the loss of Admiral Shovel, although I was mistaken as to the day, placing that accident about thirty-six hours sooner than it happened; but upon reviewing my schemes, I quickly found the cause of that error. I likewise foretold the battle at Almanza to the very day and hour, with the loss on both sides, and the consequences thereof. All which I showed to some friends many months before they happened; that is, I gave them papers sealed up, to open at such a time, after which they were at liberty to read them; and there they found my predictions true in every article, except one or two very minute.

As for the few following predictions I now offer the world, I forebore to publish them, till I had perused the several Almanacks for the year we are now entered upon. I found them all in the usual strain, and I beg the reader will compare their manner with mine: and here I make bold to tell the world, that I lay the whole credit of my art upon the truth of these predictions; and I will be content, that Partridge, and the rest of his clan, may hoot me for a cheat and impostor, if I fail in any single particular of moment. I believe, any man who reads this paper, will look upon me to be at least a person of as much honesty and understanding, as a common maker of Almanacks. I do not lurk in the dark; I am not wholly unknown in the world; I have set my name at length to be a mark of infamy to mankind, if they shall find I deceive them.

In one point I must desire to be forgiven, that I talk more sparingly of home affairs. As it would be imprudence to discover secrets of state, so it might be dangerous to my person; but in smaller matters, and such as are not of public consequence, I shall be very free; and the truth of my conjectures will as much appear from these as the other. As for the most signal events abroad in France, Flanders, Italy, and Spain, I shall make no scruple to predict them in plain terms: some of them are of importance, and I hope I shall seldom mistake the day they will happen; therefore, I think good to inform the reader, that I all along make use of the Old Style observed in England, which I desire he will compare with that of the newspapers, at the time they relate the actions I mention.

I must add one word more: I know it hath been the opinion of several learned persons, who think well enough of the true art of astrology, that the stars do only incline, and not force, the actions or wills of men; and therefore, however I may proceed by right rules, yet I cannot in prudence so confidently assure that the events will follow exactly as I predict them.

I hope I have maturely considered this objection, which in some cases is of no little weight. For example: a man may, by the influence of an over-ruling planet, be disposed or inclined to lust, rage, or avarice, and yet by the force of reason overcome that evil influence. And this was the case of Socrates: but the great events of the world, usually depending upon numbers of men, it cannot be expected they should all unite to cross their inclinations, from pursuing a general design, wherein they unanimously agree. Besides, the influence of the stars reaches to many actions and events, which are not any way in the power of reason; as sickness, death, and what we commonly call accidents, with many more needless to repeat.

But now it is time to proceed to my predictions, which I have begun to calculate from the time that the sun enters into Aries. And this I take to be properly the beginning of the natural year. I pursue them to the time that he enters Libra, or somewhat more, which is the busy period of the year. The remainder I have not yet adjusted, upon account of several impediments needless here to mention. Besides, I must remind the reader again, that this is but a specimen of what I design in succeeding years to treat more at large, if I may have liberty and encouragement.

My first prediction is but a trifle, yet I will mention it, to show how ignorant those sottish pretenders to astrology are in their own concerns: it relates to Partridge the Almanack-maker; I have consulted the star of his nativity by my own rules, and find he will infallibly die upon the 29th of March next, about eleven at night, of a raging fever; therefore I advise him to consider of it, and settle his affairs in time.

The month of APRIL will be observable for the death of many great persons. On the 4th will die the Cardinal de Noailles, Archbishop of Paris: on the 11th, the young Prince of Asturias, son to the Duke of Anjou: on the 14th, a great peer of this realm will die at his country-house: on the 19th, an old layman of great fame for learning: and on the 23d, an eminent goldsmith in Lombard Street. I could mention others, both at home and abroad, if

I did not consider such events of very little use or instruction to the reader, or to the world.

As to public affairs: On the 7th of this month there will be an insurrection in Dauphine, occasioned by the oppressions of the people, which will not be quieted in some months.

On the 15th will be a violent storm on the south-east coast of France, which will destroy many of their ships, and some in the very harbour.

The 19th will be famous for the revolt of a whole province or kingdom, excepting one city, by which the affairs of a certain prince in the alliance will take a better face.

MAY, against common conjectures, will be no very busy month in Europe, but very signal for the death of the Dauphin, which will happen on the 7th, after a short fit of sickness, and grievous torments with the strangury. He dies less lamented by the court than the kingdom.

On the 9th, a Mareschal of France will break his leg by a fall from his horse. I have not been able to discover whether he will then die or not.

On the 11th will begin a most important siege, which the eyes of all Europe will be upon: I cannot be more particular; for, in relating affairs that so nearly concern the confederates, and consequently this kingdom, I am forced to confine myself, for several reasons very obvious to the reader.

On the 15th, news will arrive of a very surprising event, than which nothing could be more unexpected.

On the 19th, three noble ladies of this kingdom will, against all expectation, prove with child, to the great joy of their husbands.

On the 23rd, a famous buffoon of the playhouse will die a ridiculous death, suitable to his vocation.

JUNE. This month will be distinguished at home by the utter dispersing of those ridiculous deluded enthusiasts, commonly called the Prophets; occasioned chiefly by seeing the time come, when many of their prophecies were to be fulfilled, and then finding themselves deceived by contrary events. It is indeed to be admired, how any deceiver can be so weak to foretell things near at hand, when a very few months must, of necessity, discover the imposture to all the world; in this point less prudent than common almanack-makers, who are so wise to wander in generals, talk dubiously, and leave to the reader the business of interpreting.

On the 1st of this month, a French general will be killed by a random shot of a cannon-ball.

On the 6th, a fire will break out in the suburbs of Paris, which will destroy above a thousand houses; and seems to be the foreboding of what will happen, to the surprise of all Europe, about the end of the following month.

On the 10th, a great battle will be fought, which will begin at four of the clock in the afternoon; and last till nine at night, with great obstinacy, but no very decisive event. I shall not name the place, for the reasons aforesaid; but the commanders on each left wing will be killed. ——— I see bonfires, and hear the noise of guns for a victory.

On the 14th, there will be a false report of the French king's death.

On the 20th, Cardinal Portocarero will die of a dysentery, with great suspicion of poison; but the report of his intention to revolt to King Charles will prove false.

JULY. The 6th of this month, a certain general will, by a glorious action, recover the reputation he lost by former misfortunes.

On the 12th, a great commander will die a prisoner in the hands of his enemies.

On the 14th, a shameful discovery will be made of a French Jesuit, giving poison to a great foreign general; and when he is put to the torture, will make wonderful discoveries.

In short, this will prove a month of great action, if I might have liberty to relate the particulars.

At home, the death of an old famous senator will happen on the 15th, at his country-house, worn with age and diseases.

But that which will make this month memorable to all posterity, is the death of the French king, Louis the Fourteenth, after a week's sickness, at Marli, which will happen on the 29th, about six a-clock in the evening. It seems to be an effect of the gout in his stomach, followed by a flux. And in three days after, Monsieur Chamillard will follow his master, dying suddenly of an apoplexy.

In this month likewise an ambassador will die in London; but I cannot assign the day.

AUGUST. The affairs of France will seem to suffer no change for a while under the Duke of Burgundy's administration; but the genius that animated the whole machine being gone, will be the cause of mighty turns and revolutions in the following year. The new king makes yet little change either in the army or the ministry; but the libels against his grandfather, that fly about his very court, give him uneasiness.

I see an express in mighty haste, with joy and wonder in his looks, arriving by the break of day on the 26th of this month, having travelled in three days a prodigious journey by land and sea In the evening I hear bells and guns, and see the blazing of a thousand bonfires.

A young admiral of noble birth does likewise this month gain immortal honour by a great achievement.

The affairs of Poland are this month entirely settled: Augustus resigns his pretensions, which he had again taken up for some time: Stanislaus is peaceably possessed of the throne; and the King of Sweden declares for the Emperor.

I cannot omit one particular accident here at home; that near the end of this month much mischief will be done at Bartholomew Fair, by the fall of a booth.

SEPTEMBER. This month begins with a very surprising fit of frosty weather, which will last near twelve days.

The Pope having long languished last month, the swellings in his legs breaking, and the flesh mortifying, will die on the 11th instant; and in three weeks' time, after a mighty contest, be succeeded by a Cardinal of the imperial faction, but native of Tuscany, who is now about sixty-one years old.

The French army acts now wholly on the defensive, strongly fortified in their trenches; and the young French king sends overtures for a treaty of peace by the Duke of Mantua; which, because it is a matter of state that concerns us here at home, I shall speak no farther of it.

I shall add but one prediction more, and that in mystical terms, which shall be included in a verse out of Virgil:

> *Alter erit jam Tethys, & altera, quæ vehat, Argo,*
> *Delectos heroas.*

Upon the 25th day of this month, the fulfilling of this prediction will be manifest to everybody.

This is the farthest I have proceeded in my calculations for the present year. I do not pretend that these are all the great events which will happen in this period; but that those I have set down will infallibly come to pass. It may perhaps still be objected, why I have not spoke more particularly of affairs at home, or of the success of our armies abroad, which I might, and could very largely have done. But those in power have wisely discouraged men from meddling in public concerns, and I was resolved by no means to give the least offence. This I will venture to say, that it will be a glorious campaign for the Allies, wherein the English forces, both by sea and land, will have their full share of honour: that Her Majesty Queen Anne will continue in health and prosperity: and that no ill accident will arrive to any in the chief ministry.

As to the particular events I have mentioned, the readers may judge, by the fulfilling of them, whether I am of the level with common astrologers; who, with an old paltry cant, and a few pot-hooks for planets to amuse the vulgar, have, in my opinion, too long been suffered to abuse the world. But an honest physician ought not to be despised, because there are such things as mountebanks. I hope I have some share of reputation, which I would not willingly forfeit for a frolic or humour; and I believe no gentleman who reads this paper, will look upon it to be of the same last or mould with the common scribbles that are every day hawked about. My fortune has placed me above the little regard of writing for a few pence, which I neither value nor want: therefore, let not wise men too hastily condemn this essay, intended for a good design, to cultivate and improve an ancient art, long in disgrace by having fallen into mean unskilful hands. A little time will determine whether I have deceived others or myself; and I think it is no very unreasonable request, that men would please to suspend their judgments till then. I was once of the opinion with those who despise all predictions from the stars, till in the year 1686, a man of quality showed me, written in his *album*, that the most learned astronomer, Captain Halley, assured him, he would never believe anything of the stars' influence if there were not a great revolution in England in the year 1688. Since that time I began to have other thoughts, and after eighteen years diligent study and application, I think I have no reason to repent of my pains. I shall detain the reader no longer than to let him know, that the account I design to give of next year's events, shall take in the principal affairs that happen in Europe; and if I be denied the liberty of offering it to my own country, I shall appeal to the learned world, by publishing it in Latin, and giving order to have it printed in Holland.

THE ACCOMPLISHMENT
of the First of Mr. Bickerstaff's Predictions

Being an Account of the Death of Mr. Partridge, the Almanack-Maker, upon the 29th instant, in a Letter to a
Person of Honour.

MY LORD,

IN obedience to your Lordship's commands, as well as to
satisfy my own curiosity, I have for some days past enquired
constantly after Partridge the almanack-maker, of whom it was
foretold in Mr. Bickerstaff's Predictions, published about a
month ago, that he should die the 29th instant, about eleven at
night, of a raging fever. I had some sort of knowledge of him
when I was employed in the revenue, because he used every
year to present me with his almanack, as he did other gentlemen
upon the score of some little gratuity we gave him. I saw him
accidentally once or twice about ten days before he died; and
observed he began very much to droop and languish, although
I hear his friends did not seem to apprehend him in any danger.
About two or three days ago he grew ill, was confined first to his
chamber, and in a few hours after to his bed; where Dr. Case
and Mrs. Kirleus were sent for to visit, and to prescribe to him.
Upon this intelligence I sent thrice every day one servant or other
to enquire after his health; and yesterday about four in the afternoon, word was brought me that he was past hopes; upon which
I prevailed with myself to go and see him, partly out of com-
miseration, and, I confess, partly out of curiosity. He knew me
very well, seemed surprised at my condescension, and made me
compliments upon it as well as he could in the condition he was.
The people about him said he had been for some hours delirious;
but when I saw him, he had his understanding as well as ever
I knew, and spoke strong and hearty, without any seeming uneasiness or constraint. After I had told him I was sorry to see
him in those melancholy circumstances, and said some other
civilities suitable to the occasion, I desired him to tell me freely
and ingenuously whether the predictions Mr. Bickerstaff had published relating to his death, had not too much affected and worked
on his imagination. He confessed he often had it in his head, but

never with much apprehension till about a fortnight before; since which time it had the perpetual possession of his mind and thoughts, and he did verily believe was the true natural cause of his present distemper: for, said he, "I am thoroughly persuaded, and I think I have very good reasons, that Mr. Bickerstaff spoke altogether by guess, and knew no more what will happen this year than I did myself." I told him his discourse surprised me; and I would be glad he were in a state of health to be able to tell me what reason he had to be convinced of Mr. Bickerstaff's ignorance. He replied, "I am a poor ignorant fellow, bred to a mean trade; yet I have sense enough to know, that all pretences of foretelling by astrology are deceits, for this manifest reason, because the wise and the learned, who can only judge whether there be any truth in this science, do all unanimously agree to laugh at and despise it; and none but the poor ignorant vulgar give it any credit, and that only upon the word of such silly wretches as I and my fellows, who can hardly write or read." I then asked him, why he had not calculated his own nativity, to see whether it agreed with Bickerstaff's predictions? At which he shook his head, and said, "O! sir, this is no time for jesting, but for repenting those fooleries, as I do now from the very bottom of my heart." "By what I can gather from you," said I, "the observations and predictions you printed with your almanacks were mere impositions on the people." He replied, "If it were otherwise, I should have the less to answer for. We have a common form for all those things: as to foretelling the weather, we never meddle with that, but leave it to the printer, who takes it out of any old almanack as he thinks fit: the rest was my own invention to make my almanack sell, having a wife to maintain, and no other way to get my bread; for mending old shoes is a poor livelihood; and" (added he, sighing) "I wish I may not have done more mischief by my physic than my astrology; although I had some good receipts from my grandmother, and my own compositions were such, as I thought could at least do no hurt."

I had some other discourse with him, which now I cannot call to mind; and I fear I have already tired your lordship. I shall only add one circumstance, that on his death-bed he declared himself a nonconformist, and had a fanatic preacher to be his spiritual guide. After half an hour's conversation I took my leave, being almost stifled by the closeness of the room. I imagined he could not hold out long, and therefore withdrew to a little coffeehouse hard by, leaving a servant at the house with orders to come immediately and tell me, as near as he could, the minute when Partridge should expire, which was not above two hours after; when looking upon my watch, I found it to be above five minutes after seven: by which it is clear that Mr. Bickerstaff was mistaken almost four hours in his calculation. In the other circumstances he was exact enough. But whether he hath not been the cause of this poor man's death, as well as the predictor, may be very reasonably disputed. However, it must be confessed, the matter is odd enough, whether we should endeavour to account for it by chance or the effect of imagination: for my own part, although I believe no man hath less faith in these matters, yet I shall wait with some impatience, and not without some expectation, the fulfilling of Mr. Bickerstaff's second prediction, that the Cardinal de Noailles is to die upon the 4th of April; and if that should be verified as exactly as this of poor Partridge, I must own I should be wholly surprised, and at a loss, and infallibly expect the accomplishment of all the rest.

A VINDICATION

Of Isaac Bickerstaff, Esq.; against What is Objected to Him by Mr. Partridge, in his Almanack for the present Year 1709.

By the said Isaac Bickerstaff, Esq.

MR. PARTRIDGE hath been lately pleased to treat me after a very rough manner, in that which is called his almanack for the present year: such usage is very indecent from one gentleman to another, and doth not at all contribute to the discovery of truth, which ought to be the great end in all disputes of the learned. To call a man fool and villain, and impudent fellow, only for differing from him in a point merely speculative, is, in my humble opinion, a very improper style for a person of his education. I appeal to the learned world, whether in my last year's predictions, I gave him the least provocation for such unworthy treatment. Philosophers have differed in all ages, but the discreetest among them have always differed as became philosophers. Scurrility and passion, in a controversy among scholars, is just so much of nothing to the purpose; and at best a tacit confession of a weak cause: my concern is not so much for my own reputation, as that of the republic of letters, which Mr. Partridge hath endeavoured to wound through my sides. If men of public spirit must be superciliously treated for their ingenuous attempts, how will true useful knowledge be ever advanced? I wish Mr. Partridge knew the thoughts which foreign universities have conceived of his ungenerous proceedings with me; but I am too tender of his reputation to publish them to the world. That spirit of envy and pride, which blasts so many rising geniuses in our nation, is yet unknown among professors abroad: the necessity of justifying myself will excuse my vanity, when I tell the reader, that I have near an hundred honorary letters from several parts of Europe (some as far as Muscovy) in praise of my performance. Beside several others, which, as I have been credibly informed, were opened in the post office, and never sent me. It is true the inquisition in Portugal was pleased to burn my predictions,[1] and condemn the author and readers of them; but I hope at the same time, it will be considered in how deplorable a state learning lies at present in that kingdom: and with the profoundest veneration for crowned heads, I will presume to add, that it a little concerned his Majesty of Portugal to interpose his authority in behalf of a scholar and a gentleman, the subject of a nation with which he is now in so strict an alliance. But the other kingdoms and states of Europe have treated me with more candour and generosity. If I had leave to print the Latin letters transmitted to me from foreign parts, they would fill a volume, and be a full defence against all that Mr. Partridge, or his accomplices of the Portugal inquisition, will be ever able to object; who, by the way, are the only enemies my predictions have ever met with at home or abroad. But I hope I know better what is due to the honour of a learned correspondence, in so tender a point. Yet some of those illustrious persons will perhaps excuse me for transcribing a passage or two in my own vindication. The most learned Monsieur Leibnitz thus addresses to me his third letter: — *Illustrissimo Bickerstaffio astrologiæ instauratori*, &c.[2] Monsieur Le Clerc, quoting my predictions in a treatise he published last year, is pleased to say, *Ità nuperrime Bickerstaffius, magnum illud Angliæ sidus.* Another great professor writing of me, has these words: *Bickerstaffius, nobilis Anglus, astrologorum hujusce seculi facilè princeps.* Signior Magliabecchi, the Great Duke's famous library-keeper, spends almost his whole letter in compliments and praises. It is true, the renowned professor of astronomy at Utrecht seems to differ from me in one article; but it is after the modest manner that becomes a Philosopher; as, *pace tanti viri dixerim:* and, page 55, he seems to lay the error upon the printer (as indeed it ought) and says, *vel forsan error typographi, cum alioquin Bickerstaffius vir doctissimus, &c.*

If Mr. Partridge had followed these examples in the controversy between us, he might have spared me the trouble of justifying myself in so public a manner. I believe few men are readier to own their errors than I, or more thankful to those who will please to inform him of them. But it seems this gentleman, instead of encouraging the progress of his own art, is pleased to look upon all attempts of that kind as an invasion of his province.

[1] This is fact, as the author was assured by Sir Paul Methuen, then ambassador to that crown.
[2] The quotations here inserted are in imitation of Dr. Bentley, in some part of the famous controversy between him and Mr. Boyle, Esq., afterwards Earl of Orrery.

He hath been indeed so wise, to make no objection against the truth of my predictions, except in one single point relating to himself; and to demonstrate how much men are blinded by their own partiality, I do solemnly assure the reader, that he is the only person from whom I ever heard that objection offered; which consideration alone, I think, will take off all its weight.

With my utmost endeavours I have not been able to trace above two objections ever made against the truth of my last year's prophecies: the first is of a Frenchman, who was pleased to publish to the world, that the Cardinal de Noailles was still alive, notwithstanding the pretended prophecy of Monsieur Biquerstaffe: but how far a Frenchman, a Papist, and an enemy, is to be believed in his own cause, against an English Protestant, who is true to the government, I shall leave to the candid and impartial reader.

The other objection is the unhappy occasion of this discourse, and relates to an article in my predictions, which foretold the death of Mr. Partridge to happen on March 29, 1708. This he is pleased to contradict absolutely in the almanack he hath published for the present year, and in that ungentlemanly manner (pardon the expression) as I have above related. In that work he very roundly asserts, that he is not only now alive, but was likewise alive upon that very 29th of March, when I had foretold he should die. This is the subject of the present controversy between us; which I design to handle with all brevity, perspicuity, and calmness: in this dispute, I am sensible the eyes, not only of England, but of all Europe, will be upon us; and the learned in every country will, I doubt not, take part on that side where they find most appearance of reason and truth.

Without entering into criticisms of chronology about the hour of his death, I shall only prove that Mr. Partridge is not alive. And my first argument is thus: above a thousand gentlemen having bought his almanacks for this year, merely to find what he said against me, at every line they read, they would lift up their eyes, and cry out, betwixt rage and laughter, they were sure no man alive ever writ such damned stuff as this. Neither did I ever hear that opinion disputed; so that Mr. Partridge lies under a dilemma, either of disowning his almanack, or allowing himself to be no man alive. But now, if an uninformed carcass walks still about, and is pleased to call itself Partridge, Mr. Bickerstaff does not think himself anyway answerable for that. Neither had the said carcass any right to beat the poor boy, who happened to pass by it in the street, crying, "A full and true account of Dr. Partridge's death," &c.

Secondly, Mr. Partridge pretends to tell fortunes, and recover stolen goods; which all the parish says he must do by conversing with the devil, and other evil spirits: and no wise man will ever allow he could converse personally with either till after he was dead.

Thirdly, I will plainly prove him to be dead, out of his own almanack for this year, and from the very passage which he produces to make us think him alive. He there says, he is not only now alive, but was also alive upon that very 29th of March, which I foretold he should die on; by this, he declares his opinion, that a man may be alive now who was not alive a twelvemonth ago. And, indeed, there lies the sophistry of his argument. He dares not assert he was alive ever since that 29th of March, but that he is now alive, and was so on that day: I grant the latter, for he did not die till night, as appears by the printed account of his death, in a letter to a lord; and whether he be since revived, I leave the world to judge. This indeed is perfect cavilling, and I am ashamed to dwell any longer upon it.

Fourthly, I will appeal to Mr. Partridge himself, whether it be probable I could have been so indiscreet, to begin my predictions with the only falsehood that ever was pretended to be in them; and this in an affair at home, where I had so many opportunities to be exact; and must have given such advantages against me to a person of Mr. Partridge's wit and learning, who, if he could possibly have raised one single objection more against the truth of my prophecies, would hardly have spared me.

And here I must take occasion to reprove the above-mentioned writer of the relation of Mr. Partridge's death, in a Letter to a Lord; who was pleased to tax me with a mistake of four whole hours in my calculation of that event. I must confess, this censure, pronounced with an air of certainty, in a matter that so nearly concerned me, and by a grave judicious author, moved me not a little. But although I was at that time out of town, yet several of my friends, whose curiosity had led them to be exactly informed, (for as to my own part, having no doubt at all in the matter, I never once thought of it,) assured me I computed to something under half an hour; which (I speak my private opinion) is an error of no very great magnitude, that men should raise clamour about it. I shall only say, it would not be amiss, if that author would henceforth be more tender of other men's reputation, as well as his own. It is well there were no more mistakes of that kind; if there had, I presume he would have told me of them with as little ceremony.

There is one objection against Mr. Partridge's death, which I have sometimes met with, although indeed very slightly offered, that he still continues to write almanacks. But this is no more than what is common to all of that profession; Gadbury, Poor Robin, Dove, Wing, and several others, do yearly publish their almanacks, although several of them have been dead since before the Revolution. Now the natural reason of this I take to be, that whereas it is the privilege of other authors to live after their death, almanack-makers are alone excluded; because their dissertations, treating only upon the minutes as they pass, become useless as those go off. In consideration of which, Time, whose registers they are, gives them a lease in reversion, to continue their works after their death.

I should not have given the public or myself the trouble of this vindication, if my name had not been made use of by several persons to whom I never lent it; one of which, a few days ago, was pleased to father on me a new set of predictions. But I think these are things too serious to be trifled with. It grieved me to the heart, when I saw my labours, which had cost me so much thought and watching, bawled about by common hawkers of Grub-Street, which I only intended for the weighty consideration of the gravest persons. This prejudiced the world so much at first, that several of my friends had the assurance to ask me whether I were in jest? to which I only answered coldly, "that the event will show." But it is the talent of our age and nation, to turn things of the greatest importance into ridicule. When the end of the year had verified all my predictions, out comes Mr. Partridge's almanack, disputing the point of his death; so that I am employed, like the general who was forced to kill his enemies twice over, whom a necromancer had raised to life. If Mr. Partridge has practised the same experiment upon himself, and be again alive, long may he continue so; but that does not the least contradict my veracity; for I think I have clearly proved, by invincible demonstration, that he died at farthest within half an hour of the time I foretold, and not four hours sooner, as the above-mentioned author, in his letter to a lord, has maliciously suggested, with design to blast my credit, by charging me with so gross a mistake.

THE TATLER

NUMBER CCXXX

Thursday, September 28, 1710.

From my own Apartment, Sept. 27.

The following letter hath laid before me many great and manifest evils in the world of letters which I had over-looked; but they open to me a very busy scene, and it will require no small care and application to amend errors which are become so universal. The affectation of politeness is exposed in this epistle with a great deal of wit and discernment; so that whatever discourses I may fall into hereafter upon the subjects the writer treats of, I shall at present lay the matter before the World, without the least alteration from the words of my correspondent.

To ISAAC BICKERSTAFF, *Esq;*
SIR,
There are some abuses among us of great consequence, the reformation of which is properly your province; although as far as I have been conversant in your papers, you have not yet considered them. These are the deplorable ignorance that for some years hath reigned among our English writers, the great depravity of our taste, and the continual corruption of our style. I say nothing here of those who handle particular sciences, divinity, law, physic, and the like; I mean the traders in history and politics, and the *belles lettres;* together with those by whom books are not translated, but (as the common expressions are) 'done out of French, Latin,' or other language, and 'made English.' I cannot but observe to you, that until of late years a Grub-Street book was always bound in sheepskin, with suitable print and paper, the price never above a shilling, and taken off wholly by common tradesmen, or country pedlars. But now they appear

in all sizes and shapes, and in all places: they are handed about
from lapfuls in every coffeehouse to persons of quality, are
shown in Westminster-Hall and the Court of Requests. You may
see them gilt, and in royal paper of five or six hundred pages, and
rated accordingly. I would engage to furnish you with a catalogue of English books published within the compass of seven
years past, which at the first hand would cost you an hundred
pounds, wherein you shall not be able to find ten lines together of
common grammar or common sense.

These two evils, ignorance and want of taste, have produced a
third; I mean the continual corruption of our English tongue,
which, without some timely remedy, will suffer more by the false
refinements of twenty years past, than it hath been improved in
the foregoing hundred. And this is what I design chiefly to enlarge upon, leaving the former evils to your animadversion.

But instead of giving you a list of the late refinements crept
into our language, I here send you the copy of a letter I received
some time ago from a most accomplished person in this way of
writing, upon which I shall make some remarks. It is in these
terms.

   'SIR,
'I *cou'dn't* get the things you sent for all *about Town.* — I *thot*
to *ha'* come down myself, and then *I'd ha' bro't 'um;* but I *ha'n't
don't,* and I believe I *can't do't,* that's *pozz* — *Tom* begins to
gi'mself airs, because *he's* going with the *plenipo's.* — 'Tis said the
French King will *bamboozel us agen,* which *causes many speculations.* The *Jacks,* and others of that *kidney,* are very *uppish*
and *alert upon't,* as you may see by their *phizz's.* — *Will Hazard*
has got the *hipps,* having lost *to the tune of* five hundr'd pound,
tho' he understands play very well, *nobody better.* He has
promis't me upon *rep,* to leave off play; but you know 'tis
a weakness *he's* too apt to *give into, tho'* he has as much wit as any
man, *nobody more.* He has lain *incog* ever since. — The *mob's*
very quiet with us now. — I believe you *tho't* I *banter'd* you in
my last like a *country put.* — I *shan't* leave Town this month, &c.'

This letter is in every point an admirable pattern of the present
polite way of writing; nor is it of less authority for being an
epistle: you may gather every flower of it, with a thousand more
of equal sweetness, from the books, pamphlets, and single papers,
offered us every day in the coffeehouses: and these are the
beauties introduced to supply the want of wit, sense, humour,
and learning, which formerly were looked upon as qualifications

for a writer. If a man of wit, who died forty years ago, were to rise from the grave on purpose, how would he be able to read this letter? And after he had got through that difficulty, how would he be able to understand it? The first thing that strikes your eye is the *breaks* at the end of almost every sentence; of which I know not the use, only that it is a refinement, and very frequently practised. Then you will observe the abbreviations and elisions, by which consonants of most obdurate sound are joined together, without one softening vowel to intervene; and all this only to make one syllable of two, directly contrary to the example of the Greeks and Romans; altogether of the Gothic strain, and a natural tendency towards relapsing into barbarity, which delights in monosyllables, and uniting of mute consonants; as it is observable in all the Northern languages. And this is still more visible in the next refinement, which consists in pronouncing the first syllable in a word that hath many, and dismissing the rest; such as *phizz, hipps, mobb, pozz, rep,* and many more; when we are already overloaded with monosyllables, which are the disgrace of our language. Thus we cram one syllable, and cut off the rest; as the owl fattened her mice after she had bit off their legs to prevent their running away; and if ours be the same reason for maiming of words, it will certainly answer the end, for I am sure no other nation will desire to borrow them. Some words are hitherto but fairly split, and therefore only in their way to perfection, as *incog* and *plenipo's:* but in a short time it is to be hoped they will be further docked to *inc* and *plen.* This reflection has made me of late years very impatient for a peace, which I believe would save the lives of many brave words, as well as men. The war hath introduced abundance of polysyllables, which will never be able to live many more campaigns. *Speculations, operations, preliminaries, ambassadors, palisadoes, communication, circumvallation, battalions,* as numerous as they are, if they attack us too frequently in our coffeehouses, we shall certainly put them to flight, and cut off the rear.

The third refinement observable in the letter I send you, consists in the choice of certain words invented by some *pretty fellows,* such as *banter, bamboozle, country put,* and *kidney,* as it is there applied; some of which are now struggling for the vogue, and others are in possession of it. I have done my utmost for some years past to stop the progress of *mob* and *banter;* but have been plainly borne down by numbers, and betrayed by those who promised to assist me.

In the last place, you are to take notice of certain choice phrases scattered through the letter; some of them tolerable

enough, till they were worn to rags by servile imitators. You
might easily find them, although they were not in a different
print; and therefore I need not disturb them.

These are the false refinements in our style which you ought
to correct: first, by arguments and fair means; but if those
fail, I think you are to make use of your authority as Censor, and
by an annual *Index Expurgatorius* expunge all words and phrases
that are offensive to good sense, and condemn those barbarous
mutilations of vowels and syllables. In this last point the usual
pretence is, that they spell as they speak: a noble standard for
language! to depend upon the caprice of every coxcomb, who,
because words are the clothing of our thoughts, cuts them out,
and shapes them as he pleases, and changes them oftener than his
dress. I believe, all reasonable people would be content that such
refiners were more sparing of their words, and liberal in their
syllables. On this head I should be glad you would bestow some
advice upon several young readers in our churches, who coming
up from the University, full fraught with admiration of our
Town politeness, will needs correct the style of their Prayer-
Books. In reading the absolution, they are very careful to say
"*Pardons and absolves;*" and in the Prayer for the Royal Family,
it must be *endue'm*, *enrich'um*, *prosper'um*, and *bring'um*. Then
in their sermons they use all the modern terms of art; *sham*,
banter, *mob*, *bubble*, *bully*, *cutting*, *shuffling*, and *palming*, all
which, and many more of the like stamp, as I have heard them
often in the pulpit from some young sophisters, so I have read
them in some of those sermons that have made a great noise of
late. The design, it seems, is to avoid the dreadful imputation of
pedantry, to show us, that they know the Town, understand men
and manners, and have not been poring upon old unfashionable
books in the University.

I should be glad to see you the instrument of introducing into
our style that simplicity which is the best and truest ornament of
most things in human life, which the politer ages always aimed
at in their building and dress, *(simplex munditiis)* as well as their
productions of wit. It is manifest, that all new affected modes of
speech, whether borrowed from the Court, the Town, or the
theatre, are the first perishing parts in any language, and, as I
could prove by many hundred instances, have been so in ours.
The writings of Hooker, who was a country clergyman, and of
Parsons the Jesuit, both in the reign of Queen Elizabeth, are in a
style that, with very few allowances, would not offend any
present reader; much more clear and intelligible than those of
Sir H. Wotton, Sir Robert Naunton, Osborn Daniel the historian,

and several others who writ later; but being men of the Court, and affecting the phrases then in fashion, they are often either not to be understood, or appear perfectly ridiculous.

What remedies are to be applied to these evils I have not room to consider, having, I fear, already taken up most of your paper. Besides, I think it is our office only to represent abuses, and yours to redress them.

I am, with great respect,

Sir,
Yours, &c.

THE EXAMINER

No. 14

November 9, 1710

E quibus hi vacuas implent sermonibus aures,
Hi narrata ferunt alio: mensuraque ficti
Crescit, et auditis aliquid novus adjicit autor,
Illic Credulitas, illic temerarius Error,
Vanaque Laetitia est, consternatique Timores,
Seditioque recens, dubioque autore susurri.

I am prevailed on, through the importunity of friends, to interrupt the scheme I had begun in my last paper, by an Essay
upon the Art of Political Lying. We are told, "the Devil is
the father of lies, and was a liar from the beginning"; so that,
beyond contradiction, the invention is old: and which is more,
his first essay of it was purely political, employed in undermining
the authority of his Prince, and seducing a third part of the subjects from their obedience. For which he was driven down from
Heaven, where (as Milton expresseth it) he had been viceroy of
a great western province; and forced to exercise his talent in inferior regions among other fallen spirits, or poor deluded men,
whom he still daily tempts to his own sin, and will ever do so till
he be chained in the bottomless pit.

But although the Devil be the father of lies, he seems, like
other great inventors, to have lost much of his reputation, by the
continual improvements that have been made upon him.

Who first reduced lying into an art and adapted it to politics,
is not so clear from history, although I have made some diligent
enquiries: I shall therefore consider it only according to the
modern system, as it hath been cultivated these twenty years past
in the southern part of our own island.

The poets tell us, that after the giants were over-thrown by
the gods, the earth in revenge produced her last offspring, which

was Fame. And the fable is thus interpreted; that when tumults and seditions are quieted, rumours and false reports are plentifully spread through a nation. So that by this account, lying is the last relief of a routed, earth-born, rebellious party in a state. But here, the moderns have made great additions, applying this art to the gaining of power, and preserving it, as well as revenging themselves after they have lost it: as the same instruments are made use of by animals to feed themselves when they are hungry, and bite those that tread upon them.

But the same genealogy cannot always be admitted for political lying; I shall therefore desire to refine upon it, by adding some circumstances of its birth and parents. A political lie is sometimes born out of a discarded statesman's head, and thence delivered to be nursed and dandled by the rabble. Sometimes it is produced a monster, and licked into shape; at other times it comes into the world completely formed, and is spoiled in the licking. It is often born an infant in the regular way, and requires time to mature it: and often it sees the light in its full growth, but dwindles away by degrees. Sometimes it is of noble birth; and sometimes the spawn of a stock-jobber. Here, it screams aloud at opening the womb; and there, it is delivered with a whisper. I know a lie that now disturbs half the kingdom with its noise, which although too proud and great at present to own its parents, I can remember in its whisper-hood. To conclude the nativity of this monster; when it comes into the world without a sting, it is still-born; and whenever it loses its sting, it dies.

No wonder, if an infant so miraculous in its birth, should be destined for great adventures: and accordingly we see it hath been the guardian spirit of a prevailing party for almost twenty years. It can conquer kingdoms without fighting, and sometimes with the loss of a battle: it gives and resumes employments; can sink a mountain to a mole-hill, and raise a mole-hill to a mountain; hath presided for many years at committees of elections; can wash a blackamoor white; make a saint of an atheist, and a patriot of a profligate; can furnish foreign ministers with intelligence; and raise or let fall the credit of the nation. This goddess flies with a huge looking-glass in her hands to dazzle the crowd, and make them see, according as she turns it, their ruin in their interest, and their interest in their ruin. In this glass you will behold your best friends clad in coats powdered with *flower-de-luces* and triple crowns; their girdles hung round with chains, and beads, and wooden shoes: and your worst enemies adorned with the ensigns of liberty, property, indulgence, moderation, and a cornucopia in their hands. Her large wings, like those of a flying fish, are of no use but while they are moist; she therefore dips them in mud, and soaring aloft scatters it in the eyes of the multitude, flying with great swiftness; but at every turn is forced to stoop in dirty ways for new supplies.

I have been sometimes thinking, if a man had the art of the second sight for seeing lies, as they have in Scotland for seeing spirits, how admirably he might entertain himself in this town; to observe the different shapes, sizes and colours, of those swarms of lies which buzz about the heads of some people, like flies about a horse's ears in summer: or those legions hovering every afternoon in Exchange Alley, enough to darken the air; or over a club of discontented grandees, and thence sent down in cargoes to be scattered at elections.

There is one essential point wherein a political liar differs from others of the faculty; that he ought to have but a short memory, which is necessary according to the various occasions he meets with every hour, of differing from himself, and swearing to both sides of a contradiction, as he finds the persons disposed, with whom he hath to deal. In describing the virtues and vices of mankind, it is convenient upon every article, to have some eminent person in our eye, from whence we copy our description. I have strictly observed this rule; and my imagination this minute represents before me a certain great man famous for this talent, to the constant practice of which he owes his twenty years' reputation of the most skilful head in England, for the management of nice affairs. The superiority of his genius consists in nothing else but an inexhaustible fund of political lies, which he plentifully distributes every minute he speaks, and by an unparalleled generosity forgets, and consequently contradicts the next half-hour. He never yet considered whether any proposition were true or false, but whether it were convenient for the present minute or company to affirm or deny it; so that if you think to refine upon him, by interpreting every thing he says, as we do dreams by the contrary, you are still to seek, and will find yourself equally deceived, whether you believe or no: the only remedy is to suppose that you have heard some inarticulate sounds, without any meaning at all. And besides, that will take off the horror you might be apt to conceive at the oaths wherewith he perpetually tags both ends of every proposition: although at the same time I think he cannot with any justice be taxed for perjury, when he invokes God and Christ, because he hath often fairly given public notice to the world, that he believes in neither.

Some people may think that such an accomplishment as this,

can be of no great use to the owner or his party, after it hath
been often practised, and is become notorious; but they are
widely mistaken: few lies carry the inventor's mark; and the
most prostitute enemy to truth may spread a thousand without
being known for the author. Besides, as the vilest writer hath
his readers, so the greatest liar hath his believers; and it often
happens, that if a lie be believed only for an hour, it hath done its
work, and there is no farther occasion for it. Falsehood flies, and
Truth comes limping after it; so that when men come to be
undeceived, it is too late, the jest is over, and the tale has had
its effect: like a man who has thought of a good repartee when
the discourse is changed, or the company parted: or, like a physician who hath found out an infallible medicine after the patient is
dead.

Considering that natural disposition in many men to lie, and in
multitudes to believe, I have been perplexed what to do with that
maxim, so frequent in everybody's mouth, that "Truth will at
last prevail." Here, has this island of ours, for the greatest part
of twenty years lain under the influence of such counsels and
persons, whose principle and interest it was to corrupt our manners, blind our understandings, drain our wealth, and in time
destroy our constitution both in Church and State; and we at last
were brought to the very brink of ruin; yet by the means of
perpetual misrepresentations, have never been able to distinguish
between our enemies and friends. We have seen a great part of
the nation's money got into the hands of those, who by their
birth, education and merit, could pretend no higher than to wear
our liveries. While others, who by their credit, quality and fortune, were only able to give reputation and success to the
Revolution, were not only laid aside, as dangerous and useless;
but loaden with the scandal of Jacobites, men of arbitrary principles, and pensioners to France; while Truth, who is said to lie
in a well, seemed now to be buried there under a heap of stones.
But I remember it was a usual complaint among the Whigs, that
the bulk of landed men was not in their interests, which some
of the wisest looked on as an ill omen; and we saw it was with
the utmost difficulty that they could preserve a majority, while
the court and ministry were on their side; till they had learned
those admirable expedients for deciding elections, and influencing
distant boroughs by powerful motives from the city. But all this
was mere force and constraint, however upheld by most dexterous
artifice and management; until the people began to apprehend
their properties, their religion, and the monarchy itself in danger;
then we saw them greedily laying hold on the first occasion to

interpose. But of this mighty change in the dispositions of the people, I shall discourse more at large in some following paper; wherein I shall endeavour to undeceive or discover those deluded or deluding persons, who hope or pretend, it is only a short madness in the vulgar, from which they may soon recover. Whereas I believe it will appear to be very different in its causes, its symptoms, and its consequences; and prove a great example to illustrate the maxim I lately mentioned, that "Truth" (however sometimes late) "will at last prevail."

Qui sunt boni cives? Qui belli, qui domi de patriâ bene merentes, nisi qui patriae beneficia meminerunt?

I WILL employ this present paper upon a subject, which of late hath very much affected me, which I have considered with a good deal of application, and made several enquiries about, among those persons who I thought were best able to inform me; and if I deliver my sentiments with some freedom, I hope it will be forgiven, while I accompany it with that tenderness which so nice a point requires.

I said in a former paper (Numb. 13) that one specious objection to the late removals at court, was the fear of giving uneasiness to a general, who hath been long successful abroad: and accordingly, the common clamour of tongues and pens for some months past, hath run against the baseness, the inconstancy and ingratitude of the whole kingdom to the Duke of Marlborough, in return of the most eminent services that ever were performed by a subject to his country; not to be equalled in history. And then to be sure some bitter stroke of detraction against Alexander and Cæsar, who never did us the least injury. Besides, the people who read Plutarch come upon us with parallels drawn from the Greeks and Romans, who ungratefully dealt with I know not how many of their most deserving generals: while the profounder politicians have seen pamphlets where Tacitus and Machiavel have been quoted to show the danger of too resplendent a merit. If a stranger should hear these furious outcries of ingratitude against our general, without knowing the particulars, he would be apt to enquire where was his tomb, or whether he were allowed Christian burial, not doubting but we had put him to some ignominious death. Or, hath he been tried for his life,

and very narrowly escaped? Hath he been accused of high crimes
and misdemeanours? Has the prince seized on his estate, and
left him to starve? Has he been hooted at as he passed the
streets, by an ungrateful rabble? Have neither honours, offices,
nor grants, been conferred on him or his family? Have not he
and they been barbarously stripped of them all? Have not he
and his forces been ill paid abroad? And doth not the prince by
a scanty, limited commission, hinder him from pursuing his own
methods in the conduct of the war? Hath he no power at all of
disposing commissions as he please? Is he not severely used by
the ministry or Parliament, who yearly call him to a strict account? Has the senate ever thanked him for good success, and
have they not always publicly censured him for the least miscarriage? Will the accusers of the nation join issue upon any of
these particulars, or tell us in what point our damnable sin of ingratitude lies? Why, it is plain and clear; for while he is commanding abroad, the Queen dissolves her Parliament, and changes
her ministry at home: in which universal calamity, no less than
two persons allied by marriage to the general, have lost their
places. Whence came this wonderful sympathy between the civil
and military powers? Will the troops in Flanders refuse to fight,
unless they can have their own lord keeper, their own lord president of the council, their own chief Governor of Ireland, and
their own Parliament? In a kingdom where the people are free,
how came they to be so fond of having their councils under the
influence of their army, or those that lead it who in all well
instituted states, had no commerce with the civil power, further
than to receive their orders, and obey them without reserve?

When a general is not so popular, either in his army or at home,
as one might expect from a long course of success, it may perhaps be ascribed to his wisdom, or perhaps to his complexion.
The possession of some one quality, or a defect in some other,
will extremely damp the people's favour, as well as the love of
the soldiers. Besides, this is not an age to produce favourites of
the people, while we live under a Queen who engrosses all our
love, and all our veneration; and where the only way for a great
general or minister to acquire any degree of subordinate affection
from the public, must be by all marks of the most entire submission and respect to her sacred person and commands; otherwise, no pretence of great services, either in the field or the
cabinet, will be able to screen them from universal hatred

But the late ministry was closely joined to the general, by
friendship, interest, alliance, inclination, and opinion, which cannot be affirmed of the present; and the ingratitude of the nation
lies in the people's joining as one man to wish that such a

ministry should be changed. Is it not at the same time notorious to the whole kingdom, that nothing but a tender regard to the general was able to preserve that ministry so long, until neither God nor man could suffer their continuance? Yet in the highest ferment of things, we heard few or no reflections upon this great commander, but all seemed unanimous in wishing he might still be at the head of the confederate forces; only at the same time, in case he were resolved to resign, they chose rather to turn their thoughts somewhere else than throw up all in despair. And this I cannot but add in defence of the people, with regard to the person we are speaking of, that in the high station he hath been for many years past, his real defects (as nothing human is without them) have in a detracting age been very sparingly mentioned, either in libels or conversation, and all his successes very freely and universally applauded.

There is an active and a passive ingratitude; applying both to this occasion, we may say the first is when a prince or people returns good services with cruelty or ill usage; the other is when good services are not at all, or very meanly rewarded. We have already spoke of the former; let us therefore in the second place examine how the services of our general have been rewarded; and whether upon that article, either prince or people have been guilty of ingratitude.

Those are the most valuable rewards which are given to us from the certain knowledge of the donor, that they fit our temper best: I shall therefore say nothing of the title of Duke, or the Garter, which the Queen bestowed the general in the beginning of her reign; but I shall come to more substantial instances, and mention nothing which hath not been given in the face of the world. The lands of Woodstock may, I believe, be reckoned worth 40,000*l.* On the building of Blenheim Castle 200,000*l.* have been already expended, although it be not yet near finished. The grant of 5,000*l. per annum* on the post-office is richly worth 100,000*l.* His principality in Germany may be computed at 30,000*l.* Pictures, jewels, and other gifts from foreign princes, 60,000*l.* The grant at the Pall-Mall, the rangership, &c. for want of more certain knowledge, may be called 10,000*l.* His own, and his duchess's employments at five years' value, reckoning only the known and avowed salaries, are very low rated at 100,000*l.* Here is a good deal above half a million of money, and I dare say, those who are loudest with the clamour of ingratitude will readily own that all this is but a trifle in comparison of what is untold.

The reason of my stating this account is only to convince the world that we are not quite so ungrateful either as the Greeks or the Romans. And in order to adjust this matter with all fairness, I shall confine myself to the latter, who were much the more generous of the two. A victorious general of Rome in the height of that empire, having entirely subdued his enemy, was rewarded with the larger triumph; and perhaps a statue in the Forum, a bull for a sacrifice, an embroidered garment to appear in, a crown of laurel, a monumental trophy with inscriptions; sometimes five hundred or a thousand copper coins were struck on occasion of the victory, which doing honour to the general, we will place to his account; and lastly, sometimes, though not very frequently, a triumphal arch. These are all the rewards that I can call to mind, which a victorious general received after his return from the most glorious expedition, conquered some great kingdom, brought the king himself, his family and nobles to adorn the triumph in chains, and made the kingdom either a Roman province, or at best a poor depending state, in humble alliance to that empire. Now of all these rewards, I find but two which were of real profit to the general; the laurel crown, made and sent him at the charge of the public, and the embroidered garment; but I cannot find whether this last were paid for by the senate or the general: however, we will take the more favourable opinion, and in all the rest, admit the whole expense, as if it were ready money in the general's pocket. Now according to these computations on both sides, we will draw up two fair accounts, the one of Roman gratitude, and the other of British ingratitude, and set them together in balance.

A BILL OF ROMAN GRATITUDE.

Imprimis	l.	s.	d.
For frankincense and earthen pots to burn it in	4	10	0
A bull for sacrifice . . .	8	0	0
An embroidered garment	50	0	0
A crown of laurel	0	0	2
A statue	100	0	0
A trophy	80	0	0
A thousand copper medals value half pence a piece	2	1	8
A triumphal arch	500	0	0
A triumphal car, valued as a modern coach . .	100	0	0
Casual charges at the triumph	150	0	0
	994	11	10

A BILL OF BRITISH INGRATITUDE.

Imprimis	l.	s.	d.
Woodstock	40,000	0	0
Blenheim	200,000	0	0
Post-office grant . . .	100,000	0	0
Mildenheim	30,000	0	0
Pictures, jewels, &c. .	60,000	0	0
Pall-Mall grant, &c. .	10,000	0	0
Employments	100,000	0	0
	540,000	0	0

This is an account of the visible profits on both sides; and if the Roman general had any private perquisites, they may be easily discounted, and by more probable computation, and differ yet more upon the balance if we consider that all the gold and silver for safeguards and contributions, and all valuable prizes taken in the war, were openly exposed in the triumph, and then lodged in the Capitol for the public service.

So that upon the whole, we are not yet quite so bad at worst, as the Romans were at best. And I doubt those who raise this hideous cry of ingratitude, may be mightily mistaken in the consequences they propose from such complaints. I remember a saying of Seneca, *Multos ingratos invenimus, plures facimus:* We find many ungrateful persons in the world, but we make more, by setting too high a rate upon our pretensions, and undervaluing the rewards we receive. When unreasonable bills are brought in, they ought to be taxed, or cut off in the middle. Where there have been long accounts between two persons, I have known one of them perpetually making large demands and pressing for payments, who when the accounts were cast up on both sides, was found to be debtor for some hundreds. I am thinking if a proclamation were issued out for every man to send in his bill of merits, and the lowest price he set them at, what a pretty sum it would amount to, and how many such islands as this must be sold to pay them. I form my judgment from the practice of those who sometimes happen to pay themselves, and I dare affirm, would not be so unjust to take a farthing more than they think is due to their deserts. I will instance only in one article. A lady of my acquaintance, appropriated twenty-six pounds a year out of her own allowance, for certain uses, which her woman received, and was to pay to the lady or her order, as it was called for. But after eight years, it appeared upon the strictest calculation, that the woman had paid but four pounds a year, and sunk two-and-twenty for her own pocket. It is but supposing instead of twenty-six pounds, twenty-six thousand, and by that you may judge what the pretensions of modern merit are, where it happens to be its own paymaster.

AN ARGUMENT

TO PROVE THAT THE

ABOLISHING OF CHRISTIANITY IN ENGLAND

May, as Things Now Stand, Be Attended with Some Inconveniences, and Perhaps Not Produce Those Many Good Effects Proposed Thereby.

Written in the Year 1708.

I AM very sensible what a weakness and presumption it is to reason against the general humour and disposition of the world. I remember it was with great justice, and a due regard to the freedom both of the public and the press, forbidden upon severe penalties to write, or discourse, or lay wagers against the *Union*, even before it was confirmed by parliament, because that was looked upon as a design to oppose the current of the people, which, besides the folly of it, is a manifest breach of the fundamental law that makes this majority of opinion the voice of God. In like manner, and for the very same reasons, it may perhaps be neither safe nor prudent to argue against the abolishing of Christianity at a juncture when all parties appear so unanimously determined upon the point, as we cannot but allow from their actions, their discourses, and their writings. However, I know not how, whether from the affectation of singularity or the perverseness of human nature, but so it unhappily falls out that I cannot be entirely of this opinion. Nay, although I were sure an order were issued out for my immediate prosecution by the Attorney-General, I should still confess that in the present posture of our affairs at home or abroad, I do not yet see the absolute necessity of extirpating the Christian religion from among us.

This perhaps may appear too great a paradox even for our wise and paradoxical age to endure; therefore I shall handle it with all tenderness, and with the utmost deference to that great and profound majority which is of another sentiment.

And yet the curious may please to observe, how much the genius of a nation is liable to alter in half an age. I have heard it affirmed for certain by some very old people, that the contrary opinion was even in their memories as much in vogue as the other is now; and, that a project for the abolishing of Christianity would then have appeared as singular, and been thought as absurd, as it would be at this time to write or discourse in its defence.

Therefore I freely own that all appearances are against me. The system of the Gospel, after the fate of other systems, is generally antiquated and exploded; and the mass or body of the common people, among whom it seems to have had its latest credit, are now grown as much ashamed of it as their betters; opinion like fashions always descending from those of quality to the middle sort, and thence to the vulgar, where at length they are dropped and vanish.

But here I would not be mistaken, and must therefore be so bold as to borrow a distinction from the writers on the other side when they make a difference between nominal and real Trinitarians. I hope no reader imagines me so weak to stand up in the defence of real Christianity, such as used in primitive times (if we may believe the authors of those ages) to have an influence upon men's belief and actions: to offer at the restoring of that would indeed be a wild project; it would be to dig up foundations; to destroy at one blow all the wit and half the learning of the kingdom; to break the entire frame and constitution of things; to ruin trade, extinguish arts and sciences with the professors of them; in short, to turn our courts, exchanges, and shops into deserts; and would be full as absurd as the proposal of Horace, where he advises the Romans all in a body to leave their city and seek a new seat in some remote part of the world by way of cure for the corruption of their manners.

Therefore I think this caution was in itself altogether unnecessary, (which I have inserted only to prevent all possibility of cavilling) since every candid reader will easily understand my discourse to be intended only in defence of nominal Christianity; the other having been for some time wholly laid aside by general consent, as utterly inconsistent with our present schemes of wealth and power.

But why we should therefore cast off the name and title of Christians, although the general opinion and resolution be so violent for it, I confess I cannot (with submission) apprehend the consequence necessary. However, since the undertakers propose such wonderful advantages to the nation by this project, and advance many plausible objections against the system of Christianity, I shall briefly consider the strength of both, fairly allow them their greatest weight, and offer such answers as I think most reasonable. After which I will beg leave to show what inconvenience may possibly happen by such an innovation in the present posture of our affairs.

First, one great advantage proposed by the abolishing of Christianity is, that it would very much enlarge and establish liberty of conscience, that great bulwark of our nation, and of the Protestant Religion, which is still too much limited by priestcraft notwithstanding all the good intentions of the legislature, as we have lately found by a severe instance. For it is confidently reported that two young gentlemen of great hopes, bright wit, and profound judgment, who upon a thorough examination of causes and effects, and by the mere force of natural abilities, without the least tincture of learning, having made a discovery that there was no God, and generously communicating their thoughts for the good of the public, were some time ago, by an unparalleled severity, and upon I know not what obsolete law, broke only for blasphemy. And as it hath been wisely observed, if persecution once begins, no man alive knows how far it may reach, or where it will end.

In answer to all which, with deference to wiser judgments, I think this rather shows the necessity of a nominal religion among us. Great wits love to be free with the highest objects; and if they cannot be allowed a God to revile or renounce, they will speak evil of dignities, abuse the government, and reflect upon the ministry; which I am sure few will deny to be of much more pernicious consequence, according to the saying of Tiberius, *Deorum offensa diis curæ*. As to the particular fact related, I think it is not fair to argue from one instance, perhaps another cannot be produced; yet (to the comfort of all those who may be apprehensive of persecution) blasphemy we know is freely spoke a million of times in every coffeehouse and tavern, or wherever else good company meet. It must be allowed indeed, that to break an English free-born officer only for blasphemy, was, to speak the gentlest of such an action, a very high strain of absolute power. Little can be said in excuse for the general; perhaps he was afraid it might give offence to the allies, among whom, for aught I know, it may be the custom of the country to believe a God. But if he argued, as some have done, upon a mistaken principle, that an officer who is guilty of speaking blasphemy, may some time or other proceed so far as to raise a mutiny, the consequence is by no means to be admitted; for surely the commander of an English army is likely to be but ill obeyed whose soldiers fear and reverence him as little as they do a deity.

It is further objected against the Gospel System, that it obliges men to the belief of things too difficult for free-thinkers, and such who have shaken off the prejudices that usually cling to a confined education. To which I answer, that men should be cautious how they raise objections which reflect upon the wisdom of the nation. Is not every body freely allowed to believe whatever he pleases, and to publish his belief to the world whenever he thinks fit, especially if it serve to strengthen the party which is in the right? Would any indifferent foreigner, who should read the trumpery lately written by Asgill, Tindal, Toland, Coward, and forty more, imagine the Gospel to be our rule of faith, and confirmed by parliaments? Does any man either believe, or say he believes, or desire to have it thought that he says he believes one syllable of the matter? And is any man worse received upon that score, or does he find his want of nominal faith a disadvantage to him in the pursuit of any civil or military employment? What if there be an old dormant statute or two against him? Are they not now obsolete, to a degree, that Empson and Dudley themselves if they were now alive, would find it impossible to put them in execution?

It is likewise urged that there are, by computation, in this kingdom above ten thousand parsons, whose revenues added to those of my lords the bishops would suffice to maintain at least two hundred young gentlemen of wit and pleasure, and free-thinking, enemies to priestcraft, narrow principles, pedantry, and prejudices; who might be an ornament to the Court and Town: and then, again, so great a number of able (bodied) divines might be a recruit to our fleet and armies. This indeed appears to be a consideration of some weight: but then, on the other side, several things deserve to be considered likewise: as, first, whether it may not be thought necessary that in certain tracts of country, like what we call parishes, there should be one man at least of abilities to read and write. Then it seems a wrong computation that the revenues of the Church throughout this island would be large enough to maintain two hundred young gentlemen, or even half that number, after the present refined way of living; that is, to allow each of them such a rent, as in the modern form of speech, would make them easy. But still there is in this project a greater mischief behind; and we ought to beware of the woman's folly who killed the hen that every morning laid her a golden egg. For, pray what would become of the race of men in the next age, if we had nothing to trust to besides the scrofulous, consumptive productions, furnished by our men of wit and pleasure, when having squandered away their vigour, health and estates, they are forced by some disagreeable marriage to piece up their broken fortunes, and entail rottenness and politeness on their posterity? Now, here are ten thousand persons reduced by the wise regulations of Henry the Eighth, to the necessity of a low diet, and moderate exercise, who are the only great restorers of our breed, without which the nation would in an age or two become but one great hospital.

Another advantage proposed by the abolishing of Christianity is the clean gain of one day in seven, which is now entirely lost, and consequently the kingdom one seventh less considerable in trade, business, and pleasure; beside the loss to the public of so many stately structures now in the hands of the Clergy, which might be converted into theatres, exchanges, market-houses, common dormitories, and other public edifices.

I hope I shall be forgiven a hard word, if I call this a perfect cavil. I readily own there has been an old custom time out of mind for people to assemble in the churches every Sunday, and that shops are still frequently shut, in order as it is conceived, to preserve the memory of that ancient practice, but how this can prove a hindrance to business or pleasure is hard to imagine. What if the men of pleasure are forced one day in the week to game at home instead of the chocolate-house? Are not the taverns and coffeehouses open? Can there be a more convenient season for taking a dose of physic? Are fewer claps got upon Sundays than other days? Is not that the chief day for traders to sum up the accounts of the week, and for lawyers to prepare their briefs? But I would fain know how it can be pretended that the churches are misapplied? Where are more appointments and rendezvouzes of gallantry? Where more care to appear in the foremost box with greater advantage of dress? Where more meetings for business? Where more bargains driven of all sorts? And where so many conveniences or enticements to sleep?

There is one advantage greater than any of the foregoing, proposed by the abolishing of Christianity: that it will utterly extinguish parties among us, by removing those factious distinctions of High and Low Church, of Whig and Tory, Presbyterian and Church of England, which are now so many grievous clogs upon public proceedings, and dispose men to prefer the gratifying themselves, or depressing their adversaries, before the most important interest of the state.

I confess, if it were certain that so great an advantage would redound to the nation by this expedient, I would submit and be silent: but will any man say, that if the words *whoring, drinking, cheating, lying, stealing,* were by act of parliament ejected out of the English tongue and dictionaries, we should all awake next morning chaste and temperate, honest and just, and lovers of truth? Is this a fair consequence? Or, if the physicians would forbid us to pronounce the words *pox, gout, rheumatism* and *stone,* would that expedient serve like so many talismans to destroy the diseases themselves? Are party and faction rooted in men's hearts no deeper than phrases borrowed from religion, or founded upon no firmer principles? And is our language so poor that we cannot find other terms to express them? Are *envy, pride, avarice* and *ambition* such ill nomenclators, that they cannot furnish appellations for their owners? Will not *heydukes* and *mamalukes, mandarins* and *potshaws,* or any other words formed at pleasure, serve to distinguish those who are in the ministry from others who would be in it if they could? What, for instance, is easier than to vary the form of speech, and instead of the word *church,* make it a question in politics, whether the Monument be in danger? Because religion was nearest at hand to furnish a few convenient phrases, is our invention so barren, we can find no other? Suppose, for argument sake, that the Tories favoured Margarita, the Whigs Mrs. Tofts, and the Trimmers Valentini,[1] would not *Margaritians, Toftians* and *Valentinians* be very tolerable marks of distinction? The *Prasini* and *Veneti,* two most virulent factions in Italy, began (if I remember right) by a distinction of colours in ribbons, which we might do with as good a grace about the dignity of the blue and the green, and would serve as properly to divide the Court, the Parliament, and the Kingdom between them, as any terms of art whatsoever borrowed from religion. Therefore, I think, there is little force in this objection against Christianity, or prospect of so great an advantage as is proposed in the abolishing of it.

It is again objected, as a very absurd ridiculous custom, that a set of men should be suffered, much less employed and hired, to bawl one day in seven against the lawfulness of those methods most in use towards the pursuit of greatness, riches and pleasure, which are the constant practice of all men alive on the other six. But this objection is, I think, a little unworthy so refined an age as ours. Let us argue this matter calmly. I appeal to the breast of any polite freethinker, whether in the pursuit of gratifying a predominant passion, he hath not always felt a wonderful incitement by reflecting it was a thing forbidden; and therefore we see, in

---

[1] Italian singers then in vogue.

order to cultivate this taste, the wisdom of the nation hath taken special care that the ladies should be furnished with prohibited silks, and the men with prohibited wine: and indeed it were to be wished that some other prohibitions were promoted, in order to improve the pleasures of the town which for want of such expedients begin already, as I am told, to flag and grow languid, giving way daily to cruel inroads from the spleen.

It is likewise proposed as a great advantage to the public, that if we once discard the system of the Gospel, all religion will of course be banished for ever; and consequently, along with it, those grievous prejudices of education, which under the names of virtue, conscience, honour, justice, and the like, are so apt to disturb the peace of human minds, and the notions whereof are so hard to be eradicated by right reason or freethinking, sometimes during the whole course of our lives.

Here, first, I observe how difficult it is to get rid of a phrase which the world is once grown fond of, although the occasion that first produced it be entirely taken away. For several years past if a man had but an ill-favoured nose, the deep-thinkers of the age would some way or other contrive to impute the cause to the prejudice of his education. From this fountain are said to be derived all our foolish notions of justice, piety, love of our country, all our opinions of God, or a future state, Heaven, Hell, and the like: and there might formerly perhaps have been some pretence for this charge. But so effectual care has been since taken to remove those prejudices, by an entire change in the methods of education, that (with honour I mention it to our polite innovators) the young gentlemen who are now on the scene seem to have not the least tincture left of those infusions, or string of those weeds; and, by consequence, the reason for abolishing nominal Christianity upon that pretext is wholly ceased.

For the rest, it may perhaps admit a controversy, whether the banishing all notions of religion whatsoever, would be convenient for the vulgar. Not that I am in the least of opinion with those who hold religion to have been the invention of politicians to keep the lower part of the world in awe by the fear of invisible powers; unless mankind were then very different from what it is now: for I look upon the mass or body of our people here in England to be as freethinkers, that is to say as staunch unbelievers, as any of the highest rank. But I conceive some scattered notions about a superior power to be of singular use for the common people, as furnishing excellent materials to keep children quiet when they grow peevish, and providing topics of amusement in a tedious winter-night.

Lastly, it is proposed as a singular advantage, that the abolishing of Christianity will very much contribute to the uniting of Protestants, by enlarging the terms of communion so as to take in all sorts of dissenters, who are now shut out of the pale upon account of a few ceremonies which all sides confess to be things indifferent: that this alone will effectually answer the great ends of a scheme for comprehension, by opening a large noble gate at which all bodies may enter; whereas the chaffering with dissenters, and dodging about this or the other ceremony, is but like opening a few wickets, and leaving them at jar, by which no more than one can get in at a time, and that not without stooping, and sideling, and squeezing his body.

To all this I answer, that there is one darling inclination of mankind, which usually affects to be a retainer to religion, although she be neither its parent, its godmother, or its friend; I mean the spirit of opposition that lived long before Christianity, and can easily subsist without it. Let us, for instance, examine wherein the opposition of sectaries among us consists, we shall find Christianity to have no share in it at all. Does the Gospel any where prescribe a starched, squeezed countenance, a stiff, formal gait, a singularity of manners and habit, or any affected modes of speech different from the reasonable part of mankind? Yet, if Christianity did not lend its name to stand in the gap, and to employ or divert these humours, they must of necessity be spent in contraventions to the laws of the land, and disturbance of the public peace. There is a portion of enthusiasm assigned to every nation which, if it hath not proper objects to work on, will burst out and set all into a flame. If the quiet of a state can be bought by only flinging men a few ceremonies to devour, it is a purchase no wise man would refuse. Let the mastiffs amuse themselves about a sheep's skin stuffed with hay, provided it will keep them from worrying the flock. The institution of convents abroad seems in one point a strain of great wisdom, there being few irregularities in human passions, that may not have recourse to vent themselves in some of those orders, which are so many retreats for the speculative, the melancholy, the proud, the silent, the politic and the morose, to spend themselves, and evaporate the noxious particles; for each of whom we in this island are forced to provide a several sect of religion to keep them quiet. And whenever Christianity shall be abolished, the legislature must find some other expedient to employ and entertain them. For what imports it how large a gate you open, if there will be always left a number who place a pride and a merit in refusing to enter?

Having thus considered the most important objections against

Christianity, and the chief advantages proposed by the abolishing thereof, I shall now with equal deference and submission to wiser judgments as before, proceed to mention a few inconveniences that may happen, if the Gospel should be repealed; which perhaps the projectors may not have sufficiently considered.

And first, I am very sensible how much the gentlemen of wit and pleasure are apt to murmur, and be shocked at the sight of so many daggled-tail parsons, who happen to fall in their way, and offend their eyes: but at the same time, these wise reformers do not consider what an advantage and felicity it is for great wits to be always provided with objects of scorn and contempt, in order to exercise and improve their talents, and divert their spleen from falling on each other or on themselves; especially when all this may be done without the least imaginable danger to their persons.

And to urge another argument of a parallel nature: if Christianity were once abolished, how could the free-thinkers, the strong reasoners, and the men of profound learning, be able to find another subject so calculated in all points whereon to display their abilities? What wonderful productions of wit should we be deprived of, from those whose genius by continual practice hath been wholly turned upon raillery and invectives against religion, and would therefore never be able to shine or distinguish themselves upon any other subject. We are daily complaining of the great decline of wit among us, and would we take away the greatest, perhaps the only topic we have left? Who would ever have suspected Asgill for a wit, or Toland for a philosopher, if the inexhaustible stock of Christianity had not been at hand to provide them with materials? What other subject, through all art or nature, could have produced Tindal for a profound author, or furnished him with readers? It is the wise choice of the subject that alone adorns and distinguishes the writer. For, had an hundred such pens as these been employed on the side of religion, they would have immediately sunk into silence and oblivion.

Nor do I think it wholly groundless, or my fears altogether imaginary, that the abolishing of Christianity may perhaps bring the Church in danger, or at least put the senate to the trouble of another securing vote. I desire I may not be mistaken; I am far from presuming to affirm or think that the Church is in danger at present, or as things now stand; but we know not how soon it may be so when the Christian religion is repealed. As plausible as this project seems, there may a dangerous design lurk under it. Nothing can be more notorious, than that the Atheists,

Deists, Socinians, Anti-trinitarians, and other subdivisions of freethinkers, are persons of little zeal for the present ecclesiastical establishment: Their declared opinion is for repealing the Sacramental Test; they are very indifferent with regard to ceremonies; not do they hold the *jus divinum* of Episcopacy. Therefore this may be intended as one politic step towards altering the constitution of the Church established, and setting up Presbytery in the stead, which I leave to be further considered by those at the helm.

In the last place, I think nothing can be more plain, than that by this expedient, we shall run into the evil we chiefly pretend to avoid; and that the abolishment of the Christian religion will be the readiest course we can take to introduce popery. And I am the more inclined to this opinion, because we know it has been the constant practice of the Jesuits to send over emissaries, with instructions to personate themselves members of the several prevailing sects among us. So it is recorded, that they have at sundry times appeared in the guise of Presbyterians, Anabaptists, Independents and Quakers, according as any of these were most in credit; so since the fashion hath been taken up of exploding religion, the popish missionaries have not been wanting to mix with the freethinkers; among whom, Toland, the great oracle of the Anti-Christians is an Irish priest, the son of an Irish priest; and the most learned and ingenious author of a book called *The Rights of the Christian Church*, was in a proper juncture reconciled to the Romish faith, whose true son, as appears by an hundred passages in his treatise, he still continues. Perhaps I could add some others to the number; but the fact is beyond dispute, and the reasoning they proceed by is right: for, supposing Christianity to be extinguished, the people will never be at ease till they find out some other method of worship; which will as infallibly produce superstition, as this will end in popery.

And therefore, if notwithstanding all I have said, it shall still be thought necessary to have a bill brought in for repealing Christianity, I would humbly offer an amendment; that instead of the word *Christianity*, may be put *Religion* in general; which I conceive will much better answer all the good ends proposed by the projectors of it. For, as long as we leave in being a God and his providence, with all the necessary consequences which curious and inquisitive men will be apt to draw from such premises, we do not strike at the root of the evil although we should ever so effectually annihilate the present scheme of the Gospel. For, of what use is freedom of thought, if it will not produce freedom of action, which is the sole end, how remote soever in appearance, of all objections against Christianity? And therefore, the freethinkers consider it as a sort of edifice, wherein all the parts have such a mutual dependence on each other, that if you happen to pull out one single nail, the whole fabric must fall to the ground. This was happily expressed by him who had heard of a text brought for proof of the Trinity, which in an ancient manuscript was differently read; he thereupon immediately took the hint, and by a sudden deduction of a long *sorites*, most logically concluded; Why, if it be as you say, I may safely whore and drink on, and defy the parson. From which, and many the like instances easy to be produced, I think nothing can be more manifest, than that the quarrel is not against any particular points of hard digestion in the Christian system, but against religion in general; which, by laying restraints on human nature, is supposed the great enemy to the freedom of thought and action.

Upon the whole, if it shall still be thought for the benefit of Church and State, that Christianity be abolished, I conceive however, it may be more convenient to defer the execution to a time of peace, and not venture in this conjuncture to disoblige our allies, who, as it falls out, are all Christians, and many of them, by the prejudices of their education, so bigoted as to place a sort of pride in the appellation. If upon being rejected by them, we are to trust to an alliance with the Turk, we shall find ourselves much deceived: for, as he is too remote, and generally engaged in war with the Persian emperor, so his people would be more scandalized at our infidelity than our Christian neighbours. Because the Turks are not only strict observers of religious worship, but what is worse, believe a God; which is more than is required of us even while we preserve the name of Christians.

To conclude: whatever some may think of the great advantages to trade by this favourite scheme, I do very much apprehend that in six months' time after the act is passed for the extirpation of the Gospel, the Bank and East-India Stock may fall at least one *percent*. And since that is fifty times more than ever the wisdom of our age thought fit to venture for the preservation of Christianity, there is no reason we should be at so great a loss, merely for the sake of destroying it.

THE DRAPIER'S
FIRST LETTER

TO THE SHOPKEEPERS, TRADESMEN, FARMERS, AND COMMON PEOPLE OF IRELAND,

Concerning the Brass Halfpence Coined by one William Wood, Hardwareman, with a Design to Have Them Pass in This Kingdom,

Wherein is shown the power of his Patent, the value of the Halfpence, and how far every person may be obliged to take the same in payments, and how to behave himself, in case such an attempt should be made by Wood, or any other person.

(VERY PROPER TO BE KEPT IN EVERY FAMILY)

By M. B. Drapier.

Brethren, Friends, Countrymen, and Fellow-Subjects.

WHAT I intend now to say to you, is, next to your duty to God, and the care of your salvation, of the greatest concern to your selves and your children; your bread and clothing, and every common necessary of life entirely depend upon it. Therefore I do most earnestly exhort you as men, as Christians, as parents, and as lovers of your country, to read this paper with the utmost attention, or get it read to you by others; which that you may do at the less expense, I have ordered the printer to sell it at the lowest rate.

It is a great fault among you, that when a person writes with no other intention than to do you good, you will not be at the pains to read his advices: one copy of this paper may serve a dozen of you, which will be less than a farthing apiece. It is your folly that you have no common or general interest in your view, not even the wisest among you, neither do you know or inquire, or care who are your friends, or who are your enemies.

About four years ago a little book was written, to advise all people to wear the manufactures of this our own dear country. It had no other design, said nothing against the king or parliament, or any person whatsoever; yet the poor printer was prosecuted two years with the utmost violence, and even some weavers themselves, for whose sake it was written, being upon the jury, found him guilty. This would be enough to discourage any man from endeavoring to do you good, when you will either neglect him, or fly in his face for his pains; and when he must expect only danger to himself, and to be fined and imprisoned, perhaps to his ruin.

However, I cannot but warn you once more of the manifest destruction before your eyes, if you do not behave yourselves as you ought.

I will therefore first tell you the plain story of the fact; and then I will lay before you how you ought to act in common prudence, and according to the laws of your country.

The fact is thus, it having been many years since copper half-pence or farthings were last coined in this kingdom, they have been for some time very scarce, and many counterfeits passed about under the name of raps: several applications were made to England, that we might have liberty to coin new ones, as in former times we did; but they did not succeed. At last one Mr. Wood, a mean ordinary man, a hardware dealer, procured a patent under his Majesty's broad seal to coin £ 108,000 in copper for this kingdom; which patent, however, did not oblige anyone here to take them, unless they pleased. Now you must know, that the halfpence and farthings in England pass for very little more than they are worth; and if you should beat them to pieces, and sell them to the brazier, you would not lose much above a penny in a shilling. But Mr. Wood made his halfpence of such base metal, and so much smaller than the English ones, that the brazier would not give you above a penny of good money for a shilling of his; so that this sum of £ 108,000 in good gold and silver, must be given for trash, that will not be worth above eight or nine thousand pounds real value. But this is not the worst; for Mr. Wood, when he pleases, may by stealth send over another £ 108,000 and buy all our goods for eleven parts in twelve under the value. For example, if a hatter sells a dozen of hats for five shillings apiece, which amounts to three pounds, and receives the payment in Mr. Wood's coin, he really receives only the value of five shillings.

Perhaps you will wonder how such an ordinary fellow as this Mr. Wood could have so much interest as to get his Majesty's broad seal for so great a sum of bad money to be sent to this poor country; and that all the nobility and gentry here could not obtain the same favour, and let us make our own halfpence, as we used to do. Now I will make that matter very plain. We are at a great distance from the king's court, and have nobody there to solicit for us, although a great number of lords and squires, whose estates are here, and are our countrymen, spend all their lives and fortunes there. But this same Mr. Wood was able to attend constantly for his own interest; he is an Englishman, and had great friends; and it seems knew very well where to give money to those that would speak to others that could speak to the king, and would tell a fair story. And his Majesty, and perhaps the great lord or lords who advised him, might think it was for our country's good; and so, as the lawyers express it, the king was deceived in his grant, which often happens in all reigns. And I am sure if his Majesty knew that such a patent, if it should take effect according to the desire of Mr. Wood, would utterly ruin this kingdom, which hath given such great proofs of its loyalty, he would immediately recall it, and perhaps show his displeasure to somebody or other: but a word to the wise is enough. Most of you must have heard with what anger our honorable House of Commons received an account of this Wood's patent. There were several fine speeches made upon it, and plain proofs, that it was all a wicked cheat from the bottom to the top; and several smart votes were printed, which that same Wood had the assurance to answer likewise in print; and in so confident a way, as if he were a better man than our whole parliament put together.

This Wood, as soon as his patent was passed, or soon after, sends over a great many barrels of those halfpence to Cork and other seaport towns; and to get them off, offered a hundred pounds in his coin for seventy or eighty in silver: but the collectors of the king's customs very honestly refused to take them, and so did almost everybody else. And since the parliament hath condemned them, and desired the king that they might be stopped, all the kingdom do abominate them.

But Wood is still working underhand to force his halfpence upon us; and if he can by help of his friends in England prevail so far as to get an order that the commissioners and collectors of the king's money shall receive them, and that the army is to be paid with them, then he thinks his work shall be done. And this is the difficulty you will be under in such a case; for the common soldier, when he goes to the market or alehouse, will offer this money; and if it be refused, perhaps he will swagger and hector, and threaten to beat the butcher or alewife, or take the goods by force and throw them the bad halfpence. In this and the like cases, the shopkeeper or victualer, or any other tradesman, has no more to do, than to demand ten times the price of his goods, if it is to be paid in Wood's money: for example, twenty pence of that money for a quart of ale, and so in all things else, and not part with his goods till he gets the money.

For suppose you go to an alehouse with that base money, and

the landlord gives you a quart for four of these halfpence, what must the victualer do? His brewer will not be paid in that coin, or, if the brewer should be such a fool, the farmers will not take it from them for their bere, because they are bound, by their leases, to pay their rents in good and lawful money of England, which this is not, nor of Ireland neither; and the squire, their landlord, will never be so bewitched to take such trash for his land; so that it must certainly stop somewhere or other; and wherever it stops it is the same thing, and we are all undone.

The common weight of these halfpence is between four and five to an ounce; suppose five, then three shillings and fourpence will weigh a pound, and consequently twenty shillings will weigh six pounds butter weight. Now there are many hundred farmers, who pay two hundred pounds a year rent; therefore when one of these farmers comes with his half-year's rent, which is one hundred pounds, it will be at least six hundred pounds weight, which is three horses' load.

If a squire has a mind to come to town to buy clothes and wine and spices for himself and family, or perhaps to pass the winter here, he must bring with him five or six horses loaden with sacks as the farmers bring their corn; and when his lady comes in her coach to our shops, it must be followed by a car loaded with Mr. Wood's money. And I hope we shall have the grace to take it for no more than it is worth.

They say Squire Conolly has sixteen thousand pounds a year; now if he sends for his rent to town, as it is likely he does, he must have two hundred and fifty horses to bring up his half-year's rent, and two or three great cellars in his house for stowage. But what the bankers will do I cannot tell. For I am assured, that some great bankers keep by them forty thousand pounds in ready cash, to answer all payments; which sum in Mr. Wood's money would require twelve hundred horses to carry it.

For my own part, I am already resolved what to do; I have a pretty good shop of Irish stuffs and silks, and instead of taking Mr. Wood's bad copper, I intend to truck with my neighbors the butchers and bakers and brewers, and the rest, goods for goods; and the little gold and silver I have, I will keep by me like my heart's blood till better times, or until I am just ready to starve, and then I will buy Mr. Wood's money, as my father did the brass money in King James's time, who could buy ten pounds of it with a guinea, and I hope to get as much for a pistole, and so purchase bread from those who will be such fools as to sell it me.

These halfpence, if they once pass, will soon be counterfeited, because it may be cheaply done, the stuff is so base. The Dutch likewise will probably do the same thing, and send them over to us to pay for our goods; and Mr. Wood will never be at rest, but coin on: so that in some years we shall have at least five times £ 108,000 of this lumber. Now the current money of this kingdom is not reckoned to be above four hundred thousand pounds in all; and while there is a silver sixpence left, these blood-suckers will never be quiet.

When once the kingdom is reduced to such a condition, I will tell you what must be the end: the gentlemen of estates will all turn off their tenants for want of payment; because, as I told you before, the tenants are obliged by their leases to pay sterling, which is lawful current money of England; then they will turn their own farmers, as too many of them do already; run all into sheep where they can, keeping only such other cattle as are necessary; then they will be their own merchants, and send their wool, and butter, and hides, and linen beyond sea for ready money, and wine, and spices, and silks. They will keep only a few miserable cottagers. The farmers must rob or beg, or leave their country. The shopkeepers in this and every other town must break and starve; for it is the landed man that maintains the merchant, and shopkeeper, and handicraftsman.

But when the squire turns farmer and merchant himself, all the good money he gets from abroad, he will hoard up to send for England, and keep some poor tailor or weaver, and the like, in his own house, who will be glad to get bread at any rate.

I should never have done, if I were to tell you all the miseries that we shall undergo, if we be so foolish and wicked as to take this cursed coin. It would be very hard, if all Ireland should be put into one scale, and this sorry fellow Wood into the other; that Mr. Wood should weigh down this whole kingdom, by which England gets above a million of good money every year clear into their pockets: and that is more than the English do by all the world besides.

But your great comfort is, that as his Majesty's patent does not oblige you to take this money, so the laws have not given the Crown a power of forcing the subject to take what money the king pleases; for then by the same reason we might be bound to take pebblestones, or cockleshells, or stamped leather for current coin, if ever we should happen to live under an ill prince; who might likewise by the same power make a guinea pass for ten pounds, a shilling for twenty shillings, and so on; by which he would in a short time get all the silver and gold of the kingdom into his own hands, and leave us nothing but brass or leather, or what he pleased. Neither is anything reckoned more cruel or oppressive in the French government, than their common practice of calling in all their money after they have sunk it very low, and then coining it anew at a much higher value; which however is not the thousandth part so wicked as this abominable project of Mr. Wood. For the French give their subjects silver for silver, and gold for gold; but this fellow will not so much as give us good brass or copper for our gold and silver, nor even a twelfth part of their worth.

Having said thus much, I will now go on to tell you the judgments of some great lawyers in this matter, whom I fee'd on purpose for your sakes, and got their opinions under their hands, that I might be sure I went upon good grounds.

A famous lawbook, called *The Mirror of Justice,* discoursing of the charters (or laws) ordained by our ancient kings, declares the law to be as follows: "It was ordained that no king of this realm should change or impair the money, or make any other money than of gold or silver, without the assent of all the counties"; that is, as my Lord Coke says, without the assent of parliament.

This book is very ancient, and of great authority for the time in which it was wrote, and with that character is often quoted by that great lawyer my Lord Coke. By the laws of England the several metals are divided into lawful or true metal, and unlawful or false metal: the former comprehends silver or gold, the latter all baser metals. That the former is only to pass in payments, appears by an act of parliament made the twentieth year of Edward the First, called the *Statute Concerning the Passing of Pence;* which I give you here as I got it translated into English; for some of our laws at that time were, as I am told, written in Latin: "Whoever in buying or selling presumeth to refuse a halfpenny or farthing of lawful money, bearing the stamp which it ought to have, let him be seized on as a contemner of the king's majesty, and cast into prison."

By this statute, no person is to be reckoned a contemner of the king's Majesty, and for that crime to be committed to prison, but he who refuseth to accept the king's coin made of lawful metal; by which as I observed before, silver and gold only are intended.

That this is the true construction of the act, appears not only from the plain meaning of the words, but from my Lord Coke's observation upon it. By this act (says he) it appears, that no subject can be forced to take, in buying or selling or other payments, any money made but of lawful metal; that is, of silver or gold.

The law of England gives the king all mines of gold and silver;

but not the mines of other metals: the reason of which prerogative or power, as it is given by my Lord Coke, is because money can be made of gold and silver; but not of other metals.

Pursuant to this opinion, halfpence and farthings were anciently made of silver, which is evident from the act of parliament of Henry the Fourth, chap. 4, whereby it is enacted as follows: "Item, for the great scarcity that is at present within the realm of England of halfpence and farthings of silver, it is ordained and established, that the third part of all the money of silver plate which shall be brought to the bullion, shall be made in halfpence and farthings." This shows that by the words "halfpenny and farthing of lawful money," in that statute concerning the passing of pence, is meant a small coin in halfpence and farthings of silver.

This is farther manifest from the statute of the ninth year of Edward the Third, chap. 3, which enacts "that no sterling halfpenny or farthing be molten for to make vessels, or any other thing, by the goldsmiths, nor others, upon forfeiture of the money so molten" (or melted).

By another act in this king's reign, black money was not to be current in England. And by an act made in the eleventh year of his reign, chap. 5, galley halfpence were not to pass. What kind of coin these were I do not know; but I presume they were made of base metal. And these acts were no new laws, but further declarations of the old laws relating to the coin.

Thus the law stands in relation to coin. Nor is there any example to the contrary, except one in Davis's Reports, who tells us that in the time of Tyrone's rebellion, Queen Elizabeth ordered money of mixed metal to be coined in the Tower of London, and sent over hither for the payment of the army, obliging all people to receive it; and commanding that all silver money should be taken only as bullion; that is, for as much as it weighed. Davis tells us several particulars in this matter too long here to trouble you with, and that the privy council of this kingdom obliged a merchant in England to receive this mixed money for goods transmitted hither.

But this proceeding is rejected by all the best lawyers, as contrary to law, the privy council here having no such legal power. And besides it is to be considered, that the queen was then under great difficulties by a rebellion in this kingdom assisted from Spain. And whatever is done in great exigencies and dangerous times, should never be an example to proceed by in seasons of peace and quietness.

I will now, my dear friends, to save you the trouble, set before you, in short, what the law obliges you to do; and what it does not oblige you to.

First, you are obliged to take all money in payments which is coined by the king, and is of the English standard or weight, provided it be of gold or silver.

Secondly, you are not obliged to take any money which is not of gold or silver; not only the halfpence or farthings of England, but of any other country. And it is merely for convenience, or ease, that you are content to take them; because the custom of coining silver halfpence and farthings hath long been left off; I suppose on account of their being subject to be lost.

Thirdly, much less are we obliged to take those vile halfpence of that same Wood, by which you must lose almost eleven pence in every shilling.

Therefore, my friends, stand to it one and all: refuse this filthy trash. It is no treason to rebel against Mr. Wood. His Majesty in his patent obliges nobody to take these halfpence: our gracious prince hath no such ill advisers about him; or if he had, yet you see the laws have not left it in the king's power to force us to take any coin but what is lawful, of right standard, gold and silver. Therefore you have nothing to fear.

And let me in the next place apply myself particularly to you who are the poorer sort of tradesmen; perhaps you may think you will not be so great losers as the rich, if these halfpence should pass, because you seldom see any silver, and your customers come to your shops or stalls with nothing but brass, which you likewise find hard to be got. But you may take my word, whenever this money gains footing among you, you will be utterly undone. If you carry these halfpence to a shop for tobacco or brandy, or any other thing that you want, the shopkeeper will advance his goods accordingly, or else he must break, and leave the key under the door. Do you think I will sell you a yard of tenpenny stuff for twenty of Mr. Wood's halfpence? No, not under two hundred at least; neither will I be at the trouble of counting, but weigh them in a lump. I will tell you one thing further, that if Mr. Wood's project should take, it will ruin even our beggars; for when I give a beggar a halfpenny, it will quench his thirst, or go a good way to fill his belly; but the twelfth part of a halfpenny will do him no more service than if I should give him three pins out of my sleeve.

In short, these halfpence are like the accursed thing, which as the Scripture tells us, the children of Israel were forbidden to touch. They will run about like the plague and destroy everyone who lays his hands upon them. I have heard scholars talk of a man who told the king that he had invented a way to torment people by putting them into a bull of brass with fire under it, but the prince put the projector first into his own brazen bull to make the experiment. This very much resembles the project of Mr. Wood; and the like of this may possibly be Mr. Wood's fate; that the brass he contrived to torment this kingdom with, may prove his own torment, and his destruction at last.

N.B. The author of this paper is informed by persons, who have made it their business to be exact in their observations on the true value of these halfpence, that any person may expect to get a quart of twopenny ale for thirty-six of them.

I desire that all families may keep this paper carefully by them, to refresh their memories whenever they shall have farther notice of Mr. Wood's halfpence, or any other the like imposture.

F ROM frequently reflecting upon the course and method of educating youth in this and a neighbouring kingdom, with the general success and consequence thereof, I am come to this determination, that education is always the worse in proportion to the wealth and grandeur of the parents; nor do I doubt in the least, that if the whole world were now under the dominion of one monarch (provided I might be allowed to choose where he should fix the seat of his empire) the only son and heir of that monarch, would be the worst educated mortal, that ever was born since the creation; and I doubt, the same proportion will hold through all degrees and titles, from an emperor downwards, to the common gentry.

I do not say that this hath been always the case; for in better times it was directly otherwise, and a scholar may fill half his Greek and Roman shelves with authors of the noblest birth, as well as highest virtue. Nor do I tax all nations at present with this defect, for I know there are some to be excepted, and particularly Scotland, under all the disadvantages of its climate and soil, if that happiness be not rather owing even to those very disadvantages. What is then to be done, if this reflection must fix on two countries, which will be most ready to take offence, and which of all others it will be least prudent or safe to offend?

But there is one circumstance yet more dangerous and lamentable: for if, according to the *postulatum* already laid down, the higher quality any youth is of, he is in greater likelihood to be worse educated, it behoves me to dread, and keep far from the verge of *scandalum magnatum*.

Retracting therefore that hazardous *postulatum*, I shall venture no further at present than to say, that perhaps *some* additional care in educating the sons of nobility and principal gentry might not be ill employed. If this be not delivered with softness enough, I must for the future be silent.

In the mean time, let me ask only two questions which relate to a neighbouring kingdom, from whence the chief among us are descended, and whose manners we most affect to follow. I ask first, how it comes about, that for above sixty years past, the chief conduct of affairs in that kingdom hath been generally placed in the hands of *new-men*, with few exceptions? The noblest blood of England having been shed in the grand Rebellion, many great families became extinct, or supplied only by minors. When the King was restored, very few of those lords remained who began, or at least had improved their education, under the happy reign of King James, or King Charles I., of which lords the two principal were the Marquis of Ormond and the Earl of Southampton. The minors having, during the Rebellion and Usurpation, either received too much tincture of bad principles from those fanatic times, or coming to age at the Restoration, fell into the vices of that dissolute reign.

I date from this era, the corrupt method of education among us, and the consequence thereof, in the necessity the Crown lay under of introducing *new-men* into the chief conduct of public affairs, or to the office of what we now call prime ministers, men of art, knowledge, application and insinuation, merely for want of a supply among the nobility. They were generally (though not always) of good birth, sometimes younger brothers, at other times such, who although inheriting good estates, yet happened to be well educated, and provided with learning. Such under that king, were Hyde, Bridgeman, Clifford, Osborn, Godolphin, Ashley-Cooper; few or none under the short reign of King James II. Under King William; Sommers, Montague, Churchill, Vernon, Boyle, and many others: under the Queen; Harley, St. John, Harcourt, Trevor, who indeed were persons of the best private families, but unadorned with titles. So in the following reign Mr. Robert Walpole was for many years Prime Minister, in which post he still happily continues; his brother Horace is Ambassador Extraordinary to France. Mr. Addison and Mr. Craggs, without the least alliance to support them, have been Secretaries of State.

If the facts have been thus for above sixty years past (whereof I could, with a little further recollection, produce many more instances) I would ask again, how it hath happened, that in a nation plentifully abounding with nobility, so great a share in the most important parts of public management, hath been for so long a period chiefly entrusted to commoners, unless some omissions or defects of the highest import may be charged upon those to whom the care of educating our noble youth hath been committed. For, if there be any difference between human creatures in the point of natural parts, as we usually call them, it should seem that the advantage lies on the side of children born from noble and wealthy parents; the same traditional sloth and luxury which render their bodies weak and effeminate, perhaps refining and giving a freer motion to the spirits, beyond what can be expected from the gross, robust issue of meaner mortals. Add to this, the peculiar advantages which all young noblemen possess by the privileges of their birth, such as a free access to courts, and a deference paid to their persons.

But as my Lord Bacon chargeth it for a fault in princes, that they are impatient to compass ends without giving themselves the trouble of consulting or executing the means, so perhaps it may be the disposition of young nobles, either from the indulgence of parents, tutors and governors, or their own inactivity, that they expect the accomplishments of a good education without the least expense of time or study, to acquire them.

What I said last, I am ready to retract. For the case is infinitely worse; and the very maxims set up to direct modern education, are enough to destroy all the seeds of knowledge, honour, wisdom and virtue among us. The current opinion prevails, that the study of Greek and Latin is loss of time; that the public schools by mingling the sons of noblemen with those of the vulgar engage the former in bad company; that whipping breaks the spirits of lads well born; that universities make young men pedants; that to dance, fence, speak French, and know how to behave your self among great persons of both sexes, comprehends the whole duty of a gentleman.

I cannot but think this wise system of education hath been much cultivated among us by those worthies of the army, who during the last war, returning from Flanders at the close of each campaign, became the dictators of behaviour, dress, and politeness, to all those youngsters who frequent chocolate-coffee-gaming-houses, drawing-rooms, operas, levees and assemblies; where a colonel by his pay, perquisites and plunder, was qualified to outshine many peers of the realm; and by the influence of an exotic habit and demeanor, added to other foreign accomplishments, gave the law to the whole town, and was copied as the standard-pattern of whatever was refined in dress, equipage, conversation, or diversions.

I remember in those times, an admired original of that vocation, sitting in a coffee-house near two gentlemen, whereof one was of the clergy, who were engaged in some discourse that savoured of learning; this officer thought fit to interpose, and professing to deliver the sentiments of his fraternity, as well as

his own (and probably did so of too many among them) turning
to the clergyman, spoke in the following manner, 'D———n me,
Doctor, say what you will, the army is the only school for gentlemen. Do you think my Lord Marlborough beat the French with
Greek and Latin. D———n me, a scholar when ne comes into
good company, what is he but an ass? D———n me, I would be
glad by G-d to see any of your scholars with his nouns, and his
verbs, and his philosophy, and trigonometry, what a figure he
would make at a siege or blockade, reconoitring——D———n
me,' &c. After which he proceeded with a volley of military
terms, less significant, sounding worse, and harder to be understood than any that were ever coined by the commentators upon
Aristotle. I would not here be thought to charge the soldiery
with ignorance and contempt of learning, without allowing exceptions, of which I have known a few; but however, the worse
example, especially in a great majority, will certainly prevail.

I have heard that the late Earl of Oxford in the time of his
ministry never passed by White's Chocolate-House (the common rendezvous of infamous sharpers and noble cullies) without
bestowing a curse upon that famous academy as the bane of half
the English nobility. I have likewise been told another passage
concerning that great minister, which, because it gives a humorous idea of one principal ingredient in modern education, take
as followeth. Le-Sac, the famous French dancing-master, in
great admiration, asked a friend whether it were true that Mr.
Harley was made an Earl and Lord-Treasurer? And finding it
confirmed, said; 'Well, I wonder what the devil the Queen could
see in him; for I attended him two years, and he was the greatest
dunce that ever I taught.'

Another hindrance to good education, and I think the greatest
of any, is that pernicious custom in rich and noble families of
entertaining French tutors in their houses. These wretched
pedagogues are enjoined by the father to take special care that
the boy shall be perfect in his French; by the mother that master
must not walk till he is hot, nor be suffered to play with other
boys, nor be wet in his feet, nor daub his clothes; and to see that
the dancing-master attends constantly and does his duty, she further insists that the child be not kept too long poring on his
book, because he is subject to sore eyes, and of a weakly constitution.

By these methods, the young gentleman is in every article as
fully accomplished at eight years old as at eight and twenty, age
adding only to the growth of his person and his vices; so that if
you should look at him in his boyhood thro' the magnifying end

of a perspective, and in his manhood through the other, it would be impossible to spy any difference; the same airs, the same strut, the same cock of his hat, and posture of his sword (as far as the change of fashions will allow) the same understanding, the same compass of knowledge, with the very same absurdity, impudence, and impertinence of tongue.

He is taught from the nursery that he must inherit a great estate, and hath no need to mind his book, which is a lesson he never forgets to the end of his life. His chief solace is to steal down and play at span-farthing with the page, or young black-a-moor, or little favourite foot-boy, one of which is his principal confident and bosom-friend.

There is one young lord in this town, who, by an unexampled piece of good fortune, was miraculously snatched out of the gulf of ignorance, confined to a public school for a due term of years, well whipped when he deserved it, clad no better than his comrades, and always their play-fellow on the same foot, had no precedence in the school, but what was given him by his merit, and lost it whenever he was negligent. It is well known how many mutinies were bred at this unprecedented treatment, what complaints among his relations, and other great ones of both sexes; that his stockings with silver clocks were ravished from him; that he wore his own hair; that his dress was undistinguished; that he was not fit to appear at a ball or assembly, nor suffered to go to either; and it was with the utmost difficulty that he became qualified for his present removal to the university, where he may probably be farther persecuted, and possibly with success, if the firmness of a governor and his own good dispositions will not preserve him. I confess I cannot but wish he may go on in the way he began, because I have a curiosity to know by so singular an experiment, whether truth, honour, justice, temperance, courage, and good sense, acquired by a school and college education, may not produce a very tolerable lad, although he should happen to fail in one or two of those accomplishments which in the general vogue are held so important to the finishing of a gentleman.

It is true, I have known an academical education to have been exploded in public assemblies; and have heard more than one or two persons of high rank declare they could learn nothing more at Oxford and Cambridge than to drink ale and smoke tobacco; wherein I firmly believed them, and could have added some hundred examples from my own observation in one of those universities; but they all were of young heirs sent thither, only for form; either from schools where they were not suffered by their careful parents to stay above three months in the year, or from under the management of French family-tutors, who yet often attended them in their college, to prevent all possibility of their improvement: but I never yet knew any one person of quality, who followed his studies at the university, and carried away his just proportion of learning, who was not ready upon all occasions to celebrate and defend that course of education, and to prove a patron of learned men.

There is one circumstance in a learned education, which ought to have much weight, even with those who have no learning at all. The books read at schools and colleges are full of incitements to virtue, and discouragements from vice, drawn from the wisest reasons, the strongest motives, and the most influencing examples. Thus, young minds are filled early with an inclination to good, and an abhorrence of evil, both which encrease in them, according to the advances they make in literature; and, although they may be, and too often are, drawn by the temptations of youth and the opportunities of a large fortune into some irregularities when they come forward into the great world, it is ever with reluctance and compunction of mind because their bias to virtue still continues. They may stray sometimes out of infirmity or compliance, but they will soon return to the right road, and keep it always in view. I speak only of those excesses which are too much the attendants of youth and warmer blood; for, as to the points of honour, truth, justice, and other noble gifts of the mind, wherein the temperature of the body hath no concern, they are seldom or never known to be misled.

I have engaged my self very unwarily in too copious a subject for so short a paper. The present scope I would aim at is to prove that some proportion of human knowledge appears requisite to those, who, by their birth or fortune, are called to the making of laws, and in a subordinate way to the execution of them; and that such knowledge is not to be obtained without a miracle under the frequent, corrupt, and sottish methods of educating those who are born to wealth or titles. For I would have it remembered that I do by no means confine these remarks to young persons of noble birth, the same errors running through all families where there is wealth enough to afford that their sons (at least the eldest) may be good for nothing. Why should my son be a scholar, when it is not intended that he should live by his learning? By this rule, if what is commonly said be true, that money answereth all things, why should my son be honest, temperate, just, or charitable, since he hath no intention to depend upon any of these qualities for a maintenance?

When all is done, perhaps upon the whole, the matter is not so

THE INTELLIGENCER

bad as I would make it; and God, who worketh good out of evil, acting only by the ordinary course and rule of Nature, permits this continual circulation of human things for his own unsearchable ends. The father grows rich by avarice, injustice, oppression; he is a tyrant in the neighbourhood over slaves and beggars, whom he calleth his tenants. Why should he desire to have qualities infused into his son, which himself never possessed, or knew, or found the want of in the acquisition of his wealth? The son bred in sloth and idleness, becomes a spendthrift, a cully, a profligate, and goes out of the world a beggar, as his father came in; thus the former is punished for his own sin, as well as for those of the latter. The dunghill having raised a huge mushroom of short duration, is now spread to enrich other men's lands. It is, indeed, of worse consequence where noble families are gone to decay, because their titles and privileges outlive their estates: and politicians tell us that nothing is more dangerous to the public than a numerous nobility without merit or fortune. But even here, God hath likewise prescribed some remedy in the order of Nature, so many great families coming to an end by the sloth, luxury, and abandoned lusts which enervated their breed through every succession, producing gradually a more effeminate race, wholly unfit for propagation.

A MODEST PROPOSAL

FOR

PREVENTING THE CHILDREN OF POOR PEOPLE IN IRELAND FROM BEING A BURDEN TO THEIR PARENTS OR COUNTRY, AND FOR MAKING THEM BENEFICIAL TO THE PUBLIC

I T is a melancholy object to those who walk through this great town, or travel in the country, when they see the streets, the roads and cabin-doors crowded with beggars of the female sex, followed by three, four, or six children, all in rags, and importuning every passenger for an alms. These mothers, instead of being able to work for their honest livelihood, are forced to employ all their time in strolling, to beg sustenance for their helpless infants, who, as they grow up, either turn thieves for want of work, or leave their dear native country to fight for the Pretender in Spain, or sell themselves to the Barbadoes.

I think it is agreed by all parties that this prodigious number of children, in the arms, or on the backs, or at the heels of their mothers, and frequently of their fathers, is in the present deplorable state of the kingdom a very great additional grievance; and therefore whoever could find out a fair, cheap, and easy method of making these children sound and useful members of the commonwealth would deserve so well of the public as to have his statue set up for a preserver of the nation.

But my intention is very far from being confined to provide only for the children of professed beggars; it is of a much greater extent, and shall take in the whole number of infants at a certain age who are born of parents in effect as little able to support them as those who demand our charity in the streets.

As to my own part, having turned my thoughts for many years upon this important subject, and maturely weighed the several schemes of other projectors, I have always found them grossly mistaken in their computation. It is true a child just dropped from its dam may be supported by her milk for a solar year with little other nourishment, at most not above the value of two shillings, which the mother may certainly get, or the value in scraps, by her lawful occupation of begging, and it is exactly at one year old that I propose to provide for them, in such a manner as, instead of being a charge upon their parents, or the parish, or wanting food and raiment for the rest of their lives, they shall, on the contrary, contribute to the feeding and partly to the clothing of many thousands.

There is likewise another great advantage in my scheme, that it will prevent those voluntary abortions, and that horrid practice of women murdering their bastard children, alas, too frequent among us, sacrificing the poor innocent babes, I doubt, more to avoid the expense than the shame, which would move tears and pity in the most savage and inhuman breast.

The number of souls in Ireland being usually reckoned one million and a half, of these I calculate there may be about two hundred thousand couples whose wives are breeders, from which number I subtract thirty thousand couples who are able to maintain their own children, although I apprehend there cannot be so many under the present distresses of the kingdom, but this being granted, there will remain an hundred and seventy thousand breeders. I again subtract fifty thousand for those women who miscarry, or whose children die by accident or disease within the year. There only remain an hundred and twenty thousand children of poor parents annually born: the question therefore is, how this number shall be reared, and provided for, which, as I have already said, under the present situation of affairs is utterly impossible by all the methods hitherto proposed, for we can neither employ them in handicraft or agriculture; we neither build houses (I mean in the country), nor cultivate land: they can very seldom pick up a livelihood by stealing until they arrive at six years old, except where they are of towardly parts, although I confess they learn the rudiments much earlier, during which time they can however be properly looked upon only as probationers, as I have been informed by a principal gentleman in the County of Cavan, who protested to me that he never knew above one or two instances under the age of six, even in a part of the kingdom so renowned for the quickest proficiency in that art.

I am assured by our merchants that a boy or a girl before twelve years old, is no saleable commodity, and even when they come to this age, they will not yield above three pounds, or three pounds and half-a-crown at most on the Exchange, which cannot turn to account either to the parents or the kingdom, the charge of nutriment and rags having been at least four times that value.

I shall now therefore humbly propose my own thoughts, which I hope will not be liable to the least objection.

I have been assured by a very knowing American of my acquaintance in London, that a young healthy child well nursed is at a year old a most delicious, nourishing and wholesome food, whether stewed, roasted, baked, or boiled, and I make no doubt that it will equally serve in a fricassee, or a ragout.

I do therefore humbly offer it to public consideration, that of the hundred and twenty thousand children already computed, twenty thousand may be reserved for breed, whereof only one fourth part to be males, which is more than we allow to sheep, black-cattle, or swine, and my reason is that these children are seldom the fruits of marriage, a circumstance not much regarded by our savages, therefore one male will be sufficient to serve four females. That the remaining hundred thousand may at a year old be offered in sale to the persons of quality, and fortune, through the kingdom, always advising the mother to let them suck plentifully in the last month, so as to render them plump, and fat for a good table. A child will make two dishes at an entertainment for friends, and when the family dines alone, the fore or hind quarter will make a reasonable dish, and seasoned with a little pepper or salt will be very good boiled on the fourth day, especially in winter.

I have reckoned upon a medium, that a child just born will weigh twelve pounds, and in a solar year if tolerably nursed increaseth to twenty-eight pounds.

I grant this food will be somewhat dear, and therefore very proper for landlords, who, as they have already devoured most of the parents, seem to have the best title to the children.

Infant's flesh will be in season throughout the year, but more plentiful in March, and a little before and after, for we are told by a grave [1] author, an eminent French physician, that fish being a prolific diet, there are more children born in Roman Catholic countries about nine months after Lent than at any other season; therefore reckoning a year after Lent, the markets will be more glutted than usual, because the number of Popish infants is at least three to one in this kingdom, and therefore it will have one other collateral advantage by lessening the number of Papists among us.

I have already computed the charge of nursing a beggar's child (in which list I reckon all cottagers, labourers, and four-fifths of the farmers) to be about two shillings *per annum*, rags

[1] Rabelais.

included, and I believe no gentleman would repine to give ten shillings for the carcass of a good fat child, which, as I have said, will make four dishes of excellent nutritive meat, when he hath only some particular friend or his own family to dine with him. Thus the Squire will learn to be a good landlord and grow popular among his tenants, the mother will have eight shillings net profit, and be fit for work until she produces another child.

Those who are more thrifty (as I must confess the times require) may flay the carcass; the skin of which artificially dressed, will make admirable gloves for ladies, and summer boots for fine gentlemen.

As to our city of Dublin, shambles may be appointed for this purpose, in the most convenient parts of it, and butchers we may be assured will not be wanting, although I rather recommend buying the children alive, and dressing them hot from the knife, as we do roasting pigs.

A very worthy person, a true lover of his country, and whose virtues I highly esteem, was lately pleased, in discoursing on this matter to offer a refinement upon my scheme. He said that many gentlemen of this kingdom, having of late destroyed their deer, he conceived that the want of venison might be well supplied by the bodies of young lads and maidens, not exceeding fourteen years of age, nor under twelve, so great a number of both sexes in every county being now ready to starve, for want of work and service: and these to be disposed of by their parents if alive, or otherwise by their nearest relations. But with due deference to so excellent a friend, and so deserving a patriot, I cannot be altogether in his sentiments. For as to the males, my American acquaintance assured me from frequent experience that their flesh was generally tough and lean, like that of our schoolboys, by continual exercise, and their taste disagreeable, and to fatten them would not answer the charge. Then as to the females, it would, I think with humble submission, be a loss to the public, because they soon would become breeders themselves: and besides, it is not improbable that some scrupulous people might be apt to censure such a practice (although indeed very unjustly) as a little bordering upon cruelty, which I confess, hath always been with me the strongest objection against any project, howsoever well intended.

But in order to justify my friend, he confessed that this expedient was put into his head by the famous Psalmanazar, a native of the island Formosa, who came from thence to London, above twenty years ago, and in conversation told my friend that in his country when any young person happened to be put to death, the executioner sold the carcass to persons of quality, as a prime dainty, and that, in his time, the body of a plump girl of fifteen, who was crucified for an attempt to poison the emperor, was sold to his Imperial Majesty's Prime Minister of State, and other great Mandarins of the Court, in joints from the gibbet, at four hundred crowns. Neither indeed can I deny that if the same use were made of several plump young girls in this town who, without one single groat to their fortunes, cannot stir abroad without a chair, and appear at the playhouse and assemblies in foreign fineries, which they never will pay for, the kingdom would not be the worse.

Some persons of a desponding spirit are in great concern about that vast number of poor people, who are aged, diseased, or maimed, and I have been desired to employ my thoughts what course may be taken to ease the nation of so grievous an encumbrance. But I am not in the least pain upon that matter, because it is very well known that they are every day dying, and rotting, by cold, and famine, and filth, and vermin, as fast as can be reasonably expected. And as to the younger labourers they are now in almost as hopeful a condition. They cannot get work, and consequently pine away from want of nourishment, to a degree that if at any time they are accidentally hired to common labour, they have not strength to perform it; and thus the country and themselves are in a fair way of being soon delivered from the evils to come.

I have too long digressed, and therefore shall return to my subject. I think the advantages by the proposal which I have made are obvious and many, as well as of the highest importance.

For first, as I have already observed, it would greatly lessen the number of Papists, with whom we are yearly over-run, being the principal breeders of the nation, as well as our most dangerous enemies, and who stay at home on purpose with a design to deliver the kingdom to the Pretender, hoping to take their advantage by the absence of so many good Protestants, who have chosen rather to leave their country than stay at home and pay tithes against their conscience to an idolatrous Episcopal curate.

Secondly, the poorer tenants will have something valuable of their own, which by law may be made liable to distress, and help to pay their landlord's rent, their corn and cattle being already seized, and money a thing unknown.

Thirdly, whereas the maintenance of an hundred thousand children, from two years old, and upwards, cannot be computed at less than ten shillings a piece *per annum*, the nation's stock will be thereby increased fifty thousand pounds *per annum*, besides the profit of a new dish, introduced to the tables of all gentlemen of fortune in the kingdom, who have any refinement in taste, and the money will circulate among ourselves, the goods being entirely of our own growth and manufacture.

Fourthly, the constant breeders, besides the gain of eight shillings sterling *per annum*, by the sale of their children, will be rid of the charge of maintaining them after the first year.

Fifthly, this food would likewise bring great custom to taverns, where the vintners will certainly be so prudent as to procure the best receipts for dressing it to perfection, and consequently have their houses frequented by all the fine gentlemen, who justly value themselves upon their knowledge in good eating; and a skilful cook, who understands how to oblige his guests, will contrive to make it as expensive as they please.

Sixthly, this would be a great inducement to marriage, which all wise nations have either encouraged by rewards, or enforced by laws and penalties. It would increase the care and tenderness of mothers towards their children, when they were sure of a settlement for life, to the poor babes, provided in some sort by the public to their annual profit instead of expense. We should soon see an honest emulation among the married women, which of them could bring the fattest child to the market. Men would become as fond of their wives, during the time of their pregnancy, as they are now of their mares in foal, their cows in calf, or sows when they are ready to farrow, nor offer to beat or kick them (as it is too frequent a practice) for fear of a miscarriage.

Many other advantages might be enumerated. For instance, the addition of some thousand carcasses in our exportation of barrelled beef; the propagation of swine's flesh, and improvement in the art of making good bacon, so much wanted among us by the great destruction of pigs, too frequent at our tables, are no way comparable in taste or magnificence to a well-grown, fat yearling child, which roasted whole will make a considerable figure at a Lord Mayor's feast, or any other public entertainment. But this and many others I omit, being studious of brevity.

Supposing that one thousand families in this city would be constant customers for infants flesh, besides others who might have it at merry meetings, particularly weddings and christenings; I compute that Dublin would take off annually about twenty thousand carcasses, and the rest of the kingdom (where probably they will be sold somewhat cheaper) the remaining eighty thousand.

I can think of no one objection that will possibly be raised against this proposal, unless it should be urged that the number of people will be thereby much lessened in the kingdom. This I freely own, and it was indeed one principal design in offering it to the world. I desire the reader will observe, that I calculate my remedy *for this one individual Kingdom of* Ireland, *and for no other that ever was, is, or, I think, ever can be upon earth.* Therefore let no man talk to me of other expedients: *Of taxing our absentees at five shillings a pound: Of using neither clothes, nor household furniture, except what is of our own growth and manufacture: Of utterly rejecting the materials and instruments that promote foreign luxury: Of curing the expensiveness of pride, vanity, idleness, and gaming in our women: Of introducing a vein of parsimony, prudence, and temperance: Of learning to love our country, wherein we differ even from* Laplanders, *and the inhabitants of* Topinamboo: *Of quitting our animosities and factions, nor act any longer like the* Jews, *who were murdering one another at the very moment their city was taken: Of being a little cautious not to sell our country and consciences for nothing: Of teaching landlords to have at least one degree of mercy towards their tenants.* Lastly, *of putting a spirit of honesty, industry, and skill into our shopkeepers, who, if a resolution could now be taken to buy only our native goods, would immediately unite to cheat and exact upon us in the price, the measure and the goodness, nor could ever yet be brought to make one fair proposal of just dealing, though often and earnestly invited to it.*

Therefore I repeat, let no man talk to me of these and the like expedients, till he hath at least a glimpse of hope that there will ever be some hearty and sincere attempt to put them in practice.

But as to myself, having been wearied out for many years with offering vain, idle, visionary thoughts, and at length utterly despairing of success, I fortunately fell upon this proposal, which as it is wholly new, so it hath something solid and real, of no expense and little trouble, full in our own power, and whereby we can incur no danger in disobliging England. For this kind of commodity will not bear exportation, the flesh being of too tender a consistence to admit a long continuance in salt, *although perhaps I could name a country which would be glad to eat up our whole nation without it.*

After all I am not so violently bent upon my own opinion as to reject any offer, proposed by wise men, which shall be found equally innocent, cheap, easy and effectual. But before something of that kind shall be advanced in contradiction to my scheme, and offering a better, I desire the author, or authors, will be pleased maturely to consider two points. First, as things now stand, how they will be able to find food and raiment for a hundred thousand useless mouths and backs? And secondly, there being a round million of creatures in human figure, throughout this kingdom, whose whole subsistence put into a common stock would leave them in debt two millions of pounds sterling; adding those who are beggars by profession, to the bulk of farmers, cottagers, and labourers with their wives and children, who are beggars in effect; I desire those politicians who dislike my overture, and may perhaps be so bold to attempt an answer, that they will first ask the parents of these mortals whether they would not at this day think it a great happiness to have been sold for food at a year old, in the manner I prescribe, and thereby have avoided such a perpetual scene of misfortunes as they have since gone through, by the oppression of landlords, the impossibility of paying rent without money or trade, the want of common sustenance, with neither house nor clothes to cover them from the inclemencies of weather, and the most inevitable prospect of entailing the like, or greater miseries upon their breed for ever.

I profess in the sincerity of my heart that I have not the least personal interest in endeavouring to promote this necessary work, having no other motive than the *public good of my country, by advancing our trade, providing for infants, relieving the poor, and giving some pleasure to the rich.* I have no children by which I can propose to get a single penny; the youngest being nine years old, and my wife past child-bearing.

POEMS

To Their Excellencies The Lords Justices of Ireland.
THE HUMBLE PETITION OF FRANCES HARRIS,
WHO MUST STARVE, AND DIE A MAID IF IT MISCARRIES.
Anno. 1700.

Humbly sheweth.
That I went to warm my self in Lady Betty's chamber, because
    I was cold,
And I had in a purse, seven pound, four shillings and six pence,
    besides farthings, in money, and gold;
So because I had been buying things for my Lady last night,
I was resolved to tell my money, to see if it was right:
Now you must know, because my trunk has a very bad lock,
Therefore all the money I have, which, *God* knows, is a very
    small stock,
I keep in a pocket ty'd about my middle, next my smock.
So when I went to put up my purse, as *God* would have it, my
    smock was unript,
And, instead of putting it into my pocket, down it slipt:
Then the bell rung, and I went down to put my Lady to bed,
And, *God* knows, I thought my money was as safe as my maiden-
    head.
So when I came up again, I found my pocket feel very light,
But when I search'd, and miss'd my purse, *Lord!* I thought I
    should have sunk outright:
Lord! Madam, says Mary, how d'ye do? Indeed, says I, never
    worse;
But pray, Mary, can you tell what I have done with my purse!
Lord help me, said Mary, I never stirr'd out of this place!
Nay, said I, I had it in Lady Betty's chamber, that's a plain case.
So Mary got me to bed, and cover'd me up warm,

However, she stole away my garters, that I might do my self no
    harm:
So I tumbl'd and toss'd all night, as you may very well think,
But hardly ever set my eyes together, or slept a wink.
So I was a-dream'd, methought, that we went and search'd the
    folks round,
And in a corner of Mrs. Dukes's box, ty'd in a rag, the money
    was found.
So next morning we told Whittle, and he fell a-swearing;
Then my dame Wadgar came, and she, you know, is thick of
    hearing;
Dame, said I, as loud as I could bawl, do you know what a loss I
    have had?
Nay, said she, my Lord Collway's folks are all very sad,
For my Lord Dromedary comes a Tuesday without fail;
Pugh! said I, but that's not the business that I ail.
Says Cary, says he, I have been a servant this five and twenty
    years, come spring,
And in all the places I liv'd, I never heard of such a thing.
Yes, says the steward, I remember when I was at my Lady
    Shrewsbury's,
Such a thing as this happen'd, just about the time of goosberries.
So I went to the party suspected, and I found her full of grief;
(Now you must know, of all things in the world, I hate a thief.)
However, I was resolv'd to bring the discourse slily about,
Mrs. Dukes, said I, here's an ugly accident has happen'd out;
'Tis not that I value the money three skips of a louse;
But the thing I stand upon, is the credit of the House;
'Tis true, seven pound, four shillings, and six pence, makes a
    great hole in my wages,
Besides, as they say, service is no inheritance in these ages.
Now, Mrs. Dukes, you know, and every body understands,
That tho' 'tis hard to judge, yet money can't go without hands.
The *devil* take me, said she (blessing her self,) if I ever saw't!
So she roar'd like a Bedlam, as tho' I had call'd her all to naught;
So you know, what could I say to her any more,
I e'en left her, and came away as wise as I was before.
Well: but then they would have had me gone to the cunning
    man;
No, said I, 'tis the same thing, the chaplain will be here anon.
So the chaplain came in; now the servants say, he is my sweet-
    heart,
Because he's always in my chamber, and I always take his part;
So, as the devil would have it, before I was aware, out I blunder'd,

Parson, said I, can you cast a nativity, when a body's plunder'd?
(Now you must know, he hates to be call'd *Parson*, like the
    devil.)
Truly, says he, Mrs. Nab, it might become you to be more civil:
If your money be gone, as a learned divine says, d'ye see,
You are no *text* for my handling, so take that from me:
I was never taken for a conjurer before, I'd have you to know.
Lord, said I, don't be angry, I'm sure I never thought you so;
You know, I honour the cloth, I design to be a parson's wife,
I never took one in your coat for a conjurer in all my life.
With that, he twisted his girdle at me like a rope, as who should
    say,
Now you may go hang your self for me, and so went away.
Well; I thought I should have swoon'd; *Lord*, said I, what shall
    I do?
I have lost my money, and shall lose my true-love too.
Then my Lord call'd me; Harry, said my Lord, don't cry,
I'll give something towards thy loss; and says my Lady, so will I.
Oh but, said I, what if after all the chaplain won't *come to?*
For that, he said (an't please your Excellencies) I must petition
    you.

The premises tenderly consider'd, I desire your Excellencies
    protection,
And that I may have a share in next Sunday's collection:
And over and above, that I may have your Excellencies letter,
With an order for the chaplain aforesaid; or instead of him, a
    better:
And then your poor petitioner, both night and day,
Or the chaplain (for 'tis his trade) as in duty bound, shall ever
    pray.

A DESCRIPTION OF THE MORNING

1709

Now hardly here and there an hackney-coach
Appearing, show'd the ruddy morn's approach.
Now Betty from her master's bed had flown,
And softly stole to discompose her own.
The slipshod prentice from his master's door,
Had par'd the dirt, and sprinkled round the floor.
Now Moll had whirl'd her mop with dext'rous airs,
Prepar'd to scrub the entry and the stairs.

The youth with broomy stumps began to trace
The kennel-edge, where wheels had worn the place.
The small-coal man was heard with cadence deep,
'Till drown'd in shriller notes of chimney-sweep,
Duns at his lordship's gate began to meet,
And brickdust Moll had scream'd through half the street.
The turnkey now his flock returning sees,
Duly let out a-nights to steal for fees:
The watchful bailiffs take their silent stands;
And school-boys lag with satchels in their hands.

A DESCRIPTION OF A CITY SHOWER

[In Imitation of Virgil's Georgics]

1710

Careful observers may foretell the hour
(By sure prognostics) when to dread a show'r:
While rain depends, the pensive cat gives o'er
Her frolics, and pursues her tail no more.
Returning home at night, you'll find the sink
Strike your offended sense with double stink.
If you be wise, then go not far to dine,
You'll spend in coach-hire more than save in wine.
A coming show'r your shooting corns presage,
Old aches throb, your hollow tooth will rage.
Sauntring in coffee-house is Dulman seen;
He damns the climate, and complains of spleen.

Meanwhile the South rising with dabbled wings,
A sable cloud a-thwart the welkin flings,
That swill'd more liquor than it could contain,
And like a drunkard gives it up again.
Brisk Susan whips her linen from the rope,
While the first drizzling show'r is borne aslope,
Such is that sprinkling which some careless quean
Flirts on you from her mop, but not so clean.
You fly, invoke the gods; then turning, stop
To rail; she singing, still whirls on her mop.
Not yet, the dust had shunn'd th' unequal strife,
But aided by the wind, fought still for life;
And wafted with its foe by violent gust,
'Twas doubtful which was rain, and which was dust.
Ah! where must needy poet seek for aid,
When dust and rain at once his coat invade;

His only coat! where dust confus'd with rain,
Roughen the nap, and leave a mingled stain.

   Now in contiguous drops the flood comes down,
Threat'ning with deluge this *devoted* town.
To shops in crowds the daggled females fly,
Pretend to cheapen goods, but nothing buy.
The Templar spruce, while ev'ry spout's a-broach,
Stays till 'tis fair, yet seems to call a coach.
The tuck'd-up sempstress walks with hasty strides,
While streams run down her oil'd umbrella's sides.
Here various kinds by various fortunes led,
Commence acquaintance underneath a shed.
Triumphant Tories, and desponding Whigs,
Forget their feuds, and join to save their wigs.
Box'd in a chair the beau impatient sits,
While spouts run clatt'ring o'er the roof by fits;
And ever and anon with frightful din
The leather sounds, he trembles from within.
So when Troy chair-men bore the wooden steed,
Pregnant with Greeks impatient to be freed,
(Those bully Greeks, who, as the moderns do,
Instead of paying chair-men, run them thro.)
Laocoon struck the outside with his spear,
And each imprison'd hero quaked for fear.

   Now from all parts the swelling kennels flow,
And bear their trophies with them as they go:
Filth of all hues and odours seem to tell
What street they sail'd from, by their sight and smell.
They, as each torrent drives, with rapid force
From Smithfield, or St. Pulchre's shape their course,
And in huge confluent join at Snow-hill ridge,
Fall from the conduit prone to Holborn-bridge.
Sweepings from butchers' stalls, dung, guts, and blood,
Drown'd puppies, stinking sprats, all drench'd in mud,
Dead cats and turnip-tops come tumbling down the flood.

STELLA'S BIRTHDAY

[1718/9]

Stella this day is thirty-four,
(We shan't dispute a year or more)
However Stella, be not troubled,
Although thy size and years are doubled,

Since first I saw thee at sixteen
The brightest virgin of the green,
So little is thy form declin'd;
Made up so largely in thy mind.

   Oh, would it please the gods, to split
Thy beauty, size, and years, and wit,
No age could furnish out a pair
Of nymphs so graceful, wise, and fair
With half the lustre of your eyes,
With half your wit, your years, and size.
And then, before it grew too late,
How should I beg of gentle Fate,
(That either nymph might have her swain)
To split my worship too in twain.

PHYLLIS, OR, THE PROGRESS OF LOVE

1719

Desponding Phyllis was endu'd
With ev'ry talent of a prude;
She trembled when a man drew near;
Salute her, and she turn'd her ear;
If o'er against her you were plac'd,
She durst not look above your waist:
She'd rather take you to her bed
Than let you see her dress her head;
In church you heard her thro' the crowd,
Repeat the Absolution loud;
In church, secure behind her fan,
She durst behold that monster, *man*;
There practis'd how to place her head,
And bit her lips to make them red;
Or, on the mat devoutly kneeling
Would lift her eyes up to the ceiling,
And heave her bosom unaware
For neighb'ring beaux to see it bare.

   At length a lucky lover came,
And found admittance from the dame.
Suppose all parties now agreed,
The writings drawn, the lawyer fee'd,

The vicar and the ring bespoke;
Guess how could such a match be broke.
See then what mortals place their bliss in!
Next morn, betimes, the bride was missing.
The mother scream'd, the father chid;
Where can this idle wench be hid?
No news of Phil! The bridegroom came,
And thought his bride had skulk'd for shame,
Because her father us'd to say,
The girl had such a bashful way.

Now John the butler must be sent,
To learn the way that Phyllis went.
The groom was wish'd to saddle Crop;
For John must neither light nor stop,
But find her wheresoe'er she fled,
And bring her back, alive or dead.

See here again, the devil to do;
For, truly, John was missing too.
The horse and pillion both were gone;
Phyllis, it seems, was fled with John.

Old Madam, who went up to find
What papers Phil had left behind,
A letter on the toilet sees,
To my much honour'd father — these:
('Tis always done, romances tell us,
When daughters run away with fellows)
Fill'd with the choicest common-places,
By others us'd in the like cases;
'That, long ago, a fortune-teller
Exactly said what now befell her,
And in a glass had made her see
A serving-man of low degree.
It was her fate; must be forgiven;
For marriages are made in heaven:
His pardon begg'd, but to be plain,
She'd do't if 'twere to do again.
Thank God, 'twas neither shame nor sin,
For John was come of honest kin.
Love never thinks of rich and poor,
She'd beg with John from door to door.

Forgive her, if it be a crime,
She'll never do't another time.
She ne'er before in all her life
Once disobey'd him, maid nor wife.
One argument she summ'd up all in,
The thing was done, and past recalling;
And therefore hop'd she should recover
His favour when his passion's over.
She valued not what others thought her,
And was — his most obedient daughter.'

Fair maidens all, attend the Muse,
Who now the wand'ring pair pursues.
Away they rode in homely sort,
Their journey long, their money short;
The loving couple well bemir'd;
The horse and both the riders tir'd;
Their victuals bad, their lodging worse;
Phil cry'd, and John began to curse;
Phil wish'd that she had strained a limb
When first she ventur'd out with him;
John wish'd that he had broke a leg,
When first for her he quitted Peg.

But what adventures more befell 'um,
The Muse hath now no time to tell 'um;
How Johnny wheedled, threatened, fawn'd,
Till Phyllis all her trinkets pawn'd;
How oft she broke her marriage vows
In kindness, to maintain her spouse,
Till swains unwholesome spoil'd the trade,
For now the surgeon must be pay'd,
To whom those perquisites are gone,
In Christian justice due to John.

When food and raiment now grew scarce,
Fate put a period to the farce,
And with exact poetic justice;
For John is landlord, Phyllis hostess;
They keep, at Staines, the Old Blue Boar,
Are cat and dog, and rogue and whore.

A SATIRICAL ELEGY

On the Death of a Late Famous General

1722

His Grace! impossible! what, dead!
Of old age too, and in his bed!
And could that mighty warrior fall?
And so inglorious, after all!
Well, since he's gone, no matter how,
The last loud trump must wake him now;
And, trust me, as the noise grows stronger,
He'd wish to sleep a little longer.
And could he be indeed so old
As by the newspapers we're told?
Threescore, I think, is pretty high;
'Twas time in conscience he should die.
This world he cumber'd long enough;
He burnt his candle to the snuff;
And that's the reason, some folks think,
He left behind so great a st– –k.
Behold his funeral appears,
Nor widow's sighs, nor orphan's tears,
Wont at such times each heart to pierce,
Attend the progress of his hearse.
And what of that, his friends may say,
He had those honours in his day.
True to his profit and his pride,
He made them weep before he died.

Come hither, all ye empty things,
Ye bubbles rais'd by breath of kings;
Who float upon the tide of state,
Come hither, and behold your fate.
Let pride be taught by this rebuke,
How very mean a thing's a duke;
From all his ill-got honours flung,
Turn'd to that dirt from whence he sprung.

STELLA'S BIRTHDAY

March 13, 1726/7

This day, whate'er the Fates decree,
Shall still be kept with joy by me:

This day then, let us not be told,
That you are sick, and I grown old,
Nor think on our approaching ills,
And talk of spectacles and pills;
To-morrow will be time enough
To hear such mortifying stuff.
Yet, since from reason may be brought
A better and more pleasing thought,
Which can in spite of all decays,
Support a few remaining days:
From not the gravest of divines,
Accept for once some serious lines.

Although we now can form no more
Long schemes of life, as heretofore;
Yet you, while time is running fast,
Can look with joy on what is past.

Were future happiness and pain,
A mere contrivance of the brain,
As atheists argue, to entice,
And fit their proselytes for vice;
(The only comfort they propose,
To have companions in their woes),
Grant this the case, yet sure 'tis hard,
That virtue, styled its own reward,
And by all sages understood
To be the chief of human good,
Should acting, die, nor leave behind
Some lasting pleasure in the mind,
Which by remembrance will assuage,
Grief, sickness, poverty, and age;
And strongly shoot a radiant dart,
To shine through life's declining part.

Say, Stella, feel you no content,
Reflecting on a life well spent?
Your skilful hand employ'd to save
Despairing wretches from the grave;
And then supporting with your store,
Those whom you dragg'd from death before:
So Providence on mortals waits,
Preserving what it first creates,

Your gen'rous boldness to defend
An innocent and absent friend;
That courage which can make you just
To merit humbled in the dust:
The detestation you express
For vice in all its glitt'ring dress;
That patience under tort'ring pain,
Where stubborn Stoics would complain.

Must these like empty shadows pass,
Or forms reflected from a glass?
Or mere chimaeras in the mind,
That fly, and leave no marks behind?
Does not the body thrive and grow
By food of twenty years ago?
And, had it not been still supplied,
It must a thousand times have died.
Then, who with reason can maintain,
That no effects of food remain?
And, is not virtue in mankind
The nutriment that feeds the mind?
Upheld by each good action past,
And still continued by the last?
Then, who with reason can pretend,
That all effects of virtue end?

Believe me Stella, when you show
That true contempt for things below,
Nor prize your life for other ends
Than merely to oblige your friends;
Your former actions claim their part,
And join to fortify your heart.
For Virtue in her daily race,
Like Janus, bears a double face;
Looks back with joy where she has gone,
And therefore goes with courage on.
She at your sickly couch will wait,
And guide you to a better state.

Oh then, whatever heav'n intends,
Take pity on your pitying friends;
Nor let your ills affect your mind,
To fancy they can be unkind.

Me, surely me, you ought to spare,
Who gladly would your suff'rings share;
Or give my scrap of life to you,
And think it far beneath your due;
You, to whose care so oft I owe,
That I'm alive to tell you so.

VERSES ON THE DEATH OF DR. SWIFT, D.S.P.D.

Occasioned by reading a Maxim in Rochefoucault

*Dans l'adversité de nos meilleurs amis nous trouvons quelque chose,
qui ne nous deplaist pas.*
In the adversity of our best friends, we find something that doth not
displease us.

Written by Himself, November 1731

As Rochefoucault his maxims drew
From nature, I believe 'em true:
They argue no corrupted mind
In him; the fault is in mankind.

This maxim more than all the rest
Is thought too base for human breast;
"In all distresses of our friends
We first consult our private ends,
While nature kindly bent to ease us,
Points out some circumstance to please us."

If this perhaps your patience move
Let reason and experience prove.

We all behold with envious eyes,
Our equal rais'd above our size;
Who wou'd not at a crowded show
Stand high himself, keep others low?
I love my friend as well as you,
But would not have him stop my view;
Then let me have the higher post;
I ask but for an inch at most.

If in a battle you should find,
One, whom you love of all mankind,
Had some heroic action done,
A champion kill'd or trophy won;

Rather than thus be over-topt,
Would you not wish his laurels cropt?

Dear honest Ned is in the gout,
Lies rackt with pain, and you without:
How patientiy you hear him groan!
How glad the case is not your own!

What poet would not grieve to see,
His brethren write as well as he?
But rather than they should excel,
He'd wish his rivals all in hell.

Her end when emulation misses,
She turns to envy, stings and hisses:
The strongest friendship yields to pride,
Unless the odds be on our side.

Vain human kind! Fantastic race!
Thy various follies, who can trace?
Self-love, ambition, envy, pride,
Their empire in our hearts divide:
Give others riches, power, and station,
'Tis all on me an usurpation.
I have no title to aspire;
Yet, when you sink, I seem the higher.
In Pope, I cannot read a line,
But with a sigh, I wish it mine:
When he can in one couplet fix
More sense than I can do in six:
It gives me such a jealous fit,
I cry, pox take him, and his wit.

Why must I be outdone by Gay,
In my own hum'rous biting way?

Arbuthnot is no more my friend,
Who dares to irony pretend;
Which I was born to introduce,
Refin'd it first, and shew'd its use.

St. John, as well as Pultney knows,
That I had some repute for prose;

And till they drove me out of date,
Could maul a minister of state:
If they have mortify'd my pride,
And made me throw my pen aside;
If with such talents heav'n hath blest 'em
Have I not reason to destest 'em?

To all my foes, dear fortune, send
Thy gifts, but never to my friend:
I tamely can endure the first,
But, this with envy makes me burst.

Thus much may serve by way of proem,
Proceed we therefore to our poem.

The time is not remote, when I
Must by the course of nature die:
When I foresee my special friends,
Will try to find their private ends:
Tho' it is hardly understood,
Which way my death can do them good,
Yet, thus methinks, I hear 'em speak;
"See, how the Dean begins to break:
Poor gentleman, he droops apace,
You plainly find it in his face:
That old vertigo in his head,
Will never leave him, till he's dead:
Besides, his memory decays,
He recollects not what he says;
He cannot call his friends to mind;
Forgets the place where last he din'd:
Plyes you with stories o'er and o'er,
He told them fifty times before.
How does he fancy we can sit,
To hear his out-of-fashion'd wit?
But he takes up with younger fokes,
Who for his wine will bear his jokes:
Faith, he must make his stories shorter,
Or change his comrades once a quarter:
In half the time, he talks them round;
There must another set be found.

"For poetry, he's past his prime,
He takes an hour to find a rhime:

His fire is out, his wit decay'd,
His fancy sunk, his muse a jade.
I'd have him throw away his pen;
But there's no talking to some men."

And, then their tenderness appears
By adding largely to my years:
"He's older than he would be reckon'd
And well remembers Charles the Second.

"He hardly drinks a pint of wine;
And that, I doubt, is no good sign.
His stomach too begins to fail:
Last year we thought him strong and hale;
But now, he's quite another thing;
I wish he may hold out till spring."

Then hug themselves, and reason thus;
"It is not yet so bad with us."

In such a case they talk in tropes,
And, by their fears express their hopes,
Some great misfortune to portend,
No enemy can match a friend.
With all the kindness they profess,
The merit of a lucky guess
(When daily howd'y's come of course,
And servants answer; worse and worse)
Wou'd please 'em better than to tell,
That, God prais'd, the Dean is well.
Then he who prophecy'd the best,
Approves his foresight to the rest:
"You know, I always fear'd the worst,
And often told you so at first":
He'd rather chuse, that I should die,
Than his prediction prove a lie.
Not one foretells I shall recover;
But, all agree, to give me over.

Yet shou'd some neighbour feel a pain,
Just in the parts, where I complain;
How many a message would he send?
What hearty prayers that I should mend?

Enquire what regimen I kept;
What gave me ease, and how I slept?
And more lament, when I was dead,
Than all the sniv'llers round my bed.

My good companions, never fear,
For though you may mistake a year;
Though your prognostics run too fast,
They must be verify'd at last.

Behold the fatal day arrive!
"How is the Dean? He's just alive.
Now the departing prayer is read:
He hardly breathes. The Dean is dead."
Before the passing-bell begun,
The news thro' half the town has run.
"O, may we all for death prepare!
What has he left? And who's his heir?
I know no more than what the news is,
'Tis all bequeath'd to public uses.
To public use! A perfect whim!
What had the public done for him!
Mere envy, avarice, and pride!
He gave it all: — But first he dy'd.
And had the Dean, in all the nation,
No worthy friend, no poor relation?
So ready to do strangers good,
Forgetting his own flesh and blood?"

Now Grub-street wits are all employ'd,
With elegies, the town is cloy'd:
Some paragraph in ev'ry paper,
To curse the Dean or bless the Drapier.[1]

The doctors tender of their fame,
Wisely on me lay all the blame:

[1] [The notes to this poem were prepared by Swift himself, except that
occasionally he left some blanks — a characteristic device. His omissions
were supplied in later editions of the poem and in some manuscript versions.]
    The author supposes that the scriblers of the prevailing party, which
he always opposed, will libel him after his death; but that others who
remember the service he had done to Ireland, under the name of M. B.
Drapier, by utterly defeating the destructive project of Wood's half-pence,
in five Letters to the People of Ireland, at the time read universally, and
convincing every reader, will remember him with gratitude.

"We must confess his case was nice:
But he would never take advice:
Had he been rul'd, for ought appears,
He might have liv'd these twenty years:
For when we open'd him we found,
That all his vital parts were sound."

From Dublin soon to London spread,
'Tis told at Court, the Dean is dead.[2]
Kind Lady Suffolk[3] in the spleen,
Runs laughing up to tell the Queen,
The Queen so gracious, mild, and good,
Cries, "Is he gone? 'Tis time he shou'd.
He's dead you say; Why, let him rot;
I'm glad the medals were forgot.[4]
I promis'd him, I own, but when?
I only was a Princess then;
But now as consort of a king
You know 'tis quite a different thing."

Now, Chartres[5] at Sir Robert's levee,
Tells, with a sneer, the tidings heavy:

  [2] The Dean supposeth himself to dye in Ireland.
  [3] Mrs. Howard, afterwards Countess of Suffolk, then of the Bedchamber
to the Queen, professed much favour for the Dean. The Queen then
Princess, sent a dozen times to the Dean (then in London) with her
command to attend her; which at last he did, by advice of all his friends. She
often sent for him afterwards, and always treated him very graciously. He
taxed her with a present worth ten pounds, which she promised before
he should return to Ireland, but on his taking leave, the medals were not
ready.
  [4] The medals were to be sent to the Dean in four months, but she forgot,
or thought them too dear. The Dean being in Ireland sent Mrs. Howard a
piece of plaid made in that kingdom, which the Queen seeing took it from
her and wore it herself, and sent to the Dean for as much as would clothe
herself and children — desiring he would send the charge of it. He did
the former; it cost 35l. but he said he would have nothing except the
medals: he went next summer to England and was treated as usual, and she
being then Queen, the Dean was promised a settlement in England but
return'd as he went, and instead of receiving of her intended favours or the
medals hath been ever since under her Majesty's displeasure.
  [5] Chartres is a most infamous, vile scoundrel, grown from a foot-boy, or
worse, to a prodigious fortune both in England and Scotland: he had a
way of insinuating himself into all Ministers under every change, either as
pimp, flatterer, or informer. He was tried at seventy for a rape, and came
off by sacrificing a great part of his fortune (he is since dead, but this
poem still preserves the scene and time it was writ in.)

"Why, is he dead without his shoes?
(Cries Bob [6]) "I'm sorry for the news;
Oh, were the wretch but living still,
And, in his place my good friend Will;[7]
Or, had a mitre on his head
Provided Bolingbroke [8] were dead."

Now, Curl [9] his shop from rubbish drains;
Three genuine tomes of *Swift's Remains*.
And then, to make them pass the glibber,
Revis'd by Tibbalds, Moore, and Cibber.[10]
He'll treat me as he does my betters.
Publish my will, my life, my letters.[11]
Revive the libels born to die;
Which Pope must bear, as well as I.

[6] Sir Robert Walpole, Chief Minister of State, treated the Dean in 1726, with great distinction, invited him to dinner at Chelsea, with the Dean's friends chosen on purpose; appointed an hour to talk with him of Ireland, to which kingdom and people the Dean found him no great friend; for he defended Wood's project of half-pence, &c. The Dean would see him no more; and upon his next year's return to England, Sir Robert on an accidental meeting, only made a civil compliment, and never invited him again.

[7] Mr. William Pultney, from being Mr. Walpole's intimate friend, detesting his administration, became his mortal enemy, and joyned with my Lord Bolingbroke, to expose him in an excellent 'paper, called the *Craftsman*, which is still continued.

[8] Henry St. John, Lord Viscount Bolingbroke, Secretary of State to Queen Anne of blessed memory. He is reckoned the most universal genius in Europe; Walpole dreading his abilities, treated him most injuriously, working with King George who forgot his promise of restoring the said lord, upon the restless importunity of Sir Robert Walpole.

[9] Curl hath been the most infamous bookseller of any age or country; his character in part may be found in Mr. Pope's *Dunciad*. He published three volumes all charged on the Dean, who never writ three pages of them; he hath used many of the Dean's friends in almost as vile a manner.

[10] Three stupid verse writers in London, the last to the shame of the Court, and the highest disgrace to wit and learning, was made Laureat. Moore, commonly called Jemmy Moore, son of Arthur Moore, whose father was jaylor of Monaghan in Ireland. See the character of Jemmy Moore, and Tibbalds, Theobald in the *Dunciad*.

[11] Curl is notoriously infamous for publishing the Lives, Letters, and last Wills and Testaments of the nobility and Ministers of State, as well as of all the rogues, who are hanged at Tyburn. He hath been in custody of the House of Lords for publishing or forging the letters of many peers; which made the Lords enter a resolution in their Journal Book, that no life or writings of any lord should be published without the consent of the next heir at law, or licence from their House.

Here shift the scene, to represent
How those I love, my death lament.
Poor Pope will grieve a month; and Gay
A week; and Arbuthnot a day.

St. John himself will scarce forbear,
To bite his pen, and drop a tear.
The rest will give a shrug, and cry,
I'm sorry; but we all must die.
Indifference clad in wisdom's guise,
All fortitude of mind supplies:
For how can stony bowels melt,
In those who never pity felt;
When *We* are lash'd, *They* kiss the rod;
Resigning to the will of God.

The fools, my juniors by a year,
Are tortur'd with suspence and fear.
Who wisely thought my age a screen,
When death approach'd, to stand between:
The screen remov'd, their hearts are trembling,
They mourn for me without dissembling.

My female friends, whose tender hearts,
Have better learn'd to act their parts,
Receive the news in doleful dumps,
"The Dean is dead, (and what is trumps?)
Then Lord have mercy on his soul.
(Ladies I'll venture for the vole.)
Six deans they say must bear the pall.
(I wish I knew what king to call.)
Madam, your husband will attend
The funeral of so good a friend.
No madam, 'tis a shocking sight,
And he's engag'd to-morrow night!
My Lady Club wou'd take it ill,
If he shou'd fail her at quadrill.
He lov'd the Dean. (I led a heart.)
But dearest friends, they say, must part.
His time was come, he ran his race;
We hope he's in a better place."

Why do we grieve that friends should die?
No loss more easy to supply.

One year is past; a different scene;
No further mention of the Dean;
Who now, alas, no more is missed,
Than if he never did exist.
Where's now this fav'rite of Apollo?
Departed; and his works must follow:
Must undergo the common fate;
His kind of wit is out of date.
Some country Squire to Lintot [12] goes,
Enquires for SWIFT in Verse and Prose:
Says Lintot, "I have heard the name:
He dy'd a year ago." The same.
He searches all his shop in vain;
"Sir you may find them in Duck-Lane: [13]
I sent them with a load of books,
Last Monday, to the pastry-cooks.
To fancy they cou'd live a year!
I find you're but a stranger here.
The Dean was famous in his time;
And had a kind of knack at rhyme:
His way of writing now is past;
The town hath got a better taste:
I keep no antiquated stuff;
But, spick and span I have enough.
Pray, do but give me leave to shew'em,
Here's Colley Cibber's Birth-day poem.
This ode you never yet have seen,
By Stephen Duck, upon the Queen.
Then, here's a Letter finely penn'd
Against the Craftsman and his friend;
It clearly shews that all reflection
On ministers, is disaffection.
Next, here's Sir Robert's *Vindication*, [14]
And Mr. Henly's last Oration: [15]

[12] Bernard Lintot, a bookseller in London, *Vide* Mr. Pope's *Dunciad*.

[13] A place where old books are sold in London.

[14] Walpole hath a set of party scriblers, who do nothing else but write in his defence.

[15] Henly is a clergyman who wanting both merit and luck to get preferment, or even to keep his curacy in the Established Church, formed a new conventicle, which he calls an Oratory. There, at set times, he delivereth strange speeches compiled by himself and his associates, who share the profit with him: every hearer pays a shilling each day for admittance. He is an absolute dunce, but generally reputed crazy.

The hawkers have not got 'em yet,
Your Honour please to buy a set?

"Here's Woolston's [16] tracts, the twelfth edition;
'Tis read by ev'ry politician:
The country members, when in town,
To all their boroughs send them down:
You never met a thing so smart;
The courtiers have them all by heart:
Those Maids of Honour (who can read)
Are taught to use them for their creed.
The rev'rend author's good intention,
Hath been rewarded with a pension:
He doth an honour to his gown,
By bravely running priest-craft down:
He shews as sure as God's in *Gloc'ster*,
That Jesus was a grand impostor:
That all his miracles were cheats,
Perform'd as jugglers do their feats:
The Church had never such a writer:
A shame, he hath not got a mitre!"

Suppose me dead; and then suppose
A club assembled at the Rose;
Where from discourse of this and that,
I grow the subject of their chat:
And, while they toss my name about,
With favour some, and some without;
One quite indiff'rent in the cause,
My character impartial draws.

"The Dean, if we believe report,
Was never ill receiv'd at Court.
As for his Works in Verse and Prose,
I own my self no judge of those:
Nor, can I tell what critics thought 'em;
But, this I know, all people bought 'em;
As with a moral view design'd
To cure the vices of mankind;
His vein, ironically grave,
Expos'd the fool, and lash'd the knave:

[16] Woolston was a clergyman, but for want of bread, hath in several treatises, in the most blasphemous manner, attempted to turn Our Saviour and his miracles into ridicule. He is much caressed by many great courtiers, and by all the infidels, and his books read generally by the Court Ladies.

To steal a hint was never known,
But what he writ, was all his own.

"He never thought an honour done him,
Because a duke was proud to own him:
Would rather slip aside, and chuse
To talk with wits in dirty shoes:
Despis'd the fools with Stars and Garters,
So often seen caressing Chartres:[17]
He never courted men in station,
Nor persons had in admiration;
Of no man's greatness was afraid,
Because he sought for no man's aid.
Though trusted long in great affairs,
He gave himself no haughty airs:
Without regarding private ends,
Spent all his credit for his friends:
And only choose the wise and good;
No flatt'rers; no allies in blood;
But succour'd virtue in distress,
And seldom fail'd of good success;
As numbers in their hearts must own,
Who, but for him, had been unknown.

"With princes kept a due decorum,
But never stood in awe before 'em:
He follow'd David's lesson just,
In Princes never put thy Trust.
And, would you make him truly sour;
Provoke him with a slave in power:
The Irish Senate, if you nam'd,
With what impatience he declaim'd!
Fair LIBERTY was all his cry;
For her he stood prepar'd to die;
For her he boldly stood alone;
For her he oft expos'd his own.
Two kingdoms, just as faction led,
Had set a price upon his head;[18]

17 See the notes before on Chartres.
18 In the Year 1713, the late Queen was prevailed with by an Address of
the House of Lords in England, to publish a Proclamation, promising three
hundred pounds to whatever person would discover the author of a pamphlet
called *The Publick Spirit of the Whiggs;* and in Ireland, in the year 1724,
my Lord Carteret at his first coming into the Government, was prevailed on

But, not a traitor cou'd be found.
To sell him for six hundred pound.

"Had he but spar'd his tongue and pen,
He might have rose like other men:
But, power was never in his thought;
And, wealth he valu'd not a groat:
Ingratitude he often found,
And pity'd those who meant the wound:
But, kept the tenor of his mind,
To merit well of human kind:
Nor made a sacrifice of those
Who still were true, to please his foes.
He labour'd many a fruitless hour
To reconcile his friends in power;[19]
Saw mischief by a faction brewing,
While they pursu'd each others ruin.
But, finding vain was all his care,
He left the court in mere despair.

"And, oh! how short are human schemes!
Here ended all our golden dreams.
What St. John's skill in state affairs,
What Ormond's valour, Oxford's cares,
To save their sinking country lent,
Was all destroy'd by one event.
Too soon that precious life was ended,[20]
On which alone, our weal depended.

"When up a dangerous faction starts,[21]
With wrath and vengeance in their hearts;

---

to issue a Proclamation for promising the like reward of three hundred pounds, to any person who could discover the author of a pamphlet called, *The Drapier's Fourth Letter*, &c. writ against that destructive project of coining half-pence for Ireland; but in neither kingdoms was the Dean discovered.

[19] Queen Anne's Ministry fell to variance from the first year after their Ministry began: Harcourt the Chancellor, and Lord Bolingbroke the Secretary, were discontented with the Treasurer Oxford, for his too much mildness to the Whig Party; this quarrel grew higher every day till the Queen's death: the Dean, who was the only person that endeavoured to reconcile them, found it impossible; and thereupon retired to the country about ten weeks before that fatal event: upon which he returned to his Deanry in Dublin, where for many years he was worryed by the new people in power, and had hundreds of libels writ against him in England.

[20] In the height of the quarrel between the Ministers, the Queen died.

[21] Upon Queen Anne's death the Whig faction was restored to power,

By solemn League and Cov'nant bound,
To ruin, slaughter, and confound;
To turn religion to a fable,
And make the Government a Babel:
Pervert the law, disgrace the gown,
Corrupt the senate, rob the crown;
To sacrifice old England's glory,
And make her infamous in story.
When such a tempest shook the land,
How could unguarded virtue stand?

"With horror, grief, despair the Dean
Beheld the dire destructive scene:
His friends in exile, or the Tower,
Himself within the frown of power;[22]
Pursu'd by base envenom'd pens,
Far to the land of slaves and fens;[23]
A servile race in folly nurs'd,
Who truckle most, when treated worst.

"By innocence and resolution,
He bore continual persecution;
While numbers to preferment rose;
Whose merits were, to be his foes.
When, ev'n his own familiar friends
Intent upon their private ends;
Like renegadoes now he feels,
Against him lifting up their heels.

"The Dean did by his pen defeat
An infamous destructive cheat.[24]

---

which they exercised with the utmost rage and revenge; impeached and
banished the chief leaders of the Church party, and stripped all their
adherents of what employments they had, after which England was
never known to make so mean a figure in Europe: the greatest preferments
in the Church in both kingdoms were given to the most ignorant men.
Fanatics were publicly caressed; Ireland utterly ruined and enslaved; only
great Ministers heaping up millions; and so affairs continue to this 3rd. of
May 1732, and are likely to remain so.

[22] Upon the Queen's death, the Dean returned to live in Dublin, at his
Deanry-house: numberless libels were writ against him in England, as a
Jacobite; he was insulted in the street, and at nights he was forced to be
attended by his servants armed.

[23] The Land of slaves and fens, is Ireland.

[24] One Wood, a hardware-man from England, had a patent for coining
copper half-pence in Ireland, to the sum of £108,000 which in the consequence, must leave that kingdom without gold or silver (See *Drapier's
Letters.*)

Taught fools their int'rest how to know;
And gave them arms to ward the blow.
Envy hath own'd it was his doing,
To save that helpless land from ruin;
While they who at the steerage stood,
And reapt the profit, sought his blood.

"To save them from their evil fate,
In him was held a crime of state.
A wicked monster on the bench,[25]
Whose fury blood could never quench;
As vile and profligate a villain,
As modern Scroggs, or old Tressilian;[26]
Who long all justice had discarded,
Nor fear'd he God, nor man regarded;
Vow'd on the Dean his rage to vent,
And make him of his zeal repent;
But Heav'n his innocence defends,
The grateful people stand his friends:
Nor strains of law, nor judges frown,
Nor topics brought to please the crown,
Nor witness hir'd, nor jury pick'd,
Prevail to bring him in convict.

"In exile[27] with a steady heart,
He spent his life's declining part;
Where folly, pride, and faction sway,
Remote from St. John,[28] Pope, and Gay.

"His friendship there to few confin'd,[29]
Were always of the midling kind:

[25] One Whitshed was then Chief Justice: he had some years before prosecuted a printer for a pamphlet writ by the Dean, to perswade the people
of Ireland to wear their own manufactures. Whitshed sent the jury down
eleven times, and kept them nine hours until they were forced to bring
in a special verdict. He sat as judge afterwards on the tryal of the printer
of the *Drapier's Fourth Letter;* but the jury, against all he could say or
swear, threw out the bill: all the kingdom took the Drapier's part, except
the courtiers, or those who expected places. The Drapier was celebrated
in many poems and pamphlets: his sign was set up in most streets in Dublin
(where many of them still continue) and in several country towns.

[26] Scroggs was Chief Justice under King Charles the Second: his judgment
always varied in state tryals, according to directions from Court. Tressilian
was a wicked judge, hanged above three hundred years ago.

[27] In Ireland, which he had reason to call a place of exile; to which country nothing could have driven him, but the Queen's death, who had determined to fix him in England, in Spight of the Dutchess of Somerset, &c.

[28] Henry St. John, Lord Viscount Bolingbroke, mentioned before.

[29] In Ireland the Dean was not acquainted with one single Lord Spiritual

No fools of rank, a mungril breed,
Who fain would pass for Lords indeed;
Where titles give no right or power,
And peerage is a wither'd flower,[30]
He would have held it a disgrace,
If such a wretch had known his face.
On rural squires, that kingdom's bane,
He vented oft his wrath in vain:
Biennial squires, to market brought;[31]
Who sell their souls and votes for naught;
The nation stripp'd go joyful back,
To rob the Church, their tenants rack,
Go snacks with rogues and rapparees[32]
And, keep the peace, to pick up fees:
In every job to have a share,
A jail or barrack to repair;[33]
And turn the tax for public roads
Commodious to their own abodes.

    "Perhaps I may allow, the Dean
Had too much satire in his vein;
And seem'd determin'd not to starve it,
Because no age could more deserve it.
Yet, malice never was his aim;
He lash'd the vice, but spar'd the name.
No individual could resent,
Where thousands equally were meant.
His satire points at no defect,
But what all mortals may correct:
For he abhorr'd that senseless tribe,
Who call it humour when they jibe:

or Temporal. He only conversed with private gentlemen of the clergy or laity, and but a small number of either.

[30] The peers of Ireland lost their jurisdiction by one single Act, and tamely submitted to the infamous mark of slavery without the least resentment or remonstrance.

[31] The Parliament, as they call it, in Ireland meet but once in two years, and after having given five times more than they can afford return home to reimburse themselves by all country jobs and oppressions of which some few only are mentioned.

[32] The highwaymen in Ireland, are, since the late wars there, usually called Rapparees, which was a name given to those Irish soldiers who in small parties used at that time to plunder Protestants.

[33] The army in Ireland are lodged in barracks, the building and repairing whereof and other charges have cost a prodigious sum to that unhappy kingdom.

He spar'd a hump, or crooked nose,
Whose owners set not up for beaux.
True genuine dullness mov'd his pity,
Unless it offer'd to be witty.
Those, who their ignorance confess'd,
He ne'er offended with a jest;
But laugh'd to hear an idiot quote,
A verse from Horace, learn'd by rote.

"He knew an hundred pleasant stories,
With all the turns of Whigs and Tories:
Was cheerful to his dying day,
And friends would let him have his way.

"He gave the little wealth he had,
To build a house for fools and mad:
And shew'd by one satiric touch,
No nation wanted it so much:
That kingdom[34] he hath left his debtor,
I wish it soon may have a better."

[34] Meaning Ireland, where he now lives, and probably may dye.

CORRESPONDENCE

Journal to Stella

LETTER VI.

London, Oct. 10, 1710.

So, as I told you just now in the letter I sent half an hour ago, I dined with Mr. *Harley* to-day, who presented me to the attorney-general sir *Simon Harcourt*, with much compliment on all sides, *&c. Harley* told me he had shewn my memorial to the queen, and seconded it very heartily; and he desires me to dine with him again on *Sunday*, when he promises to settle it with her majesty, before she names a governor; and I protest I am in hopes it will be done, all but the forms, by that time; for he loves the church: this is a popular thing, and he would not have a governor share in it; and, besides, I am told by all hands, he has a mind to gain me over. But in the letter I writ last post (yesterday) to the archbishop, I did not tell him a syllable of what Mr. *Harley* said to me last night, because he charged me to keep it secret; so I would not tell it to you, but that before this goes, I hope the secret will be over. I am now writing my poetical *Description of a Shower in London*, and will send it to the *Tatler*. This is the last sheet of a whole quire I have written since I came to town. Pray, now it comes into my head, will you, when you go to Mrs. *Walls*, contrive to know whether Mrs. *Wesley* be in town, and still at her brother's, and how she is in health, and whether she stays in town. I writ to her from *Chester*, to know what I should do with her note; and I believe the poor woman is afraid to write to me: so I must go to my business, *&c.*

11. To-day at last I dined with lord *Montrath*, and carried

lord *Mountjoy* and sir *Andrew Fountain* with me; and was looking over them at ombre till eleven this evening like a fool: they
played running ombre half crowns; and sir *Andrew Fountain*
won eight guineas of Mr. *Coote*: so I am come home late, and
will say but little to *MD* this night. I have gotten half a bushel of
coals, and *Patrick*, the extravagant whelp, had a fire ready for me;
but I pickt off the coals before I went to-bed. It is a sign *London*
is now an empty place, when it will not furnish me with matter
for above five or six lines in a day. Did you smoak in my last how
I told you the very day and the place you were playing at
ombre? But I interlined and altered a little, after I had received a
letter from Mr. *Manley*, that said you were at it in his house,
while he was writing to me; but without his help I guess'd within
one day. Your town is certainly much more sociable than ours.
I have not seen your mother yet, &c.

12. I dined to-day with Dr. *Garth* and Mr. *Addison*, at the
Devil tavern by *Temple-bar*, and *Garth* treated; and 'tis well I
dine every day, else I should be longer making out my letters:
for we are yet in a very dull state, only enquiring every day after
new elections, where the *Tories* carry it among the new members six to one. Mr. *Addison's* election has passed easy and
undisputed; and I believe, if he had a mind to be chosen king, he
would hardly be refused. An odd accident has happened at
Colchester: one captain *Lavallin* coming from *Flanders* or *Spain*,
found his wife with child by a clerk of *Doctors Commons*,
whose trade, you know, it is to prevent fornications: and this
clerk was the very same fellow that made the discovery of *Dyet's*
counterfeiting the stamp paper. *Lavallin* has been this fortnight
hunting after the clerk to kill him; but the fellow was constantly
employed at the *Treasury* about the discovery he made: the wife
had made a shift to patch up the business, alledging that the
clerk had told her her husband was dead, and other excuses; but
t'other day somebody told *Lavallin* his wife had intrigues before
he married her: upon which he goes down in a rage, shoots his
wife through the head, then falls on his sword; and, to make the
matter sure, at the same time discharges a pistol through his own
head, and died on the spot, his wife surviving him about two
hours; but in what circumstances of mind and body is terrible to
imagine. I have finished my poem on the *Shower*, all but the
beginning, and am going on with my *Tatler*. They have fixt
about fifty things on me since I came: I have printed but three.
One advantage I get by writing to you daily, or rather you get, is,
that I shall remember not to write the same things twice; and
yet I fear I have done it often already: but I'll mind and confine

myself to the accidents of the day; and so get you gone to ombre, and be good girls, and save your money, and be rich against *Presto* comes, and write to me now and then: I am thinking it would be a pretty thing to hear sometimes from sawcy *MD*; but don't hurt your eyes, *Stella*, I charge you.

13. O Lord, here's but a trifle of my letter written yet; what shall *Presto* do for prittle prattle to entertain *MD*? The talk now grows fresher of the duke of *Ormond* for *Ireland*, though Mr. *Addison* says he hears it will be in commission, and lord *Gallaway* one. These letters of mine are a sort of journal, where matters open by degrees; and, as I tell true or false, you will find by the event whether my intelligence be good; but I don't care two-pence whether it be or no. — At night. To-day I was all about *St. Paul's*, and up at the top like a fool, with sir *Andrew Fountain* and two more; and spent seven shillings for my dinner like a puppy: this is the second time he has served me so; but I'll never do it again, though all mankind should persuade me, unconsidering puppies! There's a young fellow here in town we are all fond of, and about a year or two come from the university, one *Harrison*, a little pretty fellow, with a great deal of wit, good sense, and good nature; has written some mighty pretty things; that in your 6th *Miscellanea*, about the *Sprig of an Orange, is* his: he has nothing to live on but being governor to one of the duke of *Queensbury's* sons for forty pounds a year. The fine fellows are always inviting him to the tavern, and make him pay his club. *Henley* is a great crony of his: they are often at the tavern at six or seven shillings reckoning, and always makes the poor lad pay his full share. A colonel and a lord were at him and me the same way to-night: I absolutely refused, and made *Harrison* lag behind, and persuaded him not to go to them. I tell you this, because I find all rich fellows have that humour of using all people without any consideration of their fortunes; but I'll see them rot before they shall serve me so. Lord *Halifax* is always teazing me to go down to his country house, which will cost me a guinea to his servants, and twelve shillings coach hire; and he shall be hanged first. Is not this a plaguy silly story? But I am vext at the heart; for I love the young fellow, and am resolved to stir up people to do something for him: he is a *Whig*, and I'll put him upon some of my cast *Whigs*; for I have done with them, and they have, I hope, done with this kingdom for our time. They were sure of the four members for *London* above all places, and they have lost three in the four. Sir *Richard Onslow*, we hear, has lost for *Surry;* and they are overthrown in most places. Lookee, gentlewomen, if I write long letters, I must

write you news and stuff, unless I send you my verses; and some
I dare not; and those on the *Shower in London* I have sent to the
Tatler, and you may see them in *Ireland*. I fancy you'll smoak
me in the *Tatler* I am going to write; for I believe I have told
you the hint. I had a letter sent me to-night from sir *Matthew
Dudley*, and found it on my table when I came in. Because it is
extraordinary I will transcribe it from beginning to end. It is as
follows [Is the *Devil* in you? *Oct.* 13, 1710.] I would have
answered every particular passage in it, only I wanted time.
Here's enough for to night, such as it is, *&c.*

14. Is that tobacco at the top of the paper*, or what? I don't
remember I slobbered. Lord, I dreamt of *Stella*, &c. so confus-
edly last night, and that we saw dean *Bolton* and *Sterne* go into a
shop; and she bid me call them to her, and they proved to be two
parsons I know not; and I walked without till she was shifting,
and such stuff, mixt with much melancholy and uneasiness, and
things not as they should be, and I know not how: and it is now
an ugly gloomy morning.—At night. Mr. *Addison* and I dined
with *Ned Southwell*, and walkt in the *Park;* and at the *Coffee-
house* I found a letter from the bishop of *Clogher*, and a pacquet
from *MD*. I opened the bishop's letter; but put up *MD*'s, and
visited a lady just come to town, and am now got into bed, and
going to open your little letter: and God send I may find *MD*
well, and happy, and merry, and that they love *Presto* as they do
fires. Oh, I won't open it yet! yes I will! no I won't; I am going;
I can't stay till I turn over†: What shall I do? My fingers itch;
and now I have it in my left hand; and now I'll open it this very
moment. — I have just got it, and am cracking the seal, and can't
imagine what's in it; I fear only some letter from a bishop, and it
comes too late: I shall employ nobody's credit but my own. Well,
I see though — Pshaw, 'tis from sir *Andrew Fountain:* What, another! I fancy this is from Mrs. *Barton;* she told me she would
write to me; but she writes a better hand than this: I wish you
would enquire; it must be at *Dawson's* office at the *Castle*. I fear
this is from *Patty Rolt*, by the scrawl. Well, I'll read *MD*'s letter.
Ah, no; it is from poor lady *Berkeley*, to invite me to *Berkeley-
castle* this winter; and now it grieves my heart: she says she hopes
my lord is in a fair way of recovery; poor lady. Well, now I go

* The upper part of the letter was a little besmeared with some such stuff;
the mark is still on it. [This and the following notes are by Deane Swift,
Swift's relative, who first printed this portion of the *Journal*. Additional
notes may be found at the end of this volume.]

† That is, to the next page; for he is now within three lines of the bottom
of the first.

to *MD*'s letter: faith, 'tis all right; I hoped it was wrong. Your letter, *N.* 3, that I have now received, is dated *Sept.* 26, and *Manley's* letter, that I had five days ago, was dated *Oct.* 3, that's a fortnight difference: I doubt it has lain in *Steele's* office, and he forgot. Well, there's an end of that: he is turned out of his place; and you must desire those who send me pacquets, to inclose them in a paper directed to Mr. *Addison*, at *St. James's Coffee-house:* not common letters, but pacquets: the bishop of *Clogher* may mention it to the archbishop when he sees him. As for your letter, it makes me mad: slidikins, I have been the best boy in *Christendom,* and you come with your two eggs a penny.— Well; but stay, I'll look over my book: adad, I think there was a *chasm* between my *N.* 2 and *N.* 3. Faith, I won't promise to write to you every week; but I'll write every night, and when it is full I will send it; that will be once in ten days, and that will be often enough: and if you begin to take up the way of writing to *Presto,* only because it is *Tuesday,* a *Monday* bedad, it will grow a task; but write when you have a mind. — No, no, no, no, no, no, no, no — Agad, agad, agad, agad, agad, agad; no, poor *Stellakins.* Slids, I would the horse were in your — chamber. Have not I ordered *Parvisol* to obey your directions about him? And han't I said in my former letters, that you may pickle him, and boil him, if you will? What do you trouble me about your horses for? Have I any thing to do with them? — Revolutions a hindrance to me in my business; Revolutions — to me in my business? If it were not for the revolutions, I could do nothing at all; and now I have all hopes possible, though one is certain of nothing; but to-morrow I am to have an answer, and am promised an effectual one. I suppose I have said enough in this and a former letter how I stand with [the] new people; ten times better than ever I did with the old; forty times more caressed. I am to dine to-morrow at Mr. *Harley's;* and if he continues as he has begun, no man has been ever better treated by another. What you say about *Stella's* mother, I have spoken enough to it already. I believe she is not in town; for I have not yet seen her. My lampoon is cried up to the skies; but nobody suspects me for it, except sir *Andrew Fountain:* at least they say nothing of it to me. Did not I tell you of a great man who received me very coldly? That's he; but say nothing; 'twas only a little revenge: I'll remember to bring it over. The bishop of *Clogher* has smoaked my *Tatler* about shortening of words, &c. But, God so! &c.

15. I will write plainer if I can remember it; for *Stella* must not spoil her eyes, and *Dingley* can't read my hand very well; and I am afraid my letters are too long: then you must suppose

one to be two, and read them at twice. I dined to-day with Mr. *Harley*: Mr. *Prior* dined with us. He has left my memorial with the queen, who has consented to give the *First-Fruits* and *Twentieth Parts*, and will, we hope, declare it to-morrow in the cabinet. But I beg you to tell it to no person alive; for so I am ordered, till in publick: and I hope to get something of greater value. After dinner came in lord *Peterborow*: we renewed our acquaintance, and he grew mightily fond of me. They began to talk of a paper of verses called *Sid Hamet*. Mr. *Harley* repeated part, and then pulled them out, and gave them to a gentleman at the table to read, though they had all read them often: lord *Peterborow* would let nobody read them but himself: so he did; and Mr. *Harley* bobbed me at every line to take notice of the beauties. *Prior* rallied lord *Peterborow* for author of them; and lord *Peterborow* said, he knew them to be his; and *Prior* then turned it upon me, and I on him. I am not guessed at all in town to be the author; yet so it is: but that is a secret only to you. Ten to one whether you see them in *Ireland*; yet here they run prodigiously. *Harley* presented me to lord president of *Scotland*, and Mr. *Benson*, lord of the treasury. *Prior* and I came away at nine, and sat at the *Smyrna* till eleven, receiving acquaintance.

16. This morning early I went in a chair, and *Patrick* before it, to Mr. *Harley*, to give him another copy of my memorial, as he desired; but he was full of business, going to the queen, and I could not see him; but he desired I would send up the paper, and excused himself upon his hurry. I was a little baulkt; but they tell me it is nothing. I shall judge by next visit. I tipt his porter with a half crown; and so I am well there for a time at least. I dined at *Stratford*'s in the city, and had *Burgundy* and *Tockay*: came back afoot like a scoundrel; then went with Mr. *Addison* and supt with lord *Mountjoy*, which made me sick all night. I forgot that I bought six pound of chocolate for *Stella*, and a little wooden box: and I have a great piece of *Brazil* tobacco for *Dingley*, and a bottle of palsy water for *Stella*: all which, with the two handkerchiefs that Mr. *Sterne* has bought, and you must pay him for, will be put in the box directed to Mrs. *Curry*'s, and sent by Dr. *Hawkshaw*, whom I have not seen; but *Sterne* has undertaken it. The chocolate is a present, madam, for *Stella*. Don't read this, you little rogue, with your little eyes; but give it to *Dingley*, pray now; and I'll write as plain as the skies: and let *Dingley* write *Stella*'s part, and *Stella* dictate to her, when she apprehends her eyes, *&c.*

17. This letter should have gone this post, if I had not been taken up with business, and two nights being late out; so it must stay till *Thursday*. I dined to-day with your Mr. *Sterne*, by

invitation, and drank *Irish* wine; but, before we parted, there came in the prince of puppies, colonel *Edgworth;* so I went away. This day came out the *Tatler* made up wholly of my *Shower,* and a preface to it. They say 'tis the best thing I ever writ, and I think so too. I suppose the bishop of *Clogher* will shew it you. Pray tell me how you like it. *Tooke* is going on with my *Miscellany.* I'd give a penny the letter to the bishop of *Killaloe* was in it: 'twould do him honour. Could not you contrive to say you hear they are printing my *Thing*s together; and that you wish the bookseller had that letter among the rest: but don't say any thing of it as from me. I forgot whether it was good or no; but only having heard it much commended, perhaps it may deserve it. Well, I have to-morrow to finish this letter in, and then I'll send it next day. I am so vext that you should write your third to me, when you had but my second, and I had written five, which now I hope you have all: and so I tell you, you are sawcy, little, pretty, dear rogues, *&c.*

18. To-day I dined, by invitation, with *Stratford* and others, at a young merchant's in the city, with *Hermitage* and *Tockay,* and staid till nine, and am now come home. And that dog *Patrick* is abroad, and drinking, and I can't get my night-gown. I have a mind to turn that puppy away: he has been drunk ten times in three weeks. But I han't time to say more; so good night, *&c.*

19. I am come home from dining in the city with Mr. *Addison,* at a merchant's; and just now, at the *Coffee-house,* we have notice that the duke of *Ormond* was this day declared lord lieutenant, at *Hampton-court,* in council. I have not seen Mr. *Harley* since; but hope the affair is done about *First-Fruits.* I will see him, if possible, to-morrow morning; but this goes to-night. I have sent a box to Mr. *Sterne,* to send to you by some friend: I directed it for Mr. *Curry,* at his house; so you have warning when it comes, as I hope it will soon. The handkerchiefs will be put in some friend's pocket, not to pay custom. And so here ends my sixth, sent when I had but three of *MD*'s: now I am beforehand, and will keep so; and God Almighty bless dearest *MD, &c.*

LETTER VII.

London, Oct. 19, 1710.

O Faith, I am undone! this paper is larger than t'other, and yet I am condemned to a sheet; but since it is *MD*, I did not value though I were condemned to a pair. I told you in my letter to-day where I had been, and how the day past; and so, &c.

20. To-day I went to Mr. *Lewis,* at the secretary's office, to know when I might see Mr. *Harley;* and by and by comes up Mr. *Harley* himself, and appoints me to dine with him to-morrow. I dined with Mrs. *Vanhomrigh,* and went to wait on the two lady *Butlers;* but the porter answered, They were not at home: the meaning was, the youngest, lady *Mary,* is to be married to-morrow to lord *Ashburnham,* the best match now in *England,* twelve thousand pounds a year, and abundance of money. Tell me how my *Shower* is liked in *Ireland:* I never knew any thing pass better here. I spent the evening with *Wortley Montague* and Mr. *Addison,* over a bottle of *Irish* wine. Do they know any thing in *Ireland* of my greatness among the *Tories?* Every body reproaches me of it here; but I value them not. Have you heard of the verses about the *Rod of Sid Hamet?* Say nothing of them for your life. Hardly any body suspects me for them, only they think nobody but *Prior* or I could write them. But I doubt they have not reached you. There is likewise a *Ballad,* full of puns, on the *Westminster Election,* that cost me half an hour: it runs, though it be good for nothing. But this is likewise a secret to all but *MD.* If you have them not, I'll bring them over.

21. I got *MD*'s fourth to-day at the *Coffee-house.* God Almighty bless poor dear *Stella,* and her eyes and head: What shall we do to cure them, poor dear life? Your disorders are a pull-back for your good qualities. Would to heaven I were this minute shaving your poor dear head, either here or there. Pray do not write, nor read this letter, nor any thing else, and I will write plainer for *Dingley* to read, from henceforward, though my pen is apt to ramble when I think who I am writing to. I will not answer your letter until I tell you that I dined this day with Mr. *Harley,* who presented me to the earl of *Sterling,* a *Scotch* lord; and in the evening came in lord *Peterborow.* I staid till nine before Mr. *Harley* would let me go, or tell me any thing of my affair. He says, the queen has now granted the *First-Fruits* and *Twentieth Parts;* but he will not yet give me leave to write to the archbishop, because the queen designs to signify it to the bishops in *Ireland* in form, and to take notice, That it was done upon a memorial from me, which Mr. *Harley* tells me he does to make it look more respectful to me, &c. and I am to see him on *Tuesday.* I know not whether I told you, that in my memorial which was given to the queen, I begged for two thousand pounds a year more, though it was not in my commission; but that Mr. *Harley* says cannot yet be done, and that he and I must talk of it

further: however, I have started it, and it may follow in time. Pray say nothing of the *First-Fruits* being granted, unless I give leave at the bottom of this. I believe never any thing was compassed so soon, and purely done by my personal credit with Mr. *Harley*, who is so excessively obliging, that I know not what to make of it, unless to shew the rascals of the other party that they used a man unworthily, who had deserved better. The memorial given to the Queen from me speaks with great plainness of lord *Wharton*. I believe this business is as important to you as the *Convocation* disputes from *Tisdall*. I hope in a month or two all the forms of settling this matter will be over, and then I shall have nothing to do here. I will only add one foolish thing more, because it is just come into my head. When this thing is made known, tell me impartially whether they give any of the merit to me, or no; for I am sure I have so much, that I will never take it upon me. — Insolent sluts! because I say *Dublin, Ireland*, therefore you must say *London, England*: that's *Stella*'s malice *. — Well, for that I won't answer your letter till to-morrow-day, and so and so: I'll go write something else, and it won't be much; for 'tis late.

22. I was this morning with Mr. *Lewis*, the under-secretary to lord *Dartmouth*, two hours talking politicks, and contriving to keep *Steele* in his office of stampt paper: he has lost his place of *Gazetteer*, three hundred pounds a year, for writing a *Tatler*, some months ago, against Mr. *Harley*, who gave it him at first, and raised the salary from sixty to three hundred pounds. This was devilish ungrateful; and *Lewis* was telling me the particulars: but I had a hint given me, that I might save him in the other employment; and leave was given me to clear matters with *Steele*. Well, I dined with Sir *Matthew Dudley*, and in the evening went to sit with Mr. *Addison*, and offer the matter at distance to him, as the discreeter person; but found *Party* had so possessed him, that he talked as if he suspected me, and would not fall in with any thing I said. So I stopt short in my overture, and we parted very dryly; and I shall say nothing to *Steele*, and let them do as they will; but if things stand as they are, he will certainly lose it, unless I save him; and therefore I will not speak to him, that I may not report to his disadvantage. Is not this vexatious? and is there so much in the proverb of proffered service? When shall I grow wise? I endeavour to act in the most exact points of

---

* There is a particular compliment to *Stella* couched in these words. *Stella* was herself an *Englishwoman*, born at *Richmond* in *Surry*; nevertheless she respected the interest and the honour of *Ireland*, where she had lived for some years, with a generous patriotic spirit.

honour and conscience, and my nearest friends will not understand it so. What must a man expect from his enemies? This would vex me, but it shall not; and so I bid you good night, &c.

23. I know 'tis neither wit nor diversion to tell you every day where I dine, neither do I write it to fill my letter; but I fancy I shall, some time or other, have the curiosity of seeing some particulars how I passed my life when I was absent from *MD* this time; and so I tell you now that I dined to-day at *Molesworth*'s, the *Florence* envoy, then went to the coffee-house, where I behaved myself coldly enough to Mr. *Addison*, and so came home to scribble. We dine together to-morrow and next day, by invitation; but I shall alter my behaviour to him, till he begs my pardon, or else we shall grow bare acquaintance. I am weary of friends, and friendships are all monsters, but *MD*'s.

24. I forgot to tell you, that last night I went to Mr. *Harley*'s, hoping — faith, I am blundering, for it was this very night at six; and I hoped he would have told me all things were done and granted: but he was abroad, and come home ill, and was gone to bed, much out of order, unless the porter lied. I dined to-day at Sir *Matthew Dudley*'s with Mr. *Addison*, &c.

25. I was to-day to see the duke of *Ormond;* and coming out, met lord *Berkeley* of *Stratton*, who told me, that Mrs. *Temple*, the widow, died last *Saturday*, which, I suppose, is much to the outward grief and inward joy of the family. I dined to-day with Mr. *Addison* and *Steele*, and a sister of Mr. *Addison*, who is married to one Monsr. *Sartre*, a *Frenchman*, *Prebendary* of *Westminster*, who has a delicious house and garden; yet I thought it was a sort of monastick life in those cloisters, and I liked *Laracor* better. *Addison*'s sister is a sort of a wit, very like him. I am not fond of her, &c.

26. I was to-day to see Mr. *Congreve*, who is almost blind with cataracts growing on his eyes; and his case is, that he must wait two or three years, until the cataracts are riper, and till he is quite blind, and then he must have them couched; and besides he is never rid of the gout, yet he looks young and fresh, and is as chearful as ever. He is younger by three years or more than I, and I am twenty years younger than he. He gave me a pain in the great toe, by mentioning the gout. I find such suspicions frequently, but they go off again. I had a second letter from Mr. *Morgan;* for which I thank you: I wish you were whipt for forgetting to send him that answer I desired you in one of my former, that I could do nothing for him of what he desired, having no credit at all, &c. Go, be far enough, you negligent baggages. I have had also a letter from *Parvisol*, with an account

how my livings are set, and that they are fallen, since last year, sixty pounds. A comfortable piece of news. He tells me plainly, that he finds you have no mind to part with the horse, because you sent for him at the same time you sent him my letter; so that I know not what must be done. 'Tis a sad thing that *Stella* must have her own horse, whether *Parvisol* will or no. So now to answer your letter that I had three or four days ago. I am not now in bed, but am come home by eight; and it being warm, I write up. I never writ to the bishop of *Killala*, which, I suppose, was the reason he had not my letter. I have not time, there's the short of it. — As fond as the dean is of my letter, he has not written to me. I would only know whether dean *Bolton* paid him the twenty pounds; and for the rest, he may kiss ———. And that you may ask him, because I am in pain about it, that dean *Bolton* is such a *whipster*. 'Tis the most obliging thing in the world in dean *Sterne* to be so kind to you. I believe he knows it will please me, and makes up, that way, his other usage. No, we have had none of your snow, but a little one morning; yet I think it was great snow for an hour or so, but no longer. I had heard of *Will Crowe*'s death before, but not the foolish circumstance that hastened his end. No, I have taken care that captain *Pratt* shall not suffer by lord *Anglesea*'s death. I'll try some contrivance to get a copy of my picture from *Jervas*. I'll make Sir *Andrew Fountain* buy one as for himself, and I'll pay him again and take it, that is, provided I have money to spare when I leave this. — Poor *John!* is he gone? and madam *Parvisol* has been in town? Humm. Why, *Tighe* and I, when he comes, shall not take any notice of each other; I would not do it much in this town, though we had not fallen out. — I was to-day at Mr. *Sterne*'s lodging; he was not within, and Mr. *Leigh* is not come to town, but I will do *Dingley*'s errand when I see him. What do I know whether china be dear or no? I once took a fancy of resolving to grow mad for it but now 'tis off; I suppose I told you so in some former letter. And so you only want some salad dishes, and plates, and &c. Yes, yes, you shall. I suppose you have named as much as will cost five pounds. — Now to *Stella*'s little postscript; and I am almost crazed that you vex yourself for not writing. Can't you dictate to *Dingley*, and not strain your little dear eyes? I am sure 'tis the grief of my soul to think you are out of order. Pray be quiet, and if you will write, shut your eyes, and write just a line, and no more, thus [Hᴐw do you do, Mrs. *Stella?*] That was written with my eyes shut. Faith, I think it is better than when they are open*: and then *Dingley* may

* It is actually better written, and in a plainer hand.

stand by, and tell you when you go too high or too low. — My letters of business, with pacquets, if there be any more occasion for such, must be inclosed to Mr. *Addison*, at *St. James's Coffee-house:* but I hope to hear, as soon as I see Mr. *Harley*, that the main difficulties are over, and that the rest will be but form. — Make two or three nutgalls, make two or three — galls, stop your receipt in your —— I have no need on't. Here's a clutter! Well, so much for your letter, which I will now put up in my letter-partition in my cabinet, as I always do every letter as soon as I answer it. Method is good in all things. Order governs the world. The Devil is the author of confusion. A general of an army, a minister of state; to descend lower, a gardener, a weaver, *&c.* That may make a fine observation, if you think it worth finishing; but I have not time. Is not this a terrible long piece for one evening? I dined to-day with *Patty Rolt* at my cousin *Leach*'s, with a pox, in the city: he is a printer, and prints the *Postman*, oh ho, and is my cousin, God knows how, and he married Mrs. *Baby Aires* of *Leicester;* and my cousin *Thompson* was with us: and my cousin *Leach* offers to bring me acquainted with the author of the *Postman;* and says, he does not doubt but the gentleman will be glad of my acquaintance, and that he is a very ingenious man, and a great scholar, and has been beyond sea. But I was modest, and said, May be the gentleman was shy, and not fond of new acquaintance; and so put it off: and I wish you could hear me repeating all I have said of this in its proper tone, just as I am writing it. 'Tis all with the same cadence with oh hoo, or as when little girls say, I have got an apple, miss, and I won't give you some. 'Tis plaguy twelve-penny weather this last week, and has cost me ten shillings in coach and chair hire. If the fellow that has your money will pay it, let me beg you to buy *Bank Stock* with it, which is fallen near thirty *per cent.* and pays eight pounds *per cent.* and you have the principal when you please: it will certainly soon rise. I would to God lady *Giffard* would put in the four hundred pounds she owes you, and take the five *per cent.* common interest, and give you the remainder. I will speak to your mother about it when I see her. I am resolved to buy three hundred pounds of it for myself, and take up what I have in *Ireland;* and I have a contrivance for it, that I hope will do, by making a friend of mine buy it as for himself, and I'll pay him when I can get in my money. I hope *Stratford* will do me that kindness. I'll ask him to-morrow or next day.

27. Mr. *Rowe* the poet desired me to dine with him to-day. I went to his office (he is under-secretary in Mr. *Addison*'s place

that he had in *England*) and there was Mr. *Prior;* and they both
fell commending my *Shower* beyond any thing that has been
written of the kind: there never was such a *Shower* since
Danäe's, *&c.* You must tell me how 'tis liked among you. I
dined with *Rowe; Prior* could not come: and after dinner we
went to a blind tavern, where *Congreve*, Sir *Richard Temple*,
Eastcourt, and *Charles Main* were over a bowl of bad punch.
The knight sent for six flasks of his own wine for me, and we
staid till twelve. But now my head continues pretty well; I have
left off my drinking, and only take a spoonful mixt with water,
for fear of the gout, or some ugly distemper; and now, because
it is late, I will, *&c.*

28. *Garth* and *Addison* and I dined to-day at a hedge tavern;
then I went to Mr. *Harley*, but he was denied, or not at home:
so I fear I shall not hear my business is done before this goes.
Then I visited lord *Pembroke;* who is just come to town, and we
were very merry talking of old things, and I hit him with one
pun. Then I went to see the ladies *Butler*, and the son of a
whore of a porter denied them: so I sent them a threatening message by another lady, for not excepting me always to the porter.
I was weary of the *Coffee-house*, and *Ford* desired me to sit
with him at next door, which I did, like a fool, chatting till
twelve, and now am got into bed. I am afraid the new ministry
is at a terrible loss about money: the *Whigs* talk so, it would give
one the spleen; and I am afraid of meeting Mr. *Harley* out of
humour. They think he will never carry through this undertaking. God knows what will come of it. I should be terribly vexed
to see things come round again: it will ruin the church and clergy
for ever; but I hope for better. I'll send this on *Tuesday*, whether
I hear any further news of my affair or not.

29. Mr. *Addison* and I dined to-day with lord *Mountjoy;*
which is all the adventures of this day. — I chatted a while
to-night in the *Coffee-house*, this being a full night; and now
am come home to write some business.

30. I dined to-day at Mrs. *Vanhomrigh*'s, and sent a letter to
poor Mrs. *Long*, who writes to us, but is God knows where, and
will not tell any body the place of her residence. I came home
early, and must go write.

31. The month ends with a fine day; and I have been walk-
ing, and visiting *Lewis*, and concerting where to see Mr. *Harley*.
I have no news to send you. *Aire*, they say, is taken, though the
Whitehall letters this morning say quite the contrary: 'tis good,
if it be true. I dined with Mr. *Addison* and *Dick Stuart*, lord
Mountjoy's brother; a treat of *Addison*'s. They were half

fuddled, but not I; for I mixt water with my wine, and left them together between nine and ten; and I must send this by the bell-man, which vexes me, but I will put it off no longer. Pray God it does not miscarry. I seldom do so; but I can put off little *MD* no longer. Pray give the under note to Mrs. *Brent*.

I'm a pretty gentleman; and you lose all your money at cards, sirrah *Stella*. I found you out; I did so.

I'm staying before I can fold up this letter, till that ugly *D* is dry in the last line but one. Don't you see it? O Lord, I'm loth to leave you, faith ——— but it must be so, till next time. Pox take that *D*: I'll blot it to dry it

LETTER L.

Kensington. July. 17. 1712.

I am weary of living in this Place, and glad I am to leave it so soon. The Qu— goes on Tuesday to Windsor, and I shall follow in 3 or 4 days after. I can do nothing here, going early to London, and coming late from it and supping at Ldy Mashams. I din'd to day with the D. of Argyle at Cue, and would not go to the Court to night because of writing to Md. the Bp of Clogher has been here this fortnight; I see him as often as I can. poor Master Ash has a sad Redness in his Face, it is St Anthony's fire, his face all swelld; and will break in his Cheek, but no danger. — Since Dunkirk has been in our Hands, Grubstreet has been very fruitfull: pdfr has writt 5 or 6 Grubstreet papers this last week.. Have you seen Toland's Invitation to Dismal, or a Hue & cry after Dismal, or a Ballad on Dunkirk, or an Argument that Dunkirk is not in our Hands Poh, you have seen nothing. — I am dead here with the Hot weathr, yet I walk every night home, & believe it does me good. but my Shouldr is not yet right, itchings, & scratchings, and small akings. Did I tell you that I have made Ford Gazeteer, with 200ll a year Salary, besides Perquisites. I had a Lettr lately from Parvisol, who says my Canal looks very finely; I long to see it; but no Apples; all blasted again. He tells me there will be a Triennial Visitation in August. I must send Raymd another Proxy. So now I will answr ee Rettle N. 33. dated Jun. 17. Ppt writes as well as ever for all her waters I wish I had never come here, as often and as heartily as Ppt, what had I to do here? I have heard of the Bp's making me uneasy, but I did not think it was because I never writt to him. A little would

make me write to him; but I don't know what to say. I find I
am obliged to the Provost for keeping the Bp from being impertinent. — Yes Maram Dd, but oo would not be content with
Letters flom pdfr of 6 lines, or 12 either fais. I hope Ppt will
have done with the waters soon, and find benefit by them; I believe if they were as far off as Wexford they would do as much
good; For I take the Journy to contribute as much as any thing.
I can assure you the Bp of Cloghers being here does not in the
least affect my staying or going. I never talkt to Higgins but
once in the Street; and I believe he and I shall hardly meet but
by chance. What care I whethr my Lettr to Ld Treasr be commended there or no? why does not somebody among you
answer it, as 3 or 4 have done here (I am now sitting with
nothing but my Nightgown for heat). Ppt shall have a great
Bible. I have put it down in my memlandums, just now. and
Dd shall be repaid her tother Book; but patience, all in good
time; you are so hasty a dog would &c. So Ppt has neither won
nor lost. Why mun, I play sometimes too, at Picket that is,
Picquett I mean; but very seldom. — Out late, why 'tis onely at
Ldy Mashams, and that's in our Town: but I never come late
here from London, except once in rain when I could not get a
Coach.—We have had very little Thunder here; none these 2
Months; why pray, Madam Philosopher, how did the Rain
hinder the Thunder from doing harm, I suppose it ssquencht it.
— So here comes ppt aden with her little watry postscript; o
Rold, dlunken Srut drink pdfrs health ten times in a molning;
you are a whetter, fais I sup Mds 15 times evly molning in milk
porridge. lele's fol oo now, and lele's fol ee Rettle, & evly kind
of sing; and now I must say something else. — You hear Secty St
John is made Vicount Bullinbrook; I could hardly persuade him
to take that Title, because the eldest Branch of his Family had
it in an Earldom, & it was last Year extinct; If he did not take it
I advised him to be Ld Pomfret, wch I think is a noble Title;
you hear of it often in the *Chronicles* Pomfret Castle: but we
believed it was among the Titles of some other Ld. Jack Hill
sent his Sister a Pattern of a head-dress from Dunkirk; it was
like our Fashion 20 years ago, onely not quite so high, and lookt
very ugly. I have made Trap Chapln to Ld Bullinbroke, and he
is mighty happy & thankfull for it. — Mr Addison returnd me my
visit this morning; He lives in our Town.. I shall be mighty
retired and mighty busy for a while at Windsor. Pray why dont
Md go to Trim, and see Laracor; and give me an Account of the
Garden & the River, & the Holly, & the Cherry trees on the River
walk. ———

19. I could not send this Lettr last Post, being called away before I could fold or finish it. I dined yestrday with Ld Treasr, satt with him till 10 at night, yet could not find a Minute for some Business I had with him. He brought me to Kensington, and Ld Bulingbrook would not let me go away till 2, and I am now in bed very lazy and sleepy at nine. I must shave head & Face, & meet Ld Bullinbrook at 11; and dine again with Ld Tr. To day there will be another Grub; a Letter from the Pretendr to a Whig Ld. Grubstreet has but ten days to live, then an Act of Parlmt takes place, that ruins it, by taxing every half sheet at a halfpenny: We have news just come, but not the Particulars, that the Earl of Albermarle at the head of 8 thousd Dutch is beaten lost the greatest part of his men, & himself a Prisoner. This perhaps may cool their Courage, & make them think of a Peace. the D. of Ormd has got abundance of Credit by his good Conduct of Affairs in Flanders. We had a good deal of Rain last night, very refreshing — Tis late & I must rise. Don't play at Ombre in your waters Sollah — Farewel deelest Md Md Md Md FW FW Me Me Me lele lele lele —

Address: To Mrs Dingley, att
her Lodgings over against St
Marys Church near Capel street
Dublin.
Ireland

Swift to John Gay

Dublin, January 8, 1722–23.

COMING home after a short Christmas ramble, I found a letter upon my table, and little expected when I opened it to read your name at the bottom. The best and greatest part of my life, until these last eight years, I spent in England: there I made my friendships, and there I left my desires. I am condemned for ever to another country; what is in prudence to be done? I think to be *oblitusque meorum, obliviscendus et illis.* What can be the design of your letter but malice, to wake me out of a scurvy sleep, which however is better than none? I am towards nine years older since I left you, yet that is the least of my alterations:

my business, my diversions, my conversations, are all entirely
changed for the worse, and so are my studies and my amusements
in writing. Yet, after all, this humdrum way of life might be
passable enough, if you would let me alone. I shall not be able
to relish my wine, my parsons, my horses, nor my garden, for
three months, until the spirit you have raised shall be dispos-
sessed. I have sometimes wondered that I have not visited you,
but I have been stopped by too many reasons, besides years and
laziness, and yet these are very good ones. Upon my return after
half a year amongst you, there would be to me, *Desiderio nec
pudor nec modus*. I was three years reconciling myself to the
scene, and the business, to which fortune has condemned me,
and stupidity was what I had recourse to. Besides, what a
figure should I make in London, while my friends are in poverty,
exile, distress, or imprisonment, and my enemies with rods of
iron? Yet I often threaten myself with the journey, and am
every summer practising to ride and get health to bear it; the
only inconvenience is, that I grow old in the experiment.

Although I care not to talk to you as a divine, yet I hope you
have not been author of your colic. Do you drink bad wine, or
keep bad company? Are you not as many years older as I? It
will not be always: *Et tibi quos mihi dempserit apponet annos*.
I am heartily sorry you have any dealings with that ugly distemper, and I believe our friend Arbuthnot will recommend you
to temperance and exercise. I wish they would have as good an
effect upon the giddiness I am subject to, and which this moment
I am not free from. I should have been glad if you had length-
ened your letter by telling me the present condition of many of
my old acquaintance — Congreve, Arbuthnot, Lewis, etc., but
you mention only Mr. Pope, who, I believe, is lazy, or else he
might have added three lines of his own. I am extremely glad
he is not in your case of needing great men's favour, and could
heartily wish that you were in his.

I have been considering why poets have such ill success in
making their court, since they are allowed to be the greatest and
best of all flatterers. The defect is, that they flatter only in print
or in writing, but not by word of mouth: they will give things
under their hand which they make a conscience of speaking.
Besides, they are too libertine to haunt ante-chambers, too poor
to bribe porters and footmen, and too proud to cringe to second-
hand favourites in a great family. Tell me, are you not under
original sin by the dedication of your Eclogues to Lord Bolingbroke? I am an ill judge at this distance; and besides, am, for my

ease, utterly ignorant of the commonest things that pass in the world; but if all Courts have a sameness in them, as the parsons' phrase is, things may be as they were in my time, when all employments went to Parliament-men's friends, who had been useful in elections, and there was always a huge list of names in arrears at the Treasury, which would take up at least your seven years' expedient to discharge even one half.

I am of opinion, if you will not be offended, that the surest course would be to get your friend who lodges in your house, to recommend you to the next chief governor who comes over here, for a good civil employment, or to be one of his secretaries, which your Parliament-men are fond enough of, when there is no room at home. The wine is good and reasonable; you may dine twice a week at the Deanery House; there is a set of company in this town sufficient for one man; folks will admire you, because they have read you, and read of you; and a good employment will make you live tolerably in London, or sumptuously here; or if you divide between both places, it will be for your health. The Duke of Wharton settled a pension on Dr. Young. Your landlord is much richer. These are my best thoughts after three days' reflections. Mr. Budgell got a very good office here, and lost it by a great want of common politics. If a [Whig] recommendation be hearty, and the governor who comes here be already inclined to favour you, nothing but *fortuna Trojanae* can hinder the success.

If I write to you once a quarter, will you promise to send me an answer in a week, and then I will leave you at rest till the next quarter-day; and I desire you will leave part of a blank side for Mr. Pope. Has he some *quelque chose* of his own upon the anvil? I expect it from him since poor Homer helped to make him rich. Why have not I your works, and with a civil inscription before it, as Mr. Pope ought to have done to his, for so I had from your predecessors of the two last reigns. I hear yours were sent to Ben Tooke, but I never had them. You see I wanted nothing but provocation to send you a long letter, which I am not weary of writing, because I do not hear myself talk, and yet I have the pleasure of talking to you, and if you are not good at reading ill hands, it will cost you as much time as it has done me. I wish I could do more than say I love you. I left you in a good way both for the late Court, and the successors; and by the force of too much honesty or too little sublunary wisdom, you fell between two stools. Take care of your health and money; be less modest and more active; or else turn parson and get a bishopric

here. Would to God they would send us as good ones from
your side! I am ever, with all friendship and esteem,

Yours.

Mr. Ford presents his service to Mr. Pope and you. We keep
him here as long as we can.

Swift to Alexander Pope

September 29, 1725.

SIR,

I CANNOT guess the reason of Mr. Stopford's management, but
impute it at a venture to either haste or bashfulness, in the latter
of which he is excessive to a fault, although he had already gone
the tour of Italy and France to harden himself. Perhaps this second journey, and for a longer time, may amend him. He treated
you just as he did Lord Carteret, to whom I recommended him.

My letter you saw to Lord Bolingbroke has shown you the
situation I am in, and the company I keep, if I do not forget some
of its contents, but I am now returning to the noble scene of
Dublin, into the *grand monde*, for fear of burying my parts, to
signalise myself among curates and vicars, and correct all corruptions crept in relating to the weight of bread and butter,
through those dominions where I govern. I have employed my
time, besides ditching, in finishing, correcting, amending, and transcribing my Travels, in four parts complete, newly augmented,
and intended for the press, when the world shall deserve
them, or rather when a printer shall be found brave enough to
venture his ears. I like the scheme of our meeting after distresses
and dispersions; but the chief end I propose to myself in all my
labours is to vex the world rather than divert it; and if I could
compass that design, without hurting my own person or fortune,
I would be the most indefatigable writer you have ever seen,
without reading. I am exceedingly pleased that you have done
with translations. Lord Treasurer Oxford often lamented that a
rascally world should lay you under a necessity of misemploying
your genius for so long a time. But since you will now be so
much better employed, when you think of the world give it one
lash the more at my request. I have ever hated all nations, profes-
sions, and communities, and all my love is toward individuals: for

instance, I hate the tribe of lawyers, but I love Counsellor Such-a-one, and Judge Such-a-one: so with physicians — I will not speak of my own trade — soldiers, English, Scotch, French, and the rest. But principally I hate and detest that animal called man, although I heartily love John, Peter, Thomas, and so forth. This is the system upon which I have governed myself many years, but do not tell, and so I shall go on till I have done with them. I have got materials toward a treatise, proving the falsity of that definition *animal rationale*, and to show it would be only *rationis capax*. Upon this great foundation of misanthropy, though not in Timon's manner, the whole building of my Travels is erected; and I never will have peace of mind till all honest men are of my opinion. By consequence you are to embrace it immediately, and procure that all who deserve my esteem may do so too. The matter is so clear that it will admit of no dispute; nay, I will hold a hundred pounds that you and I agree in the point.

I did not know your Odyssey was finished, being yet in the country, which I shall leave in three days. I shall thank you kindly for the present, but shall like it three-fourths the less, from the mixture you mention of another hand; however, I am glad you saved yourself so much drudgery. I have been long told by Mr. Ford of your great achievements in building and planting, and especially of your subterranean passage to your garden, whereby you turned a blunder into a beauty, which is a piece of *ars poetica*.

I have almost done with harridans, and shall soon become old enough to fall in love with girls of fourteen. The lady whom you describe to live at court, to be deaf, and no party woman, I take to be mythology, but know not how to moralise it. She cannot be Mercy, for Mercy is neither deaf, nor lives at Court. Justice is blind, and perhaps deaf, but neither is she a Court lady. Fortune is both blind and deaf, and a Court lady, but then she is a most damnable party woman, and will never make me easy, as you promise. It must be Riches, which answers all your description. I am glad she visits you, but my voice is so weak that I doubt she will never hear me.

Mr. Lewis sent me an account of Dr. Arbuthnot's illness, which is a very sensible affliction to me, who, by living so long out of the world, have lost that hardness of heart contracted by years and general conversation. I am daily losing friends, and neither seeking nor getting others. Oh! if the world had but a dozen Arbuthnots in it, I would burn my Travels. But, however, he is not without fault. There is a passage in Bede highly commending the piety and learning of the Irish in that age, where, after abundance of praises he overthrows them all, by lamenting that, alas! they kept Easter at a wrong time of the year. So our Doctor has every quality and virtue that can make a man amiable or useful; but, alas! he has a sort of slouch in his walk. I pray God protect him, for he is an excellent Christian, though not a Catholic, and as fit a man either to live or die as ever I knew.

I hear nothing of our friend Gay, but I find the Court keeps him at hard meat. I advised him to come over here with a Lord Lieutenant. Mr. Tickell is in a very good office. I have not seen Philips, though formerly we were so intimate. He has got nothing and by what I find will get nothing, though he writes little flams, as Lord Leicester called those sorts of verses, on Miss Carteret. It is remarkable, and deserves recording that a Dublin blacksmith, a great poet, has imitated his manner in a poem to the same Miss. Philips is a complainer, and on this occasion I told Lord Carteret that complainers never succeed at Court, though railers do.

Are you altogether a country gentleman, that I must address to you out of London, to the hazard of your losing this precious letter, which I will now conclude, although so much paper is left. I have an ill name, and therefore shall not subscribe it, but you will guess it comes from one who esteems and loves you about half as much as you deserve, I mean as much as he can.

I am in great concern, at what I am just told is in some of the newspapers, that Lord Bolingbroke is much hurt by a fall in hunting. I am glad he has so much youth and vigour left, of which he has not been thrifty, but I wonder he has no more discretion.

Swift to Miss Martha Blount

Dublin, February 29, 1727–8.

DEAR PATTY,

I AM told you have a mind to receive a letter from me, which is a very undecent declaration in a young lady, and almost a confession that you have a mind to write to me; for as to the fancy of looking on me as a man *sans consequence*, it is what I will never understand. I am told likewise you grow every day younger, and more a fool, which is directly contrary to me, who grow wiser and older, and at this rate we shall never agree. I long to see you a London lady, where you are forced to wear whole clothes, and visit in a chair, for which you must starve next summer at Petersham, with a manteau out at the sides; and sponge once a week at our house, without ever inviting us in a whole season to a cow-heel at home. I wish you would bring Mr. Pope over with you when you come, but we will leave Mr. Gay to his beggars and his operas till he is able to pay his club. How will you pass this summer for want of a squire to Ham Common and Walpole's Lodge; for as to Richmond Lodge and Marble Hill, they are abandoned as much as Sir Spencer Compton, and Mr. Schutz's coach, that used to give you so many a set-down, is wheeled off to St. James's. You must be forced to get a horse, and gallop with Mrs. Janssen and Miss Bedier.

Your greatest happiness is, that you are out of the chiding of Mrs. Howard and the Dean, but I suppose Mr. Pope is so just as to pay our arrears, and that you edify as much by him as by us, unless you are so happy that he now looks upon you as reprobate and a castaway, of which I think he hath given me some hints. However, I would advise you to pass this summer at Kensington, where you will be near the Court, and out of his jurisdiction, where you will be teased with no lectures of gravity and morality, and where you will have no other trouble than to get into the mercer's books, and take up a hundred pounds of your principal for quadrille. Monstrous, indeed, that a fine lady, in the prime of life and gaiety, must take up with an antiquated Dean, an old gentlewoman of fourscore, and a sickly poet. I will stand by my dear Patty against the world; if Teresa beats you for your good, I will buy her a fine whip for the purpose. Tell me, have you been confined to your lodging this winter for want of chair-hire? (Do you know that this unlucky Dr. Delany came last night to the Deanery, and being denied, without my knowledge, is gone to England this morning, and so I must send this by the post. I bought your opera to-day for sixpence, so small printed that it will spoil my eyes. I ordered you to send me your edition, but now you may keep it till you get an opportunity.) Patty, I will tell you a blunder: I am writing to Mr. Gay, and had almost finished the letter; but by mistake I took up this instead of it, and so the six lines in a hook are all to him, and therefore you must read them to him, for I will not be at the trouble to write them over again. My greatest concern in the matter is, that I am afraid I continue in love with you, which is hard after near six months' absence. I hope you have done with your rash and other little disorders, and that I shall see you a fine young, healthy, plump lady, and if Mr. Pope chides you, threaten him that you will turn heretic.

Adieu, dear Patty, and believe me to be one of your truest friends and humblest servants; and that, since I can never live in England, my greatest happiness would be to have you and Mr. Pope condemned, during my life, to live in Ireland, he at the Deanery, and you, for reputation sake, just at next door; and I will give you eight dinners a-week, and a whole half dozen of pint bottles of good French wine at your lodgings, a thing you could never expect to arrive at, and every year a suit of fourteen-penny stuff that should not be worn out at the right side; and a chair costs but sixpence a job; and you shall have Catholicity as much as you please, and the Catholic Dean of St. Patrick's, as old again as I, for your confessor. Adieu again, dear Patty.

Swift to Miss Hoadly

June 4, 1734.

MADAM,

WHEN I lived in England, once every year I issued out an edict, commanding that all ladies of wit, sense, merit, and quality, who had an ambition to be acquainted with me, should make the first advances at their peril; which edict, you may believe, was universally obeyed. When, much against my will, I came to live in this kingdom, I published the same edict; only the harvest here being not altogether so plentiful, I confined myself to a smaller compass. This made me often wonder how you came so long to neglect your duty; for if you pretend ignorance, I may produce legal witnesses against you.

I have heard of a judge bribed with a pig, but it was discovered by the squeaking, and therefore, you have been so politic as to send me a dead one, which can tell no tales. Your present of butter was made with the same design, as a known court practice, to grease my fist that I might keep silence. These are great offences, contrived on purpose to corrupt my integrity. And besides I apprehend that if I should wait on you to return my thanks, you will deny that the pig and butter were any advances at all on your side, and give out that I made them first; by which I may endanger the fundamental privilege that I have kept so many years in two kingdoms, at least make it a point of controversy.

However, I have two ways to be revenged: first, I will let all the ladies of my acquaintance know, that you, the sole daughter and child of his Grace of Dublin, are so mean as to descend to understand housewifery, which every girl of this town, who can afford sixpence a month for a chair, would scorn to be thought to have the least knowledge in, and this will give you as ill a reputation, as if you had been caught in the fact of reading a history, or handling a needle, or working in a field at Tallaght. My other revenge shall be this; when my Lord's gentleman delivered his message, after I put him some questions, he drew out a paper containing your directions, and in your hand: I said it properly belonged to me, and, when I had read it, I put it in my pocket, and am ready to swear, when lawfully called, that it is written in a fair hand, rightly spelt, and good plain sense. You now may see I have you at mercy; for, upon the least offence given, I will show the paper to every female scrawler I meet, who will soon spread about the town, that your writing and spelling are ungenteel and unfashionable, more like a parson than a lady.

I suppose, by this time, you are willing to submit, and therefore, I desire you may stint me to two china bowls of butter a week; for my breakfast is that of a sickly man, rice-gruel, and I am wholly a stranger to tea and coffee, the companions of bread and butter. I received my third bowl last night, and I think my second is almost entire. I hope and believe my Lord Archbishop will teach his neighbouring tenants and farmers a little English country management; and I lay it upon you, Madam, to bring housewifery in fashion among our ladies, that by your example they may no longer pride themselves on their natural or affected ignorance. I am, with the truest respect and esteeem, Madam,

Your most obedient and obliged, etc.

I desire to present my most [humble respects] to his Grace and the ladies.

Swift to Mrs. Pendarves

Dublin, February 22, 1734-5.

MADAM,

I HAVE observed among my own sex, and particularly in myself, that those of us who grow most insignificant expect most civility, and give less than they did when they possibly were good for something. I am grown sickly, weak, lean, forgetful, peevish, spiritless, and for those very reasons expect that you, who have nothing to do but to be happy, should be entertaining me with your letters and civilities, although I never return either. Your last is dated above two months ago, since which time, as well as a good while before, I never had one single hour of health or spirit to acknowledge it. It is your fault; why did you not come sooner into the world or let me come later? It is your fault for coming into Ireland at all; it is your fault for leaving it. I confess your case is hard, for if you return you are a great fool to come among beggars and slaves, and if you do not, you are a great knave in forsaking those you have seduced to admire you.

The complaint you make of a disorder in one of your eyes will admit no raillery, it is what I was heartily afflicted to hear, but since you were able to write, I hope it hath entirely left you. I am often told that I am an ill judge of ladies' eyes, so that I shall make you an ill compliment by confessing that I read in yours all the accomplishments I found in your mind and conversation, and happened to agree in my thoughts with better judges. I only wish they could never shine out of Dublin, for then you would recover the only temporal blessings this town affords, I mean sociable dinners and cheerful evenings, which, without your assistance, we shall infallibly lose; for Dr. Delany lives entirely at Delville, the town air will not agree with his lady, and in winter there is no seeing him or dining with him but by those who keep coaches, and they must return the moment after dinner. But I have chid him into taking a house just next to his, which will have three bedchambers, where his winter visitants may lie, and a bed shall be fitted up for you. Your false reasons for not coming hither are the same in one article for my not going among you. I mean the business of expense; but I can remove yours easily, it is but to stay with us always, and then you can live at least three times better than at home, where everything is thrice as dear, and your money twelve in the hundred better, whereas my sickness and years make it impossible for me to live at London. I must have three horses, as many servants, and a large house, neither can I live without constant wine, while my poor revenues are sinking every day.

I am very sorry for the death of your cousin Lansdown. His son Graham is ruining himself as fast as possible, but I hope the young lady has an untouchable settlement. I am very much obliged to your care about that business with the Duke of Chandos: I hear he told a person he would grant my request, but that he had no acquaintance with me. I had a letter lately from Mrs. Donnellan, and I command you to let her know that I will answer it with the first hour of tolerable health. Pray, Madam, preserve your eyes, how dangerous soever they may be to us; and yet you ought in mercy to put them out, because they direct your hand in writing, which is equally dangerous. Well, Madam, pray God bless you wherever you go or reside! May you be ever as you are, agreeable to every Killala curate and Dublin Dean, for I disdain to mention temporal folks without gowns and cassocks. I will wish for your happiness, although I shall never see you, as Horace did for Galatea when she was going a long voyage from home; pray read the verses in the original.

> Sis licet felix, ubicunque mavis,
> · Et memor nostri, Galatea, vivas, etc.

A year or two ago I would have put the whole into English verse and applied it to you, but my rhyming is fled with my health, and what is more to be pitied is even my vein of satire upon ladies is lost. Dear Madam, believe me to be, with the truest respect and esteem,

Your most obedient, humble servant,

J. SWIFT.

NOTES

GULLIVER'S TRAVELS (1726)

THE TITLE. It may come as a surprise that the title of the work referred to as *Gulliver's Travels* is in fact *Travels into Several Remote Nations of the World*. The name of the author as given on the title page when the book was published was Lemuel Gulliver, not Jonathan Swift. Curiously, the name *Gulliver* does not appear in the actual text, but merely on the title page, underneath an engraved portrait used as a frontispiece, and in two preliminary pieces, one of which was not printed until 1735. Swift, as well as the few friends who knew the work was in progress, referred to it as the *Travels*, and it is possible, as Professor Frederick Bracher has suggested, that "Lemuel Gulliver" himself did not come into existence until the book was ready for the printer. Any hypothesis about the origin of the name or its meaning must be viewed with scepticism, including the significance attached to the first four letters.

"A Letter . . . to his Cousin Sympson": This letter, though dated 1727, was first printed as a preface to *Gulliver's Travels* in 1735, in the Dublin edition of Swift's *Works*. The date of its composition is a matter of controversy. Gulliver's cousin was possibly named Sympson to suggest a family connection with William Symson, author of *A New Voyage to the East-Indies* (1715). But Swift may have had in mind Richard Simpson, publisher of some of Sir William Temple's works.

3. 6 "Dampier": William Dampier (1652–1715), a famous buccaneer and explorer. He wrote extensively of his voyages and was widely read.

3. 23–25 "omitted . . . changed . . . I do hardly know my own work": After the first publication of *Gulliver's Travels* Swift complained bitterly that portions of his manuscript had been tampered with, that some passages had been blotted out, others changed and mangled. He endeavored to insure corrections and alterations in subsequent editions.

4. 17 "Smithfield": a locality in London, site of a cattle market for several centuries and a place where a number of martyrs and heretics had been put to the flame.

4. 32 "keys . . . second parts": Gulliveriana began to appear at once, e.g., *A Key, being Observations and Explanatory Notes upon*

the Travels of Lemuel Gulliver, by *Signor Corolini* (1726) and *Travels into several Remote Nations of the World*, by *Captain Lemuel Gulliver, vol. III* (1727). This latter work contained "A Second Voyage to Brobdingnag".

4. 38–39 "author . . . stranger": In the course of his life (and even afterwards) many works in which Swift had no hand were attributed to him, some actually published under his name or initials. His own works, except two, were published anonymously or with pseudonyms.

4. 40–41 "confound the times, and . . . dates": Swift apparently attempted to achieve accuracy in the time-scheme and dates of Gulliver's voyages, and to obtain a realistic geography within the limits of his fantasy, but either slips by the printer or himself or both have caused some confusion. There is no evidence that Swift was responsible for the maps. The geography and chronology of the *Travels* are discussed by Professor Arthur Case in his *Four Essays on "Gulliver's Travels"* (1945).

15. 3 "at fourteen years old": Students commonly attended the universities at earlier ages in Swift's day. He was himself 14 when he entered Trinity College, Dublin.

15. 15 "physic": Gulliver studied "physic" (i.e., medicine) at the famous center of medical studies, the University of Leyden in Holland.

15. 20 "Levant": the eastern Mediterranean, particularly the coastal areas and adjacent regions.

15. 24 "Old Jury": i.e., Old Jewry, a street in the old City of London, the Jewish quarter of medieval London.

15. 25 "Mrs.": In Swift's day this title (Mistress) was applied to adult women whether married or single.

16. 26–27 "Van Diemen's Land": Tasmania, then believed to be part of the Australian mainland.

17. 26 "six inches high": The sizes of things are reduced roughly to a twelfth in Lilliput and multiplied by twelve in Brobdingnag. Much has been made of Swift's accuracy in keeping to his scale, not only in linear measurements but also in areas and solids (see, for example, William A. Eddy, *Gulliver's Travels: A Critical Study*, 1923, pp. 92 ff.).

17. 34–35 "admiration": i.e., wonderment.

17. 35 "*Hekinah degul*": The languages of the various lands visited by Gulliver have been analyzed by several commentators, who believe that Swift constructed these languages carefully according to certain logical, ascertainable principles (see, for example, Paul Odell Clark, "A *Gulliver* Dictionary," *Studies in Philology*, L [1953], 592 ff.). The more traditional view is that these languages are merely nonsense, revealing Swift's characteristic verbal playfulness, so often exhibited in his puns, anagrams, and other verbal games, such as he and his friends delighted in. For aspects of Swift's interest in language, see his contribution to *The Tatler*, No. 230, and his Letter to Harley, *A Proposal for Correcting . . . the English Tongue*, 1712.

18. 13 "buff jerkin": a close-fitting leather jacket.

21. 26 "engines": mechanical contrivances.

22. 21–22 "an ancient temple": apparently intended to suggest Westminster Hall, in which Charles I had been condemned to death. For Swift's attitude towards Charles I and the political and religious implications of the beheading of that monarch, see his *Sermon Upon the Martyrdom of K. Charles I*, 1726.

23. 13 "stang": a rood or one-fourth of an acre.

23. 34 "in point of cleanliness": These lines reflect what Middleton Murry, in a rather foolish and misleading chapter, has referred to as Swift's "excremental vision" (see his *Jonathan Swift: A Critical Biography*, 1954). Swift's use of naturalistic detail in both prose and poetry (in such poems as "A Beautiful Young Nymph Going to Bed" and "The Lady's Dressing Room") has excited considerable comment, much of it unacceptable, as in Aldous Huxley's essay on Swift in *Do What You Will*, 1929. For a refutation, see the Introduction, p. xii. An intelligent approach to the matter may be found in Maurice Johnson, *The Sin of Wit: Jonathan Swift as a Poet*, 1950, and in Irvin Ehrenpreis, *The Personality of Swift*, 1958, as well as in works by other Swift scholars, such as Professor Herbert Davis and Sir Harold Williams. The latter's edition of Swift's *Poems* is authoritative.

24. 4 "The Emperor": In the political allegory the Emperor represents George I, though the descriptive details are not accurate. As Professor Arthur Case remarks, Swift is either being ironical in these details about the Emperor or guarding against prosecution, or both. The political allegory in Part I reflects some of the circumstances of the last years of Queen Anne when Swift was an active journalist in the Tory cause (see the Introduction, p. xvi), and some of the events of the early part of George I's reign. This was the period just after the close of the War of the Spanish Succession, ended by the Treaty of Utrecht in 1713.

25. 9 "High and Low Dutch": i.e., German and Dutch.

25. 9–10 "Lingua Franca": a mixed jargon or language used by traders in the Mediterranean ports.

27. 12 "to search me": The search and the inventory which follow are generally interpreted as Swift's allegorical treatment of The Committee of Secrecy formed in 1715 by the triumphant Whigs to investigate members of Queen Anne's last ministry. The leaders of that ministry, Robert Harley and Viscount Bolingbroke, were Swift's close friends, and he himself was under suspicion. The charges were sympathy with the Jacobites and betrayal of the nation by making peace with France. In Part I, Gulliver in the political allegory stands for a composite figure, Swift, Harley, and Bolingbroke.

31. 25 "Flimnap . . . is allowed to cut a caper": Flimnap represents the famous Whig statesman, Sir Robert Walpole, head of the government from 1715 to 1717 and from 1721 to 1742. His political dexterity is here satirized. Swift disliked him both as a man and a politician. See the references to him in Swift's *Verses on the Death of Dr. Swift*, 1739.

31. 29 "Reldresal": possibly Lord Carteret, Secretary of State in 1721 and later Lord-Lieutenant of Ireland, a good friend of Swift's who nevertheless in his official capacity offered a reward for the discovery of the Drapier (i.e., Swift) in 1724 (see Swift's amusing essay, *A Vindication of His Excellency John, Lord Carteret, from the Charge of Favouring None but Tories, High-Churchmen and Jacobites*, 1730). Also suggested as Reldresal: Lord Townshend, Secretary of State and a chief ally of Walpole.

31. 41 "one of the King's cushions": the Duchess of Kendal, a mistress of George I, by whose influence it was believed Walpole was restored to power in 1721. He had resigned his offices in 1717.

32. 2 "blue . . . red . . . green": the colors of the ribbons of the Orders of the Garter, the Bath, and the Thistle (see Swift's *Verses on the Revival of the Order of the Bath*, written against Walpole).

33. 9 "close chair": sedan chair.

34. 29 "Skyresh Bolgolam": the Earl of Nottingham, whom Swift had lampooned as "Dismal" and who is reported to have referred in Parliament to Swift as "a certain Divine . . . hardly suspected of being a Christian [yet] is in a fair way of being a Bishop". He was First Lord of the Admiralty from 1680 to 1684. Although a Tory, he opposed Harley and the Tory ministry at times and thus came under Swift's indictment.

35. 7 "most mighty Emperor": The pretentious titles accorded to the Emperor of Lilliput presumably parody the manner of glorifying oriental rulers in popular travel books.

37. 7 "sideling": sideways.

38. 40 "*Tramecksan* and *Slamecksan*": Tory and Whig or High Church and Low Church.

39. 2–3 "imperial heels are lower": George I favored the Whigs and Low Churchmen throughout his reign.

39. 11 "hobble in his gait": The Prince of Wales, later George II, cultivated friends among Whigs and Tories. Hence the hobble in his gait. He surrounded himself with men who opposed his father and Walpole, but to the disappointment of Swift and his friends, the prince retained Walpole in office after coming to the throne.

39. 13   "Blefuscu": France.

39. 26   "primitive way of breaking eggs": The Big-Endians and the Little-Endians represent Catholics and Protestants, whose controversies are here adumbrated. Swift's brief allegorical treatment of the religious struggles seems to include Henry VIII (who broke from the Pope, i.e., commanded his subjects to eat their eggs at the small end), Charles I (who lost his life), and James II (who lost his throne). France (Blefuscu) as a center of Catholicism fomented rebellions in England (Lilliput). Swift has not attempted, apparently, to achieve historical exactitude.

39. 41–43   "Big-Endians . . . incapable by law of holding employments": a reference to the Test Act passed by the English Parliament after the Restoration, which prevented Catholics and nonconformists from holding civil and military offices unless they received the sacrament according to the rites of the Anglican Church. Swift strongly supported this policy.

42. 17   "arrived safe at the royal port of Lilliput": Gulliver's destruction of the Blefuscudian fleet appears to represent the presumed destruction of French naval power in the War of the Spanish Succession, 1701–1713. The Tory ministry of Harley and Bolingbroke laid claim to this achievement. Professor Case suggests that Swift symbolized the culmination of the War by a *naval* victory to offset the Whig claims for the exploits of their great general, the Duke of Marlborough. For Swift on the subject of Marlborough, see *The Examiner*, No. 16 and *A Satirical Elegy on the Death of a Late Famous General* (1722).

43. 14   "a peace": The Treaty of Utrecht, signed April 11, 1713, brought the War to a close but left Whigs and Tories a heritage of bitter conflicts, as Gulliver's involvements reveal.

45. 20–22   "it is capital . . . to make water within the precincts of the palace": The Queen's resentment of Gulliver's method of putting out the fire is generally thought to refer to Queen Anne's dislike of *A Tale of a Tub* for its coarseness and presumed profaneness. She resisted endeavors to make him a dean or a bishop in the Church of England. Swift referred to the Queen as "A Royal Prude" in his poem, *The Author Upon Himself* (1714).

46. 16   "manner of writing is very peculiar": Professor R. W. Frantz suggests that Swift has modeled this paragraph on a passage in William Symson's *New Voyage to the East-Indies*, 1715.

46. 19   "The Cascagians": possibly invented by Swift.

50. 41   "domestic": i.e., household.

52. 5–6   "white staff": the symbol of office of the Lord Treasurer.

52. 23   "jealous of his wife": Flimnap's jealousy, Sir Charles Firth supposes, is "an ironical hit at Walpole, whose first wife, Catherine

Shorter, was not above suspicion, while Walpole's indifference to her levities was notorious."

54. 20 "articles of impeachment": The political allegory is still concerned with events rising out of the Treaty of Utrecht. The Committee of Secrecy with Walpole as its chairman (see note to p. 27, l. 12) made its report, and both Oxford and Bolingbroke were impeached for high treason. Swift is here satirizing the charges brought against the ousted Tory ministers.

56. 21 "to put out both your eyes": a reference, possibly, to the proposal in Parliament that Oxford and Bolingbroke be impeached for a lesser crime than high treason, in which instance they would forfeit their property and civil rights but not their lives.

58. 17 "great lenity and tenderness": perhaps an ironic comment on an Address to the King by the House of Lords in 1716, praising him for his "endearing tenderness and clemency." Soon afterwards some distinguished Jacobites were executed despite the pleas of "the mercy men."

59. 17–18 "arrived at . . . Blefuscu": Gulliver's escape parallels Bolingbroke's flight to France just before his trial. The charges against Harley, who did not flee, were dropped after two years.

61. 23 "sent back to Lilliput": The English made diplomatic protests to the French for harboring fleeing Jacobites.

63. 17 "ancient": i.e., ensign or flag.

63. 25–26 "North and South Seas": i.e., North and South Pacific.

63. 44 "the Downs": a roadstead in the English Channel, off the coast of Kent — the approach to England.

64. 25 "upon the parish": i.e., impoverished and dependent upon the charity of the parish.

67. 25 "to overblow": Swift parodies the excessive use of nautical terms. The passage is taken, almost verbatim, from Samuel Sturmy's *Mariners Magazine*, 1669.

68. 30 "Great Tartary . . . frozen sea": i.e., Siberia and the Arctic Ocean.

70. 28 "great or little . . . comparison": Among the philosophers known to Swift who discussed the relativity of size and vision was George Berkeley, in his *New Theory of Vision*, 1709.

77. 1 "baby": i.e., her doll.

77. 20 "*nanunculus . . . homunceletino*": apparently Swift's own coinages.

78. 28–29 "ignominy of being carried about for a monster": The public exhibition of Gulliver reflects the common practice of the times in displaying (for a small sum) human oddities, such as dwarfs, and various animal monstrosities. Swift refers to these "monster-mongers" in *A Tale of a Tub* (see Aline M. Taylor, "Sights and Monsters and Gulliver's Voyage to Brobdingnag," in *Tulane Studies in English*, vol. vii, pp. 29 ff., 1957).

79. 36 "pumpion": pumpkin.

81. 7 "Sanson's *Atlas*": Sanson was a famous French map-maker of the seventeenth century.

83. 12 "philosophy": in our terminology, science.

84. 7 "*lusus naturæ*": a sport or freak of nature.

84. 10 "followers of Aristotle": Note that the indictment is of the *followers* of Aristotle, not Aristotle himself (see Pt. III, ch. viii, pp. 159–60.

86. 21 "*Royal Sovereign*": one of the largest ships of the English navy in the seventeenth century.

86. 40 "birthday clothes": Custom decreed new finery for royal birthdays. Cf. Pope's "Youth more glitt'ring than a *Birthnight Beau*" in *The Rape of the Lock*, Canto I, l. 23.

89. 3 "Gresham College": the home of the Royal Society of London for Improving Natural Knowledge, usually referred to as the Royal Society, or the Royal Society of Scientists.

90. 31 "a square of Westminster Hall": i.e., a square of the same area as Westminster Hall. The Great Hall was used as a court of justice and on state occasions.

90. 44 "through a microscope": The world revealed by the microscope fascinated contemporaries. See the excellent study by Marjorie H. Nicolson, "The Microscope and English Imagination," in *Science and Imagination*, 1956.

92. 6 "Salisbury steeple": The spire of Salisbury Cathedral is over 400 feet high.

92. 21 "cupola at St. Paul's": The dome of St. Paul's Cathedral is well over 100 feet in diameter.

94. 24 "stoop": swoop.

95. 11 "maids of honour": Soon after the appearance of *Gulliver's Travels* Gay and Pope wrote an amusing letter to Swift about its reception in London. They reported to him that "among lady critics, some have found that Mr. Gulliver had a particular malice to maids of honour" (see F. Elrington Ball, *The Correspondence of Jonathan Swift*, III, 358–61). In 1711 Dr. John Arbuthnot and Swift had engaged in a hoax at the Court of Queen Anne. They circulated an announcement among the maids of honor of a forthcoming book entitled *A History of the Maids of Honour since Harry the Eighth*, for which the deceived maids of honor paid in advance (see the *Journal to Stella*, Sept. 19, 21, 23, 1711).

96. 21–22 "*jet d'eau* at Versailles": The largest fountain in the Gardens of Versailles threw its water over 70 feet in the air. Executions were popular public spectacles in Swift's day.

97. 15 "closet": small private room.

100. 23 "levee": It was customary in the period for people of distinction to receive visitors on rising from bed. Though Swift pretended to scorn levees, he sometimes appeared at Harley's.

103. 3 "plantations": colonies.

103. 12 "highest court of judicature": i.e., the House of Lords, in Swift's day the final court of appeal in legal cases.

103. 19 "holy persons": Bishops are members of the House of Lords as spiritual peers.

104. 9–10 "cultivate . . . our young nobility": for Swift's view of the education of the nobility, see his essay, *The Intelligencer*, No. IX.

104. 26–27 "prostitute chaplains to some nobleman": Dignities in the Church of England (deans and bishops) were as often as not considered political appointments. Swift was bitter over the excessive number of Low-Churchmen appointed to bishoprics by George I. He particularly showed his disrespect for the bishops of the Church of Ireland.

105. 36 "generals . . . richer than our kings": an obvious reflection on Marlborough, who profited greatly by the War of the Spanish Succession (see *The Examiner*, No. 16).

105. 39–40 "mercenary standing army . . . peace": proscribed by the Bill of Rights (1689) except with the consent of Parliament, and generally opposed by the Tories.

107. 26–27 "Dionysius Halicarnassensis": A Greek writer who lived in Rome in the days of Augustus. His *Archaeologia* is designed to show the true greatness of Rome.

108. 12 "a certain powder": In the controversy between the Ancients and the Moderns, which preoccupies Swift in *A Tale of a Tub* and *The Battle of the Books,* the Moderns boasted of the perfection of gunpowder as one of their achievements. It had led, they maintained, to the conquest of colonies and thus to the extension of Christianity, trade, and knowledge. If Gulliver's defence of gunpowder is placed in the context of the Ancient-Modern controversy, Swift's irony takes on added sharpness and meaning, as an indictment of the Moderns.

110. 2–3 "entities . . . transcendentals": Swift reacted strongly against so-called "terms of art," that is, the jargon of philosophy, science, and theology, which obscured meaning rather than clarified it (see his *Letter to a Young Gentleman lately entered into Holy Orders,* 1720).

110. 13 "art of printing": Swift is possibly reflecting an aspect of the Ancient-Modern controversy in limiting the king's library to not above a thousand volumes. The Moderns maintained that they

had a distinct advantage in knowledge by virtue of the art of printing. Sir William Temple, in defence of the Ancients, remarked that the spread of learning is not dependent on books, that in certain countries tradition has been a better preserver of history and knowledge. He argued also that the invention of printing has not necessarily multiplied books, only copies of them, i.e., that *numbers* of volumes are not a measure of learning.

110. 34 "style . . . not florid": A plain style had become an ideal by Swift's day.

111. 6–7 "nature was degenerated": The idea of the decay of nature was pervasive in seventeenth-century thought. It held that both man and civilization had declined from their earlier excellence, that just as man passes through a cycle of youth, old age, and death, so do nature and human culture in all of their aspects. This concept of universal decay came under attack as the idea of progress developed. The two chief antagonists of the controversy before 1650 were Godfrey Goodman and George Hakewell, both of whom influenced later writers. Swift's reference to the abortive births of these later times as contrasted with the giants of former ages can be found in Goodman's *The Fall of Man*, 1616, where he maintains that men of the past were stronger and larger, demonstrably so from the discovery of the large bones and weapons of early times. The two opposed concepts — the decay of nature and the idea of progress — were fundamental ones in the Ancient-Modern controversy, the first for the Ancients, the second for the Moderns.

111. 31 "tradesmen . . . farmers": Observe that the army in Brobdingnag is a citizens' militia, not the type of professional standing army that the Tories opposed.

112. 26 "tumbril": cart.

120. 21 "conceit": a witty thought or turn of expression.

120. 22 "Tonquin": Tongking, a port in French Indo-China.

120. 26 "coasting New Holland": sailing along the coast-line of Australia.

120. 34 "freight": passage.

123. 26–27 "Fort St. George": established by the East India Company; the area grew into Madras.

124. 29–30 "countries in strict alliance": At this time England and Holland were joined in the Grand Alliance and were at war with France. They were, nevertheless, strong commercial rivals. For Swift's attitude towards the Dutch, see the note to p. 175, ll. 8–9.

126. 26 "an island in the air": As in earlier ages so in Swift's day, there was great interest in the possibility of flying machines. Many parallels to Swift's Laputa have been noted, from Lucian's *True*

History to Defoe's *The Consolidator.*

127. 32 "fiddles, flutes . . .": Swift's satire of the Laputans (who are the English of the reign of George I) reflects the current enthusiasm for abstract science and the theory of music, and the tendency (particularly among scientists) to find analogies between music and mathematics. The main point of the satire, as Professor Marjorie Nicolson points out, is "that the Laputans are concerned with the theory, not with the application, of both mathematics and music" (*Science and Imagination*, p. 121).

128. 21 "kennel": gutter.

128. 33 "the King": George I, a patron of music and, to a lesser extent, of science, but he was not credited with much personal knowledge of or interest in either.

129. 12 "hospitality to strangers": a thrust at George I, much criticized for partiality to Hanoverians who had followed him to England.

129. 20 "hautboys": oboes.

130. 4–5 "the true etymology": Swift here mocks contemporary philology.

130. 20–21 "mistake a figure in the calculation": This is usually considered a reference to an error in one of Newton's publications made by the printer, who had added a cipher to Newton's calculation of the sun's distance from the earth. Swift's attitude towards Newton and Newtonian science is complex. In 1724 he had occasion to be displeased with Newton, who, as Comptroller of the Mint, had made a favorable report on Wood's copper coinage. Swift's second *Drapier's Letter* comments on Newton's assay of the controversial copper coins.

132. 12–14 "earth . . . swallowed up": The Laputans believe, pessimistically, in some of the implications of Newtonian science. Newton's analysis of planetary motion recognized at least the possibility that the earth might after "an immense tract of time" fall into the sun. (This and other notes on the scientific aspects of Pt. III are based on the brilliant article by Marjorie Nicolson and Nora Mohler, "The Scientific Background of Swift's *Voyage to Laputa*," reprinted in Professor Nicolson's *Science and Imagination*, 1956).

132. 14–15 "sun . . . effluvia": a reference to contemporary discussions concerning sun-spots.

132. 38 "avoid the stroke of the approaching comet": an allusion to Halley's comet, due to appear again in 1758. Halley and others had considered the possibility that the earth might be struck and "reduced into its ancient chaos."

134. 4–5 "a philosophical account": The "factual and learned" description which follows mimics the manner of the scientific papers contributed to the *Transactions of the Royal Society*. Swift's use of magnetism as the propelling power of the Flying Island reflects scientific interests of the day, stemming from William Gilbert's *De Magnete*, 1600.

138. 7–8 "deprive them of . . . sun and the rain": Swift is almost certainly thinking here of England's oppressive laws in restraint of Irish trade.

138. 43 "About three years": The account which follows is an allegory of Ireland's resistance to Wood's copper coinage. Swift played an important part in the controversy with his *Drapier's Letters* (1724). Lindalino is Dublin.

140. 11–12 "forced . . . their own conditions": The English government under pressure cancelled Wood's patent.

140. 18 "to leave the island": A clause in the Act of Settlement (1701) provided that the king could leave the country only with the consent of Parliament. George I secured the repeal of this clause Swift is here glancing at the repeated visits of the king to Hanover, the first of which, in 1716, lasted for six months.

141. 5 "great lord at court": possibly the Prince of Wales, later George II, who was indifferent to the arts and learning. He did, however, become a patron of the famous composer, Handel.

141. 44 "Munodi": variously identified as Bolingbroke, who ostensibly went into rural retirement on his return from exile in 1723, or as Harley, who similarly retired into the country and abstained from public life after charges of treason were dropped in 1717.

143. 37–38 "all arts, sciences . . . upon a new foot": Swift's bias against innovations and the Moderns is reflected in the treatment of Munodi and his estate. The "new rules and methods of agriculture" may be an allusion to the changes in cultivation, manuring, and crop rotation then being introduced.

143. 39 "an academy of Projectors in Lagado": The Grand Academy of Lagado is Swift's satiric representation of the Royal Society, given a royal charter in 1662. The experiments presented in the following pages are in some instances based upon actual experiments of the times, distorted by Swift to achieve his comic intentions (see Marjorie Nicolson, *Science and Imagination*, pp. 110 ff.). The word "projector" in the period meant one addicted to impractical or speculative activities. Professor Case thinks that the foolish experiments of the academicians of Lagado satirize the impractical political and economic schemes of the Whig administration as well as contemporary scientists. Swift is following a well-established tradition in English literature of satirizing the excesses and corruptions of scientific learning.

145. 9 "I was received": Swift himself visited Gresham College, home of the Royal Society, in 1710. In a letter to Stella (Dec. 13) he reports a day's activity which included a visit to the Tower of London, Bedlam, Gresham College, and a puppet-show — an odd mixture, perhaps inspired in some way by "the rainiest day that ever dript" (so he remarked of it).

146. 15–17 "colours . . . by feeling and smelling": The Great Scriblerus "first found out the palpability of colours" — so we are told in *The Memoirs of Scriblerus* (ch. viii), a satiric work in which Swift had a hand, along with Pope, Gay, Dr. Arbuthnot, and others (see the excellent edition of *The Memoirs*, edited by Charles Kerby-Miller, 1950, with valuable notes). A story of a blind man who could distinguish colors is related by the great scientist Robert Boyle, in his "Experiments and Observations upon Colour."

147. 35–36 "the universal artist": possibly an allusion to Robert Boyle, whose experiments touched many fields; but it may reflect, more generally, the pretensions of some contemporaries in the spirit of Bacon, to take all knowledge for their province. The Baconian spirit was strong among scientists.

148. 19–20 "how laborious the usual method": Compare this painless way of achieving learning with that attributed to the Moderns in *A Tale of A Tub*, sec. vii — "without the fatigue of reading or thinking."

150. 26 "school of languages": Swift gibes at the many suggestions, from scientists and others, for the formation of a philosophical or universal language. Comenius and John Wilkins, both influenced by Bacon, were perhaps the most influential of those who wrote on the subject, Wilkins's *Essay Towards a Real Character and a Philosophical Language* being published by the Royal Society in 1668. One of the ideals was that the *name* of a thing should in itself disclose the *nature* of the thing. Swift laughs at this notion by eliminating names altogether, reducing "language" to things.

155. 5 "at stool": thought to be a reference to papers found in Bishop Atterbury's close-stool and presented at his trial for Jacobite intrigues in 1722. Francis Atterbury, Bishop of Rochester and a good friend of Swift's, was found guilty of treason and fled to France. Like Swift, he was a Tory High-Churchman; but, unlike Swift, he actively supported the Pretender.

155. 18–19 "Tribnia . . . Langden": anagrams of "Britain" and "England."

155. 34 "mysterious meanings of . . . letters": Swift, who never believed Atterbury guilty, ridicules here the evidence against the bishop, particularly the endeavor to extract secret meanings from his correspondence. See note to p. 155, l. 5.

158. 37 "he was not poisoned": Plutarch in his *Lives* denies the story that Alexander the Great was poisoned by his cup-bearer. He died of a fever at Babylon in 323 B.C., at the age of 32.

158. 39–40   "Hannibal . . . vinegar in his camp": The progress of Hannibal's army over the Alps in Italy was blocked by a rock. The rock was heated, saturated with vinegar, and then easily cut. The story comes from Livy, Bk. XXI, ch. 37.

158. 44   "a modern representative": i.e., the British parliament.

160. 6   "Didymus and Eustathius": an Alexandrian (fl. 10 A.D.) and a Byzantine (12th century) who wrote commentaries on Homer.

160. 10   "Scotus and Ramus": Duns Scotus, from whose name the word "dunce" originated, was a leading scholastic philosopher (d. 1308) and author of a commentary on Aristotle. Pierre de la Ramée, an influential thinker of the sixteenth century, was a critic of Aristotle.

160. 17–18   "Gassendi . . . made Epicurus . . . palatable": Pierre Gassendi (1592–1655) supported Epicurean physics against Aristotelian and Cartesian physics. Although Epicurean ethics found defenders in the seventeenth and eighteenth centuries, the Epicurean system of physics was much attacked as atheistic and materialistic. In *A Tale of A Tub*, sec. ix, Swift uses Epicurean ideas for satiric purposes.

160. 19   "the *vortices* of Descartes": The physical theories of the great French philosopher and mathematician, René Descartes (1596–1650) were highly controversial in England in the late seventeenth and early eighteenth centuries. Particularly his theory of vortices, basic in his physics, came under fire. Swift refers to it in *A Tale of a Tub*, sec. ix, as a "romantick system."

160. 20   "*attraction*": i.e., Newton's theory of gravitation.

160. 23   "pretend to demonstrate them from mathematical principles": These words reflect the struggle between the natural philosophers (scientists) and the moral philosophers (humanists) in the period. Gulliver as Swift's spokesman expresses the scepticism of the moral philosophers over the claims of the scientists that mathematics, or the sciences founded on it, could arrive at certitude or ultimate truths. The humanists insisted that the most valuable knowledge was the knowledge of man, not of nature. The struggle between these two groups is one of the organizing principles of eighteenth-century thought.

160. 25   "determined": concluded.

160. 28   "Eliogabalus's cooks": Heliogabalus, Roman Emperor of the third century A.D., whose gluttony is proverbial.

161. 8   "Polydore Virgil": an Italian cleric of the sixteenth century who lived in England and wrote a history of England in Latin.

161. 17   "disgusted with modern history": Swift refers to the modern historians in *The Battle of the Books* as "mercenaries." His disgust with historical writers who have falsified the past can be better understood if we keep in mind the idealistic Ciceronian conception of

history which prevailed, history as the mistress of man's life, time's witness, the herald of antiquity, the light of truth, and life of memory. The exposure of "prostitute writers" at this point in *Gulliver* recalls Voltaire's remark that "history is only a pack of lies we play on the dead."

164. 27–28 "Dutch . . . the only Europeans permitted": After anti-Christian uprisings in 1638, some Dutch and Chinese traders remained as Japan's sole contact with the outside world. See below, note to p. 175, ll. 2–3.

167. 9–10 "*struldbruggs* or *immortals*": Cf. Swift's remark in his *Thoughts on Various Subjects:* "Every man desires to live long, but no man would be old."

169. 39–40 "revolutions of states and empires": In this paragraph Swift puts into Gulliver's mouth the prevalent conception of cyclical history, the view that nations, letters, the arts, knowledge in general, rise, flourish, languish, and die, only to begin a new cycle in another part of the world. This philosophy of history was opposed to two other theories of history also prevalent, one embodied in the phrase "decay of nature" and the other in the phrase "the idea of progress" (see above, note to p. 111, ll. 6–7). In his *Essay upon the Ancient and Modern Learning* Swift's patron, Sir William Temple, used the cyclical theory to counter the Moderns, who argued that civilization has maintained a steady and cumulative progress from ancient to modern times. The cyclical view of history reaches back to ancient Greece and Rome, and even beyond.

170. 2 "discovery of the longitude": Many attempts were made in the period to discover a simple, accurate method of determining the longitude at sea. The stimulus came in part from a large sum offered by parliament at the close of Anne's reign. "I am told," Swift wrote to Archbishop King in 1712, "it is a thing as improbable as the philosopher's stone, or perpetual motion." Some of the foolish proposals were satirized in Swift's circle.

170. 2–3 "perpetual motion": The idea of a perpetual motion machine had teased the imagination of scientists and others in England from the time of Bacon, who had included such machines in Solomon's House in *The New Atlantis,* 1627. By the time of *Gulliver* they were the subject of satire. Some scientists still toyed seriously with the idea; others felt that, given the laws of matter and motion, the construction of such a machine was impossible.

170. 3 "the universal medicine": another name for the elixir of life, which the alchemists maintained would prolong life indefinitely. In *A Tale of a Tub* Swift refers to Artephius, an alchemist who is reputed to have lived a thousand years or more by virtue of the *elixir vitae.* The editor of this volume does not know the elixir used by

Artephius. He offers the following as a substitute: "Take ten parts of celestial slime; separate the male from the female, and each afterwards from its earth, but physically, mark you, and with no violence. Conjoin after separation in due harmonic, vital proportion. Straightway the soul, descending from the pyroplastic sphere, shall restore, by a vivific embrace, its dead and deserted body. The conjoined substances shall be warmed by a natural fire in a perfect marriage of spirit and body. Proceed according to the Vulcanico-magical theory till they are exalted into the fifth metaphysical rota. This is that world-renowned medicine of which so many have scribbled, and yet so few have known" (from A. E. Wait, *The Hermetic and Alchemical Writings of Aureolus Philippus Theophrastus Bombast, of Hohenheim, called Paracelsus the Great*, 1894, II, 384).

170. 9–10 "desire of endless life": As a divine, Swift could hardly have been unaware that the concept of an earthly immortality ran counter to the Christian view of death as coming in with the Fall and being the inevitable lot of man.

170. 40–41 "disadvantages which old age brings": The subject of old age, with its attendant physical and moral deterioration, had been a convention in literature from the time of the ancients. Cicero in *De Senectute* (c. 44. B.C.) depicted the compensations and consolations of age, but perhaps the preponderance of literature up to Swift's day had been less favorably disposed. Swift should be seen in the latter tradition, very strong in his time.

174. 20 "Yedo": Tokyo.

175. 2–3 "*trampling upon the crucifix*": the *Jefumi* or "figure treading" was a test apparently used in certain localities to detect Japanese suspected of being converts to Christianity. There is no evidence that it was applied to the Dutch, as Swift indicates.

175. 8–9 "suspected I must be a Christian": Swift's bias against the Dutch resulted in part from the commercial rivalry between England and Holland and in part from the danger to the established Church in England from Holland as a symbol of a nation where religious toleration prevailed, to the benefit of domestic tranquility and commercial prosperity. Holland was also politically anathema as a republic and as an obstructive ally in the Grand Alliance against France.

175. 23 "*Amboyna*": As Mr. William Brown points out, Swift did not innocently choose the name of this ship. He is trying to keep alive English belief in the cruelty of the Dutch, who had tortured some Englishmen at Amboyna, in the East Indies in 1623. Dryden had revived memories of the Amboyna massacre in a play in 1673.

175. 39 "skipper": seaman.

179. 11 "Tenariff": Teneriffe, largest of the Canary Islands.

179. 12 "Campechy": on the coast of Yucatan. The logwoods, called campeachy wood, brought in from that area were used for making dyes.

181. 6–7   "shape . . . singular, and deformed": Swift's description of the Yahoos may have been suggested, according to Professor R. W. Frantz, by the accounts of large apes or of the Hottentots to be found in contemporary voyage literature. The word "Yahoo" derives, possibly, from two common expressions of disgust in the period, "yah" and "ugh" (Morley).

183. 12–13   "coat . . . wonder": The antithesis between nature and art, the natural and the artificial, a dominant theme in Pt. IV, is thus suggested early, when the Houyhnhnms who discover Gulliver are bewildered by his clothes, an artifice which does not exist among those who live according to nature. See below, note to p. 190, l. 2.

184. 14   "*Houyhnhnm*": generally accepted as an imitation of the whinny of a horse.

186. 14–15   "in this abominable animal a perfect human figure": Swift's denigration here, and elsewhere in Pt. IV, of the human body may be a satirical reaction to the physico-theologists of the times, who were lyrical in praising the body's perfection as evidence of God's handiwork and of design in the universe.

188. 19–20   "insipid diet": Gulliver's remarks on his simple diet and the good health which resulted contain more than meets the eye. It touches Swift personally in that he experimented much with diets for reasons of health, but it is also a reflection of contemporary primitivistic thought. The simple, health-giving diet of peoples living in a state of nature was often contrasted with the rich, harmful food of people in artificial societies. Furthermore, the passage reflects medical and theological tradition, particularly with respect to the concept of temperance, a virtue that man lost in the Fall. It was believed that disease (a result of repletion) and sin (as gluttony: intemperance in diet) went hand in hand. The diet of the Houyhnhnms, the very essence of temperance, is part and parcel of their rational behavior and moral perfection, in sharp contrast to the diet of the Yahoos, which is immoderate and in good part proscribed under the Levitical code of the Old Testament.

188. 29   "salt": Many commentators have noted the inaccuracy of Gulliver's remark that no animal except man is fond of salt.

189. 14–15   "speak to his horse . . . in High Dutch": i.e., German. Charles V is credited with the remark that he would address his God in Spanish, his mistress in Italian, and his horse in German.

190. 2   "not the least idea of books": Like clothes, books have no place in a "natural" society. Here again the Houyhnhnms reflect the primitivistic strain in eighteenth-century thought. See above, the note to p. 183, ll. 12–13.

195. 39–40 "find fault with . . . my body": See above, note to p. 186, ll. 14–15.

198. 24 "difference in opinions": There follow four references to contemporary religious controversies — over the consecrated elements of bread and wine in the Eucharist, the use of music in church services, the veneration of the Crucifix, and the nature of ecclesiastical vestments. Cf. the controversy in Pt. I between the Big and Little Endians. In *A Tale of a Tub* Swift gives elaborate treatment to sectarian differences.

199. 19–20 "beggarly princes . . . hire out their troops": an allusion to the mercenaries of George I when Elector of Hanover.

199. 37–38 "a description of cannons": See Pt. II, ch. vii, p. 108 and note.

201. 30 "faculty": the profession.

202. 34–35 "the use of money": For a contemporary comment on the power of money, see Bernard Mandeville's *Fable of the Bees*, Part II, Sixth Dialogue, where Cleomenes remarks that "nothing is more universally charming than Money."

203 .14–15 "especially those who presided over the rest": The ambiguity of this statement has been noted. Case suggests persuasively that it means "especially that species which presided over the rest."

203. 23 "female yahoos . . . breakfast": In this passage Swift reflects the contemporary mercantilist animus against imports, especially of luxuries. He complained that Ireland imported tea, coffee, and chocolate at an annual cost of £150,000; and he agreed with Bishop Berkeley that an Irish woman of fashion dressed in imported clothes is a public enemy.

204. 1 "wine": In 1729 Swift argued amusingly against Ireland's increasing the duty on the importation of wine "because there is no nation yet known, in either hemisphere, where the people of all conditions are more in want of some cordial, to keep up their spirits, than this of ours" (*A Proposal that all the Ladies . . . of Ireland should appear constantly in Irish Manufactures*, 1729).

213. 8–9 "seeds of spleen": Spleen was the fashionable malady of the early eighteenth century, all the more socially acceptable because Queen Anne suffered from it. The term was used rather loosely to describe vapors, hypochondria, ennui, lowness of spirits, and particularly melancholy, which was thought by both Englishmen and foreigners to be a special characteristic of the English — "a kind of demon that haunts the island" — so Addison remarked (*Spectator*, No. 387; see also Pope's Cave of Spleen in *The Rape of the Lock*). For an excellent study consult "The English Malady," in Cecil A. Moore's *Backgrounds of English Literature, 1700–1760*, 1953.

216. 20 "as Plato delivers them": an allusion, possibly, to *The*

Republic (bk. v), where *opinion* and *real knowledge* are distinguished.

216. 31 "fondness": foolish doting.

226. 26 "devoted": doomed.

226. 29 "temper": calmness.

227. 19 "artificially": skilfully.

228. 17 "February 15, 1714–15": i.e., 1715 in our reckoning. In Swift's day the English New Year began not on Jan. 1, but on March 25.

229. 26 "Mr. Herman Moll": a famous map-maker of the period.

231 b.–232. 1 "three years' residence": The chronology of Pt. IV is inconsistent or erroneous, by fault perhaps of the printer, perhaps of Swift himself. Gulliver resided in Houyhnhnmland for 3 years, 9 months, and 6 days. See the discussion of the chronology of *Gulliver's Travels* by Arthur E. Case in *Four Essays on "Gulliver's Travels,"* 1945.

232. 40 "backwards": situated at the rear.

234. 15 "stone-horses": stallions.

235. 23–24 "*Nec . . . finget*": Although vile Fortune has made Sinon wretched, she has not made him false and a liar (Virgil, *Aeneid,* II, 79–80).

236. 44 "*Recalcitrat . . . tutus*": He kicks backward, secure on every side (Horace, *Satires,* II, i, 20).

The Text. The collected edition of Swift's *Works,* Dublin, 1735, published by George Faulkner, with Swift's approval and containing his own corrections, revisions, and suggestions to improve the editions printed by Motte in 1726 and 1727. Some readings have been adopted from the Motte editions and from the various corrections and additions made by Swift's friend, Charles Ford, at the time of the first publication of *Gulliver* in 1726. Faulkner's italics, spelling, capitalization, and punctuation have been normalized amply enough, I trust, so that the text should present no difficulty to the student from "accidentals."

A Tale of a Tub (1704)

The *Apology* and the Notes. The *Apology* appeared for the first time in the fifth edition of *A Tale of a Tub* in 1710. Swift intended it as an answer to critics of the work.

All unsigned notes at the bottom of the pages were either written or approved by Swift, probably the former.

The notes signed "W. Wotton" Swift humorously extracted from the attack on *A Tale of a Tub* in 1705 by William Wotton (see below, note to p. 243, ll. 5–6).

Other notes at the bottom of the pages are from later editors and annotators. A few are from the edition of 1720 and from Swift's friend, Will Pate, whom he called "a learned woolendraper." The majority are from the editions of John Hawkesworth (signed "H") and Sir Walter Scott (signed "Scott"). The most complete annotation of *A Tale* is to be found in the edition of A. C. Guthkelch and David Nichol Smith, Clarendon Press, second edition, 1958.

242. 1 "Treatises . . . by the same Author": Swift did not write any of the treatises mentioned and probably had no intention of writing most of them. The titles are intended as part of his comic apparatus of pretense. He did, however, have some incipient plans for writing on two of the topics, the ninth and tenth in the list.

243. 5–6 "treatises written . . . against it": The most effective attack on *A Tale of a Tub* came from William Wotton, a clergyman, whose *Observations upon the Tale of a Tub* (1705) viewed Swift's work as a crude banter upon "all that is esteemed as sacred . . . among men." Perhaps more than any of the attacks, Wotton's *Observations* prompted Swift to pen this "Apology," which first appeared in the fifth edition of *A Tale*, in 1710. Amusingly Swift took advantage of his enemy's lengthy analysis of the *Tale* by including many of Wotton's interpretations in the notes of the fifth edition, with Wotton given full credit by name.

245. 2 "men in the weightiest stations": a reference, possibly, to John Sharp, Archbishop of York, whom Swift blamed for hindering his preferment in the Church of England. In his poem, "The Author Upon Himself," Swift says that Sharp showed Queen Anne "A dang'rous treatise writ against the Spleen" — i.e., *A Tale of a Tub*. Presumably he represented to the Queen that the author of this work was unfit to be a bishop.

245. 30 "L'Estrange": Sir Roger L'Estrange (1616–1704), journalist, miscellaneous writer, translator, and violent controversialist.

Knighted by James II, he was imprisoned for a time after the Revolution of 1688.

246. 17 "number Three . . . a dangerous meaning": Swift shows himself sensitive to the accusation that he had reflected on the doctrine of the Trinity.

247. 28 "a person of graver character": William Wotton. See above, note to p. 243, ll. 5–6.

247. 39 "drawn his pen against a . . . great man": Wotton defended the Moderns, in his *Reflections upon Ancient and Modern Learning* (1694), against the strictures of Sir William Temple, a proponent of the Ancients in the famous Ancient-Modern controversy, which is the subject of Swift's *Battle of the Books*. Swift now refers to Wotton as "the Reflecter."

253. 13–14 "a prostitute bookseller": Edmund Curll, the most notorious publisher of the eighteenth century, who regularly printed private letters and other works without authorization. He published *A Complete Key to The Tale of a Tub* in 1710 (reprinted in the Appendix of the Guthkelch-Nichol Smith edition of *A Tale*).

254. 3 DEDICATION. "Lord Somers": a distinguished Whig statesman, one of the four Swift defended in his early political pamphlet, *Contests and Dissensions between the Nobles and Commons*, 1701. Somers attempted without success to help Swift advance in the Church. They remained friends until Swift allied himself with the Tories in 1710.

256. 33 "Bookseller": the eighteenth-century term for "publisher."

261. 22 "a certain poet, called John Dryden": Swift's satire of Dryden here and in the *Battle of the Books* has traditionally been attributed to personal animosity, inspired by a presumed remark Dryden once made to Swift: "Cousin Swift, you will never be a poet." But Professor Maurice Johnson has effectively combatted the legend (in *PMLA*, LXVII, 1952, pp. 1024ff.). There is no satisfactory evidence that Dryden ever made the remark and no reason in Swift's treatment of Dryden for ascribing a personal animus. The political and literary career of Dryden was not without certain oddities which made him fair game for the satirist. Added to this he was an obvious target for Swift because of his desertion of Protestantism and his association with the Royal Society of Scientists and the Moderns.

261. 25 "Nahum Tate": the poet-laureate, appointed in 1692.

263. 22 "Hobbes's *Leviathan*": From the vantage of the controversies he stirred up, Hobbes was the most influential philosopher of the century, along with Locke. The *Leviathan*, his most controversial work, appeared in 1651.

264. 14 "Hobby-horses": hobbies.

265. 16 "the sublime": an aesthetic concept of the period, the subject of extensive analysis, stimulated by *Longinus on the Sublime*. The "sublime" was concerned with the rapturous and transporting passions generated by the contemplation of any sublime object, whether in nature, poetry, music, architecture, or painting.

265. 35–36 "devoted servant of all modern forms": In several sections of *A Tale* Swift makes ironical use of a Modern as a *persona*, who in praising the Moderns actually undermines their position.

269. 24 "Covent-Garden": This famous area of London acquired notoriety in the eighteenth century for its brothels, thieveries, and general dissoluteness.

269. 26 "Whitehall": then a royal palace.

269. 27 "city": The City of London, usually referred to simply as the City, was that part of London situated within the ancient boundaries. It contained the Exchange and the Bank of England. Swift uses the word in its common implication as the center of commerce or the business community.

271. 14–15 "Socrates . . . in a basket": from *The Clouds* of Aristophanes, where Socrates has a school or "Thinking-Shop."

273. 14–18 "ascending orators . . . British eloquence": The orators are condemned criminals ascending the gallows (i.e., the ladders), whose dying speeches were published (and sometimes composed) by the chaplain of Newgate prison, Paul Lorrain (d. 1719). Swift tried his hand at composing the "dying" speech of an Irish criminal, *The Last Speech and Dying Words of Ebenezor Elliston*, 1722.

273. 19 "John Dunton": a prolific journalist and hack writer, 1659–1732 (see the interesting study of him in C. A. Moore, *Backgrounds of English Literature, 1700–1760*).

273. 23 "engine . . . stage itinerant": "engine" in the sense of a mechanical contrivance. The stage itinerant, as Swift later explains, is a symbol of Grub Street (see the next note but one).

274. 36–37 "our modern saints": Anglican writers often derisively called puritans and dissenters "saints."

275. 17–18 "writers of and for *Grub Street*": Grub Street is the contemporary term applied to literary hacks and all ephemeral writing. Swift refers to the writers as Grubaean Sages. Actually there was a street so named, near Moorfields in London, inhabited, according to Dr. Johnson, "by writers of small histories, dictionaries, and temporary poems."

276. 36 "harlots": Swift's note identifying "harlots" as "modern comedies" reflects the contemporary attack, led by Jeremy Collier, upon the drama as immoral and profane. In his *Project for the*

Advancement of Religion (1709) Swift devotes a vigorous paragraph to the corruptions of the theater.

278. 10 *"adeptus":* This word and other obscure terms in this paragraph are from the jargon of alchemy. Swift satirizes or uses for other comic purposes a considerable body of terminology and ideas from mysticism, cabalism, alchemy, and Rosicrucianism. An *adeptus* is one who has attained the great secret of alchemy, the method of converting base metal into gold. Artephius, here credited by Swift with writing *Dr. Faustus* and living to the age of a thousand, is presumed to have reached his great age by taking the elixir of life. (Instances of Swift's use of alchemical and other "dark" authors have been collected in an Appendix in the Guthkelch-Nichol Smith edition of *A Tale*. See also the discussion by Miriam K. Starkman, in *Swift's Satire of Learning in "A Tale of a Tub"* [1950], pp. 44ff.). For the universal medicine or *elixir vitae*, see the note to p. 170, l. 3.

278. 19–21 *"The Hind and the Panther* . . . schoolmen": Dryden's famous poem is related to scholasticism because it reflects his conversion to Catholicism.

280. 16–17 "three sons by one wife": Wotton remarked that this was an instance of Swift's looking "asquint at the Trinity."

280. footnote 6. "Lambin": a French classical scholar of the sixteenth century. The anachronistic use of his name as an annotator of *A Tale* is a characteristic device of Swift's foolery.

281. 3–4 "live . . . in one house like brethren": "By the old man's advice to his son . . . unity is enjoined" (Curll's *Complete Key*).

281. 9 "the first seven years": the first seven centuries of Christianity, before corruptions of doctrine and practice set in.

281. 32 "Levee": the name given to the fashionable custom of receiving visitors early in the day.

282. 14–15 "a goose . . . from Jupiter": a tailor's smoothing-iron, so called because the handle is shaped like a goose's neck. Jupiter Capitolinus refers to the temple of Jupiter on the summit of the Capitoline Hill at Rome. The Capitol was saved from the Gauls in 390 B.C. when its defenders were awakened by the cries of the sacred geese.

282. 16 "Hell": a place into which a tailor throws shreds of cloth.

283. 34 *"ex traduce":* The theological doctrine of traduction held that the soul of a child, like the body, is propagated by or inherited from the parents.

288. 26–27 "a mystery . . . not to be . . . pried into": Swift reacted sharply against theological controversies in which the religious mysteries were learnedly analyzed. His sermon *On the Trinity* is a characteristic indictment of those who would explain the mysteries by subtle speculations and philosophical intricacies. See also his *Letter to a Young Gentleman lately entered into Holy Orders* (1720).

290. 31 "caution . . . through Edinburgh streets": The "effluvia of Edinburgh" (Boswell's phrase) was notorious, a result of the custom of throwing filth from the windows into the streets.

291. 17 "Momus and Hybris": In Greek divinity Momus is the god of ridicule, hence a captious critic; Hybris is the personification of pride or insolence.

292. 7 "Stymphalian birds": In mythology, Stymphalus, a district in Arcadia, was inhabited by some odious birds of prey. Their destruction was the sixth of the labors of Hercules.

294. 21–22 "our Scythian ancestors": One current theory held that the Scots were descended from the ancient Scythians.

297. 25–26 "he was their elder": " . . . an allusion to the Pope's setting up for the Supremacy, taking to himself the title of *Papa & Dominus Dominorum*, and finding ways and means to raise a fund for supporting his grandeur" (Curll's *Complete Key*).

299. 13–14 "our friendly societies": a phrase applied to insurance companies and benefit-clubs in the eighteenth century.

300. 29 "squibs and crackers": fireworks.

301. 40 "man's man": "i.e. Servus Servorum Dei, being the words us'd at the conclusion of a pardon granted by the Pope" (Curll's *Complete Key*).

303. 3 "pick up . . . strollers": permitting concubinage.

307. 25 "*utile . . . dulce*": Horace's famous remark that poetry is intended to instruct and please, in the *Ars Poetica*.

307. 30 "whether there have been ever any ancients": Swift refers to the insistence by defenders of the Moderns that, after all, the true Ancients are those who live in the later ages of the world, i.e., the Moderns. Cf. *A Battle of the Books*, p. 364, for this "Modern Paradox" and note to p. 364, ll. 23–24.

308. 1 "a certain curious receipt": The recipe which follows is another instance of Swift's satiric use of occultism, possibly reflecting Rosicrucianism whose devotees, as Mrs. Starkman points out, were "*adepti* at alchemical formulae and universal knowledge," with obscure recipes to achieve their ends. Thomas Vaughan, the Hermetic philosopher, called his endeavor to find a universal formula a "celestial hydro-pyro-magical art." Sir William Temple, who lumped the alchemists and the Rosicrucians together as examples of the Moderns, wrote: "I should as soon fall into the study of the Rosycrusian philosophy, and expect to meet a nymph or a sylph, for a wife or a mistress, as with the elixir for my health, or philosopher's stone for my fortune" (*Some Thoughts upon Reviewing an Essay of Ancient and Modern Learning*, 1731 ed., I, 299).

308. 20–21 *"abstracts, summaries . . . extracts"*: One of Swift's favorite themes, the superficiality of the Moderns ("their prudent method, to become scholars and wits, without the fatigue of reading or of thinking" [sec. vii]), is here related to the contemporary vogue of publishing readers' digests in the form of abstracts, summaries, and extracts. John Dunton's *Young Students Library*, referred to by Mrs. Starkman, contained "extracts and abridgments" of books printed in England and on the Continent. Charles Gildon, a minor writer of the day, praised the practice as being useful to those who "have no time to peruse so many large volumes" (quoted by Mrs. Starkman, p. 83). Swift's Modern *persona* recommends his own work, *My New Help of Smatterers, or the Art of being Deep-learned and Shallow-read.* Cf. Sir William Temple's remarks on the "airy speculations" of the Moderns, who expect to discover a means by which men will have a "knowledge of one another's thoughts, without the grievous trouble of speaking" (*Some Thoughts . . .* , 1731 ed., I, 303).

309. 6 "save-all": a contrivance for holding candle-ends in a candlestick, so that they may burn to the end.

309. 17 "flies and spittle": In ridiculing the Moderns, Temple remarked that he was unable to appreciate the value of some of their discoveries, for example, "the admirable virtues of that noble and necessary juice called spittle" (*Some Thoughts . . .* , 1731 ed., I, 303).

313. 8–9 "hardly a thread of the original coat . . . seen": that is, Christianity in its primitive purity has been submerged beneath innovations and ceremonies which were, in the contemporary phrase, "the inventions of men." Theologians and others in the period frequently called for a revival of primitive Christianity. A prevailing philosophy of history held that all institutions were purer in their original state, that they accumulated corruptions as they grew older.

314. 17–19 "zeal . . . the most significant word . . . in any language": Swift uses the word nearly always in a pejorative sense, particularly in religious controversy, to mean a highly irrational or emotional behavior, well beyond the bounds of common sense. He often applied it to the dissenters. Thus we find in this section that Jack's zeal makes him carry the Reformation to excessive lengths.

314. 25 "modern way of subscription": a reference to the frequent and much-abused practice of gathering subscribers to literary works in advance of publication, with the names of the subscribers to be listed in the front of the book. Swift himself actively solicited subscriptions for Pope's translation of the *Iliad* and Prior's *Poems on Several Occasions.*

316. 7 "garnish": slang for the money extorted from a new prisoner by the jailer or by the other prisoners (as drink-money). The custom was abolished by law in the reign of George IV.

317. 6 "an *Iliad* in a nutshell": As Guthkelch and Nichol Smith point out, Swift may have taken this phrase from either Pliny, who attributes it to Cicero, or from Rabelais. ". . . though it were written in characters as small as those in which were penned Homer's Iliads, which Tully tells us he saw enclosed in a nutshell" (from Rabelais, *Pantagruel*, V. xx).

318. 29–30 "like Hercules's oxen, by tracing them backwards": In Roman legend the brigand Cacus stole from Hercules some of the cattle of Geryon. He tried to avoid discovery by drawing them into his cave tail foremost.

321. 1 "æolists": Wotton characterized this section as a banter of inspiration and "a mixture of impiety and immodesty." Swift intended it to be a satire of what he might call a carnal or physical ecstasy, mechanically induced, rather than a true spiritual inspiration. Anglicans often were critical of the "divine seizures" exhibited by members of certain nonconformist sects. Swift gives an extended treatment to this subject in *The Mechanical Operation of the Spirit* (1704). This section of *A Tale* will be better understood if a reader keeps in mind certain fundamental differences between the Anglicans and some nonconformists groups. The Anglican articles acknowledged the divine inspiration of the scriptures but did not presume that members of the Anglican communion were so gifted. Secondly, the Anglican clergy tended to read their sermons and had set forms of prayers, whereas the dissenters frequently used extemporaneous preaching and praying, often in a highly emotional rhetoric.

323. 3–4 "in his nostrils . . . the choicest . . . belches": A common criticism of dissenting preachers was directed at their uncultivated nasal tones. In *The Mechanical Operation of the Spirit* Swift relates the "Twang of the Nose" to the "Snuffle of a Bag-Pipe," thus indicating that he has in mind the Scottish Presbyterians. He promises to consider the matter of Presbyterian pulpit eloquence in his *Critical Essay upon the Art of Canting, Philosophically, Physically, and Musically Considered.*

326. 30–33 "new empires . . . new schemes in philosophy . . . new religions": Swift's bias against innovations here is repeated in *Gulliver's Travels*, Bk. III, ch. iv.

327. 5 "if the vapour . . . into the brain": In this section Swift toys with the current view that madness resulted from vapors reaching the brain. As Mrs. Starkman points out (*Swift's Satire on Learning in "A Tale of a Tub,"* pp. 24ff.), the word "vapor" in the period was used in a variety of senses. It had some relationship (in the medical view of madness) to the animal spirits, which controlled man's rational powers, to the four humors of traditional physiology, and to the conception of the body as a fine and precise machine — a conception set forth in the speculations of Descartes and the Iatrophysical school of medicine.

329. 29–30 "Epicurus . . . fortuitous concourse": Although the Epicurean moral philosophy had defenders in the period, Epicurean physics, summed up in the materialistic conception that the world had been formed by a chance collocation of atoms, was constantly attacked. In this respect Epicurus, along with Lucretius, was viewed as the arch-atheist.

329. 34–36 "Cartesius . . . his romantic system . . . his own vortex": Though Cartesian physics, with its theory of vortices, was at first favorably received in England, a strong reaction had set in by the last two decades of the seventeenth century and the theory of the vortex was attacked as atheistic or materialistic. Swift refers to the theory in *Gulliver's Travels* (Pt. III, ch. viii) and in *The Battle of the Books* (p. 373). It was often termed pure romance. Temple wrote that "Descartes, among his friends, always called his philosophy, his romance" (*Some Thoughts . . .* , 1731 ed., I, 291).

330. 39–40 "enthusiasm": In the pejorative use of this word the eighteenth century embodied a sharp distrust of man's irrational nature. It meant variously fancied inspiration, a delusion of divine favor or communication, ill-regulated religious emotion or speculation, a heated imagination, from any or all of which, as Hume remarks in his essay, *Of Superstition and Enthusiasm*, "arise raptures, transports, and surprising flights of fancy," reaching to a frenzy in which human reason and morality "are rejected as fallacious guides."

331. 12 "Jack of Leyden": a tailor named Jan Bocklesan or Buckholdt, an Anabaptist, who in the religious struggles of the sixteenth century seized the city of Münster and made himself king and prophet under the title of John of Leyden. To Swift he represents a religious fanatic or enthusiast.

332. 1 "cant": The word signifies, according to *The Spectator*, No. 147, "all sudden exclamations, whinings, unusual tones, and in fine all praying and preaching like the unlearned of the Presbyterians."

333. 27–29 "with Epicurus content . . . with the . . . images . . . from the superficies of things": a reference to the infallibility of the senses and sensations in Epicurean thought, as contrasted with fallible reason. Swift's "happy Epicure" (Mrs. Starkman's phrase) hugs his delusions and is thus serene and happy.

334. 28 "Bedlam": the Bethlehem Hospital for the insane.

335. 7 "furnished . . . with a green bag": Lawyers customarily carried green bags for their documents. One contemporary remarked on the young barristers whose green bags "have as little in them as their noodles."

335. 18 "the city": See above, note to p. 269, l. 27.

336. 9 "society of Warwick-lane": the Royal College of Physicians.

339. 39 "republic of dark authors": occult writers. See above, note to p. 278, l. 10.

342. 29–30 "philosopher's stone, and the universal medicine": See above, note to p. 278, l. 10.

345. 3–4 "Gothic structure upon Salisbury plain": Stonehenge.

349. 23 "the saints": See above, note to p. 274, ll. 36–37.

350. 25 "spunging-house": a house kept by a bailiff as a place of preliminary confinement for debtors.

352. 15 "to write upon *Nothing*": By the time of *A Tale* a considerable body of literature had already been produced on the subject of "nothing." It reached back to the twelfth century on the Continent; in England poems and essays in praise of nothing began as early as 1585. In Swift's time perhaps the best known was Lord Rochester's poem, "Upon Nothing" (c. 1680), but John Dunton, Pope, and others gave the topic some attention. The vogue continued throughout the century, the most notable contribution coming from Fielding, whose "Essay on Nothing" appeared in 1743. These literary bagatelles formed a distinct tradition or literary type, deriving from ancient rhetoric, the paradoxical encomium, in which panegyrics were applied to unworthy or trivial matters, as maggots, dullness, knavery, dumplings, avarice. For an excellent study of the subject, see Henry Knight Miller, "The Paradoxical Encomium with Special Reference to its Vogue in England, 1600–1800," *Modern Philology*, LIII (1956), 145–78.

(The text. The fifth edition of 1710, with occasional readings from the first four editions. In *A Tale of a Tub* and throughout this volume, with one exception to be noted, I have freely brought the spelling, punctuation, capitalization, and italics into conformity with modern usage where the original practices might prove a hindrance to students.)

THE BATTLE OF THE BOOKS (1704)

357. 4–5 "the controversy took its rise": *The Battle of the Books* is Swift's defense of his patron, Sir William Temple. Temple entered the controversy over the respective merits of the Ancients and the Moderns in 1690 with his *Essay upon the Ancient and Modern*

Learning. His defense of the Ancients was answered by the clergy-man William Wotton in *Reflections Upon Ancient and Modern Learning,* 1694. In the second edition of this work, 1697, Dr. Richard Bentley, noted Greek scholar and Librarian of the Royal Library in St. James's Palace, entered the fray: he utilized the Appendix for his *Dissertation* attacking the authenticity of two renowned Ancients, Phalaris and Aesop, the first of whom had recently been edited by Charles Boyle. Thus, as Wotton and Bentley were aligned with the Moderns and Boyle with the Ancients, Swift treats them accordingly. Wotton's *Defence* of his work in 1705 contained the famous attack on Swift's *Tale of a Tub.* For a scholarly study of the controversy between the Ancients and the Moderns, see Richard Foster Jones, *Ancients and Moderns: A Study of the Background of the "Battle of the Books,"* 1936.

357. 7–8 "to destroy the credit of Aesop and Phalaris": Bentley denied the antiquity and authenticity of the fables ascribed to Aesop. Phalaris, a Sicilian tyrant of the 6th century B.C., was credited with the authorship of some epistles, though they were suspected generally as being forgeries of a later period. That they were in fact of a later period Bentley ably demonstrated, thus partially undermining Temple's position, who had eulogized them as the work of an Ancient.

357. 10–11 "a new edition of Phalaris . . . by . . . Boyle": Charles Boyle (later Earl of Orrery) not yet 20, was a promising young scholar at Christ Church, Oxford. He was induced to edit Phalaris by Dean Aldrich of Christ Church. His edition, 1695, had some help from other scholars of the College. Boyle was by no means committed to the view that the epistles of Phalaris were genuine.

357. 12–13 "Mr. Boyle replied . . . the doctor . . . rejoined": In the Preface to his edition of Phalaris, Boyle originated a personal quarrel by referring to Bentley's refusal to permit him ample time in collating a manuscript in the Royal Library. He wrote that Bentley had refused further use of the manuscript *pro singulari sua humanitate* [with that courtesy which distinguishes him]. Bentley rendered this literally as "out of his singular humanity" (see Swift's note, p. 363). In his *Dissertation Upon the Epistles of Phalaris . . . and the Fables of Aesop* (1697, 1699), Bentley replied to this public affront.

357. 13–14 "In this dispute, the town . . . resented": Swift seems to make Sir William Temple the center of the dispute. Actually the dispute was more fully confined to the two principals and their defenders. It was both scholarly and personal. In the first of these Bentley more than held his own, but in the personal aspect he was

perhaps less effective than Boyle's friends at Christ Church, who entered zealously into the fight. Their characterization of Bentley as an index-hunter, a critic without taste or breeding, a walking dictionary, created a conception of Bentley as the archetype of a pedant, a view that Swift, Pope, Arbuthnot, and other writers helped to perpetuate.

359. footnote 1. "*Ephem. de Mary Clarke;* opt. edit.": *Ephemeris* of Mary Clarke; best edition — as Nichol Smith points out, this is Swift's humorous description of a popular sheet, a tabular almanac, printed by Mary Clarke.

363. 8–9 "guardian . . . renowned for his humanity": See above, note to p. 357, ll. 12–13. Swift reflects ironically the complaint that Bentley had acted churlishly towards Boyle "out of his singular humanity." Boyle's defenders made much of the word "humanity" — notably in an anonymous pamphlet entitled *A Short Account of Dr. Bentley's Humanity and Justice* (1699). As R. C. Jebb points out (*Bentley*, 1882, p. 78), if Bentley was the victor with respect to scholarship, Boyle won a victory in the realm of taste and breeding.

363. 9–10 "a fierce champion for the Moderns": Why should Bentley, a classical scholar, be found siding with the Moderns? It has been suggested that Bentley was influenced in part by his friendship with Wotton and Newton, in part by his feeling that the spirit of the Royal Society and of scientific research was more congenial to his own work than the spirit of the classical humanists who opposed him. But see below, note to p. 377, ll. 24–25.

364. 2 "Withers": George Wither (1588–1667), poet and pamphleteer, often referred to as a poetaster.

364. 23–24 "Moderns . . . the more ancient": Bacon had insisted that the Moderns have an advantage over the Ancients "inasmuch as the Modern age is a more advanced age of the world, and stored and stocked with infinite experiments and observations" (*Novum Organum,* Aphorism LXXXIV). Charles Perrault, defender of the Moderns in France, wrote: ". . . il est très-vray que c'est nous qui sommes les Anciens" (*Parallèle des anciens et des modernes,* 1688).

366. 31–32 "my improvements in the mathematics": Although some of the zealous defenders of the Moderns were willing to grant that the Ancients were superior in poetry or oratory or music, they insisted that the Moderns had far excelled the Ancients in the realm of the physical and mathematical sciences, and in all areas dependent on mathematics, as navigation and fortifications. The new science as represented by the Royal Society was predominantly mathematical (See *Gulliver's Travels,* Pt. III, ch. ii, for Swift's satiric treatment of mathematicians). Temple would not admit the superiority of the Moderns in science: "Have the studies, the writings, the productions of Gresham College, or the late academies of Paris, outshined or eclipsed the Lyceum of Plato, the Academy of Aristotle, the Stoa of Zeno, the Garden of Epicurus?" He thought not. (See *An Essay upon the Ancient and Modern Learning*, 1731 ed., I, 165).

367. 29–30 "Aesop . . . most barbarously treated": See above, note to p. 357, ll. 7–8.

368. 36 "sweetness and light": This famous phrase was used by Matthew Arnold in *Culture and Anarchy* (1869).

369. 12–13 "Harvey": In maintaining the superiority of ancient science Temple suggested that Harvey owed his discovery of the circulation of the blood to the Ancients. Also he was not convinced of its truth. Even if true, Temple said, it has "been of little use to the world" (*An Essay upon the Ancient and Modern Learning*, 1731 ed., I, 162).

369. 17 "heavy-armed foot, all mercenaries": These are modern historians. Swift attacks those who falsify history in *Gulliver's Travels*, Pt. III, ch. viii.

369. 19–20 "engineers . . . Regiomontanus and Wilkins": "engineers" in the sense that they constructed or wrote about mechanical devices. John Wilkins, one of the founders of the Royal Society, wrote enthusiastically about the possibility of a "flying chariot" in his *Discovery of a New World* (1638) and *Mathematical Magic* (1648). He was associated with Robert Hooke, brilliant secretary of the Royal Society, who made many experiments in flying. Regiomontanus, a German scientist of the fifteenth century, had constructed a wooden eagle.

370. 7–9 "Momus . . . Pallas": Since the Moderns have "a large vein of wrangling and satire" (see p. 368), it is proper that Momus, god of ridicule, the celestial ancestor of modern critics (see *A Tale of a Tub*, p. 291) should be the patron of the Moderns. By the same token Pallas, goddess of wisdom, is made the patroness of the Ancients.

371. 37–38 "seminaries of Gresham and Covent Garden": Gresham College, where the Royal Society met, is linked with Covent Garden, whose coffee-houses and taverns, such as Will's, Button's, and the Cock, were frequented by wits, poets, and men of fashion.

372. 36 "Paracelsus . . . observing Galen": Perhaps the most bitter and relentless controversy between Ancients and Moderns was in the realm of medicine. Swift reflects this phase of the struggle by having Paracelsus and Galen engage in combat. Paracelsus and John Baptist Van Helmont, the famous Dutch scientist, were great pioneers of "chemical medicine" and medical practice based upon experiment and observation. In the seventeenth century a running fight went on between the Paracelsians and the Helmontists on the one side and the more conservative practitioners, who clung to the theories of Galen, on the other. The Royal College of Physicians was a stronghold of the Galenists, though some of its members yielded to the more advanced views. Sir William Temple thought Hippocrates and Galen superior to "Paracelsus and his chemical followers." For the medical controversy, see Richard Foster Jones, *Ancients and Moderns: A Study of the Background of the "Battle of the Books,"* 1936.

373. 4–6 "Bacon . . . the valiant Modern": Temple paid his respects to three great "modern wits": Sir Philip Sidney, Bacon, and Selden.

373. 10–11 "into his own *vortex*": See above, note to p. 329, ll. 34–36.

373. 33–34 "Perrault . . . Fontenelle": Charles Perrault (1628–1703) and Bernard le Bovier de Fontenelle (1657–1757) were two of the most ardent defenders of the Moderns in France.

374. 15 "the lady in a lobster": "the calcareous structure in the stomach of a lobster, fancifully supposed to resemble the outline of a seated female figure" (*OED*).

374. 18–19 "Dryden . . . soothed up the good Ancient, called him father": Dryden translated Virgil and acknowledged him as his master in Latin. See the note to p. 261, l. 22, for Dryden and Swift.

375. 7–11 "Creech . . . Ogleby": Thomas Creech and John Ogleby had translated various classical writers, including Horace (by Creech) and Homer (by Ogleby).

375. 13 "Pindar slew . . . Oldham . . . and Afra": Both John Oldham (1653–1683) and Mrs. Aphra Behn (1640–1689) modeled their odes after Pindar.

375. 16 "Cowley": Swift uses Abraham Cowley (1618–1667) in the role of poet because Cowley was the most acclaimed writer of pindarics of the time, but Cowley was also an enthusiastic supporter of the new science and of the Royal Society. His poem, "To the Royal Society," was printed at the beginning of Thomas Sprat's *History of the Royal Society*, 1667.

377. 13–14 "thy study of humanity": i.e., of the ancient Greek and Latin classics.

377. 24–25 "his beloved W–tt–n": "beloved" because Bentley's *Dissertation* was first printed as an appendix to Wotton's *Reflections* (2d ed., 1697). But Bentley, it should be noted, insisted that he was not taking up the cudgels for Wotton in the controversy over the Ancients and the Moderns; he was concerned with the authenticity of certain writings, particularly of Phalaris and Aesop.

378. 13–15 "Phalaris . . . his bull": Phalaris, whose cruelty was

proverbial, burned his enemies in a brazen bull, including the
Athenian who had presented him with the bull. Nichol Smith mentions a contemporary caricature of Bentley with the pun: "I had
rather be roasted than boyled."

378. 23–24 "a fountain . . . called . . . Helicon": Helicon is actually the mountain in Boeotia, sacred to the muses, on which were
the springs or fountains of Aganippe and Hippocrene.

380. 1–2 "helmet and shield of Phalaris . . . lately with his own
hands new polished": a reference to Boyle's edition of the *Epistles of
Phalaris* (1695).

380. 16–19 "Boyle . . . darted the weapon": The weapon is *Dr.
Bentley's Dissertations on the Epistles of Phalaris Examined* (1698),
in which Boyle attacked both Bentley and Wotton, the former much
more severely.

(The text. Faulkner's edition of Swift's *Works*, Dublin, 1735, with
a few readings from earlier editions.)

BICKERSTAFF PAPERS (1708–9)

382. 8 "Partridge's Almanack": John Partridge, a cobbler turned
astrologer, was a preëminent practitioner of astrological quackery
from as early as 1679. He mingled medicine, astrology, and politics
profitably, and even gained some royal recognition. He and his annual almanac, *Merlinus Liberatus*, had been satirized before Swift's
attack, by Tom Brown and Ned Ward; and Swift was joined in the
jest by Congreve, Steele, Addison, Prior, and Arbuthnot. For the
contributions by some of these, see Swift's *Prose Works*, edited by
Herbert Davis, Vol. II, Appendix B. Professor Davis suggests con-
vincingly that Swift's attack on Partridge was inspired in part by
the violent assaults the astrologer made on High Churchmen. A
pleasant account of the various exposures of Partridge is that by
William A. Eddy, "The Wits vs. John Partridge, Astrologer,"
Studies in Philology, XXIX (1932), 29ff.

Swift is presumed to have found the name Isaac Bickerstaff on a
sign over the dwelling of a locksmith. Steele took it over for his
Tatler.

382. 10 "Gadbury": John Gadbury was perhaps the chief rival of
Partridge, from whom Partridge learned his quackery but whom he
later attacked.

384. 1 "the Old Style observed in England": England did not
adopt the reformed calendar of Gregory XIII until 1752. The dates
which prevailed in England were known as Old Style, those abroad
as New Style. In the eighteenth century the difference was eleven
days. Jan. 1 (O.S.) was thus Jan. 12 (N.S.).

385. 34 "the Prophets": The French Prophets were a fanatical

sect in England started by refugee Protestants from France, the
Camisards, who believed they possessed the power of prophecy. The
chief member of the cult was John Lacy, very active at the time
Swift was writing about Partridge and much in the public eye.

387. 12–13 "Bartholomew Fair": held on St. Bartholomew's Day
(Aug. 24), for trade and pleasure, from the time of Henry II until
1855.

387. 27 "Virgil": Eclogue IV, 34–5.

389. 6 "die the 29th instant": On the 30th of March, one day
after the predicted date of Partridge's death, Swift published *The
Accomplishment . . . of Mr. Bickerstaff's Predictions*. Curiously, at
his "death" Partridge was struck from the role of the Company of
Stationers and denied at law the right to publish his Almanac. He
continued to dispense quack medicines.

389. 15–16 "Dr. Case and Mrs. Kirleus": two famous London
quacks at this time.

390. 38–39 "on his death-bed . . . a nonconformist": Swift glances
at Partridge's religious extremism by turning him into a fanatical dis-
senter on his death-bed.

392. 1–2 "to treat me . . . rough": In his Almanac for 1709
Partridge protested that he was still alive: "the same villain
[Bickerstaff] told the world I was dead, and how I died . . . I thank
God . . . that I am still alive, and (excepting my age) as well as
ever I was in my Life; as I was also at that 29th of March. And
that paper was said to be done by one Bickerstaffe, Esq., but that
was a sham-name; it was done by an impudent lying fellow. But
his prediction did not prove true."

392. 29–393. 1 "inquisition in Portugal . . . burn my predictions":
Swift's biographer, his relative Deane Swift, reported this as coming
from the English ambassador to Portugal. Some later biographers
have accepted the story as true.

393. 19 "Leibnitz": German philosopher and mathematician, 1646–
1716.

393. 20 "Le Clerc": Jean Le Clerc, 1657–1736, a Swiss theologian
who championed Arminianism.

393. 25 "Magliabecchi": a learned Florentine scholar, 1633–1714,
librarian to the Grand Duke of Tuscany.

396. 16 "a new set of predictions": probably *A Continuation of
the Predictions for the Remaining Part of the Year 1708*, by Isaac
Bickerstaff, Esq. The person who took over Swift's jest in this
paper wrote that Partridge was busy "composing a medicine called
Elixir Lethifugum, or the *Death-driving Elixir*," to avert his fate,
but to no avail.

396. 20 "Grub-Street": See above, note to p. 275, ll. 17–18.

(The texts. Faulkner's edition of Swift's *Works*, Dublin, 1735, with a few readings from earlier editions.)

THE TATLER, No. CCXXX (1710)

397. 1–11 "The following letter . . . *To* Isaac Bickerstaff, *Esq;*": Richard Steele issued the *Tatler* papers from 1709 to 1711 as *The Lucubrations of Isaac Bickerstaff, Esq.*, using Swift's pseudonym to take advantage of the popularity of the Bickerstaff Papers. Swift and Steele were warm friends before Swift abandoned the Whigs, and Swift is presumed to have written several *Tatlers* and given hints for others. No. CCXXX, however, is the only one definitely known to be his. In addition he contributed two poems to *The Tatler*. The subject of this paper, the corruptions of the English language, greatly preoccupied Swift (see below, note to p. 398, l. 11).

397. 24–25 "Grub-Street": See above, note to p. 275, ll. 17–18.

398. 3 "Court of Requests": courts established in the reign of Henry VIII, to decide claims under 40 shillings.

398. 11 "corruption of our English tongue": Like many of his contemporaries, Swift was concerned over the presumed deterioration of the language. In 1712 he published *A Proposal for Correcting, Improving and Ascertaining the English Tongue*, addressed to Robert Harley, in which he pleaded for the founding of an English Academy authorized to sanction usages. His proposal was immediately attacked by Whig journalists, who denounced Swift as a lewd, irreverent cleric, a political turncoat, and a partisan scribbler.

398. 25 "plenipo's": plenipotentiaries.

398. 27 "Jacks": Jacobites, supporters of James II, or the Stuart dynasty.

398. 29 "hipps": hypochondria, i.e., spleen or melancholy. See above, note to p. 213, ll. 8–9.

398. 35 "Country Put": slang for a lout or bumpkin.

399. 10 "Gothic": often used in the period in the sense of "medieval" and, by extension, "barbarous" or "unrefined."

400. 6 *Index Expurgatorius*: an authoritative specification of passages to be expunged or altered in works otherwise permitted. Swift has in mind as a parallel the *Index librorum prohibitorum*, a list published by authority of books which Roman Catholics are forbidden to read or may read only in expurgated editions.

400. 25 "sophisters": students at Cambridge in the second or third year.

(The text. Faulkner's edition of Swift's *Works*, Dublin, 1735.)

THE EXAMINER, Nos. 14 AND 16 (1710)

"No. 14": Swift had begun to conduct *The Examiner* in the preceding week, with No. 13. The earlier numbers of this Tory journal,

founded to present sympathetically the policies of the new ministry
headed by Robert Harley, were written by some of Swift's recently
acquired friends as he broke away from the Whigs, among them
Bolingbroke, Atterbury, and Prior. The first two of these men
appear significantly in the political allegory of *Gulliver's Travels*.
Swift wrote the *Examiners* from Nov. 2, 1710, to June 14, 1711, numbers 13 through 43, and gave hints for some later ones. He was much
attacked by the opposition as "Mr. Examiner." For the circumstances
which led to his appointment to the important task of chief journalist for the Harley ministry, see the Introduction, pp. xvi–xvii. See
also below, note to p. 407, l. 11.

402. 1 *"E quibus"*: Ovid, *Metamorphoses*, xii, 56–61.

402. 9 "the Art of Political Lying": In 1712 Dr. John Arbuthnot,
Swift's friend and physician to Queen Anne, published a brief treatise
entitled *The Art of Political Lying*. It was a mock proposal for a
two-volume work on this subject. Swift himself arranged for the
printing.

402. 15–16 "viceroy of a great western province": intended to
bring to the reader's mind the Earl of Wharton, who is the object of
Swift's attack in this essay. Wharton was then the viceroy or Lord
Lieutenant of Ireland. He had recently returned to England, to begin active opposition to the ministry of Harley and Bolingbroke,
which *The Examiner* was defending. Swift knew him to be both
dangerous and effective; and he attacked Wharton again in *The Examiner*, No. 17, and in *A Short Character of His Excellency Thomas
Earl of Wharton*, published in Dec., 1710.

403. 1 "Fame": "Fame" in the sense of rumor, depicted as a
monster in Virgil, *Aeneid*, iv, 173–78.

403. 29 "a prevailing party": the Whigs.

403. 34–35 "make . . . a patriot of a profligate": Swift dwells on
Wharton's notorious profligacy in *A Short Character*, mentioned
above in note to p. 402, ll. 15–16.

403. 40–41 *"flower-de-luces* and triple crowns"*: emblems of
France, a Catholic nation which favored the Pretender, and of Roman
Catholicism. Swift's point is that a political lie falsely depicts good
citizens or patriots (i.e., the Tories) as Jacobites.

404. 11 "Exchange-Alley": a center of the commercial interests —
the trading interest which Swift thought was dominating the landed
interest, to the disadvantage of the nation.

404. 23 "a certain great man": the Earl of Wharton.

404. 41–43 "God and Christ . . . believes in neither": Stories of
Wharton's blasphemous behavior were current. Swift recounts one
in *The Examiner*, No. 22, the desecration of an altar; and in *A Short
Character* he writes: Wharton "goeth constantly to prayers in the
forms of his place, and will talk bawdy and blasphemy at the chapel

door. He is a Presbyterian in politics, and an atheist in religion; but he chooseth at present to whore with a papist."

405. 22 "destroy . . . Church": As Lord Lieutenant of Ireland, Wharton endeavored to have the Test Act repealed, to ease the lot of the dissenters. Swift viewed this Whig policy as a threat to the Established Church. Even when he was allied with the Whigs, he was adamant against any measure which in his view would impair the strength of Anglicanism. See the Introduction, p. xv.

405. 40 "powerful motives from the city": bribery; the City is the old part of London where the financial and commercial interests were paramount.

407. 1 "Qui sunt": Cicero, *Pro Plancio*, xxxiii, 80.

407. 11 "the late removals at court": The ministry dominated by the Earl of Godolphin and the Duke of Marlborough fell in August, 1710, to be replaced by the ministry of Harley and Bolingbroke. Swift, who shortly thereafter became the leading journalistic defender of this ministry, began writing the *Examiner* papers in November. His chief task in *The Examiner* was to defend the change in ministries and to justify the policies of the new one, a task that could be fully successful only if the great popularity of Marlborough, whose victories at Blenheim, Ramillies, and elsewhere had made him a national hero, could be lessened. Swift addresses himself to this undertaking, particularly in *Examiners* Nos. 16 and 27.

407. 15 "ingratitude . . . to the Duke of Marlborough": Attacks on Marlborough by partisans of the new ministry brought defenses from his supporters, who declaimed against the ingratitude of the nation to a man who had done so much. Typical defenses may be seen in *The Medley*, Nos. 6 and 7 (a journal which often attacked Swift).

408. 1 "Hath he been accused of high crimes": Marlborough was not accused of crimes at this time, but a year later two charges were brought against him in the House of Commons, that he had been paid commissions of more than £63,000 on bread contracts for the allied army and had appropriated a much larger sum from the pay of foreign troops in English employ. His able defense, in the light of practices of the times, was to no avail, and he was dismissed from all of his employments by the Queen at the end of 1711.

408. 4–5 "honours, offices . . . grants . . . conferred on . . . his family": The long and sometimes stormy friendship of Queen Anne and the Duchess of Marlborough is a fascinating story in itself. Before her dismissal early in 1711, she held a number of employments — Groom of the Stole, Ranger of Windsor Park, Mistress of the Robes, Keeper of the Privy Purse — amounting to over £6000 annually. Swift has been much blamed for a reference to her as the mistress of the Earl of Godolphin.

408. 12 "Has the senate ever thanked him": In 1706 both Houses of Parliament conveyed thanks to Marlborough for his great services to the nation. Earlier, in 1702, the Tory House of Commons voted that he had "retrieved the ancient honour and glory of the English nation."

408. 19 "two persons allied by marriage": Godolphin, the Lord Treasurer, whose son was married to Marlborough's daughter, Henrietta, and the Earl of Sunderland, Secretary of State, who was married to another daughter, Anne.

408. 38–39 "submission and respect to her sacred person": Anne gave as one reason for her dismissal of Godolphin that he displayed a want of respect to her dignity in the council. Harley wrote that the Earl "every day grows sourer and indeed ruder to [the queen]," in a letter dated a few days before the queen acted.

409. 6–7 "in wishing he might still be . . . head . . . forces": At the time of this *Examiner* Marlborough was still Captain General. Swift does not denigrate his greatness as a military man. He wrote to Stella a month later (Dec. 31): "I hope he will continue his command."

409. 24–26 "rewards . . . that . . . fit our temper best": The crux of the accusation against Marlborough is his avarice, a point fully developed in *The Examiner*, No. 27. Privately Swift expressed pity for Marlborough, but did not condone his faults as he conceived them: "He is covetous as hell, and ambitious as the Prince of it: he would fain have been general for life, and has broken all endeavours for Peace, to keep his greatness and get money" (*Journal to Stella*, Dec. 31, 1710).

409. 26–27 "Duke, or the Garter": Anne raised Marlborough from Earl to Duke in Dec., 1702, and granted him at the same time a pension of £5000 for her life out of the revenues of the post-office, as Swift mentions. The Queen's desire that this pension should be settled on his posterity after him forever was voted down in 1702 but carried in 1706. He was elected a knight companion of the Order of the Garter within a week of her accession to the throne; and within a month he was made captain-general of the army and sent to Holland as an ambassador extraordinary.

409. 30–31 "Woodstock . . . Blenheim Castle": In 1705 Anne, with the consent of Parliament, granted to Marlborough the ancient royal manor of Woodstock. The gift of Blenheim Palace soon followed, along with a pension of £5000 per annum, settled on him and his posterity. The Queen herself selected the famous dramatist and architect, Sir John Vanbrugh, as the architect for Blenheim Palace. Marlborough did not live to see it fully completed. Swift's estimate that it had cost £200,000 is perhaps high as of the date he wrote. By June of 1710 £134,000 had been spent and it was only half completed (Sir Winston Churchill, *Marlborough*, IV, 317).

409. 34 "principality in Germany": Soon after the Battle of Blenheim the grateful Emperor Leopold of the Holy Roman Empire made Marlborough a Prince of the Empire and gave him the little principality of Mindelheim. *The Medley*, No. 10, points out that Mindelheim, not being an English gift, should not be included in a list designed to show England's gratitude.

409. 36 "grant at the Pall-Mall": a reference to Marlborough House in Pall Mall, dating from 1709–10. Wren designed it.

409. 36 "the rangership": of Windsor Park.

411. 1 "visible profits on both sides": In *The Medley*, No. 10, Swift was accused of exaggerating the sums set down in his Bill of British Ingratitude. The writer of that paper drew up his own account of the value of Marlborough's services to the nation and of what he had received. By this calculation England was in debt to Marlborough for an additional seven and one half million pounds.

411. 12 "a saying of Seneca": *De Beneficiis*, I, i. This moral treatise is appropriate to Swift's purpose since it is much concerned with ingratitude.

411. 28 "A lady of my acquaintance": *Supposed to be her late Majesty Queen Anne* (note in *Works*, 1738).

411. 30 "her woman": *The Duchess of Marlborough* (note in *Works*, 1738).

(The text. Faulkner's edition of Swift's *Works*, Dublin, 1738.)

AN ARGUMENT AGAINST ABOLISHING CHRISTIANITY IN ENGLAND (1711)

"Abolishing of Christianity": For this phrase, to understand Swift's intention, substitute "repeal of the Test Act." The Test Act of 1673, passed at a time when the Anglicans deemed the Church in danger, was designed to safeguard the Anglican Establishment. Its chief provision was that holders of civil and political offices should be restricted to communicants of the Anglican faith. The "test" was the taking of the sacrament of the Lord's Supper according to the usage of the Church of England. This requirement was fiercely contested by the nonconformists and was felt to be oppressive by some Anglicans. But Swift felt keenly that the Church of England and of Ireland needed the protection the Test Act afforded. He wrote this ironical tract in 1708, when he was allied with the Whigs, who were then agitating for a repeal of the Test in Ireland and who looked forward to similar action in England. Swift's break with the Whigs resulted in part from his fear that their policies would weaken the Church. For some unknown reason the tract was not published at the time he wrote it, though others stating his

NOTES

539

views were. For aspects of Swift's career at the time of this tract, see the Introduction, p. xv.

412. 6 "the *Union*": In 1707 the Act of Union merged England and Scotland into one kingdom. The union was violently opposed in certain quarters, particularly by the Jacobites in Scotland and, for a time, by many Presbyterians. Swift was concerned that the union might weaken the security of the Anglican Church in a country dominated by the Scottish Kirk (Presbyterian).

413. 10 "system . . . other systems": In the light of the pejorative implications of the word "system" in Swift's day, the reduction of Christianity to a system like any other system carries special satiric meaning. See *A Tale of a Tub*, p. 329. Shaftesbury declared that "the most ingenious way of becoming foolish is by a system" (*Advice to an Author*, pub. 1710).

413. 19–20 "nominal and real Trinitarians": a passing reference to the contemporary controversies over the nature of the Trinity, a topic which Swift considered in his sermon *On the Trinity*.

413. 21–22 "Christianity . . . in primitive times": Both orthodox and heterodox thinkers of the period agreed that many corruptions had crept into the Christian religion from the time of its apostolic or primitive purity.

413. 25 "all the wit": Cf. *A Tale of a Tub*, p. 263, where Swift repeats the frequent accusation against the wits, that they utilized their wit against religion.

413. 29–30 "proposal of Horace": *Epode* XVI.

413. 36 "nominal Christianity": Swift's nominal Christian, though the phrase has wider implications, is one who evades the Test Act by occasionally conforming (i.e., taking communion) in the Anglican Church, in order to hold office. See above, the first note on this tract.

413. 38–39 "inconsistent with . . . wealth": Swift opposed the argument, widely disseminated by nonconformists and others, that only a full religious toleration would enable England to realize its potentialities as a wealthy and powerful nation. Economic writers in particular pointed to Spain as a nation in decline, a result of religious intolerance, and Holland as a nation in ascendancy, a result of relaxed ecclesiastical laws.

413. 43 "undertakers": promoters of business enterprises. The word had unpleasant connotations, suggesting schemers or impractical men.

414. 9 "liberty of conscience": This phrase was used by the dissenters in pleading for equality of their faiths under the law. Swift maintained that too often it meant an intention to subvert the law and, if granted, would create "convulsions and disturbance in a state."

He did not deny the dissenters the right to *believe* what they liked, but he insisted that they had no right to exercise political power, which under the laws of England was the exclusive right of Anglicans (see his *Thoughts on Religion* and his sermon "On the Testimony of Conscience," *Prose Works,* edited Herbert Davis, IX, 151, 263).

414. 10–11 "limited by priestcraft": Swift parrots the contention of the deists and others, that the Anglican clergy, desiring to retain their power, are responsible for corrupting religion and maintaining intolerant legislation.

414. 12 "a severe instance": probably a reference to the agitation in Ireland, in 1708, to abolish the Test Act.

414. 28 "ministry": here and elsewhere used in the political sense, roughly, the cabinet.

414. 29 "saying of Tiberius": slightly misquoted from Tacitus, *Annals,* I, 73: "deorum injurias dis curae" ("insults to the gods are the concern of the gods"). Swift liked this saying. He used it three times.

414. 39 "allies": England's allies in the War of the Spanish Succession were Holland, Austria, Savoy, Prussia and other German states, and Portugal.

415. 5 "free-thinkers": The term was applied primarily to the deists, who believed in a religion of nature or reason and rejected or were critical of any supernatural dispensation or revelation. Matthew Tindal and John Toland, named below, were two of the better known deists in Swift's time. Deism was the most dangerous heterodoxy of the period.

415. 13 "Asgill": John Asgill (1659–1738). His heresy was his conviction that a man might achieve eternal life without passing through death.

415. 20–21 "an old dormant statute or two": a reference, possibly, to the Corporation Act (1661) and the Test Act (1673), neither of which had been repealed by the Act of Toleration in 1689. Both prevented a person from holding civil and military offices unless he was a communicant of the Anglican Church.

415. 22 "Empson and Dudley": agents of Henry VII, notorious for lending legal support to that king's rapacity by reviving obsolete statutes.

415. 25 "ten thousand parsons, whose revenues": The argument that the income of the clergy would be more useful to the nation if transferred to the wits is Swift's satiric comment upon a view at times expressed by laymen — that the wealth of the Church of England had grown excessive and should be limited. Swift and many other clerics felt that the laymen too often cast greedy eyes on church possessions.

415. 40 "rent": revenue or income.

416. 6–7 "reduced by the wise regulations of Henry the Eighth": Anglican clergymen did not admire Henry VIII. They justified his attack on the Roman Catholic Church but felt that the seized possessions should have been turned over to the Anglican Establishment. Instead Henry had given church properties to many laymen and invested them with the right to tithes. Thus, he had, Swift and others felt, despoiled the Anglican clergy of their rights and was responsible particularly for the impoverishment of the parochial clergy. "I wish," Swift wrote of him, "he had been flayed, his skin stuffed and hanged on a gibbet, his bulky guts and flesh left to be devoured by birds and beasts, for a warning to his successors for ever. Amen." (See Louis A. Landa, *Swift and the Church of Ireland*, 1954, pp. 161ff.)

416. 16–17 "common dormitories": lodging houses.

416. 25 "chocolate-house": The allusion to gambling at chocolate houses would bring to mind the most famous of these, White's, which Swift characterized as "the common rendezvous of infamous sharpers and noble cullies" (see *Intelligencer*, No. IX, pp. 432ff.).

416. 35 "enticements to sleep": One of Swift's few surviving sermons is *Upon Sleeping in Church*. He remarks that too often on Sundays men divide "the time between God and their bellies, when after a gluttonous meal, their senses dozed and stupified, they retire to God's house to sleep out the afternoon."

417. 20 "Monument": the memorial, designed by Christopher Wren, to the Great Fire of London, 1666.

417. 23–24 "Margarita . . . Valentini": singers in the Italian opera, then in vogue. Since Valentini was a male soprano, Swift is sly in suggesting that he would find support among the Trimmers, i.e., those who compromise or take an in-between position.

417. 25–26 "*Prasini* and *Veneti*": two of the chief rivals in the Roman chariot races, whose rivalry led to a civil war.

418. 2–3 "prohibited silks and . . . wine": The war with France affected certain imports, but smugglers helped to maintain supplies.

418. 7 "spleen": See above, note to p. 213, ll. 8–9.

418. 36 "religion . . . the invention of politicians": This old view of religion as a "trick invented by statesmen to awe the credulous vulgar" (from the deist Toland, *Christianity not Mysterious*, 1696) was frequently remarked on, though not always defended, by unorthodox writers, as Hobbes, Mandeville, Spinoza. In *The Examiner*, No. 29, Swift refers to it as a "common atheistical notion."

419. 7 "scheme for comprehension": The dream that all Protestants might be united into one body swayed many clergymen in the seventeenth and eighteenth centuries, to no avail. As a staunch defender of the Anglican Establishment, Swift was not sympathetic.

419. 26 "enthusiasm": See above, note to p. 330, ll. 39–40.

421. 5 "*jus divinum*": The divine right or authority of Anglican bishops derived presumably from the Apostles. Swift was not wholly certain that this view was defensible. He felt more comfortable with the view that the authority of Episcopacy rested in law, as the established religion of the state. His contempt for many bishops may have influenced his attitude.

421. 22–23 "Toland . . . an Irish priest": Though born a Roman Catholic, John Toland (1670–1722) became a Protestant by the age of 16. His *Christianity not Mysterious* (1696) was one of the most violently attacked deistic works of this period.

421. 24 "ingenious author": Matthew Tindal. At the time of James II he did profess Catholicism but early in 1688 he renounced it. Swift wrote some violent remarks on Tindal, both the man and his work.

(The text. Faulkner's edition of Swift's *Works*, Dublin, 1735, with occasional readings from the *Miscellanies. The First Volume*, 1727.)

The Drapier's First Letter (1724)

In the first of seven letters written by Swift in the guise of a drapier (a dealer in cloth), he assumes the role he was increasingly to play, that of Hibernian Patriot. This *Letter* is the second of his significant Irish tracts, the first being *A Proposal for the Universal Use of Irish Manufacture* (1720). That tract had come under legal interdiction, and a reward was to be offered by the English viceroy in Ireland, one of Swift's good friends, for the discovery of the Drapier. The circumstance which led to the writing of the *Drapier's Letters* was a relatively minor affront to the Irish, a patent granted to William Wood, without consultation with anyone in Ireland, for coining and distributing copper halfpence. The patent came at a moment when Ireland was feeling unusually oppressed by England; and Swift's *Drapier's Letters* widen out beyond the initial incident into a general denunciation of English treatment of Ireland. Swift is not unmindful of the gratifying fact that he has caught his old enemy, Sir Robert Walpole, the Lord Treasurer, in an untenable position; and Walpole was to capitulate. The patent was withdrawn. But a more important aspect of the *Drapier's Letters* is that Swift uses them to set forth what he and many of the Anglo-Irish felt should be the proper relationship between England and Ireland, that of co-equals, as opposed to the colonial status Ireland had been reduced to, with all of the harsh restrictive policies attendant on that status. For the allegorical treatment of the Wood controversy, see *Gulliver's Travels*, pp. 138–40.

423. 9 "the printer to sell it at the lowest rate": Swift bore the printer's costs in the hope that an insignificant charge for his *Letter*

NOTES

would make for wider distribution. It was offered in lots of three dozen for two English shillings. The printer was John Harding, who was imprisoned in November, 1724, for printing the Fourth *Drapier's Letter*.

423. 17 "a little book was written": Swift's *Proposal for the Universal Use of Irish Manufacture* (1720).

423. 20 "the poor printer was prosecuted": Whitshed, the Chief Justice of Ireland, tried to force a reluctant jury to bring in a verdict against Edward Waters, who printed the pamphlet. Swift describes the situation at length in a letter to Pope, Jan. 10, 1721–22. See also Swift's note (p. 471) to *Verses on the Death of Dr. Swift*.

424. 14–16 "copper half-pence . . . scarce": Ireland possessed no mint. Coins were supplied under royal patents to private individuals. Swift and others admitted that "small change in copper money" was needed but far less than Wood was to supply. The animus against Wood resulted partially from earlier abuses in the system of coinage by private patent and partially from the excessive sum he was to coin and circulate.

424. 19–20 "one Mr. Wood": William Wood of Wolverhampton (1671–1730) was not, as Swift represents him, a mere hardware dealer. He seems to have had mining interests and had engaged in some rather extensive business projects, some of which cast doubt on his integrity.

424. 22–23 "not oblige . . . to take them": The legality of Swift's position — his insistence that the coin might be rejected by the Irish people — rested in part on the reading of the patent granted to Wood, that the coins were to "be received as current money by such as shall be willing to receive the same."

424. 27 "of such base metal": Swift's attack on the quality and value of Wood's coin is extreme. As Comptroller of the Mint in England Sir Isaac Newton reported that an assay showed the coins of good quality. In later *Drapier's Letters* Swift endeavors to discredit the assay.

425. 2–4 "Wood . . . had great friends": a reference to the current rumor that the King's mistress, the Duchess of Kendal, had been granted the patent, which she sold to Wood for £10,000.

425. 18–19 "several smart votes": Both Houses of the Irish parliament made "humble addresses" to the King in opposition to the patent.

425. 30 "Wood is still working underhand": He had appealed for support to Walpole and to the Duke of Grafton, then Lord Lieutenant of Ireland. Later, as Herbert Davis points out in his excellent edition of the *Drapier's Letters*, Wood offered to cease uttering the coins until objections had been met.

426. 4 "bere": "a sort of barley in Ireland" (1735 edition).

426. 13 "butter weight": formerly 18 or more ounces to the pound.

426. 25 "Squire Conolly": William Conolly, Speaker of the Irish House of Commons at the time, was at odds with the nation in his support of Wood's patent. Swift later described him to John Gay as a fellow who "from a shoe-boy, grew to be several times one of the chief governors, wholly illiterate, and with hardly common sense" (*Corres.*, Aug. 28, 1731).

427. 13–14 "run all into sheep": See below, note to p. 440, l. 31.

428. 13 *"Mirror of Justice"*: a compilation by Andrew Horn in the reign of Edward I.

428. 18 "Lord Coke": Sir Edward Coke (1552–1634), the famous jurist, from whose *Institutes* Swift quotes.

429. 20 "black money": money made of base metal.

429. 27 "Davis's Reports": Sir John Davis, whose *Le Primer Report* was published in 1615.

429. 28 "Tyrone's rebellion": The insurrection in Ireland, led by the Earl of Tyrone, broke out in 1598 and ended in 1603.

430. 41 "the accursed thing": see Joshua vi.18.

431. 1 "the king": Phalaris, a Sicilian tyrant of the 6th century, B.C. See above, note to p. 378, ll. 13–15.

(The text. Faulkner's edition of Swift's *Works*, Dublin, 1735, with a few earlier readings.)

THE INTELLIGENCER, No. IX (1728)

432. 1–2 "method of educating youth": This essay is one of seven Swift contributed to *The Intelligencer*, a short-lived journal written by him and his friend, Thomas Sheridan, in 1728, the purpose being — Swift wrote — "to inform, or divert, or correct, or vex the town." His disillusionment with the nobility, who traditionally were supposed to be the "governors" of the nation, had already been expressed in *Gulliver's Travels*. In this essay he traces their failure to a faulty education and assesses the impact of the prevalent "corrupt methods of education" upon the national culture. The topic was at the time the subject of much painful discussion. (See Swift's treatment of the education of the young among the Lilliputians and the Houyhnhnms in *Gulliver's Travels*, Pt. I, ch. vi; Pt. IV, ch. viii.) The essay had two different titles in Swift's day: "The Foolish Methods of Education among the Nobility" and "An Essay on Modern Education."

433. 6–7 "the grand Rebellion": the Civil War.

433. 14 "those fanatic times": Swift's customary use of "fanatic" as synonymous with "Puritan."

434. 10 "Bacon chargeth it": in his essay, "Of Empire."

434. 21 "Greek and Latin is loss of time": Critics of contemporary education seldom called for the elimination of Greek and Latin; they deplored the excessive emphasis on these subjects. Particularly they were critical of the methods used in teaching them. Defoe's view, that a gentleman might be a scholar without the classical languages, was perhaps extreme.

435. 17 "Earl of Oxford": Swift's friend, Robert Harley, died in 1724.

435. 31–32 "custom . . . of entertaining French tutors": The reaction against French tutors was in part nationalistic, the fear that the sturdy English character was being effeminated by alien influences. A common complaint held that both the French and the Italians stressed external good form. Swift treats this subject in his *Treatise on Good Manners and Good Breeding* (date uncertain), where he also observes the harmful influence of a notable practice of the day, the Grand Tour of the Continent, by which young men of quality customarily "finished" their education.

435. 37 "dancing-master": Swift reflects the current criticism of the emphasis placed on dancing, but many writers in the period seriously defended instruction in dancing as vital in training the young. It was recommended less for the pleasure afforded than for the social grace and ease it inculcated, the development of "a handsome presence," as one writer put it. Thus the duties of the dancing master went beyond his title, to involve genteel behavior as a whole. The art of dancing "shows the genteel and most proper attitudes of body, and without which no person can be said to be well bred; . . . a fine [dancing] master not only teaches his scholar a becoming grace and deportment in the disposition and turns of body, but every attitude that is most particularly adapted to such and such motions in his general conduct and behaviour. . . ." (John Littleton Costeker, *The Fine Gentleman: Or, The Compleat Education of a Young Nobleman*, 1732, pp. 42–43). This is only one of many anticipations of the Earl of Chesterfield, the *arbiter elegantiarum* of the later eighteenth century. See an amusing essay on the subject in *The Spectator*, No. 334.

436. 10 "span-farthing": a very simple game in which a player attempts to throw his farthings so close to those of his opponents that the distance between them can be spanned with the hand.

436. 32 "a school . . . education": Contemporaries disagreed over what Mr. Spectator (No. 313) called "that famous question, whether the education at a public school, or under a private tutor is to be preferred." By "public school" is meant such private institutions as Eton, Harrow, and Westminster. Swift clearly disagrees with John Locke, who maintained that education by tutor has the advantage.

Locke's *Thoughts Concerning Education* (1693) was highly influential.

(The text. Faulkner's edition of Swift's *Works*, Dublin, 1735, with
a few emendations from earlier editions.)

A MODEST PROPOSAL (1729)

The "modest proposal" is cannibalism, the use of the children of
the poor as food, a plan well calculated, Swift maintains, to reduce
over-population, increase the national income, and tickle the palates
of gourmets by a new dish. In the greatest of his Irish tracts and
one of the finest pieces of irony in any language, Swift's premise
is that a country so desperate as Ireland cannot afford such luxuries as parental love and the sanctity of human life. As an (ironic)
economic planner Swift presents this cure for the ills of Ireland,
to call attention by its extremity to the folly, greed, and oppression
which have produced the impoverishment of a nation. Both Ireland
and England share the blame. Shortly before he produced *A Modest
Proposal* Swift wrote to Pope: "As to this country, there have
been three terrible years' dearth of corn, and every place strewed
with beggars" (Aug. 11, 1729). But the evils, he said, were much
deeper than the failure of crops in a nation already at a low level
of subsistence; and, he added, "the kingdom is absolutely undone, as
I have been telling often in print these ten years past."

439. 1–2 "this great town": Dublin.

439. 3 "crowded with beggars": Arthur Dobbs, one of Swift's
contemporaries, estimated the number of strolling beggars alone in
Ireland at 34,425, among whom "not 1 in 10 [are] real objects of
charity." Swift and other citizens of Dublin complained that they
might well care for the deserving indigent of their own city if
swarms of beggars from other parts of the country could be kept
out of Dublin. He therefore proposed that every parish be responsible for its own poor, each of whom could be recognized as
a deserving object of charity if he were provided with a badge (see
his *A Proposal for Giving Badges to the Beggars in all the Parishes
of Dublin*, 1737).

439. 9–10 "fight for the Pretender in Spain": Irish Catholics were
recruited for service in the armies of Spain and France, to fight
against England. Swift's old friend, the Duke of Ormonde, had Irish
troops in an ill-fated expedition, planned by Cardinal Alberoni of
Spain in 1719, to restore the Pretender to the English throne.

439. 10 "sell themselves to the Barbadoes": Emigration to the
West Indies troubled the Irish authorities at the time Swift was
writing *A Modest Proposal*. The numbers leaving the country
tended to increase in direct ratio to the failure of harvests, but some

were induced to emigrate by the glowing tales of agents from the colonies in America and by ship masters.

439. 13–14 "present deplorable state of the kingdom": a reference to the three years of poor harvests.

439. 26 "schemes of other projectors": The word "projector" had pejorative connotations as one who proposed impractical or foolish projects. Thus the reference by the *persona* to himself as a projector would be the first hint to Swift's readers that the proposal to follow is ironic.

440. 17–18 "I calculate . . . breeders": Swift here and elsewhere in the essay adopts for ironic purposes the methods of the political arithmeticians of the period with their unemotional statistical approach to problems of poverty, labor, and national wealth (see George Wittkowsky, "Swift's *Modest Proposal:* the Biography of an Early Georgian Pamphlet," *Journal of the History of Ideas,* IV, 1943, 75–104).

440. 31 "nor cultivate land": England had applied restrictive legislation to Irish agriculture. One consequence was that much arable land was left fallow or converted to pasturage for sheep, to supply the woollen industry. Thus the country's capacity for producing food was reduced.

440. 32–33 "seldom pick up a livelihood by stealing until . . . six": Swift's great contemporary, the philosopher Bishop Berkeley, who wrote of Ireland in much the same vein as Swift, remarked that "in Holland a child five years old is maintained by its own labour; in Ireland many children of twice that age do nothing but steal, or encumber the hearth and dunghill." Berkeley thought that the sloth of the native Irish was in part due to the dirt which encompassed the child from birth: ". . . alas! our poor Irish are wedded to dirt upon principle. It is with them a maxim that the way to make children thrive is to keep them dirty" (*A Word to the Wise*).

441. 15 "our savages": In the Seventh *Drapier's Letter* and elsewhere Swift remarked on the need to civilize the native Irish and redeem them from their "ignorance, barbarity and poverty," as a consequence of which they give themselves "wholly up to idleness, nastiness, and thievery."

441. 29–30 "landlords . . . devoured most of the parents": In his Irish tracts Swift indulged in many bitter diatribes against the large landowners as being responsible, in great measure, for Ireland's dire condition. He accused them of demanding exorbitant leases, oppressing small farmers, converting arable land into pasturage, resisting tithes to the Established Church, and absenting themselves from Ireland, which sorely needed their talents.

441. 33 "a grave author": Rabelais (1494?–1553), the great

French satirist, much admired by Swift. Pantagruel maintained (Bk. V, ch. xix) that the Lenten diet was deliberately devised to "forward the propagation of mankind."

441. 37–38 "Popish infants . . . three to one": Swift glances at the high birth rate among the native Catholic population, viewed with alarm by the Protestants. Suggestions were made that the Irish parliament should pass measures to restrict marriages among the poor. Swift wrote: ". . . many thousand couples are yearly married, whose whole united fortunes, bating the rags on their backs, would not be sufficient to purchase a pint of buttermilk for their wedding supper. . . ." (*A Proposal for Giving Badges to the Beggars in all the Parishes of Dublin*, 1737).

442. 41 "Psalmanazar": a contemporary imposter who published a fictitious account of Formosa in 1704.

443. 9 "chair": sedan chair.

443. 37 "tithes against their conscience": Nonconformists often resisted, on the plea of freedom of conscience, paying tithes to the Established Church.

443. 39 "liable to distress": subject to seizure for payment of debt.

445. 1–2 "number of people . . . lessened": The argument of the *persona* that he offers his "modest proposal" to reduce the population of Ireland runs counter to a firmly implanted economic doctrine of the times — that people constitute the wealth of a nation. The greater the population, the greater the riches of a country. In his *Maxims Controlled* [i.e., confuted] *in Ireland* (c. 1729), Swift wrote: "It is another undisputed maxim in government, 'That people are the riches of a nation'; which is so universally granted, that it will be hardly pardonable to bring it in doubt. And I will grant it to be so far true, even in this island, that if we had the African custom, or privilege, of selling our useless bodies for slaves to foreigners, it would be the most useful branch of our trade. . . ." (see Louis A. Landa, "*A Modest Proposal* and Populousness," *Modern Philology*, XL (1942), 161ff.).

445. 7 "other expedients": The "expedients" which follow are the measures Swift proposed in his various tracts as remedies for Ireland's economic ills.

445. 8–10 "using . . . our own growth and manufacture": Swift had elaborated this plea for a restriction of imports in one of his better Irish tracts, *A Proposal for the Universal Use of Irish Manufacture . . . utterly Rejecting and Renouncing Everything Wearable that comes from England* (1720).

445. 12 "pride, vanity . . . in our women": In 1729 Swift wrote to Pope that the pride of the Irish women "will not suffer them to

wear their own manufactures, even where they excell what comes
from abroad" (*Corres.*, ed. F. E. Ball, IV, 90).

445. 37–38 *"perhaps I could name a country"*: Swift's bitterness
against England breaks out here. However much he blamed the
people of Ireland, England was in his eyes the chief cause of Ireland's
difficulties by virtue of the restrictions she imposed on Ireland's
commerce. "The chief cause of our misery," Swift said in his sermon *On the Wretched Condition of Ireland*, "is the intolerable
hardships we lie under in every branch of our trade, by which we
are become as hewers of wood, and drawers of water, to our rigorous
neighbours" (i.e., England).

(The text. Faulkner's edition of Swift's *Works*, Dublin, 1735, with
a few emendations from earlier editions.)

POEMS

Although he was not a poet of any pretensions to greatness, Swift's
verses are often both pleasing and interesting. He refused to attempt anything in the grand manner; and in fact much of his poetry
is likely to be thought trivial. Certainly much of it was private,
deliberately composed for the eyes of a few friends and concerned
with some intimate occasion or highly personal relationship. But
even here he sometimes rises above the trivial and the private to a
delightful comment on human relations, as in the birthday verses
to Stella, in which tenderness and wit mingle so effectively; or as in
The Humble Petition of Frances Harris, in which the loss of a
purse is turned into an amusing vignette and depiction of character.
His best poems have some of the qualities and intentions of his prose
— intensely-felt comment on man and society; the desire to expose
folly, injustice, greed, and hypocrisy; indignant reflections on public
events; and above all, wit, playfulness of mind, and lucidity. Whether
he is versifying on the morning, the death of the Duke of Marlborough, the progress of love, or his own death, we are likely to
find, as in the prose, his characteristic comic and satiric vision, along
with his customary tonic and astringent realism.

TO THEIR EXCELLENCIES . . .

"Lords Justices": The setting of this poem is the household of the
Earl of Berkeley, one of the Lord Justices of Ireland. Swift at the
time (1699–1701) was chaplain to Berkeley, and Frances Harris was
one of Lady Berkeley's gentlewomen.

447. 2 "Lady Betty's chamber": Lady Betty Berkeley, later Lady
Betty Germain, was the eldest daughter of Lord Berkeley and a life-
long friend and correspondent of Swift's. At the time of Mrs. Harris's
lost purse Lady Betty was a girl of about 16.

447. 21 "Mary": Among the domestics mentioned by Swift are the housemaid, the footman's wife, the valet, the housekeeper, the clerk of the kitchen, the steward.

448. 14 "Lord Collway's folks'": the Earl of Galway, one of the Lord Justices.

448. 15 "Lord Dromedary": the Earl of Drogheda, recently appointed one of the Lord Justices.

448. 38–39 "cunning man": fortune teller.

449. 29 "the chaplain": i.e., Swift.

A Description of the Morning (1709)

Steele published this poem in *The Tatler*, No. IX. He recognized Swift's intention to parody the romantic and hackneyed descriptions of the morning by introducing the poem as by a poet who has "run into a way perfectly new, and described things as they happen: he never forms fields, or groves where they are not...."

450. 1–2 "broomy stumps ... kennel-edge": A youth with a worn broom scavenges in the kennel (open drain in the street).

450. 3 "small-coal man": a street vendor of small pieces of coal. Any reader of this poem in 1709 would almost certainly think of Thomas Britton (d. 1714). Swift may have had him in mind. Britton was unquestionably the only person of this lowly occupation in the period to become famous. He held musical concerts at his shop for 40 years, attended by noted artists (as Handel and Pepusch) and titled aristocrats. He was also a book collector, particularly interested in the occult sciences.

450. 6 "brickdust Moll": a vendor of powdered brick, used for cleaning knives. For London street vendors and their cries, see *The Spectator*, No. 251.

450. 8 "fees": It was customary for gaolers to exact fees from prisoners in return for certain prison privileges.

A Description of a City Shower (1710)

The poet Matthew Prior commended this poem to Swift: "there never was such a shower since Danae's." Swift probably thought of it as a burlesque imitation of Virgil's *Georgics*. Published in *The Tatler*, No. 238, it is another instance of Swift's mockery of romantic and hackneyed nature poetry.

450. 13 "depends": impending.

450. 18 "spend in coach-hire": A frugal man in personal expenditures, Swift complained frequently of what he spent in coach-hire. His frugality did not extend to his charitable contributions.

450. 20 "aches": pronounced "aitches."

450. 22 "spleen": see note to p. 213, ll. 8–9.

450. 29 "quean": a jade or wench.

451. 5 "daggled females": i.e., with skirts wet or bemired.

451. 7 "Templar": a barrister from the Inner or Middle Temple.

451. 10 "oil'd umbrella": umbrellas were made of oiled silk.

451. 13 "Triumphant Tories": The Tories had recently come into power.

451. 15 "chair": sedan chair.

451. 23 "Laocoon": Virgil, *Aeneid*, ii, 50–53.

451. 33–35 "Sweepings . . . flood": The last three lines are intended to mock the use in poetry of the triplet and the alexandrine — a line of six iambic feet, such as Dryden used.

STELLA'S BIRTHDAY (1719)

"Stella" was Swift's poetic name for Esther Johnson, for whom see the introductory note to the Correspondence, p. 552. He wrote birthday verses to her each year from 1719. Born March 13, 1681, she was actually 38, not 34 as stated in the opening line. Swift was often inaccurate in referring to Stella's age, here deliberately so.

A SATIRICAL ELEGY (1722)

The "Famous General" was the Duke of Marlborough. He died June 16, 1722. This poem was not published in Swift's lifetime. For Swift and the Duke of Marlborough, see *The Examiner*, No. 16, p. 407.

VERSES ON THE DEATH OF DR. SWIFT (1731)

La Rochefoucauld's *Reflexions ou sentences et maximes morales* were published anonymously in 1665. When Swift was putting the final touches to *Gulliver's Travels*, he wrote to Pope that Rochefoucauld "is my favorite, because I found my whole character in him" (Nov. 26, 1725).

459. 35 "St. John": Swift's friend, Henry St. John, Viscount Bolingbroke, outlived Swift by six years.

459. 35 "Pultney": Sir William Pulteney, later Earl of Bath (1684–1764), first a supporter and after 1721 a bitter political enemy of Sir Robert Walpole. He and Swift became friends and correspondents in 1726. Pulteney was a brilliant speaker in the House of Commons.

462. 27 "Grub-street wits": See above, note to p. 275, ll. 17–18.

464. 9 "glibber": i.e., to be moved (sold) the more easily.

465. 26 "vole": in quadrille a "slam."

466. 16 "pastry-cooks": Old paper was disposed of to small shopkeepers, such as pastry cooks.

466. 26 "Colley Cibber's Birth-day poem": As poet laureate (appointed in 1730) Cibber dutifully supplied birthday poems in commemoration of the king.

466. 28   "Stephen Duck": a thresher turned poet, considered in his day to be a "natural poet" whose genius was unmarred by education. He won the favor of Queen Caroline.

466. 30   "the Craftsman": the journal of the dissident Whigs who attacked Walpole. Bolingbroke and Pulteney were leaders of this group after 1726.

467. 22   "the Rose": a fashionable tavern.

468. 29   "The Irish Senate": Swift had attacked both houses of the Irish parliament on occasions; but his most devastating attack was yet to be written, *The Legion Club*, 1736, directed at the Irish House of Commons, which was making one of its periodic attempts to reduce tithes claimed by the Anglican clergy.

469. 22   "Ormond": the Duke of Ormonde, long Swift's friend, who fled abroad and actively conspired to restore the Stuart line to the throne of England. His distinguished early career contrasts sharply with his later activities; and his last years were spent as a Jacobite exile.

470. 1   "By solemn League and Cov'nant": Swift links the Whigs to this infamous covenant (in the eyes of Anglicans) which in 1643 was imposed by the Scots on a desperate England. It demanded, for the price of support, that the Anglican Establishment be reformed in the direction of Presbyterianism.

473. 14   "a house for fools and mad": a reference to his greatest charitable act. Swift left most of his fortune for the founding of a hospital for the treatment of mental illnesses. It is today a flourishing institution.

(The texts. *The Humble Petition of Frances Harris*: Swift's *Miscellanies in Prose and Verse*, 1711; *A Description of the Morning*: *Miscellanies*, 1711; *A Description of a City Shower*: *Miscellanies*, 1711; *On Stella's Birthday*, [1718/9]: *Miscellanies in Prose and Verse*, 1727; *Phyllis, or The Progress of Love*: *Miscellanies*, 1727, with emendations from the manuscript version, with grateful acknowledgments to Harold Williams and the Clarendon Press, Oxford (see *The Poems of Jonathan Swift*, ed. Harold Williams, Clarendon Press, second edition, 1958, I, 221ff.); *A Satirical Elegy on the Death of a Late Famous General*: Deane Swift, *Works*, 1765; *Stella's Birthday, March 13, 1726–27*: *Miscellanies*, 1727; *Verses on the Death of Dr. Swift*: Faulkner's version of 1739, with some omissions and additions to the notes from manuscript versions and later editions, by courtesy of Harold Williams and the Clarendon Press.)

CORRESPONDENCE

The Journal to Stella is the title given to a series of letters written in journal form and addressed jointly to Esther Johnson

NOTES

(Stella) and her companion, Mrs. Rebecca Dingley. The journal dates from September, 1710, to June, 1711, that fascinating period in Swift's life when he was associated with the Harley cabinet and moved among the great figures of the nation. He recorded for the two ladies in Ireland his day-by-day activities and observations in the most intimate and informal manner. Stella is the poetic name Swift applied to Esther Johnson, whom he first knew about 1689 when she was a little girl, aged eight, living in the household of Sir William Temple. He had a hand in her education ("a person of my own rearing and instructing, from childhood," he once said), and she came to live in Ireland in 1700 or 1701 at his suggestion, when she was about twenty — a young woman of unusual charm. Swift remarked later that she was "a little too fat." Unquestionably of all the people who entered his life, she was the one he most loved. Their relationship was in the eighteenth century and has continued to be the subject of speculation and downright absurd comment, with Stella at one time or another credited with being Swift's mistress, his half-sister, his wife, none of which is supported by credible evidence. Scholarly and restrained treatment may be found in the following: *The Correspondence of Jonathan Swift*, ed. F. Elrington Ball, IV, Appendix I, 1913; Herbert Davis, *Stella: A Gentlewoman of the Eighteenth Century*, 1942; *Jonathan Swift: Journal to Stella*, ed. Harold Williams, Vol. I, xxiiiff., 1948.

The same authorities may be consulted for the famous "little language" Swift used at times in the *Journal to Stella*, examples of which will be found in the excerpts included in this volume. Next to the relationship between Swift and Stella, the "little language" has excited most attention. It has startled and bewildered commentators. Was it a later-day imitation of Esther Johnson's talk as a child? Was it lover's prattle? Was it a refuge from the formality of Swift's daily routine or an escape from the strains of his political career? These questions and others have been asked and answered without a final completely satisfying solution. What is clear, is that the "little language" is an expression of the playfulness which was so essential an aspect of Swift's character, an aspect too often ignored in the attempts to understand him.

LETTER VI. **475. 4–5** "my memorial to the queen": Acting as agent for the Irish bishops Swift memorialized the Queen for remission to the Irish clergy of the First Fruits and Twentieth Parts (levies by the crown on clerical benefices). Through the influence of Harley, now heading the ministry, he succeeded. It was Harley's willingness to aid Swift in this enterprise that won Swift over to support the Tories and to write for the Harley cabinet. See the Introduction, p. xvi.

475. 7 "a governor": i.e., a lord lieutenant of Ireland. Swift's friend, the Duke of Ormonde, was appointed.

475. 12 "the archbishop": William King, Archbishop of Dublin, with whom Swift frequently had difficulties. King was an ardent Whig, and his supporters in the chapter of St. Patrick's often opposed Swift after he had become dean. But Swift and King joined hands at times, as in the crisis over Wood's copper coinage in 1723–24 and in their endeavors to solve Ireland's economic troubles.

475. 16 *"Description of a Shower"*: See pp. 450–51.

476. 5 *"MD"*: My Dear or My Dears. By these two letters Swift designates Stella and Mrs. Dingley.

476. 6 *"Patrick"*: Swift's Irish servant, the subject of constant vexation to Swift, for drunkenness and other faults.

476. 9 "smoak": detect.

476. 11 "ombre": Both Swift and Stella played the fashionable game of ombre. In the *Journal* he frequently twits Stella on her losses at cards and on her inept playing of a hand.

476. 16 "Dr. *Garth*": Dr. Samuel Garth (1661–1719), physician and poet, a Whig in politics.

476. 21 *"Addison's* election": Addison was a member of Parliament from 1708 until his death in 1719.

477.3 *"Presto"*: Swift. The Duchess of Shrewsbury, of Italian birth, had called Swift by this Italian word meaning "swift." It is an editor's insertion. Swift referred to himself in the *Journal* as pdfr (i.e., poor dear fellow *or* poor dear foolish rogue).

477. 19–20 "one *Harrison*": William Harrison, who edited a continuation of *The Tatler* after Steele gave it up.

477. 33 *"Halifax"*: later the Earl of Halifax, a prominent Whig politician, to become First Lord of the Treasury on the accession of George I. Swift's first political tract, *Contests and Dissensions* (1701), in defense of the Whigs, led to friendly relations between the two. Halifax was President of the Royal Society, 1695–98, and a patron of poets.

478. 11 "tobacco at the top": Deane Swift, who saw the manuscript, observed a little smear on the upper part of the letter, possibly from snuff.

478. 13 *"Sterne"*: John Stearne, the Dean of St. Patrick's, Dublin, whom Swift was to succeed in 1713. Also a friend and a companion-at-cards of Stella. Swift quarrelled with him on several occasions.

479. 4 *"Steele's* office": Steele was still Gazetteer (editor of *The London Gazette*) when Swift arrived in London in September, 1710. Swift had used Steele's office in the Cockpit as a mailing address. The friendship between the two was soon to end. See below, note to p. 483, l. 23.

479. 20–21 "horse . . . *Parvisol*": Like Swift, Stella enjoyed riding.

Parvisol, Swift's steward and tithe collector, had suggested selling Stella's horse. She refused.

479. 35 "My lampoon": Swift's poem, *The Virtues of Sid Hamet the Magician's Rod*, directed against the fallen Lord Treasurer, Earl of Godolphin, who had refused to aid Swift in obtaining remission of the First Fruits and Twentieth Parts. See the Introduction, p. xv.

479. 40 "my *Tatler* about . . . words": See p. 397ff.

480. 2 "*Prior*": Matthew Prior, the poet (1664–1721), was also a diplomatist. He had earlier (1702) changed from Whig to Tory. He was impeached and imprisoned after Queen Anne's death.

480. 7 "lord *Peterborow*": the third Earl of Peterborough, (d. 1735), long a friend and correspondent of Swift's, a gifted aristocrat at home among soldiers and poets. Pope, Gay, and Arbuthnot were among his friends.

480. 21 "*Smyrna*": a coffee house in Pall Mall. Steele refers to it amusingly in *The Tatler*, No. 78, where he invited those who wish instruction in "the noble sciences of music, poetry, and politics" to appear at night after preparing "their bodies with three dishes of bohea, and [purging] their brains with two pinches of snuff."

480. 33–34 "*Brazil* tobacco": for grating into snuff. As was customary in the times, Swift, Stella, and Mrs. Dingley all took snuff. In the *Journal* for June 7, 1711, Swift writes to the two ladies: "And are you as vicious in snuff as ever?" A few months later he sent a roll of tobacco to Dingley and an ivory snuff-rasp for grating it.

480. 34 "palsy water": or palsy drops, another name for compound tincture of lavendar, admitted to the London Pharmacopoeia in 1721. Swift sent several bottles to Stella from London. This medicinal water contained 27 ingredients, mostly aromatics, among which were cowslips, flowers of lavendar, sage, rosemary, as well as citron, ambergris, and nutmeg, all "digested" in French brandy. It served variously as a carminative, for languors, weakness of the nerves, and as a reviving cordial.

480. 39 "your little eyes": Stella's weak eyes were Swift's constant concern.

481. 1 "*Irish* wine": curiously, the name was applied to claret.

481. 7 "my *Miscellany*": Swift's *Miscellanies in Prose and Verse*, published early in 1711.

LETTER VII. 482. 3 "*Lewis*": Erasmus Lewis — "This Lewis is a cunning shaver/And very much in Harley's favour." So Swift wrote of him in 1713. He had been Harley's private secretary in 1704 and later became an Under-Secretary of State. He introduced Swift to Harley in Oct., 1710 — a turning point in Swift's life.

482. 6 "Mrs. *Vanhomrigh*": Mrs. Vanhomrigh's daughter, Esther, is the Vanessa of Swift's poetry. Vanessa at this time was about 22 years of age and was soon to fall in love with Swift. She followed him to Ireland in 1714, where the progress of the relationship can be followed in their correspondence and in Swift's poem, *Cadenus and Vanessa.* He repulsed her romantic, impetuous advances and she died, an unhappy and frustrated woman, in 1723. Like Stella, she has been the subject of much comment and speculation.

482. 12 "*Wortley Montague*": a member of Parliament and later the husband of Lady Mary Wortley Montagu, the authoress, who is best known for her letters and her quarrel with Alexander Pope.

483. 8–9 "lord *Wharton*"; See *The Examiner*, No. 14, pp. 402ff., and notes.

483. 10 "*Tisdall*": Dr. William Tisdall, a clergyman, who had "entertained" Stella with convocation disputes and had proposed marriage. Swift's letter to him about the proposal (April 20, 1704) has been much analyzed for the light it presumably throws on Swift's relations with Stella (see F. Elrington Ball, *Corres. of Swift,* I, 45).

483. 23 "to keep *Steele* in his office": Steele indiscreetly printed an attack on Harley and the new ministry in *The Tatler*, No. 193, July 4, 1710. Despite his Whig affiliations, he was permitted to retain his place as Commissioner of the Stamp Office, due in part probably to Swift's plea in his behalf. But Swift's good intentions did not preserve the friendship.

484. 26 "*Prebendary* of *Westminster* . . . delicious house and garden": A decade earlier Swift had eagerly sought appointment to a prebend of Westminster, which he maintained had been promised him. He would have been settled comfortably for life, with "a delicious house and garden" and easy duties — a sinecure in both the theological and popular sense of the word.

484. 28 "*Laracor*": In 1700 when Swift failed to be appointed Dean of Derry, as he had hoped, he was presented to the livings of three country parishes, of which Laracor was the chief one. He held these along with the deanery of St. Patrick's, using, as was customary, curates to perform the parochial duties. For Laracor he had great fondness, and it became a kind of country retreat for him.

484. 31 "*Congreve*": William Congreve (1670–1729), the dramatist, had been at Kilkenny Grammar School and Trinity College, Dublin, at the same time as Swift.

485. 1 "my livings are . . . fallen": a reference to his income, in the form of tithes, from his country parishes. Swift was always bitterly eloquent on the difficulties faced by the clergy in collecting their tithes from laymen. He once wrote to Pope that "although

tithes be of divine institution, they are of diabolical execution"
(Feb. 26, 1729–30).

485. 8–9 "I write up": The weather being warm, Swift in this
instance was not following his usual practice of writing the journal
while warm and snug in bed.

485. 23 "my picture from *Jervas*": Charles Jervas, the artist, finished a portrait of Swift at this time. It is thought to be the one
now hanging in the Bodleian Library at Oxford.

485. 27 "*Tighe*": Richard Tighe, a violent Whig from Ireland,
whom Swift cordially disliked and lampooned in verse.

486. 43 "Mr. *Rowe*": Nicholas Rowe (1674–1718), dramatist and
poet, became poet-laureate in 1715.

487. 6 "blind": obscure.

487. 13 "hedge tavern": of mean or third-rate quality.

487. 16 "lord *Pembroke*": The Earl of Pembroke, a distinguished
statesman and cultivated nobleman, was Lord Lieutenant of Ireland,
1707–9, at which time Swift came to know him well. They prized
each other as inveterate punsters.

487. 21 "*Ford*": Charles Ford, of Woodpark, Co. Meath, Ireland,
an Irish absentee but one of Swift's most cherished friends and correspondents. He also knew Stella, who made a visit to Woodpark
(see Swift's poem, *Stella at Woodpark*, 1723). See below, the note
to p. 488, ll 28–29.

LETTER L. 488. 15 "Ldy Mashams": Lady Masham, a cousin of
Robert Harley, became an intimate of Queen Anne as the Duchess
of Marlborough was losing favor. She played an important part in
court intrigue, helping to undermine the Godolphin ministry and
bring Harley into power. She and Swift became close friends.

488. 17 "Bp of Clogher": St. George Ashe, the Bishop of
Clogher, had been tutor to Swift at Trinity College, Dublin. He
and Swift were warm friends over many years.

488. 21–22 "Dunkirk . . . Grubstreet . . . fruitfull": Swift goes
on to list several occasional pieces he wrote on the subject of the
French port of Dunkirk and its fortifications, the destruction of
which was an objective of the English negotiators in the Treaty
of Utrecht (1713). Dunkirk provided a base for French privateers
to prey on English ships in the Channel and for raids on the southern coast. The subject of its destruction became an inflammatory
topic in politics between the Harley ministry and the opposition,
with Swift doing his share for the ministry.

488. 22 "pdfr": These letters stand probably for "poor dear fellow" or "poor dear foolish rogue" — that is, Swift himself.

488. 28–29 "I have made Ford Gazeteer": i.e., writer of the official government journal, *The London Gazette*, which dated back to

the middle of the seventeenth century. Swift persuaded the Earl of Dartmouth, Secretary of State for the Southern Department, to offer the editorship to Ford. Salary plus perquisites amounted to about £300 annually, but Swift complained to Stella that though "it is the prettiest employment in England for its bigness, yet the puppy does not seem satisfied with it" (*Journal to Stella*, July 1, 1712).

488. 30 "my Canal": At Laracor, his country parish, Swift had a canal and a garden which gave him great satisfaction.

488. 34 "Ppt": This is the designation for Stella. It stands for Poppet or Poor Pretty Thing. Swift did not use the name Stella for Esther Johnson in these letters. It was inserted, along with other revisions, by those who first printed the letters.

489. 3 "Maram Dd": Madam Dingley.

489. 11–13 "my Lettr to Ld Treasr . . . answer it": a reference to Swift's tract on the English language in a Letter to Harley, published in May, 1712, and to the attacks on it. Swift's tract was titled *A Proposal for Correcting, Improving and Ascertaining the English Tongue* (see Swift, *Prose Works*, ed. Davis, IV, 5–21). For a reprinting of two answers to Swift, see The Augustan Reprint Society, series 6, no. 1: "Poetry and Language" (1948).

489. 15 "memlandums": memorandums.

489. 25–26 "ppt aden . . . o Rold, dlunken Srut": These words illustrate a common principle in Swift's "little language" — the substitution of *r* for *l* and of *l* for *r*. The words are to be read: "poppet again . . . o Lord, drunken Slut."

489. 28–29 "lele's fol oo now": In the "little language": "there's for you now, and there's for your letter, and every kind of thing."

490. 8 "another Grub": This is Swift's usual method of indicating to Stella that he has written an occasional pamphlet — a Grub Street production.

490. 18 "Sollah": sirrahs.

490. 18–19 "deelest . . . FW Me . . . lele": dearest . . . Farewell (or Foolish Wenches), Madam Elderly (i.e., Mrs. Dingley) . . . dears (?). "Lele" is a puzzler. This closing sentence illustrates what Sir Harold Williams calls Swift's delight "in the use of alphabetical symbols as fond tokens of farewell at the end of his letters."

SWIFT TO GAY. 491. 5 "my garden": a reference to a field, to the south of St. Patrick's Deanery, which Swift named Naboth's Vineyard. He refers to it often in his correspondence. In 1724 he had the field enclosed by a stone wall, against the southern exposure of which he planted fruit trees. Here he kept his horses. He built the wall, he wrote to Pope, because he was "tired with the knavery

of grooms, who foundered all my horses and hindered me from the
only remedy [i.e., riding] against increasing ill health" (Feb. 26, 1729–
30).

491. 11–12 "three years reconciling myself to the scene": When
Swift returned to Ireland in 1714, depressed over the fall of his
friends from power, he found the political atmosphere antagonistic.
His personal disappointment, tension within his cathedral chapter,
and the interception of his mail, with the possibility that he might
be returned to England to testify about Jacobite activities, all contrasted painfully with the previous years of brilliant activity when
he was close to Harley's ministry.

491. 14–15 "my friends are in . . . exile . . . or imprisonment":
Atterbury was at this time imprisoned in the Tower, awaiting trial
as a Jacobite plotter; Ormonde and Bolingbroke were in exile on
the Continent, though the latter was shortly to return to England.

491. 26 "the giddiness I am subject to": From his early years,
possibly before he was 20, Swift was subject to giddiness, resulting,
he thought, from an occasion when he surfeited himself on fruit.
Actually his difficulty was labyrinthine vertigo, or Ménière's Syndrome, a malady that attacks the inner ear and causes deafness and
vertigo.

491. 42 "by the dedication of your Eclogues to . . . Bolingbroke":
In April, 1714, Gay published his pastorals, *The Shepherd's Week*,
with the Prologue addressed to Bolingbroke. In 1715 Bolingbroke
fled to France, to join the Pretender.

492. 30 "poor Homer helped to make him rich": Pope's translation of Homer's *Iliad* (1715–20), published by subscription, was
both a financial and a literary success. Later he translated the
Odyssey (with assistance), and the two together brought him, possibly, as much as £9000.

493. 1–2 "as good ones from your side!": Swift's jesting remark to
Gay that he should "turn parson and get a bishopric" in Ireland
is followed by one of his frequent remarks about the inferior quality
of the episcopal appointments to the Church of Ireland. Swift was
often in conflict with the bishops, in both ecclesiastical and political
matters, particularly with the ones from England, who were strong
Whigs.

SWIFT TO POPE. 493. 19 "those dominions where I govern": As
Dean of St. Patrick's Cathedral, Swift had civil authority in the
adjacent area, known as the Liberty of St. Patrick's.

493. 23–24 "a printer . . . brave enough to venture his ears":
Printers of earlier works by Swift had been prosecuted (see p. 423,
note to l. 20). The printer of the first edition of *Gulliver's Travels*,

Benjamin Motte, sought to lessen the chance of prosecution by altering Swift's manuscript in some instances and even by omissions, much to Swift's disgust. These changes were later rectified, and the revisions are included in the text printed in this volume.

494. 17 "your Odyssey": See above, note to p. 492, l. 30.

494. 23–24 "subterranean passage to your garden": a reference to Pope's famous grotto at his home in Twickenham. He built it with loving care, to connect divided sections of his grounds and serve as an entrance to his garden. Pope was an enthusiastic gardener, much concerned with both theory and practice in the art of landscaping and gardening. His literary works and letters abound in horticultural references.

494. 27–28 "the lady . . . at court": Mrs. Howard, afterwards Countess of Suffolk and mistress of George II, with whom Swift carried on an extensive correspondence. See the *Verses on the Death of Dr. Swift*, p. 463.

SWIFT TO MISS MARTHA BLOUNT. Patty Blount was an intimate friend of Alexander Pope for many years, whom Swift had seen on his recent visit to Pope in Twickenham. She is eulogized in Pope's *Moral Essay, Epistle II: To a Lady*. At the time of this letter she was 36; Swift was approaching 60.

496. 4 "cow-heel": a dish made of the foot of a cow or an ox stewed into a jelly.

496. 5–6 "leave Mr. Gay to his beggars": Gay's *Beggar's Opera* was then running in London.

496. 25 "an old gentlewoman of fourscore": Pope's mother.

496. 30 "Dr. Delany": an Irish clergyman, a friend of Swift's and later his biographer.

SWIFT TO MISS HOADLY. This letter was written to the daughter of John Hoadly, Archbishop of Dublin. He and Swift had several clashes, but in the main their relations appear to have been without undue friction.

SWIFT TO MRS. PENDARVES. Swift and Mrs. Pendarves (later Mrs. Delany and one of the Blue Stockings) became acquainted in 1733 and soon began to correspond. Swift was 66; she was 33. After their first meeting she described Swift as "a very odd companion, if that expression is not too familiar for so extraordinary a genius; he talks a great deal and does not require many answers; he has infinite spirits, and says abundance of good things in his common way of discourse." Later, after dining in Swift's presence again, she wrote: "The Dean of St. Patrick's was there, in very good humour;

he calls himself 'my master,' and corrects me when I speak bad English, or do not pronounce my words distinctly. I wish he lived in England; I should not only have a great deal of entertainment from him, but improvement" (see Swift's *Corres.*, ed. F. E. Ball, V, 436n.).

499. 36 "my poor revenues are sinking": To Gay, in 1732, Swift had written: ". . . all my revenues which depend on tithes are sunk almost to nothing, and my whole personal fortune is in the utmost confusion." Complaints about the decrease in his income abound in Swift's correspondence from 1730 on. Losses from tithes he certainly suffered, as did all clergymen, and he may have had some reduction in rents or interest from mortgages. Nevertheless, Swift was far from impoverished. His comfortable fortune was increasing from sound investments. Perhaps one explanation of his complaints is that he conscientiously set aside about two-thirds of his income for charity. The increase in his creature comforts and reasonable indulgences as he grew older might well have taxed the remaining third.

499. 40–41 "that business with the Duke of Chandos": Six months before, Swift had solicited some manuscripts owned by the Duke for the University of Dublin (Trinity College, Dublin). The Duke had not replied. At Swift's instigation Mrs. Pendarves, then in England, found an emissary to approach Chandos.

500. 8–9 "Horace . . . Galatea . . . a long voyage": Since Mrs. Pendarves was leaving Ireland and he never expects to see her again, Swift quotes appropriately from Horace's *Ode to Galatea* (Bk. iii, ode 27) in which the poet wishes Galatea favorable omens and a happy voyage, at the same time that he represents the dangers to which she is exposing herself.

(The texts. Letters VI and VII are reprinted from Swift's *Works*, Vol. XII, 1768. These letters were first published by Swift's relative, Deane Swift, who possessed the originals, now lost. Although he made certain unwarranted alterations, all subsequent editors have had to depend on his text. Except for one typographical change, elimination of the long "s", I have left the eighteenth-century usages unaltered as a sample of certain contemporary practices, in spelling and italics, for instance. Letter L is reprinted from the *Journal to Stella*, edited by Harold Williams, Clarendon Press, Oxford, 1948, the authoritative edition. Here the editor had access to Swift's original letter now in the British Museum and he has reproduced what Swift wrote "as exactly and as closely as is possible in printed form" except for one or two minor orthographical peculiarities. The most obvious differences from Deane Swift's text are the absences of italics and the retention of Swift's many contractions, which Deane Swift filled in. For an account of the way in which Swift's letters to Stella were changed by the first editors, see the Introduction to the Williams edition of the *Journal* or the more detailed study in *Essays on the Eighteenth Century Presented to David Nichol Smith*, Clarendon Press, Oxford, 1945, pp. 33–48. I am greatly obliged to Sir Harold Williams and to the Clarendon Press for permitting me to reprint Letter L from his scholarly edition. The remaining correspondence is reprinted from *The Correspondence of Jonathan Swift*, D.D., edited by F. Elrington Ball, London, 1910–14, 6 vols. This edition is published by G. Bell & Sons, Ltd., to whom I am grateful for permission to reprint.)

SELECT BIBLIOGRAPHY

A. EDITIONS. These are authoritative editions and have valuable introductions, notes, and appendices.

The Prose Works of Jonathan Swift, edited by Herbert Davis, Oxford, 1939–68. 14 vols. *Index*, by Irvin Ehrenpreis and others.

The Correspondence of Jonathan Swift, D.D., edited by F. Elrington Ball, London, 1910–14. 6 vols.

A Tale of a Tub, to which is added The Battle of the Books and The Mechanical Operation of the Spirit, edited by A. C. Guthkelch and D. Nichol Smith, Oxford, 1929; second edition, 1958.

The Drapier's Letters to the People of Ireland against receiving Wood's Halfpence, edited by Herbert Davis, Oxford, 1935.

The Letters of Jonathan Swift to Charles Ford, edited by David Nichol Smith, Oxford, 1935.

The Poems of Jonathan Swift, edited by Harold Williams, Oxford, 1937; second edition, 1958. 3 vols.

Swift: Poetical Works, edited by Herbert Davis, London, 1967.

Journal to Stella, edited by Harold Williams, Oxford, 1948. 2 vols.

The Correspondence of Jonathan Swift, second edition, edited by Harold Williams, Oxford, 1958. 3 vols.

B. BIOGRAPHICAL AND CRITICAL. The following list is confined to books. Much of the best commentary on Swift's life and works is to be found in articles. For the title of many of these the student may consult Louis A. Landa and James Edward Tobin, *Jonathan Swift: A List of Critical Studies Published from 1895 to 1945*, New York, 1945, where the more valuable articles are designated, and James J.

Stathis, *A Bibliography of Swift Studies, 1945–1965*, Nashville, Tenn., 1967, which gives useful brief indications of content. The indispensable and most extensive appraisal of Swiftian criticism is Milton Voigt's *Swift and the Twentieth Century*, Detroit, 1964. For articles published after 1965, consult "English Literature, 1660–1800: A Current Bibliography," published annually in *Philological Quarterly*. Two brief appraisals of the commentaries on Swift may save a student from undiscriminating reading: (1) Herbert Davis, "Recent Studies of Swift: A Survey," *University of Toronto Quarterly*, VII (1938), 273–88; (2) George Sherburn, "Methods in Books about Swift," *Studies in Philology*, XXXV (1938), 635–56. See also the "Guide" by Louis Landa in A. E. Dyson, *The English Novel*, Oxford, 1974.

Brady, Frank, ed. *Twentieth Century Interpretations of Gulliver's Travels*, Englewood Cliffs, N.J., 1968.

Bullitt, John M. *Jonathan Swift and the Anatomy of Satire*, Cambridge, Mass., 1953.

Burlingame, Anne. *The Battle of the Books in Its Historical Setting*, New York, 1920.

Carnochan, W. B. *Lemuel Gulliver's Mirror for Man*, Berkeley, 1968.

Case, Arthur E. *Four Essays on "Gulliver's Travels,"* Princeton, 1945.

Davis, Herbert. *Jonathan Swift: Essays on His Satire and Other Studies*, New York, 1964.

Eddy, William A. *Gulliver's Travels: A Critical Study*, Princeton, 1923.

Ehrenpreis, Irvin. *The Personality of Jonathan Swift*, London, 1958.
———. *Swift: The Man, His Works, and the Age*, vol. I, London, 1962; vol. II, 1967; vol. III in progress.

Ewald, William Bragg, Jr. *The Masks of Jonathan Swift*, Cambridge, Mass., 1954.

Foster, Milton, ed. *A Casebook on Gulliver among the Houyhnhnms*, New York, 1961.

Harth, Phillip. *Swift and Anglican Rationalism: The Religious Background of "A Tale of a Tub,"* Chicago, 1961.

Jeffares, A. Norman, ed. *Fair Liberty was all his Cry: A Tercentenary Tribute to Jonathan Swift, 1667–1745*, London, 1967.
———. *Swift: Modern Judgements*, London, 1968.

Johnson, Maurice. *The Sin of Wit: Jonathan Swift as a Poet*, Syracuse, N.Y., 1950.

Landa, Louis A. *Swift and the Church of Ireland*, Oxford, 1954.

McHugh, Roger, and Philip Edwards, eds. *Jonathan Swift, 1667–1967: A Dublin Tercentenary Tribute*, Dublin, 1967.

Murry, John Middleton. *Jonathan Swift: A Critical Biography*, London, 1954.

Nicolson, Marjorie. *Science and Imagination*, Ithaca, N.Y., 1956.

Price, Martin. *Swift's Rhetorical Art: A Study in Structure and Meaning*, New Haven, 1953.

Quintana, Ricardo. *The Mind and Art of Jonathan Swift*, London and New York, 1936 (reprinted 1953).

———. *Swift: An Introduction*, London and New York, 1955.

Rawson, Claude, ed. *Focus: Swift*, London, 1971.

Starkman, Miriam Kosh. *Swift's Satire on Learning in "A Tale of a Tub,"* Princeton, 1950.

Taylor, W. D. *Jonathan Swift: A Critical Essay*, London, 1933.

Traugott, John, ed. *Discussions of Jonathan Swift*, Boston, 1962.

Tuveson, Ernest, ed. *Swift: A Collection of Critical Essays*, Englewood Cliffs, N.J., 1964.

Van Doren, Carl. *Swift*, New York, 1930.

Vickers, Brian, ed. *The World of Jonathan Swift*, Oxford, 1968.

Williams, Kathleen. *Jonathan Swift and the Age of Compromise*, Lawrence, Kansas, 1958.

———, ed. *Swift: The Critical Heritage*, London, 1970.

(The books listed as edited by Brady, Foster, Jeffares, McHugh and Edwards, Rawson, Traugott, and Vickers and collections of critical essays, some reprinted and some original. Collectively they are extremely valuable.)